Killigrew and the North-West Passage

Jonathan Lunn

headline

First published in Great Britain in 2003
by HEADLINE BOOK PUBLISHING

First published in paperback in 2003
by HEADLINE BOOK PUBLISHING

10 9 8 7 6 5 4 3 2 1

Lunn, Jonathan

Killigrew and
the North-West
Passage /

F Pbk

1230817

ISBN 0 7472 6525 9

Typeset in Times by
Letterpart Limited, Reigate, Surrey

Printed and bound in Great Britain by
Mackays of Chatham plc, Chatham, Kent

HEADLINE BOOK PUBLISHING
A division of Hodder Headline
338 Euston Road
LONDON NW1 3BH

www.headline.co.uk
www.hodderheadline.com

For Jack Rosenthal

ACKNOWLEDGEMENTS

Thanks are due once again to the usual crew for support, encouragement, and assistance: James Hale, Sarah Keen, Yvonne Holland, and last but by no means least Alastair Wilson for invaluable advice, both technical and literary! As usual, any errors or inaccuracies remain the responsibility of the author.

Particular thanks are also due to M. Jean Verney-Carron, *Directeur Général* of Verney-Carron SA, for his kind and helpful advice on breech-loading shotguns of the mid-nineteenth century.

I should also like to thank the following for providing inspiration: Hans Christian Andersen, Peter Benchley, John Carpenter, Samuel Taylor Coleridge, James P. Delgado, Fergus Fleming, William Goldman, Jerry Goldsmith, Carl Gottlieb, Stephen Hopkins, Bill Lancaster, Barry Lopez, John McTiernan, Herman Melville, Dan O'Bannon, Ann Savours, Ridley Scott, Mary Shelley, Alan Silvestri, Steven Spielberg, Francis Spufford, Jim Thomas and John Thomas, John Williams, Ralph Vaughan Williams, and the anonymous author of *Beowulf*.

. . . In a state of nature, and in places little visited by mankind, they are of dreadful ferocity. In Spitzbergen, and the other places annually frequented by the human race, they dread its power, having experienced its superiority, and shun the conflict: yet even in those countries prove tremendous enemies, if attacked or provoked.

Barentz, in his voyages in search of a north-east passage to China, had fatal proofs of their rage and intrepidity on the island of Nova Zembla: his seamen were frequently attacked, and some of them killed. Those whom they seized on they took in their mouths, ran away with the utmost ease, tore to pieces, and devoured at their leisure, even in sight of the surviving comrades. One of these animals was shot preying on the mangled corpse, yet would not quit its hold; but continued staggering away with the body in its mouth, till dispatched with many wounds.

They will attack, and attempt to board, armed vessels far distant from shore; and have been with great difficulty repelled. They seem to give a preference to human blood; and will greedily disinter the graves of the buried, to devour the cadaverous contents . . .

Thomas Pennant, *Arctic Zoology*, 1784

The North-West Passage, 1852

Incognita

Incognita

North Devon

Baffin Bay

Baffin Land

Wellington Channel

Cornwallis Island

Beechey Island

Lancaster Sound

North Somerset

Prince Regent Inlet

Incognita

Gulf of Boothia

Melville Island

Melville Sound

Peel Sound

Prince of Wales Land

Boothia

Chantry Inlet

King William Land

Incognita

Victoria Land

Dease Strait

North-West Territories

Incognita

Charted

Uncharted

Greenland

Atlantic Ocean

Hudson Bay

Beaufort Sea

See Main Map

Great Slave Lake

North America

Pacific Ocean

0   100   200   300   400

Miles

I

The Wreck of the *Carl Gustaf*

The English whalers called Melville Bay the 'Breaking-up Yard'.

Four sounds discharged floating ice into the north end of Baffin Bay: Lancaster Sound, Whale Sound, and Smith and Jones Sounds. When the ice met the contrary winds and currents at the centre of the bay, it collected to form the Middle Pack: a field of ice nearly 150 miles across, made up of thousands of floes all jammed together. Constantly in motion, the vast mass circled in a counter-clockwise direction, and where it met the Greenland coast at Melville Bay it ground against the shore ice like a gargantuan millstone.

Each year whaling ships from Europe tried to pass through this maelstrom of ice to gain access to the open, whale-rich 'North Water' of Baffin Bay. Sometimes the pack, blown away from the Greenland coast by offshore winds, opened up to reveal a lead through which the ships could sail. But the ice was nothing if not capricious, and could close again just as easily. More than 200 whaling ships had been wrecked there in the past thirty years.

On Thursday, 17 June 1852, the name of the whaling ship *Carl Gustaf* was added to this toll of destruction.

Of 310 tons burden, the *Carl Gustaf* was a three-masted barque, measuring a little less than 100 feet from stem to stern. She had departed from Hamburg nine weeks earlier, sailing across the Atlantic Ocean to Cape Farewell at the southern

1

extremity of Greenland. Her master, Kapitän Wolfgang Weiss, was a seasoned Arctic hand, having sailed into the North Water every season since 1820. He had been captain on his last fifteen voyages, and was considered remarkable amongst the whaling fraternity in that he had never lost a ship.

The old Arctic hands working on deck doffed their caps as a mark of respect as the ship passed the Devil's Thumb: a peculiar, sheer-sided pinnacle of rock that jutted up on the Greenland coast. But such superstitious gestures would not be enough to save them.

The summer sun – shining twenty-four hours a day in those latitudes – worked upon the vast, pristine glaciers that snaked their way down from the mountainous, granite-faced plateau of Greenland, calving off huge chunks of ice to form icebergs. Sometimes these would break off the top of the glaciers to plunge into the cobalt-blue waters with an immense splash, sending up fountains of water that drenched the men working on the *Carl Gustaf*'s rolling deck, freezing at once to form icy cuirasses about their torsos. The men were employed constantly, struggling to bend sails frozen stiff or to work running rigging that had become as hard as iron, or simply trying to keep the ship's upper works free of the build-up of ice, to stop her from becoming top-heavy and capsizing.

Out of her crew of forty-eight, only sixteen survived the initial sinking, an appalling mortality that can only be accounted for by the rapidity with which the disaster occurred. The wind, blowing offshore, did not back or veer, so the only explanation for the movement of the pack was some unseen ocean current that drove it against the shore. If the lookout in the crow's nest cried a warning, none of the survivors remembered hearing it afterwards; the lookout may have dozed off, but since he was one of the first to die the truth will never be known. Indeed, so much confidence did the crew have in their captain's ability to see them through the ice that half of them were below, asleep in their hammocks in the forecastle, when the first cry of warning came from Bjørn Sørensen, the chief harpooner.

Born thirty-six years earlier on the Danish island of Rømø – famous for its whalers – Sørensen was as much a legend amongst the whaling fraternity as Weiss was himself. Six foot two in his stocking feet, he had broad shoulders, tattooed arms, blond hair and a shaggy beard that reminded his shipmates of his Viking forebears. Normally a gentle giant, put him in a barroom brawl on the Hamburg waterfront and he exploded with berserker fury, but he was never more alive than when he stood in the bows of a whaleboat, bearing down on his quarry with a harpoon in one hand.

'The ice!'

Kapitän Weiss had been on the quarterdeck, conferring with his first mate, Niklaus Jantzen, when he was alerted by Sørensen's cry. He looked up and saw that the pack, which had been a cable's length to larboard a minute ago, had already halved that distance and was closing rapidly with the *Carl Gustaf*.

'All hands on deck!'

'All hands on deck!' Sørensen repeated the captain's order in a roar, clanging the ship's bell frantically. 'Tumble up!'

In these waters, the men did not need to be told to sleep in their clothes. Even if it had not been for the cold, the constant fear of a disaster like this would have been enough for them to take that basic precaution. Even so, they may not have realised the immediacy of the impending disaster, and many paused to put on their boots before ascending the companion ladder. The third man to emerge was still climbing up through the fore hatch when the ice pack slammed into the *Carl Gustaf*'s port side.

A terrific shudder ran through the ship. The men of the watch above – including several topmen working in the rigging – were thrown to the deck. One of the men climbing the companion ladder to the fore hatch lost his footing and was hurled down on to the men behind him. The *Carl Gustaf*'s hull, reinforced with triple layering against shocks such as this, withstood the initial onslaught.

But the pack kept on coming.

The *Carl Gustaf* was being pushed sideways through the water now, heeled over at thirty degrees to port. The men on deck struggled to their feet, fighting to keep their balance on the slippery, canting deck. Some of them scrambled over the gunwale and jumped for the relative safety of the ice at once; others, only slightly more cool-headed, scrabbled for their kitbags first.

3

Some grabbed the first kitbag that came to hand; others wasted precious seconds making sure that they got their own belongings. Two men even squabbled over a kitbag that each was convinced was his own.

As soon as the *Carl Gustaf* had rounded Cape Farewell at the southern extremity of Greenland, Weiss had ordered his crew to keep a spare kitbag with a change of clothes stowed on deck: a standard practice on board Arctic whalers, in case the ship was 'nipped' by the floes and the men had to jump on to the ice. The *Carl Gustaf*'s six whaleboats were already hoisted in their davits, each loaded with an emergency medicine chest and enough food to keep eight men alive for two weeks. The whaler was by no means the only ship trying to reach the Northern Water that summer, and two weeks should have been more than enough time for the men to reach the safety of another vessel.

'Wait for it!' roared Weiss, who knew that jumping on to the ice prematurely was even more dangerous than lingering on the doomed ship. He had taught them this in the many drills they had performed during the voyage up the west coast of Greenland, but in their panic the raw hands forgot his warnings.

Weiss knew instinctively that the ship was doomed, and he had a more pressing concern than the welfare of his men: his wife. Like the wives of many skippers on the Greenland fishery, she accompanied her husband on his voyages into the Arctic.

Ursula Weiss would have had to be deaf not to hear Sørensen's warning and the ringing of the bell. Twenty years younger than her husband, she had been married to him for nine years, and this was the ninth time she had accompanied him on one of his voyages, so she knew better than to delay. She jumped out of the bunk and hurried to pull a fox-skin jumper over the shirt she had been wearing in bed, made from the down of hundreds of auks. She had plenty of European clothes, but when venturing on the ice she preferred a full suit of Inuit apparel she had purchased from one of the natives at Lively harbour, their clothes being warmer and more hard-wearing than anything manufactured by Europeans.

Kapitän Weiss was crossing the great cabin aft when the *Carl Gustaf* was thrust against the shore ice to starboard. A second shudder ran through the deck, and this time the ship heeled

4

violently to starboard, almost thrown on her beam-ends. In the stateroom, Frau Weiss was hurled back across the bunk, bumping her head badly on the bulkhead. The heavy wooden bureau at which Weiss did his paperwork was thrown across the great cabin, smashing into his back, slamming him against the side and crushing him instantly.

The ice did not hesitate, but sliced through the ship's hull from both sides to meet amidships below decks. Many of the men fighting to clamber out of the forecastle must have been crushed before they had a chance to be frozen by the icy water that now gushed in through the breaches in the hull.

The foremast was smashed at its base and its forestays, frozen brittle, snapped under the impact. The mast toppled, bouncing against the rigging that supported the mainmast. The crow's nest broke free from the foretop and splintered against the upper deck, killing the lookout instantly. Then the foremast came down a second time, slicing through the rigging and landing across many of the men who crowded the port bulwark. Their screams were drowned out by the crunching of the ship's timbers and the awful screeching of the grinding ice.

As the pack ice met the shore ice, the floe on to which many of the crew had already jumped snapped under the immense pressure of the pack behind it with a crack like a peal of thunder. Two chunks of the floe rose up out of the water in an inverted V, the men on the ice sliding down it into the closing gap between the floe and the ship. Some fell into the water and drowned as the sub-zero temperature of the water paralysed them with cramp; others were crushed against the ship's side. Then the split floe fell across the upper deck, knocking down the mainmast, which in turn dragged the mizzen-mast after it. The screams and groans of terribly injured men mingled with the sound of water rushing into the hold.

Committing himself to divine providence, Third Mate Dietrich Ziegler made his way to the great cabin and knocked on the door of the captain's stateroom. There was no reply: for all he knew, Frau Weiss had already left the ship. But he had to be sure. He kicked the door in, and found her sprawled unconscious across the bunk.

There was no time to fetch some hartshorn to try to revive her, even if it was possible to reach the sick-berth in the stricken ship: for now, the only thing that stopped the *Carl Gustaf* from sinking was the ice that impaled her sides. Ziegler slapped the captain's wife into consciousness. She recovered quickly, realising without a word from him that they needed to get off the ship fast. She pulled a pair of bearskin breeches over her Turkish pantaloons – a new garment, popularised by Mrs Bloomer – worn more because of their practicality than as a conscious statement of any belief in women's rights.

Ziegler looked away, embarrassed at the sight of her undergarments. 'Come on!'

She pulled a hooded sealskin jacket over her head and followed him out of the stateroom. But she came to a dead halt when she saw the corpse of her husband, crushed against the bulkhead by the bureau.

'There's nothing you can do for him,' Ziegler told her. He was twenty-seven, the same age as she, and had served as an officer on many merchant ships plying between Hamburg and London. But this was his first voyage on board a whaler and his experiences so far had made him doubt he was cut out for the life of a 'spouter'.

Frau Weiss allowed Ziegler to drag her from the great cabin and the two of them made their way to the companion ladder, but they could not raise the after hatch: it was pinned down from above by wreckage. Seeking to escape via the main hatch, they opened a door leading forward to find themselves face to face with a solid wall of ice.

Feeling panic rise within him, Ziegler led the way back to the great cabin. The mizzen-mast had fallen across the skylight above, and the carpet below was covered with shards of glass, but there was a chance he could smash away enough of the remaining frame for the two of them to climb up on deck. They were moving the table to the centre of the cabin when they heard a tapping on the window that looked out astern, and saw the end of a boat-hook.

Ziegler ran to the window and saw Sørensen below them, in one of the whaleboats with half a dozen other men. He could have kissed the harpooner, but given that Sørensen was not inclined to such displays of emotion, even under circumstances

6

such as this, it was probably just as well that the glass was between them.

There was no chance of simply opening the window: it had been sealed with oakum to keep out the cold and the water. 'Get back!' shouted Ziegler. 'I'm going to smash the glass!'

Sørensen nodded and ordered his crew to back water. The third mate did not wait for them to get clear, snatching up a chair and smashing at the glass with the legs. The first blow shattered the panes, but it took five more to knock out the leading. He swept the legs around the frame to knock out the remaining shards, and then Sørensen and his men brought the boat back in closer so that Ziegler could lower Frau Weiss to them. Sørensen caught her, and once she was safely in the boat the third mate lowered himself from the window. The glass sliced through his mittens and lacerated the fingers within, but that was the least of his concerns. Two more of the men in the boat caught him and lowered him gently to the bottom boards.

'The captain?' asked Sørensen.

Ziegler shook his head. 'He's with God now.'

Jakob Kracht laughed. The *Carl Gustaf*'s blacksmith, he was a brawny fellow who could repair anything from a twisted whaling iron to a cooking stove. 'With God! I don't share your certainty in an afterlife, Herr Ziegler; but if there is a heaven, I very much doubt that old bastard has gone to it.'

The third mate scowled and flicked his eyes to where Ursula sat in the stern sheets, but she had a dazed expression on her face and had not apparently heard Kracht denigrate her husband.

Sørensen ordered his crew to row away from the ship. Even as they got clear, the ice started to part again and the wrecked whaler, pulled free of the projecting shelf of shore ice that had skewered her, began to sink.

They rowed to one of the larger floes, now the pack was quiescent, and saw another six men from the *Carl Gustaf* picking their way across the ice to rendezvous with them, two of them carrying a third between them, while a fourth limped and was forced to lean against a companion for support. With the help of the boat's crew, Ziegler and Sørensen dragged the boat up on to the ice, and turned to greet the other survivors. Ziegler was pleased to recognise the second mate, Konrad Liebnitz, among them – it meant that responsibility for these men no longer rested on his shoulders alone – and Dr Bähr, carrying his rifle slung from one shoulder. In his early fifties, Bähr was a tall, lean man with a balding head, spiky eyebrows, liver-spotted hands and a scrawny neck that had earned him the nickname '*das Geier*' amongst the hands: 'the Vulture'.

'The captain?' Liebnitz asked Ziegler.

'Didn't make it. Jantzen?'

'The same.' Liebnitz was silent while he contemplated their situation. 'All right, let's get organised,' he said at last, and gestured to where several barrels floated on the water where the *Carl Gustaf* had gone down. Dozens of large tuns, freed from the whaler's hold, floated high on the water: the empty tuns in which they had hoped to transport the oil from any whales they had caught. Others, almost submerged, might carry victuals from the ship's stores. 'Sørensen, take the boat and see what you can salvage.'

'First things first,' said Bähr. 'We must light a fire before we freeze to death. We've got four injured men here. They need to be kept warm—'

'Light a fire?' Liebnitz seemed amused. 'With what, *Herr Doktor*?'

Bähr looked abashed. Liebnitz clapped him on the back. 'Never fear, *Herr Doktor*. Sørensen will get you your firewood.' He noticed the rifle slung from Bähr's shoulder. 'I see you brought your shooting stick. Did you think to salvage your medicine chest from the sick-berth?'

'There wasn't time. There's a medicine chest in the boat, isn't there?'

Sørensen lifted the chest out of the boat. It was much smaller than the one Bähr had had in the sick-berth, containing only the bare essentials, and precious few of those. The harpooner threw the chest at the doctor, who caught it awkwardly.

'Besides, a medicine chest won't be much good to us if a polar bear comes by,' Bähr said defensively.

'Him and his damned polar bears!' muttered the blacksmith.

'Stow it, Kracht,' snapped Liebnitz. 'You can help Sørensen salvage what he can. That goes for you too, Eisenhart, Arndt, Glohr and Ohlsen.'

'Aren't you forgetting something?' sneered Kracht. 'The ship's sunk. The articles we signed are hereby null and void. That means we don't have to take orders from you or anyone else any more—'

Liebnitz caught him by the throat, and threw him down on the ice. 'Now you listen to me, you scrimshanker! You may not be answerable to me any longer, but as far as I'm concerned I'm still responsible for you! Thirty-two men died today, and there isn't one of them I wouldn't rather have before me in your place. But I'm damned if I'll lose any more men before we get to safety, so we're going to have to work together to stay alive. Someone's got to take responsibility for your miserable hides. I'm the senior officer, so that means me. Don't think I welcome the responsibility: I don't. But that's the way it's got to be, so you'd better learn to like the idea. And until we get to safety you obey my orders, understand?'

'*Jawohl, mein Herr,*' Kracht said sarcastically. But he picked himself up and followed Sørensen and the others to where the boat had been drawn up on the ice.

Liebnitz turned to Bähr, who was now attending to the injured. 'How bad are they?' he asked in a low voice.

'Fischbein's shattered his elbow, Immermann's got a compound fracture of the tibia, Tegeder is suffering from concussion, and as far as I can tell Noldner's got three broken ribs. I'd say one of them has punctured a lung, judging from the blood on his lips. I doubt he'll last the night.'

Sitting up cradling his arm, Fischbein overheard him. 'And what about the rest of us? We're going to die here, aren't we?'

Liebnitz smiled. 'Don't lose heart, lad. There's plenty of Arctic whalers that have been in worse pickles than this, and have lived to tell the tale. Things could be worse, believe me.'

'We mustn't lose faith,' Ziegler told him. The third mate was a devout Lutheran. 'The Good Lord will deliver us.'

'I wouldn't be too sure about that,' muttered Kracht. 'He put us in this mess in the first place, didn't He?'

'I suggest we pray, offering thanks to the Lord for our preservation thus far, and hoping that if it is not part of His plan to deliver us from these straits, then that at least our souls may be saved. "The name of the Lord is a strong tower: the righteous runneth into it, and is safe." '

'To hell with your prayers, Herr Reverend! Right now I'd rather have a strong ship than any damned tower.' The blacksmith could be trusted to take a pragmatic view of any situation.

'Be silent, you blasphemous wretch!' said Liebnitz. 'Ziegler's right: we should pray.'

The two mates got down on their knees and clasped their hands. Sørensen and Fischbein joined them, the half-deck boy putting his hands together as best he could with one arm splinted and in a sling. Ziegler led them in reciting Psalm 23: 'The Lord is my shepherd . . .'

When they had finished praying, Sørensen and the others salvaged what they could from the water, including some empty barrels they could use to build a bonfire. The wood was soaked through, but with the encouragement of a liberal amount of lamp-oil they were able to get a bonfire going. The damp wood produced a lot of smoke, but that was all to the good: if any other ships in the vicinity saw the smoke, they would realise a vessel had been nipped in the ice, and try to help.

Liebnitz took an inventory of what they had been able to salvage, before addressing the men huddled before the bonfire. 'We've got plenty of victuals,' he told them. 'Enough to last us weeks, so we won't starve to death. Another ship is bound to come this way sooner or later: the whole whaling fleet is behind us.'

'What if they can't get through?' asked Kracht.

'We have Dr Bähr's rifle, plenty of ammunition, and some irons,' Liebnitz told him. 'So we can hunt – kill seals and wildfowl to supplement our victuals. If we ration the food, I think there's enough to last us for two months, although I doubt we'll have to wait that long. Even so, I agree it would be foolish of us to wait when we all know there's a danger no other ships will get through this season, which is why I'm going to propose that eight of us take the boat and try to make it back to Upernavik.' The northernmost settlement on the western coast of Greenland, Upernavik was the last outpost of civilisation in the Arctic.

'Upernavik!' scoffed Kracht. 'Upernavik's more than two

10

hundred miles away, Herr Liebnitz. You're going to row two hundred miles to Upernavik?'

'If necessary,' said the second mate. 'The one boat we were able to salvage has a sail, so whoever goes won't have to row all the way.'

'And if the ice gets in their way, as it's wont to do?'

'Then they drag the boat behind them. It's a chance, but it's one I'm willing to take. Besides, the likelihood is they'll meet another ship long before they get to Upernavik. It's better than sitting here doing nothing.'

'We can get more than eight in that boat,' said Bähr.

'Yes, but she'll be overloaded,' said Liebnitz. 'If some of us can get to safety, they can send help. They won't be able to do that if the boat sinks before it gets there.'

'So who goes?' asked Kracht.

'I think it's more a question of who stays.' Liebnitz knew as well as Ziegler – as well as any of them – that on balance, whoever set off for Upernavik stood a better chance of survival than the ones who were left behind. Even if they could get to Upernavik, there was no guarantee that a rescue was possible, or that any of those who stayed behind would still be alive by the time the rescuers reached them. 'I suppose it's up to me to set a good example, so I'm volunteering to be one who stays behind.' He turned to where Ziegler was holding his hands out while Bähr tended to his lacerated palms. 'That means you'll be in charge of the boat, Herr Ziegler.'

'You're joking,' said Ziegler. 'With these hands? Whoever goes in the boat, officer or rating, is going to have to pull his weight. I can't pull an oar: my fingers are cut to pieces.' He hated to admit it; he wanted to be in that boat more than anything else in the world. But he knew there was no escaping the reality of the situation.

'He's right,' said Bähr.

Ziegler grinned ruefully. 'Looks like I drew the short straw, eh, Herr Liebnitz?'

The second mate scowled, as if he had been cheated of a chance to be a hero.

'Don't worry,' Ziegler told Liebnitz. 'The Lord will protect those of us who stay behind.'

11

'All right. I'll take the boat back towards Upernavik. Herr Ziegler is in charge of those who remain here. Who's staying with him?'

'Immermann, Noldner, Fischbein and Tegeder aren't going anywhere,' said Bähr. 'You can't afford to be held back by carrying sick men in that boat. And if they're staying, I suppose that means I have to stay behind to take care of them.'

Liebnitz grinned. 'Don't try to play the hero, Bähr. You know as well as I do that you're only staying behind because you think you'll get a chance to catch that polar bear you've got your heart set on while we're gone.'

Bähr just scowled.

'All right, that's six staying behind. We need one more.'

'I'll stay,' said Ursula.

Liebnitz shook his head. 'You're coming with me, Frau Weiss.'

'I've got nothing left to live for, now that Wolfgang's dead.'

Ziegler did not believe that for an instant. She still had the faint traces of a black eye from the latest beating her husband had given her, something he had seemed to do on a regular basis as far as Ziegler could tell. Perhaps she felt she had nothing left to live for because of Jantzen, but not because of her husband. As much as he would have liked her to stay with him, he knew that was just being selfish. He did not want her to die with him. 'Herr Liebnitz's right, Frau Weiss. You must go with him.'

'No. Didn't the doctor say you needed able-bodied men, if you were going to make it to Upernavik?'

'You can help me navigate, if you want to make yourself useful,' Liebnitz told her. 'But useful or not, you're coming with me. That's final.'

If Ursula had lost the will to live, she certainly did not have the will to argue with Liebnitz.

'I'll stay,' Sørensen volunteered at once.

'Thank you.' Ziegler said it quietly, but he meant it. God might have been his refuge and strength, but the tough harpooner was a very present help in time of trouble.

'Good for you, Sørensen,' said Liebnitz.

'When do we leave?' asked Kracht.

'Tomorrow, at six,' Liebnitz told him. There was no point in saying 'at dawn'. In the land of the midnight sun, dawn had no meaning at this time of year. 'It's late, and we've had a rough day. We could all do with some sleep. I want us fully refreshed before we set out.'

Sørensen and the others had salvaged two buffalo-hide robes from the water, and had managed to dry them out, more or less, in front of the bonfire. If they were still a little damp, at least it was better than sleeping on the ice itself. The sixteen of them huddled together for warmth, Frau Weiss gladly abandoning the modesty of her sex in the interests of survival by nestling between Liebnitz and Ziegler. The latter, who would have been delighted to snuggle next to Frau Weiss under happier circumstances, could only think about the forthcoming day, and the prospect of being abandoned on the ice by Liebnitz and the others.

The darkless, bitterly cold night seemed to last for ever, yet morning came all too soon. While Kracht got a fire going to prepare a breakfast of pickled herrings and tea, Bähr checked his charges. Noldner had been contrary and defied the doctor's prognosis that he would not last the night, but Tegeder had given up the ghost: his frozen body was as stiff as a board. After seeing so many of the crewmates die the preceding evening, none of them could summon any last reserves of emotion at the discovery, but the mood over breakfast was muted. Whether they had been chosen to go to Upernavik, or to stay behind with the injured, there could be no doubt they were all weighing up their chances of survival.

While Liebnitz supervised his men as they loaded their share of the victuals on board the boat, Ziegler took Frau Weiss to one side. 'Don't worry about us,' he told her. 'We'll be fine. The important thing is that you get safely back to Upernavik; then perhaps you can send someone for the rest of us. We'll start heading back ourselves, so that even if they can't send help, there's every chance we'll be all right. All we have to do is follow the coast of Greenland down, and . . .'

He tailed off. She knew as well as he did that they had been condemned to death.

She remained silent, no hint of emotion showing on her face. He wanted to say more. 'Frau Weiss . . . I know we've only

13

known one another a short time, but . . . in that time I've come to hold you in the highest regard.' As he started to unburden himself, the words came tumbling out. 'I would like to think that if things had turned out differently, we should—'

'Don't say it!'

'I love you,' he blurted. He knew it was not the most tactful thing to say to a widow on the day after her husband had died, but he knew there had been no love lost between Kapitän Weiss and his wife. Besides, what other chance would he get? 'I've never believed in love at first sight. It's irrational, it makes no sense to become besotted with a woman about whom I know nothing, and yet . . . I've loved you from the first time I laid eyes on you.'

He paused for breath, trying to gauge her reaction. Her eyes met his steadily, and yet there was no hint of emotion in them as she stared back blankly as if his words were meaningless to her. Somehow, even pity, contempt or derision might have been preferable to her silence.

'Frau Weiss!' called Liebnitz. He and his men had finished loading the boat, and were ready to shove off.

'I must go,' she said, and turned her back on him. She walked across to where the boat waited without so much as a backward glance.

Ziegler and some of the others followed her to wish the men in the boat good luck.

'Whatever you do, don't give up hope!' Liebnitz called to them from the stern sheets. 'I'll bring help, or die trying. I'll be back. Just make sure you're all still alive when I get here.' He erected the boat's mast and its single sail to take advantage of the breeze that blew offshore.

'The Good Lord go with you and protect you,' Ziegler called after them. He stood at the edge of the floe and raised a hand in a forlorn gesture of farewell. He watched the boat as the six men with Liebnitz rowed it slowly down the lead, until they disappeared around a hummock in the pack ice. Then he was left with Sørensen, Bähr, and the four injured men.

'That's the last we'll see of them, I suppose,' grumbled the doctor.

'Now what do we do?' asked Fischbein.

'Do?' Sørensen regarded the youth with amusement, then hawked and spat a tobacco-stained gobbet on to the ice. 'We stay alive.'

An eerie whistling sound filled the air as Liebnitz, Frau Weiss and the six men with them rowed the boat through the broad lead between the Middle Pack and the cliffs of craggy, white ice that towered over them where a glacier several miles wide entered the sea. The noise started out as a high note, gradually dying away to a low tone beyond the limits of human hearing.

'What the hell is that?' Ib Ohlsen asked fearfully. He was the youngest and least experienced member of the boat's crew.

'They say it's the sound of dead whalers, killed in these straits, keening a warning for those that would follow them,' Franz Eisenhart said with a wink at his shipmates, who grinned. 'They say it presages a death.'

'Belay that!' snorted Liebnitz. 'No one says any such thing, and if they do it's only fools who believe it. It's just a sound, Ohlsen, nothing more. The sound of the Arctic.'

'But where's it coming from, *min herre*?' persisted Ohlsen.

'From the air itself.' Liebnitz shrugged. 'It's just the sound of the wind.'

Ursula knew the second mate was guessing, but for an explanation to set Ib Ohlsen's mind at rest, it would do for now. She had heard it herself enough times to know that whatever it was, it could not hurt them.

It was nearly thirty hours since they had left Ziegler and the others on the pack ice, and almost as many miles behind them. They travelled at a leisurely pace: they had another 175 miles left to cover before they reached Upernavik, so there was no point in exhausting themselves by rowing frenetically when both they and the men they had left behind them had plenty of food. Ziegler and the others would be all right, as long as they kept their heads and the weather remained mild.

The sea was mirror-smooth and the only sounds were the plashing of the oars and the oarsmen's rasping breath. Even the loons that perched on the crags to port were silent, until suddenly they all took wing at once, swooping low over the boat after their plunge from the icy cliffs. At first Ursula thought it must have been the appearance of the boat that had startled them, but then there came a sound from the cliffs, like the crash and rumble of thunder. As one, the oarsmen stopped rowing and turned to stare at the cliffs.

It took Ursula a second to realise what was happening: the shadows lengthening amongst the crags on the cliff face, the laws of perspective seemingly in abeyance, a downdraught of icy wind; and then she understood.

The cliff face was collapsing, falling towards them.

She parted her lips to scream, but no sound would come; even if it had, it would have done little good. All they could do was sit and stare in mesmerised horror as that vast wall of ice toppled forwards. Water surged and foamed at the foot of the cliff, and the next thing she knew she was flying through the air. She saw the boat spin end over end, another body flying through the air, whiteness all around her, a roaring in her ears, and then she plunged into the water.

It was like falling into a lake of fire. Ten thousand red-hot needles stabbed into her flesh, the intense burning snatching her breath away. She opened her mouth to cry out and water filled it as the waves closed over her head. Cramp tried to seize up her joints, but instinct overruled the shock and she struggled back to the surface without even thinking about it. The heavy swell that surged back and forth in the wake of the collapsing cliff lifted her up, and she found herself treading water in the lee of a ledge of ice at what she took to be the foot of the cliffs. Eisenhart was already on the ledge, Ohlsen climbing up out of the water beside him. She knew she had to get out of the water fast, and struck for the ledge, vaguely conscious of another figure swimming along-side her. He overtook her and scrambled up on the ledge; she was seconds behind him, and even as he turned to help her – it was Kracht – Eisenhart and Ohlsen was already hauling her up after him.

The four of them crouched on the narrow ledge, their backs pressed to the wall of ice behind them, limbs shivering, teeth chattering. Ursula looked about for the others but saw no one, no sign of the boat except for a single oar adrift in the water.

'Where are the others?' asked Ohlsen.

'They're gone, lad,' said Eisenhart.

16

'What do you mean, gone?'

'Gone. Drowned, crushed. Dead.'

Ohlsen just shook his head and stared down into the water a couple of feet below them.

'Now what do we do?' asked Ursula. 'We'll freeze if we don't get out of these wet clothes soon.'

'We'll have to head back to where we left the others,' said Kracht.

'Go back!' protested Eisenhart. 'It's almost thirty miles!'

'It's more than a hundred and seventy to Upernavik,' the blacksmith pointed out. 'Would you rather head south?'

'He's right,' said Ursula. 'It's our only chance.'

'We'll freeze to death before we even get halfway!'

'We'll freeze to death sooner if we sit here and do nothing.' Kracht stood up and looked about for a way off the narrow ledge, but the wall of ice was sheer above them.

'We're not even on the right side of the lead!'

'We'll have to swim for it, anyhow,' said Kracht. 'There's no other way off this ledge.'

'Swim!' Ohlsen gazed mournfully across to the floating pack ice on the other side of the lead, at least a quarter of a mile away. 'We'll never make it.'

'We've got to do something,' said Eisenhart. 'We can't just sit here!'

'The lad's right,' said Kracht. 'Trying to swim that far in these temperatures is certain death.'

'And sitting here in sopping wet clothes isn't?'

'Perhaps another ship will come by,' suggested Ohlsen.

'Perhaps,' agreed Eisenhart. 'But I wouldn't count on it.'

'Maybe we don't have to swim all the way across to the pack.' Kracht leaned out from the ledge, trying to spy a place where they could climb up further along the foot of the cliff. 'Perhaps we can—'

A judder ran through the ledge. The four of them exchanged glances. 'What the hell was that?' asked Ohlsen. 'Don't tell me this part of the cliff is about to fall away again – with us on it!'

'No fear of that,' said Eisenhart.

'How can you be so sure?'

'Because we're not on the cliffs, my lad. We're on an iceberg. When the cliffs fell on our boat? An iceberg, calving away from the glacier.'

The four of them stared at one another in horror. Kracht swore.

Another judder ran through the berg. 'That's the bottom of the berg scraping across the sea floor,' explained Eisenhart.

'So we're stranded?'

'It could be worse.' Eisenhart took out his tobacco pouch and pipe, realised the tobacco was soaked through and hurled the pouch into the water below with a sigh. He gestured with his pipe across to where the Middle Pack seemed to drift past them. 'I reckon the current's taking us north at . . . what? A quarter of a knot? Half a knot? Sooner or later it'll take us back to where we left the others.'

'Later rather than sooner,' said Kracht. 'Even if we're travelling at half a knot, it'll be sixty hours before we reach the others. We'll be dead in sixty minutes, if we don't find some shelter and get out of these clothes—'

Another shudder ran through the iceberg, and then the whole world seemed to spin around them. Ursula felt herself lifted up with a sickening lurch, spray hissing from the icy crags and dripping into the water that plunged away vertiginously beneath them. She clutched at the ice instinctively, bracing herself in the angle of the ledge as the wall behind her became the ground, and then started to tilt in the opposite direction. Kracht and Ohlsen slithered across the ice, dropping out of sight. Ursula and Eisenhart heard a scream, fading away into a distant splash as someone plunged into the icy seas on the other side. Then the iceberg swung back, swaying gently to and fro on the ocean swell as it found a new equilibrium.

Ursula hardly dared move. She knew it was ridiculous to suppose that any motion on her part might upset the balance of an iceberg of several million tons' mass, yet she had seen enough bergs roll and capsize in the water to understand how precarious their position was. The next roll might so easily plunge her and Eisenhart to the sea floor.

'Are you all right?' Eisenhart asked her.

She nodded, too breathless to speak.

He eased himself gingerly into a sitting position. 'I think we're safe for now.'

Ursula laughed weakly.

'What's so funny?'

'We're stranded on a drifting iceberg, a hundred and seventy-five miles from civilisation, slowly freezing to death, and you say we're safe for now?'

'Massage your fingers and wriggle your toes in your boots,' he told her. 'Got to keep frostbite at bay.' He stood up and looked around. Now they were on top of the iceberg, they could see the Greenland coast to the east, already a few hundred yards away. It was at least sixty feet from where they crouched close to the peak of the berg to the water far below, but even so, the granite cliffs seemed to tower over them.

'We have to find a way down to the water,' said Eisenhart. 'Now we've got to swim for it: the pack or the shore, there's not much in it. At least the pack is smooth; we'll be hard-pressed to find a way up those cliffs . . .'

'You couldn't give me a hand first, could you?' asked Kracht, his voice strained as he tried to pull himself up the frictionless ice to join Eisenhart and Ursula on the ledge beneath the peak.

'Jakob!' exclaimed Eisenhart. 'I thought we'd lost you.'

Kracht's head dropped out of sight as he lost his footing, but his gloved hands remained in view where they gripped the ledge. 'There's time yet!'

Eisenhart pulled him up. 'Ib?'

Kracht shook his head. 'I didn't see what happened to him. Must've gone straight under.'

The iceberg was out of shoal water now, no longer scraping its bottom on the sea bed but floating freely. The three of them explored the narrow space on the top of the berg tentatively, searching for a way down. The sides of the berg were not sheer, but so steep that they might as well have been. 'That's it, then,' Kracht said glumly. 'We're trapped up here.'

'Maybe,' said Eisenhart. He edged across to where the sides of the berg were steepest, almost a straight drop into the water below. 'I think we could dive from here.'

'Dive!' spluttered Kracht. 'Are you crazy? It's got to be a hundred feet!'

'Nearer sixty, I'd say.'

'There could be a projecting ledge just under the water; you'll break your neck! And even if there isn't, you'll freeze to death before you get halfway to the pack ice.'

'We'll freeze to death anyhow if we don't do something.' Eisenhart sighed. 'Look, I'll admit it's not much of a choice. If you don't think you can make it, wait here. I'll make my way across the pack ice to where we left the others. Perhaps we can salvage another boat, bring some dry clothes for you, something to make a fire with.'

Kracht clasped him by the hand. 'I don't know if you're the bravest man I ever met or just the biggest fool, but . . . well, good luck.'

'Just try to stay alive until I get back.' Without another word, Eisenhart took a run up and dived over the precipice. It was a perfectly executed dive and he cleaved the water like a knife, a trail of bubbles rising in his wake.

Ursula and Kracht watched and waited, but Eisenhart did not resurface.

Kracht swore. Ursula buried her face in her hands. The blacksmith sat down next to her and put an arm around her shoulders. He tried to draw her close to him, but she shied away.

'Forgive the familiarity, Frau Weiss, but it's the only way to keep warm. I've got a wife waiting for me back in Hamburg, and I happen to love her very much.'

She grudgingly accepted his embrace. 'You do not care for me much, do you, Kracht?'

'That's neither here nor there now,' he replied evasively.

'We're going to die here, aren't we?'

'Let's hang on to life just that little bit longer, shall we? You never know your luck. Maybe Ib was right: perhaps another ship will come by. What's the date today?'

'Thursday . . . no, Friday. The eighteenth.'

'Then by now I've probably got a child waiting for me at home, as well as a wife. And I intend to hold that baby boy in my arms before I die.'

Ursula managed a smile. 'What makes you think it's a boy?'

'Oh, it's a boy, all right! Gerda will have some explaining to do if it isn't. Are you a religious woman, Frau Weiss?'

'I suppose so. You?'

'Never been a devout churchgoer. But right now I'd become a Mohammedan, if Allah stood a better change of getting us out of this pickle than God!'

'Whatever God we pray to, we'd better pray for a miracle.'

'*Allahu akbar*!' breathed Kracht. Ursula looked up at his face, and saw he was staring off towards the cliffs of the coast. 'Look!'

She followed his gaze, and saw eight figures dragging a sledge across the top of another glacier that entered the sea up ahead of them. 'Who can they be?' she asked. 'Esquimaux?'

'They can be damned Chinamen for all I care, as long as they get me off this damned iceberg and into some warm, dry clothes.' Kracht leaped to his feet and started waving his arms over his head. 'Hey! Over here! Help! Help!'

But Ursula knew it was hopeless. 'Even if they do see us, what good can it do? There's no way they can reach us.'

'Maybe they've got kayaks nearby.'

'Even if they have, how can that help? There's still no way down to the water's edge.'

'Perhaps they can get help . . .' Even as he spoke, Kracht must have realised how ridiculous his words were. But he refused to relinquish his grip on the slender thread of hope presented by the distant figures. 'Damn it! There must be *something* they can do.'

The men on top of the glacier had seen them now, and had stopped dragging the sledge to stand and stare, sizing up the situation. Kracht's face crumpled as he realised the truth of Ursula's warning: even if these men were willing to help, there was simply nothing they could do.

Then the tallest of the figures was galvanised into action. He must have been their leader, for when he turned to address his fellows it was obvious from his gestures he was giving orders. They were obeyed promptly too. One man took some things from the sledge and started to sprint as fast as he dared across the ice, towards the precipice where the far edge of the glacier's face overhung the water, jutting out like the prow of a massive ship. Even as the man moved, the leader was giving orders to the remaining six men, who started to pull equipment from the sledge.

'It looks like they're doing something,' said Kracht.

'But what?'

The man who had broken away from the group had reached the precipice now and crouched down, attacking the ice with a Norwegian axe. Ursula saw that one of the things he had taken from the sledge was a coil of rope, and realised that the iceberg's path was going to take them to within a few yards of where the prow of the glacier jutted out over the sea.

'They're going to try to lower a rope to us!' Kracht exclaimed excitedly.

Six of the men were now dragging the sledge across the ice at the double, heading away for the far side of the glacier, while the leader hurried to join the first man at the precipice. As the ocean current carried the berg on its ponderous way towards the overhang, Ursula and Kracht were close enough to see that these men did not wear Esquimaux clothes, but European apparel, adapted for the Arctic: box-cloth jackets, sealskin caps and boots, mittens and comforters. The leader carried a shotgun slung across his back.

'Who *are* they?' wondered Ursula.

'Angels,' asserted Kracht. 'Angels sent from heaven!'

The two men at the precipice fixed an ice-anchor, S-shaped like a butcher's hook, in the ice, and rove one end of the rope to it. They lowered the other end of the rope over the ice-cliff, and Ursula and Kracht moved to the opposite side of the narrow space on top of the berg so they would be closer to it.

'When we pass under that rope, you grab it and pull yourself up,' Kracht told Ursula. 'Don't worry about me.'

They both knew that the rope would not be secure enough to take the weight of both, and as slowly as the iceberg drifted, there would not be time for each to climb up separately. 'What about you?' she asked. 'You've got a wife and a child waiting for you back in Hamburg. Now that Wolfgang is dead, I have no one.'

'Ladies first,' insisted Kracht, and grinned. 'Besides, you never—'

He broke off as another judder passed through the berg, and the smile was frozen on his face. The berg spun slowly in the water, moving away from the precipice: only a few yards, but far enough to make it clear they would never be able to reach the dangling rope. 'Oh, God in heaven!' moaned the blacksmith, realising that their last chance of survival was about to be snatched away from them.

On top of the precipice – now almost immediately overhead – the leader of the strangers pulled in the rope and retreated out of sight. The berg drifted past the overhang, only a few yards too far away. Kracht sank to his knees on the ice, sobbing.

On the other side of the precipice, Ursula looked up and saw the leader running along the side of the overhang, away from the iceberg, the rope – still secured at one end to the ice-anchor – wrapped tightly around his leather-gauntleted fists, a Norwegian ice-axe dangling by its thong from one wrist.

When there was no more slack left on the rope, he turned and, without even hesitating, launched himself off the edge.

He swung low beneath the precipice, swooping around in a great arc, the skirts of his mackintosh greatcoat flapping. Ursula's heart was in her mouth as he swept over the iceberg. He released the rope, flying free to plummet the last few feet on to the top of the berg, about a dozen yards from where she stood next to Kracht. He smacked against the iron-hard ice with a sickening thud that made her wince, and lay still, spread-eagled. At first Ursula thought he was dead, but then he began to slither down the cambered ice towards the edge and was galvanised into life. He gripped his ice-axe and swung it against the ice, halting his slide even as his long legs shot out over the precipice from which Eisenhart had plunged to his death only minutes earlier.

The man managed to get a grip on an outcrop of ice with his left hand, and swung the ice-axe again. It bounced off; a second swing gave him firmer purchase. But his feet scrabbled uselessly against the ice below and he was unable to pull himself up.

Heedless of her own safety, Ursula hurried across the top of the berg to where he dangled. She seized him by the arm and tried to drag him up. Then Kracht was beside her, and the two of them managed to drag the stranger up to safety. He lay on his back, condensation billowing from his mouth as he clutched his arms about his ribs, evidently winded and in considerable pain. He wore a pair of wire-mesh snow-goggles over his bronzed, wedge-shaped face, like a couple of tea-strainers strapped over his eyes.

'Are you crazy?' Ursula asked him furiously. 'You almost got yourself killed!'

'I don't suppose you speak English, do you?' the stranger asked in that language, and managed a grin as he pulled his goggles down around his neck, revealing a pair of warm brown eyes with a hint of mischief in them. 'I'm afraid I don't speak German. The name's Killigrew, by the way. Lieutenant Kit Killigrew, of Her Majesty's navy, at your service.'

II

The *Venturer*

'I'm Frau Weiss,' the woman responded, too stunned by Killigrew's sang-froid to do anything but introduce herself in turn. 'This is Herr Kracht.'

'A foolhardy thing you did just now,' said Kracht, who spoke English as well as Frau Weiss, if with a heavier accent. 'And while I wouldn't want you to think me ungrateful, I hardly see how it helps. Now there are three of us trapped on this iceberg, instead of just two.' He nodded to where the overhang of the glacier from which Killigrew had swung was swiftly falling astern as the current carried them northwards.

Killigrew sat up with a wince, and unlooped the coil of rope he had slung from one shoulder, laid it carefully on the ice so there was no danger of it slipping from the iceberg, and took an ice-anchor from his belt and put it in the centre of the coil of rope along with his ice-axe. 'Three of us,' he said, 'and one ice-anchor, one Norwegian axe, and a coil of rope.'

He took off his greatcoat and handed it to Ursula, and then removed the frock-coat underneath it and passed it to Kracht. 'Strip off those wet clothes and put those on, before you freeze to death,' he told them, standing there in trousers of twilled cotton *de Nîmes*, a cable-knit Guernsey, woollen comforter, leather gauntlets and sealskin cap.

'You want us to undress?' protested Ursula, glancing across to where the seven men who had been left on the glacier were following the iceberg. They had cleared the sledge of all but a

25

few objects, unidentifiable at that distance, and two of them were pulling it ahead at speed while the remaining five carried the rest of their equipment between them. 'Out here in the open?'

'I'm afraid the necessity of survival will have to overrule your modesty, Frau Weiss,' said Killigrew, starting to explore the top of the iceberg. As cold as they would be wearing nothing but coats, better that than standing around in wet clothes that were already freezing on their bodies. 'Besides, my men are too far away to see anything. You and Herr Kracht will just have to turn your backs to one another and get it over and done with as quickly as possible.'

'What about you?' asked Kracht.

'I shan't peep, I promise.' Killigrew found the least steep part of the iceberg's sides and crouched over it to study it more closely.

'I mean, are you not cold?'

'I'll be fine. At least I'm dry. And working will keep me warm.' He began to dig a hole in the ice with a succession of blows from his ice-axe, in which to secure the ice-anchor. 'I suppose you're whalers?' he asked, working with his back to Kracht and Ursula as they stripped off their sodden clothes, the fabric crackling as pieces of ice broke off.

'Yes. Our ship was crushed in the ice. Eight of us set out in a boat for Upernavik, but we were sunk by this iceberg when it calved off the glacier. Kracht and I were the only ones to survive.'

'Ågård – one of our ice-quartermasters – guessed that a whaler had gone down when we saw smoke somewhere north of here yesterday,' explained Killigrew. 'Commander Pettifer suggested I set out with a sledge team to see if we could bring succour to any survivors.'

'You have a ship?'

'Indeed, ma'am – Her Majesty's exploring ship *Venturer*. She's south of here, waiting for a lead to open. We set out intending to follow the shore ice northwards, but we had to head inland when we came to the glacier. It's just as well we did: we might never have seen you, otherwise.'

'How far is it to your ship?' asked Kracht.

'About a dozen miles. But don't worry – we'll have you out of this wind and in some dry clothes within a quarter of an hour.' And not a moment too soon, Killigrew might have added: the exposed parts of Kracht and Ursula's bodies were already turning blue. 'Massage yourselves, keep the blood flowing. Noses, ears, fingers and toes especially.'

'You are looking for Franklin?' guessed Ursula, rubbing her face.

Killigrew nodded. 'We're with Sir Edward Belcher's squadron. Six ships – our biggest effort to find Franklin yet.'

It was seven years since Captain Sir John Franklin had sailed into the Arctic in search of the fabled North-West Passage. The Royal Navy had been engaged in mapping the ice-choked islands and channels of the Canadian Arctic ever since the end of the great war with France thirty-seven years earlier. Because the season of open water in the Arctic was only three months long, it was standard practice for such exploring ships to overwinter in the polar seas, and three years had gone by before anyone had expressed alarm at the failure of Franklin's two ships – HMS *Erebus* and *Terror* – to return. Since then there had been no fewer than ten expeditions to try to rescue Franklin's party, presumed to be trapped in the ice in the heart of the Arctic: five by the navy itself, three sponsored by Lady Franklin, one by the Hudson's Bay Company and one by a wealthy American philanthropist.

Killigrew hammered the ice-anchor home with the haft of the ice-axe, then rove one end of the rope through it, tying it fast and throwing the other end down the side of the iceberg. It reached almost down to the water. 'There! Think you can climb down, Frau Weiss? If not, I'm sure Kracht here and I can lower you down.'

'What good will it do? We still have to swim to the shore. Or do you happen to have a boat in your back pocket?'

'No.' Killigrew grinned. 'But I know a man who does.'

Ursula and Kracht followed Killigrew's gaze as he glanced back to the glacier, where the two men who had gone on ahead with the sledge had reached the crest of a ridge. On the other side, the ground – if ground there was beneath that thick layer of ice – sloped down gently to the shore ice perhaps half a mile north of the drifting iceberg. The two men sat astride the sledge, the equipment wedged between them. They pushed off, and the sledge began to move as gravity carried it down the slope, slowly at first but quickly gathering momentum. The man in front thrust his legs out before him, occasionally digging his heels against the ice to guide them or check their headlong rush.

It was not long before the men on the sledge had overtaken the ponderously drifting iceberg. As they slalomed in and out between the hummocks of ice that dotted the slope, sometimes shooting over the lower ones and flying several feet through the air, Killigrew was sure they must be pitched from the sledge and break their necks. But the man driving the sledge knew what he was doing and did not once lose control, even if the man seated behind him looked as if he were clinging on for dear life.

At last they reached the bottom of the long incline, a furlong ahead of the iceberg, and the man at the front of the sledge guided it on to the shore ice, braking with a sharp turn that almost pitched them over. The two of them sprang up, the man who had been clinging to the back setting up a portable stove while the other picked up a large, black object like a sausage and carried it across to the water's edge along with two paddles and what looked like a stirrup pump. He removed a couple of straps from the sausage-like bundle and unrolled it, revealing something not unlike a black, oval hearth rug. Then he fiddled about with the stirrup pump for a moment, attaching one end of it to the oval shape, and began to pump it. The black oval began to swell as it was filled with air.

'What in God's name is that?' Kracht demanded incredulously.

'A new invention,' explained Killigrew. 'A Halkett inflatable India-rubber boat: no well-equipped Arctic explorer should be without one. Just be careful where you stick your hatpins! Bundle up your clothes, Frau Weiss and Herr Kracht, and we'll take them with us. As soon as we get back on board the *Venturer*, I'll have them laundered, dried and restored to you.'

The iceberg was almost level with the two men on the shore ice by the time the man with the stirrup pump finished inflating the Halkett boat. He pushed it into the water, climbed confidently into it, and began to paddle across to meet the iceberg, dipping his paddle into the water first on one side of the peculiar boat, then on the other. He paddled strongly and before long he was keeping the boat in position immediately beneath the rope. Killigrew drew it up, tied one end around Ursula's torso, and then he and Kracht lowered her down to the man in the boat. The man looked up, saw what Ursula was not wearing under the greatcoat, and looked away again hurriedly.

Once Ursula was level with the man, he helped her into the boat, and then waved for the next person to follow. 'After you, Herr Kracht,' said Killigrew. He had intended to take the bundle of clothes himself, but the German picked them up, slung them from one shoulder by the belt he had used to tie them together, swung himself nimbly over the edge of the precipice and rappelled down the rope. Killigrew waited until he too was safely in the boat before following, almost as nimbly. He suspected he had cracked a rib or two when he had landed on the iceberg, and the descent gave him a tight pain in the chest, but there was nothing for it but to grit his teeth and bear it.

Soon all three of them were in the boat with the man who had paddled it across from the shore ice. In his late twenties or early thirties – even he did not know for certain – Petty Officer Wes Molineaux was one of the two boatswain's mates on board HMS *Venturer*, a black man who had grown up on the back streets of London.

Molineaux took up his paddle again, Killigrew took the other, and the two of them began to paddle the Halkett boat back to the shore ice. 'Where did you learn to sledge like that?' Killigrew asked the petty officer.

'Primrose Hill, sir, when I was a chavy,' replied Molineaux, as if to say: *isn't that how everyone learns to sledge?*

By the time they reached the shore ice, the man with the portable stove had brewed up some tea and he came across the ice with a couple of steaming mugs that he thrust at Ursula and Kracht. He lifted his own wire-mesh goggles to reveal a pair of china-blue eyes, and fumbled for his spectacles. 'Jings!' he exclaimed, when he saw Ursula's face. 'A woman!'

'It's good to see you learned something from those anatomy lectures at the Edinburgh School of Medicine,' Killigrew said with a smile. 'Frau Weiss, Herr Kracht: permit me to introduce Mr Strachan, our assistant surgeon. Strachan, perhaps you could heat up some soup for our guests while Molineaux and I erect the tent?'

'Of course!' said Strachan, and took a couple of tin canisters – specially designed for keeping preserved food in on Arctic expeditions – from a haversack. 'Mulligatawny?' he asked Ursula and Kracht.

'I beg your pardon?'

'Mulligatawny soup. Highly seasoned, just the thing for a cold winter's day. Or a summer's day in the Arctic, for that matter.'

'I am too grateful to be safe and alive to care what I eat,' said Kracht.

Killigrew and Molineaux set up four cut-down boarding pikes in a pair of inverted Vs, eleven feet apart and joined at the top by a horsehair clothes-line. Three more ropes acted as guys to hold the frame up, well secured to the sledge at the back and to an ice-axe buried in the snow at the front. They finished the tent by throwing a cloth of brown holland over the top and banking snow along the sides at the bottom to hold it down. Inside they spread an oilskin canvas to keep out the wet, and over that a buffalo-robe carpet.

By the time they had finished, the remaining five men of Killigrew's party had joined them. 'Endicott, you're about Frau Weiss' size,' Killigrew remarked to one of them. 'Perhaps you'd be so good as to lend her your spare set of dry clothes.'

'Aye, aye, sir.' A tall, lanky Liverpudlian, Able Seaman Seth Endicott handed Ursula a kitbag. 'There you go, ma'am. They're clean, I washed 'em myself only last Monday.' He pulled aside one of the tent flaps for her. 'I'll stand guard while you're getting changed, make sure no one disturbs you.'

'Thank you.' She crawled into the tent with the kitbag and fastened the opening behind her.

Killigrew turned to one of the other men. 'O'Houlihan, perhaps you'd be so good as to extend the same courtesy to Herr Kracht?'

'My pleasure, sir,' replied the Irish seaman. Like Endicott, he seemed genuinely pleased to be of service to the two Germans. He handed his kitbag to Kracht, who clutched it to his chest and waited for Ursula to finish getting changed so he could use the tent. He did not have long to wait; it was too cold to linger in a state of undress.

'Were there no other survivors from your crew, ma'am?' Killigrew asked Ursula while Kracht was dressing in the tent.

She shook her head. 'There are others: Herr Ziegler, Dr Bähr . . . six in all. Three of them are badly injured.'

'What about the captain? I presume you are the captain's wife?'

'He's dead.'

The pain in Killigrew's eyes was genuine enough, the pain of a man who knew what it was like to lose a loved one. 'I'm most dreadfully sorry . . .'

'Thank you.' Ursula spoke dully, nothing more than a formal acknowledgement of Killigrew's commiserations. He told himself she was probably in a state of shock after the terrible ordeal she had been through.

'What about the others? Where are they?'

'About thirty miles north of here. We only had the one boat. Herr Liebnitz thought we should make for Upernavik, try to get help for the men we left behind—'

'The others – they have shelter, food, warm clothing?'

'No shelter; plenty of food and warm clothing.'

'Then they'll have to fend for themselves, for the next few hours at least. Still, the weather's warm. Our first priority must be to get you safely on board our ship.'

'Warm, he calls it!' exclaimed Molineaux, who had been deflating the Halkett boat so he could roll it up once more. 'It's cold enough to freeze the balls on a brass monkey.'

'By Arctic standards, this is positively balmy,' said Strachan.

'You want my opinion, sir? This whole damned expedition is barmy!'

Killigrew grinned. Molineaux could be an insubordinate dog when he put his mind to it – which was most of the time – but he was one of the finest sailors Killigrew had ever known. After coming through several adventures together in which the seaman had saved the lieutenant's life too many times to count, Killigrew had decided that Molineaux had earned the right to be given some leeway, provided he remembered not to be quite so familiar in the presence of other officers. For his own part,

Molineaux saw a kindred spirit in the lieutenant: a fellow rebel with a firm sense of justice and mischievous sense of humour. Descended from a long line of naval officers stretching back to the sixteenth century, when the Killigrews had been notorious pirates in Cornwall, the lieutenant was born to command, although he never forgot that respect from his men was a privilege rather than a right.

One of them an officer and a gentleman – albeit the sort of gentleman who was considered a little too 'fast' for the liking of some of his more staid peers – the other a common seaman born the wrong side of Regent Street, Killigrew and Molineaux were not exactly friends, but they were joined by a bond far stronger than mere friendship: the mutual respect of two men who knew they could rely on one another, no matter what.

After Ursula and Kracht had had a chance to rest, Killigrew asked them if they were ready to make their way to where the *Venturer* was moored. Feeling much better now that they were in warm, dry clothes and had some hot soup inside them, both consented, mindful that the longer they lingered where they were, the longer Ziegler and the other survivors of the *Carl Gustaf* would be stranded on the ice without proper shelter. Killigrew gave the order: 'Down house – break up!' and the tent was dismantled and all the equipment stowed back on the sledge. While Killigrew and Strachan hauled the sledge along with the rest of their men, Ursula and Kracht walked alongside them.

The first half a mile – back up the side of the glacier – was the worst. After that, it was level, and then downhill at the other side of the glacier to the smooth shore ice beyond. They travelled at a leisurely pace out of consideration for the two exhausted Germans, covering a mile in fifty minutes and using the remaining ten minutes in each hour to stop and brew tea. At six o'clock they stopped an hour for supper: preserved meat and pemmican – pulverised lean, sun-dried beef mixed with animal fat and leavened with chocolate – thawed out over the portable stove to the point where it was as palatable as it was ever likely to be.

Taking advantage of the ever-present sun, Killigrew decided that they should push on and put a couple more miles behind them, but by nine it was clear that Ursula and Kracht had had enough for one day – even though it was equally clear that neither would admit it – and the lieutenant gave the order to make camp for the night. They erected the tent once more, and Killigrew and Strachan gave up their chrysalis bags for the two Germans, wrapping themselves up in warm clothes instead. As his seniority demanded, Killigrew took the place of honour at the rear of the tent, where he acted as a highly paid draught excluder, the tent having been set up with its mouth out of the cold wind that blew down from the Greenland icecap.

Killigrew and his men took turns to keep watch – not that they expected to meet any human enemies in that frozen wasteland, but there was always a risk from marauding polar bears – and at six O'Houlihan, who had taken the last watch, roused Endicott, whose turn it was to make breakfast. They set out at seven, with only four more miles to cover before they reached the *Venturer*.

They heard the Middle Pack grinding against the shore ice long before they saw it. A mountainous headland jutted from the coast; when the *Carl Gustaf* had sailed this way two days previously, the gap between the headland and the pack ice had been wide open, but in the usual capricious manner of the Arctic, the gap had now closed and the constantly shifting pack ice ground against the shore ice. Floes would sometimes break off, or smash the shore ice, or rise up over it, angular chunks piling up over one another to form the pressure ridges that crisscrossed the surface of the pack. Sometimes a chunk of ice would be hurled thirty feet or more into the air by the tremendous pressure, crashing down again with an explosion like a mortar shell.

Dragging the sledge over the shore ice, Killigrew and his party were able to avoid this peril with ease, and about a quarter of a mile beyond they saw the *Venturer* moored in a dock sawn in the ice in the manner pioneered by Arctic whalers, waiting for a lead to open.

Half as long again as the *Carl Gustaf* – about 150 feet from stem to stern – HMS *Venturer* was a bluff-bowed, two-masted, brig-rigged vessel with a funnel amidships betraying the presence of an engine deep in her bowels. Ursula saw that she had no paddlewheels, so she must have been one of the newer steamers, driven by a screw-propeller, that were gradually replacing paddle steamers.

While Killigrew's men unloaded the sledge, the lieutenant escorted Ursula and Kracht up the gangplank to the upper deck. This was the first time she had ever been on board a naval vessel. She had expected to see cannon lining the bulwarks, but there were none: she reminded herself this was an exploring ship, not a man-o'-war. Her husband had kept a smart ship, by whaling standards at least, but the neatness and orderliness of the *Venturer* put the *Carl Gustaf* to shame. Nonetheless, there was so much stowed on the upper deck, she could not help looking a little chaotic: spare spars stacked against the bulwarks, water casks around the sides of the quarterdeck, and dozens of sacks of coal heaped wherever space permitted. There were also two closet-like structures – one on the forecastle, the other on the quarterdeck – that looked like privies.

'Frau Weiss, may I introduce our captain, Commander Orson Pettifer?' asked Killigrew. 'Sir, this is Frau Ursula Weiss, a survivor of the *Carl Gustaf*, a whaler that was nipped in the ice the day before yesterday; and this is Herr Jakob Kracht, the *Carl Gustaf*'s blacksmith.'

A huge, barrel-chested bear of a man, Pettifer took one of Ursula's delicate hands in a massive paw and kissed it with surprising delicacy. 'It's a pleasure to meet you, ma'am. You are to be congratulated on your fortunate escape. Anything you require to make your stay with us more comfortable while you are a guest on board the *Venturer*, you have only to ask.'

'Thank you,' Ursula said distantly. 'You are too kind.'

Pettifer turned to Petty Officer Jake Unstead, the *Venturer*'s other boatswain's mate. 'Take Herr Kracht down to the mess deck and see to it he gets some hot tea. Make arrangements for him to berth with the hands until we can put him on another whaler.'

'Aye, aye, sir,' said Unstead.

'Thank you, *Herr Kapitän*.'

'This way, *mein Herr*.' The boatswain's mate led Kracht to the forward hatch.

Pettifer turned to Ursula. 'Let's get you below out of the cold, ma'am.' He motioned for Ursula to precede him down the after hatch. 'Were there no other survivors?' Pettifer asked Killigrew as they followed her down.

'There are six others, sir, about thirty miles north of here. Three of them are badly injured.'

'Only eight survived in all? Most Arctic whalers carry a complement of forty or fifty men. What happened to the others? Surely they can't all have died when the ship went down?'

In a short corridor on the lower deck, Killigrew briefly explained what Ursula had told him the night before about the ill-fated voyage of Liebnitz's boat. 'With your permission, sir, I should like to lead another sledge party on to the ice to search for the rest of the survivors from the *Carl Gustaf*,' he concluded.

'Not granted, Killigrew,' said Pettifer. 'At the rate the pack is moving, they're probably nearer forty miles north of here by now. Even if you do find them, how will you get three injured men back here? Besides, the way the ice is shifting, there's no guarantee we'll be able to stay here. You might get back and find we've had to retreat to Upernavik.'

'That's a chance I'm prepared to take, sir. And I'll lay odds I can find seven men in the crew willing to take that chance with me.'

'I can't spare eight of you. We'll just have to wait for the pack to open, and pray for the deliverance of those poor fellows on the ice. Now be a good chap and ask Armitage to make some soup and a hot drink for the lady.'

'Yes, sir. Tea or coffee, ma'am?'

'Tea, please.'

'Tea it is.' Killigrew headed forwards.

'Second door on your left, ma'am.' Pettifer nodded aft, to where a Royal Marine stood on duty at the end of the corridor. The marine opened the door for them, and Ursula ducked through into a compartment about sixteen feet across and twelve feet deep, with bookshelves lining two bulkheads and lockers lining the others. A large table dominated the centre of the room, with six chairs arranged around it, and a bowl of assorted nuts set in the middle of the tablecloth.

As Pettifer followed her in, a dachshund leaped from a basket and scampered across the room to jump up at him excitedly, yipping madly. The commander lifted the dog up in his arms and cradled her like a newborn babe while she licked his face.

'Yes, yes, Horatia! No need to make such a fuss. Anyone would think I'd been on the ice for four hours with Mr Killigrew and his men, instead of just up on deck for a few minutes.' He smiled apologetically at Ursula. 'A gift from Mrs Pettifer, to keep me company,' he explained, nodding to a framed calotype of a pinch-faced woman that hung from the side.

'She's adorable,' said Ursula, referring to the dog. She tried to sound enthusiastic, because she knew that was what Pettifer wanted to hear. She had never had much time for dogs, or indeed animals of any description.

'Isn't she?' Pettifer tickled Horatia's stomach, and the bitch squirmed with delight. He crossed to the door on the far side of the day-room and opened it to reveal a small but well-furnished cabin. 'There are plenty of cabins on board, but all the ones that aren't being used for accommodation are full of stores at present. I'm sure we've used up sufficient stores to be able to make space for you, but until then do please feel free to use mine, if you wish to lie down. You must be exhausted after your ordeal.'

'Thank you, but I am not tired. However, I would be grateful for a chance to . . . make myself fresh?'

'Freshen up, you mean. By all means, ma'am. There's a washstand in my cabin, and you'll find a . . . ahem . . . a "seat of ease" on the quarterdeck.'

By the time she had attended to her ablutions, a white-coated steward had arrived with a pot of tea and a bowl of steaming chicken broth.

The steward poured out the tea. 'Milk and sugar, *signora*?'

'Sugar, no milk,' she told him.

He nodded. 'One spoon or two?'

'One, please.'

The steward did not have to ask Pettifer how he took his tea. 'Thank you, Orsini,' said the commander.

As the steward bowed and withdrew, a young officer squeezed past him and rapped on the open door with his knuckles. At first Ursula did not recognise him as the young man who had come to their rescue on the pack ice earlier that day. Gone were the mackintosh greatcoat, comforter, and the sealskin cap with its ridiculous if practical ear flaps: now he wore an epauletted frock coat with all the elegance of a dandy, and had a peaked cap on his thick, black hair at a jaunty angle. She had to admit he looked quite dashing.

'Come in, Killigrew!' said Pettifer.

The lieutenant stepped smartly into the room and saluted the commander before bowing to Ursula. 'Sir, would I be correct in thinking you intend that Frau Weiss should dine with you at supper tonight?'

Pettifer smiled. 'Indeed, Mr Killigrew. Unless you have some objection?' he added archly.

'Of course not, sir. But in that event, as president of the wardroom mess I have been instructed by my fellow officers to request the pleasure of Frau Weiss' company at supper tomorrow night.'

Pettifer turned to Ursula. 'If you feel up to it, of course?'

'I'd be delighted,' she found herself saying.

'Then we shall look forward to your joining us at five o'clock *post meridiem*, or *post* whatever passes for *meridiem* in these latitudes,' Killigrew said with a smile. 'Just one thing. Dress is formal in the wardroom.'

Ursula felt herself blushing. 'Mr Killigrew, you'll have to acknowledge that I hardly came on board equipped with formal evening wear . . .'

'Then if I may be so bold, ma'am? Sir?'

Ursula hardly knew what to expect, so she merely nodded her assent.

Killigrew snapped his fingers, and Able Seamen Seth Endicott and Mick O'Houlihan marched into the room with a large quantity of clothing bundled in their arms. The lieutenant took one of the articles from Endicott and held it up for Ursula's inspection: a magnificent gown of bright emerald silk, lavishly trimmed with ribbon, lace, and artificial flowers.

'It is beautiful!' she gasped. 'But where in the world did you get it?'

'Our mate, Mr Cavan, purchased it from a dressmaker of my acquaintance,' explained Killigrew. 'He's about your size, ma'am – perhaps a little broader in the shoulders. I think blue would suit your eyes better, but the green will compliment your auburn hair superbly, and it was this or Mr Latimer's gown, which is bright yellow with scarlet trimmings.'

'Such things are not . . . not standard issue in the British navy, I trust?' she stammered.

Pettifer smiled. 'I fear Mr Killigrew is making game of you, Frau Weiss. I suspect this is merely one of the costumes Mr Cavan had brought on board for our amateur theatricals. Just one of the ways we plan to keep ourselves amused while we're frozen into our winter quarters during the long Arctic night.' He turned to Endicott and O'Houlihan. 'You can lay those out on the bunk in my cabin.'

'Sir?'

'Don't look at me like that, O'Houlihan! Frau Weiss is using my cabin until one of the cabins we're using as a storeroom has been cleared out.'

'Aye, aye, sir.' Endicott and O'Houlihan trooped through into the cabin and disappeared for a few moments.

'What play were you thinking of putting on, Mr Killigrew?' asked Ursula.

'*The Winter's Tale*, ma'am. I believe Mr Cavan was thinking of taking the role of Perdita.'

'You have a devilish sense of humour, Mr Killigrew,' said Pettifer. 'Are you sure Shakespeare isn't a little too . . . shall we say elevated . . . for the hands?'

'We were going to do *The Silent Woman*, sir, but Petty Officer Molineaux has been reading *Julius Caesar* to them and now they want *aut* Shakespeare *aut nihil*. I thought we'd do it with all the knockabout comedy, the way it was originally performed in the Bard's day.'

'With men taking the female parts,' observed Ursula. 'I wish I could be there to see it.'

'We'd be delighted to perform for you, ma'am,' said Killigrew, 'but we haven't even begun rehearsals yet. We were planning to do it for our Christmas Eve entertainment. By then I expect you'll be safely home in Germany, with any luck. Not that we shan't be sorry to lose your company, of course, but we can hardly take you with us into the heart of the Arctic. We'll be putting you on board the first whaler we encounter.'

She nodded absently, rearranging the teapot, sugar bowl and

her cup and saucer on the table before her so they formed the points of an equilateral triangle. Endicott and O'Houlihan emerged from the cabin and were heading for the door when Pettifer called after them.

'You two! Since you're so concerned about Frau Weiss' sleeping arrangements, perhaps you'd be good enough to offer your services to Mr Latimer so he can get a cabin ready for her.'

'Aye, aye, sir,' they chorused wearily, and Endicott punched O'Houlihan on the arm as they went out.

'Will you have a cup of tea, Mr Killigrew?' invited Pettifer.

'Thank you, sir, but I'm due on deck in half an hour, and I really ought to pay a visit to the sick-berth beforehand.'

'Nonsense, man, nonsense! The sick list can wait. Sit down. You could do with a hot drink inside you before you go back out into the cold. Orsini!'

At Pettifer's roar, the steward returned within seconds, and was instructed to fetch a third cup for the lieutenant.

'Herr Killigrew said you were with Sir Edward Belcher's squadron?' Ursula said, when the steward had gone.

'Indeed, ma'am,' confirmed Pettifer. 'It's a great honour to be serving as part of one of Her Majesty's Arctic expeditions.'

'Forgive me for asking, but . . . I did not see any other ships when I came on board. The others are nearby?'

'You mean you haven't seen them?' Killigrew asked in some surprise. 'We thought they were only a few hours ahead of us . . .'

'It's rather embarrassing, actually,' said Pettifer. 'As we were leaving the Whalefish Islands last week, we had the misfortune to get on shore. There was no serious damage, thank heavens, but it took us the best part of a week to get her off: we had to unload all our supplies to float her, and as you can probably imagine we have no shortage of those. Sir Edward was eager not to waste time waiting for us, the sailing season being so short here in the Arctic, so he pressed on and signalled us to rendez-vous with him at Lievely Harbour. By the time we reached Lievely, we discovered that we had missed the rest of the squadron by a matter of hours: Sir Edward had waited for us for the best part of a week before losing patience and sailing without us. We've been trying to catch up with them ever since.

Are you quite sure you haven't seen them? Not even the smoke from their funnels, in the distance?'

'No other steamships have passed this way, Captain Pettifer, I assure you. We were at Lievely ourselves three weeks ago, and no steamships have passed us since then. You must have passed them. You have made good time to have travelled so far in so short a space of time yourselves.'

'Yes, we have been pushing the engines rather,' Killigrew said drily, glancing at Pettifer. Ursula sensed this was a sore point between them.

'Sir Edward is not a man who is noted for his tolerance of the misfortunes of those serving under his command,' Pettifer reminded his lieutenant, and shook his head in bewilderment. 'I cannot comprehend it. How could we have passed them without realising it? I know we've been caught in several fogs since we left Lievely, but even so, one would have expected to have heard something if we passed them in a fog: signal guns, perhaps, or ships' bells.'

'Perhaps the rest of the squadron stopped at Upernavik?' suggested Ursula.

Killigrew shook his head. 'We looked in the harbour. There was no sign of the other ships.' He glanced at Pettifer. 'If we are ahead of the rest of the squadron, sir, perhaps we should wait here for it? Sir Edward won't thank us for entering the Middle Pack ahead of him, and the fate of the *Carl Gustaf* is a timely reminder of the danger of ships travelling alone in the Arctic.'

'You're forgetting those poor devils out there on the ice, aren't you, Killigrew?' said Pettifer. 'If a lead opens, I intend to take it at once, the sooner to bring succour to Frau Weiss's shipmates, regardless of whether or not the rest of the squadron has caught up with us. Besides, it's not as if we don't know where the rest of the squadron is heading. We can rendezvous with them there.'

Ursula arched her eyebrows quizzically.

'Beechey Island, ma'am,' explained Killigrew. 'The Admiralty has instructed us to make it our base of operations.'

'It was part of Franklin's plan to spend his first winter in the Arctic there, and proof that he did so lies in the three graves discovered by Captain Austin's rescue expedition two years ago,' said Pettifer. 'Sir Edward plans to search up Wellington

Channel with *Assistance* and *Pioneer*. He'll be wasting his time, of course.'

'Why do you say that?' asked Ursula.

'The Admiralty's instructions to Sir John were to investigate Wellington Channel for a possible North-West Passage; but Lady Franklin has confided in me that her husband was always convinced that if there was a passage, it lay to the south, along the north coast of the American mainland. Perhaps Peel Sound links to Dease Strait; Lady Franklin is convinced that her husband may have disregarded Admiralty instructions and sailed that way rather than up Wellington Channel.'

'Not that it makes any difference to us, sir,' put in Killigrew. 'Our instructions are to remain at Beechey Island as a tender to the *North Star*. Our depot ship,' he added, for Ursula's benefit.

'No need to remind me, Killigrew.' Pettifer grimaced, as if he had hoped for a more active role for his ship in the search for Franklin.

'You said there were six ships in the squadron in total,' said Ursula. 'If Sir Edward plans to sail north with the *Assistance* and the *Pioneer*, and your instructions are to remain at Beechey Island with the *North Star*, what will the other two ships be doing?'

'The *Resolute* and the *Intrepid*?' said Pettifer. 'They're to sail west in the hope of linking up with *Enterprise* and *Investigator*.'

'*Enterprise* and *Investigator*?' asked Ursula, losing track of all the different ships the Royal Navy had sent into the Arctic.

Pettifer nodded. 'The two ships that were sent into the Arctic via the Bering Strait two years ago, in the hope of finding a North-West Passage from the west, and linking up with Franklin's ships. They haven't been heard from since, either.'

Killigrew grinned ruefully. 'You might say that we're the men who've been sent to find the men who were sent to find men who were sent to find the North-West Passage.'

'The Arctic seems to be swallowing ships at an alarming rate,' agreed Ursula. 'Will anyone be sent to rescue *you*, if you become trapped in the ice?'

As Molineaux made his way on to the mess deck, one of the huskies leaped at him, barking furiously. Startled, the petty officer threw himself sideways against the bulkhead to his left before he remembered that the dogs were secure behind the wooden, straw-filled cages the carpenter's mate had built on the lower deck.

A city boy born and bred, Wes Molineaux had never had much time for animals. He had a particular phobia about dogs, ever since he had broken into a big house in London as a boy and been badly bitten by the Alsatian that lived there. Molineaux had known about the dog – that was why he had gone in armed with a drugged steak – but the dog had decided it preferred live meat and gone straight for his throat. He had got his arm up in time, an arm that still bore the scars of that encounter twenty years later.

Able Seaman Erlend McLellan was working his way along the row of cages, feeding them fresh seal-meat.

'Damn it, Mac, can't you keep these bloody monsters under control?'

The Orcadian looked up with a hurt expression, as if by insulting the dogs Molineaux was insulting him, but said nothing. A taciturn man, McLellan had kept himself to himself during the voyage from Woolwich, as far as it was possible for an able seaman to keep himself to himself on one of Her Majesty's ships. He seemed to prefer the company of the twelve huskies – bartered from the Inuit at the Whalefish Islands – to that of his shipmates.

In fact, the *Venturer* was not as crowded as any of the other ships Molineaux had served on in the fourteen years since he had given up a life of crime to become a seaman. The crew of thirty was tiny; a sloop of comparable size might have a complement of a hundred men. The steam tender had more than its fair share of officers, so there were only ten petty officers, six able seamen and five marines to share the capacious mess deck.

Except that much of the space of the mess deck was taken up with the dogs' cages, and with barrels of salt junk or water, and crates of food preserved in the tin canisters that had been specially developed for the navy's Arctic explorations. Not to mention the special equipment they were carrying for their expedition: sledges, sledge-boats, Halkett boats, scientific equipment, galvanic batteries, even barrels of chemicals for generating lighter-than-air gases. One of the more harebrained schemes that the Admiralty had taken up was a special fuse attached to an unmanned balloon. When they sent up the balloon, attached to the fuse would be hundreds of scraps of brightly coloured paper bearing printed messages to Franklin, telling him where they would be looking for him. As the fuse burned down, the papers would be scattered across the Arctic. There was even a printing press on board for printing the messages to tell Franklin where he could meet up with the men searching for him.

To Molineaux it was all junk. If anything were going to find Franklin, it would be guts and determination, not newfangled gadgets.

Born on the back streets of Saint Giles' parish – one of the most notorious rookeries in London – Molineaux was the son of a layabout and a washerwoman. The layabout had abandoned his family when the going had got tough, and Molineaux had learned to fend for himself at an early age. He was six when he had taken part in his first burglary, and by the time he was twelve he had been the toast of the swell mob as the most skilled snakesman in England. But when he was seventeen a burglary had gone wrong and he had been forced to go on the run. Joining the crew of HMS *Powerful* had seemed like a good way of lying low until the hue and cry died down. By the time the 84-gun ship of the line had paid off after active service in the Levant, Molineaux had discovered a new way to make a living. Serving in the navy might not bring the same financial rewards as being a first-rate snakesman, but it brought rewards of a different kind: the satisfaction of doing something worthwhile, something that would benefit people other than himself, something that his mother could be proud of him for.

He had been in the navy for fourteen years now and had finally earned himself a petty officer's badge of distinction on the sleeve of his blue jacket. His shipmates jeered at him when he told them that one day he would be a boatswain; they had never heard of a black warrant officer. Molineaux knew he could do the job as well as any white man, if they let him; perhaps *better* than any white man. He was sick of white coves looking down on him simply because of the colour of his skin, treating

43

him as if he was ignorant, despite the fact he read poetry by Milton and Coleridge when they struggled to reach the end of the 'Naval Intelligence' column in *The Times*. He would become a boatswain, and prove to the Admiralty there was nothing a white man could do that a black man could not do better.

Beyond the dogs' cages, he joined his messmates at one of the tables suspended from the deck head outside the galley. There were no gunports in the *Venturer*'s sides, and with the hatches sealed against the cold the only light came from the guttering pusser's dips that flickered fitfully in lanterns hung at strategic points around the mess deck, casting pools of thin yellow light that only seemed to emphasise the darkness around them.

Seth Endicott was holding forth on the subject of Frau Weiss' sexuality, which a few minutes spent in her presence made him an expert on, while Mick O'Houlihan decorated an ivory cheroot case he had carved with scrimshaw work and pretended to listen by occasionally saying, 'Uh-huhn.' They both acknowledged Molineaux with a nod, and Endicott resumed his discourse.

'Don't be fooled, Mick. She may come across as a frosty bitch, but I'll bet she's as randy as a rabbit in bed.'

'I thought you always said it was quiet, sweet gals that turned out to be the most passionate,' O'Houlihan said with a smile. Like Molineaux, he knew Endicott well enough to take the Liverpudlian's self-proclaimed carnal expertise with a bushel of salt.

'Same difference,' Endicott retorted dismissively. 'She was giving me the eye, Mick. I could tell.'

'Don't talk daft, man,' said Able Seaman Hughes. 'A woman like that wouldn't look twice at a cove like you. And do you know why?'

'Here we go,' groaned O'Houlihan.

'Because – in the eyes of the likes of her – you're inferior. It's all right for oppressed working-class proletarians to work and slave so that bourgeois capitalists like her can benefit from the fruits of your labours, but if you should aspire to share in those fruits she'll slap you down soon enough.'

'Bloody hell, he's off again!' groaned Endicott. 'Someone stuff a sock in his trap!'

'It's true, I tell you!' protested Hughes, and reached inside his

44

jacket to draw out a well-thumbed copy of a political pamphlet he was constantly quoting at his shipmates. 'You should read this, Seth. You might learn something.'

Molineaux snatched the pamphlet from his hand. Hughes tried to grab it back, but Endicott and O'Houlihan seized him, giving Molineaux a chance to peruse the pages. 'Oi! Give it back, you thieving pig!' squealed Hughes.

'You told us we should read it, didn't you?' said Molineaux. 'Let me read it out to the others.' As he scanned the pages, the other men on the mess deck gathered round. 'Here's a good bit. Listen to this, lads: "The Bourgeoisie substituted shameless, direct, open spoliation, for the previous system of spoliation concealed under religious and political illusions. They stripped off that halo of sanctity which had surrounded the various modes of human activity, and had made them venerable, and venerated. They changed the physician, the jurisprudent, the priest, the poet, the philosopher, into their hired servants . . ." '

'What's a juris-whatsit when it's at home?' asked Endicott.

'Highfalutin' word for a land-shark, shipmate. And I bet you'd have to look a long time to find one with a halo.' Molineaux tucked the pamphlet inside his jacket. 'I think I'll hang on to this, Red. I've a feeling it'll come in handy next time I visit the head.'

'Give it back!' repeated Hughes, struggling to free himself from Endicott and O'Houlihan. 'That's my personal property, that is!'

'But sure, Red, are ye not the one who's always tellin' us that all property is theft?' O'Houlihan pointed out.

'Yur,' agreed Molineaux. 'And I'm thieving it. So put that in thi' pipe and smoke it!' he added, borrowing one of the boatswain's favourite phrases – not to mention his broad Yorkshire vowels. Molineaux's skilled mimicry never failed to reduce his shipmates to tears of laughter.

'You bastard!' yelled Hughes. 'I'll report you to the cap'n, so I will!'

'And won't he be impressed when he finds out ye brought seditious material on board?' said O'Houlihan. 'Sure, the man'll like as not be congratulatin' Wes here for consficatin' it, so.'

Molineaux took the pamphlet out again and threw it at

Hughes. 'Keep your bloody book. I don't want it anyhow. I'll wipe my flanky on good British oakum, none of your foreign gammon, thank you very much!'

'Bastards!' Once Endicott and O'Houlihan had released him, Hughes bent down to retrieve his pamphlet. 'You're nothing but lackeys of your own capitalist oppressors. I'm telling you, boys, the day will come when the likes of those bourgeois pigs are strung up from the lampposts of London!' He flung an arm in the direction of the officers' quarters. Before it could reach its fullest extent, however, it met an immovable barrier: the chest of Mr Thwaites, the boatswain.

'All right, lads, simmer down. What's all this about? What's the book, Hughes?'

'It's mine, Mr Thwaites.' Hughes tried to thrust the pamphlet inside his Guernsey, where he wore it next to his heart, but in his panic to hide it from the boatswain's view as quickly as possible, he repeatedly caught it against the neck of his shirt underneath.

Thwaites laid his cherriculum – a short cane covered with the cured hide of a bull's pizzle, the boatswain's staff of office – across Hughes' chest. 'I didn't ask *whose* it were, I asked *what* it were.' He held out his left hand. 'Let me see.'

Realising he had no choice but to obey, Hughes placed the pamphlet in Thwaites' hand. The boatswain tucked his cherriculum under one arm so he could leaf through the pages until he came to a passage that caught his eye. ' "We have followed the more or less concealed Civil War pervading existing Society, to the point where it must break forth in open Revolution, and where the Proletarians arrive at the supremacy of their own class through the violent fall of the Bower-jee-oysee." '

'It's pronounced *Bourgeoisie*, Mr Thwaites,' Molineaux explained helpfully. 'It's French. It means "the middling sort".'

Thwaites glared at him. 'I know what it means, Molineaux. This is seditious material, Hughes. Where did thee get this?'

The Welshman hung his head. An awkward silence settled over the mess deck: the other hands knew that Hughes was in trouble this time and no mistake. While some felt his comeuppance was long overdue, they were sorry for it: apart from his tedious parroting of Communist dogma, Hughes was not such a bad cove.

But the seaman was oblivious to their sympathy as he quailed before the boatswain's glare. 'Well, lad? Speak up! Did thee bring this book on board?'

'Is everything all right here, Bosun?' As everyone watched Thwaites browbeat Hughes, no one had seen Mate Sebastian Cavan enter the main deck.

'I caught Hughes wi' this, sir,' explained the boatswain. 'Seditious material, sir, intended to foment mutiny on one of Her Majesty's ships.'

Only recently commissioned, Cavan was not yet twenty, a handsome young man with all the self-assurance of one to the manor born – his father owned large swathes of Ireland, by all accounts – who had served as a midshipman on Molineaux's last ship. He had been a shy, awkward, downy-cheeked youth of fifteen when HMS *Tisiphone* had sailed from Portsmouth in October 1848. By the time the sloop had returned from a cruise of the Far East and the South Seas lasting two and a half years, Cavan had been a self-assured young man, tried and tested in skirmishes with pirates and other desperadoes. But he wore his self-assurance lightly, maintaining an easy command over men three times his age, neither looking down on them as his social inferiors nor earning their contempt by trying to be overly familiar.

He took the pamphlet from the boatswain and glanced at the flyleaf. ' "The Manifesto of the German Communist Party". Oh, it's all right, Bosun. I lent it to him. It's mine.'

'*Yours*, sir?' Thwaites said dubiously.

'Yes. All a load of gammon, of course, but one needs to read these things to keep abreast of what the enemy that lurks on the fringes of our society is up to. Isn't that right, Hughes?'

'Yes, sir!' Hughes tugged his forelock furiously.

From the expression on Thwaites' face, it was clear he was not taken in, but he could hardly gainsay an officer. Nonetheless, Cavan had gone out on a limb for Hughes. As a commissioned officer – albeit a junior one – he might outrank the boatswain, but Thwaites would not look kindly at being made to look a fool in front of the men. He could make trouble for the mate if he wanted to, and he was just vindictive enough to do so. As much as Molineaux admired Cavan's sand, he could not help wondering if the mate appreciated how danger-ous an enemy he had made.

Cavan's next words probably did not help either. 'Well done, though, Bosun. We need to be vigilant at all times. You never know when the enemy within will strike next. Carry on.'

'Aye, aye, sir,' rumbled Thwaites, and from that moment onwards Molineaux knew that the boatswain would be looking for any opportunity to pay Cavan back.

Dismissed, Thwaites made his way topsides. Cavan turned to head aft.

'Sir?'

Cavan turned back. 'Yes, Hughes?'

'Can I have my book back, sir?'

Molineaux suppressed a groan. The Welshman just did not know when to keep his trap shut.

But Cavan only smiled. 'I think I'd better hold on to this for now, don't you?' He tucked the book inside his coat. 'We don't want you getting into any more trouble, do we? Next time I may not be able to bail you out.'

'Aye, aye, sir,' Hughes grovelled obsequiously. 'Thank you, sir. God bless you, sir.'

Cavan headed aft.

'They're the devil, aren't they, those capitalist bourgeois oppressors?' Molineaux remarked laconically.

'I just used him, the way his kind have been using us working-class proletarians for centuries,' sneered Hughes. 'When the revolution comes, the likes of him will be the first to be strung up from the nearest lamppost.'

Molineaux smiled. 'Yur, right.'

III

A Piece of Cake

Killigrew winced as Strachan probed his bruised chest with his fingers. 'No bones broken, at any rate,' opined the assistant surgeon. 'You may have cracked a couple of ribs, though. How in the world did you do it?'

'I think it happened when I dropped on that iceberg.'

'When you dropped on that iceberg? That was yesterday afternoon! And you helped haul the sledge for a dozen miles after that. Faiks, man! Why did you no' say something?' As always when he was agitated, Strachan's native Perthshire accent crept more strongly into his voice.

'Didn't want the hands to think I was scrimshanking, did I? What can you do for me?'

'Apart from recommend a doctor who specialises in mental cases? I'll bind you up; it's the standard treatment for cracked ribs, though I'm dubious of the benefit. As with most injuries, the best medicine is time. You'll heal soon enough. I'd better tell the Old Man that you'll not be fit for duty for a couple of weeks—'

'Don't you dare! Pettifer needs all the help he can get, until we rejoin the rest of the squadron. I can't afford to spend time on the sick list.'

Strachan sighed. 'Will you at least try to get some rest, stop pushing yourself all the time?'

Killigrew smiled. 'I'll try.'

Strachan set to work winding a bandage tightly around the

lieutenant's chest. 'How's the lassie settling in?'

'Fine, I think. Difficult to tell – she's not what I'd call garrulous.'

'Hardly surprising. English isn't her first language, she's probably in a state of shock after her ordeal on the ice, and now she finds herself on a naval ship of a foreign power, surrounded by strangers. I don't suppose she happened to mention how she got that blue eye?'

'I'd assumed that she fell and bruised her face when the *Carl Gustaf* was nipped.'

Strachan shook his head. 'That bruise is at least four days old. I know contusions, Killigrew. By the hookie! I should do the number of times I've treated you after you got into a fight, or fell off a mountain, or . . . or swung on to a passing iceberg like something out of a Walter Scott novel! You know I only volunteered to come on this expedition with you because I thought this would be the only place on earth where you could steer clear of trouble? More fool me!'

'You only volunteered to come on this expedition because you want to write a book on Arctic zoology,' Killigrew corrected him.

'It's nearly seventy years since Pennant wrote the standard reference. And some of it is, frankly, nonsensical. Besides, with the advances in methods of scientific investigation made in the intervening years, I'm sure I can shed new light on the various little-known, little-studied species that inhabit the Arctic wilderness.'

Strachan had first come into contact with the flourishing world of science while studying to become a fellow of the Royal Society of Apothecaries at the Edinburgh School of Medicine. His studies had included courses on anatomy, botany, chemistry, *materia medica*, and the theory and practice of physic; but there were other, new fields of investigation opening up for those of an enquiring mind.

The Admiralty had equipped the ships of Belcher's squadron with all manner of scientific instrumentation, but in its infinite wisdom it had not thought to appoint the *Venturer* with a science officer. It had been thanks to Killigrew – who had mentioned Strachan's scientific interests to Pettifer when the commander had asked him if he could recommend anyone as an assistant surgeon – that the Scotsman had been offered the position. When Strachan had tried to assure the captain that he would not let his scientific investigations interfere with his duties as assistant surgeon, Pettifer had pooh-poohed the suggestion. 'Nonsense, nonsense! Let us hope your duties as assistant surgeon do not interfere with your scientific investigations!'

Strachan had almost finished binding Killigrew's chest when there was a knock at the door. 'Come in!'

The *Venturer*'s clerk entered. In his early twenties, Nicodemus Latimer had a soft, pink face beneath an unruly thatch of hair so fair it was almost white. Killigrew had heard Strachan described as having a schoolboyish enthusiasm for science, although he could not see it himself; he doubted there were many schoolboys as studious and hardworking as Strachan. Latimer, on the other hand, fit the bill far better: feckless, idle, work-shy, scruffy, inky-fingered; if there was an overgrown schoolboy on board the *Venturer*, it was the clerk.

'Sick parade is at half-past eight in the morning, Latimer,' sighed Strachan.

'It's an emergency, Pills!' protested the clerk. 'I think my teeth are coming loose. They're all wobbly!' Latimer opened his mouth so that Strachan could feel for himself.

The assistant surgeon sighed. 'All right, let's have a look, shall we?' He took a dentist's probe from a drawer. 'Open wide.'

Strachan poked and prodded about inside Latimer's mouth with the probe, while the clerk whimpered at the slightest touch of probe against gum. 'You have the healthiest teeth on board, Latimer,' he said at last. 'The only thing you're suffering from is an acute case of chronic hypochondria.'

'But they're all wobbly!'

'Of course they are. Teeth are supposed to give a little in their sockets. Otherwise they'd break every time you bit down on something hard.'

The clerk looked disappointed. 'You don't think it's scurvy, then?'

Strachan smiled patiently. 'I think it's a little early in the expedition for any of us to be coming down with scurvy.' He turned to Killigrew. 'Some fool thought of including a medical dictionary amongst the books we have in the ship's library, and Latimer here's been reading it.' He turned back to the clerk. 'Have you been suffering from any other symptoms?' He pulled Latimer's head down so he could root around in his hair. 'Blood seeping from the hair follicles? Skin haemorrhages? Jaundice? Swollen legs? Pain in the joints?'

'That's it!' exclaimed Latimer. 'I've got this terrible pain in my knees. Give it to me straight, Strachan. I can take it. It's scurvy, isn't it?'

'Drop your pantaloons, let's take a look at your legs.'

Rubicund at the best of times, Latimer turned beetroot. 'In front of Mr Killigrew?'

'I'll avert my gaze, if it will make you feel better,' offered the lieutenant. 'I know it will make *me* feel better to look away!'

'Now drop your pantaloons.'

The clerk complied.

'The knobbliest knees in the navy,' said Strachan.

'They're not knobbly,' said Latimer. 'It so happens I have water on the knee.'

'Water on the brain, more like. Pull up your pantaloons. There's nothing wrong with you.'

'Tell them they can put that on my tombstone.'

'Certainly,' said Strachan. ' "Nicodemus Latimer, eighteen thirty to nineteen ten. There was nothing wrong with him, except knobbly knees. His loss will be greatly mourned by many a bookmaker." '

'You'll be laughing on the other side of your face when I'm dead because you were blind to my symptoms!' said Latimer. 'I ought to report you to the Royal Society of Apothecaries!'

'No, I ought to report *you* to the RSA. They can send a circular to all their other members, warning them about you. For any favour, Latimer, will you stop bothering me with imaginary ailments and find something constructive to do? Away with you! I've work to do. Unless you'd like to help me with the dispensary returns . . .?'

Latimer vanished.

Strachan chuckled. 'I shouldn't complain. If it weren't for Latimer – and your propensity for getting into scrapes – I'd be going off my head with the boredom. This is the most disgustingly healthy crew I've ever had the misfortune to sail with.'

'I'd've thought that would please you,' said Killigrew. 'Doesn't it leave you more time for your scientific investigations?'

'Precious little opportunity I've had for those! Since we left the Whalefish Islands, we haven't touched anywhere long enough for me to go ashore.'

'The Old Man's in a hurry to catch up with the rest of the squadron. Don't worry: I should imagine we'll be at Beechey Island for a year or two. That should give you plenty of opportunity for investigations.'

'Beechey Island? That fly-speck on the maps! As if it hasn't been picked over by enough explorers already. When I volunteered for this expedition, I thought we'd be sailing into uncharted waters, not nurse-maiding a depot ship for two years!'

' "They also serve who only stand and wait",' Killigrew reminded him, although secretly he shared his disappointment. Everyone in the *Venturer*'s crew had volunteered. They had signed up for different reasons: some out of a feeling of duty to the men of Franklin's expedition, fellow seamen; others keen for the double pay of Arctic discovery. But however noble or cynical their motives, everyone on board must have considered the glory and adventure of having a chance to be the ones who discovered the North-West Passage. From Commander Pettifer to young Private of Marines Andy Phillips, there was not a man on board who did not resent the fact that Sir Edward had failed to assign them a more exciting role to play in this expedition.

Killigrew took his leave of Strachan and made his way up on deck to relieve Cavan as officer of the watch. There was little to be done while the *Venturer* was moored to the ice waiting for a lead to open, so Cavan was practising his pistol-shooting with Bombardier Osborne of the Royal Marine Artillery. Armed with their new Deane and Adams revolvers, the two of them were taking it in turns to shoot at bottles swinging from the foreyard. Cavan was cheerfully humiliating Osborne by blasting into smithereens every bottle that he got in his sight without even troubling to aim, or so it seemed. Taking his time, lining up each shot with all the careful aplomb of a clerk defending his honour on Calais Sands, Osborne was having less luck.

The noise of gunfire and shattering bottles was drowned out by the groaning, creaking, screeching and cracking of the ice pack where it ground against the shore ice. Killigrew crossed to where Petty Officer Ågård stood on the quarterdeck. 'Any sign of a lead opening up?' he asked him in Swedish.

The ice quartermaster shook his head. 'Normally we could hope for this wind to push the Middle Pack away from the shore, sir, but it doesn't seem to be working,' Ågård replied in the same language. 'There must be strong ocean currents at work.'

A brawny, blond-haired Swede with blue eyes narrowed from years of squinting across the wide oceans, Olaf Ågård spoke perfectly good English – albeit with the East Riding accent of the Hull whalers he had first gone to sea on – but whenever Killigrew served with a foreigner he made a point of paying for lessons in that man's language. This was his third voyage with Ågård, and he was becoming fluent in the tongue.

Ågård had served as a quartermaster on their last voyage together, and with the Arctic experience he had gained during the ten years he had spent on the Greenland fishery he was well qualified for his current role of ice quartermaster, guiding the ship between the floes from the crow's nest at the foretop and advising the captain on the quirks and perils of the ice.

'Those poor devils out on the ice, Ågård – the survivors of the *Carl Gustaf* – what chance do they stand?'

'Difficult to say, sir. If they've got warm clothes, vittles . . . they could stand every chance. I remember back in eighteen thirty there were nineteen ships sunk trying to get through the Middle Pack, including mine – a fifth of the entire whaling fleet. And not a man came to any harm. Baffin's Fair, we called it: there were football matches on the ice, drinking and dancing, more like a celebration than a disaster. But the Arctic's a capricious place, sir. You never know what she's going to throw at you next. Those survivors from the *Carl Gustaf* might freeze to death, be attacked by polar bears, or go crazy and start killing one another. It's been known to happen.' Ågård shook his head again. 'Why don't we just send a sledge party to pick them up, sir?'

'I've already suggested that,' said Killigrew. 'The Old Man's

54

against it. Says it's too dangerous: he can't risk losing that many men.'

'I admit it would be risky, sir,' agreed the ice quartermaster. 'But if we wanted to avoid danger, none of us should have come to the Arctic in the first place. It's better than doing nothing.'

Killigrew glowered at the deck. Ågård was right. He sighed. 'I want seven volunteers for a sledging party to try to rescue the men on the ice. Ask Orsini to fetch my pepperboxes. And for God's sake, be discreet.'

Understanding, Ågård grinned. '*Ja, min herre.*'

'How are the Danish lessons coming along, sir?' Osborne asked Killigrew.

'That's not Danish, that's Swedish,' said Cavan. 'Although why a man would want to learn either language is beyond me. Most Danes and Swedes speak pretty good English, anyhow.'

'A naval officer cannot know too many foreign languages, Mr Cavan,' said Killigrew.

The steward came up on deck a couple of minutes later, bearing Killigrew's brace of six-barrelled revolving pistols. 'Your pepperboxes, *signore.*'

'Much obliged, Orsini.'

'Are you going to join us for a little target practice, sir?' asked Osborne, indicating the latest empty bottle that swung from the yard-arm.

Killigrew had no such intention: his marksmanship was almost as bad as Osborne's, and he suspected the bombardier knew it. But since Orsini had brought him the pistols rather sooner than he had anticipated, he had to do something to account for them rather than risk having Cavan and Osborne guess he intended to lead a sledging party on to the ice without Pettifer's permission. One way or another, he knew that disobeying a direct order would lead to his court martial, but he would have preferred it to happen after he had a chance to rescue the remaining survivors of the *Carl Gustaf.*

He drew a bead on the swinging bottle with one of his pepperboxes.

'You're not still using those antiques, are you, sir?' asked Osborne.

'They've given me perfectly good service until now,' replied

Killigrew. 'Besides, my Coopers have six shots to your Deane and Adams' five.'

'Maybe so, sir, but the Deane and Adams is a lot lighter than one of your pepperboxes; and the trigger action isn't as stiff either.' Osborne held out one of his revolvers. 'Why don't you give it a try, sir?'

Killigrew swapped his pepperbox for the bombardier's revolver and drew a bead on the swinging bottle. The trick was to aim for the bottle where it reached the outmost extent of each oscillation, where it hung still for a split second before swinging back. He waited, getting the timing right in his head, took a deep breath, and as the bottle started to swing back into his line of fire he squeezed the trigger. As the hammer came back, the cylinder rotated through seventy-two degrees, bringing the next primed and loaded chamber into line with the barrel . . .

He had a blinding flash of inspiration.

The hammer came down and the gun went off. The bottle swung back across the deck, untouched.

'I've got it!' exclaimed Killigrew.

'Er . . . I don't think so, sir,' said Cavan.

'No, you blockhead! I mean, I've just thought of a way to get through the Middle Pack into the North Water!' He tossed the revolver back at Osborne – who clutched it awkwardly to his chest and exchanged bewildered glances with Cavan – and ran across the deck to the fore hatch.

'Doc!'

It was a long-standing tradition, dating back to the time when ships had carried no surgeons and the ship's cook had had charge of the medicine chest, that the cook was known as 'the doctor'. Tommo Armitage was no exception, although such was the quality of his cooking that he was more likely to send a man to a sick bed than help him out of it. Not that anyone would have dared to say as much to his face: the cook had a violent temperament, and a habit of gesticulating with whatever he was holding at the time – usually a meat cleaver.

Armitage pulled aside the curtain of Fear-Nought cloth across the entrance to the galley below and looked up to where Killigrew stood over the fore hatch. 'Sir?'

'That cake you're baking to celebrate the anniversary of the

Queen's accession – is it round?'

'Round, sir? Yes, sir. Don't know that I know any other shape for a cake, 'cepting maybe square for weddings.'

'Bring it to the captain's day-room.'

'Now, sir? It ain't finished.'

'Doesn't matter. And on your way, could you tell Ågård to forget the instructions I gave him a couple of minutes ago? And tell him to join me outside the captain's quarters.'

'Aye, aye, sir.' Armitage was bewildered, but he knew better than to waste time with stupid questions when the lieutenant was in this frame of mind.

Killigrew made his way back to the quarterdeck. 'Mr Cavan, would you be so good as to take the watch?'

Cavan nodded.

Killigrew turned to Osborne. 'Come with me.'

The two of them descended aft, and the lieutenant thrust his head into the chart-room, where he found the master working on his charts. 'Could you join us, Yelverton?' asked Killigrew. 'I want your opinion on something.'

'Certainly.' The master joined Killigrew and Osborne in the corridor, where the lieutenant knocked on the door to Pettifer's quarters. The sound set Horatia off barking at once. Killigrew glanced over his shoulder at the other two and all three of them rolled their eyes: it did not take much to set the dachshund off barking. The twelve husky dogs put together did not make half as much noise as Horatia on her own.

'Who is it?' called Pettifer.

'Lieutenant Killigrew, sir, with Mr Yelverton and Bombardier Osborne. I think I may have thought of a way to get us through the ice.'

'Come in, come in!'

The three of them entered the day-room where they found Pettifer going through some papers at his desk.

Killigrew knew that this expedition was the first time Pettifer had had a command since he had been promoted to commander. He had been a lieutenant at the time of the China War, and had served with distinction by all accounts. His promotion had effectively ended his career: the navy had more captains than it had ships for them to command. Like Killigrew, Pettifer lacked 'interest' – perhaps that was one reason why he got on so well with his lieutenant: they both disdained the politicking that went on at the Admiralty – so when it came to handing out commands his name was always a long way down the list. But last year Pettifer had met Lady Franklin at an Admiralty levee, and she had decided that he was just the man to rescue her husband. Some said that when it came to Arctic expeditions, Lady Franklin carried more political weight than all the Lords of the Admiralty combined.

No one could say that Pettifer was not qualified for command of an exploring ship. As a midshipman, he had taken part in surveying the Great Lakes of North America after the great war with France, and afterwards had helped Lieutenant Owen carry out his great survey of Africa: charting the Dark Continent's coasts from the Gambia to the Horn of Africa, an exercise that had taken five years and lost so many lives to yellow fever that someone had once commented that the 300 charts prepared by the expedition had been drawn and coloured with blood. Killigrew was not concerned that this was Pettifer's first voyage to the Arctic – he was in the same boat himself – but it did give him pause for thought that this was the commander's first command in nearly ten years. A good deal had changed in that time.

Pettifer stood up and crossed to the table, gesturing for them to join him. 'Be seated, gentlemen. A way through the ice? I'm intrigued, Mr Killigrew!'

'With your permission, sir, I'd like to wait until Ågård's joined us. I'd like to hear his opinion on this matter, if I may.'

They sat down at the table and presently Armitage stumped in on his wooden leg, with the base of a sponge cake on a plate. 'It ain't finished yet, sir. I've still got to put the icing on it.'

'It's all right, Doc, we don't need that great a degree of verisimilitude. Put it on the table,' Killigrew told him. 'With your permission, sir?'

'What's this for, Killigrew?' asked Pettifer.

'I need this to explain my idea, sir. Sorry, Doc: looks like you're going to have to bake another cake for the anniversary of Her Majesty's accession.'

'Aye, aye, sir.' The cook placed the cake on the table with a sigh, and stumped out.

The door from the captain's cabin opened and Ursula Weiss emerged, her auburn hair tousled, sleep in her blue eyes. 'What is going on?' she asked.

'Sorry to have disturbed you, ma'am,' said Pettifer. 'Mr Killigrew thinks he may have thought of a way to get us through the ice.'

'Perhaps Frau Weiss would be good enough to join us, sir?' suggested Killigrew. 'She must have sailed through the Middle Pack a number of times. I'd value her opinion.'

Ursula looked stunned; clearly she was not used to being consulted about anything. But she took the chair that Killigrew pulled out for her at the table. Pettifer was too polite to comment when she started straightening the edges of some of his papers, lining them up so they were exactly parallel with the sides of the table.

Ågård arrived and was invited to join the others at the table. 'All right, Killigrew,' said Pettifer. 'Now we're all here . . . what the deuce is all this about?'

'It's so simple, sir, I wonder I didn't think of it before.' Killigrew reached behind him, took a weighty tome down from the bookshelves, and placed it on the table. 'Imagine, if you will, this book is the shore ice.' He pushed the plate with the cake on it up against the book. 'This cake is the Middle Pack. And this nut . . .' he took a walnut from the bowl at the centre of the table, '. . . is the *Venturer*.' He placed it in the angle between the cake and the book. 'As we all know, the Middle Pack rotates anti-clockwise, rubbing up against the shore ice.' Killigrew turned the plate.

'Try not to get crumbs on Sir John Franklin's first *Narrative*,' chided Pettifer.

'Sorry, sir.' Killigrew realised that Armitage had neglected to bring a cake slice. 'May I borrow your letter opener, sir?'

'By all means.'

'We cut a dock in the pack ice, thus.' Killigrew cut two parallel lines into the cake, opposite the walnut, about three inches apart. He then cut a third line, joining the tops of the first two cuts, and lifted out the oblong of sponge cake. 'We sail the *Venturer* into the dock, thus.' He put the walnut in the middle of the indentation in the sponge cake. 'And then we just wait for the rotation of the Middle Pack to carry us round until we can sail out into the North Water.' He turned the cake so that the indentation passed Sir John's *Narrative*, and then pushed the walnut out again on the other side. Then he put the piece of cake he had cut out into his mouth and munched it. His smug expression faded rapidly: Armitage's sponge could have been used for ballast.

'By George!' said Pettifer. 'It's quite insane, of course. But it might just work.' He turned to the ice quartermaster. 'What do you think, Ågård?'

'The ice isn't one cohesive mass, sir. It's made up of masses of separate floes, all jumbled together. When the mouth of that dock grinds against the shore ice, we may find that the whole thing collapses. And you know what will happen then.' He picked the walnut off the table, put it in his mouth and cracked it between his teeth. The graphic demonstration made Yelverton wince.

'But if we chose a strong section of the floe?' Pettifer asked eagerly.

Yelverton shook his head. 'It won't work, sir. Let's see, the edge of the pack moves at about a quarter of a knot. We'd want the dock to be deep: the mouth of it will almost certainly collapse, but if we're far enough back, that shouldn't make any odds. Say, four times the length of the *Venturer*, about two hundred yards. How thick would you say the ice is here, Ågård?'

'It varies, sir. About four or five feet, I should say.'

'Let's assume the worst and say five; better to go too far back than not leave ourselves enough time to finish cutting the dock and get the *Venturer* inside before the mouth passes the shore ice. Even if we have two teams cutting the ice, it'll take about a minute to cut through a foot of ice of that thickness – again, let's play it safe and say two minutes. With the men taking ten-minute breaks every hour, we're going to have to allow at least thirty hours to cut the dock, I should say. With the pack rotating at half a knot an hour, that means we need to sail back for seven and a half nautical miles to give ourselves a sufficiently narrow margin of error. I'm sorry, Killigrew. It was a good notion, but we simply don't have enough open water.'

The lieutenant cleared his throat. 'There is a quicker way to cut a dock in the ice . . .'

'You've been itching to do this ever since we saw Ned Belcher blow up them empty tar barrels on the parade ground at Woolwich, ain't you, sir?' Petty Officer Molineaux commented with a grin.

'That's "Sir Edward" to you,' Killigrew chided him, stripping the gutta-percha covering from the copper wires. He had had to take off his chamois-lined leather gauntlets to handle the knife, but the weather continued to be mild and there was little danger of frostbite. He connected the wires to the tin canister – six inches in diameter, containing two and a half pounds of gunpowder – and carefully lowered it into the hole drilled in the ice, about three feet deep. 'Gather this snow off the top of the ice and pack it in the hole, tightly. Be careful not to break the connection with the canisters.'

'Aye, aye, sir.'

Killigrew picked up the reel of wire and spooled it out, retreating to where Pettifer stood with Osborne, Ågård, Endicott and O'Houlihan by the galvanic batteries. 'All ready, Killigrew?' asked Pettifer.

'Molineaux's just finishing the last one now, sir.'

They had placed no fewer than eight charges in the ice, strategically positioned at points in the dock that the carpenter's mate had mapped out on the ice. Killigrew handed the red end of the last wire to Osborne, who connected it to another. 'Now, you're sure this will work?' Killigrew asked him.

'The galvanic batteries will explode the charges, sir,' asserted the bombardier. 'Whether or not they successfully blast out a dock sufficiently large to take the *Venturer* – and strong enough to resist the pressures of the pack where it meets the shore ice – remains to be seen.'

More of an engineer than an artilleryman, Bombardier Bernard Osborne had been assigned to the *Venturer* to work the various newfangled devices they had brought with them in their quest to find Franklin. He had great faith in modern technology, and believed there was nothing that could not be achieved by technical know-how. Killigrew preferred to reserve his judgement: it puzzled him that a civilisation that could invent the telegraph and the steam-engine could not come up with a better plan for finding Franklin than an unmanned balloon for scattering useless messages.

Molineaux had finished packing in the last charge and was walking across the ice towards them. Pettifer waved impatiently for him to get a move on, and the petty officer broke into a gentle trot, taking care not to slip on the ice.

'Are you sure you used enough gunpowder?' asked Pettifer.

'In my experience, sir,' Ågård said, grinning, 'the danger with Mr Killigrew is not whether he used too little explosive, but too much.'

'We *are* safe here, aren't we?' asked the commander. 'I mean, we're not too close?'

'Trust me, sir,' said Killigrew. 'I've been blowing things up for years.'

'Is everyone else clear?' Pettifer asked as Molineaux approached.

Ågård handed Killigrew a telescope so he could sweep the ice to make sure that everyone else was back on board the *Venturer*, anchored to the pack ice a safe distance away. 'Looks clear, but let's make sure, shall we? A shrill warning blast on your call, Molineaux, if you please.'

Molineaux blew into his call. 'All clear,' he announced.

'Everyone knows to stay where they are until we signal the all clear?' asked Pettifer.

'Everyone knows, sir.'

'All right, let's, er . . . let's do it.'

Osborne crouched over the galvanic batteries. 'Now, I've connected the charges in parallel, so they should all explode simultaneously when you touch these two wires together.' He offered the wires to Pettifer.

The commander shook his head. 'Good Lord, no! Gunpowder I don't mind, but this dashed electricity stuff . . . Killigrew, perhaps you'd care to do the honours?'

'With pleasure, sir.'

'Your hands are wet, sir,' observed Osborne. 'Dry them with your handkerchief. Salt water is an electrical conductor. There. Now, be sure to hold the wires by the covering; don't touch the wires themselves or you'll get a shock.'

'Ready?' asked Killigrew.

Everyone nodded. Osborne turned his back on the charges, folding his arms over his ears, eyes screwed shut.

Killigrew touched the wires together.

Nothing happened.

He tried again, and again. Still nothing.

'Get on with it, man!' said Pettifer.

'It's not working, sir,' said Killigrew. He tapped Osborne on the shoulder.

The bombardier looked up. 'Did it work?'

Killigrew touched the wires together in front of his face. 'No.'

Osborne peered towards the charges. 'I don't understand it . . . There must be a break in the circuit.'

'Can you find it?'

'Of course! We'll have to test each of the wires individually, mind you . . .'

'Oh, for heaven's sake!' snapped Pettifer. 'How long will that take?'

'A few hours at the most, sir,' Osborne assured him.

'In a few hours, sir, the dock we've laid out will be level with the shore ice,' warned Ågård.

'Suggest we proceed with Bickford's, sir?' said Killigrew.

'I agree,' said Pettifer. 'Damn your blasted newfangled galvanic batteries, Osborne! We'll do it the old-fashioned way.'

'Fetch a spool of Bickford's safety fuse from the *Venturer*, O'Houlihan,' ordered Killigrew. 'And ask for four volunteers: it'll take eight of us to light all the fuses at once.'

'Why not have all the fuses connected to a central point, where you can light them all at once?' asked Pettifer.

Killigrew smiled. 'I'd have to check, sir, but I'm fairly certain we don't have eight hundred yards of safety fuse on board. Disconnect those batteries, Osborne, Molineaux, Endicott – you two start digging up those charges so we can connect the fuses to them.'

Molineaux and Endicott started to walk towards the charges, but Endicott stopped after a couple of paces and turned back. 'Begging your pardon, sir, but how can we be sure the charges won't go off while we're digging them up?'

'The wires are disconnected from the batteries, Endicott,' Osborne assured him. 'There's no possibility of the charges going off.'

'Mightn't there be a delayed reaction, sir?'

'You're quite safe,' Pettifer assured him, and glowered at Osborne. 'The entire point of igniting gunpowder by galvanic charge is that the explosion is instantaneous.'

Molineaux and Endicott were still leery about returning to the charges, until Killigrew going with them helped to put their minds at ease. They dug the charges out of the ice, and O'Houlihan returned, carrying the safety fuse and accompanied by Able Seamen Hughes, Smith and Smith. The last two – both baptised John, differentiated by their shipmates as Jacko and Johnno – even looked alike, despite the disparity in their ages; they might have been mistaken for father and son. They were not related, but they had served as shipmates together for so long that sometimes they caught themselves talking in unison.

Measuring the safety fuse between his outstretched arms, Killigrew cut it into eight lengths. When he had finished, all that was left was a five-inch length of fuse that he thrust into one of his pockets. 'These should give us three minutes to get clear,' he told the men, handing out the fuses. 'I don't suppose you thought to bring any slow matches, O'Houlihan?'

'Right here, sir.'

'Well done.'

They fixed the fuses to the charges, and gathered around Killigrew at the centre. The lieutenant struck an ordinary match, and lit eight slow matches. 'I'll give the signal by firing a shot from my pepperbox,' he told them, handing out the smouldering matches. 'When you hear that, light your fuse and move back to where the captain's waiting. Walk, don't run, hoist in? If anyone slips and cracks his skull on the ice, he needn't expect me to come back for him. You've got three minutes to get clear: that's all the time in the world, so there's no hurry. All right, cut along.'

He waited until they were all in position. 'Ready?' he called.

'Aye, aye, sir!' they chorused.

'Stand by!' Killigrew drew his pepperbox and aimed it at the ice by his feet. He pulled the trigger and the report echoed through the Arctic silence. The ratings lit their respective fuses and set off back to where Pettifer waited with Osborne and Ågård. Killigrew lingered, making sure all eight of them were ahead of him, so that if anyone did stumble and injure himself, he would see and be able to go to the man's assistance before it was too late.

'I said walk, don't run, Smith!' he bellowed.

'I *am* walking, sir!' protested Johnno.

Killigrew grimaced. 'The other Smith!'

Jacko checked his pace.

Once they were clear of the charges, Molineaux fell into step beside him. 'Reckon it'll work this time, sir?'

'I don't see why not.'

The charges did not explode simultaneously – using fuses instead of the galvanic batteries had made that impossible – but it was a testament to the efficiency of Bickford's safety fuse that they all went off within a couple of seconds of one another. There was a succession of overlapping blasts, flames shooting fountains of ice spicules high into the air, and the roar of the explosions echoed off the granite, snow-capped cliffs on the Greenland shore. A great cheer went up from the men watching on the deck of the *Venturer*.

Travelling through the floe like a ripple through water, the shock wave hit the men standing on the ice a moment later. They were all thrown to the ice. Killigrew sat up and let out a whoop of exhilaration.

'All right, Killigrew, try to show some decorum,' chided Pettifer.

The lieutenant grinned boyishly. 'Sorry, sir. Got caught up in the excitement of the moment.'

Pettifer picked himself up and rubbed his posterior gingerly. 'Is everyone all right?'

They all replied in the affirmative.

'Good! Let's see if that's done the trick.'

As they approached, Killigrew's heart sank when he could see no difference except some holes blown in the ice. 'It hasn't worked!' protested Osborne, disappointed.

'Yes it has – look!' Ågård pointed. The ice had fractured throughout the area they had marked off, the great chunks resting where they had started like the pieces of a jigsaw.

It was the work of an hour to float all the pieces out of the dock, erecting masts on some of the larger chunks so they could sail them out like rafts. One segment had not been blown free of the surrounding ice, but it took only three hours for two teams of a dozen men each to cut away the remaining chunks using ice-saws suspended from tripods and weighted at the bottom.

The dock was less than half a mile from where the pack ground against the shore ice by the time they manoeuvred the *Venturer* inside under steam. The men on the ice packed up all their gear and passed it back to the ship, which moored to the ice at the rear of the dock using ice-anchors. Killigrew was making sure no one had been left behind when he saw Ågård wandering about on the ice behind the mouth of the dock.

'Everything all right, Ågård?'

'You realise, sir, that if the explosive charges have fractured the surrounding ice, then dock or no dock, the floes will collapse on the ship and crush her as if she were made of balsa?'

Killigrew smiled thinly. 'I was trying not to think about it.'

IV

The North Water

They returned on board the *Venturer*. Now there was nothing to do but wait for the pack itself to carry them through to the North Water – or else crush them like an egg in a meat-grinder.

The moving pack seemed to take for ever to carry them round to where it ground against the shore. Everyone was on deck, wrapped up in their warmest clothing, watching, waiting to see what would happen, well aware of how badly things might go wrong. Like the crew of the *Carl Gustaf*, the *Venturer*'s men had had spare sets of clothes stowed on the upper deck in kitbags ever since they had rounded Cape Farewell, and the ship's boats were all in their davits ready for any emergency.

Cavan stood at the bulwark and watched the grinding ice approach in the distance, squinting against the glare of the sun on the snow. 'What do you reckon our chances of making it through are, Latimer?'

'Oh, I should say about three to one,' the clerk replied cheerfully. Despite his chronic hypochondria, Latimer was a young man of sanguine temperament, one of life's eternal optimists. Perhaps because he spent so much time worrying about imaginary ailments, he had no fear left when it came to real dangers.

Or perhaps he was just too daft to realise how much danger they were in.

Killigrew turned to Pettifer. 'I suggest we start bringing some provisions up from the hold, sir, in case we have to "do a flit".'

'Good thinking,' acknowledged Pettifer. 'Latimer! Organise the men into work parties. I want six months' victuals brought up on deck.'

'Aye, aye, sir.'

The boatswain set the men to their work. Whether or not it would do them any good if the *Venturer* was nipped remained to be seen: if they went down as fast as the *Carl Gustaf* must have done, they were probably wasting their time. But at least it kept the men from watching the maelstrom of ice drawing ever closer and dwelling on thoughts of what might go wrong if luck was against them.

'Here comes the moment of truth.' Ågård nodded to where they approached the grinding ice. The cacophony was awful as the edges of the pack twisted, buckled, bent, rose up over one another and then crashed down again, shattering into smithereens. Standing nearby on deck, Molineaux began to recite Coleridge in a doom-filled monotone:

> '*The ice was here, the ice was there,*
> *The ice was all around:*
> *It cracked and growled, and roared and howled,*
> *Like noises in a swound!*'

Even with a hull reinforced with three overlapping layers of wood that made it a total of ten inches thick, and strengthened with iron stanchions as opposed to more conventional wooden ones, the *Venturer* was not immune to a nip. Throughout the voyage from England, Pettifer had put his men through countless drills so that each and every man knew his role in the event of an emergency. But in their present position, there was nothing for them to do but wait and watch tensely, praying it never came.

Killigrew remembered reading the *Argonautica* of Apollonius of Rhodes when he had been a boy, including how the *Argo* had sailed through the Symplegades – the clashing rocks – and wondering how he could have passed such a test had he been in Jason's shoes; or his single sandal, at any rate. This was the closest equivalent he was ever likely to encounter in the real world; he wondered if he had found the right solution.

The ice creaked all around them under the strain of the massive pressure. Osborne was muttering the Lord's Prayer under his breath, over and over again, while Marine Private Arthur Walsh told the beads on his rosary. Killigrew thrust his hands in his pockets so he could cross his fingers without anyone noticing. Ågård stood a short way in front of the lieutenant, his hands clasped behind his back, his knuckles white. Could it possibly be that even the fearless Swede was worried?

Killigrew had known stress before – pursuing slavers off the Guinea Coast, the drawn-out tension of a prolonged stern-chase that could end in a bloody skirmish – but nothing like this. It was always the helplessness that got to him, and he had never felt more helpless than he did now: the die was cast, and he could only wait to see how it fell.

Minutes crawled past like hours. Where the floes ground against one another, the edges of the iron-hard ice crumbled into powder. Then a loud screech – like the crack of doom – sounded above the groans of the grinding floes, and a chunk of ice broke away from the pack to the immediate left of the dock.

'The ice!' yelled someone. 'It's giving way!'

Something snapped inside Ågård. 'That's it!' he screamed. 'Abandon ship!'

Killigrew was so stunned by the ice quartermaster's outburst that at first all he could do was stare open-mouthed. Then Ågård started to run for the side, galvanising the lieutenant into action. He strode across the deck and caught up with the ice quartermaster by the bulwark, seizing his arm and holding him cast.

'Belay that, Ågård!' said Killigrew. 'We're not nipped yet!' Normally he would not have been able to restrain a man as big as the Swede, but one glare into Ågård's fear-filled eyes warned the ice quartermaster to get a grip on himself. 'Stand fast, lads!' he called to the men.

Everyone on deck – which was everyone on board, the *Venturer*'s entire crew of thirty plus Frau Weiss and Jakob Kracht – was staring at Ågård. Killigrew knew what the hands were thinking: if Ågård had cause to be afraid, then perhaps they really were in trouble.

In spite of the cold weather, he could feel sweat trickling down his spine as he watched the huge chunk of ice – a right-angled triangle fifty feet on its longest side – being forced into the mouth of the dock by the shore ice. One angle of the floe came within ten yards of the *Venturer*'s bows, thrusting towards them like the blade of a dagger. Then the triangle was caught in the mouth of the dock, wedged, unable to come any deeper. The shore ice got under the far edge of the triangle somehow, tipping it up with a ghastly crackling noise so that the angle towards the ship was forced under the water. There was another loud snap, like the blast of a carronade, and then the pack was floating free of the shore ice. On the other side of the triangle of ice, a lead of open water threaded its way northwards between the pack and the shore ice.

Killigrew breathed again.

'That's it,' said Petty Officer Qualtrough, the senior ice quartermaster. 'We're through.'

A huge cheer went up from the men on the deck. 'We made it!' exclaimed Yelverton. 'By God, we actually made it!'

In his excitement, Osborne forgot himself and grasped Killigrew by the hand, pumping it vigorously. 'Well done, sir! My hat off to you. It actually worked!'

Killigrew took out his handkerchief to mop away the sweat that trickled down from beneath the brim of his cap, before it froze on his face. 'Did you ever doubt it?' he asked with a sickly grin.

He turned to where Ågård stood. Crimson-faced, the petty officer stumbled below deck.

'Very disappointed in Ågård, Mr Killigrew,' Pettifer remarked as soon as the *Venturer* was underway once more, threading her way through the lead between the pack and the shore ice.

'I know what you mean, sir. But before you take any action, I feel I should point out that Olaf Ågård is one of the bravest men I've ever known. He's served on every ship I have. He was with me when we stormed the walls of Chinkiang-fu. He was at my side when we attacked the Dyak stronghold at Karangan. I've seen him board pirate junks in the South China Seas as calmly as you or I would board an omnibus.'

'I don't doubt what you're telling me is true, Killigrew. But you'll own that it's a little difficult to square that image of him with the scene we've just witnessed. Clearly the fellow's lost his nerve.'

'I confess I'm astonished, sir. I can only hope it was a one-off.'

'Hoping isn't good enough. It's fortunate for us that the rest of our lads are more stout-hearted. He might have sparked off a panic; and then where would we be? Cowardice like that could get us all killed: if he hasn't the sand, he should never have volunteered for this expedition.'

'He volunteered reluctantly, sir. I had to talk him into it. I was puzzled at the time . . . Sir, I was the one who recommended him to you. If you're going to blame anyone, you should blame me.'

'Don't castigate yourself, Killigrew. We all make mistakes. I was not obliged to accept your recommendation.'

'Exactly, sir. We all make mistakes – well, I tell the men under my command that they're entitled to one mistake and one mistake only. In the fifteen years I've known Ågård, that's the first time I've ever known him put a foot wrong.'

'You think I should give him another chance?'

'Let me talk to him, sir.'

Pettifer sighed. 'Very well.' He grimaced. 'It's not as if I can dismiss him now. Where would I find a replacement around here?'

'Thank you, sir,' Killigrew said with feeling.

Pettifer returned below deck. 'You have the watch, Mr Cavan,' said Killigrew.

'Aye, aye, sir.'

Killigrew turned to Molineaux. 'Would you ask Ågård to join me in the chart-room?' No need to ask the boatswain's mate to be discreet: Molineaux understood.

The lieutenant made his way below. He found Yelverton in the chart-room, staring at a framed calotype of his wife and children. The master quickly tried to conceal it, but Killigrew was not going to let him off so easily. 'Feeling homesick so soon, Mr Yelverton?'

The master grinned. A beefy-faced salt-horse squire who had come aft through the hawse-hole to gain promotion to the

71

quarterdeck, Giles Yelverton had been the master on Killigrew's last two commissions. Although the two of them were too far apart in both age and class to be friends, they respected one another for their ability at their different jobs, and it was a great reassurance to have the dependable Yelverton in charge of the *Venturer*'s navigation on this voyage into the great unknown.

'Every time I find myself regretting coming on this expedition, I look at that calotype to remind me of what I left behind . . .' he grinned ruefully, '. . . and then the Arctic doesn't seem so bad.'

Killigrew laughed. 'Mind if I borrow the chart-room for a few minutes?' Although as first lieutenant he had the right to go wherever he pleased on board the *Venturer*, barring the captain's quarters, the chart-room was Yelverton's domain just as much as the sick-berth was Strachan's, and Killigrew considered it courteous to get his permission before evicting him, no matter how temporarily.

'By all means.' Yelverton stood up. 'Going to have a word with Ågård?' he guessed shrewdly.

The lieutenant nodded.

'Go easy on him, Killigrew. We were all scared; Ågård was the only one who showed it, that's all. It would be wrong to punish him because we've come to expect him to be so fearless, when really he's just as human as the rest of us. And you owe him.'

'I hadn't forgotten it.'

As Yelverton squeezed out of the chart-room, Ågård arrived and knocked on the open door. 'Come in, Ågård,' said Killigrew. 'Close the door behind you.'

The ice quartermaster complied. 'May I speak, sir?'

Killigrew nodded.

Ågård took off his cap and twisted it in his hands before him, the very image of contrition. 'I just wanted to say I'm sorry, sir, that's all. I lost my head. There was no excuse for it.'

There was no point in berating the ice quartermaster. Ågård had made a fool of himself, and he knew it. For the rest of this voyage he would have to live with that knowledge; and for a man like Ågård, that was punishment enough.

'There was every excuse for it, Ågård. But as ice quartermaster, you of all people should be the one to keep his head in a situation like that. If the others see you panic, what can they be expected to think?'

'I know, sir. I should never have volunteered for this expedition. Whatever punishment the captain sees fit to give me, I'll accept it.'

'Of course you will. But I've spoken to the captain: he's prepared to give you another chance.'

If Killigrew had expected Ågård to be effuse in his gratitude, he was disappointed. 'I'm not sure I deserve it, sir.'

'The fact of the matter is, until we rejoin the rest of the squadron, Qualtrough and yourself are the only men with experience of the ice we have access to. But I think the captain would be prepared to give you a second chance even if that were not the case. You've never let me down in the past. Make sure it never happens again.'

'I will, sir. Thank you.'

'Don't thank me, Ågård. Thank Commander Pettifer.'

'Yes, sir. I will.' The ice quartermaster started to turn to leave.

'Wait a moment, Ågård. There's just one thing I want to know.'

'Sir?'

'Of all the men on board the *Venturer* who might have panicked . . . why you?'

Ågård considered the question, and then shrugged. 'Perhaps because apart from Qualtrough, sir, I'm the only one who really understands the dangers.'

'He's dead.' Bähr took off Lenz Noldner's woollen cap and draped it over his face.

'Better put him with Tegeder, then.' Sørensen gestured to where they had laid Stephan Tegeder out on the ice a short distance away from their camp.

'Shouldn't we bury them?' asked Ziegler.

'Bury them in the ice?' Bähr said incredulously. 'We haven't got the tools, and even if we did, I suggest we'd be better off conserving our energy. I think it's reasonable to assume we're going to need it.'

'I meant bury them at sea.' Ziegler gestured to the open

water nearby. 'The least we can do is give them a Christian burial.'

'I wouldn't recommend it,' said Sørensen. 'For one thing, we haven't got anything to put them in or anything to weigh them down with. And for another, we might need them later.'

'*Need* them?' Ziegler echoed. 'They're *dead*, Bjørn! What possible good can they do . . . Oh!' The colour drained from his face.

'You're not suggesting we . . .?' asked Fischbein. Kapitän Weiss' nephew, Ignatz Fischbein had been one of the half-deck boys, apprenticed to his uncle to learn the craft of whaling. A freckle-faced, snub-nosed youth, he was not yet out of his teens and far too young to be stranded on the ice pack with a shattered elbow, waiting to die.

'The custom of the sea, lad,' Sørensen told him. 'Sacrifice the dead to spare the living.'

Fischbein shook his head. 'I couldn't do it. Not . . . not poor Stephan and Lenz. I know their families, Herr Sørensen! How could I ever look them in the face again, with such a crime against nature on my conscience?'

'Not now, perhaps,' agreed Sørensen. 'But you'll change your mind soon enough when the hunger pangs start to gnaw at your innards.'

'Well, that's a long way in the future, if it ever even comes to that,' said Ziegler. 'For now we have plenty of food to keep us going. What day is it today, Dr Bähr?'

'Tuesday, I think.'

Ziegler nodded. 'Four days since Liebnitz left us.'

'Early days yet,' said Sørensen.

'How's Immermann doing?' Ziegler asked Bähr.

'Not good.' The doctor lowered his voice. 'He's got a bad fever. He's not long for this world, I'm afraid.'

'May I speak, sir?' Sørensen asked Ziegler. The third mate nodded. 'I do not think we should pin all our hopes on Herr Liebnitz, sir. Even if by some miracle he does make it to Upernavik, there's no guarantee that any ship that he can persuade to come looking for us will make it through the ice. We can't wait here for ever for a rescue that might never come. We can't make it to Upernavik on foot, but if we can get far enough

74

south, there's a chance we'll reach some whalers waiting to take the ice at the Devil's Thumb.'

'And what about him?' Ziegler gestured at Immermann. 'Are you suggesting we drag him over the ice?'

'No, sir,' said Sørensen. 'We leave him here. You heard what the doctor said: he's dead already. We sacrifice the dead to spare the living.'

'What about the provisions?' Ziegler indicated the barrels of victuals they had salvaged from the water. 'We can't carry all that with us. Even if we only take enough to get us as far as the Devil's Thumb, what if we get there and find there aren't any ships? We'll be no better off than we are now. In fact we'll be worse off: at least here we're in no danger of running out of food.'

Immermann muttered something under his breath.

'That food isn't going to last for ever, *mein Herr*,' warned Sørensen.

'Wait a moment,' said Fischbein. 'Eugen's trying to say something!'

'Leave me,' rasped Immermann. 'No sense you all dying, just because I didn't have the sense to get out of the way of a falling spar . . .' He tried to say more, but a fit of coughing racked his body and blood bubbled up between his lips. He closed his eyes and lay still.

'Is he dead?' asked Ziegler.

Bähr felt for Immermann's wrist. 'No, but his pulse is damned weak.'

'What's that?' asked Fischbein, gazing off towards the south. No one paid any attention to him.

'I said: his pulse is damned weak,' repeated Bähr.

'No!' said Fischbein. 'Look! Over there!'

Ziegler stared in the direction Fischbein indicated. 'Smoke!'

'Another ship crushed in the ice, most likely,' said Sørensen. Even when a whaler that was nipped did not sink immediately, it was the custom on the Greenland fishery to burn a wrecked ship once it had been stripped of anything salvageable.

'There must be others stranded on the ice like us,' said Fischbein. 'Perhaps we can reach them . . .'

'Aye,' agreed Sørensen. 'Maybe they weren't able to salvage

75

as much food as we were. Maybe we'd find ourselves having to share what food we have with fifty of them.' He glanced speculatively towards the distant column of smoke. 'Wait a moment!' he exclaimed. 'That's not a burning ship! That's smoke from a funnel: a steamer!'

'Don't be crazy,' sighed Bähr. 'There aren't any steamers in the Arctic. Whoever heard of a steam-powered whaler?'

'Shows how much you know, Herr Know-Better!' said Sørensen. 'It's not just whalers that come to the Arctic. What about the British naval ships that come to search for Franklin?'

'He's right,' said Ziegler, getting his hopes up again. 'It's a ship all right! It must be a British ship! Look, I can see the tops of her masts now!'

Those who could waved their arms frantically above their heads. 'Over here!' they yelled, even though they knew full well that the men on the ship would not be able to hear them at so great a distance.

Ziegler fired the rifle into the air. A couple of minutes later, the ship sent up a signal rocket.

'They've seen us!' The third mate was ready to sob with relief. 'We're saved!'

Two hours later Dietrich Ziegler found himself sipping coffee in the captain's day-room on board the *Venturer* with Pettifer and Killigrew.

Ziegler flushed when Ursula joined them. '*Guten Tag, Frau Weiss*,' he mumbled.

'*Guten Tag, Herr Ziegler*,' she returned. '*Wie geht's?*'

'*Danke, gut. Und Ihnen?*'

'*Gut, gut.*' She smiled apologetically. 'Perhaps out of courtesy to our guests, we should speak English, yes?'

'Please! No need to trouble on our account, Frau Weiss,' Pettifer said jovially. 'Whatever makes you feel comfortable.'

'We both speak good English, Commander Pettifer,' Ursula assured him.

The four of them sat in awkward silence. Killigrew sensed there was an atmosphere in the day-room, and not just because Ziegler and Ursula were in the company of strangers. There was more awkwardness between the two Germans than

76

between either of them and their hosts.

Ziegler cleared his throat. 'Where is Herr Liebnitz?'

Ursula lowered her eyes, rearranging the crockery on the table into some abstract geometrical pattern so she would not have to meet his gaze. 'Liebnitz did not make it, Herr Ziegler.'

He looked at her in surprise. 'What about the others? Eisenhart, Glohr, Kracht and the rest?'

'Kracht is all right. The rest ... An iceberg calved off a glacier as we rowed past, and crushed the boat. Herr Liebnitz must have been killed at once along with Bøje, Arndt and Glohr. Ohlsen managed to climb on to the iceberg with Kracht and me, but then it rolled and Ohlsen was thrown into the sea. A short while after that Eisenhart died trying to swim for the pack. Kracht and I would surely have died from the cold if Herr Killigrew and his men have not happened to chance by at that moment.'

'*Mein Gott!*' gasped Ziegler. 'I ... we are obliged to you, *Herr Leutnant*.'

It was Killigrew's turn to blush. 'Think nothing of it, Herr Ziegler. It was pure chance we happened to be passing. Anyone else would have done the same in our shoes.'

'*Gott in Himmel!*' breathed Ziegler. 'Only seven of us left? Out of forty-eight?'

'A bad business,' said Pettifer. 'But at least you're all right: that's what matters now. We'll do everything in our power to make you comfortable for as long as you are guests on board the *Venturer*. We have sufficient cabins on board for you and Dr Bähr to have one each, Herr Ziegler, once we've cleared out the stores.'

'We do not want to be any trouble, Commander Pettifer.'

'Nonsense, nonsense! No trouble at all. Delighted to be of assistance, young man. Where is Dr Bähr, Killigrew?'

'In the sick-berth, sir. Two of the men are badly injured, and the doctor insisted on going to help Strachan attend to them.'

'The rest of your men will have to sleep with the hands in the fo'c'sle,' said Pettifer. 'But there's plenty of room. We've only got a crew of thirty – most of the space is taken up with stores.'

'The chances are that the two injured men will remain in the sick-berth while they're on this ship,' said Killigrew. 'That only leaves two to sleep in the fo'c'sle: the chief harpooner and Kracht.'

'While we're on board, those of us who are able will be happy to do our fair share of any work that needs to be done,' said Ziegler. 'I'm not much of a sailor, but I can navigate; Sørensen and Kracht are both experienced hands, and I'm sure Dr Bähr will be delighted to continue helping your surgeon in the sick-berth when the need arises.'

'Not necessary, I assure you,' said Pettifer. 'You've all been through a dreadful ordeal. What you need now is rest and recuperation—' There was a knock at the door. 'Come in!'

It was Cavan. 'Sorry to intrude, sir. Ågård reports open water ahead.'

'Thank you, Mr Cavan.'

As the mate withdrew, Pettifer rose to his feet and Killigrew followed his lead. Ziegler and Ursula made to do likewise, but the captain motioned for them both to remain seated. 'Don't trouble yourselves to rise, please! Stay here for now. I must attend to some business on deck. Make yourselves at home. If there's anything you should require – anything at all – please don't hesitate to ask Orsini, our steward.' Pettifer opened the door and indicated one of the doors across the passageway. 'That's his cubby-hole. He never strays far from there for very long. If you'll come with me, Mr Killigrew . . .?'

The two naval officers put on their greatcoats and made their way up on deck to where Cavan and Yelverton waited. To the east, the open expanse of the North Water beckoned invitingly.

Pettifer took the telescope from the binnacle to survey the scene, then snapped it shut. 'Splendid, gentlemen! Well, let's get under way, shall we? Loose all sails, Mr Thwaites! Sheet home and hoist tops'ls, t'gallants'ls and royals. Free the ice-anchors.'

'We're pressing on, sir?' Killigrew asked in some surprise.

'But of course! We've come this far, haven't we? In record time too, I shouldn't wonder. Let's not squander it now.'

'I thought we might wait here for the rest of the squadron to catch up, sir.'

'We'll be waiting an awfully long time if they're ahead of us,' Pettifer pointed out with a smile.

'But no one on board the *Carl Gustaf* saw them come this way.'

'Who is to say the *Assistance* and the other ships did not find some other way through the Middle Pack?'

'Other way?' Yelverton echoed in disbelief. 'Sir, there is no other way.'

'Behind us or ahead of us, we're all bound for the same place,' Pettifer said dismissively. 'Beechey Island. Lay me a course for Lancaster Sound, Mr Yelverton.'

'Aye, aye, sir. We should be able to fetch it on a course of north-west.'

'Very good. All plain sail, Mr Killigrew. Course north-west.'

'Aye, aye, sir.'

'Forgive me for asking, sir,' said Cavan, 'but what about the spouters?'

'What about them?'

'They only came to the Arctic for a single season. It isn't fair to drag them along with us. We could be here for years.'

'What would you have me do, Mr Cavan? Sail back through the Middle Pack so we can take them back to Upernavik, after all the trouble we went to get through in the first place? Oh, don't look at me like that, Cavan! I'm not suggesting we keep them on board indefinitely. It's still early in the season. We're bound to encounter a whaler or two on our way to Beechey Island. We'll put our guests on board the first one we meet.'

'We'd stand a better chance of falling in with another whaler if we waited here for the rest of the squadron, sir,' Killigrew pointed out.

'I've already told you once: for all we know, the rest of the squadron is already well on its way to Beechey Island.'

'And if we get as far as Beechey Island without falling in with any more whalers?'

'Then what we do with our guests will be up to Sir Edward.'

'And what if you're wrong, sir? What if the squadron isn't ahead of us? What if they don't make it through the Middle Pack?'

'If they don't make it through, we'll do no more good waiting here for them than we will waiting at Beechey Island. This is a naval expedition, Mr Killigrew, and I don't intend that we should waste time at the British taxpayer's expense simply on account of seven shipwrecked whalers who can count themselves lucky we chanced by to rescue them. We have a schedule to meet, a rendezvous to make.'

The men who had descended to the ice pack to free the ice-anchors now returned to the ship. 'Anchor's aweigh, sir,' reported Molineaux.

'Hoist the jib, Mr Thwaites!' ordered Pettifer. He watched to see that all canvas was drawing, and once the *Venturer* was under way again he turned to Yelverton. 'Set course for Beechey Island.'

'Strachan, Strachan . . .' Dr Bähr mused as the two of them worked on Fischbein and Immermann respectively in the sickberth. 'No relation to the Reverend Donald Strachan, are you?'

'His son,' Strachan replied curtly. He was not proud of the association. The Reverend Donald Strachan had lived by blind faith; his son was an atheist, dedicated to rationalism and scientific observation. The fields of geology and palaeontology in particular appealed to him as demolishing his father's conviction that God had created the Universe on 26 October 4004 BC.

'Good Lord! I'm honoured. I've no children myself – ghastly things, can't abide them – but I always recommend your father's book to the husbands of expectant mothers.'

Strachan smiled thinly. He too detested children, but having been raised according to the precepts laid down in his father's best-selling work *Spare the Rod, Spoil the Child*, he would not have recommended it to anyone.

'I must congratulate you on your English, *Herr Doktor*,' Strachan told Bähr, to change the subject. 'Where did you learn it?'

'Spent twenty years doing missionary work with the British in Burma and India. Nowadays my English is better than my German. When I go back to Hanover, I have people ask me if I'm British!' He took a step back from Immermann's cot. 'Well, I've done all I can for this fellow. Not that that's much.' He glanced around the sick-berth. 'I must say, you seem to have an awful lot of stuff in here.' He cast an eye over the books on the shelves, and picked one out. '*On the Vestiges of the Natural History of Creation*. Very impressive-sounding!'

80

'It created quite a stir in the scientific community back home when it was published a few years ago.'

'What's it about?'

'It expands some of Lamarck's theories on the chain of being. About how animals seem to evolve into more developed species.'

'Orthogenesis, eh? All gammon, if you ask me. Why would God create a creature that required nature to improve on it?'

Strachan decided that now was not the time to get into a debate as to whether or not there was a God. 'Well, until someone can posit an explanation of the unknown mechanism that leads different species to develop in different ways, I'm afraid orthogenesis is just going to remain a theory, and a tenuous one at that. But one that I adhere to, nonetheless. One of the reasons I enjoy studying wildlife is that I hope it will enable me to come up with an explanation myself.'

'You're interested in wildlife?' asked Bähr. 'So am I!'

Strachan perked up. Perhaps he had misjudged the doctor. 'Really?'

'I should say so! Got a taste for it in Burma. Managed to bag myself a couple of tigers. Got quite a collection on the walls of my library, now: lions, tigers, bears . . . but never a polar bear. That's one of the reasons I decided to get a job as ship's doctor on board a whaler working the Greenland fishery. My practice seems to be more or less running itself now, and I needed a holiday. Signing on with Captain Weiss seemed like the easiest way to get passage to the polar regions. If I can bag meself a fine specimen of an *Ursus maritimus*, I shall return to Germany a happy man.'

Strachan's smile became sickly. 'Oh.' He turned to Fischbein. 'I'm afraid I'm going to have to operate on this elbow immediately.'

'*Ich verstehe nicht,*' said Fischbein. '*Ich spreche kein Englisch.*'

'*Er sagt, er muß an Ihrem Ellbogen operieren,*' Bähr told him.

'*Operieren? Wird es weh tun?*'

'*Na klar wird es weh tun. Das will ich wohl sagen!* He wants to know if it will hurt,' Bähr explained for Strachan's benefit.

'Not if I use an anaesthetic. Doctor, I wonder if you'd help me with the chloroform?'

'Chloroform, eh? I don't know, all this newfangled stuff. Everything seems to be changing. And now they tell me they have woman doctors in America. Woman doctors! Scandalous! Only in America . . .' He sighed and shook his head. 'What do you want me to do?'

'I'll show you.' The assistant surgeon took a bottle from the dispensary and tipped some chloroform on to a gauze pad. He held it over Fischbein's mouth and nose. 'Tell him to breathe normally.'

'*Normal atmen.*'

Fischbein nodded and closed his eyes.

Strachan handed the bottle to Bähr. 'I'd be grateful if you'd drip this – very slowly – on to the gauze pad.'

'We didn't have any anaesthetics when I was your age,' sniffed the doctor. 'When I performed amputations in India, we had to use a bottle of brandy, if there was one available.'

'And if there wasn't?'

'Bless you, then I'd have to perform the operation sober!'

' "Forasmuch as it hath pleased Almighty God of His great Mercy to take unto himself the soul of our dear brother here departed, we therefore commit his body to the deep, to be turned into corruption . . ." '

Pettifer was interrupted by an explosive, hacking cough. Glaring about the *Venturer*'s upper deck, he saw the assembled marines part to reveal Yelverton wiping his nose and mouth with his handkerchief. The master gazed at the contents of his handkerchief with a slight frown on his face; then he became aware of the stares of Pettifer and everyone else on deck, which was the entire crew and the six surviving whalers. He hurriedly thrust the handkerchief into a pocket and mouthed the word 'Sorry!' with a suitably abashed expression.

Pettifer gave Yelverton another bushy-browed glare for good measure, and then cleared his throat to resume the service.

' "We therefore commit his body to the deep, to be turned into corruption, looking for the resurrection of the body, when the sea shall give up her dead, and the life of the world to come through our Lord Jesus Christ; who at his coming shall change our vile body, that it may be like unto his glorious body, according to the mighty working, whereby he is able to subdue all things to himself." '

The hatch cover on which Immermann's shrouded corpse lay was hoisted at one end, tipping his weighted body over the bulwark and into the sea with a splash.

' "I heard a voice from Heaven",' read Ziegler, ' "saying unto me, Write, From henceforth blessèd are the dead which die in the Lord: even so saith the Spirit; for they rest from their labours".'

It was 8 July, two weeks and two days since the *Venturer* had picked up the survivors of the *Carl Gustaf* in the Middle Pack. They had left Greenland behind, sailing around the northern edge of the pack, and were now hove-to off Cape Walter Bathurst on the northern coast of Baffin Land, close to the entrance to Lancaster Sound.

No one had been surprised when Immermann had passed away. Of the four men who had been left injured on the ice when the *Carl Gustaf* went down, Immermann had been the most grievously hurt, and it was a miracle he had outlasted Noldner and Tegeder. Of the four, now only Ignatz Fischbein survived, but he at least was well on the road to recovery. Back on his feet, he stood with his splinted arm in a sling next to Dr Bähr, Sørensen, Kracht, and Frau Weiss in her Inuit clothes. In spite of the solemnity of the occasion, and the fact she was recently widowed, Killigrew could not help thinking that they made her look damned fetching.

As Pettifer led them in the recitation of the Lord's Prayer, Killigrew cast his eyes over his fellow mourners. Thickly muffled against the cold, the hands all looked suitably solemn: even in peacetime, death was never far from the life of a sailor, and it was not something they treated lightly. The officers, too, had composed their features into suitably grave expressions; all except Latimer, who looked as if he was bored and did not care who knew it. The sorrow on the faces of Ziegler, Kracht and Fischbein was very real, however, and the fact that he was the forty-second member of their crew to die in three weeks only added to their grief. Bähr looked aloof: an inveterate snob, he made no secret of the fact he was sufficiently well connected to be able to look down on everyone on board.

Ursula looked stony-faced, but then she had looked stony-faced ever since Killigrew had met her, her expression giving away nothing. He had not expected her to cease mourning her husband all at once; but the occasional hint of a smile, no matter how wan, would have been healthy. Indeed, he was starting to wonder if she had *begun* to mourn, let alone finished.

' "The grace of our Lord Jesus Christ, and the love of God, and the fellowship of the Holy Ghost, be with us all evermore," ' concluded Pettifer, closing his prayer book.

'Amen,' said Ziegler, and a murmur of 'Amens' ran round the deck. In the silence that followed, Hughes sang 'Amazing Grace' in a surprisingly good tenor: Killigrew had always acknowledged the Welsh to be the finest singers in the world, but somehow he had always supposed that if any Welshman should be the exception that proved the rule to be false, it would be Hughes. When he had finished, the assembled men remained on deck in contemplative silence out of respect for the deceased, for as long as the bitterly cold weather would allow, which was about five seconds. Then Pettifer nodded to Molineaux.

The boatswain's mate piped 'up spirits' and the men were served their grog. 'Drinks in the wardroom, sir,' Killigrew murmured to Pettifer. 'That goes for you too, Doctor.'

'Capital!' said Bähr. 'Don't mind if I do.' He followed Pettifer, Yelverton, Strachan and Latimer below. Killigrew was about to follow them – as president of the wardroom mess, it was his duty to play host – when he saw Ziegler and Ursula standing on the quarterdeck. He wanted to invite them too, but something about the way they were conversing in low tones suggested that his invitation would be an intrusion.

Ziegler laid a hand on Ursula's arm, but she shrugged him off. '*Lassen Sie mich!*'

Ziegler hesitated, and then bowed away and headed for the after hatch.

'Drinks in the wardroom, Herr Ziegler,' Killigrew told him as he passed. The whaler ignored him, storming past with a face as black as thunder. Killigrew stared after him until he had disappeared below, and then contemplated Ursula. She stood at the taffrail with her back to him, staring out across the sea astern.

He crossed the deck, instinctively removing his greatcoat. When he joined her at the taffrail, he tried to press it on her.

She regarded him with an amused smile – a smile devoid of humour – and shook her head. 'My Esquimaux clothes are perfectly adequate, thank you. I do not feel the cold.'

'My condolences, Frau Weiss. This must have been especially painful for you, coming so soon after the death of your husband. A pity he could not enjoy the luxury of a funeral service, but I'd like to think that—'

'What difference does it make? They're both in the same place now, along with the other men killed when the *Carl Gustaf* went down.'

Killigrew was a little shocked by her apparently callous attitude, but he thought he understood: she was using bitterness to armour herself against grief. 'It's all right to cry, you know.'

She laughed – the first time he had heard her do so – and under the circumstances it was not the pleasantest sound he had heard. 'Cry? For that *Schweinhund*?' She moved her face closer to Killigrew's, so that the rim of her hood almost touched the peak of his cap. 'Permit me to let you into a little secret, Herr Killigrew: I hated that pig. Do you understand me? I *hated* him. I am glad he is dead.'

Killigrew's feeling of shock increased, but at the same time it was mixed with a sense of appreciation for her refreshing honesty, a feeling he knew should be out of place. 'I take it you're not referring to Herr Immermann?'

She regarded him with a scathing expression of contempt. 'Now you know what a monster I am,' she said, and left him at the taffrail, clutching his coat and shivering in the cold.

'Unfeeling devil, *ja*?'

Killigrew turned and saw Kracht standing nearby. His first instinct was to upbraid the man for speaking out of turn, but that would have been hypocritical; Kracht had done no more than voice what Killigrew had been thinking.

'On the *Carl Gustaf* we used to call her the Snow Queen – you know, like in Hans Andersen's fairy tales? Oh, I don't blame her for feeling no sorrow at Kapitän Weiss' death: the *Scheißkerl* used to abuse her. Not just beat her – which is bad enough – but also be horrid to her. Always calling her a *Schlampe* – in English you would say "trollop"? – and telling her she was no good, she was a burden to him, she was lucky to have a husband like him

85

who was willing to put up with her and look after her. Perhaps once she was a warm, caring woman; but she hears that kind of thing often enough, sooner or later she starts to believe it. I overheard them rowing about it in the great cabin more than once; I'm not a *Lauscher*. . . one who listens?'

'Eavesdropper?'

'*Ja*, eavesdropper. But it was difficult not to hear sometimes. Well, you must know what it's like on board ship. Bulkheads thin as paper; the *Kapitän* made no attempt to keep his voice down. Then there would be smacks, sobs, and then she wouldn't appear on deck for a few days so that we wouldn't see the bruises. You know why he took her to sea with him? Because he was frightened that if he left her in Hamburg she would be unfaithful to him. The irony was, she and Herr Jantzen were at it like rabbits every time the *Kapitän*'s back was turned. Reckon he drove her into Jantzen's arms. Everyone on board knew except the *Kapitän*, and he was bound to find out sooner or later; when he did, it would have been the worse for Jantzen: Weiss was insanely jealous. Take my advice, Herr Killigrew: never marry a beautiful woman twenty years your junior.'

Killigrew smiled. 'At my age, I think it's illegal.'

'It's Jantzen I feel sorry for, *schlecht Saukerl*. She was using him: I think she *wanted* her husband to catch them at it. You think she shed a tear when she heard he was dead as well as her husband?' Kracht shook his head. '*Kalte Luder*; the Arctic suits her.'

He nodded to an iceberg drifting slowly past perhaps a mile to starboard. It was immense – perhaps half a mile across; it was impossible to be sure at that distance – yet as far away as it was it still managed to tower over the *Venturer*, dwarfing the tiny ship. Its centre was a deep indigo, its colour shading off from a deep blue to white where it grew thin and transparent towards the edges and the snow-covered top. The crevices of its irregular mass were thrown into deep shade, in sharp contrast with the way the pinnacles glittered in the sun. A deep rumbling and cracking sounded from it constantly, and chunks of ice broke off it to tumble down into the water with great splashes.

'See that iceberg, *mein Herr*? There's more warmth in the centre of that than there is in Frau Weiss's heart.'

V

Terregannoeuck

'A desolate place to spend eternity,' remarked Strachan.

Killigrew hunkered down on the barren shore of Beechey Island and stared at the three headstones as if they held the secret of Franklin's fate. There had been 129 men on the *Erebus* and *Terror* when they had sailed into the Arctic, never to be seen again; by the time they had sailed from Beechey Island some time after 3 April 1846 – the date on the last of the graves – that number had been reduced to 126.

'They've gone to a better place.' Killigrew stood up and lit a cheroot. 'And if they haven't, at least they've gone to a warmer one.'

'You believe that?' asked the assistant surgeon. 'All that Heaven and Hell nonsense?'

Killigrew smiled. 'We all have to believe in something, Mr Strachan. Religion may not hold all the answers, but then neither does your science.'

'True. But at least science permits us . . . no, *requires* us . . . to look for those answers. As far as I can see, religion provides no answers at all; it all rests on blind faith. Put that in your pipe, and smoke it!' he added, using a catchphrase he had overheard the boatswain use.

Killigrew did not reply, disturbed by the thought that Strachan might be right. The assistant surgeon had argued religion with his father; if the Reverend Donald Strachan could not defeat his son in theological debate, what chance did the lieutenant stand?

Less than two miles wide, Beechey Island was dominated by steep slate and granite cliffs that rose up to a plateau 800 feet above sea level. At the foot of these cliffs, a low shore land of dark gravel surrounded the island, which was linked to its larger neighbour – Devon Island, to the north-east – by a low gravel isthmus. Unlike the treeless coasts to the north and south of Lancaster Sound – which had been ablaze at that time of year with purple saxifrage, low-bush cranberry, blue harebells, and acres of dog lichen and green moss – Beechey Island was utterly barren. It was without a doubt the most desolate place that Killigrew had ever seen; compared to this, the deserts of Syria had been the garden of Eden. There was simply nothing here: just rock, shingle, and the three graves.

The names of the occupants of the graves were clearly marked on the wooden headboards: Leading Stoker John Torrington of HMS *Terror*, who had died on New Year's Day 1846; Able Seaman John Hartnell of the *Erebus*, who had died three days later. After that there had been a gap of three months to the day before Private of Marines William Braine had died. How they had died remained a mystery; Strachan had offered to carry out a post mortem, but Pettifer refused to disturb the dead with an exhumation.

There was no indication where the *Erebus* and *Terror* might have gone after they left Beechey Island. It had long been standard practice for Royal Naval vessels exploring the Arctic to build cairns on prominent headlands, containing messages in watertight canisters giving details of when they had been there and where they were bound. Someone had built a cairn on the summit of the island, and it was presumed to be the handiwork of Franklin's men, but the searchers who had come to the island two years ago had dismantled it and searched all around without finding any trace of a message.

It was Thursday 22 July, a week since the *Venturer* had dropped anchor in the natural harbour to the north-east of the island. There had been no sign of the rest of Sir Edward Belcher's squadron when she had arrived. Nor, indeed, had her crew seen any other vessels in the uneventful voyage through Lancaster Sound. A fortnight after they had buried Immermann at sea, the survivors of the *Carl Gustaf* remained inadvertent guests on board the *Venturer*.

Strachan waggled the geologist's hammer he had brought ashore with him. 'I'm going to look for fossils,' he said. Killigrew nodded, and the assistant surgeon headed off in the direction of the slate cliffs.

Killigrew, meanwhile, followed a precipitous path that led up the side of the cliffs to the plateau. There he paused for a few minutes, smoking another cheroot and gazing off to the east in the direction of Lancaster Sound, expecting the rest of the squadron to heave in sight at any moment.

The *Venturer* looked tiny below him, dwarfed by the vast immensity of the nothingness that stretched in all directions. To the north-west and the south, the open waters of Wellington Channel and Barrow Strait respectively showed cobalt blue beneath the pale sky; to the north-east, Devon Island, like Beechey itself, was denuded of snow by the summer thaw, but every bit as barren. A trick of the sharp, clear Arctic light enabled him to see further than the earth's curvature should have permitted, making this wilderness seem even larger than it was. Cornwallis Island, more than twenty-eight miles away on the opposite side of Wellington Channel, looked so close it seemed that he could reach out and touch it.

Killigrew felt as though he was gazing into eternity, and he had never been more aware that he was nothing more than a flyspeck on the face of God's creation; and not a very large flyspeck, at that. The sensation was not humbling – growing up with his grandfather, a cold man who had no time for children, after his parents had died, Killigrew had learned at an early age that the universe did not revolve around him – so much as unnerving. But most striking of all was the oppressive silence. The only sound was the gentle soughing of the wind across that barren landscape. The endless sky seemed to swallow up all other noises.

He heard scrunching on the gravel behind him, and whirled round in time to see O'Houlihan – one of the crewmen in the dinghy that had brought Killigrew and Strachan ashore – clambering up to join him on the plateau. The seaman looked surprised to discover him there. 'Begging your pardon, sir. Didn't mean to startle ye.'

'That's all right, O'Houlihan. I was miles away. Not playing football with your shipmates?'

'The ground's too hard for a decent game of footie, sir . . . I can leave you be, if ye like, sir . . .'

'No, no. You've come this far, you might as well enjoy the view.'

'It's a beauty, though, is it not, sir?'

'Is it what you expected?'

O'Houlihan shook his head. 'I'm not sure what it was I was after expecting, sir. Snow and ice, I am thinking. Isn't that what everyone thinks of when they're thinking o' the Arctic?'

Killigrew smiled. 'You wait until winter comes, O'Houlihan. We'll have all the snow and ice a man could wish for.'

'Aye, I s'pose you're right, sir.' He crouched down, seized a fistful of gravel and began to pick out pebbles, pitching them into space. 'I don't know, sir. Somehow it don't seem right.'

'The lack of snow, O'Houlihan?'

The seaman shook his head. 'Not that, sir. Us being here, I mean. You go to a place like New Zealand, the climate's good and the soil's rich, and you think: God meant this place for man. Sure, and it'd be an insult to the Almighty if ye didn't cultivate it, as if the Big Man upstairs had given you a gift and you were turning your nose up at it. And then you come to a place like this.' He sighed and shook his head, before letting the last few pieces of gravel in his hand cascade through his splayed fingers. 'God never meant for us to be here, sir.'

'The Esquimaux manage to survive here.'

'Maybe so, sir. But they've got their way of life, and we've got ours. And ours was never meant for a place like this.'

Even though Killigrew could not claim to have O'Houlihan's appreciation for the soil, he felt he knew what the Irishman meant. He told himself he had come here with the noblest of motives – to rescue Sir John Franklin and his men – but when he had volunteered for this expedition, he had secretly half hoped he would be part of that happy band to whom fell the honour of discovering the North-West Passage. Now he felt that the Passage was not something God intended Man to find. Which begged the question, what was he really doing here? Seeking new lands for Queen Victoria, lands that no one but the Esquimaux had any use for? Suddenly, for the first time since the *Venturer* had sailed from Greenwich, he did not want to be where he was. He wanted to be warm and safe in his rooms in Paddington, or on the quarterdeck of a ship cruising the Tropics. Where did not matter; anywhere but here would be an improvement.

The two of them stood in silence for a while, lost in their own thoughts. 'Come on,' Killigrew said at last. 'Time we got back to the ship. You go on ahead, O'Houlihan. I'll follow you shortly.'

'As you will, sir.'

While O'Houlihan preceded him down the precipitous path, Killigrew lingered on the summit, gazing in the direction of Lancaster Sound. The wide, open, empty sea mocked his hopes.

Days turned into weeks without any sign of Belcher and the rest of his squadron. The hours – the very minutes – dragged slowly. Pettifer and his officers tried to keep the men busy with drills, exercises and boat races. In the evenings Killigrew gave those hands who wished for them lessons in reading and writing – no easy task, when the literary skills of the men ranged from Stoker Jemmy Butterwick, who had signed the ship's articles with a cross, to Molineaux, who could quote Milton and Coleridge. On Sundays, Strachan gave lectures on topics that took in botany, zoology, chemistry, geology, vulcanology and palaeontology. These lectures were invariably packed out, and not simply because there was nothing better to do. Strachan had an enthusiasm for science that he was able to impart to his audience, and a skill for talking about the more abstruse aspects of the natural world in a way that even the most ill-educated of seamen could understand, and yet at the same time even the best-informed of the officers could attend and come away having learned plenty.

Yet these provided only brief respite from the tedium. Like all the officers on board, Killigrew had not joined the navy for a quiet life, and although his service had inured him to long periods of boredom, at least on a long voyage on the open sea he could usually count on occasional fits of rough weather to liven things up. Yet while the *Venturer* was anchored at Beechey Island, the weather remained mild and unchallenging. The monotony of the dreary, oppressive landscape served only to emphasise the monotony of their dreary day-by-day existence.

When the lookout in the crow's nest spied a sail on the first Saturday in August, it was enough of an event to bring the whole crew on deck.

'Where away?' asked Killigrew, taking the telescope from the binnacle.

'Fine off the port bow!'

Killigrew and Cavan exchanged glances. The *Venturer* was anchored on a west–east axis, so that any vessels coming from Lancaster Sound should have appeared astern.

'I can't see anything yet.' Killigrew lowered the telescope.

'Perhaps the squadron *did* get here ahead of us,' suggested Cavan. 'Perhaps it's *Resolute* and *Intrepid* returning from Melville Island.'

'So soon?' Killigrew was sceptical. 'If the squadron's already been here, then where's the *North Star*?'

'Perhaps the rest of the squadron got split up too,' said Cavan, as Latimer emerged from the after hatch. 'Or perhaps it's *Enterprise* and *Investigator*. Perhaps the summer thaw has freed them from whatever icy prison held them, and they are continuing their eastward voyage.'

'Or perhaps it's *Erebus* and *Terror*!' said Latimer.

'Perhaps it's Cleopatra's barge,' said Killigrew. 'But more likely it's a whaler that got through Melville Bay ahead of us.'

A gutta-percha speaking tube ran from the crow's nest to the binnacle. Killigrew handed the telescope to Cavan and blew into the brass mouthpiece, sounding the whistle at the other end. Then he lifted the mouthpiece to his ear to listen for the lookout's response.

'Crow's nest,' Endicott responded in his unmistakable Liverpudlian accent.

'Can you see what kind of ship it is?' asked Killigrew, before transferring the speaking tube to his ear.

'You're not going to believe me, sir.'

'Try me.'

'Well, sir, unless I'm very much mistaken . . . it looks like a paddle-steamer, sir!'

'In the Arctic?' exclaimed Killigrew. 'Impossible. No one would be foolish enough to take a flapper into the Arctic. The ice would break off her paddles in a brace of shakes.' He lowered the mouthpiece and turned to Cavan and Latimer. 'He says it's a paddle-steamer!'

'A paddle-steamer?' Cavan echoed incredulously. 'In the Arctic? Who's in the crow's nest?'

'Endicott.'

'Endicott? Not like him to make a mistake.'

'I see it!' Latimer said excitedly. He was pointing the telescope forward. 'He's right, sir! It *is* a paddle-steamer!'

'Give me that telescope.' Killigrew looked for himself. It took him a moment to locate the ship; it was little more than a speck, and should have been too far away to see – only the peculiar refraction of the Arctic light made it visible, he supposed. And there was no mistaking the plashing of her paddles. 'Good God! It *is* a flapper!'

'What the devil's going on?' asked Bähr, coming on deck with Pettifer and Ziegler.

'There's a paddle-steamer approaching from the west, sir,' said Cavan.

'A paddle-steamer?' echoed Pettifer. 'In the Arctic?'

'Take a look, sir.' Killigrew handed him the telescope.

'Good gracious! She must be lost.'

'That's putting it mildly, sir,' said Killigrew.

'May I see, sir?' asked Ågård. In the seven weeks since they had passed through the Middle Pack, the ice quartermaster had recovered himself, and his shipmates – officers and ratings alike – had forgiven his moment of panic. But now there was a niggle at the back of Killigrew's mind, a doubt about Ågård's reliability. He hated that niggle, but he could not ignore it.

Pettifer handed Ågård the telescope. 'What do you think?' he asked Killigrew. 'Could she have seen us? Perhaps we should send up a rocket to get her attention.'

'Good thinking, sir.' Killigrew was about to order Thwaites to prepare a signal rocket when Ågård spoke again.

'Yes . . . yes, there's no mistaking it,' said the ice quartermaster. 'It's a kayak.'

Pettifer smiled tolerantly. 'I've been at sea since I was twelve, Ågård. I think I can tell a paddle-steamer from a kayak when I see one.'

'See for yourself, sir.' Ågård held out the telescope. Pettifer seemed reluctant to question his own conviction, so Killigrew took the glass and raised it to his eye.

'It's a paddle-steamer,' he asserted. 'No question. It is, without doubt, incontrovertibly and incontestably, a . . . a *kayak*?'

'What? Give that to me!' Pettifer snatched the telescope from Killigrew and levelled it once more.

'The *fata morgana*, sir,' said Ågård. 'The Arctic mirage.'

The ship's library was well stocked with the journals of previous Arctic explorers, and all the assembled officers had read enough to know the Arctic had a way of producing images that put desert mirages to shame, making a few rocks on a distant shore look like a range of mountains, or turning a walrus into a whale, but the deceptive effects of the *fata morgana* had to be seen to be believed.

'I'll be a Dutchman!' said Pettifer. 'It *is* a kayak. Yet I was certain . . .'

'If it's any consolation, better men than ourselves have been caught out by the *fata morgana*,' said Killigrew. 'Sir John Ross, for one.'

'Unusual, to see a single kayak,' mused Ågård. 'Usually the Esquimaux travel in bands of a dozen or so, the men in their kayaks, the women and children in an umiak.'

'Is it coming this way?' asked Pettifer.

'Making a beeline straight towards us, sir.'

The kayak was much the same as those they had seen at the Whalefish Islands. Twirling his double-bladed paddle, the oarsman scudded the canoe across the water. Dressed in typical Inuit clothing, he paddled right up to the *Venturer*, trailing the blade of his paddle in the water to slow his light craft as he drew near to the side.

'Good day to you!' Pettifer called down to him.

The Inuk seemed to ignore him, making his kayak fast to the *Venturer*'s accommodation ladder.

'Perhaps he doesn't understand English,' suggested Cavan.

Pettifer nodded. 'Does anyone on board speak Esquimau?'

Sørensen shouldered his way to the front of the men crowded round the entry port. 'I speak a little. *Tunnga-sugitsi*,' he called down. '*Kinauvit?*'

The Inuk did not reply at first, but climbed nimbly up the accommodation ladder and through the entry port to stand on deck, his eyes slowly searching the faces of the men who stood in a circle around him. Dressed in sealskin boots and bearskin breeches, he peered out of the deep hood of a buttonless sealskin jacket from behind a set of Inuk snow-goggles: made from a strip of whalebone tied across his face, with two horizontal slits cut on either side of his nose to reduce the amount of painful glare reaching his eyes. A bear's tooth – an incisor, at least two inches long – hung on a thong around his neck, presumably some kind of talisman.

He looked at Killigrew. 'You are the captain?' He spoke slowly and ponderously, but his English was perfect.

The lieutenant shook his head and indicated Pettifer standing next to him.

'You speak English!' exclaimed the captain.

The Inuk arched an eyebrow, as if to suggest that confirming what they already knew would be a waste of words.

Pettifer remembered his manners. 'Commander Orson Pettifer, of Her Majesty's navy, at your service. And you are?'

The Inuk thumped his chest with the flat of his hand. 'Terregannoeuck.'

'We're looking for two ships,' said Pettifer. 'Big ships, much like this one, with many *kabloonas* on board. Have you seen such ships?'

'*Erebus* and *Terror*?' asked Terregannoeuck.

The officers on deck exchanged glances. 'You know of the *Erebus* and the *Terror*?' asked Pettifer.

'Terregannoeuck meet them six years ago. Cap'n Franklin take Terregannoeuck on board, give him vittles and grog. Terregannoeuck like Cap'n Franklin very much.'

'You met Sir John Franklin?' Pettifer said eagerly. 'Where?'

'Terregannoeuck very hungry.' The Inuk rubbed his stomach theatrically. 'Bad year for seals, poor hunting. Terregannoeuck not eat in three days.'

Pettifer could take a hint as well as the next man. 'Have some hot food and some grog brought to my day-room at once, Mr Cavan!' he ordered. 'Mr Terregannoeuck, perhaps I can tempt you to partake of our hospitality in my quarters . . .?'

'Is that one of my calves' heads, Mr Cavan?' asked Pettifer.

'I took the liberty of ordering Armitage to take it from your private stock, sir,' the mate replied disingenuously. 'I assumed you'd want him to have the best, under the circumstances.'

'I just hope the wretched fellow appreciates it. I'd've thought that after a lifetime of dining on seal-meat and whale blubber, even salt-horse and hard tack would make a pleasant change.'

Seated at the table in the captain's day-room, Terregannoeuck looked up. With his sealskin jacket taken off and the goggles removed, they could see his angular face more clearly: leathery brown skin stretched taut over high cheekbones, his hollow cheeks pitted by the ravages of smallpox, and deeply incised scars all over his head, disappearing behind his beard and his hairline.

He did not smile – it was impossible to imagine a smile cracking that scarred, leathery face – but he seemed pleased. '*Mamaqtualuk!*' he pronounced, pouring himself a second glass of claret. '*Kabloona* vittles very good!'

The Inuk ate with his fingers, occasionally using his own knife – made of steel, clearly of European origin – to carve a chunk of meat from the calf's head. He seemed to be oblivious to the half a dozen officers who stood around the table, waiting for him to tell them where he had seen Franklin, like Hindu disciples waiting for words of wisdom to fall from the lips of a guru. The last people known to have seen Franklin and his men alive were the crews of two whalers that had met the *Erebus* and *Terror* in Baffin's Bay in the summer of 1845; Terregannoeuck was claiming to have seen them a year later, after the deaths of the three men buried on Beechey Island.

'You speak English very well,' said Killigrew.

Terregannoeuck nodded. 'I was harpooner on *kabloona* ship *Cora Benchley* for two summers.'

Yelverton pulled a large chart of the known Arctic and spread it on the table beyond Terregannoeuck's plate. Showing the Inuk the chart had been Killigrew's idea: from what he had read in Ross's journals, the Inuit had a marvellous facility for understanding the *kabloonas*' maps.

'This ... is ... a ... map,' the master told Terregannoeuck. 'You savvy "map"?'

The Inuk nodded, impatient with being patronised, and wiped grease from his chops with the back of his sleeve. 'Cap'n Franklin show Terregannoeuck many maps. He seek way to west, to great ocean there.'

'Did you show him?'

Terregannoeuck nodded. 'Many ways to west, over land, sea and ice. Terregannoeuck show him ways by sea, on map.'

'Can you show us?' Pettifer asked eagerly.

Killigrew cleared his throat. 'Perhaps Mr Terregannoeuck should start by showing us where he met the *Erebus* and *Terror*.'

Pettifer nodded. Terregannoeuck studied the map, and then jabbed at Beechey Island with a finger. 'We here?'

'That is correct,' said Killigrew.

'Terregannoeuck meet Cap'n Franklin here.' The Inuk indicated one of the blank patches on the map, south of where Prince of Wales Land and North Somerset Land flanked the unexplored southern end of Peel Sound.

Yelverton shook his head. 'You must be mistaken. Franklin's orders were to sail north, up Wellington Channel. Here.' The master indicated the channel on the map.

The Inuk nodded, impatient to finish chewing the piece of meat he had bitten off the calf's head and swallow it so he could reply. 'He tell Terregannoeuck he sail up this channel, all the way around north of this island here. Then he turn south and enter this channel, here. This is where Terregannoeuck meet him. Terregannoeuck stay on board for a day, tell him there is way to the west, but for kayak, not for *kabloona* ship: too much ice. Him not listen. Terregannoeuck leave *Erebus*, fearing danger. Him sail on.'

'What danger?' asked Killigrew.

The Inuk hunched his head over his meal. 'Many dangers, in Arctic.'

Pettifer jerked his head towards one corner of the day-room and huddled there with his officers, leaving Terregannoeuck to finish his meal in peace. 'You think this fellow is telling the truth?' he asked in a low voice.

'Difficult to see why he should lie,' said Killigrew.

97

'Peel Sound has never been explored.'

'It's always been choked with ice,' explained Yelverton.

'Perhaps it wasn't choked with ice in 1846,' said Pettifer. 'Perhaps Franklin found it open and sailed down it, hoping it would link with Dease Strait. That would complete the North-West Passage.'

'It's possible, sir,' agreed Killigrew. 'We can put it to Sir Edward when he arrives. A piece of intelligence like this is just what we need to divert his anger towards us for getting separated.'

'Sir Edward, yes . . .' mused Pettifer.

'From what I've heard of Sir Edward, he's more likely to be angry with us for finding this vital clue instead of him,' said Yelverton.

'If we hadn't been here ahead of the rest of the squadron, the chances are we'd never have met Terregannoeuck to find this out,' Killigrew pointed out.

'You think Sir Edward will see it that way?' asked Yelverton. Killigrew had to admit the master had a good point.

'Sir Edward!' Pettifer snorted impatiently. 'And what do you think he'll do when he gets here? *If* he gets here? Order us to remain here with the *North Star*, while he explores Peel Sound and gets all the glory of being the one to find the North-West Passage, I shouldn't wonder!' He shook his head. 'Do you think it is mere coincidence that *we* were the only ones to get through Melville Bay; that *we* were here at Beechey Island when our Esquimau friend happened by? No, gentlemen. There is a higher purpose at work here. Fate, one might almost dare say.'

'What are you suggesting, sir?' asked Killigrew. 'That we explore Peel Sound without waiting for the rest of the squadron?'

'Why not?' asked Pettifer. 'Gentlemen, we've been sent a God-given opportunity. For all we know, the rest of the squadron might not get even this far. It's over three weeks since we arrived here. Even if we did somehow get ahead of the rest of the squadron, they've had more than enough time to catch up with us by now. But still there is no sign of them.'

'Anything could have happened to them on the way through Melville Bay, sir,' said Yelverton. 'We were lucky to get through so quickly. They may still be trying to get through. They may be past the Middle Pack and sailing to meet us even as we speak.'

'They may also have been nipped in the ice, or have given up and sailed back to England,' snorted Pettifer. 'Are we to spend the entire winter waiting for ships that may never arrive, when we have this opportunity to achieve the object of our expedition? Nothing less than the discovery of the North-West Passage!'

'With all due respect, sir, I thought our purpose was to find Franklin's expedition?' said Yelverton.

'Don't you see?' Pettifer replied tetchily. 'If what our Esquimau friend tells us is correct, then it's all one and the same thing!'

'Then if *Erebus* and *Terror* sailed down Peel Sound to find it, sir, how come they never emerged on the other side?'

'We'll never know if we don't try to follow them,' Pettifer pointed out reasonably. 'What do you say, Mr Killigrew?'

'I can see no harm in sailing as far as Peel Sound. It can't be more than a hundred miles from here. We could check to see if it's open, or choked with ice, and then sail back here to see if the rest of the squadron's arrived yet. It wouldn't take us more than a week at the most.'

'Terregannoeuck come with you,' the Inuk announced from the far side of the room. 'You need *krauyimatauyok* – guide. Terregannoeuck show you the way.'

'We don't need a guide to show us as far as Peel Sound,' muttered Yelverton. 'The charts do that clearly enough.'

'Assuming the charts are correct,' said Pettifer. 'The men who charted them two years ago could have made all kinds of mistakes, thanks to the *fata morgana*. If Sir John Ross marked mountains where there are no mountains across Lancaster Sound, perhaps the men who charted Peel Sound charted a continuation of a sound where there were only mountains. Besides, suppose we find Peel Sound open? If we come back here to see if the rest of the squadron has arrived, and Sir Edward decides he wishes to send a ship or two to examine the sound, they'll need a guide. We can't ask this fellow Terre-whatsisname to wait here until we get back from Peel Sound.'

'Many *tonrar* lie that way,' said the Inuk. 'You need Terregannoeuck, to protect you.'

'*Tonrar*?' asked Pettifer.

Sørensen shrugged. 'Evil spirits, sir.'

'Superstitious nonsense,' snorted Strachan.

'What do you think, Killigrew?' asked Pettifer.

The lieutenant smiled. 'About superstitions, sir?'

'About taking Terregannoeuck along as a guide.'

'The Esquimaux have lived and survived in the Arctic for hundreds if not thousands of years,' said Killigrew. 'I'm not afraid of evil spirits, but there will be other dangers. It wouldn't hurt to have an Esquimau around to advise us.' He turned to Terregannoeuck. 'If you help us, what will you want in return?'

The Inuk picked up one of the forks on the table. '*Savirajak*.'

'A fork?' Pettifer asked in bewilderment.

'Steel,' said Sørensen. 'Saws and knife-blades. To the Inuit, it's more precious than gold.'

'I think we can spare him all the saws and knives he wants,' said Latimer. They had brought a plentiful supply of such things, specifically for the purpose of bartering with the Inuit.

'Then it's decided,' said Pettifer. 'Welcome to the crew of the *Venturer*, Mr Terrewhatsyername. Mr Yelverton! Be so good as to chart a course for Peel Sound.'

Peel Sound was open.

The *Venturer* sailed ninety miles into the sound, as far as Cape Coulman: the point reached by Sir James Ross with the *Enterprise* and *Investigator* in 1848, the first year of the Franklin search, before ice had blocked his way. Two other expeditions had tried Peel Sound since then: the *Prince Albert*, a schooner hired by Lady Franklin, in 1850, and some of Captain Austin's men in a sledging expedition only the previous year; but neither had got even this far.

Now the sound was wide open; as it had been six years ago when Franklin had sailed down it, if Terregannoeuck's story was to be believed.

The channel between Prince of Wales Land to the west and North Somerset Land to the east was some twenty-five miles wide. The shore ice that clung to the coast to port stretched out for more than a mile, while a red sandstone headland at the other side of the channel, a thousand feet high, was just visible in the distance.

Pettifer ordered the *Venturer* hove-to while the officers gathered on deck to gaze at something none of them had ever seen before: uncharted waters, stretching invitingly away before them. Perhaps as far as King William Land, and the channel linked to the Beaufort Sea by Dease Strait: the North-West Passage.

'Wide open.' Killigrew spoke in tones of hushed reverence, conscious that he was looking at something no man – no white man, at least – had looked upon since Franklin had sailed down this channel six years earlier.

'A heaven-sent opportunity,' said Pettifer. He hesitated, as if aware he was on the threshold of something remarkable. This was not a decision to be taken lightly. 'Gentlemen, it behoves us to take full advantage of it. Make all plain sail, Mr Killigrew: course due south.' Without another word, he descended the after hatch.

Killigrew exchanged glances with Yelverton, Cavan and Strachan.

'Is he crazy?' The master kept his voice low so the hands working nearby would not overhear. 'I thought we were going back to Beechey Island as soon as we'd established that this sound was open.'

'This sound was open in 1846 when Franklin sailed down it, if Terregannoeuck is to be believed,' said Cavan. 'And I for one believe him, sir. Every expedition that has come this way since Franklin and his ships disappeared has found this way blocked; we're the first to find it open. The Old Man's right, sir. We can't miss this opportunity.'

Yelverton shook his head. 'The sound may be open now, but supposing the ice closes in after we've entered it? We might be trapped in there for months; years, possibly.'

'Not afraid, are you? We knew the risks when we signed on for this expedition.'

Yelverton bridled; he did not care to be accused of cowardice by a young mate, no matter how far Cavan had his tongue pushed into his cheek. 'We knew the risks, aye. But with all due respect, Mr Cavan, you're forgetting one thing: we have civilians on board. They never signed on to spend two or three years in the Arctic.' He turned to Killigrew. 'Damn it, sir! We may never get out of here alive. I'm not afraid to take that chance, but I'm damned if I'll risk the lives of civilians—' Yelverton broke off, coughing doubled up with a handkerchief over his mouth until the fit had passed.

'Are you all right?' Killigrew asked him, concerned.

The master straightened, wiping tears from his eyes with his sleeve. He smiled wanly and thrust his handkerchief into the pocket of his greatcoat. 'Bit of a cold, that's all. It's hardly surprising. In this weather, it's a wonder we're not all sniffling and sneezing.'

'That sounds nasty to me,' said Strachan. 'Come to the sick-berth at the end of the watch and I'll give you some syrup of squills.'

'Mr Yelverton's quite right, of course,' Killigrew told Cavan. 'I'll ask the Old Man what his intentions are towards the whalers.'

He descended the after hatch and made his way to the captain's quarters. Private Phillips was on duty outside the door; he slammed the stock of his side-arm – one of the new Minié rifled muskets – against the deck. 'Lieutenant Killigrew to see you, sah!'

'Send him in, Phillips.'

'Very good, sah!' The marine opened the door and ushered Killigrew through.

The lieutenant found Pettifer crouched over Horatia's basket in his day-room, feeding the dachshund titbits. 'Yes, Mr Killigrew, what is it?' he asked without looking up.

Killigrew closed the door behind him. 'I was under the impression that it was our intention to return to Beechey Island as soon as we had established that the sound was open.'

'I've changed my mind, Mr Killigrew.' Pettifer chuckled jovially. 'Captain's prerogative.'

'Sir, the *Venturer*'s just a steam tender. I'm sure I need hardly remind you we were never intended to spend so long away from the *North Star*. We're not equipped to pass a winter in the Arctic alone. And we didn't leave a message for Sir Edward at Beechey Island. If anything goes wrong, no one's going to come looking for us.'

'Not equipped, Mr Killigrew? We have provisions enough to see us through three winters in the Arctic, if necessary.' Pettifer shook his head. 'We came here to find Franklin, as Mr Yelverton was so quick to remind me the day before yesterday. We knew the risks when we volunteered for this expedition. Do you expect us to balk now, when we are so close to the end of our quest?'

'We didn't have civilians on board then, sir,' said Killigrew. 'Including a woman. Perhaps it would be better to sail back to Beechey Island and see if the rest of the squadron has turned up yet. If it has, we can leave Frau Weiss on board the *North Star* and—'

'You know as well as I do that if we go back to Beechey and find the rest of the squadron there, we'll have to report to Sir Edward. Do you really think he's going to let us drop off our passengers and come back to explore this sound? He'll order us to stay at the island with the *North Star*, while he explores this sound for himself.'

Outside, Private Phillips crashed the stock of his musket against the deck. 'Mr Ziegler to see you, sah!'

'Send him in, Phillips.'

'Very good, sah!'

The door opened and Ziegler stormed in, looking very red in the face. 'Forgive the intrusion, *Herr Kapitän*, but there is a rumour on board that it is not your intention to turn back to Beechey Island, but to press on deeper into the Arctic. I just wanted your assurance that—'

'No rumour, Herr Ziegler,' said Pettifer. 'We are standing on the threshold of history. The Good Lord has vouchsafed to us an opportunity to learn the fate of the Franklin expedition and to be the ones to discover the North-West Passage. It is not my intention to pass up that opportunity.'

'And what of us, *Herr Kapitän*? We were to be put on board the first whaler you encountered . . .'

'But we have encountered no whalers since the *Carl Gustaf* sank, as you are well aware.'

'Then take us back to Beechey Island, damn you!'

'And waste precious time which we could be using to explore this sound? And supposing we get back to Beechey Island and find that Sir Edward and the rest of the squadron have not yet arrived? Perhaps they will never arrive. Am I to spend the whole winter waiting here, achieving nothing? No, Herr Ziegler. We must press on. It is our duty. I am sorry for the inconvenience, but I cannot allow the work of one of Her Majesty's exploring ships to be held up – indeed, prevented altogether – by the accidental presence of civilians on board.'

'Inconvenience?' exploded Ziegler. '*Inconvenience?* You could be gone for three years! What of our loved ones in Hamburg? They were expecting us back before the end of the autumn. What are they to think, if no one is to bring them word of the tragedy that befell the *Carl Gustaf*? And what if you never come back, like Franklin and his men? Are we to be frozen in the ice for eternity along with you? This is kidnapping, damn you! If by some miracle we ever do make it back to Germany, you may be sure that my Government shall protest to your Admiralty concerning your actions in the strongest terms imaginable!'

'Kidnapping!' Pettifer retorted icily. 'You ungrateful swine! Might I remind you, Herr Ziegler, that had it not been for the *Venturer* coming by when she did, then you and your companions would all still be stranded on the ice?'

Ziegler shook his head. 'I regret that I ever set eyes on this *verdammt* vessel! For if I had not, the chances are that we would have been picked up by another whaler on its way to the North Water: a whaler due to return to Europe in the autumn. You're *verrückt, Herr Kapitän* – insane!'

Pettifer turned puce. 'How dare you? One more word out of you, Herr Ziegler, and I shall have you clapped in irons, do you hear me?'

Ziegler marched back to the door, opened it, and then turned to face Pettifer once more. 'May God have mercy on your soul, you maniac! You're going to get us all killed!'

'Oh, don't be so damned melodramatic . . .' protested Pettifer. But Ziegler had already slammed the door behind him.

Pettifer turned to Killigrew. 'Did you hear that? That damned fellow had the impertinence to insult me! And after all we've done for them. Who would have thought that anyone could be so ungrateful?'

'With all due respect, sir, he does have a point. Not about your sanity,' Killigrew added hurriedly, 'but it really isn't fair on them to drag them into the Arctic with us.'

'What choice do we have?'

'We can sail back to Beechey Island and wait for Sir Edward to arrive; if he isn't there already. At least let's go back, build a cairn, leave a message telling him which way we're bound.'

'I can't afford to lose that much time,' Pettifer said wearily. 'We've been most fortunate to get so far so early in the season. Would you have me throw it all away just because we have a few civilians on board? They're all sailors – excepting Frau Weiss, of course, and she's spent enough time on board her husband's whaler . . . You're fretting over nothing, Killigrew. Why, if our luck holds we shall be able to sail through the passage before the winter sets in. Then Ziegler and his friends will have the privilege of being members of the first crew to sail through the North-West Passage!'

'Assuming this channel does lead us to the North-West Passage, sir. And if our luck doesn't hold?'

'I see.' Pettifer nodded gravely. 'Now I understand. Rear Admiral Napier assured me you were a bold and audacious officer, Mr Killigrew, but now I see you've lost your nerve. You're afraid to go on. That's it, isn't it? It's not Herr Ziegler and his friends you're worried about, it's yourself.'

'It's not a question of courage, sir. It's a question of common sense. With all due respect, might I remind you that Admiralty policy is for ships to sail in company in Arctic waters at all times, so that if one is nipped there is at least one other close by to take on board the shipwrecked men? It's bad enough that we've been separated from the rest of the squadron for so long, but to compound an unavoidable error by pressing deeper into the Arctic . . .?'

'I don't need you to quote Admiralty policy to me, Mr Killigrew! Might *I* remind *you* of what it says in their lordships' instructions to Sir Edward – and I quote: "We are sensible however that . . . an ardent desire to accomplish the object of your mission, added to a generous sympathy for your missing countrymen, may prevail in some degree to carry you beyond the limits of a cautious prudence." It's the twelfth of August now. The navigable season will be drawing to a close in another month or so. If we're going to take full advantage of this opportunity, I suggest we do so at once, without wasting another week in sailing back to the Beechey Island to see if the rest of the squadron has turned up. Supposing the ice closes in while we're gone?'

'If the ice closes in, sir, I'd prefer it did so when we were out of the sound rather than in it.'

Pettifer scowled. 'We've come this far. We may be ignoring the letter of our instructions if we press on, but better that than ignoring their spirit by turning back now. We came to the Arctic to search for Franklin. It is my intention that we should do just that, while we still have the chance.'

Killigrew stood stiffly to attention. 'In that case, sir, it is my duty to object formally and to request that my objection be noted in the log.'

Pettifer glared at Killigrew. Then he crossed to the door and opened it. 'Private Phillips!'

'Sah?'

'Ask Mr Latimer if he would be so good as to join us, Phillips.'

'Very good, sah.' The marine marched off to find the clerk.

'I'm disappointed in you, Killigrew,' said Pettifer. 'I had thought that you of all the men on board could understand the nobility of our quest; but now I see you are a small-minded, frightened little man, just like all the others.'

'If it pleases you to think that, sir . . .'

The clerk arrived. 'You wanted to see me, sir?'

'Ah, come in, Mr Latimer. We need you to be a witness. As you probably know by now, I have decided that we should take this opportunity to press forward into Peel Sound for as long as the ice permits. Mr Killigrew has objected to this course of action, and wishes his objection to be noted in the log.' Pettifer sat down at the bureau and took out the log. 'The date is Thursday the twelfth of August, the time . . .' he checked his fob watch, '. . . sixteen minutes past one *post meridiem*.' He laboriously entered Killigrew's objection in the log: ' "On finding Peel Sound free of all but loose floe ice, I announced my intention to press ahead in search of Franklin. Lieutenant

Killigrew objected formally to this course of action." There! Would you and Mr Latimer care to sign the entry?'

'That won't be necessary, sir.'

'Good.' Pettifer smiled. 'You'll live to rue that entry, Mr Killigrew. When the *Venturer* sails through the Bering Strait in a few weeks' time, the first ship ever to sail through the North-West Passage—'

'When that happens, sir, you shall have my full and unconditional apology.'

'That will be all, gentlemen. Carry on.'

VI

The Great Unknown

Killigrew and Latimer made their way to the wardroom. Normally the officers of a ship were divided into the senior wardroom officers, and the junior officers who messed in the gunroom; but with only five officers on board apart from Pettifer himself, it made sense for them to mess together in the wardroom, and use the gunroom for stores. That had been before they had picked up the survivors of the *Carl Gustaf*, however, and now the wardroom also acted as a saloon for Ziegler, Bähr and Ursula.

The three of them were in there now, Ziegler with his back to the door as he addressed the other two in German. Killigrew did not understand a word of it, but from his tone it was obvious that he was relating his recent interview with Pettifer, and he was not happy about it. Ursula flickered her eyes to where Killigrew and Latimer had entered. Ziegler broke off and turned. Seeing them, he blushed.

'And what about you, Herr Killigrew?' he asked. 'Do you approve of Kapitän Pettifer's course of action?'

'I am his lieutenant, Herr Ziegler. That is between the captain and myself.'

'But just between you and me, he's just objected formally,' Latimer said with a wink, earning himself a scowl from Killigrew to which he remained oblivious. 'Stood over the Old Man while he entered it in his log and everything; I was called in as a witness too. That's no small thing. Killy's really gone out on a limb for you fellows. I mean, if we do make it safely back to England, that entry will make Killy look an absolute fool. It will be the end of his career and no mistake!'

'Yes, Latimer, thank you for reminding me.' Killigrew poured himself a measure of Irish whiskey from one of the decanters. 'Does the expression "Don't wash your dirty linen in public" mean nothing to you?'

Latimer looked hurt by the rebuke. 'I was only trying to defend you. You don't want these people thinking you're insensitive to their plight, do you?'

'Is there nothing more you can do, Herr Killigrew?' asked Ziegler.

'He's my captain. I'm duty-bound to obey his orders.'

'Even when they're insane?'

'Pressing on is hardly an act of insanity. Ill judged, perhaps, but there have been times when I've been guilty of acts far more ill judged than this one. The only test of a decision is its consequences, and we shan't know those until it's too late.'

'Couldn't we put them in a boat so they could sail back to Beechey Island?' suggested Latimer. 'It's not as if we haven't got boats to spare, and I'm sure Sørensen and Kracht could handle one—'

'It would be kinder to put pistols to their heads and shoot them,' snapped Killigrew. 'It's a hundred and seventy-five miles back to Beechey Island, and there's no guarantee they'll be safe when they get there. Suppose the rest of the squadron hasn't turned up? They'll be stranded on one of the most desolate spots on earth, without food or water.' He shook his head. 'They'll be safer with us here on the *Venturer*.'

'Will we?' asked Ursula. 'Be safe, I mean? What are our chances?'

'Of finding the North-West Passage?' Latimer did not know much about Arctic exploration, but knew plenty about giving the odds. 'I'll give you ten to one. Of finding Franklin and the others? A hundred to one. But for making it back to Europe? For that I'll give us better than evens. The *Venturer* is one of the most advanced ships in the world. We have a triple-reinforced hull, iron sheathing on the bows, a retractable screw-propeller and a telescopic funnel, a Sylvester stove and pipes for keeping the ship warm—'

'We do not want to be an inconvenience,' said Ursula, adjusting the liquor decanters on the sideboard so they were aligned with geometric precision. 'If it helps to put your mind at ease, this is not my first voyage to the Arctic. Why, apart from Sørensen and Kracht, and your two ice quartermasters, I suspect I have more polar experience than everyone else on board put together.'

Killigrew smiled. 'Bravely said, ma'am. But there's no need to make apologies. If anyone should be apologising, it's us, for dragging you into this.'

'Deplorable as I find the awkward situation into which Frau Weiss has found herself thrust,' said Bähr, 'speaking for myself I'm quite looking forward to it. Not that it wouldn't have been nice if Pettifer had had the courtesy to consult us first before dragging us off along with him, but . . . supposing he's right, hey? We'll be on board the first ship to sail through the North-West Passage. That's nothing to be sniffed at. And I know Sørensen, Kracht and Fischbein are all excited by the prospect. Sorry, Ziegler, but you're in the minority.'

'Then you are as big a fool as he is,' snapped Ziegler, jerking his head towards the rear bulkhead that separated the wardroom from Pettifer's quarters. 'May God have mercy on us all.' He stormed out of the room, slamming the door behind him.

'You'll have to forgive Ziegler,' said Bähr. 'He gets terribly self-righteous sometimes. It's what comes from having God for a personal friend. I'd better have a word with him, try to calm him down. If we are going to be stuck in the Arctic together for the next three years, I think it would be as well if we all learned at least to pretend to get along, even if we secretly all loathe one another.' He followed Ziegler out.

'May I ask you a question, Herr Latimer?' asked Ursula.

'By all means.'

'If you rate your chances of finding Franklin or the North-West Passage so low, why did you volunteer for this expedition?'

Latimer grinned. 'Gaming debts. Seems as though every bookmaker in London was after me. I decided that the Arctic was the one place I could be safe from the attentions of their

111

bullies. Well, I've got paperwork to do. If you'll excuse me?' He retreated from the wardroom, leaving Killigrew alone with Ursula.

'And what about you, Herr Killigrew? From what are you running away?' asked Ursula.

'The same as Latimer,' he replied jocularly. 'Bad debts.'

'You are a gaming man?'

He shook his head. 'No, I just happen to have expensive tastes. The old, old story: I'm a victim of tradesmen who actively encouraged me to accept the lines of credit they extended me, before selling my debts to money brokers.'

'Do you really think that some men from Franklin's expedition might still be alive? After so much time?'

Killigrew met her gaze levelly. 'If they're still alive, then they need help. If they're dead, then the wives and families of the men on those ships deserve to know what happened to their loved ones.'

'But why did you *really* volunteer for this expedition? You can talk to me about duty, if you like, but you need not expect me to believe it. From listening to your fellow officers talk, I get the impression there would have been plenty of other officers foolish enough to take your place had you declined.'

'When I was a child, most of my friends wanted to be like Nelson when they grew up, but I always wanted to emulate Cook. To explore strange new lands, to seek out new peoples and new civilisations. To boldly go where no white man has gone before.'

'There are not many places you can say that about nowadays.'

'That's why I came to the Arctic. Most of my service has been spent in the Tropics: the Guinea Coast, the East Indies, the South Seas . . . but I always wanted to be an explorer. If I were an army officer, I suppose I'd want to explore inland in Africa or South America. But I'm a sailor, and when it comes to mapping coasts there's really only one great discovery left to be made: the North-West Passage.' He grinned. 'Those blank patches on the charts – they're like an itch I can't scratch.'

'That is not a very good reason for risking your life. And if you get frozen in, like Franklin and his men? If you die of cold and starvation? Will it have been worth it?'

'When Franklin was putting his expedition together seven years ago, I applied to sail on board HMS *Erebus* as a mate. I was passed over in favour of a friend of mine, Charles DesVoeux. We'd served together in the China War. If it hadn't been for Charlie I wouldn't be standing here right now. I think I owe it to him to return the favour.'

'If it had not been for your friend Charlie, you might have sailed with Franklin in his place. Did you ever think about that?'

'Since it became apparent that some disaster had befallen Franklin's expedition . . . every day of my life.'

'Of course, you realise that Pettifer's going to get us all killed, don't you?' Yelverton asked in a low, almost conversational tone when Killigrew brought him the latest rough charts they had made of the west coast of North Somerset Land in the chart-room.

'I really don't see what you're worried about. It's an open ice year. The only ice in sight is the shore ice, and that doesn't present any danger to us.'

Yelverton slammed down his pencil. 'It was an open ice year in 1846, when the *Erebus* and *Terror* sailed down this sound! Don't you understand? Open ice years are the most dangerous of all! The Arctic lures you in, like a . . . like a whore in Vauxhall Gardens, tempting you with supposedly untasted delights, when all along she's planning for her bully to bash you on the back of the head with his neddy so she can relieve you of your pocket book!'

'Sounds like the voice of experience speaking,' the lieutenant said with a grin.

Yelverton scowled. 'If we get bashed, Killigrew, we won't recover and go on our way with an empty pocket book and an aching but wiser head. We'll be stranded here until the midnight sun bleaches our bones as white as the snow they lie in.'

'We're charting undiscovered coastline here, Yelverton. It's what I've always wanted to do. Doesn't that excite you? To think that in a few years' time, you'll be able to open any atlas anywhere in the world, look at the map of the Arctic and think: I was one of the men who discovered the coastline. Now, that's what I call making your mark on the world.'

'Charting! This isn't charting, Killigrew, and you know it. We should stop to take soundings, measure the headlands by triangulation for the benefit of future navigators. This . . .' Yelverton gestured at the unfinished drawings before him, '. . . this isn't a chart, Killigrew. It's an outline. It's no good to anyone. But Pettifer's in too much of a hurry to be the one to discover the North-West Passage to worry about what lies along the route.'

'There's also Franklin and his men to consider,' Killigrew reminded him. 'If they *are* still alive, then every day's delay before we can bring them succour increases the chances they'll all be dead by the time we reach them.'

'Listen to yourself, Killigrew! You know as well as I do they're all dead by now. You can believe your own lies, if it helps you come to terms with this madness we're committing, but don't expect me to believe them.'

Before Killigrew had a chance to wonder if there was any truth in Yelverton's accusation, a shout came from the deck above: 'Sail ho!'

Killigrew and Yelverton exchanged glances. A moment later they bumped into one another as they raced for the door, the master's curiosity getting the better of his manners. Killigrew could hardly blame him: it was not every day one encountered another ship in uncharted waters.

The two of them found Cavan and Ågård on the quarterdeck, gazing off the port quarter. The coast was visible on the other side of a mile of shore ice: a low, undulating, barren landscape. 'It's not another damned kayak, is it?' asked Killigrew.

Ågård shook his head and handed him the telescope. 'See for yourself, sir.'

'Where am I supposed to be looking?'

'See those two valleys that converge on the coast? The one on the left.'

Killigrew found the ship, about five miles away, the snow heaped in drifts around its hull where it was frozen into the sea. There was no mistaking it, though: the three masts rose up from the deck, truncated, the tops taken down.

'It looks as if she's overwintered,' said Ågård. 'She must've cut her way into the inlet when the ice closed in, and hoped that the ice would release her in spring.'

'How many winters ago was that, I wonder,' mused Killigrew. 'There's no sign of life.'

Pettifer came on deck and Killigrew pointed the ship out to him. 'Is it the *Erebus* or the *Terror*?' the captain asked.

'Could be either, sir.'

'Or neither,' Yelverton pointed out. 'If she's the *Erebus*, where's the *Terror*? If the *Terror*, where's the *Erebus*?'

'Suppose one of them was nipped and sank, sir?' said Ågård. 'The other might have stopped here to overwinter with the crews of both ships on board.'

'We must investigate,' said Pettifer. 'Take her in closer, Mr Cavan. We'll anchor to the shore and send a party to the ship. You'd better take seven men, Mr Killigrew.'

'Aye, aye, sir. I'd like to take Ågård, Qualtrough, Molineaux, Bombardier Osborne, Endicott, McLellan and Terregannoeuck. And Mr Strachan also, if I may, sir. If there is anyone left alive on board that ship, they've been there a long time: a year at least, possibly much longer. They'll need medical attention.'

'Good idea. Carry on, Killigrew.' Pettifer descended the after hatch.

'Where *is* Terregannoeuck?' Killigrew asked Ågård.

The Swede pointed directly up, as if to say that the Inuk had gone to heaven, but when Killigrew raised his eyes skywards he saw Terregannoeuck sitting cross-legged at the maintop. 'What the devil's he doing up there?'

'Seems to like it up there, sir. Spends most of his time up there, at any rate.'

Killigrew took the speaking trumpet from the binnacle. 'Mr Terregannoeuck!'

The Inuk did not stir.

'Mr Terregannoeuck! We could use your assistance with the dogs, if you would oblige us . . .?'

The Inuk did not seem to hear him, even though Killigrew's voice boomed out across the water, amplified by the trumpet. 'Go up there and fetch him down, would you?' Killigrew asked Hughes with a sigh.

'Aye, aye, sir.' Hughes scrambled up the ratlines as nimbly as a monkey and joined Terregannoeuck on the maintop, first talking to him and then shaking him. 'He's asleep, sir!' he called down in astonishment.

'Then wake him up!'

Hughes shook the Inuk, gently at first, and then so vigorously he almost threw him off the maintop. 'I can't, sir!'

'Is he dead?'

'No, sir. He's breathing. It's like he's in some kind of trance.'

'A trance! Mr Terregannoeuck picked a fine time to hold his own private séance! All right, tie him to the topmast so he doesn't fall off in his sleep and climb down, Hughes. You'll have to come with us in his place. We'll leave the dogs. I'm in too much of a hurry to reach that ship to want to waste time learning how to drive a team of huskies. We'll do it the old-fashioned way: by pully-hauly. Mr Thwaites, while we're gone, perhaps you could have Terregannoeuck brought down so Dr Bähr can take a look at him? Can't have comatose Esquimaux cluttering up the tops of one of Her Majesty's ships.'

'Aye, aye, sir.'

Hughes and the others were issued with their winter clothing. Killigrew got changed in his cabin, a feeling of excitement tight in the pit of his stomach. For the past five years, the fate of Franklin's expedition had puzzled everyone: from Greenland to Van Diemen's Land, from San Francisco to Hong Kong, from the middle-class paterfamilias reading *The Times* at the breakfast table to the ploughboy supping a pot of ale in his local country inn, from the lowest guttersnipe to the Queen herself. And now he, of all people, was being given the chance to solve that mystery. Assuming, of course, the ship was indeed the *Erebus* or the *Terror*.

Not quite sure what to expect, he decided to take his pepperboxes.

Terregannoeuck had been taken down to the sick-berth and the *Venturer* was anchored to the shore ice by the time Killigrew re-emerged on deck. A gangplank was lowered to the ice, and a sledge dragged down. Ågård supervised while they loaded the equipment: cooking apparatus, food, a luncheon haversack, a spare shotgun – Killigrew already had his own Verney-Carron breach-loading double-barrelled shotgun slung across his back – and plenty of ammunition, signal rockets, Strachan's medicine chest, a shovel, pickaxe and ice-axe, and a tent.

'Do we need all this stuff?' Killigrew asked Ågård. 'We're only going five miles.'

'Five miles there, five miles back, sir,' the ice quartermaster reminded him. 'It's past noon already. If a fog comes up or the weather turns nasty, we might be stuck out there overnight. We don't want to take any chances.'

Killigrew took his place at the head of the sledge-haulers, next to Strachan; when there was no need for someone to go ahead to blaze a trail, there was no excuse for the two officers not to haul on the sledge with the rest of the men. 'Ready, lads?'

'Aye, aye, sir,' they chorused.

'Then let's shove off.' Killigrew pulled his wire-mesh snow-goggles up over his eyes and the men took up the strain on the harness.

They soon fell into step and built up a steady rhythm. After their previous venture on to the ice in Melville Bay, Killigrew had asked O'Houlihan and Kracht to jury-rig some kind of cleats for their sealskin moccasins so they could get a grip on the ice, using screws as studs; the modified footwear seemed to work a treat. The shore ice was three feet thick at least, and smooth, so the party made good time towards the coast. A chill wind swept down from the north, reminding Killigrew that the long Arctic winter was just round the corner, but they were well wrapped up, and the exertion of pulling the sledge kept them all warm.

It took them forty minutes to reach the shore. They did not venture on to the land itself, but stuck to the ice where the going was smoother. They headed into the frozen inlet. The ship was still four miles off, so after another ten minutes Killigrew signalled a break, and Molineaux brewed up some tea. No one seemed to feel like talking much: they all knew that whatever questions were preying on their minds, they would be answered soon enough when they reached the stranded ship. Behind them the *Venturer* looked surprisingly close, although Killigrew was sure they had covered a mile by now. Normally he had a good sense of distance and direction, but here in the Arctic he felt he could no longer rely on even those faculties.

After a ten-minute rest, they set out again, heading deeper into the inlet where the ship was entombed in the ice. They kept up a good pace – even Strachan did not falter – and it was exhilarating to be stretching their legs after being cooped up on ship for so long; even their walks on Beechey Island had felt claustrophobic, trapped on that tiny islet with the vastness of the sea around them. At least here they felt as if they were heading somewhere, eating up the miles. Killigrew let them rest ten minutes in every hour, and there was no grumbling.

When Killigrew called for their fourth halt, they had only one more mile to go. Now the *Venturer* looked tiny, the strange ship trapped in the ice so very near. 'Two bells,' he remarked. 'They'll be sitting down to supper on board the *Venturer*.'

Ågård glanced at the other men, who nodded, as if they had already discussed this by some kind of telepathy. 'Begging your pardon, sir, but if it's left to us I think we'd all choose to go on. We want to know what's waiting for us on that ship, and if that means having supper an hour later than usual, we don't mind.'

Killigrew concealed his pleasure; he felt exactly the same way. 'Very well,' he told them. 'One more cup of char, and we'll be on our way.' While Endicott took his turn to make the tea, the lieutenant studied the mystery ship through the telescope. The hulk looked utterly bereft of life; the eerie sight sent a shudder down his spine.

Then he realised something.

'It's not one of Franklin's ships,' he announced, unsure whether he was pleased that the *Erebus* and *Terror* had gone further than this, or disappointed that that particular mystery would have to wait to be unravelled some other day.

'How can you tell, sir?' asked Osborne.

'The mainmast is too far forward. Both the *Erebus* and the *Terror* had their mainmasts moved aft to accommodate their engines when they were converted for discovery service.' Killigrew handed the telescope to Ågård. 'What do you make of her?'

The ice quartermaster was silent for a moment. 'She's had all her upper works taken down, no clues . . . Reckon she must be a whaler, though, sir. What other ships would be found in these waters?'

'She's a little deep in these seas for a whaler, wouldn't you say?' Killigrew pointed out. 'Do whalers often sail into uncharted waters?'

'The *Elizabeth* and the *Larkins* were sailing into uncharted waters when they passed through Melville Bay thirty-five years ago; and they profited richly by it, having the whole of the North Water to themselves that season. Perhaps the master of this ship thought he could pull off the same trick.'

'If he did, it doesn't look as though he profited richly by it.'

They put the harnesses back on as soon as they had drunk their tea, and covered the last mile in three-quarters of an hour. Killigrew called a halt when they were a hundred yards from the hulk, and shrugged off the harness. He pulled his comforter down from his face and cupped his hands around his mouth.

'Hullo!'

No reply, just the gentle soughing of the wind over the treeless hills on either side of the inlet. An awning had been tented over the upper deck, but it had fallen in in places, perhaps collapsed under the weight of the snow, and here and there tatters of canvas flapped in the breeze. Somehow, the ship looked even more lifeless than the barren landscape around them.

'But answer came there none,' Molineaux muttered.

'I'm going on board,' said Killigrew. 'I want one volunteer to come with me while the rest of you wait here.'

Ågård, Osborne, Molineaux, Endicott, Hughes and McLellan all stepped forward.

'Ask a silly question,' sighed Killigrew. 'Molineaux, you come with me. The rest of you wait here.' There was not one of them whose company Killigrew would not have been glad of in a pinch, but he knew from experience there was no man he preferred to have watch his back than Molineaux. 'Take the other shotgun.'

'Aye, aye, sir.' The petty officer broke open the gun, loaded two shells and stuffed some more in his pockets. 'Just in case,' he explained.

A gangplank ran down from the ship's entry port to the ice. Killigrew and Molineaux approached it. 'Hullo!' repeated the lieutenant. 'Is there anyone there?'

There was no reply. 'Reckon that means one of three things,

sir,' said Molineaux. 'Either there's no one there; *or*, there is someone there, but they don't want to reply; *or*, there is someone there, but they can't reply on account of being dead.'

'You can be a cheerful fellow sometimes, Molineaux.'

'What were you expecting, sir? A brass-band reception?'

'A sign of life would be nice.' Killigrew raised his voice again. 'Hullo! I'm coming on board!' He led the way up the gangplank and pulled aside a flap of canvas to step under the awning. There were enough rents in the rotten material to provide plenty of light from outside. He pulled down his snow-goggles around his neck to see more clearly. Snow had banked up here and there where it had blown in through the rents, protected from the summer thaw by the shade of the awning, and a layer of rime covered everything.

'Not exactly shipshape and Bristol-fashioned, is it, sir?' said Molineaux. There were ropes everywhere, harpoons, cutting-in spades and flensing knives scattered all over the deck. 'There's a lot of blood here.'

'This is a whaling ship, Molineaux. Flensing whales is a messy business.'

'Then where's the whalebone?'

'Hm?'

'They hunt bowhead whales in these waters, right, sir? I don't need to have been a spouter like Ollie to know that. Those sperm whales the Yankees hunt in the South Seas, well, they got teeth, just like you and me. But bowheads have mouths full of whalebone. They use it for stiffening ladies' corsets; it's as valuable as the whale-oil. So if they killed a whale, where's the whalebone? It's too big to be below decks; they tie it to the masts, great big curving bits of it. I've seen it. And if they didn't kill a whale, where'd all this blood come from?'

The two of them stared at one another.

'Sir, you know that prickly feeling you get on the back of your neck, when you know something's wrong, but you can't quite say what?'

'You've got that feeling too, eh?'

'Uh-huh.' Molineaux nodded sombrely. He crossed to the try-works, slung his shotgun across his back, and climbed up to look inside one of the copper pots. 'Clean as a whistle.' He jumped down behind the try-works, and then re-emerged with a harpoon gun in his hands. 'This looks like it's been fired, sir. There's a spent percussion cap on the nipple.'

'Not lately, I'll warrant.'

'No, sir.'

There was a loud bang. The two of them whirled round, Killigrew levelling his shotgun, Molineaux brandishing the heavy harpoon gun like a club. A second, softer thud sounded as the door of the deck-house aft banged in the wind.

Molineaux chuckled humourlessly. 'Jesus! I nearly sha— That gave me quite a scare, sir.'

'Me too.' Killigrew crossed to the deck-house, and noticed a harpoon embedded deep in the planks. 'Molineaux! Come and take a look at this!'

The petty officer hurried along the deck and crouched to examine the harpoon. 'No one threw this iron, sir. Not through this bulkhead.'

Killigrew nodded. 'So now we know where the harpoon from that harpoon gun went.'

'Which kind of begs the question, what was it fired at?'

'Not a whale, that's for certain. Not unless the whale jumped out of the sea and landed on the deck. Come on. Maybe the answer to this mystery lies below.'

Molineaux made to enter the door first, but Killigrew stopped him. 'I'll go first.'

'If you insist, sir.'

The deck-house was empty. A companion ladder led down to the lower deck. Holding his shotgun before him, Killigrew tiptoed below. At the foot of the companion ladder they found themselves in the steerage. A huge hole, five feet wide, had been smashed in the flimsy bulkhead aft; there was a similar hole in the bulkhead forward.

'Jesus!' gasped Molineaux. 'Looks like a bloody rhinoceros went through here!'

'There are no rhinoceroses in the Arctic.'

'Tell me something I don't know, Sir Joseph Banks,' muttered Molineaux. 'Which way now, sir?'

'Perhaps we should split up to search the ship,' Killigrew said dubiously.

'Yur, *right*.'

The lieutenant was grateful for the contempt with which the petty officer treated the suggestion. All the indications were that whatever had happened here had taken place months if not years ago; but with his flesh crawling the way it was, the thought of wandering alone in this wreck did not appeal to him any more than it did to Molineaux.

Killigrew ducked his head to step through the hole leading to the captain's stateroom. The table that had once dominated the centre of the room was smashed, the legs broken underneath it, as if a stout party had tried to sit on it. There was a dusting of snow on the surface of the broken table, with shards of glass in it. Killigrew and Molineaux both glanced up to see that the skylight above was smashed in.

Molineaux nodded at the gun rack in one corner. 'No guns,' he remarked.

'They must have taken them with them.'

'Taken them where? There were eight boats stowed on the upper deck; I don't reckon a ship of this size would have more'n that.'

Killigrew crossed to the bureau in one corner and opened a drawer. There was a ledger within. He opened it up and glanced at the title page. The ship was the *Jan Snekker*. 'The captain's log,' he said. 'No skipper would abandon ship and leave his log behind. Not unless he was in a devil of a hurry; and the ship obviously wasn't sinking.'

'So either they didn't abandon ship, or when they did the skipper and anyone clever enough to think of bringing the log was already dead.'

Killigrew leafed through a few pages of the log. The date of the final entry was '13 Desember 1850'.

'What language is that?' asked Molineaux, peering over his shoulder at the text. 'Swedish?'

Killigrew shook his head. ' "December" is spelled with a C in Swedish, the same as in English.'

'It's got to be one of those Scandinavian languages, though,' said Molineaux. 'Look at all them lines through the Os, and the little circles over the As. Norwegian, I reckon; that, or Danish. Can you make it out, sir?'

'A few words here and there, which look the same as they do in Swedish. Not enough to make any sense of it.' Killigrew closed the ledger and tucked it under one arm.

'Maybe Sørensen can read it,' suggested Molineaux. 'He's Danish.'

'All right, we'll let him take a look at it when we get back to the *Venturer*. Shall we check the rest of the ship?'

Molineaux nodded. 'Let's get it over with.'

'Take this.' Killigrew handed him the log and found the stub of a candle resting in a saucer. He lit it with a match, and with his shotgun in one hand and the candle in the other, he ducked through the hole on the other side of the steerage and emerged into the blubber room, where a third hole was smashed through the bulkhead on the far side.

'What the devil did this?' Killigrew wondered out loud.

Molineaux shrugged. 'Sixty-eight-pound round shot?'

Killigrew shook his head. 'Too small.'

'Ninety-eight-pound?'

'Where did it enter the hull? There was no breech in the captain's stateroom, and whatever it was, it was travelling this way.' He pointed forward.

Molineaux nodded. He could see for himself that the splinters of wood smashed in the bulkheads lay forward of the holes.

Killigrew looked up at the hatch in the deck head. It had been barred from below with boards nailed across it. 'Looks as if they were determined to keep someone out.'

'Or some*thing*.' Molineaux indicated the large hatch in the centre of the deck, the hood smashed in as if some great weight had landed on it. 'I guess they didn't have much luck.'

The two of them crouched over the hatch. The light from the candle did not penetrate the inky depths of the hold. 'Shall we go down?' asked Killigrew.

'It's either that, sir, or spend the rest of our lives wondering.'

The lieutenant indicated the hole in the forward bulkhead. 'We'll check the fo'c'sle first,' he decided, telling himself he was just being methodical.

Like the rest of the ship, the forecastle was in disarray: broken crockery everywhere, upset stools, fold-down tables wrenched from the sides. The two of them found a companion way down to the hold. They were about to descend when something streaked past them, level with their ankles, making them both jump.

'Jesus!' said Molineaux. 'What was that? Ship's cat?'

'Arctic fox. Come on.'

They descended. The candle cast a flickering, eerie light about the hold, the shadows of the stacked casks dancing threateningly on the sides. Some of the casks had been stacked across the far end of the hold, but they had been pulled down and smashed to one side.

'Did I tell you about my nevvy Harry, sir? Nine years old. You know what his favourite game is, sir? Playing forts. Ever since his dad told him he was named after the Hector of Afghanistan, Harry likes to pretend he's defending Piper's Fort against the heathens, just like his namesake. He can make a fort out of just about anything. Many's the time Luther's opened up the King's Head to find that Harry's rearranged all the furniture for a re-enaction of the last stand of the Fighting Forty-Fourth. The thing is, sir, the way these barrels are stacked . . .'

'You think this is your nephew's handiwork?'

Molineaux laughed. In the echoing hold, the sound was hollow. 'No, sir. But it looks like someone was trying to build a fort here. For a last stand, know what I mean?' He peered over a stack of barrels into the space behind. 'What the hell *is* that? Sir, could you bring that light here?'

'By all means. What have you found, Molineaux?'

'I'm not sure, sir. It looks like—'

He broke off as the light of the candle fell across the space behind the barrels. Then he swore vilely, combining an obscenity and a blasphemy in one breath.

Killigrew saw it too. He set the candle down on an upright cask and struggled to choke back the bile that rose to his gorge.

VII

Into the Ice

Killigrew had seen some gruesome sights in his career: the slaughter of the innocents at Chinkiang-fu; the aftermath of a pilong attack; the effects of a sixty-eight-pound shell when it exploded in close proximity to men. But nothing could have prepared him for what he found behind those barrels. If it did not match what he had seen at Chinkiang-fu in scale, it more than matched it for sheer, grisly horror.

Bones. Unmistakably human, for all that something had torn the skeletons apart. A pelvis here; a piece of spinal column there. Crushed ribcages. Scattered jawbones. All had scraps of flesh adhering to them; not decayed – the Arctic cold had preserved them – but whoever these men had been, they had died some months, if not years, ago. Dark stains were splashed all about beneath the layer of rime that glistened in the candlelight.

'Jesus Christ!' exclaimed Molineaux. 'It's like a bloody abattoir! What d'you think happened here, sir?'

'Your guess is as good as mine.'

'Whoever did this must've been crazy, sir.'

'Not necessarily. The way the bones have been scattered may be the work of scavengers. You saw that fox. From the mess topsides, it looks to me as if at least one polar bear was also attracted by the scent of blood.'

'Then who killed these poor—' Molineaux broke off and tensed.

125

Before Killigrew could ask him what was wrong, he heard it too: a deck board creaked somewhere overhead.

Perhaps it was just Killigrew's imagination – hardly surprising that it was running wild, considering the macabre surroundings – but he thought he saw a couple of shadows fall across the hatch in the deck head.

But the footsteps that came down the companion way were real enough.

As one, both Killigrew and Molineaux ducked behind casks and unslung their shotguns, levelling them at the foot of the companion way. Killigrew belatedly realised that he had been so intent on following the trail of destruction, he had not bothered to check the rest of the cabins. Anyone could have been hiding in there.

He could feel his heart pounding in his chest. He struggled to hold his breath for fear that it would give him away. His mouth was dry, his palms moist where they gripped the shotgun.

Molineaux gesticulated insistently; Killigrew had left the candle burning on one of the casks. Whoever these men were, they would see it and know that the intruders were not far away. But there was not time to put it out now: they must have seen the flickering light through the hole in the deck above.

Two figures descended the companion way, one gripping a loaded harpoon gun, the other brandishing an ice-axe. Both were heavily muffled against the cold, their eyes hidden behind wire-mesh snow-goggles. The man with the harpoon gun was huge; he was framed by his own shadow on the bulkhead behind him, which made him look even bigger.

'Drop your weapons and raise your hands in the air!' shouted Killigrew. 'There are four shotguns lined up on you!'

The shorter man dropped his ice-axe with a Caledonian oath of fright, but his larger companion merely lowered the harpoon gun. 'Mr Killigrew? Is that you, sir?'

Killigrew and Molineaux heaved huge sighs of relief and rose to their feet as Ågård pulled down his goggles. The Swede grinned. '*Four* shotguns, sir?'

'I thought a little bluff wouldn't go amiss, under the circumstances. Who's that with you?'

'It's me,' Strachan said testily, retrieving the ice-axe from the deck. 'Damn it, Killigrew, did you have to frighten us like that? I almost dropped this confounded thing on my foot!'

'I thought I told you to wait outside with the others?'

'You were gone a mortal long time, Killigrew. We were starting to get worried.'

'It's only been ten minutes. Did you expect Molineaux and me to search the whole ship in that time? You might at least have tried calling our names when you came on board.'

'Begging your pardon, sir,' said Ågård, 'but for all we knew you and Wes had been done in by a couple of spouters who'd gone out of their minds after being trapped in the Arctic for so long. We didn't think it'd be right clever to announce our arrival.'

'If you were worried about crazed whalers, Ågård, wouldn't it have been more sensible to bring one of the others?' asked Killigrew.

'As opposed to what?' Strachan asked bitterly. 'Bringing me, I suppose you mean? I think I resent that! Just because I wear spectacles and read a lot of books, you think I can't be heroic?'

'Very heroic you looked, almost dropping that ice-axe on your foot!'

'Ah, come on now, sir,' Ågård said with a grin. 'Don't tell me you weren't scared when me and Mr Strachan came down that companion ladder? I know *I* was. Happen it were Mr Strachan's idea that we come look for you. Me, I was all for giving you another five minutes.'

'All right. My apologies to you, Strachan. You're more heroic than I gave you credit for.'

'Hmph! Don't patronise me, Killigrew. What happened here, anyhow?'

'That's what Molineaux and I were just trying to work out. As a matter of fact, I have a theory . . .'

The sound of wood splintering came from somewhere at the back of the hold. Killigrew realised that Molineaux had disappeared in that direction. 'Molineaux? Is everything all right back there?'

'Just plummy, sir. Be with you in a brace of shakes. I just want to check something, that's all.'

Strachan peered behind the barrels and blanched in the

flickering light of the candle. 'Jings! What *happened* here?'

'That's what I'd like to know,' Killigrew said grimly. 'When we get out of here, say nothing to any of the others about what we found. That goes for you and Molineaux too, Ågård. Until we can get some clue of what happened here, I'd prefer not to alarm the others. Ignorance breeds fear.'

'They'll be curious,' warned Strachan.

'Then we tell them the bare minimum: we found the ship deserted, with no obvious way of telling what happened. It's to be hoped that the solution to this mystery lies in this log.'

'You said you have a theory?'

'I fear the crew of this ship were forced to resort to anthropophagy, Mr Strachan.' Killigrew hid from the horror of it all behind the technical term, perhaps to shield himself as much as others from its grisly implications.

'Oh my word!' groaned Strachan.

All of this was lost on Ågård. 'Anthropo-what, sir?'

'The last date in that log is December eighteen-fifty,' explained Killigrew. 'Suppose this ship entered the Arctic in the season of 'forty-nine, but got trapped here in the ice? One winter would be bad enough, but if the ice didn't thaw sufficiently for the ship to break free in the following summer? Whalers only carry enough provisions for one season. By December eighteen-fifty they'd have been crazed with hunger. Desperate enough to resort to the ultimate taboo.'

'Oh! You mean cannibalism, sir.'

Killigrew nodded. 'The ones who drew the short straws didn't care for it – assuming they were given the chance to draw straws. However they decided the matter, the result was a desperate fight. The weaker party tried to barricade itself below decks, but the others broke in through the skylight in the captain's stateroom. Deranged, they smashed their way through the bulkheads. The defenders retreated here, to the hold, built themselves a barricade out of these casks and prepared to sell their lives dearly. Whoever won butchered the men they killed. Then the survivors decided to set out on foot. Who knows? Perhaps they may even have made it back to civilisation.'

'You mean the men responsible for this charnel house are still on the loose somewhere?' exclaimed Strachan. 'That's a cheering thought!'

'Don't worry. It's more than a thousand miles to civilisation. The chances that they made it are almost non-existent.'

'It's a nice, neat theory, sir.' Molineaux returned from the depths of the hold, tossing a tin can from one hand to the other. 'There's just one hole in it – a hole as big as the ones in the bulkheads on the lower deck.' He tossed the tin canister at Killigrew. 'Put that in your pipe and smoke it.'

The lieutenant caught it, thinking that if one more person told him to put something in his pipe and smoke it, he would not be answerable for the consequences. He looked at the label on the tin. ' "Boiled mutton"?'

'Crazed with hunger, sir? So crazed they forgot about the nine hundred or so tins of food they had crated at the back of the hold? And not just boiled mutton. Roast beef, roast lamb, knuckle of veal, carrots in gravy . . . lumme, sir, they even had beef *à la flamande*. So don't try to tell me they wanted a bit of variation in their vittles.'

Killigrew swallowed. The fact that they could make no sense of it all only added to the horror of the scene. Perhaps there was no sense to it. Perhaps the men on this ship, driven beyond all reason by their ordeal in the Arctic, had simply gone crazy, smashing up the ship and butchering one another. He wondered if a similar fate had befallen the crews of the *Erebus* and *Terror*. Or if the same fate awaited . . .

He shook his head. 'Whatever the explanation is, we shan't find it down here. Maybe it's in this log. The sooner we get back to the *Venturer* so Sørensen can do his best to translate it, the better.'

They made their way back up to the lower deck. Killigrew ducked through the hole in the bulkhead between the blubber room and the steerage, and then glanced back at the hole behind him as the others came through. He noticed some odd scratches in the wood: five parallel scars, each about two and a half inches apart. 'What could have made these marks, do you suppose?' he asked Strachan. 'You don't think . . .?' He broke off and shook his head.

'What?'

'Nothing. It's too ludicrous to contemplate.'

'Tell me.'

'You'll laugh.'

'I won't. I promise,' said Strachan. 'Killigrew, I'm as much at a loss here as you are. If you've got a theory, no matter how ludicrous it may seem, at least share it with us so we can let you know what we think of it.'

Killigrew took a deep breath. 'You don't think . . . well, is it possible . . . Strachan, could a polar bear have done this?'

Strachan laughed. Not one of his characteristic wry chuckles, but a deep, uncontrolled howl of laughter that doubled him up. A long laugh that left him struggling for breath so severely that at first Killigrew thought he was suffering from a seizure. At last the assistant straightened, removed his spectacles, and dabbed the tears of laughter from his cheeks with a handkerchief. 'No,' he told Killigrew gravely. 'It could not.'

'Isn't it possible that . . .?'

'That what? That an animal weighing a mere eleven hundred pounds could claw its way through four bulkheads and a hatch cover, and slaughter the entire crew of a whaler? Fifty men armed with pistols and muskets?' He shook his head. 'Forget it, Killigrew. If you're trying to come up with an explanation for what we've seen here today, you'll have to do better than that.'

On the upper deck, Molineaux opened a locker and helped himself to half a dozen harpoons and a box of percussion caps. Killigrew noticed he was carrying the harpoon gun Ågård had brought down to the hold. 'What are you doing with that thing?'

'Salvage, sir. We're allowed, ain't we?'

'What do you intend to do with it?'

'Thought it might come in handy, sir. I don't know what made them holes in the bulkheads, but if it comes after me, I aim to be ready for it!'

'Are we setting out for the ship immediately, sir?' asked Ågård.

'Would you prefer to spend the night here?' asked Killigrew. As summer drew to a close and the *Venturer* headed south, the sun had finally started to dip below the horizon at midnight, but it still did not get any darker than dusk. Nevertheless, Killigrew had no wish to spend the night in proximity to this ship in the twilight. 'Come on, let's get back. The sooner we unravel this mystery, the happier I'll be.' He pulled aside a flap of canvas and walked down the gangplank, followed by Strachan.

The two petty officers lingered. 'Did he say eleven hundred pounds?' asked Molineaux. 'That's more'n a third of a ton, ain't it?'

'Nearer a half,' agreed Ågård. He glanced at the harpoon gun Molineaux clutched, and clapped him heartily on the back. 'You're going to need a bigger gun, Wes.'

'Are you all right, Killigrew?' Pettifer asked when his lieutenant reported to him in the privacy of his day-room. 'You look as if you've seen a ghost!'

Killigrew smiled thinly. 'A ghost ship, sir. It's not the first time I've been on board a ghost ship, but they always leave me in a funk.' Searching the *Jan Snekker* had reminded him of a couple of ships he had encountered in the China Seas, victims of piracy, dredging up memories he would have preferred to forget.

Pettifer poured a couple of glasses of sherry from a crystal decanter. 'Perhaps a drink will help calm your nerves.'

'Thank you, sir.' Killigrew tossed his back in one go.

'Good gracious! You *are* shaken up, aren't you? I overheard Ågård tell the bosun it wasn't the *Erebus* or the *Terror*. What was it?'

'Norwegian whaler, sir. Must've got trapped in the ice back in 'forty-nine.'

'Any survivors?'

'No, sir. At least, none on the ship. A few corpses, though. What was left of them. They'd been pretty badly mauled by scavengers, from the look of it. Whatever happened there, it must've been an utter massacre. If there were any survivors, they must've set out for the mainland on foot. With your permission, sir, I'd like to go back to the whaler tomorrow and see what else I can learn.'

'Go back?' Pettifer gave him a puzzled smile. 'Why?'

'I want to know what happened on that ship, sir. If there's one thing I can't abide, it's a mystery without an explanation.'

'One mystery at a time, Mr Killigrew. Our mission is to find Franklin and the others. Naturally, we'll report the whaler when

131

we get back to England; someone must've reported it missing. I dare say there'll be some women in Norway as yet unaware they are widows.'

'And can we tell them that they are?'

'You say you found no survivors; whoever was on that whaler is either dead or long gone. There's nothing more we can do for them. We'll set sail immediately.'

'In which direction, sir?'

'South, of course. You say you abhor a mystery. Don't you want to know where this sound leads? We're on the verge of discovering the North-West Passage. Surely you don't want to turn back now, just because you found a stranded whaler?'

'Something strange happened on that whaler, sir. How do we know the same thing won't happen to us?'

'Now you're just being foolish, Killigrew. Mind you, from what you've told me of what you saw on that whaler, I can appreciate that you might be unnerved. You get back to your cabin and have a good night's rest. I'm sure you'll feel better in the morning.'

'I suppose you're right, sir.'

'Of course I am!'

Killigrew put down his sherry glass. 'One other thing, sir. Only I, Strachan, Ågård and Molineaux went aboard the whaler. The rest didn't see what we saw, and I told the others to make no mention of the human remains. I thought it best not to spread panic and alarm through the crew. You know how superstitious seamen can be.'

'Very wise, Killigrew. Did you get the log?'

'Yes, sir. It's in Norwegian; Sørensen's doing his best to translate it.'

'All right. Perhaps it will solve the mystery of what happened. But we have bigger fish to fry.'

Killigrew took his leave of the captain. As he passed through the wardroom, Yelverton, Ziegler and Bähr confronted him, demanding to know what he'd found on the mysterious ship.

'Nothing,' Killigrew told him. 'We didn't find anything. The crew must've abandoned ship when they realised the ship was permanently trapped in the ice.'

'Then how come they left the log behind?' demanded Yelverton.

'I don't know,' Killigrew retorted impatiently. He felt he could confide in the master what he had discovered on the ship, but he was too tired, too drained to do it tonight, and he did not want to discuss it in front of Ziegler and Bähr. 'Perhaps we'll know when Sørensen's finished translating it. By the way, doctor, did you get a chance to examine Terregannoeuck?'

'Up to a point,' said Bähr. 'They brought him into the sick-berth and I was just starting to look at him when the damned fellow woke up on me. Refused to let me examine him properly and went back up on deck without so much as a by-your-leave, let alone an explanation.'

'Anything wrong with him?'

'Not that I could see – apart from his deuced rum behaviour, of course. Rather put me in mind of a Hindu holy man I saw in India once,' he added thoughtfully.

'Oh?'

'A fakir, I think he was called. This fellow could put himself in a trance for hours on end. Some of the natives said he could go for months on end like that, without eating, although I didn't get a chance to confirm that with my own eyes. Or rather, I had better things to do than to sit around watching some emaciated, diaper-wearing Indian doing nothing at all for days at a time.'

Killigrew entered his cabin, where Sørensen was laboriously transcribing the log into English in a fresh ledger provided by Latimer. The Danish harpooner rose to his feet as soon as the lieutenant entered.

'Making any progress?' Killigrew kept his voice low, not wanting the others in the wardroom to overhear through the louvred slats in the door, and Sørensen had sense enough to do the same.

'Not much, *min herre*. I've only just begun. But I have found one thing out.'

'What's that?'

'You checked the date of the final entry; maybe you should have checked the date of the first. They sailed from Trondheim in April eighteen-fifty.'

'Eighteen-*fifty*? You're sure?'

'See for yourself.'

'So they probably weren't trapped in the ice for more than three months.'

The harpooner nodded. 'Hardly enough time to go insane, *min herre*. Not for seasoned whalers who were used to spending time cooped up on board a ship.'

'All right, Sørensen. You can continue in the morning. I'm going to try to get some sleep now.' Although Killigrew very much doubted he would sleep restfully, after what he had seen on the *Jan Snekker*.

'Ice, dead ahead!'

On the quarterdeck, Killigrew levelled his telescope, but could see nothing of this new ice. Not that there was not plenty of ice in evidence all around them: shore ice clinging to the coasts on either side of the channel, and 'growlers' – so named from the noise they made as they ground against the *Venturer*'s iron-sheathed bows – floating in the open water between. He picked up the speaking tube to address the ice quartermaster in the crow's nest.

'What does it look like, Ågård?'

'Pack ice, sir. Lots of it. From one side of the channel to the other.'

Peel Sound had narrowed, and then opened up again, until the sea stretched out as far as the eye could see to starboard; but most of that was covered in irregular chunks of pack ice. The *Venturer* continued her voyage through the lead between this pack ice and the shore ice to port, following the coast southerly. According to Yelverton, they were now following the west coast of the Boothia. Discovered by Sir John and Sir James Ross more than twenty years earlier, Boothia had been named after Felix Booth, the philanthropic gin magnate who had funded their voyage, which made the peninsula the largest advertisement for mother's ruin – or indeed any other commodity that Killigrew could think of – in the world. Although the Rosses' ship had only touched at the more accessible east coast of the peninsula, James Ross had undertaken many sledge journeys across the neck of land. On one such journey he had discovered the

Magnetic North Pole; the *Venturer* had passed it the previous day.

The compass had not gone crazy – at least, as crazy as a compass could go, by spinning wildly – as some had suggested it would. It had simply become even more sluggish, and refused to point in any particular direction with a sense of conviction. Strachan had wanted to stop for a few hours so he could carry out some measurements with his magnetometer and his dip circle, but Pettifer flatly refused. They were too close to discovering the North-West Passage.

Strictly speaking, they were back on *mare cognita* for now, although they had connected Peel Sound with the waters off the north coast of King William Land. The latter had also been discovered by James Ross, although it had not been entirely mapped out. Was it connected to Victoria Land, to the west, or was it an island? The explorers Dease and Simpson had discovered a strait between the south of King William Land and the north coast of the Canadian mainland during an overland expedition, but did King William Land connect to the mainland to the south-east? Yelverton refused to be drawn into making any guesses, but Pettifer was convinced that there must be a way around the east and south of King William Land that connected with Dease Strait. If he was right, they were on the threshold of discovering the North-West Passage.

They were passing through a channel between King William Land and Boothia, no more than twenty-seven miles wide, although two miles of shore ice on either side cut that down to a channel twenty-three miles across. After half an hour, Killigrew could see the ice ahead through the telescope: thick pack ice, unmoving, anchored by the several icebergs embedded in it that must have been grounded in shoal water. He sent Cavan below to report this to the captain. The mate returned a minute later with fresh instructions.

'He says to proceed under tops'ls only and order Varrow to get steam up, sir.'

'Get steam up?' Killigrew echoed. 'Has he forgotten how much of our coal we've already used up?'

'That's what he said, sir.'

'I don't doubt it, Mr Cavan. But would you remind him

135

that . . . Oh, never mind. I'll tell him myself. You have the watch while I'm below, Mr Cavan. Tell the bosun to heave-to.'

'Aye, aye, sir.'

Killigrew descended the after hatch. On being ushered into Pettifer's day-room by the marine sentry, he found the captain bundling up in warm clothes. The lieutenant himself was wrapped up warmly in his greatcoat, comforter and leather gauntlets: the days when they could stroll about the deck in frock-coat and cap were gone until the spring.

'Is there a problem, Killigrew?'

'No, sir. I just thought I ought to remind you that we're down to forty-nine tons of coal; nearly half what we had on board when we set out. Are you certain you wish to proceed under steam?'

'That's what I told Mr Cavan, is it not? Or did he relay my instructions imprecisely?'

'Not at all, sir.'

'I'm well aware of how much coal we have left, Killigrew. We brought the coal to be used, not simply as ballast.'

'Yes, sir. But you mustn't forget, we have one, perhaps two winters in the Arctic ahead of us. We'll need coal to fuel the stoves.'

'Perhaps if we can push through the Dease Straight before the end of September, there'll be no need for us to spend a winter in the Arctic at all.' Pettifer was clearly in high spirits, buoyed up by the thought of not only discovering the North-West Passage, but also of sailing through it in a single season.

'I'm not sure that's something I'd care to gamble on, sir.'

'Pish! You worry too much, Killigrew.' Pettifer wound his comforter around his neck and led the way up on deck. 'Unbox the sails, Mr Thwaites!' he ordered the boatswain. 'Proceed under tops'ls only. Instruct Varrow to get steam up, Mr Killigrew.'

Killigrew took the speaking tube from the binnacle. 'Mr Varrow? Fire the boilers.'

'Fire the boilers?' The engineer's voice, thick with a Geordie accent. 'Are you off your head?'

'Those are the captain's orders.'

'Is *he* off his head?'

'Ahem! Make it so, Mr Varrow.' Killigrew replaced the stopper in the brass mouthpiece, stifling a torrent of Geordie imprecations.

While waiting for the engineer to get steam up, the *Venturer* followed the edge of the pack under sail, searching for a lead, but the ice stretched from one side of the channel to the other.

'How far does this ice go, Qualtrough?' Pettifer asked the senior quartermaster, a Manxman who had spent most of his life serving as an officer on board whalers before being recruited into the navy for his Arctic experience.

'As far as the eye can see from the crow's nest, sir. But there's open water somewhere on the other side: you can see it reflected in the "water sky".' He pointed to the dark shadow on the underside of the cloud over the south side of the pack ice.

'Can we force our way through?'

'I don't know, sir. There's a lot of brash ice – it's soft, sludgy stuff, but it can solidify in no time, if the temperature drops . . .'

'The thermometer has already fallen seven degrees in as many days; unusually early in the season, I might add. How much further is it likely to drop?'

'Who can say, sir? These are little-known waters; the only people who've been here before us are Sir James Ross with his sledge parties, twenty-two years ago, and the *Erebus* and *Terror* – maybe. Who's to say what's usual for this part of the world?'

'Then it can be done?' Pettifer asked brightly.

Qualtrough glanced at Killigrew, as if to say: *Am I no longer speaking English?*

'Well?' demanded the captain.

'Yes, but—'

'Capital! As soon as Mr Varrow has steam up, we shall try to force our way through the ice. See if you can find a weak spot, Qualtrough.'

'I beg your pardon, sir. I said, yes, it *could* be done. I did *not* say it *should* be done. If the ice closes in on us while we're in the midst of it, the brash ice between the floes will solidify, freezing us in like a fly in amber. I cannot in all conscience advise you to proceed any further.'

'What would you have me do, Qualtrough? Turn back now,

when we've come so far? When we're but a few miles from mapping the North-West Passage?'

'I don't see what else we can do, sir.'

'Then you have no vision, Qualtrough. You have the watch, Mr Killigrew.'

'Aye, aye, sir.'

But Pettifer was already descending the after hatch.

Qualtrough lit his clay pipe. 'Tell me, sir, what was the purpose in bringing me along if Commander Pettifer has no intention of heeding my advice?'

'Advice is all it is, Qualtrough. You've given it, you've done your duty. The captain is responsible for this ship and the decision rests with him.'

'Does my advice count for nothing, then, even if by ignoring it the captain risks the lives of all on board?'

'The captain is aware of his responsibilities. I'm sure he's weighed up all the consequences of his decision. It's not for you or me to gainsay him.'

'Even though I've got more than thirty years' experience of sailing in the Arctic, and this is his first voyage in polar seas?'

'You said it was possible.'

'A mistake. Yes, I suppose it's possible. Anything's possible. It's possible to flap your arms and fly to the moon. You've just got to flap hard enough.'

'Is that normal, Ågård?' asked Pettifer, perturbed. Great clouds of condensation billowed from his mouth as he spoke.

The ice quartermaster smiled thinly. 'You tell me, sir. I have no experience of steam-driven vessels in the Arctic.'

Pettifer was referring to the odd glugging noise made by the *Venturer* as its screw drove her through the mushy brash ice. The floes were thick but consisted mostly of snow, and were soft. The ship steamed through the leads between them, ploughing through brash ice the consistency of porridge.

'What rate are we making, Mr Cavan?' asked Pettifer.

'A little over two knots, sir,' replied the mate who, assisted by Jacko Smith and Johnno Smith, had just finished measuring the ship's speed with log and line.

'You see?' Pettifer told the ice quartermaster triumphantly.

'We're making good time. You should have more faith in modern technology, Ågård.'

A slight thud ran through the *Venturer*'s deck as the bows collided with something that gave at first, but slowed their progress until they had come to a halt. Beneath the surface of the soupy brash ice that closed in astern, the screw continued to make glugging noises.

Whatever they had collided with, they had certainly not hit anything with enough force for anyone to even think of sending someone below to make sure the hull had not been breeched. Ågård hurried forward to peer over the bows to see what the problem was. 'We're wedged between two floes,' he reported. 'They've not nipped us – there's no pressure on them – but they're big enough to bar our passage.'

'See if we can force them aside, Mr Killigrew,' ordered Pettifer.

'Aye, aye, sir.' The lieutenant took the speaking tube from the binnacle. He noticed that the pliable gutta-percha was now brittle with cold and laced with tiny fracture lines. 'Can you give us full power, Mr Varrow?'

'I'll do me best, sir.'

The deck throbbed more urgently as Varrow increased revolutions. The *Venturer* pushed forward a couple of feet, and then the floes seemed to assert themselves and the ship was pushed back.

'We're not getting through,' said Ågård.

'We'll see about that,' snorted Pettifer. 'We'll take a run-up.'

'Aye, aye, sir. Mr Varrow? Turn ahead, full speed.'

The *Venturer* surged forwards through the sludgy brash, gathering way: half a knot, one knot, a knot and a half . . .

The bows bore down on the two floes ahead. The *Venturer* was not accelerating fast enough. Then she hit the floes. She came to an abrupt halt and the men on deck staggered as a shudder ran through the hull. At first it seemed as if the floes had baffled them a second time, but a moment later something gave and the ship was moving forwards once more, pushing aside the floes. Then they were through, glugging through the ice at a knot and a half.

'Didn't I tell you to have more faith in modern technology,

Ågård?' Pettifer crowed, patting the *Venturer*'s bulwark. 'She'll see us through, never fear.'

'We're not through yet, sir,' warned the ice quartermaster.

Within half an hour more floes blocked their path. This time the *Venturer* had to back up and run at them three times before they broke through. Now they were making no more than a knot through the thickening ice.

'This will never do,' grumbled Pettifer. 'Tell Varrow I want more speed.'

'We're at full ahead as it is, sir,' said Killigrew.

'More speed, damn your eyes!' snapped Pettifer, startling the lieutenant with his uncharacteristic anger.

'Aye, aye, sir.' Killigrew picked up the speaking tube. 'More speed, Mr Varrow.'

'We're already at full ahead!'

Killigrew took a deep breath. 'The captain's aware of that, Mr Varrow. Give her all you can.'

'We're using up a lot of coal, Mr Killigrew. Maybe a quarter of a ton in the past two hours.'

'Stick to it, Mr Varrow. There's open water up ahead somewhere.'

'Aye – the Pacific Ocean, two thousand miles to the west!'

Killigrew replaced the speaking tube. 'Mr Varrow reports that we're getting through a lot of coal, sir.'

'Duly noted, Mr Killigrew,' Pettifer replied blithely.

Strachan came on deck and handed Killigrew his notebook. The lieutenant glanced at the last page of his notes and nodded, understanding. He handed the notebook back to Strachan, and turned to the captain. 'May I speak with you, sir?'

'By all means.' Pettifer gestured for him to step on to the port side of the quarterdeck, away from the others gathered around the helm. 'What is it, Mr Killigrew?'

'Sir, Mr Strachan reports that the temperature has dropped two degrees in as many hours.'

'What of it? We're still making progress, aren't we?'

'Deeper and deeper into the ice. And an hour ago we were making three knots, not one. Perhaps we should heed Qualtrough's advice and turn back.'

'Turn back? When we're so close to completing the North-West

Passage? Where's your spirit, Killigrew?'

'Sir, the longer we leave it, the less our chance of making it out of this brash ice before we become beset. We should turn back now, make for the open water behind us and anchor to the ice, wait for a lead to open. Either that, or prepare to overwinter in the ice. We've come further into the Arctic in a shorter time than any ship that has preceded us. We'll be superbly placed to complete the passage when the thaw comes next spring.'

'No, Killigrew. We shall press on. You heard what Qualtrough said: there's open water somewhere ahead of us.'

Twice more the *Venturer*'s iron-shod bows had to batter their way through the floes. As the temperature dropped, young ice grew outwards from the surrounding pack, choking the narrow channels with oncoming slabs of drift ice. The thicker the brash ice became, the more their progress was blocked by smaller floes that she would easily have nuzzled aside in open water. She was advancing at little more than a snail's pace.

'Sir, we cannot go on like this!' Ågård protested at last. 'We'll never get through! You're driving us to destruction!'

'Belay that, Ågård!' snapped Pettifer.

Killigrew had only ever seen the captain as angry as this once before, when he had returned from the *Assistance* at Greenhithe to report that Sir Edward intended the *Venturer* to stay with the *North Star* at Beechey Island throughout the search for Franklin.

'Sir, as ice quartermaster, it's my duty to warn you about the ice. I must formally protest at your current course of action. Turn back now, or else—'

'You may be one of my ice quartermasters, Ågård, but I am captain. One more word out of you, and I shall have you placed under arrest and removed from the quarterdeck!'

Ågård turned to Killigrew. 'For God's sake, sir! Tell him! Tell him we'll be caught in the ice, and crushed! We have to stop *now*!'

'Private Jenkins!' bellowed Pettifer.

The marine approached the quarterdeck. 'Sir?'

'You will place Ågård under arrest.'

'Sir?'

'Take him below and confine him to his cabin,' Pettifer elaborated impatiently.

'Very good, sir.' Jenkins turned to Ågård with an apologetic shrug. 'If you'll come with me?'

Ågård backed away, shaking his head. 'Are you all mad? Do you want to destroy us all?'

'Come along now.' Jenkins tried to take Ågård by the arm, but the ice quartermaster broke free, dodged past the marine and lunged at Pettifer. Before he could reach the captain, however, Jenkins caught him from behind and pinioned him against the binnacle. 'Calm down now. The cap'n knows what he's doing.'

'You bloody fools! He has no notion! None of you does!'

'Put Ågård in irons in the lazaretto, Jenkins,' ordered Pettifer.

Jenkins was a big man, but even he struggled to cope with the ice quartermaster's frenzy. 'Give us a hand, Walsh!'

Walsh abandoned his post by the ship's bell and came to his assistance. The two of them frog-marched Ågård to the after hatch and forced him below.

'Perhaps we should heed his advice, sir,' said Killigrew. 'He's got more Arctic experience than the rest of us put together, Qualtrough excluded; and Qualtrough wasn't too happy about the thought of pressing on.'

'Experienced he may be, Mr Killigrew, but the man's clearly lost his nerve,' said Pettifer. 'You remember how he squealed with terror as we came through the Middle Pack – came through unscathed, I might add. Besides, he said so himself: he has no experience of steamers in the Arctic.'

'Perhaps we should ask Sørensen what he thinks.'

'Damn it, Killigrew! I will not turn to a Danish spouter for advice! Now pipe down, mister, unless you wish to find yourself in irons in the lazaretto alongside our pusillanimous Mr Ågård! We push on, damn you!'

Pettifer was still glaring at Killigrew when the speaking tube leading to the crow's nest whistled shrilly. Neither the captain nor the lieutenant made a move.

'Do you want me to get that, sir?' asked Cavan.

Neither Pettifer nor Killigrew gave any indication that they had heard him. After a pause, the mate picked up the speaking tube and listened. Then he hooked the brass mouthpiece back on the binnacle.

Pettifer turned away from Killigrew abruptly. 'Well?' he demanded of Cavan.

'Qualtrough reports clear water less than two miles ahead, sir.'

Pettifer smiled. 'Well, mister? Didn't I tell you we'd make it? The North-West Passage is ours for the taking, gentlemen!'

The ship lurched under their feet as the bow collided with something solid, throwing the helmsman against the wheel and the rest of them to the deck. Killigrew leaped to his feet and went to help Pettifer up, but the captain waved him away.

'I'm all right, Killigrew,' he snapped pettishly. 'Go below, Mr Cavan. I want a full damage report immediately!'

'Aye, aye, sir.' Cavan scurried below.

Pettifer snatched the speaking tube from the binnacle and blew into it. 'What the devil was that, Qualtrough? . . . Didn't you see it, man? . . . Spare me your pathetic excuses! If we're holed, I'll have you disrated, damn your eyes! Pay more attention in future.'

If we're holed, thought Killigrew, *then being disrated will be the least of Qualtrough's worries.*

'What happened, sir?' the helmsman, Endicott, asked groggily, still dazed from his fall.

'We ran into a floe,' snapped Pettifer.

'Are we holed, sir?' asked McLellan.

'I don't think so,' said Killigrew. There was no sound of water rushing into the hull, no list in the deck.

Presently Cavan returned on deck. 'No sign of damage in the bows, sir. I think we're all right.'

'We'd better check the outside of the hull,' said Killigrew. 'With your permission, sir?'

Pettifer nodded and followed him forward. The two of them peered over the bulwark, but it was impossible to see the bow clearly from that angle. 'We'll have to put a boat in the water to check,' said Pettifer.

The hull had rebounded a few feet from the floe, but what filled the gap between the foot of the prow and the floe could hardly be called water: it was brash ice, thick and sludgy. 'A boat will make slow progress through that, sir, and there's not much room for manoeuvre. Besides, if the wind changes and that floe closes in, we'll be short a boat and possibly her crew besides.'

'You have a better suggestion, Killigrew?'

'I'll go over myself on a lifeline.'

'Very well. Reeve a bowline through the tackle on that cathead, Hughes!'

'Aye, aye, sir.'

Killigrew secured the bowline around his waist and scrambled over the bulwark, his feet braced against the side. The soles of his boots slipped and slithered on the rime-covered timbers. If he fell into the brash ice below him, it would be like falling into an icy quagmire: his limbs would cramp and the thick sludge would suck him under before he had a chance to freeze to death. He inspected the iron plates riveted to the bows, then climbed back on deck to go over on the other side of the prow to check for damage there as well.

'No sign of damage above the waterline, sir,' he reported to Pettifer. 'Some scratching on the plates, that's all. She's hardly dented.'

'Didn't I tell you?' the captain exulted as they walked back to the quarterdeck. 'This tub can take anything the Arctic's got to throw at her, and worse.'

'There could be worse damage below the waterline, sir,' warned Killigrew. 'I can't see more than an inch below the surface. And we can hardly send a diver over to check: he'd freeze to death in a minute.'

'We can't very well careen her in this ice,' said Pettifer. 'It'll have to wait until we've broken out on the other side. Order Varrow to turn astern, half speed.'

'Sir, if some of the iron plates have broken off the stem and we try to ram those floes, we might just finish what the floes started!'

'I'm aware of the risk. I'm disappointed in you, Mr Killigrew. You're starting to display an alarming tendency to faint-heartedness.' He took the speaking tube from the binnacle. 'Mr Varrow! Turn astern, full speed.'

As the *Venturer* reversed through the brash ice, Killigrew glanced astern and saw another floe had closed in behind her. 'Stop her, sir!'

'Damn your eyes, mister! How dare you countermand one of my orders?'

'For God's sake, sir! The floe!' Killigrew gestured, and snatched the speaking tube from Pettifer. 'Turn ahead full, Varrow! *Now!*'

VIII

Beset

The edge of the floe had already disappeared beneath the stern when Varrow stopped the engine so he could turn ahead. Even with the brash ice sucking at the hull, the ship continued to drift backwards under her own momentum and then another shudder ran through the deck, accompanied by the unmistakable sound of splintering wood.

Thrown to the deck a second time, Killigrew scrambled for the speaking tube he had dropped. 'Everything all right down there, Mr Varrow?'

'Me dignity's bruised, but I think I'll live. Sounds like the rudder took a basting, though. What happened?'

'We reversed against another floe.'

'Damage report, Mr Cavan!' roared Pettifer.

The hull had not been breeched, but the rudder had been smashed and when they tried to haul the screw up into the iron well on the orlop deck they found that one of the blades had been bent.

'Kracht thinks he can beat it back into shape, but it's going to take time, sir,' Killigrew reported when Pettifer had gathered his officers in his day-room to discuss the situation. 'Time, and a lot of coal. Coal we can't spare. It will be quicker to replace the screw with the spare. Kracht thinks he can have it fitted within a few hours.'

'Very well,' said Pettifer. 'See to it.'

'I'm most concerned about the loss of the rudder,' said Killigrew.

'Riggs has sufficient timber to build a new one, hasn't he?'

'He says it's going to take forty-eight hours to build it. But the difficult part is going to be fixing it to the sternpost. I wouldn't care to be the one who has to dive into this brash ice to fix the pintles to the gudgeons below the waterline.'

'If we shift some of the ballast forward, that may bring one more of them close enough to the surface to reach from a boat. Tell him to see what he can jury-rig. Once we're free of this ice, we can effect more permanent repairs.'

Killigrew and Cavan made their way on deck where Qualtrough approached them, relieved from his duties in the crow's nest by Sørensen. 'Forgive me, sir. I just wanted to apologise for not seeing that first floe in time. From the crow's nest, it's almost impossible to tell where the brash ice ends and the floes begin.'

'That's all right, Qualtrough,' Killigrew assured him. 'No one's blaming you. If anyone's to blame for the fix we're in, it's me for not seeing the second floe astern. Don't worry, though: Chips thinks we can jury-rig a temporary rudder within forty-eight hours.'

'Forty-eight hours, eh?'

'What's the matter, Qualtrough? You look dubious.'

'It's getting colder by the minute, sir. If this north wind keeps up it'll only pack the ice in around us closer. I just hope that forty-eight hours is soon enough.'

'Then we'd better get to work at once, hadn't we?'

'Yes, sir.' The ice quartermaster turned away to return to his duties.

'Qualtrough?' Killigrew called after him.

'Sir?'

'Don't worry. The captain knows what he's doing.'

Qualtrough nodded and went away.

'You seem pretty confident of that, sir,' said Cavan.

The lieutenant shrugged. 'He's the captain, Mr Cavan,' he explained with an ironic smile. 'The captain is always right.'

'Sir?'

'Yes, Mr Cavan?'

'Did you ever wonder what would happen if the captain were ever wrong?'

Killigrew grimaced. 'Then we'd be in damned hot water.'

The young man grinned. 'Chance would be a fine thing.'

Killigrew had to haul O'Houlihan up out of the sludge and into the dingy in the *Venturer*'s stern. 'One more pintle, sir,' gasped the seaman. 'I've almost got it.'

'Belay that, O'Houlihan. You're turning blue as it is. You go back on board, change into some dry clothes and warm yourself by the galley stove. Get a hot mug of tea inside you.'

'Please, sir.' O'Houlihan was shivering uncontrollably. 'Another thirty seconds will do it.'

'Another thirty seconds will kill you, man! Back on board this instant, O'Houlihan. That's an order.'

Seeing what had needed to be done, O'Houlihan had volunteered to work in the brash ice without the promise of an extra ration of grog – if they could not repair the rudder, they would all be in trouble – and Killigrew had reluctantly agreed, against his better judgement.

O'Houlihan was in no state to climb one of the lifelines to the quarterdeck above them, but it was not necessary: a boatswain's chair was already waiting. 'Take him straight to the galley, Molineaux!' Killigrew called up to the petty officer at the taffrail overhead once O'Houlihan had been swung inboard. 'And put some rum in his tea: he's earned it!'

'Aye, aye, sir!' Molineaux saluted and disappeared from view.

'Do you want me to get that last pintle?' asked Kracht, who had offered to help with the repairs, and sat in the dinghy next to Killigrew.

The lieutenant shook his head. 'If anyone else is going over the side into that filthy stuff, it's me.' He was thinking he should have gone in the first place, instead of letting O'Houlihan do it.

'Maybe it bain't necessary, sir,' said the carpenter's mate, on the other side of Killigrew. 'We got eleven of the twelve pintles fixed now.' Just as Strachan was an assistant surgeon without a surgeon to assist, so Jeremiah Riggs was a carpenter's mate without a carpenter to be a mate to. The Admiralty did not think the *Venturer* large enough to warrant a full-blown carpenter, or was trying to pinch pennies at any rate; but Killigrew had no complaints about Riggs, and it was a mystery to him why the carpenter's mate was not rated higher.

'You think she'll hold, Chips?'

'Four would hold her, sir. It be a question of how much punishment she can take. Twelve'd be better than eleven, sir, but then thirteen would be better than twelve. Reckon eleven'll do for now.'

Killigrew lifted his face towards the taffrail. 'Mr Cavan!'

The mate appeared above them. 'Sir?'

'Hard a-starboard, Mr Cavan!'

'Aye, aye, sir.' The mate turned to someone behind him. 'Hard a-starboard, Endicott!'

The rudder moved soundlessly to port on well-oiled hinges, churning through the brash ice.

'Now to port!'

'Hard a-port, Endicott!'

The rudder swung across to starboard.

'How does she handle?' Killigrew called up.

Cavan turned to Endicott and repeated the question. 'He says "sluggish", sir,' the mate reported.

'That's just the brash ice,' said Killigrew. 'She'll do . . . for now. She'll have to.' Kracht had already replaced the bent-bladed screw with the spare, and Riggs had excelled himself, assembling the parts of the spare rudder in twenty-four hours rather than forty-eight. But all the while the thermometer had dropped, turning the brash ice the consistency of 'mushy peas', as Thwaites put it, and the north wind had increased, packing the floe ice tightly on all sides of the *Venturer*. If they could not get out now, they would be stuck there in the pack until the spring thaw came in eight months' time, if the ice did not crush the hull in the meantime.

The men in the boat climbed up the lifelines to the deck so the dinghy could be hoisted back into its davits. Black smoke billowed from the funnel as the stokers shovelled coal into the furnace to get steam up, but instead of rising into the sky the smoke dropped to the deck as soon as it met the cold air, and only the breezes gusting in from the starboard quarter prevented the men on the forecastle from being choked.

'Tell the captain we're ready when he is,' Killigrew told Cavan. Even as the mate descended the after hatch, Killigrew spoke into the speaking tube. 'Stand by in the engine room.'

'Aye, aye, sir,' replied Varrow.

Pettifer came on deck. 'Well, gentleman, if you're ready? We shall endeavour to break out of our icy cage. Instruct Varrow to set on, Killigrew. Turn ahead, full speed.'

'Aye, aye, sir.' Killigrew took the speaking tube from the bulwark. The gutta-percha had split now, and he had to cup one hand over the hole to blow the whistle at the other end. 'Full ahead, Mr Varrow.'

'Full ahead it is, Mr Killigrew.'

They felt the deck throb beneath their feet as the engine started up: slowly at first, but accelerating with every second as Varrow increased revolutions. Killigrew could hear the floes of ice squeak in protest as the *Venturer* strained against them, but they did not give. Astern, the screw churned the brash ice and pushed it about ineffectively.

'She's not budging, sir,' Killigrew said when the engine reached the plateau of its power.

'We need more revolutions,' said Pettifer.

'We're already going full ahead, sir.'

'That's not good enough!' snapped the captain. 'Go below and see if anything can be done.'

Killigrew hesitated, knowing it would be a wasted journey. But he preferred Varrow's company in the dark, filthy and noisy sweatbox of the *Venturer*'s engine room than he did being on deck with Pettifer in his present frame of mind, demanding the impossible. He shed some of his Arctic clothes in his cabin on the way below and descended to the engine room.

'The captain wants more!' he told Varrow, shouting to make himself heard above the clamour of the engine.

The engineer shook his head. A squat, neckless man with thinning hair, a wide mouth and bulging eyes that gave him a toad-like appearance, Assistant Engineer (First Class) Walter Varrow was the first engineer Killigrew had met who never seemed ill at ease in his filthy overalls when surrounded by officers in their epauletted frock coats. Varrow had a uniform of his own somewhere, but only wore it when he had to, and could be relied on to get it rumpled so quickly that somehow it looked even filthier than his overalls.

'The pressure gauge is in the red as it is. And the lads are

151

shovelling coal in at an alarming rate.' Varrow nodded to where the three stokers were hard at work, stripped to the waists, the sweat running in rivulets over muscular bodies filthy with coal dust.

Killigrew nodded. Now he understood what had happened to the Franklin expedition as clearly as he ever would. There had been no unexplained disaster, no mystery, just the ice creeping in around them, freezing them in for eternity. They had challenged the Arctic and lost, just as it now seemed that the *Venturer* had made the same gamble and faced the same end. Feeling slightly sick, trying to tell himself it was not all over yet, he made his way back on deck.

'They're doing all they can down there, sir, but it's no good. We're just wasting coal – coal we can ill afford to spare.'

'Turn astern, full speed,' ordered Pettifer.

Killigrew relayed the order to the engine room via the speaking tube. Varrow put her in reverse, but they made no more progress astern than they had done ahead.

They tried stopping the engines and starting them again suddenly. They tried stopping them, and slowly bringing them up to full revolutions. They called all hands on deck and ordered them to run from one side to the other, in the hope that the rocking motion they set up would break up the ice around them. They tried attaching ice-anchors to one of the thickest floes ahead of them and turning about the capstan to kedge through the ice. In desperation, they even broke out more gunpowder charges and tried to blast their way through the ice. Nothing worked: the *Venturer* was stuck fast.

Less than two miles from open water, and they could not budge her an inch.

Pettifer's shoulders slumped. He seemed to have shrunk six inches. 'Let fires die out,' he ordered.

'What do we do now, sir?' asked Cavan.

Pettifer looked at him. 'Do? We do nothing, Mr Cavan. We wait.' He turned and stalked down the after hatch, a broken and defeated man.

'Wait for what?' muttered Cavan.

'A miracle, sir,' Qualtrough told him. 'Because that's what it's going to take to get us out of here.'

Molineaux sat down to dinner on the mess deck and listened to the crackling of the ice outside. In contrast to the oppressive silence of Beechey Island, the pack was a cacophony. The jumbled floes shifted constantly, jostling one another, sometimes cracking, sometimes rising in slabs that slithered upwards to form weird, angular pressure ridges that crisscrossed the pack, separating the fields of ice like hedgerows in the countryside.

Sometimes the floes screeched eerily as they ground against one another, now like a nighthawk, now like the squealing wheels of a steam train; at other times they boomed like distant artillery as they were snapped by the weight of the floes pressing up behind them. And all that pressure was building up around the *Venturer*'s hull. The ship responded to the pressure with her own protests, the bolts and fastenings cracking like pistol shots in the cold. To make matters worse, Pettifer's dachshund responded to the unearthly sounds by adding her own keening howls to the ululating threnody of the wind. It was bad enough in the mess deck, at the opposite end of the ship; Christ only knew how Pettifer could put up with it.

It was not so bad during the day, when one's duties distracted from the sound, and the constant hubbub of voices and the clump of footsteps helped to cover it. But at night, as the men lay in their hammocks, Molineaux could hear the ice scratching against the outside of the hull, less than a foot from his head. After what he had seen on the *Jan Snekker*, it did not take too much imagination to conjure up images of a polar bear scratching its claws on the planks outside, trying to get in. But a polar bear could be shot, he told himself; there was no defence against the ice. He sensed they were alive because the Arctic permitted them to live this long; but it was only a matter of time before the capricious environment changed its mind and crushed them in its icy grip.

The noise and the tension robbed everyone of sleep, which only made them tenser, and the men quarrelled over the smallest things.

'What the hell's this?' Corporal Naylor demanded when Able Seaman Johnno Smith, who was mess cook for the day, started to dole out their victuals. On most ships, the marines would have been carefully segregated from the sailors – whom they would have to shoot in the event of a mutiny – and messed separately. But space was at a premium on board an exploring ship, even compared to other naval vessels, and with as small a crew as the *Venturer* had, it made no sense to waste space for a second mess for the five marines on board.

'Salt pork and split peas,' said Smith. 'Same as it always is on Wednesdays.'

'I can see that,' snapped Naylor. 'Don't tell me there's three-quarters of a pound of pork there, cooked or raw.'

'We're on six-upon-four until further notice. Cap'n's orders. In case we get stuck in the ice for longer than we anticipated.'

'Bloody marvellous, isn't it?' said Hughes. 'We need proper full meals inside us in weather like this, not six-upon-four. I'll bet the bloody officers aren't on six-upon-four. I'll bet they're bloody gorging themselves on beef tongues and rice in the wardroom.'

'They have corned beef on Wednesdays,' Johnno told them. 'And Vinny says they're on reduced rations, the same as the rest of us.'

'Corned beef, huh?' said Molineaux. 'I'd rather have salt pork and split peas.' He would rather have had a full ration too, but that went without saying.

'Easy for them,' sneered Hughes. 'They've got their private stocks of food from Fortnum and bloody Mason. They won't go hungry. Their kind never does. Typical! The capitalists exploiting the working class as always.'

'I'd hardly describe you as *working* class, Red,' said O'Houlihan, getting a laugh from the other seamen. Hughes was notorious for scrimshanking when there was work to be done.

'Hold on a moment, Mick,' said Naylor. 'I'm starting to think Red's got a point. Cap'n Carney and the others are happy enough to lead us all to our deaths, but if they get a chance to get out of it, you think they won't leave us behind if they have to?'

'You don't know them very well if you think they'd do that,' scoffed Molineaux.

'Oh, no?' said Naylor. 'You can trust them if you like, Wes, but I'm with Red here. I trusted Cap'n Carney when he told us that with all the newfangled dooflickers on this ship, there was no way we could get trapped in the ice. Speaking tubes that disintegrate in the cold air. Steam engines that are supposed to be able to drive through the ice. Where's that got us?'

'Stow it, Naylor,' said Molineaux. 'You volunteered for this expedition, same as the rest of us. There were never any guarantees. Anyhow, we're stuck now, so there's no point whining about it. We've just got to knuckle down and hope that the pack loosens enough for us to break free.'

'And if it don't loosen? What if we're stuck here for the rest of our lives, like Franklin and them others?'

Molineaux stood up. 'You got any better suggestions, Naylor?'

The corporal also stood up. 'Cap'n Carney and those others aren't going to get us out of this, I know that much.'

Osborne caught Naylor by the sleeve and tried to pull him back down to his seat. 'Sit down, Dick. It's not worth it.'

Naylor jerked his arm free of Osborne's grip. 'You keep out of this, Bernie. You heard Ågård tell the cap'n we shouldn't enter the ice. Well, the cap'n ignored him and none of the other officers did owt about it, and now we're stuck. But did they let Ågård out of the lazaretto and apologise to him? Did they hell as like!'

'Ollie spoke out of turn,' said Molineaux. 'Same as you're speaking out of turn now.'

'I'll speak out of turn when I like, Wes Molineaux. Maybe it's time we took charge of things.'

Everyone on the mess deck stopped talking at once. Naylor had just proposed building a tower of Babel.

'That's mutinous talk,' Molineaux said softly.

'I'd rather be a live mutineer than a dead lapdog like you!'

'Aye, I'm with you, Corporal!' said Hughes. 'We'll show those capitalist bastards, eh?'

'Shut up, Red,' said Naylor. 'This ain't about your bloody working-class struggle. This is about us living long enough to see old England again. Because we won't if we leave things to those bastards!' He gestured angrily towards the officers' accommodation aft.

'Which bastards are those then, Corporal Naylor?' Thwaites stepped up beside the marine and laid his cherriculum across his brawny chest. 'Did I hear thee inciting mutiny?'

'You must've misunderstood, Bosun,' Molineaux said quickly. 'The corporal didn't say anything about—'

'Pipe down, Molineaux! I wasn't speaking to thee! Well, Naylor? What does tha' say? Perhaps I should take thee down t' cap'n's quarters and we'll let him see what he thinks we should do with a mutinous dog like thee.'

Naylor refused to back down. 'Aye, take me to see the cap'n. I'll tell him what I think. I'll tell him—'

They never found out what Naylor was going to tell the captain, because Molineaux chose that moment to drive a fist into the corporal's jaw. Naylor tripped over the seat-locker behind him and sprawled across a table, scattering mugs and pannikins.

'What did tha' do that for, Molineaux?' demanded Thwaites.

'He called my blower a whore, Bosun.'

'Thi' blower *is* a whore, Molineaux.'

'Maybe she is, Mr Thwaites. But it ain't for the likes of him to say so.'

'The cap'n takes a dim view of brawling, Molineaux. I've half a mind to take thee before him instead of Naylor here.' He glanced at the corporal, who had slithered to the floor and was fingering his jaw gingerly. 'But I reckon he was asking for it. Not for calling thi' lass a whore, mind thee.'

The boatswain turned to address the whole mess deck. 'The next man I hear talking of mutiny, I'll have him strung up from t' yard-arm, just thee see if I don't! What started all this? Being put on six-upon-four, I suppose.' He shook his head in disgust. 'Call thissen British tars? Tha'art supposed to be the best, aren't thee? Tha's volunteered for discovery service, dreaming of glory and riches, and at t' first hint of hardship tha' start to grumble! Tha' think that things are tough now, tha's not lived, boys. Tha' wait until t' winter sets in, then we'll be able to separate t' sheep from t' goats. British tars in my eye! That's nowt. Tha's dung. Tha's worse'n dung. Thee'd defile dung if thee licked it. Tha' don't hear Sørensen or Kracht whingeing, does thee? And them isn't even British! Buck up th' ideas sharpish, or I'll have to give thee all a taste of real hardship! Put that in tha' pipes, and smoke it!' He stalked off.

Naylor glared at Molineaux. 'Hell of a punch you pack, Wes. I wonder if you can take them as well as you dish them out?'

'Why don't you try me, Dicky boy?' Molineaux said softly, his fists clenched by his sides.

'Pack it in, the pair o' yez!' said O'Houlihan. 'Grown men acting like kidgers, so yez are! The bosun's right; it's going to get a lot worse before it gets better, so we'd better stop grumbling and brace ourselves. And as for you, Dicko, I reckon you can count yourself lucky you didn't get yourself a flogging. You can thank Wes for that.'

'Aye,' sneered Naylor. 'Maybe one day I'll get a chance to return the favour.'

Killigrew knocked on the door to Strachan's cabin.

'Come in!'

It was two bells in the first watch, after 'ship's company's fire and lights out', and Killigrew expected to find the assistant surgeon in his bunk. But Strachan was at his desk, reading a book by candlelight.

'Hullo, Killigrew. What can I do for you?'

The lieutenant slipped inside the cabin and closed the door behind him. He held out one of the ship's ledgers to Strachan. 'I'd like you to take a look at this.'

'What is it?'

'Sørensen's translation of the log we found on board the *Jan Snekker*. It makes interesting reading. I'd like your opinion on it. As a zoologist.'

'As a zoologist?' Intrigued, Strachan opened the ledger and glanced at the first page.

'You can save time and start at the entry for September eighteen-fifty,' Killigrew told him. 'But later.' He kept his voice low, not that there was much point: the groaning of the ship's timbers as the ice pressed against her sides would have drowned out a chorus. 'I can't sleep with the racket that damned dog is making. Is there something you can give me for it?'

'Laudanum, you mean? Are you sure that's wise, with your history?'

'It's not for me, it's for the dog.'

Strachan blinked. 'Are you suggesting we *drug* Horatia?'

'Orsini thinks he can slip something in her food.'

'Absolutely not, Killigrew. I will *not* be responsible for turning a poor wee animal into an opium addict!'

'It's the bitch or us, Strachan. It's driving everyone insane!'

'Even if you could silence Horatia, that wouldn't silence the ice, would it? And let's face facts, that's what's really getting everyone so worked up, isn't it? The thought of all that ice out there, pressing against the hull?' Strachan shook his head. 'It's the ice you want to silence, but you can't, so you want to take it out on the dog. Come in!' he added, as someone else knocked on the door.

It was Private Phillips. 'Mr Killigrew! I've been looking for you. It's Ågård, sir. He's been taken queer.'

'Taken queer? What the devil do you mean, taken queer?'

'I can hear him in the lazaretto, sir, moaning and groaning. I keep asking him if anything's the matter, but he won't answer.'

'I'll get the keys.' Killigrew entered the gunroom and knocked on the door to Latimer's cabin.

'Come in,' the clerk called wearily. He squinted blearily at Killigrew from his bunk. 'Who's that?'

'Killigrew.'

'Uhn. Have you spoken to Strachan about shutting that damned dog up yet, sir?'

'Just now. He refuses. He doesn't want the dog to become an opium addict.'

'I forgot he was a rotten animal lover. Tell him if he doesn't get that dog to shut up one way or another, one of us is going to kill it. My money's on Dr Bähr. And if it's still alive when we get back to civilisation, I'm going to kidnap the confounded brute and take it to a sporting gentleman of my acquaintance who keeps rats.'

'Horatia isn't a trained ratter.'

'Exactly!' There was a dark glint in Latimer's eyes.

'Have you got the keys to the lazaretto?'

'Shelf.' Latimer gestured vaguely across the cabin.

The shelf above the clerk's desk was cluttered with enough bottles of medicines and pills to rival the dispensary. It was a wonder Latimer did not have any laudanum of his own: he had just about everything else.

Killigrew found the keys amongst the various medications. 'Much obliged.'

'Don't mention it. You can return them in the morning.' Latimer buried his head under the pillow.

Killigrew, Strachan and Phillips made their way down to the orlop deck. The marine had not been exaggerating when he said that Ågård had been moaning and groaning: the ice quartermaster sounded like a soul in torment. Killigrew unlocked the door.

'Careful, sir,' said the marine. 'It might be a trick. Maybe he's planning to do a runner.'

'Don't be ridiculous, Phillips. Where's he going to go? We're more than a thousand miles from civilisation. No one knows that better than Ågård.'

He opened the door. The ice quartermaster was rolling about on the floor, writhing spastically, rattling the chains of his irons like Marley's ghost. His unshaven face was ashen in the light of Phillips' lantern, bathed in sweat, his eyes moving rapidly beneath closed eyelids.

'He's having a nightmare,' said Strachan.

Killigrew crouched over Ågård and gently shook him awake. The ice quartermaster's eyelids flicked up and he stared wild-eyed at the lieutenant, clenching fistfuls of his frock coat. 'We're all going to die!' he moaned. 'Don't you see? *We're all going to die!*'

'No one's going to die, Ågård. Pull yourself together, man! You were having a nightmare, that's all.'

The ice quartermaster lowered his gaze and his shoulders heaved as he laughed and cried hysterically at the same time. When he looked up again, he seemed a little calmer. 'You've got to let me out of here, sir! For the love of God, let me out of here!'

'I'm sorry, Ågård. The Old Man's orders . . .'

The ice quartermaster seized Killigrew by the throat. 'Let me out of here now! I don't want to die down here!'

Phillips thrust the lantern into Strachan's hands and moved to help the lieutenant, but by then Killigrew had already pulled Ågård's hands away, and he motioned for the marine to stay back. There was no sense in making Ågård feel even more claustrophobic by crowding around him.

'All right.' Killigrew started to unlock Ågård's irons. 'Ten minutes on deck. That's all.'

'Sir, the cap'n's orders . . .' protested Phillips.

'I'll take full responsibility,' said Killigrew. 'Go with him while he gets his coat from his cabin, then take him topsides.'

'Very good, sir.'

There was no point in rousing Commander Pettifer from his cabin at such a late hour; Killigrew would tell him what he had done in the morning. He made his way to his own cabin, wrapped up warmly, and then went on deck. Cavan met him at the top of the after hatch.

'Mr Strachan and Private Phillips have brought Ågård up on deck, sir. They say that you—'

'Yes, Cavan, it's all right,' Killigrew told him. 'I gave them permission.'

'Does the Old Man know, sir?'

'It's after nine, Cavan, and the captain needs his sleep.' Assuming Pettifer *could* sleep, with the ice crackling all around the ship and Horatia howling endlessly in the day-room right next to his cabin. How could one small dachshund have so much breath in her lungs? 'I'll tell him in the morning.'

'Aye, aye, sir.'

Killigrew crossed to where Strachan and Phillips flanked Ågård at the bulwark, the ice quartermaster gulping the fresh, sharp air into his lungs like a man saved from drowning. Despite the late hour, it was still no darker than dusk, and in the half-light they could see the jumbled pack that stretched out on all sides of the ship.

'Feel better now?' Strachan asked Ågård.

The ice quartermaster smiled wanly. 'Yes. Thank you, sir.'

Strachan proffered him a cigarillo. 'Have one of these. It will help soothe your nerves. You're claustrophobic?'

Ågård shook his head and lit the cigarillo from a match Strachan struck for him before replying. 'Sixteen years ago, when I was specksnyder on a whaler, she was caught in the ice returning through the Middle Pack. The skipper sent me below with three shipmates to bring up some casks of vittles, in case the hull was crushed and we were left stranded on the ice. Well, she was crushed right enough, but a lot sooner than any of us expected. The cover fell over the hatch and the sides were pressed in so hard it got wedged there. We shouted for help, but all we could hear was the thunder of our shipmates' feet on the deck above us as they scrambled for the upper deck to do a flit. We threw ourselves at the hatch cover, attacked it with our crowbars, but it wouldn't shift. Then pressure of the ice opened the seams.'

White-faced in the moonlight, Ågård trembled as he spoke. 'For nine hours we were trapped in that hold while it slowly filled with ice-cold water. We only had the stub of a candle; it burned away in half an hour and left us in the darkness. All we could do was sit there and wonder how we'd die: by freezing, drowning or crushing.

'Bob Jameson was the first to lose his head. I think we all went a little bit crazy – who wouldn't? – but Bob just lost his mind, lost it completely, started screaming his head off. First we tried to calm him down, then gave up and concentrated on trying to get that hatch cover up, though we knew it were hopeless. We thought he'd run out of breath sooner or later. But he didn't. He just went on screaming, on and on, until finally Johnny Harper couldn't take it any longer. I don't know how he killed Bob; used his clasp-knife, I s'pose, for he was always handy with it. We could hear Bob gurgling as he died. And then it was just me, Alex and Johnny, trapped in there and one of us a murderer.

'We were sitting up high on the barrels, our heads and shoulders against the deck head, trying to keep ourselves out of the water as it slowly rose around us. All we could hear was the groaning of the ship's timbers – as you hear them groaning now – and the chattering of our teeth.

'The end came sudden like. There was a crash, like being in a thunderclap, and gallons of cold water flooding through the holes. I thought I were a dead man. To this day I'm still not sure how I got out; the ship's bottom seemed to fall away beneath me, and I were swimming in that icy water, drowning, and the next thing I knew t'others were hauling me out on to the ice. We never did find out what happened to Alex and Johnny, if they were crushed or drowned; we never even found their bodies.

'We were only on the ice a few days. Then another whaler

came by, the *Norfolk*. She picked us up, took us back to Stromness. I swore I'd never go to the Arctic again. So I signed on board HMS *Dreadful* and . . . well, you know the rest, sir.'

'Why in the world didn't you say something sooner?' asked Killigrew. 'If I'd known you had an experience like that in your past, I would never have pressed you to join us on this expedition.'

Ågård grinned ruefully. 'Didn't want you thinking I was funky, sir, did I? Besides, I thought if I could face the Arctic again, it would help me overcome the nightmares. Looks like I were wrong, don't it?'

'Mr Killigrew!' a voice roared from the quarterdeck.

The four of them whirled from the bulwark to see Commander Pettifer striding towards them.

'Mr Killigrew! What is that prisoner doing on the upper deck?'

The lieutenant had never seen the captain so angry. He kept his voice calm, hoping to calm Pettifer down by example. 'I said he could come up for fresh air for ten minutes, sir.'

'Did you, sir? Did you, by God?'

'Yes, sir. He was in a state of some distress, as I can well understand after the story he's just told me.'

'I'm not interested in his tales, Mr Killigrew.'

Killigrew felt himself colouring. If Pettifer wanted to weigh him off for disobeying him that was his privilege, but he would have preferred it if the captain had done so in the privacy of his day-room. 'Sir, if you'd only let me explain—'

'And I'm not interested in your explanations!' snarled Pettifer. 'I gave explicit instructions that Ågård was to be kept in irons in the lazaretto. By ignoring those instructions you have defied me!'

'My apologies, sir. I did not want to disturb you, but it was obvious that Ågård was very much in need of—'

'I don't care what Ågård was in need of! He was being punished!'

Killigrew could rein his temper in no longer. 'For what, sir? For doing his job? For warning us against entering the ice? For being *right*, sir?'

He thought Pettifer was going to have a seizure. 'Why . . .

you . . . you impertinent damned pup, you! How dare you answer me back? How dare you! By God, I ought to—'

A crash like distant thunder cut him off. A deep, ominous rumble sounded off to starboard, and they all turned to stare across the ice. 'What in God's name was that?' demanded Pettifer, pale-faced.

Ågård gestured helplessly. 'The ice . . .' A dubious note in his voice suggested they had heard something beyond even his experience.

Killigrew stared out across the pack, his eyes straining against the gathering gloom. He saw nothing at first, but then fancied he detected some movement amongst the floes at the edge of their visibility.

Soon there was no mistaking it: a shockwave passing through the ice like a ripple through a still pond, lifting up a broad band of floes as it passed. It was hurtling towards the *Venturer* at an appalling rate. Even as the wave passed through the pack, they could hear the floes squealing and crackling in protest. The floes were lifted up, thrust over one another as the shockwave forced them together, the whole pack surging towards the trapped ship.

'Oh, dear God!' moaned Ågård.

Killigrew felt he should do something – shout an order, call hands on deck – but it was impossible to see what could be done to avert the oncoming wave. He could not even guess what would happen when it reached them. Would it pass harmlessly beneath them, or crush the hull in the blink of an eye? Not that it mattered either way: it was only two hundred . . . a hundred and fifty . . . fifty yards away . . .

He grabbed hold of the bulwark. 'Brace yourselves!'

The floes next to the hull were slammed against the side and a shudder ran through the whole ship. Pettifer and Strachan, who had been too slow to grab hold of anything, were thrown to the deck. Pushed by some unseen pressure far to the north, the floes just kept on coming, slithering over one another with eldritch screeches as they piled up against the *Venturer*'s starboard side. The timbers of the hull groaned dreadfully in protest at the vicelike tightening of the ice.

IX

Nipped!

The *Venturer* was tilted twenty degrees to port. Killigrew listened for the sound of splintering planks as the ice staved in the sides, but it never came. In the frightened silence that followed, the only sound that could be heard was the creaking of the ship's timbers. Even Horatia had been stunned into silence by the shock. Killigrew could almost feel the immense pressure of the ice crushed against the side.

When the bitch started yapping somewhere below, the familiar sound was almost a relief. 'Is everyone all right?' asked Killigrew.

Phillips helped Pettifer to his feet; Strachan was left to fend for himself. 'No bones broken here,' he said, dusting himself down.

The groaning of the ship's timbers, far from dying down, took on a more ominous tone. 'She's going to go!' moaned Ågård.

'She can't!' Pettifer protested, like a petulant child who had been promised a treat and then discovered his parents had lied to him. His face was as white as a sheet. 'She's built to take this kind of pressure!'

'Not *this* kind of pressure, sir,' said Killigrew. 'Nothing could be built to withstand this kind of pressure. Unstead!'

'Sir?'

'Call all hands on deck.'

'Aye, aye, sir.'

Even as Killigrew gave the order, the first of the men came

rushing up from the lower deck to find out what was going on, but Boatswain's Mate Unstead blew into his call anyway, in case there were any slugabeds who underestimated the gravity of the situation.

Killigrew was not sure if the Germans on board would understand the boatswain's pipes: the other hands would alert Sørensen, Kracht and Fischbein, but Ziegler and Bähr shared one cabin, while Ursula had another to herself. He was about to send Cavan below to fetch them when he saw Ziegler escorting Ursula out of the after hatch.

'Where's Bähr?' he asked them.

'He wasn't in his cabin,' said Ziegler.

'Over there, sir.' Ågård nodded towards the forecastle. Following the gesture, Killigrew was relieved to see the doctor had emerged from the fore hatch with Fischbein.

A look of panic crossed Ursula's face, and she turned and went back down the after hatch.

'Frau Weiss!' Killigrew called after her. 'Come back! Whatever you've forgotten, there isn't time to . . .'

Ziegler started to follow her down, but Killigrew caught him by the arm. 'Oh, no you don't, *mein Herr*! One of you below decks is more than enough for me to worry about. Wait here.'

He clattered down the companion ladder and caught up with Ursula halfway to the door to Pettifer's quarters. Catching her by the arm, he whirled her back to face him. 'What the devil d'you think you're doing?'

She looked at him with fire blazing in her eyes. 'Commander Pettifer's dog!'

The door to Pettifer's quarters opened and Orsini emerged with Horatia bundled in his arms; ironically, since the steward had been one of those most voluble in his protests to the lieutenant about the noise the dog made. Failing to appreciate that Orsini was trying to rescue her, Horatia writhed in his arms and tried to sink her jaws into his wrist, but the steward had enough experience of handling her to avoid being bitten.

'Orsini will take care of her,' Killigrew promised Ursula, pushing her towards the door at the other end of the corridor.

On the other side, she stopped and stared in amazement.

'To your right, ma'am,' said Killigrew, thinking she had

become disorientated in her panic.

Then he saw it too, and gaped in horror.

Looking forward, they could see the deck bulging upwards as the ship's sides were forced together by the ice. On the deck head above, the stout wooden beams bent upwards as if they were no more than bamboo canes. The creaking they made under the pressure was tremendous; it was a miracle they had not snapped already.

He opened the door to the companion way and thrust her through. 'Up you go, ma'am.'

On deck, Cavan was already forming the men into their divisions: it was quicker to take a head count than to search the ship to make sure no one had been left behind. Killigrew guided Ursula towards Ziegler. 'Look after her.'

'I can look after myself,' she retorted sharply, but went to stand with Ziegler nevertheless, staying out of the way of the other men on deck. Orsini came on deck and handed Horatia to a thankless Pettifer.

Killigrew took a head count of the men in his division. They were all there. 'Cavan?'

'All present and accounted for,' returned the mate.

The boats were already stowed in their davits, ready to be lowered at a moment's notice: they had been that way ever since the *Venturer* had rounded Cape Farewell at the southern tip of Greenland with the rest of the squadron, ready for an eventuality such as this. The men had had spare clothes stowed in bags on the upper deck ready for the same eventuality; now they had collected them, ready to leap for the ice if the worst came to the worst. Every man knew what to do: at Killigrew's suggestion, Pettifer had drilled them all rigorously ready to do a 'flit'.

And if the ship was crushed? What then? They would be stranded on the ice, over a thousand miles from civilisation. Only now, when it was too late, did Killigrew fully appreciate the folly of a ship sailing alone in the Arctic; but he had been swept up in Pettifer's madness, deaf to the entreaties of Ågård and Yelverton, thinking only of Franklin and the North-West Passage.

He cast his eyes about the surrounding pack ice; a less inviting landscape he could not imagine. By some quirk of the pack's crazy geometry, while the pressure built up against the *Venturer*'s sides a lead had cracked open in the ice about a cable's length to the south west. But now, with the hull pinned between two floes, it might as well have been ten thousand miles away.

The ship's timbers groaned piteously. 'Do we jump yet, sir?' asked Stoker Butterwick, a tall, spud-faced Geordie lad with lank black hair. He was none too bright, and easy prey for teasing of his shipmates, but his fellow stoker, Bob Gargrave, usually kept him out of trouble. Unlike the average stoker, Gargrave was a small, wiry man, but Killigrew had seen the little Geordie at work in the boiler room, making up in energy what he lacked in muscle.

'Stow it, Jemmy!' hissed Gargrave. 'Mr Killigrew will give us the order when it's time to jump. Ain't that right, sir?' he added to the lieutenant, tugging at the air where his forelock would have been if his hair had not habitually stuck up at all angles.

'You jump when the bosun's mates pipe you over the side,' Killigrew told them.

The ship gave another groan. 'Ready when you are, sir,' said Molineaux, holding his call.

Killigrew turned to Pettifer. The captain stood at the bulwark, one hand gripping the upper strake so tightly his knuckles showed white in the moonlight, pounding it with his other fist and mumbling to himself.

'Do we jump yet, sir?' Killigrew prompted him.

Pettifer did not seem to hear him.

'Sir?'

'For God's sake!' exploded Ågård. 'Let's go now, while we still can.'

Pettifer whirled. 'Pipe down, Ågård! I give the orders on this ship! We jump when I say so, not before!'

'What the deuce is he waiting for?' Cavan hissed out of the corner of his mouth at Killigrew.

Everyone was silent, watching the captain, waiting for the order and listening to the ominous creaking of the planks. Killigrew's mouth was dry and he could feel the sweat trickling down his back, in spite of the bitter cold. Should *he* give the order? If he did, he had no doubt it would be obeyed. Pettifer would bawl him out, perhaps even have him placed under arrest pending a court martial – if his present frame of mind did not wear off – but better that than they all die needlessly when the ship was crushed in the ice.

Then the creaking stopped.

No one spoke, as if the slightest sound would be enough to set the ice off again. Even Horatia stopped barking, perhaps sensing something was wrong. The only sound was the soughing of the wind.

Killigrew exchanged nervous glances with Yelverton. 'Now what?' muttered the master.

'Ågård?'

The ice quartermaster shrugged, as much at a loss as any of them.

Killigrew started to stride across the tilting deck to the bulwark, as if a glance over the side might tell him what was going on. Perhaps the pressure was easing off . . .

He was two steps from the bulwark when the whole ship seemed to rise up with a violent lurch.

The *Venturer* heeled over to port. Killigrew's feet slipped out from beneath him on the icy deck and he landed painfully on his hip before slithering into the scuppers. He was aware of others flying around him, tumbling and sliding. The *Venturer*'s masts bent like saplings in a storm. The whole ship was heeled over at fifty degrees. Then the masts whipped back, lashing the air, and a couple of backstays snapped and cracked. Someone screamed and blood splashed across the deck.

Molineaux landed in the scuppers facing Killigrew. The two of them stared at one another, both of them wondering if these were their final moments before the *Venturer* was crushed in the ice. Then the ship gave another lurch and rolled sharply to starboard with an ugly scraping sound. Bodies slithered back to the opposite side of the deck. Killigrew had already caught hold of a lifeline and he clung there while Molineaux, wide-eyed, slipped past the helm to land against the provisions casks on the far side of the quarterdeck. Then Killigrew's gauntlet gave up its imperfect grip on the rope and he too was sliding, falling. Something crashed painfully against his side and he found himself clinging to the binnacle, the whole deck canted over to starboard now. The deck pressed hard against Killigrew and his stomach gave a lurch. The ice that was piled up on either side of the gunwales seemed to disappear, and with a dizzy sensation he realised that the *Venturer* had been lifted clean out of the water and was rising up with the ice.

The dizzying ascent was brief. Then everything on deck was still, but to starboard the ice piled up rapidly, great floes rising on top of one another, their jagged edges lancing towards the sky until they towered over the deck, stacked so haphazardly they threatened to come crashing down at any second. The ice growled and crackled, and ice spicules rained down on them, blinding them. There was a final, terrible crash and then everything was deathly silent.

Killigrew clung to the binnacle and listened to his own heart pounding in his chest. Were they safe? It was too much to hope for. He glanced down to where Ursula lay in Ziegler's arms. She looked dazed but otherwise unhurt.

Killigrew stood up unsteadily on the icy, canted deck. A second later something split with a crack like a carronade. The *Venturer* gave another lurch. She pitched forwards and he was thrown violently against the capstan. He clung on for dear life, the breath smashed from his lungs. The bows descended sharply and then came to rest with a juddering crash. There was a sound of rending metal and then the whole ship slithered forwards, gaining momentum, until her bows splashed into water. His feet shot out from beneath him once more and he spun helplessly into the waist of the ship.

He lay there, gasping for breath, hardly able to believe he was still alive. Then he realised from the gentle, rocking motion of the deck that they were afloat once more. But for how much longer?

He caught hold of a pinrail and pulled himself to his feet. 'Qualtrough?'

The ice quartermaster stood up unsteadily.

'Get below. Find out if the hull's been breached.'

'Aye, aye, sir.'

As Qualtrough clumped down the companionway Killigrew looked about them. They were on a wide stretch of open water, in no immediate peril. Horatia resumed her howling.

Killigrew surveyed the chaos of the deck. Those who could were rising to their feet. Orsini clutched his arm and looked as if he was in pain. Leading Stoker Dawton lay face down on the deck in a pool of blood: when Killigrew and Molineaux turned him over they found his throat had been ripped out by one of the backstays which had parted and slashed across the deck.

Qualtrough came back on deck with Riggs, who was limping. 'Damage report, Chips?' asked Killigrew. Pettifer was standing nearby, but he looked so dazed and confused it was too much to expect him to take charge of things.

'The timbers be cracked in a couple of places and they'm seeping, but we'll be right enough, sir.' The carpenter's mate grinned. 'Someone up there must like us.'

'What about your leg?'

'Must've twisted me ankle when we went over, sir.'

'All right, get to the sick-berth so Dr Bähr and Mr Strachan can take a look at it. You too, Orsini. That arm looks broken to me. Does anyone else need medical attention?' A few did. 'Right, you'd better get yourselves to the sick-berth, too. Thwaites, I want the backstays on the mainmast replaced. And check the stays on the foremast.'

'Aye, aye, sir. You heard him, lads! Let's look lively.'

Killigrew turned to Pettifer. 'Are you all right, sir?'

The captain was ashen-faced and trembling. He looked as though he had aged ten years in as many minutes. He nodded dumbly.

Killigrew pointed across to a large ice floe. 'I suggest we anchor the ship over there and take stock of the damage, sir.'

'Whatever you think best, Killigrew,' Pettifer said dully.

Once the *Venturer* was anchored to the floe, out of harm's way, and the officers had had a chance to assess the damage, they gathered in the captain's day-room: Pettifer, Killigrew, Yelverton, Strachan, and Cavan. Although only a warrant officer, Varrow was also present to report on the state of his engine. Pettifer's chair at the head of the table was empty: the captain sat in the easy chair in the corner of the room with Horatia curled up in his lap, absently stroking her.

171

Killigrew exchanged glances with the others. 'We're ready to start when you are, sir.'

'I can hear well enough from here.'

'As you will, sir. Shall we start with our individual reports?' When Pettifer neither agreed nor dissented, Killigrew turned to the mate. 'Perhaps you'd like to start the ball rolling, Cavan?'

'Right.' The mate referred to his notes. Killigrew knew some officers who could remember most things off the top of their heads, and acted as if they could remember everything, but he preferred to work with more methodical men like Cavan, who wrote everything down and made sure there was no possibility of forgetting anything. 'Apart from the broken stays – which have already been replaced – there's no damage to the masts: Endicott has been over them with a magnifying glass checking for cracks, and he reports that all three are sound.' Riggs should have done the job, but the carpenter's mate was in no condition to go climbing the masts.

'I've set Hughes, O'Houlihan and the two Smiths to work recaulking the seams from within. We'll need to careen the ship to do it properly, but there's no possibility of that at present. I've told Unstead to keep an eye on the amount of water in the well, but seepage seems to be minimal and I don't think we need worry too much on that account. The rest of the damage seems to be limited to broken plates and crystal in the wardroom, so from here on we'll be pouring our claret out of jugs instead of decanters.'

Killigrew smiled. 'I think we'll survive, Mr Cavan. Mr Strachan?'

'Only one dead,' the assistant surgeon announced grimly. 'Dawton seems to have been lacerated by one of the backstays whipping across the deck; it opened the carotid artery in his neck. He must've bled to death in seconds.'

'I suggest we have a burial service for Dawton tomorrow. If that's acceptable to you, sir?'

Pettifer did not look up from where he was stroking his dog. 'You must do as you see fit, Mr Killigrew.'

'Right, burial at sea it is. You'll officiate, sir?'

'Hm?'

'At the funeral. You'll lead the service?'

'Yes . . . yes, of course.'

'That takes care of the dead,' said Killigrew. 'I hate to sound brusque and callous about it, but at the moment I'm more concerned for the living. How many injured, Mr Strachan?'

'Chips has seriously sprained his ankle and Orsini has a compound fracture of the left forearm, so we'll not only be serving our claret from jugs, we'll be pouring it out ourselves too, for a while. Apart from that, it's just a few bruises and grazes. Frankly, I think we've been damnably lucky. The butcher's bill could have been worse.'

'*Should* have been worse,' muttered Yelverton. No one disagreed with him.

'Let's not throw a ball to celebrate just yet,' said Killigrew. 'Tell them about the screw, Mr Varrow.'

'We lost both blades,' the engineer explained cheerfully; he was one of those people who seemed to revel in being the bearers of ill tidings. 'Must ha' been when we were sliding across the ice. Either they're at the bottom of the sea or we left them back there on the floe, buried under tons of ice.'

'We have a spare, don't we?' asked Cavan.

'That *was* the spare, sir,' Varrow reminded him. 'The original were damaged last Saturday when we reversed into that floe.'

'Can we repair the original?' asked Killigrew.

'Why aye, man. Given time. But I'm more worried about the shaft. It's bent out o' kilter, and I'm not sure we've got the facilities to straighten it out here.'

'Improvise, Mr Varrow,' Killigrew told him. The engineer knew as well as anyone present that without the engine working, their chances of getting out of the Arctic were minimal, if not non-existent. 'That's what the navy's best at.'

'What do we do now?' asked Cavan.

Killigrew glanced across at the captain. Pettifer still did not seem to be particularly interested, so it fell to the lieutenant to propose a course of action. 'All we can do is follow this lead and see where it takes us,' he said. 'It bears to the south-east, so there's a good chance it'll take us to the west coast of Boothia. If we can make it that far, I suggest we find a nice, comfortable cove where we can sit out the winter and cut ourselves a harbour in the shore ice. Unless you have any objections, sir?' Killigrew was terrified Pettifer would insist that they press on in their search for the North-West Passage, but he had to ask: Pettifer was still the captain, after all, even if he no longer acted like one. Fortunately, even he seemed to realise the folly of pushing any deeper into the ice so late in the season, especially with their screw missing, and merely nodded his assent.

'I know it still isn't September yet, but I think that as far as we're concerned, the navigating season is over,' said Killigrew, and the others murmured their agreement with no small hint of relief. 'Well, gentlemen, I'd say we've got our work cut out for us. Shall we get cracking?'

Jakob Kracht found Varrow at the rear of the quarterdeck with stoker Gargrave, the two of them gazing mournfully down into the well for hoisting the screw out of the water and up to the upper deck. 'Is there anything I can do to help, *meinen Herren*?'

Varrow regarded him sceptically. 'I divven't know. *Is* there owt you can do to help?'

'I used to be the *Schmied* on the *Carl Gustaf*. The blacksmith, yes? Herr Killigrew thought I might be able to help repair the broken screw-propeller?'

'It's kind of you to offer, Fritz, but even if you could fix it, it wouldn't do no good anyhow.' Varrow pointed down into the well. 'See the "banjo" there – the metal guide rails running down the sides of the well? The portside one's got a kink in it; they have to be absolutely parallel if we're to bring the bearing up atwix them. So even if we did have a spare screw, we wouldn't be able to hoist the bearing to fix it on.'

Molineaux overheard them, and joined them, peering down into the well. 'You know what you want, don't you? You want a jack-brace.'

'Oh aye?' sneered Varrow. 'And what would you know about it?'

'I used one all the time, when I was a snakesman in the Big Huey. Used it to push bars apart when I was trying to get through a window. Same principle: put it between the guide rails at the kink, and push them apart. Chances are you'll push the bent rail back into shape.'

'Aye, or just end up bending the other rail.'

'It's got to be worth a try though, ha'n't it, Mr V?' said Gargrave, who had been pressed into service as the engineer's assistant.

'Oh, aye. If we had such a thing as a jack-brace on board. Which we divven't. Unless Molineaux here's got one in his locker?'

The boatswain's mate shook his head sadly.

'Could we not make one?' asked Kracht.

Varrow laughed. 'Make one? That's a good one, that is! "Make one," he says!'

'Might as well let him have a go, Mr V,' said Gargrave. 'We've got metal-working tools on board.'

'Can you draw me a picture, showing how it works?' Kracht asked Molineaux.

'Sure.'

'All right, Molineaux. Get some paper and a pencil from Mr Latimer.' Varrow sighed. 'I suppose it's better than sitting round doing nothing. While he's doing that, Fritz, you can take a look at the broken screw, see if you can do owt with it. Take him down to the workshop, Gargrave.'

'Aye, aye, Mr V.'

'And when you've shown Fritz down to the workshop, put the kettle on and we'll have a brew up, there's a good lad.'

As Molineaux, Kracht and Gargrave hurried away on their allotted tasks, Stoker Butterwick came on deck. 'Begging your pardon, Mr V, but have you got a left-handed spanner?'

Not for nothing was Butterwick known as 'Daft Jemmy' by his shipmates. In the ordinary run of things it would not have mattered: stoking furnaces required brawn, not brains, and even Butterwick had mastered the less than fine art of trimming coal. But Varrow's winger, Assistant Engineer (Second Class) Bill Ibbott had a fondness for practical jokes, and found endless amusement in sending Butterwick on wild-goose chases. Last week Butterwick had asked Varrow for a pot of tartan paint.

'A left-handed spanner,' Varrow echoed wearily. 'I suppose it's for Mr Ibbott?'

'Why, aye, Mr V. How did you guess?'

'Call it engineer's intuition, lad.' Varrow bent down to retrieve a spanner from his toolbox. 'Hold out your hand.'

Butterwick extended his right hand.

Varrow put the spanner into it. 'That's a right-handed spanner, see?'

Butterwick nodded.

Varrow took the spanner back from him. 'Hold out your other hand.'

The stoker complied. Varrow turned the spanner over and put it in his palm. 'That's a left-handed spanner.'

Butterwick looked confused. 'Hang on a min't, Mr V. I thought you said it were a right-handed spanner?'

'It's a right-handed spanner *and* a left-handed spanner,' Varrow explained patiently. 'You can use it in either hand. It's an ambidextrous spanner.'

Butterwick held up the spanner in his left hand. 'Left-handed spanner . . .' He transferred it to his other hand. 'Right-handed spanner!' Delighted, he looked up at Varrow with the light of comprehension shining in his eyes. 'Howay, Mr V! That's right canny, that is! A spanner you can use in either hand! Whatever will they think of next?'

Varrow suppressed a groan. 'I dread to think. Now take that spanner to Mr Ibbott and tell him to stick it up his nose. I've got better things to do than deal with the wild-goose chases he sends you on.'

Butterwick nodded gravely. 'Mr V says you're to stick it up your nose,' he rehearsed. He had an appalling habit of interpreting everything literally.

'Divven't bother,' sighed Varrow. 'I'll tell him misel. You can fetch me a replacement cheese coupling for the banjo.'

Butterwick nodded, turned away, and then caught himself. He turned back to Varrow with a knowing grin. 'Oh, no you divven't, Mr V.'

'Eh?'

'A replacement cheese coupling for the banjo? You must think I'm daft or summat, me.'

'What are you talking about? It's a metal disc with a slot in it, about so wide . . .'

'I'm nay falling for that one.' Butterwick made his way below.

Varrow shook his head wearily. 'God's punishing me,' he decided. 'That's what it is.'

'Frostbite, Latimer?' Strachan exclaimed in disbelief. 'How can you *possibly* have frostbite? You haven't been on the ice once, yet!'

'In my feet, Pills. The skin's gone dead in spots. I can feel it. See for yourself.' Hopping up and down on one foot, the clerk tried to hold the other up from Strachan's inspection.

'Eurgh! Good God, Latimer! That's disgusting!'

'I was right, wasn't I, sir? It's frostbite, isn't it? Please, tell me there's something you can do. Tell me you don't have to amputate.'

'How often do you wash your feet?'

'Once a month, sir. But I don't see what that's got to do with frostbite.'

'Nothing at all, Latimer. But it's got everything to do with the fact that your feet are the dirtiest and smelliest I've ever had the misfortune to encounter. You should wash them at least once a week; and if we weren't on board ship, I'd recommend you wash them every day. And cut your toenails every once in a while! You look like Shock-headed Peter! All right, you can put your socks and boots back on now.'

'But what about this, sir? This hard patch of skin here? Tell me that's not frostbite!'

'It's a corn, Latimer. Go on, get out of my sight. And take your disgusting feet with you!'

Even redder in the face than usual, Latimer laced his half-boots. On his way out of the sick-berth, he passed Killigrew coming in. 'What's he got this time?' Killigrew asked Strachan, as he closed the door after Latimer.

'Frostbite, he says. A corn, according to my diagnosis.'

'Want me to have a word with him?'

'What will you say? Tell him not to bother me with imaginary ailments? How's he to distinguish between imaginary and real? In his mind, they're all equally real. He just wants attention, that's all.'

'Then you shouldn't give it to him. Perhaps you ought to refer his next case to Dr Bähr. I can't see him putting up with any of Latimer's nonsense. He'll end up like the boy who cried wolf, if he's not careful. Got the sick list?'

Strachan handed him the list, and Killigrew cast his eye over it: a few minor cases of frostbite amongst the men who had been working on the ice, a couple of hernias, a dozen men suffering constipation, nothing out of the ordinary. 'Men's health generally good?' he asked.

'Not bad,' returned Strachan. 'But I'm not sure how long it will last. They can't stay on six-upon-four for ever. These are big, strong lads who work hard, Killigrew. They need a full ration of food each and every day. And I'm wondering how long it will be before scurvy rears its ugly head. Eating preserved vegetables out of tin canisters is all very well, but what they need are fresh greens. Did we not bring some cress seeds on board, and trays for growing it?'

Killigrew nodded. 'We can set them up down in the hold, once we've cleared some space there. Latimer can have charge of that: it seems to me that if he had more to do, he'd have less time to think up new ailments to come down with.' He handed the sick list back to Strachan.

It was early September: six days since they had escaped from the ice, and three since they had found a suitable anchorage on the west coast of Boothia – an inlet sheltered from the winds and currents that swept icebergs and bergy bits down from the north – and set to work to settle the ship in her winter quarters. The only problem was that almost a mile of shore ice lay between the *Venturer* and the inlet, so Killigrew, Ågård and Bombardier Osborne led a team of ten men on to the ice to cut a passage through. The ice was only six inches thick but it would get thicker as the winter progressed. The weather had cleared, but the air was still biting cold beneath the moonlit sky. At least at this time of year, in these latitudes, the sun behaved in a manner approximating to the normality they had grown up with in Europe, rising early in the morning and setting in the evening.

The Venturers chopped a series of holes in the ice in two lines, a little over the width of the hull apart. Tripods made from the ship's spare spars were built over these and the ice-saws were suspended from them. Then they began to cut. It took ten minutes to cut as many yards. At first the triangular slabs of ice that were cut free could be floated clear, but as the channel became deeper it became easier to submerge the slabs by tipping them up and sliding them under the ice on either side of the channel, like brushing dust under the rug.

The surface of the water they exposed formed into mottled ice within minutes and they had to work fast. As soon as the first hundred yards was clear the *Venturer* was kedged into the channel, the men still on board turning about the capstan, the bluff bows bumping against the ice. No one was allowed to spend more than two hours working on the ice; at the end of each shift they would go back aboard and change into warm, dry clothes. As they came on board Strachan and Bähr checked them all for signs of frostbite, and when they went back on to the ice they were warned to keep massaging the exposed parts of their flesh to keep the circulation going.

Working non-stop through the lengthening nights it took them three days to carve the channel through the ice. Seventy-two hours of back-breaking work in sub-zero temperatures, with the bitter winds howling across the ice pack driving snow and ice spicules into their faces, hands and feet growing numb beneath their mittens and socks. When the men started coming back on board with white, waxy faces, Strachan ordered the shifts to be reduced to an hour and a half, then an hour. Bathing tubs were filled on the mess deck and constantly replenished with hot water so that the men who came back on board could be quickly warmed up.

Following Molineaux's illustration, Kracht had constructed the jack-brace using parts cannibalised from spare tools and spare parts for the machinery, and to everyone's astonishment it had worked. True, the bearing did not glide up and down the banjo as smoothly as it had done before; in fact, it had never been all that smooth in the first place, but now it got stuck midway, and Varrow had to climb into the well and stamp on the bearing to get it past the ghost of a kink. It was not ideal, but it worked.

Repairing the damaged screw was going to take longer, however. Kracht would need a forge to hammer out the twisted metal blade, and they could not build that until they had settled into their winter quarters. The blacksmith was already making a set of bellows in preparation, using the squeeze box of O'Houlihan's concertina, to the delight of everyone on board

179

apart from the Irish seaman himself.

The men had finished cutting the channel through the ice and the *Venturer* was kedged the last few yards into its anchorage. Astern, the channel froze over fast, locking them in for who knew how many months. When the bows bumped against the ice at the end of the channel, the thud sounded to Killigrew like a knell of doom.

They moored the ship in position with an ice-anchor and set to work stripping her upper works. All the rigging was unrove, and the shrouds that remained in place to support the lower masts were slackened off. The topmasts and topgallants were taken down and stacked on the ice with the boats. The ropes and sails were put on shore to prevent them from rotting, along with the ship's provisions: the sub-zero temperatures would help to preserve the mix of salted and tinned food; and storing them on the ice made more room on the ship. And if disaster struck and the ship burned or was somehow crushed in the ice, at least they would not lose their stock of victuals.

A foot of fresh snow was spread on the upper deck to act as insulation. The lowest spars were turned fore-and-aft to form a single ridge-pole that ran the length of the ship, and plank rafters were fixed every few feet between the bulwarks and the spars. Then wadding tilt cloth was draped over the peaked framing and tacked into place to form a large tent that covered the entire deck so that only the stovepipes and one companion way amidships protruded. Finally, pylons were set in the ice all around the hull, about a hundred yards distant from it, and connected by ropes to form a perimeter fence beyond which no one was to travel without permission from an officer.

'Fetch an ice-axe and come with me,' Killigrew told O'Houlihan. The two of them descended the gangplank to the ice, and the lieutenant indicated a spot nearby. 'Dig a hole there, two feet across. That's our fire hole. If there's a fire on board, that will be our only supply of water. I'm making you responsible for ensuring the hole is free of ice at all times. I want it cleared every morning and every night, without fail. Hoist in?'

'Aye, aye, sir.' O'Houlihan went to work.

Killigrew strolled away across the ice to study the *Venturer* from about a hundred yards away. With the topmasts down and the tent of wadding tilt spread over the deck, it looked less like a modern exploring ship than an illustration of Noah's Ark in a Sunday school picture-book. It was to be the home of thirty-five men, one woman and thirteen dogs for the next few months. With the exception of Terregannoeuck, as sailors they were all used to getting along with one another in the confined spaces of a ship for prolonged periods, but at least on a ship there was always a chance of a change of scenery, and one had a good estimation of when one's next shore leave was coming up. Here there was no escape, just the men trapped in the hull with nowhere to go but the ice outside.

Killigrew sighed. He had a feeling it was going to be a long winter. Even by Arctic standards.

Strachan dreamed that he discovered a perfectly preserved dinosaur frozen in the ice: a new, previously undiscovered species. They took the dinosaur back to London, where Strachan displayed it to the leading lights of the Royal Society, not to mention the Queen and Prince Albert, at Somerset House overlooking the Thames. As they were applauding him, however, Michael Faraday revived the monster with a galvanic charge and it went on the rampage and ate the Prince. Just as Strachan saw his knighthood flying out of the window, the dinosaur turned on him. He was running through the corridors of Somerset House, his legs as heavy as lead, the dinosaur's breath hot and foul on the back of his neck.

At last he made it to the rooms of the London University and tried to barricade the door with the bookshelves. The dinosaur started to batter at the door, smashing aside the bookcases. One weighty tome flew at Strachan's head, flapping its pages like a pterodactyl, and he just had time to see it was a copy of the Bible before he woke up with a start. He was drenched with sweat, in spite of the fact it was so cold in his cabin that his breath formed clouds of condensation as it billowed from his mouth.

Someone was knocking at the door.

'Who is it?' he called sleepily.

'Orsini, *signore*. I bring you some coffee.'

'Thank you. Come on in.'

181

The steward entered, holding the mug with the hand that protruded from the sling on his arm. Strachan glanced at the porthole above his bunk; even with the curtain drawn across it he could see it was still dark outside. 'What time is it?' he asked, fumbling for his watch.

'Two bells in the morning watch, *signore*.'

Five o'clock in the morning, in other words. After the brief summer in which the sun had never set, now the days were drawing in, the nights growing longer. 'How long have you had your arm in that splint now?' he asked Orsini.

'Five weeks, *signore*.'

'Five weeks, eh? That splint will be ready to come off your arm in another week, I should say. Come to the sick-berth after breakfast and I'll take another look at it.'

'Thank you, *signore*.' Orsini withdrew.

Five weeks, mused Strachan. Five, since they had been nipped in the ice; more than four since they had settled into their winter quarters at Horsehead Bay, as they had come to name the inlet from its shape. He had expected the days to drag by, but they seemed to have flown past.

Strachan joined Killigrew, Yelverton, Cavan, Ziegler, Bähr and Ursula in the wardroom for a breakfast of bacon, bread and butter, and tea or coffee, and afterwards, bundled up warm, he made his way up on deck. He unfastened the opening in the awning, closing it again quickly behind him to keep the warm air in, and paused at the top of the gangplank. It was cold, but not intolerably so, and the sun warmed the air with its thin rays, a copper orb low over the southern horizon surrounded by a coronet jewelled with sundogs. Strachan drew a deep breath of sharp Arctic air into his lungs, and stepped on to the gangplank. His legs shot out from beneath him; he landed painfully on his backside and slithered down to the ice.

'Mind yourself, sir,' O'Houlihan said laconically, chopping with an ice-axe at the film of ice that had formed during the night over the fire hole. 'The gangplank's a bit slippery this morning.'

Strachan stood up, dusted snow from the seat of his trousers, and massaged his cheeks ruefully before making his way around the stores stacked on the ice to the 'observatory': a large wooden shack built on the ice of spare spars and wadding tilt, insulated with blocks of ice, a short distance from the ship. The barometers and magnetometers were in the observatory, at least, but the thermometers had to be kept outside and were sheltered under one of the *Venturer*'s cutters, which had been inverted and raised on spare spars to make a sort of awning. The final building in the cluster of huts beside the *Venturer* was the euphemistically named wash-house.

Strachan checked the current temperature on a standard thermometer, and then recorded highest and lowest recordings of the past sixteen hours on the maximum and minimum thermometers, correlating the results with the extremes measured by the Six's self-registering thermometer. To any normal man, it would have been tedious work, simply jotting down such statistics, but Strachan was not a normal man. His faith in science was founded on the immutable patterns in mathematics, and as a scientist he was dedicated to research through painstaking observation and note-taking.

His observations made, he turned back to the *Venturer*, where the morning's sick parade would already by queuing up outside the sick-berth. The crew were still on six-upon-four, the hands grumbling about it mightily in his presence, as if they thought he had some influence over the captain. He kept a sharp eye out for signs of malnutrition and scurvy. Neither had reared its ugly head yet, although it was early days. But the reduced rations were taking their toll. In addition to becoming increasingly fractious with every passing day, the men seemed to have an increased susceptibility to all manner of minor ailments: coughs and colds, aches and pains.

As Strachan was making his way back to the ship he caught sight of a movement out of the corner of his eye. Ivory on white, he might have missed it if it had remained motionless, even though he was passing within a few feet of it.

He froze at once, and then turned slowly, expecting to see an Arctic fox. Instead what he saw was a polar bear cub.

No – *two* polar bear cubs.

His heart pounding in his chest with excitement, he hunkered down so as not to scare them away. They backed off, hissing, but then seemed to relax, more curious than afraid. He guessed they could not be more than a few months old, and yet already they were more than five feet long: delightful, cuddly little creatures, no more menacing than his Uncle Andrew's golden retrievers. Strachan might be a scientist, but he had a weak spot for adorable mammals.

He could barely contain his excitement. Two real, live polar bear cubs, born and raised in the wild, and so close he could almost reach out and touch them. He wished he had his camera with him, but he dared not go back on board to fetch it in the hope they would remain still long enough for him to get a half-decent exposure; they would almost certainly be gone by the time he got back. So he concentrated on studying them, trying to impress every tiny detail in his mind's eye so he could draw a sketch later.

'Hullo there, ma wee bairns,' he murmured softly, soothingly. 'What are you doing here? Lost your mama and papa, eh?' He held out his hand to them, wishing he had some food on him with which he could tempt them. 'It's all right, I'm no' going to hurt you.'

Strachan's reassurance was completely unnecessary: the cubs seemed to have no fear of him whatsoever. One of them edged forwards, sniffed his outstretched hand, even licked his gauntlet. He realised he was probably the first *homo sapiens* the cubs had ever seen; who could blame them for being curious? Even as he crouched there, he felt a frisson of excitement, like the time he had been walking through a glen near his native Crieff and had encountered a magnificent stag; this was the kind of moment he knew would stay with him for ever.

Then the moment was shattered as the two cubs started at a sound from the direction of the *Venturer*, too low for Strachan to hear. They backed off, hissing.

'Mr Strachan, sir!' O'Houlihan called from the gangplank. 'Whatever you do, don't move!'

Strachan cursed inwardly at the seaman's well-intentioned blundering. 'It's all right, O'Houlihan,' he called back as loudly as he dared, not wanting to frighten the two cubs away. They stood their ground now, glaring towards O'Houlihan and bobbing their heads up and down. 'They're just bairns . . .' He backed away from the cubs to reassure them.

'*No*, sir!' The Irishman almost screamed with hysteria.

Strachan heard a snort behind him, and froze.

'There's a bear behind me, isn't there?' His cracked voice sounded high and reedy to his own ears, as if it had broken yesterday rather than fourteen years ago.

'Wes has gone to get help,' said O'Houlihan.

'Is it big?'

'Big enough, sir.'

Slowly – *very* slowly – Strachan turned. The bear was about seven feet from head to tail, weighing perhaps 550 pounds, her fur a yellowish-ivory. She drew black lips over sharp fangs and snarled at the assistant surgeon, bobbing her head up and down, muscles tensed to pounce.

Strachan swallowed hard, and whimpered. His whole life flashed before his eyes. One incident seemed to have particular resonance: he was eight years old, visiting his Uncle Andrew in London, and the two of them were in the Zoological Gardens in Regent's Park. Strachan liked his uncle – preferred him to his father, at any rate – and had always loved animals (ironic – but perhaps inevitable – that he should die at the hands ... well, *paws*... of one), so it was a day he had numbered among his happiest childhood memories, which were few. He had sat on his uncle's shoulders, the better to see the animals in their cages over the heads of the crowds.

'You know what that is, don't you, boy?' his uncle had asked him at the bear pit.

'Of course,' Strachan had replied, full of boyish impatience at such a foolish question. 'It's an *Ursus arctos*.'

'Oh, an *Ursus arctos*, is it?' his uncle had replied good humouredly. 'And there was I thinking it was a grizzly bear. You know they say you should never come between a mother bear and her cubs?'

Strachan had almost been too proud to admit his ignorance, but then as always his scientific curiosity had got the better of him. 'Why not?'

'Because mother bears are mortal protective of their bairns. If you come between a sow and her cubs, she'll tear you apart.'

At the time, it had struck Strachan as one of the most useless pieces of advice anyone could ever have given him. It was true his uncle had also told him that if you stepped on the cracks in the paving stones on Princes Street, a bear would come out and get you. In a spirit of scientific inquiry, Strachan had refuted that hypothesis in one second flat, satisfying himself that, regardless of whether or not he stepped on the cracks, the chances of him meeting one bear – let alone a mother and her cubs – in Great Britain were so slim as to be non-existent.

The mother bear growled.

A warm, wet feeling spread through Strachan's crotch. He felt afraid – more than that, he felt terrified – but most of all, he felt embarrassed. He could imagine everyone standing over his corpse, laughing because he had soiled himself.

The bear pounced. She slammed into him, all 550 pounds or so of her, with both massive paws on his chest, throwing him back down on the ice. A moment later, Strachan was not feeling much of anything at all.

X

The Transgression

Killigrew was making an inspection of the *Venturer*. In fifteen minutes' time the crew would beat to divisions, and immediately after that – while the crew jogged around the upper deck for an hour to exercise – Pettifer and Strachan would inspect the ship formally. But Killigrew liked to carry out his own inspection beforehand, making sure there was nothing for Pettifer to find fault with.

A conscientious officer, it was something he did as a matter of course, even though it had been unnecessary at the outset of the voyage. In those days – had it really been only been six months ago? – Killigrew had been able to do no wrong, in Pettifer's eyes at any rate. But ever since he had asked for his objection to continuing into the Arctic to be noted in the log, all that had changed. Now Killigrew could do no right, and if anything was amiss in the 'tween decks then he would be the one who would get an earful.

But the lieutenant's main concern was damp. Excess water vapour was a constant curse, whether exhaled from the mouths of the men as they returned from their daily exercise or billowing from the cooking pots. When Armitage prepared food, the curtain of Fear-Nought cloth that covered the door to the galley had to be kept shut tight to stop clouds of steam flooding through the mess deck and crystallising into hoarfrost on everything they touched.

Breakfast over, the hands had hoisted the mess tables up to the deck head and were fastening them in position. Killigrew noticed a dirty mess kid had been put on the deck. 'What's that?' he demanded crisply. The number on the mess kid was 4 – the number of the marines' mess. 'Corporal Naylor?'

'Mess kid, sir,' the marine responded sharply.

'What's it doing there?'

'Sir?'

'Clear it away, man! Scrub it and stow it!'

'Private Phillips is mess cook for today, sir.'

'Is Phillips here now?'

'No, sir. He's on sentry-go topsides, sir.'

'Then you do it.'

'Very good, sir.' Naylor picked up the kid with a grimace.

Feet thundered on the companion ladder leading down from the after hatch. Killigrew glanced aft to see Dr Bähr emerge from the door at a run and disappear into his cabin. Although the doctor habitually moved briskly, Killigrew had never seen him do anything so undignified as to run – with his long legs, it only made him look comical. He headed to the cabin to ask Bähr what was going on and had almost reached the door when the doctor reappeared, clutching his shotgun, at such a pace that Killigrew was forced to back off to avoid a collision.

'Dr Bähr! What the devil's going on?'

'Polar bear!' the doctor called excitedly over his shoulder, thundering back up the companion ladder.

Mildly curious – not sharing Bähr's keenness to bag a polar bear, or any other Arctic wildlife for that matter – Killigrew followed him up the ladder. He was halfway out of the hatch when he heard first one shot, then another. He had almost reached the opening in the awning when Cavan charged through, cannoning into him. Both of them reeled.

'Steady as she goes, Cavan! Where's the fire?'

'It's Mr Strachan, sir!' the mate panted, ashen-faced. 'A bear's got him!'

Killigrew ducked out from under the awning and slid gracefully down the slippery gangplank to the ice. Bähr and Molineaux were both there, holding smoking guns – the doctor his double-barrelled shotgun, the seaman a Minié rifle that Killigrew guessed he had snatched from Private Phillips, who stood beside him looking dazed. O'Houlihan clutched an ice-axe. Glancing across to where the barrels and crates of victuals were stacked on the ice, Killigrew saw a bear's hindquarters jutting out from behind the stores. He pushed between Bähr and Molineaux and dashed across the ice. He realised belatedly that he was armed with nothing more than his dress-sword: the edge honed to razor-sharpness, every bit as deadly as his cutlass, but he would have preferred his shotgun under the circumstances.

He rounded a stack of barrels, almost capsizing as he skidded on the ice, and saw the bear sprawled motionless on the ground, a couple of smaller bears standing nearby. There was no sign of Strachan at first, until he saw the assistant surgeon's boots poking out from under the adult bear.

Looking cowed and bewildered, the two cubs presented no immediate threat. 'Get him out from under there!' ordered Killigrew.

'Careful!' warned Bähr, his shotgun still levelled. 'It might be playing possum.'

O'Houlihan advanced slowly with the ice-axe raised. Killigrew ran out of patience and grabbed the bear's right forepaw. The animal was nothing but a dead weight: a bullet had drilled through its skull. Killigrew heaved. 'Pull him out!'

The Irishman dropped the ice-axe and seized Strachan's ankles, pulling him clear. Killigrew let go of the dead bear, and the two cubs moved closer, pawing uncertainly at their mother as if they thought she was just sleeping. O'Houlihan brandished the ice-axe at them. 'Shoo, yer buggers!'

'Is he all right?' Killigrew asked anxiously, as Bähr made a cursory examination of the assistant surgeon.

'No wounds that I can see. He's lost consciousness, though.'

'Concussion?'

'Fainted, I should say.'

'Fetch some smelling salts from the sick-berth, Molineaux,' ordered Killigrew. 'You'll find them in a bottle marked "sal ammoniac".'

'Don't bother,' Bähr said before the petty officer had taken a second step. 'This should do the trick.' He scooped up a handful of snow and rubbed it in Strachan's face.

The assistant surgeon spluttered his way back to semi-consciousness.

'It's all right, Strachan,' Killigrew told him, trying to drag him back to the present. 'You're all right.'

The assistant surgeon blinked at him. 'Of course I'm all right! Why shouldn't I be all right?' He massaged his ribs through his gauntlets and grimaced. 'I had the strangest dream. I dreamed I was attacked by an *Ursus maritimus*. . .'

With an apologetic expression, Killigrew nodded to the dead bear lying behind Strachan, the two cubs still nuzzling it in spite of O'Houlihan's efforts to drive them off. Strachan glanced over his shoulder and blanched; Killigrew thought he was going to faint again. But instead the assistant surgeon managed a wan grin.

'Whew! I know I came to the Arctic to study wildlife, but that's as close to nature as I care to get.' He glanced at Bähr, who still held his shotgun. 'It's fortunate for me you're a good shot, doctor. I'm obliged to you.'

Bähr scowled and turned away. 'Not Dr Bähr, sir,' explained Private Phillips. 'Molineaux. He grabbed my musket and brought the bugger down with one shot. Just as it was jumping at you too, sir.'

The petty officer looked embarrassed. 'You'd've done the same for me, sir.'

'Aye,' agreed Strachan. 'But I'd've missed.'

Bähr was evidently miffed that the first polar bear they had encountered had been killed by a common petty officer – and a negro at that – instead of himself.

'Never mind, doctor,' Killigrew tried to console him. 'I'm sure there'll be plenty of other opportunities for you to bag a bear before the winter's out.'

The doctor did not smile. He broke open his shotgun, plucked out the spent cartridge, and replaced it with a fresh one.

Terregannoeuck started talking in his own tongue, a droning monologue. Killigrew looked up to see who he was speaking to and realised that he was addressing the carcass of the dead bear.

'I don't think it can hear you, Terry,' O'Houlihan said with a grin.

Terregannoeuck glared at the interruption. 'We must thank

nanuq,' he explained, 'for allowing us to slay her.'

'Thank *nanuq* for allowing us to slay her,' echoed Killigrew. Well, if that was the Inuit custom, who was he to mock it? It could do no harm. He turned back to Strachan. 'Come on, let's get you back on board the *Venturer*. I'll wager you could use a drink.'

'A stiff one,' agreed Strachan.

Killigrew turned to the other crew members who had gathered around them. 'Come on, back to your duties,' he told them. 'There'll be plenty of time to admire Molineaux's kill later. Divisions in five minutes, everyone.'

They were halfway back to the foot of the *Venturer*'s gang-plank when they heard a shot behind them. Killigrew whirled to see one of the polar bear cubs sprawled in the ice beside its mother's carcass, its haunches a bloody mess, Bähr standing over it with his shotgun in his hands, one of the muzzles smoking. Finally realising that this was no game, the second cub turned and ran. Bähr levelled his shotgun at the cub's flanks. Terregannoeuck broke off his private ceremony and tried to stop the doctor, but it was too late: Bähr fired. A crimson splash stained the cub's ivory-coloured hide, and the cub yelped briefly, sprawled on the ice and lay still.

Terregannoeuck reached Bähr, snatched the shotgun from his hands and drove the stock into the doctor's jaw. Bähr fell on the ice and glared up at the Inuk, more humiliated than hurt.

Killigrew sprinted back across to the pair of them and grabbed the shotgun from Terregannoeuck. The Inuk made no attempt to resist.

Bähr fingered his jaw. 'What the devil was that for?'

'Not good, to kill cubs. No need. *Nanuq* should be allowed to grow old and have cubs of their own, before they are hunted. It will anger Kokogiaq.'

'The daddy bear's like to get pretty waxy about it too,' Molineaux said with a grin.

'You don't need to worry about that,' said Strachan. 'Male polar bears have no interest in raising their cubs. The dad . . . the boar bear is probably long gone. Isn't that right, Mr Terregannoeuck?'

'Usually,' the Inuk said darkly.

'Usually, my eye! It's a scientific fact. But Terregannoeuck's right about one thing. For any favour, why did you have to shoot them, Doctor?'

'It was the kindest thing to do. How long would they last without a mother?'

'They're old enough to at least stand a chance to fend for themselves. What right have we to deny them that?'

Killigrew could see that Strachan and Bähr were going to come to blows if they kept this up. 'All right, Strachan, calm down. They're dead now, and it's no use crying over spilt milk. Now, what about that drink I promised you?'

They left Bähr with Terregannoeuck and Molineaux – Killigrew knew he could trust the petty officer to handle things if the doctor and the Inuk got into a fight – and headed back to the *Venturer* once more.

'That was totally unnecessary,' Strachan muttered under his breath. 'He only shot those poor wee cubs because he was feeling left out after Molineaux bagged the mother.'

'You're not a hunting man, I take it?'

'Me? Faiks, no! I remember when I was a boy my uncle took me stag hunting one time. Ever been stag hunting? They cut it up, skin it, and give the choicest pieces of what remains to the dogs. Ghastly business. Uncle Andrew made me take part, get my hands all bloody. I just remember thinking I wanted to put it all back together again, make it live. It had looked so magnificent when it was still alive, and suddenly it was just . . . so much meat.'

'Is that why you studied medicine?'

'I wanted to be a veterinary surgeon for a while. Then my mother died . . .' He looked wistful, and then shrugged. 'I decided that if I was going to dedicate my life to making things better, I was as well looking after people as I was animals.'

Killigrew got Strachan settled in the wardroom with a mug of whisky. The lieutenant was glancing at his fob watch – at any moment now they would beat to divisions – when there was a knock on the door.

'Come in?'

Private Jenkins opened the door and thrust his head through.

'Cap'n wants to see you, sir,' he said, looking at Killigrew.

'Very good, Jenkins.'

As he followed the marine out of the wardroom, it occurred to Killigrew as peculiar that apart from the marines – who would stay at their posts come hell or high water – Pettifer was the only man on board who had not emerged from the ship to investigate the shooting on the ice. Oh, he had known captains who would not have done, showing an aloofness and trusting in their executive officers to keep them informed as soon as possible; but Pettifer was not such an officer. At least, he had not been when they had left Beechey Island.

But the captain had changed in the weeks since they had settled into their winter quarters. As if being trapped in the ice were not incarceration enough, Pettifer seemed to have confined himself to his quarters, only emerging to attend divisions each day at a quarter to nine, and to inspect the lower deck afterwards. It could not be good for a man, even a naval captain used to a degree of solitude, to shut himself off from the companionship of his fellows.

The curtains were drawn over the stern window, even though the sun was shining outside, and it was dark in the day-room. What did Pettifer do in there all day, with the lights out?

'You wanted to see me, sir?'

'What was all the shooting about?'

'Strachan was attacked by a polar bear, sir. Fortunately Petty Officer Molineaux was able to bring it down before Strachan was hurt.'

'And you did not see fit to inform me?'

'I was going to tell you, sir, but Strachan was shaken up and I thought my first priority was to look after him. I knew I'd be seeing you at divisions at any moment—'

'Your first priority, Mr Killigrew, is to keep me informed of anything that happens, no matter how trivial it might seem. Damn your eyes! I ought to place you under arrest—'

The boatswain's mates piped their calls, summoning the crew to divisions. 'You needn't think this is the end of the matter, Mr Killigrew,' growled Pettifer. 'I'll decide what's to be done with you later.'

'Aye, aye, sir. Sir, Mr Strachan is still a little shaken up by his narrow escape. Perhaps he ought to be excused divisions today . . .'

'Is he physically injured?'

'Not that I'm aware of, although I'd like Dr Bähr to examine him properly. The bear landed right on top of him.'

'Mr Strachan will attend divisions along with everyone else, Mr Killigrew. Dr Bähr can examine him later.'

'Aye, aye, sir.'

'Carry on.'

On his way out of the day-room, Killigrew looked into the wardroom to tell Strachan that he was not getting out of divisions, but the assistant surgeon was not there; he made his way up on deck and found that Strachan had decided for himself that he was fit to attend divisions.

Pettifer came up on deck and inspected the men before reading to them from the Articles of War. Afterwards he toured the lower deck with Killigrew and Strachan while the rest of the crew thundered around the upper deck over their heads. Fortunately, the hands had learned as well as Killigrew that there was no percentage in leaving anything for the captain to find fault with, no matter how trivial: the mess deck was spotless.

At ten o'clock Pettifer retired to his quarters and the ship's company marched around the outside of the ship for an hour and a half. Only the duty cooks for the day were excused this exercise: the victuals stored on the ice had to be brought on board the ship several days in advance, to give them time to thaw out ready for cooking. At half-past eleven the hands were given the first half of their daily ration of grog to wash down their ration of lemon juice and sugar, while the officers repaired to the wardroom or the gunroom for their first drink of the day.

Dinner was at midday, and in the afternoon work parties were assigned to their chores, while the rest of the hands stayed on board for a 'make and mend', carrying out repairs to worn or damaged clothing. Strachan had the dead polar bears dragged into the observatory – the door was just wide enough to get the mother through – so he could dissect them. As much as the assistant surgeon deplored the unnecessary slaughter of wild animals, once he had a fresh carcass on his hands he was too much of a practical scientist to pass up the opportunity for the study of comparative anatomy. Killigrew had some paperwork to complete – even in the Arctic, there was always paperwork – and afterwards entered the wardroom. Ursula and Ziegler were there, speaking in German. Even though they knew Killigrew hardly spoke a word of their language they both fell silent when he entered, and from the way Ziegler blushed bright crimson the lieutenant guessed they had not stopped talking in deference to him.

'I am going to my cabin,' Ursula said coldly.

Killigrew stepped aside for her and touched the peak of his cap. 'Ma'am.'

'I'm glad you're here,' Ziegler said when Ursula had closed the door behind her, although Killigrew suspected he was anything but. 'I wanted a word with you about Kapitän Pettifer . . .'

'Shall we take a walk?' suggested Killigrew.

Ziegler glanced at the thin partition that separated the wardroom from Pettifer's day-room, and nodded. The two of them put on overcoats, comforters and mittens and made their way out on to the ice. Now that the mess cooks had finished bringing the stores on board, the ice was deserted. Ziegler almost lost his footing on the slippery gangplank, but Killigrew caught him by the arm and preserved his dignity.

'Perhaps I should explain about that scene you saw when you entered the wardroom just now,' Ziegler said when they had reached the ice safely.

'It's really none of my business.'

Ziegler shook his head. 'No, I feel you deserve an explanation.'

'No explanation necessary. You love her a great deal, don't you?'

The German smiled wanly. 'Is it that obvious?'

Killigrew took out a cheroot for himself and offered one to his companion. 'I've been in love myself, once.'

Ziegler cupped his hand against the wind so the lieutenant could light his cheroot for him. 'What happened?'

'I lost her.'

'Lost her? You mean, she left you?'

'In a manner of speaking.' There seemed little point in boring Ziegler with the self-pitying details: how the woman in question had been killed largely as a result of Killigrew's carelessness; how he had subsequently thrown himself into a succession of doomed love affairs in a futile attempt to forget the one he had truly cared for. 'Have you told her? Frau Weiss, I mean.'

Ziegler grimaced. 'Yes. The day after her husband died.'

'Hmm.' Killigrew pursed his lips. 'Your timing might have been better.'

'I thought I was going to die; that I would never see her again. Besides, it is not as if there was any love lost between them. He used to beat her.'

'So I understood.'

'Who told you? Was it her?' There was a note of jealousy in Ziegler's voice at the very thought of Ursula confiding in the lieutenant.

'That hardly matters. The point is, there are certain proprieties a gentleman is expected to observe in these situations. You said you wanted to speak to me about Commander Pettifer. Or was that merely a blind for the discussion of more . . . personal matters?'

Ziegler shook his head. 'It has not escaped our attention that Kapitän Pettifer has not been . . . shall we say, himself? . . . of late.'

'The captain's been under a great deal of strain these past few weeks,' Killigrew allowed cautiously. 'We all have our own ways of dealing with these situations.'

'By shutting oneself in one's quarters, only coming out a couple of hours a day?'

'The life of a ship's captain in the Royal Navy is a lonely one. Shall we go into the observatory, see how Strachan's getting on with his specimens?'

There was a stove in the observatory, but Strachan had not lit the fire, presumably to allow the cold air to preserve the organs of the bears he was dissecting. If the observatory was not heated, at least it was out of the wind. Killigrew and Ziegler found Bähr helping Strachan with his dissection: evidently the two of them had put their earlier quarrel behind them.

'Found anything interesting?' Killigrew asked jocularly.

'I'll say!' agreed Strachan. 'Look at these paws! See how wide they are. Ideal for walking on thin ice, to spread the bear's weight; and for use as paddles, if you will, when swimming. A peculiar beast, the *Ursus maritimus*. Very similar to *Ursus arctos* in so many points of anatomical congruity, and yet so very different. It's almost as if someone had taken the grizzly bear as a blueprint, and then adapted it for life in the Arctic.'

Ziegler smiled. Already he and Strachan had enjoyed many good-natured debates about the existence of God. 'It amazes me that someone who is as fascinated in the patterns recurring in nature as you are can fail to detect the hand of God at work.'

The assistant surgeon shook his head. 'Are you familiar with Lamarck's theory of orthogenesis, Herr Ziegler?'

Ziegler shook his head.

'The theory is that all life on earth has a drive for perfection that leads all organisms to evolve to higher states on what Linnaeus called the "great chain of being". If I can only understand the mechanism that leads animals to seek perfection, I cannot help but wonder if I shan't have the key to the very nature of all life on earth. But I'm not convinced that such a secret can be learned simply by cutting up corpses. To understand animals, we have to study them alive, to study their behaviour. You can dissect the corpse of a criminal, but that won't help you understand what drove him to become a criminal.'

Killigrew stared at the dead bear. Never mind its similarity to a grizzly bear; stretched out on its back on the sturdy workbench, it looked disturbingly human. The lieutenant had been raised in the Church of England, and until he had met the assistant surgeon it had never occurred to him to question fundamental Christian teachings. But suppose what Strachan said was true? Suppose all animals were somehow related, if you went back far enough? Was man, too, just another animal, rather than made in God's image? Perhaps there was no God. Perhaps He was the product of wishful thinking, made in Man's image rather than vice versa. And if that was true, what was the purpose of existence? *Was* there a purpose, even?

There was a knock on the door. 'Come in,' called Strachan.

The door opened, bringing with it a blast of cold air, and Boatswain's Mate Unstead thrust his head inside, looking at each of them in turn until his eyes lit on Killigrew. 'Begging your pardon, sir, but the cap'n wants you in his day-room.'

'All right, Unstead.'

As he followed the boatswain's mate back across to the *Venturer*, Killigrew thought he knew what it was about. Pettifer had not forgotten his earlier threat to have his lieutenant put under arrest for failing to report the shooting of the polar bear. It was difficult to see what the captain could do to him, apart from confine him to his cabin under guard. As grim as their incarceration in ice was, being confined to his cabin in such circumstances would be even grimmer. But he knew it would not be for too long: it was not immodesty so much as common sense that told him Pettifer could not run the ship for long with his one and only lieutenant confined to his cabin.

Except that when Private Walsh ushered Killigrew into Pettifer's day-room, it immediately became apparent this had nothing to do with him: Able Seamen Jacko Smith and Johnno Smith stood to attention before the table, flanked on either side by Thwaites and Molineaux, while Orsini hovered in the background. Pettifer glared at them with contempt and fed titbits to Horatia, who sat curled in his lap, while Latimer sat next to him with some papers on the table before him.

'You're just in time, Killigrew,' Pettifer said without taking his eyes off the two able seamen. 'Smith and Smith were caught red-handed stealing food from my storeroom; furthermore, they have both admitted their culpability.'

'Culpability?' protested Johnno, alarmed. 'I never said nothing about doing any culpability!'

'He means you've admitted that you did it,' explained Killigrew.

'Oh. That. Aye.'

'Have you got anything to say for yourself?' asked Pettifer.

'We was hungry, sir.'

'That's no excuse,' said Pettifer. 'All the men are hungry. But only you chose to steal food.'

'Aye, all the men,' spat Jacko. 'What about the officers? They're not on six-upon-four, I'll bet.'

'As a matter of fact, we've been on six-upon-four just as long as you have, Smith,' Killigrew informed him. It had been his suggestion that they show solidarity with the rest of the crew in this matter.

'Not that bloody dog, though, sir,' said Jacko. 'I'll bet that bloody dog isn't on six-upon-four!'

'Horatia's just a dog, Smith,' said Killigrew. 'She didn't volunteer for this expedition; unlike you. And I hardly see what Horatia's food has got to do with this matter.'

'It was the dog's food they stole,' explained Latimer.

'A fact which makes their crime all the more contemptible,' snorted Pettifer. 'Stealing food from a poor, defenceless animal! You should both be ashamed of yourselves! I see no need for any leniency in this matter. You'll both receive thirty-six lashes.'

'May I see the warrants?' asked Killigrew.

Latimer had evidently made out two warrants for corporal punishment, one for each of them. 'Either one will do,' Pettifer told the clerk. 'The details are the same in both; even the name of the culprit!'

Killigrew glanced at the warrant Latimer handed him.

Whereas it has been represented to me by Steward Vincenzo Orsini that on Friday 1st October, Able Seaman John Smith (7 months) did steal provisions from the captain's stores valued at four shillings, and having duly investigated the manner by inquiry and having heard the evidence of Clerk Nicodemus Latimer and Steward Vincenzo Orsini in support of the charge, as also what the Prisoner had to offer in his defence, I consider the charge to be substantiated against him, and this being the 1st complaint made against him, I therefore adjudge him to receive 36 lashes, according to the custom of the Service, on Saturday 2nd October, or as soon afterwards as circumstances will admit without inconvenience to the Service.

Given under my hand, on board
Her Majesty's Ship Venturer at two o'clock
the 1st day of October 1852.
Cmdr Orson Pettifer,
Commanding Officer

'Everything in accordance with Her Majesty's regulations, as I'm sure even you will agree, Mr Killigrew?' remarked Pettifer.

'Yes, sir.' The lieutenant handed the warrant back to Latimer, who looked ashen-faced. Clearly the full implications of the document were not lost on the clerk: it was probably the first time he had ever copied out such a document; floggings were so few and far between nowadays, it would probably be the first one he had ever watched. Even Killigrew had not witnessed a flogging for over six years.

'Dismissed!' Pettifer told Smith and Smith. 'Take them away, Mr Thwaites!'

The two prisoners were marched out of the captain's day-room by Thwaites and Molineaux. Orsini followed them out, evidently glad to get out of there. The steward was not the talkative sort and it was difficult to tell what he was thinking, but Killigrew was willing to bet that had Orsini known where it would lead, he would never have reported the theft of the provisions in the first place.

'Might I speak with you *in camera*, sir?' asked Killigrew.

'Leave us,' Pettifer told Latimer. The clerk gathered up his writing things and hurried out, every bit as glad to leave as Orsini had been. 'Well?' Pettifer asked Killigrew when the door had closed behind him.

'With all due respect, sir, don't you think thirty-six lashes is a little harsh for stealing dog food?'

Pettifer turned puce. 'Are you questioning my orders, Mr Killigrew?'

'No, sir. It's just that—'

'Stealing is stealing, and I will not tolerate it aboard my ship! And I will not tolerate officers who question my orders and plot to undermine my authority.'

'I'm not trying to undermine your authority, sir—'

'Be quiet, damn your eyes! You think I don't know about you, Mr Killigrew? About how you've deliberately thwarted my attempts to sail through the North-West Passage in a single season? I can't prove it – yet. But I will. By God, I'll see you court-martialled and dismissed the service! I'm disappointed in you, Killigrew. The others – I might have expected nothing less than their treachery. But I thought I could trust you. Instead it turns out that I've been harbouring a viper in my bosom. Get out! Get out of my sight at once!'

Stunned though he was by Pettifer's accusation of sabotage,

Killigrew had sense enough to know when to stand and fight and when to withdraw gracefully. The sheer nonsense of the accusation infuriated him, and it was only by keeping a tight rein on his all-too-volatile temper and telling himself that the captain was under a lot of strain that he kept his composure.

He made his way into the wardroom and crossed straight to the sideboard, where he poured himself a generous measure of Irish whiskey and knocked it back in one.

'It that always your response to a crisis?'

Killigrew whirled guiltily and saw Ursula sitting on the couch behind the door, a novel in her lap. 'It depends on the crisis,' he told her, pouring himself a second measure, but sipping this one. 'What's the book?' he asked her.

'*The Whale*, by Herman Melville.'

'The fellow who wrote *Typee* and *Omoo*?' he asked. She nodded. 'What's it about? Apart from a whale, obviously.'

'A captain who's so obsessed with achieving an impossible goal that he drives his ship to destruction.'

'Reckon I know what attracted them bears here yesterday,' said O'Houlihan, as the hands on the lower deck dressed in their mustering rig for divisions the following morning. He winked at Hughes, and jerked his head at Endicott, who was preening himself with the aid of a tarnished hand-held looking-glass. 'Reckon they was after Seth.'

Sensing a leg-pull was imminent, Endicott did not even bother to turn. 'Don't talk daft, Mick. There's thirty-six of us on this ship. Why the hell would they pick on me?'

'Why, revenge, to be sure!'

'Revenge? What are you talking about, you chucklehead? What have I ever done to them?'

'What about all that bear's grease you plaster on your hair? How many bears have died over the years to keep your locks tidy?'

Hughes joined in the joke. 'Reckon there must be enough bear's grease in your locker to account for half a dozen bears,' he said, indicating the open seat locker where Endicott had stock-piled enough bottles of the ursine unguent to last him three years; and considering how thickly he applied the stuff, it was hardly surprising there was little room left in the locker for anything else.

'Oh, aye?' sneered Endicott. 'How would they know?'

'Bears have a powerful strong sense of smell, Seth,' said O'Houlihan. 'Reckon they can sniff it on you.'

'Aye,' said Hughes. 'You want to watch yourself, Seth. One of these days the wind's going to be blowing in the wrong direction, and the next thing you know every bear on the polar ice is going to recognise Uncle Bruin's scent, and they're going to come looking for him. And what they'll find is you.'

'Gammon!' snorted Endicott. 'I'm not falling for that humbug.'

'What the devil is that?' Pettifer demanded when he came up on deck for divisions.

'It's a polar bear bladder, sir,' explained Killigrew.

'And why is it hanging over the quarterdeck?'

'Some kind of Esquimau joss, sir. Terregannoeuck says that for five days after you kill a sow, you must act as if her *tatkoq* – that's her soul, sir – were a guest in your home. You hang up needles and brushes and women's things like that, which the sow's *tatkoq* can use in polar bear heaven, and after five days the bear's soul leaves with the spirits of the ornaments. Then, when she gets to polar bear heaven, she'll tell the spirits of unborn polar bears that Petty Officer Molineaux is a worthy hunter to be killed by . . .' He realised that Pettifer was staring at him as if kipper trees were growing out of his ears. 'I didn't see any harm in it, sir. It's supposed to be good luck, and you know how superstitious sailors are.'

'Sailors' superstitions I can put up with, Mr Killigrew, but I will not tolerate heathen superstition. It's unhygienic. Have it taken down at once, sir!'

'But, sir—'

'Don't argue with me, man! At once!'

'Aye, aye, sir. Endicott!'

'Sir?'

'Remove the bladder.'

'Terregannoeuck's not going to like it, sir,' Endicott said dubiously.

'That's Terregannoeuck's problem. Do as the captain says.'

The offending item removed, the captain inspected the men paraded before him. Where previously Pettifer had turned a blind eye to all but the scruffiest seaman – leaving Killigrew, who was himself quite relaxed about such things, to reprimand any slovenly reprobates in private later – today he was looking for faults. By the time he had finished, the boatswain had taken enough names to cover a whole page of his notebook.

'I notice several of the men have started to grow beards, Mr Killigrew,' Pettifer said when he returned to the quarterdeck.

'It's standard practice to let the men grow beards on Arctic service, sir. It reduces the risk of frostbite.'

'That may be good enough for other ships, Mr Killigrew, but I will not tolerate it on the *Venturer*! From now on I want all men clean-shaven, hoist in? I cannot abide facial hair. This is the navy, not the damned army!'

'Aye, aye, sir.'

After Pettifer had read out the Articles of War, he ordered that they proceed to the punishment of Smith and Smith, reading out the charge, conviction and sentence. Any hopes for a remittance of their sentence were dashed: it remained at thirty-six lashes. The whole crew was drawn up on the quarterdeck to witness the administration of the punishment, including Terregannoeuck, Sørensen and the Germans rescued from the ice. Only Ursula was excused: a flogging was hardly a fit sight for the eyes of a lady. *Hardly a fit sight for anyone's eyes*, Killigrew thought to himself. But Admiralty regulations demanded that the whole ship's company, officers and ratings alike, witness such punishments.

The two culprits were ordered to strip to the waist, the flesh of their backs covered in goose pimples and mottled blue in the chill autumn air. Johnno Smith was first up. A kerchief was tied around his neck, and he was bound hand and foot to a trap ribbing, spread-eagled.

Mate Cavan shuffled over to where Killigrew stood. 'You're not going to let him do this, are you?' he whispered.

'The captain's well within his rights, Mr Cavan,' Killigrew replied out of the corner of his mouth. 'By their own admission, they stole food. There isn't an admiral in the navy who'd question his right to punish them.'

'But the men are starving!'

'I know, Mr Cavan, I know. But none of the others have stolen food.'

'Yet,' muttered Yelverton.

Thwaites brought the bag that contained the cat-o'-nine-tails up on deck; and not just an ordinary cat-o'-nine-tails, but the thieves' cat at that, with its larger, crueller knots. The bag was dyed crimson so it would not show the blood. Ordinarily, floggings were delivered by the boatswain's mates, each of them delivering a dozen lashes before passing the cat on to the next man, so there was no danger of any lashes being deprived of their full force by a weary arm. But there were only two boatswain's mates in the *Venturer*'s skeleton crew, Unstead and Molineaux, so the boatswain himself had been pressed into service to deliver the first dozen as a matter of expediency. Some boatswains would have objected, but not Thwaites: he was too much of a sadist.

Private Phillips played a drum roll and Thwaites delivered the first lash. Johnno's muscles quivered visibly, and half a dozen red welts were scored across his back. While he stopped himself from crying out, his whole body shuddered in agony.

'One!' announced Phillips.

Thwaites lashed again.

'Two!'

And again.

'Three!'

At the seventh lash, Johnno cried out. Killigrew saw Molineaux flinch at each lash, and remembered that the petty officer had once received a flogging himself.

After the first dozen lashes, Thwaites handed the cat to Unstead, who did not look happy to receive it.

'Make 'em good 'uns, Unstead,' growled Pettifer, glowering from the quarterdeck. 'For every lash I think you're holding back, I'll have *you* given two!'

By now Johnno's back was a dull red mass. Unstead murmured something in Johnno's ear, and the seaman nodded.

'He'll never make the full three dozen,' muttered Strachan.

Killigrew forced himself to watch. It had revolted him when

he had seen his first flogging, at the tender age of thirteen; it revolted him not one whit less now. Not for the first time, he swore to himself that when he had command of his own ship, no flogging would stain the deck with blood.

At the eighteenth lash the skin broke and blood began to trickle down Johnno's back. By the time Molineaux's turn to take over with the cat came, Johnno had fainted. Pettifer called for the punishment to stop. 'Douse that man with sea water, Hughes!'

'Aye, aye, sir.' Hughes' tone was truculent, but he had no choice but to obey. He disappeared from under the awning with a pail, descending the gangplank to the ice to fill the pail at the fire hole. He returned and dashed the icy water across Johnno's back. Coughing and spluttering, the seaman was revived enough for the flogging to continue.

'Proceed, Molineaux,' ordered Pettifer.

'I'd rather not, if it's all the same with you, sir.'

'It is *not* all the same with me, Molineaux!'

The petty officer was heading for a flogging himself, and that would not stop Johnno from getting his remaining twelve lashes, either. 'Damn your eyes, Molineaux!' snapped Killigrew, redirecting the anger he felt towards Pettifer at the petty officer. 'Do as you're damned well ordered!'

Molineaux looked hurt. Scowling at Killigrew and Pettifer, he took the cat-o'-nine-tails from Unstead. 'God forgive me,' he muttered, and lashed away.

By the time Johnno had been given all thirty-six lashes, his whole back, from the nape to the small, was like a lump of bloody meat. He slumped in his bonds.

'And where do you think *you're* going, Mr Strachan?' Pettifer demanded when the assistant surgeon started forward.

'To have Smith removed to the sick-berth so that his back can be treated, sir.'

'Stay right where you are, mister! Smith will remain on deck until the other Smith has received his punishment.'

'Sir, if I don't treat Smith's back quickly—'

'Are you defying me, Mr Strachan?'

The assistant surgeon hung his head. 'No, sir.'

'I should think not. Have the other Smith lashed up now, Bosun.'

Jacko was bigger and younger than Johnno, but he lacked his older namesake's fortitude, and after biting back his cries for the first three lashes, he let out a howl of agony. As he screamed, the huskies on the lower deck took up the refrain, howling piteously in sympathy.

'Shut those damned dogs up!' snarled Pettifer.

McLellan went below to quiet the huskies – evidently grateful not to have to witness any more of the brutality – but the dogs went on howling.

So did Jacko. As soon as the punishment was over, Strachan ran forward and helped Unstead and Molineaux untie him. 'Get him in the sick-berth, quick, before he freezes to death! And the other one too, untie him . . .'

Molineaux started to untie one of Johnno's wrists but then paused, and felt for a pulse in his neck. He lifted an eyelid and saw only white. 'No hurry with this one.'

Strachan carried out his own examination and concurred with Molineaux's diagnosis. 'He's dead, sir.'

XI

Blood and Ice

'How do you bury a man at sea in the Arctic, anyhow?' McLellan wondered as he stood on sentry duty that night.

'Dig a hole in the ice and drop him through,' Endicott said facetiously. He was part of the anchor watch, along with Molineaux, McLellan and Private Walsh; since there was not actually anything for them to do at that time of night, the four of them were huddled around the after hatch. As officer of the watch, Yelverton paced back and forth on the quarterdeck in an effort to keep warm, but he was too far away to hear the seamen talking.

A blizzard – surprisingly rare in the Arctic – blew outside, and the howling wind beat against the awning, flapping the wadding tilt noisily against the spars. Despite the best efforts to seal up the space below the awning, icy draughts still found a way through and Molineaux wished he was tucked up in his hammock on the mess deck like everyone else. With so many bodies stuffed into such a small space, it was nice and toasty down there at night.

'What do you think, Wes?' Endicott asked Molineaux. 'Will they dig a fresh hole for him, or just drop him through the fire hole?'

Toying with his rosary, Walsh scowled. Johnno Smith had been one of his friends – as much as a seaman and a marine could be friends – and he did not appreciate the Liverpudlian's levity on the subject. 'I wish you'd shut your trap, Seth.'

'They'll bury him ashore, like those three coves that died at Beechey Island,' guessed Molineaux. 'I just hope we're not the poor bastards that have to dig the grave in that hard, frozen soil.'

'Reckon they'll give him a headstone?' wondered Endicott.

'Aye,' said Walsh. 'And I know what they can write on it: "Able Seaman John Smith, born eighteen oh-two, died eighteen fifty-two. Served on board HMS *Asia* at the battle of Navarino. Awarded the General Service Medal and the China War medal. Devoted husband and father of three. Executed . . . for stealing dog food!" '

'All right, Walsh, keep your shirt on,' said Molineaux. 'The captain wasn't to know he'd die.'

'Thirty-six lashes for an auld feller like Johnno? He must've had a fairly good idea, so!'

'It wisnae just dog food,' said McLellan. 'I heard it were hashed venison. That stuff costs two shillings a can!'

'Bloody hell!' said Endicott. 'That dog eats better'n we do.'

McLellan sighed and stamped his feet to keep the circulation going. 'This is a damned waste o' time. I mean, what are we supposed to watch for? This is the middle o' the Arctic, for Goad's sake! Who's going tae try tae sneak on board? Esquimauxs?'

'Hey, if you don't like it, complain to the Old Man,' suggested Molineaux, wrapping his box-cloth jacket more tightly around him.

'Maybe we're not on guard to stop fellers from getting on,' said Walsh. 'Maybe we're after stopping them from getting off.'

'Yur, right,' sneered Molineaux. 'Like anyone in his right mind is going to desert while we're in the middle of the Arctic.'

Footsteps sounded on the aft companion way and Horatia emerged from the hatch, pulling a tightly bundled figure on a leash. Molineaux was only able to recognise Cavan from the eyes that peeped out over his comforter in the shadows beneath a hat like a fur deerstalker with the ear flaps tied down.

Molineaux stood to attention. 'Not taking her out for a walk in this weather are you, sir?' he asked incredulously.

A smile crinkled the corner of Cavan's eyes. 'Captain's orders, Molineaux. Horatia needs her exercise.'

Molineaux grinned back. 'I wouldn't send a dog out on a

night like this. Maybe not even an officer. Why don't you just give her a couple of turns around the deck, sir? We won't tell, will we, lads?'

Endicott, McLellan and Walsh shook their heads.

'That's very kind of you, but orders are orders. Besides, I could do with some fresh air myself. It's so stuffy down there.'

'A little too fresh out for my liking, sir,' said Molineaux, as Cavan took Horatia to the sealed opening in the awning. 'Make sure you don't wander past the perimeter, sir. You can barely see your hand in front of your face, and you wouldn't have to go far to get lost.'

'I know what I'm doing, Molineaux,' Cavan said with all the confidence of youth.

'And don't stay out too long, sir. It's cold out.'

'You think this is cold? Ågård tells me it's going to get much colder before the winter is out.'

Molineaux's heart sank. 'I didn't think it *could* get colder than this.' The last time he had looked at the thermometer it had registered twenty below zero, and it had grown colder since then.

Cavan nodded. 'Ågård says it's like the way the coldest hour is before the dawn. With the sun gone, the air just gets colder and colder until it comes back again.'

'Well, don't be too long, sir, all the same.'

'Oh, stop fussing, for Heaven's sake, Molineaux! You're worse than my mama. I won't be long. Just twice round the hull. That should be more than enough for both of us. Come along, Horatia.' Cavan parted the flaps of the opening and slipped outside with the dachshund as a great gust of wind blew through with a flurry of thick snowflakes.

'Oh, that's just plummy, that is,' McLellan grumbled, when Cavan had sealed up the flaps behind him. 'I didna think there was any warm air in here, but I realise there must've been some, because it's *all* gone noo.'

Outside they heard a cry and a thump: the now-familiar sound of someone slipping on the icy gangplank and coming to grief. Molineaux, Endicott, Walsh and McLellan cheered ironically.

A muffled growling sound came from close by and Endicott looked about in alarm. 'What was that?'

'My crammer,' said Molineaux, and once again his stomach growled. He had known hunger in his childhood, but that had been a long time ago. They had been on six-upon-four for so long, he had forgotten what it was like not to be hungry all the time. Now he always felt tired and lackadaisical, and the morning run around the deck that he would normally have taken in his stride left him feeling totally drained. And he knew he was no worse off than anyone else on board. The constant cold and close confinement was making everyone fractious, and the permanent hunger only added to their irritability.

'We can't go on like this,' said Walsh, voicing Molineaux's own thoughts.

'Maybe the cap'n's right,' said Molineaux. 'Maybe we'll be stuck here for five years. You'll be glad enough the cap'n had the foresight to reduce our vittles then.'

'We'll be lucky to last one year at this rate, never mind five! What the hell are we doing here, Molineaux? Franklin's dead, we're never going to find him in all this; and as for the North-West Passage . . . even if there is one, no ship can get through with all the ice.'

'Forget Franklin and the North-West Passage. Just think of that lovely double pay we're getting for discovery service.'

'We'll never make it back to spend it on anything, if someone doesn't do something about the captain.'

'I'm sure Tom Tidley and the officers would welcome any suggestions you care to make to them.'

'A bayonet up his backside, that's what he needs,' muttered Walsh.

'Stow it, Walsh.' Despite his sympathy with the marine's sentiments, mutinous talk always made Molineaux feel nervous.

Orsini came on deck with five mugs on a tray; with his arm still in a sling, he had to balance the tray on one hand, but seemed to manage with his usual grace and élan. He took one mug to Yelverton, and carried the remaining four across to the four seamen. 'Some hot cocoa, *signores*, with Signor Armitage's compliments.'

'God bless him,' said Molineaux, as he and his three companions snatched the mugs from the tray. Walsh lifted his mug to his lips and cried out.

'What's the matter?' asked Orsini. 'Too hot?'

Glaring at him, Walsh merely upended his mug and gave the base a solid whack with the heel of his left hand. The cocoa fell out in a perfect cylinder and hit the deck with a thump.

'Now that's what I call cold,' said Molineaux.

Orsini looked puzzled. 'I no understand. I bring the drinks up from the galley right away . . .'

'You didn't bring it up fast enough then, did you?' said Walsh.

'All right, Walsh, let him alone,' said Molineaux. 'It's not his fault. Hot water freezes faster'n cold.'

'I fetch you some more,' offered Orsini, and scurried below deck once more.

All at once the dogs started howling. 'What the devil's got into them?' demanded Walsh.

'Maybe they're hungry,' suggested Endicott.

'Tell 'em they ain't alone,' said Molineaux.

McLellan shook his head. 'Something's got them in a funk,' he said, and crouched before the pens. 'What's up, boys?' he asked, studying the dogs carefully as they paced up and down behind the wooden bars.

Terregannoeuck had warned Molineaux about something he called *piblokto*, a disease affecting dogs that manifested itself in restlessness, frothing at the mouth, convulsions, lockjaw and then death, when the helpless beast was torn apart by the rest of the pack. The restlessness was there right enough, but there could have been a hundred and one other reasons for that. Molineaux was wondering if he should send Endicott below to wake Terregannoeuck to see what he thought – if there was disease amongst the dogs they would have to be separated out as quickly as possible – when he heard a scratching sound at the awning behind him.

McLellan stood up and exchanged glances with Molineaux, Endicott and Walsh. Their faces were pale. The scratching – its movement visible through the wadding tilt at the opening – became more frantic, and they could hear the sound of whimpering and snuffling.

Molineaux crossed to the opening and was about to unfasten the flaps when Hughes laid a hand on his arm. 'You don't know what's out there.'

The petty officer looked at him, and then opened the awning. At once Horatia scampered through in a flurry of snow, trailing her leash behind her. She scurried across the deck and curled up in a corner, whimpering.

'Where the devil's Mr Cavan?' wondered Walsh.

Molineaux snatched up the nearest thing he could use as a weapon: a gaff hook. 'Get Mr Killigrew, quick!' he said, and then stepped out through the opening.

If it had been freezing beneath the awning, sheltered from the wind and warmed by the heat of the boilers and the men crammed on the mess deck, then outside – exposed to the full fury of the gusting blizzard – it was a hundred times worse. Molineaux was wearing about a dozen layers and the wind seemed to cut straight through them as if he was naked. It was as dark as hell and the snow seemed almost as thick in the air as it was on the ice.

'Mr Cavan? Sir?' Molineaux stood at the top of the gangplank and leaned into the howling wind, his voice drowned out by the mournful threnody. He could not even see the foot of the gangplank and doubted his voice would carry that far. A full orchestra could have been playing the finale from a Beethoven symphony down there for all he knew, and he would have been none the wiser. He realised that if he were to have a hope of finding Cavan he was going to have to go down there.

He took one step on to the gangplank and at once his feet shot away from beneath him. He landed painfully on his backside and dropped the gaff hook as he desperately scrabbled for a handhold. He slithered down and fetched up at the foot of the gangplank, dazed, sore and winded. No orchestra, and no Cavan either: just snow, ice and biting wind.

He picked himself up. Behind him, the *Venturer* was covered in a thick drift of snow, no more than a vague outline in all the whiteness. It had become so much a part of its surroundings, it was impossible to imagine it breaking free in the spring thaw and sailing back to England.

But there was no time to worry about that now. Mr Cavan was out there somewhere. Perhaps he was safe and sound and had only let Horatia get away from him, but some instinct told Molineaux otherwise. He crawled around in the snow until he found the gaff hook and then stood up, gripping it tightly.

Twice round the hull, Cavan had said. For all his youthful bravado, the mate was a sensible lad and would have done just that and no more. Molineaux started to make his way round the stern.

The wind was even stronger on the far side of the hull. Molineaux kept on calling out Cavan's name but he began to suspect he was wasting his time. He could have passed within a couple of feet of the mate and neither of them would have realised it. He reached the bows and saw a light through the snow ahead of him, swaying back and forth, the beam of a bull's-eye lantern picking out the swirling flakes. He waved his arms above his head.

'Over here!' he bawled.

Two tightly bundled figures stumbled out of the night: Killigrew with the bull's-eye, and Walsh carrying his rifled musket, both of them heavily muffled.

'Find anything?' Killigrew yelled above the noise of the blizzard.

'Can't see a thing, sir!'

'You should've brought one of these!' Killigrew raised the bull's-eye, and then lowered its beam to pick out the set of footprints he and Walsh had been following, already almost filled in by the snow. They followed the trail back the way Molineaux had come, Molineaux's own prints occasionally crossing Cavan's.

Killigrew shone the beam of his bull's-eye a short distance ahead and it picked out something dark against the whiteness in the oval of light. All around, the snow was splashed crimson.

The three of them broke into a run.

'Jaysus Christ!' Walsh made the sign of the cross.

Molineaux had a strong stomach but, even so, he felt sick. What they had found might have been Cavan; but it could easily have been a beef carcass after all the best cuts had been carved off. The tattered, blood-soaked remnants of the mate's uniform were scattered all around. Killigrew kneeled down and picked up something from the snow: Cavan's epaulette.

'Sweet Jesus!' said Molineaux. 'What could do that to a man?'

'*Nanuq.*'

The three of them whirled. Molineaux hefted the gaff hook and Walsh raised the barrel of his musket. Terregannoeuck backed away, his harpoon in one hand and a bull's-eye in the other.

They lowered their weapons again. 'Jesus, Terry!' protested Molineaux. 'Don't you know better than to go creeping up on a cove like that?'

'*Nanuq* do this,' said Terregannoeuck. He flashed the beam of his bull's-eye over the snow and revealed some massive paw-prints in the snow, over a foot across. 'Big one.'

' "Forasmuch as it hath pleased Almighty God of his great mercy to take unto himself the souls of our dear brothers here departed, we therefore commit their bodies to the ground; earth to earth, ashes to ashes, dust to dust; in sure and certain hope of the Resurrection to eternal life, through our Lord Jesus Christ; who shall change our vile body, that it might be like unto his glorious body, according to the mighty working, whereby he is able to subdue all things to himself." '

Solemn-faced, Pettifer closed his prayer book. He looked awful: unshaven, white-faced and hollow-eyed. Shrouded in sacking, the body of Johnno Smith, and the last mortal remains of Mate Sebastian Cavan, were lowered into their respective graves on the rocky shore near where the *Venturer* was anchored in the ice. The graves were shallow: Stokers Butterwick and Gargrave had dug them, but the permafrost had defeated them less than two feet below the surface. The bodies would have to be heaped over with stones: the bigger the better, to stop any more bears from coming by and digging them up. Riggs had done both men proud, working all night to carve and inscribe two wooden headboards for the graves.

Pettifer read from the Bible: something entirely inappropriate from the Book of Revelation, but Killigrew was too distracted to pay much attention. The blizzard had died down during the night, giving way to a pale, thin sunlight that failed to warm the thickly bundled men who stood shivering on the rocky, ice-bound shore. It was too cold to stand around listening to the captain blethering on about the Whore of Babylon: 'a measure of wheat for a penny, three measures of barley for a penny, and

214

see thou hurt not the oil and the wine!'

As the rest of the ship's company folded their hands before them and gazed down in the gaping maws of the graves, Able Seaman Hughes started to sing 'Faith's Review and Expectation': one of the tunes that the band had played as Sir Edward's squadron sailed from Woolwich. Even then Killigrew had wondered at the potential irony of the line 'I once was lost, but now am found'; now it no longer even brought a smile to his lips. They could locate their position on the globe with sextant and chronometer, but it put them in a blank in the middle of the Arctic. The ice notwithstanding, Killigrew little doubted they could have found their way back to Beechey Island without those charts. But the ice was everything. It had closed in, sealing off Peel Sound, trapping the *Venturer* in its cove on the west side of Boothia.

Perhaps, somewhere not so very far away, a few survivors of the Franklin Expedition were still alive. Perhaps they too could pinpoint their location to within a minute of a degree; much good it could do them while they were trapped in the ice.

Ursula left Ziegler's side and approached Pettifer, taking one of his massive paws in her tiny mittens. 'On behalf of both myself and the men from the *Carl Gustaf*, Commander Pettifer, I should like to offer you our condolences. Herr Cavan's death was a tragedy, but the kind of tragedy that is by no means unusual in the Arctic; and as for Seaman Smith, well . . . I am sure it was not your intention that his life should end this way, and that no one on board the *Venturer* feels his loss more keenly than yourself . . .'

Pettifer raised his face from the grave at his feet and turned slightly to look into her eyes. 'You . . .' he muttered, almost to himself.

'I, *Herr Kapitän*?'

'You killed them,' said Pettifer. 'Cavan, Smith, Dawton . . . it's all your fault. Everything was going perfectly swimmingly until Mr Killigrew brought you on board. It's true what the sailors say about women being bad luck. You've jinxed this ship, as surely as you jinxed the *Carl Gustaf*.' He turned his back on her abruptly and set off back to the *Venturer*.

Killigrew remained as the others started to file back to the ship. He stared down at the limp, bloodstained sacking that lay in Cavan's shallow pit. It was impossible to accept that the cheerful, carefree young mate had been reduced to nothing more than a mess of bone and gristle. Johnno Smith's death was bad enough, but Killigrew had only known him a few months, and not very well at that. But he had known Cavan for seven years, ever since they had served together chasing slave traders on the Guinea Coast. He had watched him grow from a callow youth into a promising young officer: if Killigrew was any judge, he should have had a long and glittering career before him. Now it had been cut short, and by a passing polar bear of all things. What was he to say to Cavan's parents when he got back to England?

Worse than that, what was he to say to Lord Hartcliffe, a fellow naval officer who had been Cavan's particular friend and mentor, as well as Killigrew's best friend ever since the young aristocrat had saved his life at the taking of Chinkiang-fu ten years earlier? Hartcliffe had tried to talk Cavan out of going on this expedition, and at first he had been angry with Killigrew for getting the young man a berth on the *Venturer*. Killigrew had argued that Arctic service would improve Cavan's chances of rapid promotion. In the end there had been nothing Hartcliffe could do but plead for Killigrew to bring his young friend back alive. And Killigrew had laughed at his concerns! The young aristocrat thought that Arctic exploration was a waste of good men, and only now, when it was too late, did Killigrew see how right he was. Better that these useless channels remain uncharted for eternity, than one good man – let alone three – die in this harsh wasteland.

'Leave me,' he heard Ursula say in a low voice, and looked up to see her standing on the other side of the graves, talking to Ziegler. Everyone else had gone back to the ship, except for Butterwick and Gargrave, who were waiting a discreet distance away to fill in the graves. Ziegler shot Killigrew a suspicious glance, and then turned and walked after the others.

'Are you all right?' she asked him, when Ziegler was some distance off.

He looked up at her, dazed by the unreality of it all. He couldn't be dead – not Cavan. After all, the remains they had found could have belonged to just about anyone. But there was no escaping it: they had mustered the crew, and Cavan was the only one missing. Killigrew's conviction that he would glance up and see the mate approaching him across the ice with that big grin of his all over his face was just a delusion. He was dead.

'Why him?' he asked Ursula. 'Of all the people on board the *Venturer*, why did it have to be Sebastian? Why not that brute Thwaites, or Naylor, or . . .' He trailed off and shook his head hopelessly.

'Or you?' suggested Ursula.

Killigrew shrugged. 'At least if it had been me, there'd be no one to mourn me.'

'And you think that would make your death preferable to Herr Cavan's?'

'Don't you? Why should a self-confessed monster like you care, anyhow? You hardly knew him.'

She smiled. 'I liked what I did know about him. And I am sorry that his death makes you so sad.'

Killigrew shook his head. 'Save your pity for someone that needs it. Come on, let's get in out of the cold and let Gargrave and Butterwick attend to their duty.' He headed back to the *Venturer* with Ursula, and behind them the two stokers started to fill in the graves.

'Do you think it's true?' she asked him.

'What?'

'That I am a jinx.'

Killigrew shook his head. 'That? Don't pay any attention to Pettifer. He was upset, that's all. He didn't mean what he said. That stuff about women being bad luck on board ships. Even most sailors don't believe that, and they're as superstitious a bunch as any. I remember when I was a volunteer first class – what they call a "cadet" these days – the hands on board my first ship were never happier than when we were in port, and they could bring their wives on board. Using the word "wives" in its loosest possible sense, you understand. Not that that sort of thing is allowed nowadays.'

'But the *Carl Gustaf* sunk, all but six of us dead . . . and now your men are starting to die too, Perhaps I *am* a jinx.'

'Don't be silly. Now you listen to me: this is your ninth

voyage into the Arctic, isn't it? How many men did you see die before this voyage?'

She did not need to think about it. 'Three.'

'Three men. On eight whaling voyages into the Arctic. I'll lay odds that's a lot less than average. And as for things going wrong on board the *Venturer*, that happened long before you and your friends came on board. Our troubles started when Pettifer ran us aground at the Whalefish Islands . . .' Killigrew shook his head. 'No. They started before that. They started when Pettifer returned from having dinner with Sir Edward onboard the *Assistance* at Greenhithe, shortly before we set sail, with the news that we were to act as tender to the *North Star*. That's when the madness and idiocy first took root.'

'You think Pettifer's mad?'

'I think we're all mad, for going along with him. Never mind demanding that my objection be noted in the log at Peel Sound; I should have assumed command there and then. It was an act of madness to continue. It would have meant the end of my career, one way or another, but at least Cavan would still be alive.'

'You will assume command now?'

'I don't see the point. It's too late for Cavan.'

'But there may be more deaths, if the madness does not stop.'

He glanced around at the icy desolation. Perhaps she was right; on the other hand, perhaps it was too late for all of them.

They walked on in silence. When they finally climbed the gangplank and ducked through the opening in the awning, they found Terregannoeuck waiting for them on the upper deck.

'Where is it?' demanded the Inuk.

'Where's what?'

'*Nanuq*'s bladder.' Terregannoeuck pointed to where the bladder had hung over the stern.

'Sorry. Commander Pettifer made me take it down. Said it was unhygienic. I suppose he had a point.'

Terregannoeuck shook his head. 'Very bad. Take down bladder before five days' end, you give great offence to *nanuq*'s *tatkoq*. Father of cubs seek to avenge his honour. Perhaps,' the

Inuk added darkly, 'he already has.'

'You're saying that if I hadn't taken down the bladder, Cavan wouldn't have been attacked?' Killigrew asked incredulously.

'Poppycock!' Standing nearby talking to Strachan, Bähr overheard the Inuk. 'Polar bears are just animals, like any other. They don't form emotional attachments.'

'The seventeenth-century Arctic explorer van de Brugge once killed a female polar bear in Spitsbergen,' mused Ursula. 'Afterwards he saw a boar – presumably the sow's mate – running to and fro, clawing at her body as if he wished to make her rise again, and growling fearfully.'

'In the mating season, perhaps,' allowed Bähr. 'The father of the cubs will have vanished long before they were born.'

'Van de Brugge reported that the dead sow had already been accompanied by a cub.'

'You have wife, *Angakoq*?' Terregannoeuck asked Bähr. '*Angakoq*' was his name for the doctor; Killigrew has been amused to learn it meant 'medicine man' in Inuktitut. 'Children?'

'Of course.'

'Yet you are not with them. You do not care what happens to them?'

'That's different. I'm a human being. Humans are different from animals.' He sniffed contemptuously. 'You're not suggesting that while I'm here in the Arctic, the father of those cubs is nosing about the back streets of Hannover, are you?' He laughed at his own wit.

No one else did. 'I have a feeling the father of those cubs is a damned sight closer than Hannover,' said Ziegler.

'I'm sorry, Terregannoeuck,' said Strachan. 'But Dr Bähr does have a point. There's absolutely no scientific evidence to suggest that polar bears form any emotional attachments.'

'You *kabloonas* are wise,' said the Inuk. 'Perhaps you know more about the ways of *nanuq* than an Inuk like Terregannoeuck.' He turned and walked away.

Killigrew turned to Strachan. 'Polar bears: are they territorial or migratory?'

'Oh, migratory, I'm sure.'

'They follow seasonal patterns?'

'To some extent, perhaps. Without making a lifetime's study

219

of it, following the bears – which would be next to impossible –
one could not say for certain. In a wilderness like the Arctic,
they go where the food is likely to be found, I should imagine.'

Killigrew grimaced. 'That isn't very reassuring.'

'What do you mean . . .? Oh!'

XII

Mørkesyke

Everyone in the mess deck was engaged in a 'make-and-mend' when Endicott seized his chance the following afternoon. Trying to look nonchalant, he opened his locker and took out a bulging sack before heading for the companion ladder.

'Going somewhere, Seth?' asked Hughes.

'Just off for a stroll.' Endicott tried to sound airy.

'I'd've thought you'd had more than enough exercise this morning,' said O'Houlihan.

'I need some fresh air,' grumbled the Liverpudlian. 'I'm sick of being cooped up in here with you lot.'

'What's in the sack?' asked Hughes.

'Just some stuff.'

'What stuff?'

'Stuff the pill-roller asked me to look after. For his experiments.'

Hughes and O'Houlihan exchanged sceptical glances. The idea of Mr Strachan asking Endicott to look after his expensive scientific equipment was laughable.

'He asked me to take it to the observatory.'

'Sure he did, Seth.' O'Houlihan returned his attention to his needlework and Hughes took his lead from the Irishman, pretending disinterest by burying his nose in a back-issue of *Punch*.

Endicott eyed them both warily. They were a pair of nosy buggers, and he found it hard to believe his hastily improvised lies had satisfied them so easily, but even if they did follow him, it would only take him a few seconds to dispose of the sack and its contents; by the time they emerged from the ship behind him, the damning evidence would be gone for ever, and he would be out of danger.

He ascended the companion ladder to the upper deck, where Private Phillips was on sentry duty at the entry port. Endicott approached him with his heart pounding in his chest.

'I'm just taking some stuff across to the observatory,' he told the young marine.

'All right.'

Endicott's heart soared, and then his suspicion kicked in. It was too easy. He glanced back to the forward hatch, but there was no sign of Hughes and O'Houlihan following him. Remembering that the quicker he got this done, the less chance there was of being caught, he quickly untied the flaps at the entry port and slipped out from under the awning.

He paused at the top of the gangplank to survey the ice. Even though it was only one bell in the first dog watch, the sun was setting already, casting long shadows over that eerie landscape, a reminder that the long, sunless night of the Arctic winter was closing in. And somewhere out there, perhaps, was the bear that had killed Mr Cavan. The bitter wind that blew down Peel Sound from the North Pole stung his face, but Endicott was sweating inside his warm clothes and his mouth was dry. He stepped on to the gangplank and his feet shot out from beneath him. He landed painfully on his rump and dropped the sack, sliding on his backside down to the ice.

He picked himself up, rubbed his buttocks ruefully and scrambled across to where the sack had landed. Some of the contents had spilled out into the snow, and he hurriedly scooped them back into the sack, glancing around fearfully as he did so in case a bear crept up on him. He was well aware that Hughes and O'Houlihan had been pulling his leg the other day when they had teased him about the bear's grease he wore on his hair. But many a true word was spoken in jest. Surely if bears could hunt seals and reindeer for miles across the ice, they could smell the grease? And even if they could not identify it, wouldn't their infamous curiosity bring them in packs? Better safe than sorry.

He tied the mouth of the sack closed and carried it across to the fire hole. A final glance about him reassured him that no one was watching. He dropped the sack into the hole, but the ice that had formed across the surface of the water since O'Houlihan had cleared it earlier that day was already thick enough to resist the impact of the heavy sack. Cursing under his breath, Endicott sat down on the edge of the hole and kicked at the sack until the ice broke beneath it. He breathed again, and then stared in horror with his heart in his mouth when he realised the bloody thing was not sinking. He knew he should have put some round shot into the sack to weigh it down . . .

He was wondering what to do next when he heard a slight sound behind him. Remembering how Mr Strachan had been surprised – and how Mr Cavan had died – Endicott froze.

'Is that you, Mick?' he called nervously, without turning.

Whatever was behind him, it did not reply. His heart thudding like a steam hammer, Endicott started to turn when two heavy paws landed on his shoulders and an animalistic roar filled his ears.

Darkness descended over him.

'It middle of the night,' said the Inuk. 'Terregannoeuck and his brother fall asleep. Terregannoeuck dream of beautiful Inuit women when brother wake him. Brother signal for Terregannoeuck to be silent. Terregannoeuck listen.'

Molineaux listened with the other sailors who gathered in the pool of light cast by a flickering pusser's dip, hanging on Terregannoeuck's every word as the Inuk told one of his tales of hunting on the ice. On the mess deck, you could have heard a pin drop as they strained to hear every word the Inuk spoke in hushed tones.

'Outside, something moves. Something big. Brother reach for a spear. Then we hear it . . .'

At that moment, a blood-curdling roar sounded outside, making all the seamen jump in alarm. Unconcerned, Terregannoeuck glanced towards the bulkhead. 'Not *nanuq*,' he asserted.

Molineaux was not convinced. Pushing the Inuk's tale from his head and dragging himself back to the present, he hurried up on deck where he snatched up a gaff hook and headed for the entry port, followed by the others. There was no sign of a sentry there, but the flaps of the awning were untied, a chill wind blowing through them.

Gripping the gaff hook tightly, Molineaux stepped out to see Private Phillips sprawled on the ice at the foot of the gangplank, where he must have landed after slipping on the icy planks. Nearby, a body lay motionless on the ice by the fire hole while Hughes and O'Houlihan stood over it.

Molineaux swore and slid gracefully down the gangplank, running past Phillips to where the body lay. 'Who is it?' he asked O'Houlihan.

'Seth.'

'Is he dead?'

'Fainted, I think,' said Hughes.

'*Fainted*? What happened? What was that roar?'

'That was me,' admitted O'Houlihan. 'It was only meant as a joke.' The Irishman chuckled. 'You should have seen him jump when I grabbed him from behind . . .'

Hughes rubbed snow in Endicott's face. The Liverpudlian revived and spluttered. 'Bear!' he moaned. 'Bear attacked me!'

'Like this, you mean?' O'Houlihan raised his mittened hands like claws, and emitted another convincing roar.

As shaken as Endicott must have been, even he could see he had been made a fool of. 'You bastards!' he snarled, eyeing O'Houlihan malevolently. 'You lousy, rotten bastards!'

Everyone laughed, and Hughes helped Endicott to his feet. As the others trooped back on the ship, O'Houlihan caught Molineaux by the sleeve.

'He was putting something down the fire hole.'

Molineaux glanced at the sack that still floated amongst the broken ice in the hole. 'What's in it?'

'You tell me,' said O'Houlihan. 'But it looks like tin canisters to me.'

The implication was clear: Endicott had secretly been stealing food, stockpiling it in his locker. Molineaux shook his head, unwilling to believe his friend was guilty of such a crime. Amongst sailors, theft was the worst crime a shipmate could be guilty of. Even murder might be excusable, but theft? Never.

'Seth wouldn't steal,' he said uncertainly. 'Not him. Besides, why would he prig it, only to ditch it in the hogwash?'

'Maybe he got scared after what happened to Johnno and Jacko. Maybe he was trying to get rid of the evidence.'

'Only one way to find out.' Molineaux fished the sack out of the hole with the gaff hook. Lowering it to the ice, he pulled open the mouth of the sack to find it contained . . . dozens of jars of bear's grease: Endicott's entire supply, by the look of it.

Molineaux scratched his head in bewilderment, but O'Houlihan threw back his head and roared with laughter. The sound echoed off the low, distant hills. Before Molineaux could ask O'Houlihan what the big joke was, another sound came back in answer to the Irishman's laughter – a sound that wiped the smile off his face.

The howl of a large animal.

A shudder ran down Molineaux's spine. He gazed about the icescape. If there was a bear out there, he could not spot it in the gathering gloom of the Arctic dusk.

'Come on,' he told O'Houlihan. 'Let's get back on board.'

The Irishman nodded soberly and the two of them hurried up the gangplank, fastening the flaps of the awning securely behind them.

Killigrew was working on some paperwork in his cabin when there was a knock at the door. 'Come in, Orsini,' he called. With a crew of only thirty, it did not take long to learn how to distinguish one man's knock from another's.

The steward entered, looking agitated. 'Is problem, Signor Killigrew.'

'What kind of a problem?'

'Is best you come see for yourself, *signore*.'

Killigrew sighed and followed the steward out of the cabin. The two of them made their way down to the hold. 'I check the oil in the lamp in the wardroom,' explained the steward. 'Is getting low, so I go down to storeroom to get more. But is no more in the storeroom, so I come here, to hold.'

They made their way between the racks of cress, where Kracht was helping Latimer water the latest crop. As they passed, Orsini glared malevolently at Latimer, although the clerk was too busy concentrating on the task in hand to notice.

Beyond the trays of cress, they came to where several casks

were stacked. Orsini had brought a lantern and he passed it to Killigrew so the lieutenant could take a closer look. 'No more whale oil,' he explained. 'This is what I find.'

Killigrew studied the lettering painted on the side of the casks: 'Orr's Patent Burning Fluid'.

'Ah!' he said, seeing the problem at once. 'Mr Latimer!' he called down the hold. 'Could you come here a moment, please?'

'Coming!'

'So's Christmas! Chop chop, Mr Latimer.'

The clerk put down his watering can and, followed by Kracht, made his way to where Killigrew stood with Orsini.

'What's this?' Killigrew asked him, indicating the casks.

'Burning fluid,' Latimer said proudly.

'And why do we have burning fluid on board, Mr Latimer?'

'I thought I'd save the British taxpayer some money. It's much cheaper than whale-oil, and it burns brighter, too.'

'Yes, and all at once! Don't you read the newspapers, Latimer?'

'Only the *Sporting Chronicle*. Why?'

'Because if you took a proper newspaper, you would know what happens when you put burning fluid in a whale-oil lamp. There's scarcely a month goes by without some little moppet burning to death because mama thought she could save money by putting burning fluid in her lamps, not realising you need special lamps for burning fluid.'

'How much did you pay for these, *mein Herr*?' asked Kracht.

'I'd have to check the receipts,' admitted Latimer. 'But it was much cheaper than whale-oil, I know that much.'

'It is cheaper still if you mix your own. It is just four parts ethanol to one part camphene.'

'And you can burn that safely in whale-oil lamps?' Killigrew asked the blacksmith testily.

'I would not recommend it, *mein Herr*.'

'Is there no more whale-oil on board?' Killigrew asked Orsini.

'Only what's left in the lamps, *signores*.'

'I don't suppose we have enough candles on board to last us through the winter?' asked Killigrew.

'I doubt it,' said Latimer.

226

'Capital!' Killigrew said wryly. 'As if going for weeks on end without sunlight wasn't going to be depressing enough, now we've got to go without lights too!'

'I could adapt the lamps to take burning fluid, *mein Herr*.'

'Are you sure?'

'Of course! It is simple enough. All I would have to do is cut the wick tubes off the bottoms of the burners and fix them to the top, make them taper, and then make caps to put over the tubes.'

'And they'd be safe?'

'Safe enough, as long as everyone remembers to put them out with the caps, instead of blowing on them.'

'Orsini here puts out the lamps. Think you could remember that, Orsini?'

'If the alternative is being doused with blazing burning fluid?' The steward grinned. 'I think I can remember that, *signore*.'

'Better get to work then, Kracht. Mr Varrow will give you whatever you need from his workshop.'

'*Jawohl, mein Herr.*' The blacksmith hurried up the companion ladder.

Latimer grinned. 'Problem solved, then?'

'Don't push your luck, Latimer. If it wasn't for Kracht's know-how . . .' Killigrew shook his head in disgust. 'Get back to your cress. And try not to mess that up!'

Latimer beat a hasty retreat. Killigrew made his way back to the lower deck where he found Yelverton looking agitated in the corridor outside the wardroom. 'There you are!' said the master. 'Pettifer's declared the chart-room out of bounds.'

'The chart-room's always been out of bounds.'

'To the hands, maybe. But to the officers? To me, damn it! The master!'

Killigrew blinked. 'You must be mistaken.' He knew that for Yelverton to be mistaken was unthinkable, but not as unthinkable as a captain declaring the chart-room out of bounds to the master. Pettifer might as well declare the engine-room out of bounds to the engineer.

The lieutenant approached the door to the chart-room. On duty outside the door to Pettifer's quarters, Private Phillips stretched out an arm to block his path to the chart-room door. 'I'm sorry, sir. You can't go in there. Cap'n's orders.'

'It's all right, Phillips. Mr Yelverton and I just want to consult one of the charts.'

'I'm sorry, sir, but the cap'n gave me strict orders. No one but him's to go in the chart-room.'

'In that case, Phillips, I'd like to see the captain.'

'Cap'n's not to be disturbed, sir.'

'I'm giving you new orders, Phillips. Stand aside. I demand to see the captain.'

'I'm sorry, sir. I can't let you in.'

Killigrew was strongly tempted to snatch the musket from Phillips and force him aside; but there was too great a risk the gun might go off and injure someone, and Phillips was only obeying orders. 'Commander Pettifer!' he called. 'This is Killigrew, sir! I'd like to talk to you!'

On the other side of the door, Horatia started to bark, but no sound indicated Pettifer was stirring.

'I'm sorry, sir.' Phillips was squirming with embarrassment. 'But I'll have to ask you not to shout like that. The cap'n's—'

'Not to be disturbed, yes, I heard you the first time.'

'Come on, Killigrew,' said Yelverton. 'We're wasting our time here.'

'He can't stay in there for ever,' said Killigrew. 'I'll have a word with him after divisions tomorrow.'

From the restless way the crew paraded on the upper deck in their mustering rig, it was obvious they knew something was amiss. Killigrew glanced at his fob watch: five to nine. However erratic Pettifer's behaviour might be otherwise, he was always on the quarterdeck in time for divisions; yet this morning he was ten minutes late.

Yelverton caught Killigrew's eye and arched an eyebrow.

'Is something wrong?' asked Bähr. 'Is Commander Pettifer all right?'

'I wish I knew,' muttered Killigrew.

'Well?' asked Yelverton.

'We'll give him another five minutes.'

The minutes ticked by. The hands started to talk amongst themselves – doubtless speculating on Pettifer's non-appearance – until Thwaites bellowed for them to pipe down.

At nine o'clock Private Walsh rang the ship's bell twice. Killigrew made up his mind. 'Mr Latimer!'

'Sir?'

'Come here.' Killigrew retreated to the taffrail, and Latimer followed him. 'Be so good as to inform the captain that it is now two bells in the forenoon watch, and the ship's company is mustered for divisions, awaiting his pleasure.'

Latimer turned beetroot. 'Me, sir?'

'Yes, you, sir.'

The clerk swallowed, and descended the after hatch.

'When was the last time anyone actually saw the Old Man?' asked Yelverton.

'I saw him yesterday when we inspected the lower deck,' murmured Killigrew, exchanging glances with Strachan, Bähr and Ziegler. 'Has anyone seen him since then?'

Blank faces met his. 'What about Orsini?' he asked. 'Orsini!'

The steward left his place amongst the men drawn up on deck to approach the officers. The splint had come off his right arm the previous day, but now the muscles were withered and he flexed the elbow constantly, trying to get the stiffness out of it. '*Signore*?'

'You took Commander Pettifer his breakfast this morning, Orsini?'

'Yes, *signore*.'

'Did you see him?'

'Of course.'

'How did he seem to you?'

' "Seem", *signore*?'

'Did he look well, ill, was he dressed, in his nightshirt, had he shaved?'

Orsini squinted into the middle distance as he tried to picture the scene in his mind's eye. He shook his head slowly. 'No, *signore*. Now that I think, I did not see him at all.'

'Then how do you know he was there?'

'I heard him, moving around in the cabin. The door was closed, but he was in there. Private Jenkins, he let me in. I carry the breakfast in, but there is no sign of the *comandante*. I call out: "*Signore*?", and I hear the *comandante*'s voice from the cabin. He say: "Put it on the table." I put it on the table, and go.'

'All right, Orsini, thank you. Back to your division.'

'Yes, *signore*.'

Latimer re-emerged from the after hatch. 'I knocked on his door, sir,' he told Killigrew. 'He wouldn't answer.'

'Do we even know he's still in there?' wondered Yelverton.

'All right, wait here.' Killigrew made his way below deck. This time there was no one on guard outside the door to Pettifer's quarters; all five of the marines were up on deck for divisions. Killigrew knocked on the door. 'Sir?'

No reply.

'Is everything all right, sir?' Killigrew tried the handle, but the door was bolted on the other side. His patience grew short. 'Sir, if you don't answer me, you'll leave me no choice but to assume command of this vessel. Is that what you want me to do, sir?'

All was as silent as the grave on the other side of the door. Even Horatia was uncharacteristically quiet; for all Killigrew knew, Pettifer might be dead. He might have hanged himself, or slit his wrists: it was not unknown for the dreary, oppressive Arctic wastes to drive a man to such despair, but usually *mørkesyke* – Arctic madness – did not kick in before the dead of the long Arctic night had set in. On the other hand, Pettifer had been under a great deal of strain since they had become separated from the rest of the squadron. Sooner or later, any man would crack under such circumstances.

Yet Killigrew knew instinctively that Pettifer was still alive in there, quietly listening to every word he said. If Horatia was trapped in there with the corpse of her master, surely she would howl fit to wake the dead? Unless, his mind turned, Pettifer had killed her too before taking his own life. One way to find out was to kick down the cabin door. But Killigrew knew he was treading on thin ice there: the Admiralty took a dim view of an officer who broke into his captain's quarters. Better not to take any precipitate action before he had had a chance to discuss the situation with the other officers.

He made his way up on deck. 'Commander Pettifer is unwell,' he announced to the crew. 'I'll be conducting divisions today.'

A hubbub of consternation ran through the men assembled on the upper deck. 'Pipe down!' roared Thwaites.

'How do you know the Old Man's unwell?' Strachan

demanded in a low voice, as if piqued that someone without any sort of medical qualification was trying to determine his authority. 'Did you see him?'

'Meeting in the observatory after divisions,' Killigrew told him softly.

'A meeting!' exclaimed Yelverton. 'The last refuge of a man incapable of taking responsibility for anything.'

Killigrew rounded on him furiously. 'Whatever I do decide to do,' he hissed, 'it has to be done with the full backing of every officer on board. Because if the worst comes to the worst and I have to relieve Commander Pettifer of command, that will be my only chance of escaping dismissal and disgrace when the inevitable court martial follows. And even then it's a very slim chance. So before I do anything, we'll have a meeting of the officers in the observatory after divisions.'

'And what will the rest of the crew think when they see us converging on the observatory? They'll know something's wrong.'

'They already know something's wrong. If they don't see someone doing something about it, they're going to—'

'Pettifer's birthday,' said Strachan.

'What?'

'It's Pettifer's birthday on Friday.'

'Friday?' echoed Killigrew. 'The fifteenth of October?'

'Yes. Why do you ask?'

'That's the same date as my birthday.'

'Birth-date of great men,' remarked Yelverton.

'If you say so,' Strachan said dismissively. 'If we tell the hands that we're arranging a surprise for him . . .'

'Good idea,' said Killigrew. 'I'll tell Hughes, warn him to keep it under his hat. It'll be all over the ship within an hour.' He glanced across to where the other officers – the clerk and the two engineers – stood on the other side of the quarterdeck. 'Tell Latimer and Varrow, but for Christ's sake be discreet.'

As Killigrew read the crew the Articles of War, he was careful to stand a couple of feet to the right of where Pettifer usually stood, as if reluctant to be seen usurping the captain's authority. 'I have only one announcement,' he concluded. 'For the duration of the captain's illness, everything will continue as usual on board, with myself or Mr Yelverton attending to the captain's duties, until further notice. Dismissed! Bosun?'

Thwaites marched briskly across to where Killigrew stood. 'Sir?'

'The usual drill: keep them jog-trotting around the upper deck until ten, then marching round "Rotten Row" until noon, while the mess cooks bring in the stores. I'll be in the observatory with the other officers if you need me.'

'Aye, aye, sir.'

As Killigrew turned to the entry port, he almost bumped into Hughes. 'Oh, hullo, Hughes. Didn't see you there.'

'Meeting in the observatory, sir?'

Killigrew lowered his voice conspiratorially. 'It's the captain's birthday next Friday. The other officers and myself want to arrange something special for him, but we're not sure what. Keep it to yourself, though: it's going to be a surprise.'

Hughes tapped the side of his nose. 'You can rely on me, sir. The very soul of discretion, so I am.'

The lieutenant clapped him on the shoulder. 'I know you are, Hughes. That's why I'm counting on you.'

Killigrew bundled up in his warmest clothes and made his way out on to the ice. Yelverton, Strachan, Latimer and Varrow were already waiting by the time he entered the observatory.

There seemed little point in beating around the bush. 'I've called you all here to discuss a rather awkward matter, I'm afraid. One hardly knows where to begin . . .'

'It's all right, sir,' said Latimer. 'I think we all know what this is about.' He glanced around at his fellow officers, and they nodded gravely.

Killigrew was relieved that he did not have to spell it out for him. If they saw for themselves what was wrong, then surely they could not refuse to back him up? 'If any of you have any thoughts . . .?'

'I've a notion or two, sir.'

'You, Latimer?' Killigrew asked in surprise. 'Go on.'

'I thought perhaps a masquerade ball. We can make all sorts of exciting costumes, and we can get Armitage to bake him a cake—'

'You great gowk!' said Varrow. 'He's not talking about the

captain's birthday. He's talking about the fact that the captain's got a screw loose!'

'He has?'

'He's ignored his orders,' said Yelverton. 'He's imperilled the safety of this ship and her crew by ignoring the advice of his ice quartermasters. He's put the men on a starvation diet for no apparent reason. He locked himself in his quarters and refuses to come out. He's declared the chart-room off limits to everyone; even me, the master! He had Smith and Smith given three dozen lashes for stealing two canisters of dog food—'

'It *was* hashed venison,' Latimer pointed out.

'I don't care if it was a canister of bloody ambrosia!' said Yelverton, and turned pleadingly to Killigrew. 'He'll kill us all if you let him. He's obsessed with finding the North-West Passage, and now that we can't make it in a single season, he's blaming everyone but himself for his failure to achieve the impossible. We can't go on like this. Three men dead already! At this rate, there won't be anyone left alive by the time the ice thaws in spring. *If* it thaws.'

'What do you want me to do, Yelverton?' demanded Killigrew. 'Relieve the captain? Take command myself? There's a word for that: mutiny—'

There was a knock on the door. Everyone started guiltily. Killigrew put a hand in the pocket of his greatcoat to grasp the butt of the pepperbox that nestled there. 'Who is it?'

'Herr Ziegler and Herr Doktor Bähr,' Ziegler called back. 'May we come in?'

'We're a little busy at the moment, Herr Ziegler.'

'That's what we wanted to talk to you about.' The door opened and Ziegler and Bähr entered.

'Clandestine meeting, gentlemen?' asked Bähr, closing the door behind him.

'We have certain matters to discuss,' Yelverton said curtly.

'I'll say you have,' agreed the doctor.

'This isn't our ship,' acknowledged Ziegler. 'It isn't even our navy. But I think we've a right to know what's going on. We didn't ask to be dragged this far into the Arctic.'

Killigrew nodded. 'They're right. This concerns all of us, naval officers and civilians. Gentlemen, we were discussing what to do about Commander Pettifer's erratic behaviour.'

'Can you not just relieve him of command?' asked Ziegler.

'I'm afraid it isn't as simple as that.'

'The devil it isn't!' said Yelverton. 'As his lieutenant, you have a responsibility. Not only to him, but also to the men under your command. To all of us, damn you! Are you just going to turn a blind eye to his behaviour?'

'And on what grounds am I to relieve the captain of his command?' demanded Killigrew.

Yelverton rolled his eyes in derision and disbelief. 'Tell him, Strachan. Tell him the Old Man's insane.'

Strachan pursed his lips. 'Define "insane".'

'Not acting rationally. A danger to himself and the men who serve under his command.'

'I've yet to meet a naval captain who wasn't a danger to himself and the men under his command.' Strachan smiled sadly. 'As for "not acting rationally", I fear I'd be uncertain of my ground there. Walking on thin ice, as it were, no pun intended. Would you like me to define "not acting rationally"? Two hundred and fifty-two men piling into six ships bound for the most inhospitable region on earth, to search for a hundred and twenty-nine men who've already vanished in similar circumstances, searching for a strait that may or may not exist. If I were a physician with a comfortable country practice, I think I could reasonably make a case for having the whole lot of us certified insane. As it is, I'm an assistant surgeon in the Royal Navy. There are other considerations to take into account. It's not unknown for men who acted every bit as strangely as Pettifer's acting now to make a full recovery. Supposing I certify him insane, and on the way back to England he recovers? Much good my certification will do, with Pettifer speaking with perfect lucidity at our court martial!'

'Damn it, Strachan!' Yelverton exclaimed in exasperation.

'What do you want me to do, sir? Certify Pettifer insane so that Killigrew can relieve him of command?'

'Would you?'

Strachan hesitated, torn between the desire to say what he knew Yelverton and the others wanted to hear, and his own professional, scientific rationalism. 'No. I've seen nothing that satisfies me that Commander Pettifer is *non compos mentis*. I'll acknowledge there has been a marked alteration in his behaviour in the past couple of weeks. An alteration that gives me, a medical man, pause for thought. But nothing to convince me his behaviour has deteriorated to the extent where I'd be prepared to diagnose him insane.'

'I'll do it,' offered Bähr. 'If you want my considered medical opinion, your captain is as mad as a hatter.'

Killigrew smiled. 'Thank you for the offer, Doctor. But I'm afraid your opinion won't cut much ice at my court martial. I'm not denying you're better qualified than Mr Strachan here – no offence, Strachan—'

'None taken.'

'But I'm afraid you, Doctor, are a foreigner. Worse than that, you're a civilian. Nothing personal, but that's how the Admiralty will view it. Besides, all of this is academic: there is no procedure in Queen's Regulations for a lieutenant to relieve his own captain of command, with or without a medical officer having certified the captain insane.'

'What if he was badly injured?' asked Bähr. 'Rendered unconscious? Physically incapable of command. You could do it then, couldn't you?'

'Of course. But mentally incapable? That's a different kettle of fish.'

'We'd all back you up.' The doctor turned to Strachan. 'Wouldn't we? Sane or insane, there must come a point at which a captain's behaviour threatens the safety of his ship and crew.'

Killigrew shook his head. 'If Commander Pettifer accused me of mutiny, it would not matter if every man-jack on board the *Venturer* backed up my side of the story. The captain is *always* right. He's second only to God. And in this godless place, he *is* God.'

Strachan grinned humourlessly. 'A mad God. That would explain a great deal. At times like this, my atheism is a great comfort to me.'

Ziegler glared at him. 'This is hardly the time for your blasphemy, Herr Strachan. If we're going to get out of this alive, it will be thanks to the grace of God.'

'Oh, that's wonderful, that is!' spat Strachan. 'So what are we going to do? Sit around doing nothing, hoping that God will save us?'

'We must have faith, Herr Strachan.'

'Faith! I lost my faith a long time ago, Herr Ziegler. Where was God when my mother died? Where was God when the *Carl Gustaf* was nipped, or Dawton died, or the Old Man had Able Seaman Smith flogged to death, or that polar bear tore poor Mr Cavan limb from limb?'

'The Good Lord moves in mysterious ways his wonders to perform, Herr Strachan.'

'*Quem di diligunt adolescens moritur*,' said Killigrew, adding for the benefit of those who did not speak Latin: ' "Whom the Gods love die young." But Strachan's got a point. My creed has always been that the Good Lord helps those who help themselves.'

'Then stop playing the noble Dane and take charge of the situation, damn your eyes!' exploded Yelverton. 'Before anyone else gets killed—' He broke off and hurriedly reached for his handkerchief as a coughing fit seized him. He clamped it over his mouth as the spasms shook him, and tears came to his eyes.

He straightened with an apologetic smile and was about to thrust his handkerchief into his pocket when Killigrew caught him by the wrist. The two of them struggled, but Yelverton must have realised that the game was up for he finally allowed Killigrew to see the handkerchief.

The lieutenant looked up from the handkerchief at the master. Yelverton looked back at him with pleading in his eyes.

'Mr Strachan! Would you be so good as to escort Mr Yelverton to the sick-berth for a thorough medical examination? I believe he is not feeling A1 at present.' Killigrew showed him the handkerchief, the white linen stained with dark blood.

XIII

Rogue Male

'Pulmonary tuberculosis,' Strachan told Killigrew in the privacy of his cabin. 'I can't believe I didn't see it before.'

Killigrew pinched the bridge of his nose between forefinger and thumb in a vain attempt to stave off the headache he felt coming on. 'You didn't see it because Yelverton didn't want you to see it. He didn't want any of us to see it.' He opened his eyes and looked up at Strachan. 'He knew, didn't he?'

'Yes. Oh, he denies it, of course, but when you practise medicine in the navy you soon learn to tell when someone's lying.'

'Is there anything you can do for him?'

'Not a great deal. He needs rest – lots of it – clean air, of course . . . he'll get plenty of that in these parts . . . but it's at an advanced stage. There's no cure that I know of.'

'How long has he got?'

'You want an exact date? Three years, three months, who can say? I've read about cases of men and women with consumption living to a ripe old age; more often they just get progressively worse and then . . .' He shrugged helplessly. 'I most strongly advise he be relieved of duty.'

The two of them made their way to the sick-berth, where they found Yelverton still lacing up his half-boots. He saw Killigrew and smiled thinly. He suddenly looked older, as if he had suffered some defeat. He might have known how ill he was, but perhaps this was the first time his sickness had been diagnosed by a medical man, forcing him to face up to the reality. 'Strachan's told you the news, I take it?'

Killigrew nodded.

'So much for doctor-patient confidentiality.' Yelverton gestured at Strachan. 'Or apothecary-patient confidentiality.'

'Strachan would be remiss in his duty if he knew you were gravely ill and he kept it from me. What the devil were you thinking of?' Killigrew hissed angrily. 'You should be in a hospital, not acting as master on board a ship bound for the Arctic!'

'Spend the rest of my life wheezing and coughing myself into an early grave in a hospital?' Yelverton shook his head sadly. 'Have you ever looked death in the face, Killigrew?'

'We have a nodding acquaintance.'

'I look him in the face. Every morning I wake up and I look in the mirror to shave and that's when I look death in the face. *Every morning.* And I have to ask myself, should I shave off my bristles? Or just slit my throat? But life's a precious thing. You don't realise how precious until you find it's been ordained that you should be allocated less than your fair share. Every day . . . every minute, every *second* of every day . . . you become grateful for the fact that you're still alive. Can you even *begin* to imagine that, Killigrew? To know what it's like to stand on the quarterdeck watching the sand running through the glasses in the belfry and to think: That's my life slipping away? How would you want to spend that time? Rotting away in a hospital? Or on the quarterdeck of a ship, where you know you belong?'

'Somewhere where there's less chance of passing on my complaint to other, more healthy people, I hope,' Killigrew said unsympathetically. 'Just how infectious is consumption, Strachan?'

The assistant surgeon shrugged. 'As with most medical opinion, that's hotly debated.'

'Then we'll assume the worst. From now on Yelverton will avoid contact with other members of the crew, wash his own handkerchiefs and empty his own chamber pot.' Killigrew glanced at the master, and was glad to see that Yelverton did not appear inclined to argue. 'Furthermore, from now on he is to be relieved of all duties.' He turned to Strachan. 'Could you leave us a moment, please?'

'Certainly.'

As soon as the assistant surgeon had gone, Killigrew turned back to Yelverton. 'You knew, didn't you?'

The master nodded.

'It's not every man that can choose where he dies,' mused Killigrew. 'Did you think the clean air of the Arctic would prolong your life?'

'I'd rather live two days in the Arctic than one in the smoke of London. What about you, Killigrew? You can be pretty careless of your own life.'

'Isn't every man who goes to sea?'

'You take more risks than most.'

Killigrew grinned. 'Blame my upbringing. I was raised on romantic tales of swashbuckling and heroism. Lor'! Don't I wish that all I had to worry about now was slavers or pirates: something that can be dealt with cleanly with a cutlass or a pistol.'

'Romantic? Or gothic? I used to be like you once, back in the days of Algiers and Navarino. I spent so much time wanting to die a romantic death I forgot to care about how I lived. But I saw so many people killed by yellow fever when we were with the West Africa Squadron . . . that's why I got married.' He grimaced. 'I never thought we'd have a family, though. At my time of life! Coming back to England after our cruise in the Far East and the South Seas to find the house full of screaming two-year-old triplets . . . it wasn't what I'd planned. You know how to make God laugh, don't you? Tell him your plans. Well, I'd just about accepted the idea of settling down and raising a family when I discovered I had this . . . this *condition*. . . ' Yelverton gestured helplessly. 'I didn't want Babs and the kids watching me die by degrees. Then you turned up at our door with an offer of a berth on an Arctic expedition. It was the answer to my prayers.'

'If I'd known—'

'I know. That's why I didn't tell you. A word of advice, Killigrew: there's nothing romantic about death. If you make it back to England, make sure you enjoy life.'

'Flare up, man. We'll make it back to England, every one of

239

us. Strachan tells me you could still have years of life left in you. Shouldn't you be trying to make the most of them with your family, instead of coming to a dead world like the Arctic?'

'There was another reason. I suppose you'll think me an old fool, but . . .'

Killigrew shrugged, inviting him to continue.

'I wanted to see the aurora borealis.'

Ursula was crossing the deck to the entry port when she heard Ziegler call out behind her. 'Frau Weiss!'

She turned and saw him emerging from the after hatch. Like her, he was bundled up in his warmest clothes. 'Where are you going?'

'For a walk. I need to stretch my legs. I've been cooped up on this ship for too long.' She was used to spending months at a time at sea, but at least on a whaler the scenery was always changing, and in the two weeks since the two Smiths had been flogged – one fatally – and Cavan had been killed, the atmosphere on board the *Venturer* had grown increasingly sour.

'You're not going out alone, are you?' Ziegler asked jovially. 'Not with the polar bear that killed poor Herr Cavan still out there somewhere?'

Ursula smiled. 'If what Herr Strachan says about polar bears being wanderers is true, then the bear that killed Herr Cavan will be long gone by now. Besides, it is broad daylight: if there are any bears out there, they will not be able to sneak up on me in the snow and the dark and surprise me, as Herr Cavan was doubtless surprised.'

'Surprise or no surprise, you do not want to run into a polar bear without one of these.' Ziegler indicated the shotgun he carried slung over one shoulder.

'If you wish to accompany me, Herr Ziegler, simply say so. But do not pretend I need your protection. I have been to the Arctic far more times than you, and I think I have a clearer idea of the dangers than you.'

They stepped out from under the awning, tying the flaps behind them. It was mid-October, the temperature markedly colder than it had been two weeks ago, but there were still a good eight hours of daylight each day, and while the sun was above the horizon it seemed to keep away the worst bite of the Arctic winds. There was not a cloud in the sky, and the snow-covered ice glittered beneath the bright sun, giving the scenery a magical aspect.

Ziegler and Ursula picked their way carefully down to the ice, where the day's mess cooks were moving barrels and crates of victuals from the cache on the ice into the ship. The rest of the crew were marching round and round the hull on the ice, as they did every morning from ten until noon. It might have grown tedious, but they were allowed to yarn with one another as they marched, and those of them who smoked puffed away at clay pipes or cigars, depending on their rank and pockets.

'Don't go too far!' Molineaux called after them as they passed the ropes that marked the boundary of the camp. Ziegler raised an arm in acknowledgement, and then he and Ursula set out across the ice.

'Damned Englishmen!' spat Ziegler, once they were out of earshot.

'Herr Ziegler! What makes you say that?'

'I don't like the way they look at you.'

'I am a woman,' she pointed out reasonably. 'I would like to be flattered, but I am the only woman any of them has seen since they sailed from the Whalefish Islands four months ago. Can you blame them for looking? Where is the harm, if all they do is look?'

'But looks can lead to other things . . .'

'That is a terrible thing to say! There is not one of them who has not treated me with the utmost respect and deference from the moment I stepped on board.'

'Except for that madman Pettifer, Ursula. May I call you Ursula? After all we've been through together . . .'

'I would feel more comfortable with "Frau Weiss".'

'Does Herr Killigrew address you as "Frau Weiss" when you are alone?' he asked bitterly.

'Herr Ziegler! Whatever do you mean?'

'You know perfectly well! I've seen the way you look at him over the dinner table; yes, and the way you return those glances!'

'It is good manners to look someone in the eye when they

address you.' She smiled. 'Even when they are so impertinent as to make unwelcome advances such as, "Can I offer you some more parsnips, Frau Weiss?"!' She looked at him. 'Why, Herr Ziegler! Could it be that you are jealous? You are being foolish. Herr Killigrew is very charming, but his callow charms hold no interest for me.'

They walked on in silence until they were half a mile from the ship, at the foot of a pressure ridge that rose forty feet above the level of the ice field. But the jumbled lumps of ice presented no obstacle, and Ursula scrambled up them as nimbly as a mountain goat, revelling in the physical exertion after so many weeks of being cooped up on board ship.

'Ursula! What are you doing?' Ziegler called up after her. 'Where are you going?'

'Up!' she called. She reached the top, and looked out across the landscape beyond: another ice field, studded with bergy bits and stretching away to a second pressure ridge perhaps two miles off. Below her, snow had drifted against the other side of the ridge and frozen solid, producing a smooth, icy slide down to the bottom. She waited until Ziegler, climbing up after her, had almost caught her, and then slid down the other side with a whoop of delight. That was one of the reasons she loved the Arctic so much, apart from its natural beauty. Back in Hamburg, the thought of what one's neighbours might think was always a moderating influence; here in the snowy wastes, one's neighbours might be a thousand miles away. She felt she could act as outrageously as she wanted; it was supremely liberating.

Ziegler followed her down by the same route, stumbling at the bottom and rolling on his side with a curse. She hurried forward to help him up, but he knocked her hand away with a gesture of irritation: in the three years they had known one another, she had noticed that he did not like to have a woman fussing over him, as if he could not take care of himself.

He stood up, and gazed up at the smooth ice ridge above them. 'Wonderful!' he said bitterly. 'Now how do we get back?'

'Who knows? Let's have an adventure! Damn it, Herr Ziegler, doesn't it bore you to always know exactly what's going to happen next?'

'I find it reassuring.'

'The English would call you a "stick in the mud". Is that not a wonderful expression? It means someone very stuffy and boring.'

'Is that how Killigrew describes me?'

'Will you stop harping on about Killigrew? He means nothing to me. As a matter of fact, it was Herr Latimer who taught me that expression. He was using it with reference to Herr Strachan. Look, there's a way up this side of the ridge over there, if it will make you feel better.' She set off walking along the foot of the ridge to where a bergy bit, embedded in the ice-field, was close enough to the ridge to have sheltered it from aeons of gusting wind and snow, so that the jumbled blocks of ice remained exposed and climbable.

'Damn you, Ursula! Sometimes I don't know whether to kiss you or slap you.'

'That's exactly what Herr Weiss used to say to me.'

'Don't say that! Don't ever compare me to him.'

'Why not? I think you have a lot in common with him. I did love him once, you know. In a way.'

He ran to catch up with her, and caught her by the hand. 'Ursula, do you think . . .? Could you ever . . .?'

She pulled her hand away from his. 'Please, Herr Ziegler! Dietrich! Don't say it!'

'I love you, Ursula. I've loved you from the moment I first set eyes on you. It was not too difficult at first; I saw you were married to Kapitän Weiss, and told myself you could never be mine. Then I came to see how he treated you, and realised that even if a wretch like me did not deserve you, at least I deserved you more than he does . . .'

She clapped her hands over her head, pressing the sides of her hood against her ears in a futile effort to shut out his litany of love. 'Please, Dietrich! Don't do this. Do you not think that if I had felt the same about you, I might have shown it in some way?'

'But I love you!' he pleaded.

She shook her head. 'You only think you love me. You have an image of me in your head, and that is how you have seen me from the moment we have met, in spite of all that you have seen of me since we have got to know one another. Except that you have never got to know me, because you have blinded yourself to the truth about me as it does not fit in with your ideal image of me.'

'How can you say such things?'

'Because I *know*, Dietrich. I've watched you fall in love with me, as I've watched a dozen other men fall in love with me. And I've known all along it could only end in disappointment for you. Do you want to know the truth about me? The truth you've been blind to all these years? Watching you tear yourself apart falling in love with me should have torn at my heart. But it did not, because I find it pathetic.'

'Pathetic! I'll show you pathetic! Perhaps you prefer a stronger man. A man like your husband, eh? Perhaps, despite all your protestations, you're really one of those women who likes to be knocked around. Well, a real man doesn't have to hit a woman to please her. This is what a real man does . . .'

He seized her in his arms, pulled her against him, and kissed her forcefully on the lips. She kept her teeth clenched, barring the tongue that slithered between his lips, and when her efforts to push him away proved futile, she lifted her knee into his crotch. He doubled up, inadvertently bringing his forehead down against the bridge of her nose. She stumbled backwards and slipped on the ice, landing on her backside, feeling dazed and woozy.

'Oh, my God!' Ziegler wheezed in horror. 'Ursula! Are you all right? I never meant to . . .'

She found herself laughing. 'I was wrong about you, Dietrich. You are nothing like Wolfgang. He would *never* have apologised.'

'I cannot help it if I am gentlemanly.' He stepped forward to help her to her feet, proffering his hand.

She raised her head to look at him, and then her face twisted in horror.

He took a step back. 'It's all right, Ursula. I'm not going to hurt you . . .'

He saw the shadow fall from behind him and realised too late she was not looking at him. He started to turn, and then something smashed into his back, knocking him face-down on the ice. He tried to get up, but an extraordinarily heavy weight pinned him to the ground. He gasped. He felt as if the pressure must crush his ribcage.

Ursula screamed.

The weight was lifted off his back, but only briefly; then it crashed down again. He felt his ribcage snap under the weight – four-fifths of a ton – and saw blood splashed across Ursula's coat. Lots of blood. His own blood. He smelled hot, fishy breath as his assailant's maw closed over his head. Sharp teeth dug into his face and the last thing he heard was the crack of his own skull snapping like an eggshell as powerful jaws closed over it, silencing his awful screams for ever.

'They've been gone a long time,' Molineaux remarked to his shipmates when they rounded the bows of the ship for the umpteenth time that morning.

'Who have?' asked Ågård.

'Herr Ziegler and Frau Weiss.'

'Of course,' said Endicott. 'They're giving it the old . . .' The Liverpudlian demonstrated what he meant by 'the old . . .' by thrusting his hips back and forth a couple of times.

'I don't think so,' said Molineaux.

'What do you mean, you don't think so?' asked Endicott. 'What else would they be doing?'

'I don't know. But I don't think they're giving it "the old . . .".' Molineaux imitated Endicott's hip-thrusting mockingly. 'He's interested in her, but she ain't interested in him.'

'She told you that, did she?' asked O'Houlihan.

'No. But I've seen the way they look at one another. Or rather, the way he looks at her, and she avoids his gaze. And not coyly, either.'

'Is that so?' O'Houlihan said sceptically. 'So not only do I have to put up with Seth knowing what a frow's like in bed just by looking at her, but now it seems that a similar gift enables you to glance at a couple and guess immediately whether or not they're chauvering.'

'I think Wes is right,' said Ågård. 'If they are doing "t'other thing", why did they go all the way over there to do it?'

Endicott rapped his knuckles on Ågård's forehead. 'Hullo? Anyone in there? Maybe they want a bit of privacy?'

'I'm surprised they can manage it, in this cold weather,' said O'Houlihan. 'I was worried I'd get really randy, being stuck here in the Arctic without a bit of mutton to warm my belly, but I've hardly thought about it at all since we entered the Arctic Circle.'

Ågård wrapped an arm around Endicott's neck and pinned his head in his armpit, rubbing his bunched knuckles roughly over the Liverpudlian's scalp while continuing to walk around the *Venturer*'s hull. Endicott had no choice but to follow. 'How many times have I got to tell you, lad? ABs like you have got to treat POs like me with some respect.'

Endicott laughed. 'Yur, right. Ooh! Ahh! Gerroffyabugger!'

'I'm glad you said that,' Hughes responded to what O'Houlihan had said. 'I was starting to get worried. I thought maybe there was something wrong with me, like.'

'There is something wrong with you, Red,' said Molineaux. 'You're full of gammon.'

'Kiss my bum, Wes! But no, I can't remember the last time I had a dirty thought.'

'It was last night, to judge from what you were saying in your sleep.'

'Bloody hell, Ollie,' said Endicott, his head still trapped under Ågård's armpit. 'When was the last time you washed under your arms? It bloody stinks down here!'

'Give over!' protested Hughes. 'I don't talk in my sleep.'

'Why, sure ye do, Red,' said O'Houlihan. ' "Ooh, Flossie, I love you so much!" ' The Irishman did a fair imitation of Hughes' Welsh accent. ' "You're so soft and fleecy!" "Me-e-a-a-ah!" '

'Oh, yes,' Hughes said sourly. 'The "all-Welshmen-shag-sheep" joke. I haven't heard that one in at least ten minutes.'

'Make a note of that, Wes,' said O'Houlihan. 'We're not making jokes about Welshmen shagging sheep often enough. I say we step it up to once every five minutes.'

'It's not that we think *all* Welshmen shag sheep, Red,' explained Molineaux. 'Just you.'

Ågård lost interest in the limited pleasures of tormenting Endicott and finally released him. The Liverpudlian kicked the ice quatermaster in the seat of his trousers. Ågård tried to grab him, but Endicott ran off a short distance, laughing. The ice quartermaster disdained to give chase. 'It's just that, I wondered why they didn't go into the observatory to do it,' he said.

'Eh?' said Hughes. 'What are you talking about, Ollie?'

'Herr Ziegler and Frau Weiss. If they wanted a bit of privacy, why didn't they go into the observatory?'

'The pill-roller's in there, ain't he?' said O'Houlihan. 'Doing one of his experiments.'

As they rounded the stern once more, Molineaux saw a figure moving across the ice towards them. Shading his eyes against the sun, he saw it was a woman from the way she ran. 'Here comes Frau Weiss,' he remarked to the others. 'I wonder where Herr Ziegler's got to?'

They stopped and watched as she continued to run towards them, although she was still some distance off. When they saw her slip and fall on the ice, they cheered ironically.

'What's going on here?' demanded Thwaites, stepping up behind them.

'It's Frau Weiss, Bosun,' said Ågård.

'So? Tha's seen her before, hasn't thee? Keep moving . . .'

'What's that stuff on her?' asked Hughes.

'Looks like blood,' said Molineaux, suddenly feeling guilty that he had cheered when she had fallen. It looked as if she had hurt herself quite badly.

By now even Thwaites was too intrigued to tell Ågård and the others to keep moving, and he too stood with his eyes shaded against the sun.

Frau Weiss was shouting, the words torn away by the wind.

Not shouting, Molineaux realised. *Screaming*.

'That's a lot of blood,' Endicott said soberly.

She was covered in it. Molineaux was the first to start running towards her, but Ågård had the longer legs and soon outstripped him. He was about twenty yards ahead of Molineaux when she ran into his arms, sobbing hysterically and babbling in German.

'Shh!' Ågård told her. 'Rest easy, lass. It's all right. You're safe now.' He took out a clean handkerchief and started to wipe the blood from her face. 'Are you hurt? Where are you cut? It's all right, Wes. I don't think it's her blood.'

'Oh, that makes it all right, does it?' retorted Molineaux.

'Then whose blood is it? And where's Ziegler? Or have I just answered my own question?'

'Bloody hell, Wes! You don't think she's done for him, do you?'

But Ursula could only jabber hysterically in her native tongue. Molineaux caught Ziegler's name, the word '*tot*' – which he was pretty sure was German for 'dead' – and something that sounded like 'ice-bar,' whatever one of those was. Did she mean icicle?

As they took her back towards the ship, the others came across the ice to meet them, gathering solicitously around Ursula until Ågård curtly ordered them to stand back and let her breathe. 'Can you make out what she's saying?' Molineaux asked Kracht.

The German nodded. 'She says Ziegler was killed by a polar bear.'

Molineaux swore, glanced back in the direction of the pressure ridge from which she had come, and then snatched a musket from Private Phillips, who had been on sentry-go at the top of the gangplank, and turned and ran over the ice.

'Hey! That's my musket!' Phillips exclaimed lamely.

Molineaux was gasping for breath by the time he reached the pressure ridge – the sharp Arctic air stung his lungs and he could taste iron in his spit – but he did not pause. The agility that had helped him to climb in and out of other people's windows as a youth now helped him scramble up the jumbled, angular lumps of ice. At the top he paused to make sure that the musket was loaded. Then he bobbed up over the ridge, the stock of the musket hard against his shoulder, pointing the barrel this way and that in the hope that the bear that had killed Ziegler would fall in his sights.

There was no sign of the bear, just the wide ice-field studded with bergy bits.

But it was easy to see where Ziegler had died. The blood splashed on the ice a couple of hundred yards to his right stood out on the snow as only crimson on white could.

He started to scramble down the other side of the ridge, lost his footing about halfway down and slithered the rest of the way, sprawling on his back at the bottom. He lay there, muttering some ripe language under his breath, and then remembered that the bear could not be all that far away – for all he knew, it was just hiding behind one of the bergy bits – and his position was not an ideal one if the bear decided it wanted to come back for seconds. He scrambled to his feet, levelling the musket once more, but he was alone on the ice.

Downy move, Wes, he told himself. *That's the second time one of us has been cramped by a polar bear, and the second time you've run after it on your own. But at least this time you had sense enough to bring a barking iron.*

Then he remembered that Ziegler had also had a gun when he had set out from the ship; much good that had done him.

Constantly turning to make sure nothing was creeping up on him from behind, he made his way to the blood-splashed snow.

This time the bear had left even less of Ziegler than had remained of Cavan after the first attack. He found some pawprints leading away from the grisly scene. Each print was more than a foot across. *That's some big bloody bear,* Molineaux told himself. In spite of the cold, his palms were sweating inside his mittens where they gripped the musket. He glanced around the ice-field nervously. He had not met the man he could not beat in a fight – or if he had, he did not know it – but animals were another matter entirely. Even spiders scared the bejasus out of him; the thought of taking on a bloody great polar bear, even armed with a rifled musket, filled him with trepidation. He had seen how swiftly the sow had pounced on Mr Strachan; it was almost impossible to believe that such a large and lumbering animal could move so quickly. Miss with your first shot, you wouldn't have time to reload for a second.

He found the shotgun Ziegler had been carrying, covered now in his gore, and examined it distastefully. Ziegler had not even got one shot off, let alone two.

He was relieved when some of the others turned up a couple of minutes later: Killigrew, Bähr, Strachan, Terregannoeuck, Bombardier Osborne, Corporal Naylor and Private Phillips.

Bähr had fetched his hunting rifle. 'Damn it, have I missed another one?' he asked in annoyance. 'You must have scared it off, Molineaux.'

'It was gone long before I got here, sir,' the petty officer replied heavily, thinking that Ziegler's death was a far greater tragedy than Bähr's failure to add another trophy to his collection.

'Give Phillips back his musket, Molineaux,' Killigrew ordered crisply. 'What the devil did you think you were playing at, running off on your own like that? What if the polar bear had still been around? You might have ended up as another meal for it. Losing two men to polar bear attacks is quite bad enough, thank you!'

'Sorry, sir,' Molineaux replied in chagrin. 'I thought maybe Herr Ziegler might still be alive, that I could save him; and if I couldn't, at least I could make sure I stopped the bear from killing any more of us.'

'What's the point of that?' asked Osborne. 'Kill one polar bear, there are plenty more out there to take its place.'

'All right,' Killigrew allowed, in response to Molineaux's defence. 'But in future I'm sure we'd all prefer it if you reserved your initiative for times when there are no officers around to give you orders, hoist in?'

Terregannoeuck was crouching over the bear's paw-prints. 'Any chance of tracking the bugger?' Bähr asked him eagerly.

'*Nanuq* move too fast,' replied the Inuk.

'But you Esquimaux hunt bear with your dog sledges, don't you?'

'One man, one dog sledge. Terregannoeuck not fear *nanuq*. But this not *nanuq*, this Kokogiaq. Kokogiaq not die. Terregannoeuck try to kill Kokogiaq, Terregannoeuck be dead, I think.'

' "Kokogiaq"?' echoed Molineaux. 'You said that before, after Mr Strachan was attacked. What does "kokogiaq" mean?'

Terregannoeuck tapped the paw-print before him. 'Amongst my people, legends tell of Kokogiaq, ten-legged *nanuq*. When Terregannoeuck young man, one winter hunting party set out to hunt *puyee* in the land to west of Arvirtuurmiut. One man, Hoeootoerock, kill *nanuq* and two cubs. But Hoeootoerock not honour *tatkoq* of *nanuq*. He say *nanuq* dead because he kill her, not because she let him kill her. This pride makes Kokogiaq angry. For many years, all men who hunt in land to west of Arvirtuurmiut not come back. Finally, elders say matter must be settled: Hoeootoerock must appease Kokogiaq. Hoeootoerock return to land to west of Arvirtuurmiut to find Kokogiaq.

Hoeootoerock not return. But afterwards, men who hunt in land to west of Arvirtuurmiut hunt safely and successfully. And from that day on, my people always take care to honour *tatkoq* of *nanuq* they kill.'

Terregannoeuck tapped one of the paw-prints again. 'This same *nanuq* that kill Mr Cavan. This *nanuq* Kokogiaq.'

Molineaux felt a shiver run down his spine. He did not consider himself a superstitious man – he did not even believe in God, much – but he had seen some strange things in his years as a sailor, things that scientificers like Mr Strachan could not explain to his satisfaction. Could it really be that because Bähr had killed the cubs, because Pettifer had taken down the sow's bladder from inside the *Venturer* before the five days were up, this Kokogiaq was out to be avenged on them all?

It was Strachan who broke the uneasy silence. 'Piffle,' he said succinctly. 'Maybe Ziegler was killed by the same bear that killed Cavan, maybe not. We can soon find out: I took a plaster cast of one of the paw-prints by Cavan's remains; I'll take a paw-print of one of these, and we can compare the two. But I misdoubt it was the same bear. Even Pennant acknowledges that human beings aren't polar bears' natural food. If they were, then both bears and Esquimaux would have died out long ago.'

'Then why were Cavan and Ziegler killed?' demanded Killigrew.

'Perhaps it's a rogue male,' suggested Bähr. 'You get that with lions, sometimes. Something happens that means they can't hunt in the usual manner of lions, in packs; either they become too old, become outcast from their pride, or they break an incisor. It's something that no one's ever been able to explain properly . . .'

'Yet,' said Strachan, who believed that everything had a rational, scientific explanation.

'But they start to hunt alone, and sometimes they decide they prefer the taste of man flesh to wildebeest and antelope,' concluded Bähr.

Strachan shook his head. 'Polar bears don't hunt in packs.'

'So in a way, they're all rogue males?' suggested Killigrew.

Strachan glared at him. 'That doesn't explain why one would decide it preferred human flesh to seal-meat.' He shook his head

251

again. 'I think you'll find that the bear that killed Cavan was different from the one that did this.' He gestured at the mess. 'One thing is certain: whatever bear did this, it walked on four legs, not ten. And it killed Herr Ziegler not because it wanted to avenge an insult to the dead sow's soul, but because it was hungry.'

'How often do polar bears feed?' asked Killigrew.

The assistant surgeon regarded him mournfully. 'As often as they can.'

XIV

Bruin's Larder

Strachan returned to the scene of Ziegler's death as soon as he could fetch a mixing bowl, some water and some gypsum powder from the ship. Killigrew wanted to send him back with Corporal Naylor and his marines, but the assistant surgeon insisted that Ågård, Molineaux and O'Houlihan – suitably armed with rifled muskets – would be protection enough. He was quite pleased with this: it made him look braver than he was, because the truth of the matter was that he had been through several adventures with the three seamen, and he had more faith in them than he did in Naylor and his marines.

'If you don't think that Ziegler was killed by the same bear as Cavan, what's the point of taking a plaster cast, sir?' asked Ågård.

Strachan had noticed that when there were no other officers around, Ågård, Molineaux and O'Houlihan did not address him with the usual 'begging your pardon, sir' formula they might have used if they were speaking out of turn. In a way that rather pleased him: he hated mindless kowtowing, and did not care as long as there was respect. And on those rare occasions when Molineaux's natural talent for insubordination did reveal itself in a flash of disrespect, Strachan usually had to admit to himself that he had earned it.

'A plaster cast will prove that the attacks were carried out by two different bears,' he said confidently. He did not mind explaining his scientific investigations to the hands; in fact, he rather enjoyed it. He was aware that some of his fellow officers thought he could be a bore at times – perhaps they were right – but Ågård, Molineaux and O'Houlihan seemed genuinely interested, and Strachan was never happier than when he was giving one of his Sunday evening lectures to the hands. 'Besides, just look at the size of these paw-prints! Twelve and fifteen-sixteenths of an inch! I'd say we're dealing with a specimen of *Ursus maritimus* of extraordinary size. You know, I almost regret that Dr Bähr wasn't able to shoot it: stuffed, it would have made a splendid specimen to present to the British Museum. I wonder if we could take one alive? A gift to the Zoological Gardens would be even better . . .'

'Don't even *think* about it, sir,' groaned Molineaux. 'There's no way I'm sailing back to Britain with a live polar bear on board, even chained! You want my opinion, there's only one place a polar bear belongs, and that's in the Arctic.'

'You're right, of course,' acknowledged Strachan.

'Twelve and fifteen-sixteenths of an inch, you say?' mused O'Houlihan. 'That's big, for a polar bear?'

'Yes, indeed! Most polar bear prints don't measure much more than about a foot across at the very largest, and that's big males.'

'The prints of the bear that killed Mr Cavan were unusually large, were they not, sir?'

'Again, twelve and fifteen-sixteenths of an inch.'

'How many bears do you suppose there are around here with paws measuring twelve and fifteen-sixteenths of an inch, sir?'

'A good scientist isn't led into erroneous hypotheses by positing assumptions based on misleading physical evidence.'

'Come again, sir?'

'He says you're jumping to conclusions, Mick,' explained Molineaux.

'Is that so?' O'Houlihan nodded his head sagely. 'Well, you're the expert, sir.'

Molineaux looked around. 'I just don't understand it,' he said.

'What don't you understand?' asked Strachan.

'There's no cover within a hundred yards. How the hell did the bear get close enough to attack without being seen, and without Ziegler even getting a chance to get one shot off?'

'Maybe his mind was on other things,' O'Houlihan said with a wink.

'Maybe so,' agreed Molineaux. 'But you think he'd've seen *something*. I mean, polar bears are *big*. That she-bear I killed a couple of weeks back was about seven foot long, and Terregannoeuck says he-bears are much bigger.'

Strachan nodded. 'Nine feet long, usually, although specimens as large as ten feet have been recorded.'

'They're white,' said O'Houlihan. 'They don't show up against the snow.'

'The one I shot wasn't white,' said Molineaux. 'More sort of yellowy. Stood out like a sore thumb against the snow.'

'Their fur changes colour over the year,' explained Ågård, who must have seen a few polar bears himself when he was a whaler. 'It's yellowy in the summer, but it turns whiter as winter comes on.'

'Well, this bear can't have been much whiter than the one I shot two weeks ago,' said Molineaux. 'I don't care if Ziegler was spooning with Jenny Lind, never mind Frau Weiss. How could he not notice a yellow bear nine or ten feet long, weighing four-fifths of a ton, stalking him across the ice?'

Strachan could not answer that question, so he concentrated on mixing up the gypsum cement. Taking a plaster cast from ice was much trickier than working from mud or sand. The water used in the mixture – which had frozen on the walk from the ship – had to be heated up over a portable stove to melt it once more. But the mixture could not be too warm when Strachan poured it into the frame he had constructed around the print, otherwise it would melt the snow before it had a chance to set, and ruin the impression. At the same time, he had to make sure the gypsum cement set rather than simply froze, otherwise the cast would just melt when he got it back on board the *Venturer*. He had learned from the many mistakes he had made taking a cast of the first bear's foot, however, and this time got both the consistency and the temperature of the mixture just right when he poured it into the frame.

After the three seamen had shovelled what was left of Ziegler into a sack for burial the next day, O'Houlihan brewed some tea on the stove while they waited for the cast to set, and they munched some ship's biscuits. In spite of the cold, Strachan was grateful to be away from the *Venturer*, where the atmosphere had grown unbearable since Pettifer's behaviour had become increasingly erratic. Things had been relatively quiet on board over the week since Pettifer had confined himself to his cabin, and they had settled into a routine: monotonous, in a way, but Strachan liked some order in his life.

The three ratings kept glancing around them fearfully, as if they expected the polar bear to return. 'You needn't worry,' Strachan told them. 'The bear that attacked Ziegler won't be hungry again so soon.'

'Yur, well, if it *was* two different bears that attacked Mr Cavan and Herr Ziegler, maybe the bear that killed Cavan is getting peckish by now,' Molineaux pointed out.

Strachan considered the point, and then looked down at the cast, mentally trying to will it to set faster.

It was half-past four before the cast was ready to be removed, twilight at that time of year. By the time they got back to the *Venturer*, dusk had settled over the landscape and Strachan was glad to be back on board, Pettifer or no Pettifer. He took the cast to the sick-berth, where he found Frau Weiss lying in one of the cots, ashen-faced, trembling and wide-eyed.

'How is she?' he asked Fischbein.

His arm fully healed now, the young half-deck boy had been appointed sick-berth attendant, amongst other duties. He sat in the chair next to Ursula's cot, reading one of Strachan's books: Hawkins' *The Book of Great Sea Dragons*, lavishly illustrated with artists' impressions of marine dinosaurs; rather fantastic interpretations, in Strachan's opinion, but he kept it around the sick-berth for the benefit of the seamen who wanted something to occupy them but found reading an up-hill struggle.

'All right, I think, *mein Herr*,' said Fischbein. His English had improved dramatically in the four months since he had come on board the *Venturer*. 'She's not hurt, just shocked. Dr Bähr gave her some laudanum and a cup of camomile tea.'

Strachan grunted; unlike most medical men, he did not regard laudanum as a universal panacea. He crouched by Ursula's cot and looked into her eyes. 'How do you feel?'

'Still a little shaken,' she admitted.

'That's not to be wondered at. It must have been terrifying. You're a lucky lassie.'

'It was *schrecklich* – dreadful,' she admitted. 'It just appeared out of nowhere. Ziegler was standing less than two feet away when it pounced on him from behind, forced him down on to the ice. I could hear his bones cracking . . .' She shuddered. 'And then it put its jaws over his head, and closed them. His skull cracked like an egg . . . I just got up and ran. I should have helped him somehow, but I just got up and ran.' She turned away.

'Hush, now! What could you have done? If you'd lingered, the bear might well have killed you as well. You did the only sensible thing. Once the bear pounced, Ziegler was as good as dead. It doesn't sound to me as if he suffered much.'

She shook her head. 'You did not see it. So much blood . . .'

'Well, it's over now and the bear's probably long gone. You get some rest. Everything will seem so much better in the morning, I promise you.'

There was a knock on the door. Not wanting Frau Weiss to be disturbed any more than necessary, Strachan crossed to the door and opened it a crack to see Killigrew and Bähr standing there. 'You've got the second plaster cast?' asked Bähr.

'Probably best if we don't discuss this in front of Frau Weiss,' murmured Strachan.

'The wardroom?' suggested Killigrew.

Strachan nodded. 'Give me a hand with the casts, would you, Killigrew? They're not heavy, but they're big.' He found his magnifying glass, tucked it in the pocket of his frock coat, and fetched the two casts, handing one to the lieutenant so he could close the sick-berth door behind him. The two of them carried the casts down to the wardroom, where Bähr waited with Yelverton, Latimer and Varrow.

'Mind the mahogany!' Latimer said anxiously as Killigrew and Strachan put the casts down on the table.

'Bugger the mahogany!' Bähr retorted as Strachan took out his magnifying glass and scrutinised first one, then the other cast.

'Oh!' the assistant surgeon exclaimed in disappointment.

'Well?' Bähr demanded impatiently. 'Are they the same, or aren't they?'

'I'd like a second opinion, if you'd be so good, Doctor.' Strachan handed him the magnifying glass.

'Ah!' exclaimed Bähr, after a few moments' study. He looked up at Strachan, who nodded soberly.

'They're the same,' they chorused.

'What does that mean?' asked Latimer.

Killigrew took a deep breath. 'It means that all bets are off: this polar bear doesn't play according to Hoyle.'

> *. . . They are at constant enmity with the Walrus, or Morse: the last, by reason of its vast tusks, has generally the superiority; but frequently both the combatants perish in the conflict.*
>
> *They are frequently seen in Greenland, in lat. 76, in great droves; where, allured by the scent of the flesh of seals, they will surround the habitations of the natives, and attempt to break in; but are soon driven away by the smell of burnt feathers . . .*

In his cabin, Killigrew looked up from the ship's copy of Thomas Pennant's *Arctic Zoology* and rubbed his eyes wearily. All very interesting, but hardly helpful. The idea of trying to capture a walrus to use as a guard dog he dismissed out of hand: even if they had seen a walrus since they had entered Peel Sound, the idea was impractical. As for burning feathers, well . . . there were plenty of feathers on board in the officers' pillows, but not enough to burn twenty-four hours a day until the bear returned. Given the rapidity with which the bear struck, keeping feathers handy until the bear returned and then trying to burn them upwind from the bear to drive it off seemed impractical.

Normally he bowed to Strachan in all matters of zoology, but the assistant surgeon's insistence that humans were not polar bears' natural food was little reassurance after what had happened to Cavan and Ziegler. Twice the bear had killed now; the second attack was all the more worrying because it indicated that this bear had tasted human flesh and decided it liked it enough to come back for more. A third visit seemed inevitable.

In the week since Ziegler's death, Killigrew had instituted

some basic precautions with the intention of preventing any further deaths from polar bear attacks. From now on, no one was to go beyond the perimeter rope without his permission, and even then in company and well armed. Guards armed with rifles were to keep a sharp lookout for bears throughout the hours of daylight, especially when the mess cooks were bringing supplies aboard the ship from the depot on the ice. And no one – repeat, *no one* – was to leave the ship itself during the hours of darkness, or when deteriorating weather meant that visibility was poor.

It was difficult to see what else they could do. Even so, Killigrew felt a vague sense of unease. The sooner the bear made a third attempt and was dealt with, the happier he would be.

There was a knock at the cabin door. 'Come in?'

It was Private Jenkins. 'Sorry to bother you, sir. I've got orders from the cap'n to search your cabin.'

Killigrew blinked. 'To search my cabin? What for?'

'Any papers, journals, charts, that sort of thing, sir.' Jenkins squirmed with embarrassment: a seasoned marine, he must have known that this went beyond irregular. 'I don't think it's anything personal, sir. We've been given orders to search all the officers' cabins . . .'

Killigrew leaped to his feet, squeezed past Jenkins and out through the wardroom. On the other side of the passageway beyond, Private Walsh was ransacking Yelverton's cabin.

Corporal Naylor was on duty outside Pettifer's quarters. 'Stand aside, Naylor.'

'Sorry, sir.' The corporal grinned. It was obvious that, unlike Jenkins, Naylor was enjoying this immensely. 'I've orders that no one is to disturb the cap'n.'

'I'm giving you new orders, Corporal. Stand aside, damn your eyes!'

'Begging your pardon, sir –' Naylor had developed the knack of speaking respectfully, while contempt oozed from every pore, to a fine art – 'but Cap'n Pettifer's a commander, and you're only a lieutenant, which means his orders take precedence over yours.'

'Don't be a bloody fool, Naylor. Get out of my way at once!'

'I've orders not to let anyone past, using force if necessary.'

'I'm warning you, I'll have you court-martialled for this.'

'For what?' sneered Naylor. 'Obeying orders?'

Killigrew snatched his musket and rammed it back against Naylor's throat, pinning him to the door. 'This nonsense has gone quite far enough, Corporal. Trifle with me and you won't live to see a court martial, hoist in?' He pulled Naylor away from the door, swung him around and threw him to the deck. Still holding the musket, he kicked open the door to Pettifer's quarters.

The day-room was unlit, the curtain drawn over the stern window, the blinds pulled beneath the skylight – which looked up only to the covered upper deck now anyway. Horatia came scampering out of the darkness to sink her teeth into Killigrew's ankle. He gave her a kick, just hard enough to send her running back to her basket, whimpering.

'What the devil's the meaning of this?' Pettifer called from the darkness.

Killigrew slung the musket from his shoulder. Even in his anger, he knew better than to give the impression he was threatening the commander with a loaded firearm. 'You tell me, sir. What's the meaning of your ordering the marines to search all our cabins?'

'It's perfectly simple: they're looking for evidence.'

'Evidence? Evidence of what?'

'Disloyalty. Do you take me for a fool, Killigrew?'

'I'm beginning to.'

'You think I don't know that you and the others have been conspiring against me behind my back? You think I don't know about your secret meetings in the observatory? You're all in on it, aren't you? Varrow deliberately ignored my orders to stop her so we ran aground at the Whalefish Islands; Latimer falsified the records of the amount of coal that we brought on board so that we ran low. He could only have done so with your compliance!'

'What are you talking about, sir? With all due respect, the only reason we ran aground at the Whalefish Islands is because of your inexperience at conning a steam-powered ship. You were officer of the watch: what happened was your responsibility. And if we're running low on coal, it's because you used up so much in your hurry to beat the rest of the squadron to the North

Water. You knew, didn't you? You knew we were ahead of Belcher and the others, but you let the rest of us think that we'd fallen behind, and that your hurry was to catch them up. What happened when you went ashore at Lievely, sir? What did the governor really tell you? That the rest of the squadron had headed around the east side of the island? So you ordered us to sail around the west side, so that we'd be ahead of them. It's not Sir Edward who wants the glory of discovering the North-West Passage all for himself; it's you. And you don't care how many of us die to win you that honour. Well, it's over. From now on I'm assuming command of this vessel.'

Pettifer leaned forward in his chair so that the parallelogram of light from the door fell across his face. He looked awful: his cheeks unshaven, his eyes bloodshot and sunk deep within his skull. 'It's over, all right. Over for you, Mr Killigrew. You've condemned yourself out of your own mouth. Corporal Naylor!'

The corporal, who had been hovering outside the door with Private Jenkins, Phillips and Walsh to see how things panned out, now stepped into the day-room. 'Sah?'

'You will place Mr Killigrew under arrest, Naylor,' ordered Pettifer. 'The charge is mutiny. Restrain him and place him in the lazaretto in irons.'

'Don't listen to him!' Killigrew told the marines. 'You heard him: he's paranoid! He deliberately disobeyed Sir Edward's orders.'

Naylor tugged the musket urgently from Killigrew's shoulder. 'Like I said: he's the captain, and you're only a lieutenant.'

'Come along now, sir,' Jenkins said more apologetically. 'Orders is orders. No point making itself worse for you.'

Killigrew thought about resisting, but what was the point? Even if he managed to escape, there was nowhere to go.

As the lieutenant was marched from the captain's quarters, Strachan, Latimer and Varrow crowded the wardroom door to watch in disbelief. 'He's quite mad, you know,' Killigrew told them. 'It's all up to you now, Strachan: you're next in command.'

'Stow it!' Naylor rammed the stock of his musket into the small of Killigrew's back. The lieutenant stumbled and sank to his knees with a gasp. Jenkins helped him to his feet, and

Killigrew was escorted to the orlop deck, where they thrust him into the lazaretto. Phillips arrived with the irons, and they fettered him to a ring-bolt in the side.

'Sorry about this, sir,' said the young marine. 'I'm sure it's just a misunderstanding.'

'Don't waste your sympathy,' sneered Naylor. 'He's the bastard that stood by and did nothing when they flogged poor Johnno Smith to death.'

'He's going to get you all killed!' Killigrew shouted after them as they headed for the door. They closed it, plunging him into darkness. He heard a padlock click over the door, and their boots marching away down the deck.

Presently, a single pair of boots marched back. Killigrew listened as the padlock was removed again, not sure what to expect. The door opened, and Naylor was silhouetted there. After a pause, he entered the lazaretto and stood over the lieutenant.

'All my life I've had to kowtow to stuck-up bastards like you, just because you were born with a silver spoon in your gob and I wasn't. Polishing your boots, laundering your shirts, all but wiping your bloody backside for you. Now I've got you right where I want you.'

He drove a boot into Killigrew's stomach. The lieutenant doubled up in agony, retching. 'I warned you once before, Naylor,' he rasped. 'Trifle with me and you'll live to regret not being dead.'

The corporal laughed. 'See you at your court martial, *Mr* Killigrew.' He slammed the door and left Killigrew alone in the darkness with his pain.

'Forget it.' In the *Venturer*'s galley, Armitage took another tin from the crate at his feet, sliced off the top with a small axe, and tipped the contents into a large pot.

'If we do this right, Tommo, they can't touch us,' pleaded Molineaux. The condensation billowed from his mouth as he spoke. Even in the galley – one of the warmest parts of the ship – it was so cold he could not feel his toes in his boots, and he massaged his fingers to try to keep the circulation going. 'Bonesniffer will support us, and once we get Tom Tidley out of the lazaretto he can take responsibility. But we've got to be one hundred per cent behind him: all of us.'

The deck head shuddered constantly above them as the rest of the hands exercised, barring those who had gone on to the ice to bring on board more supplies. Molineaux should have been up there with them, but it had been easy enough for him to slip down the fore hatch to the galley when no one had been looking.

'What about the marines?' asked Armitage.

'I've spoken to Osborne: he's with us.'

The cook paused with his axe poised above another tin. 'What about Naylor?'

'Osborne outranks Naylor.'

'Osborne's just a specialist. Naylor takes his orders from Pettifer.'

'You let me worry about Dick Naylor. We've got to do something. We can't go on with Cap'n Carney getting more and more nuts as each day goes by.'

Armitage shrugged and chopped the top off the tin. 'Bone-sniffer's next in command. If he's agreed to support us, why can't he take the lead in this?'

'Because he hasn't got the sand, that's why. Come on, Tommo. He's a pill-roller, not an executive officer. You can't expect him to stand up to Cap'n Carney.'

'If he hasn't got the sand to stand up to Cap'n Carney now, who's to say he won't crumble when he has to face him under cross-examination at a court martial? The odds'll be stacked against us, Wes. It only takes one officer to admit there might have been two sides to the story, and our defence falls apart.' Armitage brought the axe down on another tin. 'Face it, Wes; Bonesniffer's the weakest link.'

Molineaux was staring at him, open-mouthed with horror. Armitage lowered his eyes and saw a bloody stain rapidly spreading across the front of Molineaux's box-cloth jacket. He stared as the stain grew larger and larger.

'Wes? Are you all right?'

'Am *I* all right? Tommo, you just chopped your thumb off!'

Armitage raised his mittened hand to study the blood jetting from the stump of his thumb. 'Will you look at that, now?' He giggled nervously. 'I can't feel a thing!'

Molineaux swore, snatched up a dishcloth, and clamped it over the wound. 'Come on, Tommo, let's get you to the pill-roller.'

'I'm all right, I'm all right.' Armitage was unnaturally calm as Molineaux helped him into the sick-berth, and the boatswain's mate wondered if he was speaking for his benefit, or for his own.

Strachan was sitting at one of the workbenches, hunched over a microscope, when they entered. 'Mr Strachan?' said Molineaux. 'Bit of an emergency here, sir.'

'What's the problem?'

'Armitage just cut his thumb off.'

Strachan glanced up from the microscope. 'Well, that was a fool thing to do, wasn't it? You'd better lie on the table here. Keep his arm up as high as you can while I put a tourniquet around it. Fischbein, pass me a bottle of iodine, a gauze pad and some bandages.' There was no panic in his voice: a medical emergency was something the assistant surgeon knew he was well equipped to cope with.

Assisted by Molineaux and Fischbein, Strachan cleaned and dressed the wound quickly and efficiently. Finally he sent Fischbein to fetch a beaker of water, and gave Armitage a pill. 'What is it, sir?' asked the cook.

'Codeine,' Strachan explained as Armitage washed the pill down. 'It's a new drug, to take away the pain.'

'I don't feel any pain,' protested the cook.

Strachan clapped him on the shoulder. 'You will.'

A blood-curdling scream sounded somewhere outside. It cut through the thudding footsteps of the men exercising on the upper deck and sent a shiver down Molineaux's spine.

'Now what?' he asked in exasperation.

The upper deck had fallen silent as everyone stopped to listen. Then a hubbub of yells came from outside, and the sound of a musket shot.

'I think I'd better go and see what that is,' said Molineaux.

Strachan nodded. 'Stay with Armitage, Fischbein,' he told the half-deck boy. 'Make sure he keeps that arm up.'

As Strachan followed Molineaux up the companion ladder to the fore hatch, they heard a ragged fusillade of musket shots. Both of them broke into a run.

The men who had been taking their exercise on deck now crowded around the opening in the awning, trying to get out. Latimer was there, trying to fight his way through. 'All right, stand back, stand back!'

Strachan and Molineaux fell in behind the clerk and the men parted to let them pass. The three of them stepped out through the opening to stand at the top of the gangplank.

Naylor, Walsh and Jenkins stood at the foot of the gangplank, frantically trying to reload their muskets. Phillips was there too, and even as Molineaux emerged the private raised his musket to his shoulder and fired.

Molineaux peered through the thick cloud of musket smoke and tried to see what they were shooting at. There were half a dozen men running back from where the ship's victuals were stored on the ice, and for one terrible moment Molineaux thought they were the ones the marines were shooting at. Then he saw a dark smear in the snow, and a trail leading from it. The trail seemed to grow longer even as he watched, and then he saw a dark shape moving over the snow. Even as he stared, he realised that the shape was the mangled corpse of a man gripped in the jaws of some great, pale beast, its white fur making it almost invisible against the snow.

Molineaux hurried down the gangplank, Strachan slithering awkwardly down after him to join the marines just as Naylor and Walsh fired again, but the bear was too far away now. It lolloped over the uneven ice at an incredible pace in spite of the burden in its jaws. Then Jenkins and Phillips had reloaded and they too fired. By the time the smoke cleared, the bear and its grisly burden had disappeared over a pressure ridge.

The men who had been running from the stores finally reached the foot of the gangplank. Gargrave was as white as a ghost and trembling like a sail brought too close to the wind. Molineaux grabbed him by the shoulders and stopped him. 'What happened?'

'Bear,' sobbed Gargrave. 'Big bear . . . It just snatched him . . . It came out of nowhere and snatched him . . .'

Seeing he was unlikely to get any more sense from the shocked stoker, Molineaux let him go and turned to the others. 'Who did it get?'

'It was the bosun,' said Endicott. Even he looked shaken. 'Mr Thwaites. It just grabbed him by the leg and ran off with him. And there wasn't a bloody thing we could do about it!' he added bitterly.

'All right,' Strachan told them. 'Corporal Naylor, have your men fall in.' He glanced about and saw Terregannoeuck descend the gangplank with some of the ratings. 'Get the dogs hitched to the sledge, Mr Terregannoeuck. We're going after him.'

'You're wasting your time,' Naylor said bitterly. 'He's dead.'

'You can't be certain of that . . .'

'I can. The bear just smashed his skull like you or I would crush an eggshell in the palm of our hands.'

'It was huge, sir,' said O'Houlihan. 'And I mean *huge*. Twelve foot long if it was an inch. Must've weighed nigh on a ton.'

'If it was so damned big, how the hell did it get so close without anyone seeing it?' demanded Strachan, and rounded on the marines. 'Who was on guard?'

'We were, sir,' said Walsh. He looked almost as shaken as Gargrave. 'The corporal and me. I swear to God, we were watching the whole time and the first we saw of it was when it ran out from behind the crates, dragging the bosun behind it.'

'Obviously you weren't watching closely enough,' said Strachan. 'Jings! How in the world could this have happened?' He searched their faces as if he expected them to come up with an answer, but his eyes met only blank stares.

Bähr emerged from the ship and Strachan told him what had happened. 'You're quite certain Thwaites is dead?' asked the doctor.

Endicott nodded. 'Corporal Naylor's right, sir. There's no way on earth the bosun could've survived the swipe the bear gave him. At least it must've been quick.'

'How could this happen?' sobbed Latimer. 'With so many people standing around, how come no one saw it until it was too late?'

'*Nanuq* stalk his prey, creep up on him,' said Terregannoeuck. 'He hide in dead ground and his fur match white of snow. If *nanuq* not want to be seen, you not see him.'

'All right, everyone back on board,' said Strachan. Molineaux was surprised to see the young Scotsman barking out orders so confidently. Although he could be brisk and decisive in the sick-berth, as he had so recently demonstrated, at all other times he was keenly aware of his lesser status as a civilian officer, and more than happy to let others have the responsibility of giving orders. But with no other officer present apart from Latimer – who clearly was not going to take charge of anything – Strachan just picked up the ball and ran with it. 'There's nothing more to be done here.'

'We ought to see if we can find what's left of the bosun,' said Bähr. 'With any luck we might catch the bear and kill it.'

'We ought to get the captain's permission,' Latimer said dubiously.

'Then go and get it!' suggested Strachan.

But the clerk dithered, even more terrified of Pettifer than he was of any polar bear.

Bähr sighed. 'I'll speak to him,' he said, and ascended the gangplank.

As the seamen followed Bähr back on board, Terregannoeuck found the tracks the bear had left in the snow and studied them. 'What do you see, Terry?' Molineaux asked him.

The Inuk stood up. 'Same bear.'

'The same bear!' exclaimed Strachan. 'Are you trying to tell me that Thwaites was killed by the same bear that killed Cavan and Ziegler?'

Terregannoeuck nodded. 'Kokogiaq.'

Strachan turned to the marines. 'Do you think you wounded it?'

They shook their heads. 'No, sir,' said Naylor.

'Damn it, how could you miss?' yelled Latimer. 'You're supposed to be marksmen, aren't you? I know the light was poor, but the range was less than a hundred yards!'

'I don't know, sir,' said Phillips. 'It's like our bullets went straight through it . . .'

'Don't talk nonsense, man,' barked Strachan. 'Either you hit it, or you didn't.'

'Anyhow, by then it didn't make much difference, did it, sir?' said Jenkins.

'Meaning?'

'Well, sir, you heard what Endicott said, did you not? Mr

Thwaites was dead before he knew it. So it wouldn't have made much difference whether we hit it or not.'

Strachan made a visible effort to control his temper. 'No difference?'

'Well . . . no, sir. Not that I can see.'

'Let's recap, shall we?' Strachan said heavily. 'A little less than a month ago, this bear attacked and killed Mr Cavan. Thirteen days ago, it attacked and killed Herr Ziegler. Now it's just killed the bosun and dragged the poor devil's corpse away so it can feast at its leisure. From which we can deduce two things: first, that this bear, having tried the taste of human flesh, has decided it is rather partial to it; and second that it knows where it can find an abundant supply and help itself whenever it feels like it with no difficulty whatsoever. Would you like to make a hypothesis based on these deductions?'

The marine looked puzzled. 'Sir?'

'The bear's coming back, Jenkins.' Strachan turned abruptly on his heel and ascended the gangplank.

Molineaux followed him inside. Beneath the awning, the upper deck was deserted but for the two of them. Strachan stood there and took off his cap to run his fingers through his hair in agitation.

'Maybe they did hit the bear, and didn't realise it,' Molineaux told the assistant surgeon. 'Maybe some of that blood was the bear's.' But even he did not really believe it.

'I wish we could be sure of that,' said Strachan. 'But you saw how fast it ran; and weighed down by Thwaites' body, too. That wasn't a wounded bear we saw leaving just now.'

Hughes and Kracht stepped under the awning. The Welshman was ashen-faced and trembling. 'You want to know what I think, sir?' he asked Strachan.

'Not particularly, Hughes.'

'Maybe Terregannoeuck was right, sir. Maybe that bear wants revenge for the murder of its mate and the two cubs that Dr Bähr killed.'

'Don't be ridiculous, Hughes! It's just a bear. A dumb animal. Bears don't mate for life, and they certainly don't understand concepts like revenge.'

'If I might say something, *mein Herr*?' said Kracht. 'Whether or not the bear that attacked Herr Thwaites was the father of the cubs Dr Bähr shot is irrelevant. The fact we cannot escape is that there *is* a bear out there, and now it has a taste for human blood.'

'Plummy,' sighed Molineaux. 'As if we didn't have enough to contend with, some polar bear's decided that the *Venturer* is his private larder.'

XV

Mutiny

They found what was left of the boatswain about two miles from the *Venturer*.

The bloodstained snow was trampled all around, and all that was left of the seaman were a few gnawed bones with some gobbets of flesh adhering to them. As the eight men approached, dragging a sledge behind them, an Arctic fox that had been gorging itself on the scraps of the bear's banquet reluctantly ran away, but only a short distance. It stopped and turned when it was only a hundred yards away, watching, waiting for the men to pass on so it could resume its feast. Bähr levelled his hunting rifle and killed the fox outright with a single shot.

'Got the little bugger!' he declared triumphantly.

'It's not going to look very impressive amongst all the lions, tigers and rhinos on the walls of your library, is it?' Strachan said sourly.

'Don't you get saucy with me, young man,' said Bähr. 'Anyhow, it will make a nice companion piece for the bear, when I shoot it.'

'If you shoot it.'

'Oh, I'll get it, Mr Strachan,' asserted the doctor. 'I've faced beasts more daunting than a polar bear before now. This bear's chosen the wrong ship to pick a fight with. I've been on the lookout for an *Ursus maritimus* to add to my collection, and this one's just volunteered for the honour.'

271

Strachan grunted non-committally. 'Molineaux! Endicott! Gather up the remains.'

'Keep a sharp lookout for that bear,' Molineaux told Jenkins and Phillips, as he took a shovel and a sack from the sledge. He tossed the sack to Endicott. 'You hold it open while I shovel what's left of the bosun inside.'

'There's a lot of tracks here,' observed Endicott, gazing about the snow around them. Apart from the tracks leading to and from the *Venturer*, there were at least six more sets of tracks leading to where they stood, and another six leading away. 'Looks like Rotten Row for polar bears!'

'Reckon the bastard must've had some friends round for dinner,' grunted Molineaux, trying not to gag as he shovelled up the scraps of bone and gristle.

Terregannoeuck crouched to examine the tracks.

'The question is, which tracks belong to the bear that killed Cavan, Ziegler and Thwaites?' asked Bähr.

The Inuk straightened. 'All of them.'

'What do you mean, *all* of them?' spluttered the doctor.

'*Nanuq* come here, go away. Come here, go away. Come here, go away. Come here, go away . . .'

'I think we get the point, Mr Terregannoeuck,' said Strachan.

'I don't get it, sir,' said Molineaux. 'What's so special about this place? Why did it keep coming back here?'

'Never mind that,' said Bähr. 'More to the point, which tracks do we follow?'

Terregannoeuck shrugged. '*Nanuq* make many tracks, so we not know which to follow.'

'Are you trying to tell me the bear made all these tracks to throw us off the scent?' exclaimed Bähr.

Strachan shaded his eyes against the sun. 'These tracks go for miles in every direction. The bear didn't have time to make them after it got here with poor Mr Thwaites.'

'He make them before,' said the Inuk.

'You mean, it *planned* this?' spluttered Bähr. 'It made all these tracks, planning to come and get one of us, knowing that we'd try to follow it?'

'*Nanuq* very cunning.'

'More clever than we are?' asked Bähr. 'Somehow, I doubt it!'

'It's outwitted us this time, ain't it?' muttered Molineaux.

'Which tracks do we follow?' asked Strachan.

'Let's split up,' suggested Bähr. 'We know these tracks lead back to the *Venturer*, so it must have gone in one of the other directions.'

'Split up, sir?' said Qualtrough. 'So it can pick us off one by one?'

'We've got muskets, haven't we?'

'Herr Ziegler had a barking iron when the bear got him, sir,' Molineaux pointed out. 'Much good it did him.'

'Qualtrough's right,' said Strachan. 'I doubt the bear's as clever as Terregannoeuck seems to think it is; but it's proved that it knows how to stalk and kill men. We'll stick together, I think.'

'So which tracks do we follow?'

'These ones.' Strachan pointed.

'Those ones lead back to the *Venturer*!'

'Exactly. Even if we did pick the right set of tracks, we might never catch it; and it could just lead us further and further away. I'm not playing its game.'

'Very well,' said Bähr. 'You go back to the *Venturer*, if you haven't got the pluck to press on. But I've come this far; I'm not turning back now.'

'You misunderstand me, sir. I meant we're *all* going back. That's an order.'

'Who the devil do you think you are, to order me around? I don't take orders from some squit of an assistant surgeon! You're not even a real surgeon: you're just an apothecary!'

'With all due respect, sir, I may only be qualified as an apothecary, but I also happen to be the senior officer present. And since this is a naval expedition and not an operating theatre, I'm the one who's giving the orders. I say we go back to the *Venturer* and wait.' He smiled thinly. 'Don't you fret about filling that space on the wall of your study, Doctor. I've got a feeling our bear's going to show up again sooner or later.'

Strachan was starting to think that the day could not get any worse by the time the sledging party got back to the *Venturer* at six o'clock that evening – nearly three hours after sunset as the winter nights closed in with increasing rapidity.

He was wrong.

There was no sign of the cook in the sick-berth.

'Where's Armitage gone?' he asked Fischbein.

'Herr Naylor took him.'

'Naylor took him? And you *let* him?'

Fischbein flinched, as if he had let Strachan down. 'Kapitän Pettifer's orders, *mein Herr*. I tell him Herr Armitage is too weak to be moved, he tell me he has orders. I try to stop him, he hit me in stomach. Very hard.'

'We'll see about that.'

Strachan set his jaw and marched the length of the lower deck until he reached Pettifer's quarters. There was no marine on sentry duty outside. Strachan burst through the door without knocking and found Armitage propped between Naylor and Walsh before the captain's table, his ashen face beaded with sweat in spite of the fact it was so cold in the day-room that everyone's breath billowed from their mouths. Seated next to Pettifer at the table, Latimer looked almost as sick as Armitage.

Pettifer launched himself from his chair. 'Mr Strachan! How *dare* you burst in here unannounced?'

'Never mind that!' said Strachan. 'What's this man doing out of bed?'

'By God, mister. You address your captain as "sir" – and do so in a civil tone, or I'll have you dismissed the service, by God!'

'This man is sick . . .'

'This man is on trial for drunkenness.'

'Drunkenness!' It would have been laughable had it not been so utterly insane. 'He cut his thumb off!'

'Precisely so, Mr Strachan. Would a sober man cut off his own thumb?'

'If his fingers were so numbed with cold that he could not feel them, aye!'

'I know a drunkard when I see one, Strachan. Look at him, the disgusting beast! He can hardly stand!'

'You'd have difficulty standing too, if you'd lost a pint of blood and been drugged to the back teeth with codeine.'

'Pipe down, Mr Strachan! I will not be gainsaid by my

274

officers, least of all a civilian officer – and a junior civilian officer at that!'

'Sir, I should like to speak in Armitage's defence.'

'It's too late for that, Mr Strachan. Petty Officer Armitage has already been examined by me and has failed to give an adequate explanation for his condition.'

'I'm no' surprised! In that state, he probably couldnae tell ye his own name!'

'It is my judgement that this man will be punished with two dozen lashes of the cat after divisions tomorrow.'

Strachan could not believe his ears. 'You're going to flog him? For cutting off his own thumb?' He turned pleadingly to Latimer. 'Am I the only one in this room wi' a shred o' sanity left? This is madness, damn ye! Fair madness!'

Pettifer turned puce. 'How dare you?' he spluttered. 'How dare you!'

'Aw, go to Fruchie and fry mice, ye barmpot!' Strachan turned on his heel and marched out of the room. 'This has gone far enough!'

'Mr Strachan!' Pettifer bellowed after him. 'How dare you walk out when I'm talking to you? This is intolerable behaviour, sir! I'll break you, by God I will!'

Strachan turned a deaf ear to Pettifer's imprecations and made his way back to the sick-berth.

'Is everything all right, Herr Strachan?' Fischbein asked him.

'No, Fischbein, everything is no' all right.' The assistant surgeon found a clean sheet of paper, dipped his pen in his inkwell and started to write with a trembling hand.

30th October 1852

To whom it may concern:

Having had the opportunity to observe the behaviour of Commander Orson Pettifer, captain of Her Majesty's Exploring Ship Venturer, over a period of some weeks, it has been impossible to ignore the marked deterioration in his mental stability.

Commander Pettifer is displaying classic symptoms of monomania: a morbid obsession – in this case his desire to discover the North-West Passage – combined with a state of paranoia manifesting itself in the form of a conviction that all those around him are seeking to thwart his efforts.

In this condition, he is clearly a danger not only to himself but also to those under his command and in his care. It is my painful duty not only to recommend but also to urge that his subordinate officers deprive him of command and physically restrain him until such time as his mental condition should show sufficient and sustained improvement permitting his release.

Strachan signed the letter and was reaching for the blotting paper when a scarlet-sleeved arm reached over his shoulder and plucked the letter from before him. He whirled on his stool to find Naylor standing there reading the note, flanked by Walsh.

'How dare you?' spluttered Strachan. 'That's none of your business. Give that back!' He tried to snatch at the paper, but Naylor gave him a shove in the chest that knocked him off the stool so that he landed painfully on the deck.

'None of our business, eh?' said Naylor. 'Listen to this, Arthur: "It is my painful duty not only to recommend but also to urge that his subordinate officers deprive him of command".'

'Sounds like inciting mutiny to me, Corp.'

'It does indeed, doesn't it?' Naylor reached down, grabbed Strachan by the arm and hoisted him to his feet. 'Come along, sir. It's the lazaretto for you!'

'You bloody fools!' sobbed Strachan. 'You're as mad as he is if you're going along with this insanity!' The two marines dragged him down to the orlop deck. 'You're enjoying this, aren't you, Naylor?'

The corporal grinned. 'You have no idea how much.'

When they opened the door to the lazaretto, Killigrew blinked up at them from the floor in the light of Walsh's lantern.

'Got some company for you, Mr Killigrew, sir,' said Walsh.

'Hullo, Strachan,' the lieutenant said cheerfully.

The assistant surgeon was shackled in irons alongside Killigrew, and the two marines closed the door and padlocked them in.

'Want to tell me about it?' Killigrew asked when the sound of the marines' boots had faded down the deck.

So Strachan brought him up to speed, telling him all about Thwaites' death, Armitage's accident, the abortive bear-hunt, and Armitage's impending flogging. 'He's quite mad, you know,' he concluded, referring to Pettifer.

'I know.'

'Now what are we going to do?'

The lieutenant clinked his irons. 'I'm open to suggestions.'

'Poor Armitage. He's in no fit state for a flogging. They'll kill him, as surely as they killed Smith.'

'I'm afraid it's out of our hands. It's all up to Latimer now.'

'*Latimer?*' Strachan shook his head. 'Armitage is a dead man.'

The next day – All-Hallows' Eve – was a Sunday, so the men paraded in their mustering rig for divisions. The smartness of their clothes only seemed to emphasise how awful their physical appearance was. Less than six months had passed since they had entered the Arctic Circle – a fraction of the time they had known they might have to spend in these waters – but they had been through too much in that time: the nerve-racking passage through the Middle Pack, the tension of being nipped in the ice off Boothia, and now the twin nightmares of Pettifer's erratic behaviour and the attacks of the polar bear.

Two-thirds rations was not a healthy diet for a fully grown man in ordinary conditions, and these were a long way from ordinary conditions. The men looked pale from lack of sunlight, their faces drawn and haggard with hunger. Everyone was tetchy and irritable from spending so much time cooped together, and hardly a day passed without Sørensen having to break up a fight on the mess deck. The brawny Dane had been appointed acting boatswain in the wake of Thwaites' death. Unstead, the senior boatswain's mate, had been disappointed not to be promoted, but he did not have the experience to be a boatswain just yet. As specksnyder on board the *Carl Gustaf*, Sørensen had included a similar duty amongst his functions in spite of the fact he had never served in the Royal Navy before. And the combination of his bulk and his easy-going temperament had already won him the respect of the British seamen on board the *Venturer*.

The muster was taken and Pettifer calmly read the Articles of War as if this were just another ordinary day at sea, but as Ågård stood on the quarterdeck and cast his eyes over the faces of the men paraded there he could see there was going to be trouble. After a quarter of a century at sea one learned to sense these things; the way seamen stopped holding whispered conversations the moment one approached, looked guilty all the time, avoided meeting one's eyes.

A grating was seized up. Armitage, still ashen from loss of blood, was tied spread-eagled to it with his back exposed.

Private Phillips played a drum-roll. Ågård kept an eye on the men watching, wondering which direction the trouble would come from. He kept a particularly close eye on Hughes.

Sørensen handed the scarlet bag containing the cat-o'-nine-tails to Molineaux. The boatswain's mate took the scourge out, and hesitated.

'Proceed with the punishment, Molineaux,' ordered Pettifer.

'Begging your pardon, sir, but I'm afraid I can't do that.'

Pettifer stared at him. 'I beg your pardon?'

'I beg leave to remind you of Chapter Five of Queen's Regulations, Section Two, Appendix Twenty-eight, Paragraph Five, sir? "No Officer of any description, class or age, including therefore all Subordinate and *Petty Officers*" –' the emphasis was Molineaux's – ' "is to be subjected to Corporal Punishment for any offence committed by him whilst holding such rank." Sir.'

As ship's cook, Tommo Armitage was rated petty officer. No one on board had forgotten that fact, or the fact that the flogging of petty officers was prohibited. But so extreme was the madness of having a man flogged for accidentally chopping off his own thumb, the added twist that it would be in contravention of Queen's Regulations had seemed neither here nor there.

For all he admired his friend's courage and sense of fairness, Ågård's heart sank. When a man like Molineaux refused to obey an order, you could be sure that things had gone too far. He cast his eyes at the five marines paraded on deck with their muskets, trying to gauge the expressions on their faces, but none of them gave anything away.

Pettifer had turned white with rage. 'How dare you quote Queen's Regulations at me, Molineaux? You'll deliver the first twelve lashes, by God, or I'll have you flogged next!'

'Then have me flogged, sir. I'll not flog a man for chopping off his own thumb.'

'Flogged? By God, you'll wish I *had* flogged you by the time I've finished with you. Refusing to obey orders, gross insubordination – I'll have you court-martialled for this, Molineaux! You'll swing, by God! Take the cat from him, Unstead!'

But the other boatswain's mate just folded his arms and shook his head. 'Molineaux's right, sir. I'll not be breaking Queen's Regulations.'

Pettifer quivered with barely controlled rage. Ågård could see a vein throbbing in the commander's temple as his face became suffused with blood. 'The Queen is in England and I am here, and I am giving you a direct order to give the cat to Unstead.'

'I'll give it to him if you like, sir, but he don't have no use for it,' said Molineaux. Unstead nodded firmly.

'Molineaux! Am I to take it that you are refusing a direct order?'

'Yes, sir.'

'You appreciate the seriousness of what you are saying? That refusing to obey your captain's orders is punishable by death?'

'Yes, sir.'

'Very well. Guilty by his own admission, gentlemen. I see no need to waste any time with a summary trial. Private Jenkins!'

'Sah!'

'Shoot Petty Officer Molineaux.'

Jenkins blinked. 'Sir?'

'You heard me. I'm giving you a direct order, private! You will shoot Molineaux! Do you hear me?'

Jenkins stepped forward and levelled his musket uncertainly at the petty officer. 'Come on, Wes! See sense, lad. Let Unstead have the cat.'

Molineaux held up the scourge, as if to say: *this cat*? Then he crossed to the main hatch, lifted the cover and dropped it down to the lower deck. 'You want it, you go and get it.'

'*Wes!*' hissed Jenkins. 'He's not kidding. Wes! Don't make me do it.'

'It's too late for that,' snapped Pettifer. 'Molineaux's had his chance. You will shoot him this instant.'

'You heard the cap'n, Jenkins,' Molineaux said calmly. 'What are you going to do?'

'Do you hear me, Jenkins?' screamed Pettifer. 'I'm giving you a direct order! Shoot Molineaux, or by God I'll have you strung up from the yard-arm!'

Jenkins shook his head and lowered his musket, turning away. 'Shoot him yourself, you crazy old bastard.'

'Gutless chicken-heart.' Naylor levelled his own musket at Molineaux. 'I'll do it, sir. It'll be my pleasure.'

Molineaux grabbed the musket from Jenkins and aimed it back at the corporal. 'Put the gun down, Naylor, or 'swelp me I'll drill you where you stand.'

Walsh went to his corporal's assistance, levelling his own musket at Molineaux. Ågård stepped up behind the private and seized him in a full nelson, while O'Houlihan took the musket and levelled it at Naylor. 'You shoot Wes, Dicky Boy, and ye'll be dead before he hits the deck.'

To judge from the worried expression on Naylor's face, he understood O'Houlihan was not bluffing.

Pettifer sighed and snatched Phillips' musket. 'Must I do everything myself?' he demanded, taking careful aim at Molineaux.

'Put the gun down, sir!'

Everyone turned to see Killigrew emerge from the after hatch, followed by Strachan and Yelverton, the last wearing a greatcoat over his nightshirt. The lieutenant had a pepperbox in either hand, the one in his right pointed unwaveringly at Pettifer's head, the other down by his side.

For one awful moment that seemed to stretch as far away as the eternity of snow and ice that surrounded the ship, Pettifer looked as though he was tempted to put Killigrew to the test. In the silence, you could have heard a pin drop on felt.

'You son of a bitch!' Naylor shattered the silence with his oath, and started to turn his musket on Killigrew. Without taking the pistol in his right hand off Pettifer, the lieutenant brought up his left hand and fired in the same instant as Molineaux and O'Houlihan. One bullet went wide, the second tore a chunk out of Naylor's shoulder, the third drilled a hole in his forehead and blew out the back of his skull. The corporal measured his length on the deck, the blood seeping from his body to stain the snow packed there for insulation.

Still keeping the pepperbox in his right hand on Pettifer, Killigrew tucked the other in his belt and laid hold of the barrel of the commander's musket. The two of them were frozen in a tableau: the muzzle of Pettifer's musket levelled at Killigrew's forehead, the lieutenant's left hand on the barrel while his right hand held the pepperbox an inch from the commander's face. In spite of the cold, a droplet of sweat trickled down the side of Killigrew's head.

Then Pettifer loosened his grip on the musket. The lieutenant pulled it away slowly, and then threw it to Endicott, who caught it deftly. 'Keep him covered, Endicott,' Killigrew jerked his head at the commander.

'Aye, aye, sir.'

'You've done it this time!' snarled Pettifer. 'This time you've gone too far! This is mutiny, damn you! You'll swing for this!'

'No, sir. I'm simply doing what I should have done weeks ago: my duty.'

'Your duty? Since when did the duties of a Royal naval officer include mutiny?'

'It is the duty of the senior executive officer to assume command when his captain is rendered incapable of command by injury or illness,' said Killigrew. 'Mr Strachan?'

'It is my opinion, as medical officer for this vessel, that Commander Pettifer is suffering from acute monomania and as such is a danger to himself and his crew and is unfit for command.'

'As the captain is not currently of sound mind, I hereby assume command of this vessel,' said Killigrew.

'You have no right, Mr Killigrew!' snarled Pettifer, his lips flecked with froth. 'You are in mutiny, d'you hear? In mutiny!'

The lieutenant ignored him. 'Bombardier Osborne?'

The bombardier stepped forward. 'Sir?'

'Who is in command of this vessel?'

'Awaiting your orders, sir.'

'Good. Take the captain down to his cabin and secure him. Make sure there's nothing he can use to effect his release, or to hurt himself – or anyone else, for that matter. Until such time as

281

Mr Strachan is prepared to certify him fit for duty once more, I want him kept under twenty-four-hour guard.'

'Very good, sir! Jenkins, Phillips: you two come with me.'

As the three marines escorted Pettifer below, Killigrew turned to the rest of the crew. 'Unstead, Fischbein: untie Armitage and carry him down to the sick-berth. Endicott, O'Houlihan: remove what's left of Corporal Naylor to the hold. We'll bury him tomorrow – and I pray he's the last.'

'I'd better go tend to Armitage.' Strachan hurried below after Unstead and Fischbein as they carried the cook down the fore hatch.

'What about this one, sir?' asked Ågård, who still held Private Walsh in a full nelson.

Killigrew crossed the deck and looked the marine in the eye from a couple of feet away. 'Are you going to give me any trouble, Private Walsh?'

'No, sir.'

'Good. Let him go, Ågård.' Killigrew turned to Molineaux. 'Are you all right?'

The boatswain's mate grinned. 'Yes, sir. Thank you. If you hadn't come along when you did, I hate to think what might've happened.'

Killigrew shook his head dismissively. 'When I think of the number of times you've saved my life, Molineaux . . . consider that a down payment on what I owe you. Anyhow, if you're going to thank anyone, thank Mr Yelverton. If he hadn't stolen the keys from Latimer's cabin and released Mr Strachan and myself . . .'

Yelverton shrugged. 'I've done just about everything else in my life. I thought, why not try my hand at being a mutineer before I die?'

'You'll see us all into our graves, Giles.'

'Provided he goes straight back to bed, where he belongs, before he freezes to death,' chided Bähr.

'What about the rest of the men, sir?' asked Molineaux. 'Shall I have them dismissed too?'

'Yes,' said Killigrew. 'No! I'll say a few words to them first.' He took a deep breath and addressed them with his hands behind his back.

'Some of you will think that in assuming command I have acted correctly. Some of you will not. Well, I shan't hold that against you: you may be right. But until such time as my actions are vindicated – or condemned, as the case may be – by my inevitable court martial, I require you to obey my orders as loyally and efficiently as if I'd been appointed captain of the *Venturer* by the Admiralty. So if any of you disapprove of my actions, you'd better say so now. You'll spend the rest of this expedition in the lazaretto; if I'm found to be a mutineer, you'll have nothing to worry about; if I'm vindicated, I'll bear no grudge. *But*, if there's anyone here who thinks I've acted improperly, and holds his peace, and later tries to make trouble for me, by God, I'll kick his backside from here to the South Pole and back again. So if you've anything to say, I suggest you say it now.'

'We're behind you all the way, sir,' said Gargrave, and there was a general murmur of approval.

'I'm glad to hear it; and thank you. Now, as I'm sure you can imagine, from now on there will be a few adjustments around here. Firstly, all rations will be returned to their normal portions—'

The men cheered.

'Pipe down!' commanded Killigrew. 'You think that what's happened here today is a cause for celebration? Let me assure you that *I* do not. In the sixteen years I have served in Her Majesty's navy I have seen many terrible things, but I never thought I should have to live to see such a day such as this. And for what has happened here today I must take full responsibility—'

'Not you, sir!' shouted someone. 'That bloody Bedlamite Pettifer!'

'Take that man's name, Mr Sørensen!' ordered Killigrew. 'May I remind you all that this remains one of Her Majesty's ships and I expect you all to comport yourselves like Her Majesty's sailors! There will be no relaxing of discipline, is that understood?'

The men muttered their assent.

'Just because this day has witnessed events which can only be described as . . . *irregular*. . . at best, do not think that anything has changed. I have assumed command. When we return to England – and we *shall* return to England – then there will be those who call us mutineers. I think I have done my duty, and I hope and pray that my opinion will be accepted by my court martial. Whatever happens, I intend to take full responsibility for what has happened here today. All I ask in return is that between now and then you give me your loyalty, and I hope that I may prove worthy of it.' He turned to Sørensen. 'We'll continue with the usual shipboard routine. Have the ratings jog-trot around the upper deck until ten, then out on the ice marching around the ship. Make sure you position armed guards as usual to keep an eye out for bears.'

'Aye, aye, sir.'

'The rest of the officers will convene in the wardroom for a meeting,' Killigrew added. 'That includes you, Dr Bähr.'

Killigrew, Latimer and the doctor made their way down to the wardroom, where they found Ursula. Killigrew quickly told her what had happened. She nodded dumbly, stunned by the news of yet another death on board the *Venturer*.

'Do you want me to leave you to your meeting?' she offered.

Killigrew shook his head. 'I'd be grateful if you'd stay. You've a right to know what's going on – both you and the doctor here – and the truth is that with Cavan dead, the captain confined and Mr Yelverton on the sick list, we're going to need all the help we can get.'

'What do you want me to do?' offered Ursula.

'Paperwork: mostly copying. Boring, I know, but it's how I spend much of my time off watch, and even in winter quarters watch bills and the like need to be made out. By doing so you'll free both myself and Mr Latimer for other duties.'

She nodded. 'Of course. Anything I can do to help.'

Killigrew glanced around the wardroom. 'Where's Strachan?'

'In the sick-berth, tending to the cook,' Bähr reminded him.

The lieutenant nodded. He should not have forgotten that, but so much had changed in the last few minutes, he was having difficulty keeping track of everything. 'All right, we'll proceed without him; I'll speak to him later.' He knew that if there was one officer on board he could depend on, it was the assistant surgeon. 'Firstly, I need to know now if anyone present thinks I acted improperly in relieving the captain of command?'

'If you ask me, you should have acted sooner,' said Bähr. 'But it's always easy to be wise after the event. There's no doubt in my mind: Pettifer's as mad as a hatter, and I'll gladly testify to that fact at your court martial.'

'There will be a court martial?' asked Ursula.

Killigrew nodded. 'Undoubtedly. There's no backing for what I've done in the Queen's Regulations, so technically I'm a mutineer.' He smiled wanly. 'Don't worry, it won't be the first time I've been court-martialled.'

'What was your last court martial for?' asked Bähr.

'Conduct unbecoming an officer and a gentleman.'

'I can believe it! Obviously you were found innocent, though?'

'No, as it happens I was found guilty and dismissed the service. But I was later exonerated and my commission was restored. It's a long story.' He turned back to Ursula. 'You may have to testify, although given your civilian status and the fact you are a woman, you may be exempt. If the court will accept the evidence of Dr Bähr and Mr Strachan – and if Pettifer does not recover sufficiently to employ a doctor of his own to contradict their testimony – then it should be a formality.' Killigrew was not convinced of that, but he saw no point in worrying Ursula unduly about his own problems. 'But first we've got to get back to England.'

'What happens now?' asked Bähr.

'We go on as normal. At least, as normally as possible. Jack Tar likes an orderly life and he needs to know where he stands. The less that changes, the better. We've got more than enough food to see us through the winter. We've just got to stick it until the spring comes, and with it, God willing, the thaw. When it comes, we'll sail back to Beechey Island. If the rest of the squadron made it through the Middle Pack, we should find the *North Star* there: I'll put myself under Commander Pullen's orders. If we don't meet any of the other ships of the squadron, we'll sail back to England.'

'As simple as that?' Bähr asked sceptically.

'As simple as that,' Killigrew told him. 'I'll speak to each of you later to discuss how we're going to divide up our duties, but first I've got to inspect the ship while the hands are all exercising on the upper deck. Latimer, would you run down to the sick-berth and ask Mr Strachan to join me as soon as he's finished tending to Armitage?'

'Aye, aye, sir.' Normally rubicund, Latimer was now as white as a sheet, evidently shaken by the morning's turn of events. Killigrew wondered how dependable the clerk was likely to be over the next few months.

As Latimer headed forward, Killigrew took his leave of Bähr and Ursula and made his way into the captain's quarters to make sure that Osborne, Jenkins and Phillips had secured Pettifer properly. He found Yelverton in the captain's day-room, still wearing a greatcoat over his nightshirt as he rifled Pettifer's bureau. The master had drawn the curtains back from the stern windows, and in the pale light that filtered through the snow-frosted glass he looked even more haggard than he had done on the upper deck earlier.

'I thought Bähr told you to get back to bed?'

'He also told me I needed rest, and I wasn't going to get any of that while I was wondering about the charts and logs.' Yelverton stood up and opened one of the drawers containing charts. The drawer was filled with flakes of paper. Amongst the thousands of flakes in the drawer, not one was more than half-an-inch across.

'What's that?' asked Killigrew, although in his heart he had already guessed. He felt slightly sick.

'The charts,' explained Yelverton. 'The other drawers are all the same. Must've taken him hours to tear them up this finely; days.'

'Including the charts we drew up of Peel Sound?'

'I can't find them anywhere else.'

'All right, so we'll draw fresh charts on the voyage back to Beechey Island.' Killigrew had been hoping to chart the western side of Peel Sound on the return voyage: even if they had not discovered Franklin or the North-West Passage, at least they would be able to say they had made a significant contribution to the Admiralty's charts of the Arctic. But getting the remaining men of the crew safely back to England now seemed more important than any charting.

He stared at the shreds of paper and shook his head slowly. Pettifer must have been doing that for days on end, if not weeks, to have reduced so many charts to so much mulch. 'He must have been more ill than we realised.'

'It gets worse.' Yelverton handed him the ship's log.

Killigrew opened it. The first few dozen pages had been neatly removed, sliced out with a razor by the look of it (he made a mental note to find that razor before the captain used it to cut his bonds or slash his wrists), removing all the entries made up to Saturday 9 October, the day Pettifer had declared the chart-room out of bounds. Nearly every other page left in the log was filled with doodles: a self-portrait of Pettifer being crucified, a woman being violated by a beast with seven heads and ten horns, naked bodies being torn to shreds by a razor-clawed polar bear before being plunged into a lake of fire. Images that would haunt Killigrew for the rest of his life.

'Where are the rest of the pages? The pages he cut out?'

'I was just looking for them when you came in,' said Yelverton. 'I can't find them anywhere. My guess is you'll find them mixed up with what's left of the charts.'

There was a knock at the door. 'Come in,' Killigrew called absently, turning another page in the log to survey the doodles on the next page with horror.

Strachan entered. 'You sent for me?'

Killigrew glanced up at him, and handed him the log. 'What do you make of this?'

The assistant surgeon leafed through the pages in silence, his lips pursed thoughtfully. 'Rather derivative of the work of William Blake,' he concluded. 'But the influence of Hieronymus Bosch is definitely at work here. Impressive shading, though: the way he uses hatching to give an impression of depth and perspective—'

'Never mind the artistic appraisal,' scowled Yelverton. 'What does it tell us about Pettifer's state of mind?'

'Nothing we didn't already know: he's a certifiable lunatic.' Strachan handed the log back to Killigrew. 'I suggest you take care of this, sir. This is all the evidence you'll ever need of Pettifer's insanity when it comes to that court martial. But then, I've always had my doubts about Blake and Bosch.'

'They say there's a fine line between genius and insanity,' mused Killigrew.

'It's not a fine line. It's an overlap.' Strachan noticed the shredded paper in the open drawer. 'What's that?'

'Our charts,' Yelverton said heavily.

'All of them?'

The master opened two more drawers, revealing more of the same. 'All of them.'

'We . . . we *can* find our way back, can't we?'

'Shouldn't be too difficult,' said Killigrew. 'North, straight back up Peel Sound to Barrow Strait; north-east by east to Beechey Island, then east down Lancaster Sound to Baffin Bay and the Middle Pack. We can borrow charts at Lively, copy them if we have to.'

'From Peel Sound to Disko Island from memory,' sighed Yelverton. 'He makes it sound so easy.'

'We'll manage,' Killigrew said with more conviction than he felt. 'Besides, I'll lay odds the *North Star* is waiting for us at Beechey Island. We found our way here; we can find our way back.'

The door from Pettifer's cabin opened and Osborne, Jenkins and Phillips emerged. 'We've secured the captain, sir,' reported the bombardier.

'Thank you, Osborne,' said Killigrew. 'How is he?'

'He struggled at first, but he quietened down when he saw there was no point in fighting against the three of us. He's a lot calmer now, sir.'

'Good. You may go, Bombardier. You too, Phillips: we'll need you on guard when the men go on to the ice for their exercise at ten. Not you, Jenkins: you can have first watch over the captain.'

'Very good, sir.'

As Osborne and Phillips left the captain's quarters, Killigrew and Strachan looked into the cabin to check on Pettifer, trussed like a turkey to the bunk. He stared up at them with contempt.

'I'm truly sorry about this, sir,' said Killigrew. 'But it's for your own good.'

'I know who you are, Lieutenant.'

'Of course you do, sir.'

'Mutineers!' spat the captain.

'That will be for a court martial to decide when we get back to England, sir,' said Strachan.

Pettifer shook his head. 'Court martial? You blind fool! There isn't going to be any court martial! You know he's going to get you all killed, don't you? I see it now: the scales have fallen from mine eyes. He's in league with the beast.'

'The polar bear, sir?'

'It's no ordinary beast, Mr Strachan. Don't you see? It is *the* beast: and Mr Killigrew here is its hellish spawn. He's the Anti-Christ! "And they worshipped the dragon which gave power unto the beast: and they worshipped the beast, saying, Who is like unto the beast? Who is able to make war with him?"'

Strachan touched Killigrew on the sleeve. 'We'd better leave him. I don't think we're going to get any sense out of him.'

The lieutenant nodded and closed the cabin door behind them.

Pettifer screamed after them: 'You're all going to *die*!'

Killigrew could not help thinking it was the most sensible thing Pettifer had said all month.

XVI

Ambush

Killigrew lay in his bunk and listened to the wind howling
outside. Like all the outlying parts of the ship, his cabin was
freezing in spite of the hot-water pipe running through it. For
once the hands were better off than the officers: the mess deck,
which adjoined the galley, was one of the warmest parts of the
ship.

He watched the breath billow from his mouth in the moonlight that shone through the porthole and listened to the dogs
barking. They needed more exercise: since the bear had killed
Ziegler, letting McLellan take them beyond the perimeter rope
to stretch their legs had clearly been out of the question.
Tomorrow he would take them on an expedition away from the
ship, with a party of seamen and marines. Perhaps they might
yet find some trace of the Franklin expedition.

He heard something crunching through the snow outside:
heavy footsteps, and a snuffling noise. Colder than ever, he sat
up and rubbed at the condensation frozen on the porthole, but he
could see nothing in the darkness beyond.

He tried to go back to sleep. The dogs barked for a while
longer, and then fell silent. Just when he was about to nod off a
sound in the passageway outside roused him: a creaking deck
board.

Suddenly he was wide awake. The snuffling noise had
returned, but now it was inside the ship, in the wardroom, *right
outside his cabin*.

291

His heart pounded as he leaned over the side of his bunk to ease open one of the drawers below. He located the mahogany case by touch, opened the clasp, and fumbled inside until he felt the familiar, reassuring grip of one of his pepperboxes.

He eased himself out from under the bedclothes – he had gone to bed dressed in a guernsey and an old pair of trousers – and tiptoed across the deck to the door. The snuffling immediately outside the door continued until one of the deck boards groaned beneath his foot.

The snuffling sound stopped abruptly.

Everything was silent: the preternatural silence of drawn breath. He took another step, placed his left hand on the doorknob, and levelled the pepperbox. Then he jerked the door open.

The polar bear was too fast for him. Rearing on its hind legs, it swiped the pepperbox aside effortlessly and slashed its claws at his face.

Killigrew sat up sharply. He was still in his bunk, panting for breath. He examined his body for claw-marks: it took him a while to realise it had just been a nightmare.

He looked through the porthole, but all was dark outside. Still night, he told himself. He was just about to go back to sleep again when he heard something creaking about in the passage outside.

With a distinct feeling of *déjà vu*, he took one of the pepperboxes from the drawer beneath his bunk and climbed out of the bunk. There was definitely someone or something moving about out there. Trembling with cold and fright, he laid one hand on the doorknob and jerked the door open to reveal . . .

. . . Private Jenkins standing there with a mug of coffee in one hand, the other poised to knock on the door that was already open. There was a mildly surprised look on his face when he saw Killigrew standing there in his stocking feet, hair tousled, brandishing a revolver.

'Jenkins,' said Killigrew, and straightened. 'What the devil are you doing creeping about in the middle of the night?'

'I brought you your coffee, sir. 'Tain't the middle of the night, sir, begging your pardon, but two bells in the morning watch.'

Killigrew put down the pepperbox and took the mug of

292

coffee. He was still struggling to adjust to the rapidly shortening days. 'Sorry. Thought you were a polar bear.'

Jenkins grinned. 'Easy mistake to make, sir.'

The marine left him to perform his morning ablutions in private. Killigrew got dressed and joined the other officers in the wardroom for breakfast.

It was mid-November, nearly two weeks since Killigrew had assumed command of the *Venturer*, and the crew's life had returned to a semblance of normality, if life in the Arctic could be described as 'normal' for anyone other than an Inuk. A layer of glistening rime touched surfaces everywhere except in the warmest parts of the ship, and the men would wake up to find a patch of ice on their pillows where their breath had condensed and frozen. Killigrew had given them permission to grow beards – preferring to remain clean shaven himself – and the men had cultivated their face-fungus enthusiastically, so that many of them already looked like Bohemian writers and poets.

They spent so much time below decks their faces were almost permanently tinged with soot from the lamps on board, even now that Kracht had converted the whale oil lamps to take burning fluid. Getting a proper wash was next to impossible, because although fresh-water ice was available in abundance, they could not afford to be profligate with the fuel needed to melt it down, and the sea water they used instead – hoisted in buckets from the fire hole – was too briny to get up a good lather.

With less than eight weeks until Christmas, Latimer had begun to audition the crew for their Christmas Eve concert party. With only thirty men and one woman left on board the *Venturer*, there would probably be more people taking part in the play than there were in the audience, but rehearsals, costume-making and scenery building and painting would give the men something to keep them occupied during the long weeks ahead.

After breakfast, Killigrew made his way up on deck, bundled in his warm clothes, and slipped out from under the awning, making his way down the slippery gangplank with care. It was still dark out, although the first traces of dawn silhouetted the pressure ridge to the north-east; the sun would not rise until after half-past nine. The men patrolling the perimeter rope now had a husky each on the end of a makeshift leash. Terregannoeuck had told them that huskies and polar bears were natural enemies: even if the sentries did not see the white bear against the snow, there was a good chance that the dogs would scent it and bark a warning. But the huskies did not make ideal watchdogs. Bred for sledge-pulling rather than guard duties, they accompanied the sentries reluctantly, nipping at their heels and raising false alarms by barking at anything that moved. A couple of days earlier Hughes had been dragged thirty feet across the ice, gamely refusing to relinquish his grip on his dog's leash, when the animal had spied an Arctic hare.

In the observatory, Killigrew found Strachan taking some readings from one of his magnetometers. A kettle was boiling on the stove. 'Cup of tea?' offered the assistant surgeon.

Unwinding his comforter, Killigrew shook his head.

Strachan shrugged, and poured some water into his teapot. 'How is everything?'

Killigrew removed his sealskin cap to run his fingers through his thick, black hair. Strachan was the one person on board he felt he could unburden his soul to after weeks of putting on a brave face for the rest of the crew. 'Two months ago the only thing I was worried about was whether or not anyone on the *Erebus* and *Terror* would still be alive by the time we found them.' He sighed. 'Now I'm starting to wonder how many of us will still be alive when – *if* the *Venturer* ever makes it back to England. Just between you and me, I never worried about having to spend even one winter in the ice, I was so convinced we could find the Franklin expedition and sail on through the North-West Passage to the Pacific Ocean in one season.'

'You've always got to push yourself, haven't you? Everything in life has got to be a challenge, otherwise you're not interested. And for each challenge you meet successfully, you've got to follow it up with something even more dangerous or gruelling. Why do you find it so difficult to follow the line of least resistance?'

'The thing about the line of least resistance is that it always leads downhill.' Killigrew sighed. 'When I volunteered for the Franklin Expedition, it was because I didn't know any better. I was twenty years old, I'd just been promoted to mate after

Chinkiang-fu. I thought I could conquer the world.'

'And how old are you now?'

'Twenty-eight.' He shrugged. 'Ever since it became apparent the Franklin Expedition wasn't coming back, I've had this doubt gnawing at my soul: what would have happened to me if I'd been on that expedition? Could I have survived?'

'No, you'd have died, just as the rest of them almost certainly have. Or do you suppose that your presence on that expedition would have made all the difference, that you could have led them all back to civilisation and safety where Franklin, Crozier and Fitzjames all failed?'

'No, of course not. But I needed to *know*.'

'So you volunteered for this expedition to prove to yourself you would have died with Franklin and his men if you'd gone with them?'

'In a way, I suppose.'

'No wonder you were reluctant to do anything about Pettifer. You must wonder if you're as insane as he is.'

'Do *you* think I'm insane?'

'I volunteered for this expedition too, remember. I prefer to think of us as "charmingly eccentric".'

Killigrew managed a chuckle. 'You realise you're spending far too much time in here, don't you?'

'What makes you say that? I've got everything I need in here.'

'You'll end up like Pettifer if you're not careful.'

'God forbid.'

'A curious sentiment, for an atheist.'

'Figure of speech. Can I help it if I was brought up in a religious household?'

'If you're going to spend much time out here on your own, I'd feel a lot happier if you had a firearm with you.'

'Thank you, but you know me. Can't abide guns.'

'My dear Strachan, I absolutely insist. I'll have you issued with a shotgun from the spirit room. Just be sure you only point it at polar bears.'

'Is that what you're worried about? This observatory is inside the perimeter: if that polar bear does come back, it's got to get past the patrols. And if it's as big as O'Houlihan claims it is . . . which I very much doubt—'

'O'Houlihan's not prone to exaggeration.'

'– then it couldn't fit through that doorway anyhow. I think I'm safe enough in here.'

'You saw how much damage was done on the *Jan Snekker* by scavenging bears. If this one *is* as big as O'Houlihan says, I don't think it would need to fit through the door: it could just tear down this whole shed around your ears.'

Strachan grimaced. 'That's a comforting thought.'

They heard the ship's bell clang once on the *Venturer*. 'Let's go back on board, shall we?' suggested Killigrew. 'I've got work to do; and you've got sick parade.'

They left the observatory. A light snow was falling, a few flat flakes floating down from the sky. Some of the men patrolling the perimeter rope had lit their bull's-eyes and were playing the beams across the ice-scape beyond, keeping a sharp lookout for polar bears. Both Ziegler and Thwaites had been killed in broad daylight, but the men had not forgotten that the first attack had taken place at night: the bear could return at any hour.

'Using so many bull's-eyes must be eating into our supply of candles,' Killigrew said dubiously.

'Yes, we had quite a debate about that while you were a prisoner in the lazaretto,' admitted Strachan. 'Latimer said we hadn't allowed for so many candles to be used and we're in danger of running out before the spring. And Bähr says that polar bears are incorrigibly curious and might actually be drawn by the lights. Then Osborne pointed out that our chances of persuading any of the men to stand guard without some kind of illumination – when there's a polar bear with a taste for human flesh on the prowl – are non-existent.'

'Let's just hope that Bruin shows up quickly and we get him, while there are still some candles left.'

As they approached the gangplank, two figures emerged from under the awning and descended the gangplank, one of them carrying an ice-axe. The four of them met at the bottom of the gangplank, where Killigrew recognised the two newcomers as Molineaux and O'Houlihan. 'What are you two up to?' Killigrew asked them as they saluted.

'You ordered me to keep the fire hole open, sir,' O'Houlihan reminded him, gesturing with the ice-axe.

'So I did. Carry on, O'Houlihan. What about you, Molineaux? Does it take two of you to do it?'

'I'm here to drag him out if he falls in, sir.'

'The ice is getting thicker, sir,' explained O'Houlihan. 'I'm having to lean further down into the hole to break it up. If I slip and fall in, well . . . maybe I could pull myself out. But if I got cramp . . .'

'You're right, of course,' Strachan told them both. 'You'd freeze to death in minutes in that water.'

Molineaux glanced at the snowflakes settling on his coat. 'It's starting to snow,' he remarked. 'Rum, ain't it, sir? I thought it'd snow more than it has done, here in the Arctic. Or are the blizzards still to come?'

'We might get a few blizzards come winter,' said Strachan. 'But it doesn't snow much in the Arctic as a rule. It's too cold for precipitation.'

'Precipi-what-tion?' asked O'Houlihan.

'Precipitation,' said Molineaux, adding: 'he means wet stuff falling out of the sky: rain, snow, hail.'

'Ah. Rum stuff, snow, so it is. I never understood it. I mean, when water gets cold, it freezes and turns to ice. That much I can understand. Hail I have no difficulty with. But snow? Now what the divil is all that about?'

'It has to do with the crystalline structure of the ice,' explained Strachan. 'You know they say that no two snowflakes are ever the same?'

'Is that right, sir?' asked O'Houlihan, kneeling at the edge of the fire hole to smash the skin of ice that had formed with the axe. 'How do they know?'

'What?'

'How do they know no two snowflakes are the same? All snowflakes have six points. How many different snowflake shapes can there be?'

Strachan smiled. 'I think you'd be surprised.'

'I think I would, sir! I mean, they couldn't check them all, could they? How do they know there's not a snowflake here in the Arctic which isn't the spitting image of one that settled in the Alps a hundred years ago?'

'Watch yourself, O'Houlihan,' warned Killigrew.

The seaman was leaning out over the fire hole to pick out the larger shards of the ice he smashed. 'It's all right, sir. I know what I'm after. If you think about all the snowflakes that fall in the polar regions, and on the mountains of the world, and in winter, year after year . . . there must be tens of thousand of snowflakes, right? Thousands of thousands of thousands of them. Are you going to tell me someone's been around all the snowy parts of the world and studied every single snowflake under a microscope?'

'There's a very scientific explanation for the phenomenon,' Strachan said loftily. 'I wouldn't want to confuse you with technical terms.'

'He doesn't know,' O'Houlihan said scathingly.

Molineaux nodded in agreement. 'If you ask me—'

The rest of the sentence was drowned out by a burst of spray from the fire hole. Killigrew caught a glimpse of something white and wedge-shaped emerging from the hole, but by the time he turned to look at it all he could see was O'Houlihan's feet disappearing into the water.

He blinked, not sure what he had seen, unable to believe it. One moment O'Houlihan had been kneeling by the side of the hole, the next he was gone, leaving no trace of his presence but the foamy black water sloshing about in the deep square cut in the ice.

'Faiks!' exclaimed Strachan, wide-eyed. 'Did you see that . . .?'

Molineaux swore and ran towards the hole, tearing off his mittens, unwinding his muffler and fumbling with the buttons of his coat. 'Mick!'

Still dazed by O'Houlihan's abrupt disappearance, it took Killigrew a moment to realise what the petty officer intended.

'*No!*'

Molineaux dived head-first into the fire hole, cleaving the water like a knife and disappearing after O'Houlihan.

Killigrew ran to the lip of the hole and started to tear at his own thick clothes, until Strachan grabbed him. 'Forget it, Killigrew! They're both dead.'

The lieutenant shook his head, unwilling to believe it. He had sailed with Molineaux and O'Houlihan on his last voyage, and had lost count of the number of time the black seaman had saved his life. Molineaux was so dependable – whenever things became crazy, you could always rely on him to be the voice of reason – it was impossible to believe that both he and O'Houlihan were gone together, just like that.

'There's nothing you can do,' Strachan told him.

'The devil there isn't!' Killigrew turned to the men patrolling the perimeter rope. 'You men!' he shouted. 'Bring those lights! Come on, chop chop, look lively there!'

The four nearest men ran across with their bull's-eyes bobbing. 'Which way does the wind lie?' asked one, so heavily muffled he was only recognisable as McLellan by his Orcadian accent.

'O'Houlihan . . .' said Strachan. 'He was there one minute, the next . . . the bear just came up out of the water, grabbed him by the arm and dragged him under.' It sounded as though the assistant surgeon did not believe it himself. 'Molineaux jumped in after him.'

'Jesus!' said one of the other men.

'Don't just stand there blethering!' said Killigrew. 'Point the beams into the water!'

The beams of the bull's-eyes focused on the black-looking water, which by now had ceased to ripple, but the lights did not penetrate deep.

'Can't see a thing,' grumbled Private Walsh.

'How long could a cove stay alive down there, sir?' asked Phillips.

Strachan merely shrugged, although he was probably thinking the same thing as Killigrew: one, maybe two minutes at the most, if he could hold his breath that long, and if the shock of the freezing water did not paralyse his limbs with cramp.

'They've had it,' said Hughes.

No one seemed inclined to agree or disagree. The six of them remained motionless, staring down into that black hole. Apart from Hughes, none of them wanted to be the first to suggest they were wasting their time.

A shape burst up out of the water without warning, and all six of them took a step back in alarm, fearing it might be the bear returning. But it was only Molineaux, clawing feebly at the ice at the edge of the hole, too busy gasping air into his lungs to ask for help. Killigrew grabbed one of his arms. 'Help me pull him up, Walsh!'

They dragged Molineaux up on to the ice and the petty officer lay there, coughing and spluttering. 'Couldn't see a thing, sir,' he mumbled between chattering teeth. 'It's black as the Earl of Hell's weskit down there.'

'Get him on board and below, quickly!' urged Strachan. 'Strip off his wet clothes and put him by the stove in the galley. Hot, sweet tea, and lots of it, gentlemen.'

'Hughes! McLellan! You heard Mr Strachan!' ordered Killigrew. 'The rest of you resume your patrolling.'

'What about Mick O'Houlihan?' asked McLellan.

'O'Houlihan's dead, McLellan.' Killigrew spoke wearily, his lips speaking the inescapable truth even while his brain was still too numbed with shock to accept it.

Walsh and Phillips returned to the perimeter rope, while Killigrew and Strachan followed Hughes and McLellan as they helped the shivering, sopping-wet Molineaux up the gangplank. Within a couple of minutes Molineaux sat by the stove in the warmth of the galley, his hands cupped around a steaming mug of hot chocolate, a dry blanket wrapped over his shoulders while McLellan rousted out some dry clothes from his locker. The men on the lower deck crowded around the doorway to the galley, until Killigrew chased them away, forcing them to get a garbled version of events from Hughes.

'You bloody fool!' Killigrew told Molineaux. 'Were you trying to get yourself killed? It's bad enough to lose one man; why throw your life away after his?'

In spite of his chattering teeth, Molineaux was able to lift his head and meet Killigrew's gaze steadily. 'Because he would have done the same for me, sir.'

The lieutenant forced himself to get a grip. Of course O'Houlihan would have done the same for Molineaux; just as he himself had been prepared to do for the pair of them, until Strachan had stopped him.

'You don't think it was the same bear that killed the others, do you?' he asked Strachan.

'I don't suppose we'll ever know for sure.'

'It was the same bear,' said Molineaux. His tone would admit no question of doubt. 'It killed Mr Cavan, Herr Ziegler, Mr Thwaites, and now it's got Mick O'Houlihan.' He banged his fist against the bulkhead in frustration. 'I want that bear, sir. I'll rip its guts out with my bare hands if I have to!'

'You might just get your chance,' Killigrew told him, and turned to Strachan. 'Is he going to be all right?'

'I think so. How are you feeling, Molineaux?'

'Waxy as hell, sir.'

'I mean, is the warmth returning?'

'Returning? Sir, my blood's boiling!'

'I think he'll live,' said Strachan.

Killigrew slipped out of the galley and was heading aft when Bähr and Latimer stopped him in the middle of the mess deck. 'Is it true?' asked the clerk. 'Has the bear attacked again?'

'There's been a bear attack,' admitted Killigrew. 'We don't know it was the same bear that killed the others.'

'Same bear.' Terregannoeuck sat cross-legged on one of the seat-lockers nearby with his back to the side.

Killigrew shot him a glance of annoyance – the Inuk's attempts to instil the bear with an aura of mysticism were not helping morale on the lower deck – before turning back to Bähr and Latimer. 'O'Houlihan was breaking up the ice in the fire hole when the bear surfaced below him, grabbed him by the arm and dragged him under. One moment he was there, the next . . .' Killigrew shook his head helplessly.

'I didn't know polar bears could swim,' said Latimer.

Bähr regarded him with bemusement. 'Why do you think it's called *Ursus maritimus*?'

Killigrew turned to Ågård, who stood nearby. 'Did you ever see a polar bear attack its prey that way?'

The ice quartermaster frowned. 'I once saw a bear leap out of the water to kill a seal sunning itself at the edge of an ice-floe,' he admitted. 'But I never heard of them swimming under the ice.'

'It must've held its breath a long time,' said Killigrew. 'There's no open water within miles of here.'

'When I am boy, hunting *puyee* with my father, I see hole in ice, with *nanuq*'s tracks leading to it, but no tracks lead away,' said the Inuk. 'We wait for *nanuq* to return, that we may kill it, but *nanuq* not return. Terregannoeuck go now. Must ask Nuliayuq what must do to end Kokogiaq's anger.' He abruptly sprang from the seat-locker and strode to the companion ladder.

Killigrew followed him to the upper deck. 'Who's Nuliayuq?' he asked.

Terregannoeuck did not seem to hear him. He brushed past the astonished marine on sentry duty at the entry port and slipped out from under the awning. Killigrew followed him out in time to see the Inuk step under the perimeter rope and disappear into the half-light.

'Think he's coming back, sir?' a voice asked in Killigrew's ear, startling him. It was Ågård.

'I don't know,' Killigrew said wearily. 'Not if he's got any sense. And if we had any sense, we wouldn't be standing here without overcoats, comforters, mittens and caps. Let's get back inside and seal up the flaps before we let all the warm air out.'

'Will there be a funeral for Mick O'Houlihan?'

'There's nothing left of him to bury,' Killigrew said bitterly. 'But I expect we'll have some kind of service in the morning to mark his passing. I'll leave it to you to auction off his effects. And you'll need to detail someone to take over O'Houlihan's duties at the fire hole.'

'How about Able Seaman Hughes, sir?'

'Hughes it is. Tell him to use a boat-hook instead of an ice-axe. A long one.'

Killigrew pulled himself back up the gangplank, using the hand-ropes to give him purchase against the icy incline, and made his way below. In the wardroom, he poured himself a measure of Irish whiskey with trembling hands and downed it in one.

The door opened. Ursula slipped in and closed the door behind her. 'Are you all right?'

'No, ma'am. I'm not all right. A polar bear is picking us off one by one, and there's not a damned thing I can do to stop it.' He shook his head in disbelief. 'It's eighteen fifty-two. Man can build a bridge over the Menai Strait, send a telegraph message across Europe in the blink of an eye, and navigate to the furthest reaches of the globe using steam power. But try to kill one dumb animal, with all the resources of one of Her Majesty's most up-to-date and well-equipped exploring vessels at our disposal?' He shook his head.

'It's been lucky, that's all. And you've been unlucky. Next time it comes, you'll shoot it and kill it, and that will be the end of the matter.'

'That's what we said last time, when we appointed guards to patrol the perimeter boundary. And all it had to do was swim under the ice and drag O'Houlihan through the fire hole. It's been one step ahead of us all the time. I'm starting to think Terregannoeuck was right: this is no ordinary bear . . .'

'Then think again.' Strachan came through the door behind him. 'It's not some supernatural beast seeking vengeance for the murder of the cubs that Bähr killed: it's just a dumb animal obeying its natural instincts. It's hungry, Killigrew, that's all: and I can prove it.'

'What do you mean?'

'It's a question of dates.'

'Dates?'

'Look at the calendar. The first attack was on the second of October, when Cavan was killed while taking Horatia for a walk. Ziegler was killed on the seventeenth, fifteen days later; the bosun on the thirtieth, thirteen days after Ziegler; and now O'Houlihan, exactly two weeks after the bosun.'

Killigrew pinched the bridge of his nose between forefinger and thumb. 'Is there a point to any of this, Strachan?'

'Two points. If the bear were seeking to avenge the death of the cubs by killing us all one by one, why wait between attacks? Why not just attack a couple of days later?'

'You tell me, Strachan.'

'Because it isn't hungry a couple of days after each attack. A human being gives it a feast sufficient to keep the hunger pangs at bay for two weeks. Then, when the two weeks are past, its stomach starts rumbling and it comes back to where it knows it can find a plentiful supply of food.'

Killigrew nodded thoughtfully. 'That makes sense. But I fail to see how it helps us.'

'Which brings me to my second point. Fifteen days between

the first and second attacks; thirteen between the second and third; and fourteen between the third and fourth. It's like I always say: there are patterns in nature. You've just got to study any natural phenomenon long enough for those patterns to emerge. Don't you see, Killigrew? *We can predict when the next attack will take place.* To within a couple of days, at least: that's better than nothing. Today's the thirteenth; if my hypothesis is correct, we can expect the next attack to take place between the twenty-sixth and twenty-eighth of this month.'

'And this time we'll be ready for it.' Killigrew's earlier sense of doom was dispelled by Strachan's confidence. 'If our friend Bruin thinks he can get the better of Jack Tar, he's got another think coming.'

Ursula was about to curl up in her bunk with the book she had been reading when she realised she had left it in the wardroom. She pulled a greatcoat over the pusser's slops she was wearing – guernsey and trousers – but the wardroom tended to be warmer than the surrounding cabins that insulated it.

She was surprised to find the light still on, even though it was after nine o'clock and 'ship's company's fire and lights out' had been piped more than an hour ago. She knocked hesitantly on the door.

'Come in?'

She recognised Killigrew's voice and opened the door. He was sitting at the table, poring over a ledger with a cheroot in one hand and a glass of Irish whiskey close by his elbow. He stood up as she entered. 'Good evening, Frau Weiss.'

'Good evening. I, er ... I forgot my book.' She started to move to fetch it from where she had left it on the sideboard, but he got there first. Picking it up, he glanced at the spine before handing it to her. 'Mary Shelley's *Frankenstein*? I'd've thought we had enough nightmares to deal with.'

'It seemed appropriate. I've always wanted to read it: part of it is set in the Arctic.'

Killigrew nodded. 'The explorer whose quest to reach the North Pole parallels Frankenstein's ill-fated hunger for scientific discovery. Appropriate indeed!'

She glanced at the sheaf of papers on the table: handwritten notes in the pedantic scrawl of a man who had learned to write late in life. 'What are you reading?'

He grimaced. 'More nightmares. The log of the *Jan Snekker*, the whaler we found trapped in the ice back in August.'

'Does it make interesting reading?'

'Well, either the master of the *Jan Snekker* wasn't much of a prose stylist, or his writings have lost something in the translation. But the story's gripping enough to make up for that. It's just a pity it ends rather abruptly shortly after a fourth member of the crew is killed by a polar bear.'

'It happened to them, too?'

'Apparently.'

She shook her head in disbelief. 'For nine years I have been coming to the Arctic, taking tea with the wives of other whaling captains and swapping stories. But never have I heard of a polar bear doing anything like this. And you say it's happened before? You do not suppose it could be the same bear?'

'I don't know what to think.'

'Have you spoken to Terregannoeuck about this? As an Esquimau, he must know even more about polar bears than Herr Strachan.'

'Terregannoeuck is of the opinion that the bear is a ten-legged spirit-monster out to avenge the murder of the sow and the two cubs killed by Molineaux and Bähr. I find that kind of advice less than helpful. Anyhow, Terregannoeuck's gone.'

'Gone?'

Killigrew nodded. 'Just walked off the ship and disappeared into the night shortly after O'Houlihan was killed. We haven't seen him since.'

'Like a rat deserting a sinking ship.'

'Rats are many things, Frau Weiss. Foolish is not one of them.'

'What have you got for me?' asked Killigrew.

'This, sir.' Bombardier Osborne held out the harpoon-gun, which had evidently undergone some modifications since Molineaux had found it on the *Jan Snekker*. 'It was Molineaux's idea. He says he saw something like it when he was with you in the South Seas a couple of years ago?'

'You remember, sir?' prompted Molineaux. 'That bomb-gun they had on board the *Lucy Ann*, for killing whales?'

'I'm not likely to forget!' Killigrew said with some feeling.

'The way I see it, if a gun like that could kill a whale . . . well, Bruin's not going to stand a chance, is he?'

'Kracht did all the work,' said Osborne.

'According to Herr Osborne's design,' Kracht said modestly.

The four of them stood on the ice, just outside the perimeter rope. Close by, Privates Walsh and Jenkins were keeping a sharp lookout for the bear, with huskies snapping at their heels. It was the twenty-fifth of November, and they could expect the bear to return any day now. It was five minutes to noon, only the upper half of the sun showing over the horizon, and it would sink out of sight again as many minutes after noon, not to be seen again until mid-January, if Yelverton's calculations were correct; and they usually were.

'How does it work?' asked Killigrew.

'The tail of the projectile fits into the barrel of the harpoon-gun, thus.' Osborne demonstrated. 'This tube is packed with gunpowder, the nose pointed to penetrate the bear's hide. As it does so, these two toggles on either side of the projectile catch against the sides of the wound and are rammed back against a mercury percussion cap contained within the tube. That sets off the powder charge and . . . boom! Goodbye, Bruin.'

'Have you tried it yet?'

'Not yet, sir.' Osborne nodded to where Stokers Butterwick and Gargrave had built a snowman about fifty feet away. The snowman seemed to bear a striking resemblance to Varrow, but perhaps that was only Killigrew's imagination: the stocky, neck-less engineer bore a striking resemblance to a snowman, now that he thought about it. 'With your permission, sir . . . ?'

'Fire when you're ready, Osborne.'

The bombardier raised the gun to his shoulder and took aim. Molineaux and Kracht stepped back hurriedly, in case the weapon exploded in Osborne's hands.

'Lean into it, Osborne,' warned Molineaux. 'I'll bet that thing's recoil has got a kick like a mule.'

Osborne pulled the trigger. There was a loud bang and the gun bucked in his hands, but not before the projectile had been sent

306

shrieking through the air. It plunged into the snowman's belly and there was a bright flash, dazzling in the gloom of the Arctic noon, a loud crack, and the four of them hurriedly turned away as sludge and ice spicules came flying back in their faces. When they looked again, there was nothing left of the snowman but a smoking crater in the ice.

Osborne smirked. 'As I said: goodbye, Bruin.'

'He's close, sir,' said Ågård.

'You can see him?' Killigrew did not take his eyes off the snowy landscape beneath the pink sky of the sunless noon.

The ice quartermaster shook his head. 'I feel him.'

Killigrew did not like it when Ågård spoke that way, as if the bear was some kind of mystical presence that could only be beaten by supernatural means. Crouched with Ågård and Jenkins inside a covert made from blocks of ice, igloo-style, he clutched his rifled musket and stared down to where a bunch of salted herrings, suspended from a tripod of iron pylons, roasted over a fire. The herrings had been Bähr's idea, a sure-fire way to catch a polar bear's attention, according to one of the books he had read in the ship's library.

Buried deep in the ice beneath the fire – deep enough for the heat from the flames not to set it off, according to Osborne – was a canister of gunpowder. Under a thin layer of snow, wires ran from the canister to where the bombardier crouched over the galvanic battery in another covert. Killigrew was convinced that the twenty-pound charge was excessive: the ice had grown so thick there was no danger of cracking it, yet four or even two pounds would have done the job just as well. But after losing four men to the bear, he wanted to make sure of it.

If the booby-trapped herring-pyre was the centre of a clock, then Killigrew's covert was at three o'clock and Osborne's was at noon. Bähr crouched next to the bombardier in the other covert: disdaining the makeshift bomb-gun held by Private Jenkins as newfangled, he had his double-barrelled shotgun. Between the bomb-gun, Bähr's shotgun, Killigrew's rifle and the gunpowder charge, the lieutenant had initially been confident that Bruin's next visit to the *Venturer* would be his last.

It had seemed like a good plan when he had first come up

with it. Ågård had never been especially enthusiastic about it, although he had grudgingly allowed it might work. Certainly no one had been able to come up with a better idea. After three days of freezing to death on the ice alternately with Jenkins and Phillips, Killigrew was starting to think the only thing he was going to catch was a nasty case of frostbite.

'Then where the devil is it?' he demanded irritably.

'Not far off,' said Ågård.

'You couldn't be more specific, could you?' Killigrew cast his eyes over the scene once more, squinting through the deteriorating conditions. A thick mist was drifting over the ice. He could barely see the covert where Osborne and Bähr were concealed; in a few more minutes even the fire itself would be invisible. Killigrew did not like it. The failing visibility meant there was too great a risk that he and Bähr would end up shooting at one another instead of the bear.

He heard footsteps crunching on the snow and twisted his head in time to see Phillips approaching. 'Reporting for duty, sir.'

Killigrew stood up and handed the private the rifle. 'Be on your guard, Phillips,' he said sardonically. 'Ågård says the polar bear is close. He "feels" it.'

Phillips grinned. 'I'll be sure to keep an eye out for it, sir.' He checked the rifle and huddled down next to Jenkins.

'Dinner will soon be ready, Ågård. Coming?'

'Ask the cook to keep a share warm for me, sir. I think I'll stay out here a while longer.'

Killigrew shrugged and set off back towards the long, low shape of the *Venturer*, now hidden by the thick, swirling mist that came down from the north. As the coverts were swallowed up by the fog behind him, the observatory loomed out of the murk, a light shining behind the door, and beyond it the long, low shape of the snow-cocooned *Venturer* with lights glimmering behind the frost-rimed portholes. Commander Pettifer's voice drifted from his cabin on the starboard side. They let him out once a day for two hours each morning, while two men were appointed to watch over him with muskets, but the rest of the time he was secured in his cabin.

' "Behold, he cometh with clouds"!' Pettifer recited now, his booming voice scarcely muffled by the thick snow heaped against the *Venturer*'s side. ' "And every eye shall see him, and they also which pierced him: and all kindreds of the earth shall wail because of him. Even so, Amen. I am Alpha and Omega, the beginning and the ending, saith the Lord, which is, and which was, and which is to come, the Almighty".'

The huskies – all locked in their kennels on board the *Venturer*, so they would not frighten the bear off – started to bark frenziedly, presumably upset by the deranged tone of Pettifer's ravings. The captain's continual ranting was starting to get Killigrew down as well. He wondered what sort of an effect it was having on the rest of the crew. Morale had risen briefly since he had assumed command, but he did not fool himself that was permanent. Even he could not alter the main cause of the crew's discontent, the lack of sunshine and the increasingly cold weather.

Killigrew knocked on the door of the observatory. 'Come in!' called Strachan.

After two hours on the ice, it felt swelteringly hot inside the observatory and Killigrew quickly removed his sealskin cap, unwound his comforter and unbuttoned his greatcoat. Strachan was reading the ship's log while Able Seaman McLellan kept an eye on his experiments for him. Killigrew was pleased to see a couple of muskets propped up in one corner, just in case.

'McLellan, would you be so good as to go aboard the *Venturer* and ask Private Walsh to see what he can do to keep the captain quiet? He may gag him, if necessary, but no violence.'

'Aye, aye, sir.' The Orcadian stood up and put on his muffler and greatcoat.

'And then see if you can get those dogs to pipe down. They'll scare our friend Bruin away from the trap.'

'Yes, sir.' McLellan turned up his collar and went out, closing the door behind him.

Strachan glanced up at Killigrew. 'You look awful. When did you last get any sleep?'

'I had a good long snooze yesterday afternoon,' Killigrew said absently.

'A good snooze isn't enough, Killigrew. You need eight hours.

You're pushing yourself too hard. I know you like to think you've got reserves of strength above and beyond the rest of us but – damn it! – you're only human. And these aren't normal conditions. You need all the strength you can get just to make it through the winter. We all do.'

Killigrew grunted non-committally. 'Mind if I help myself?' he asked, indicating the bottle of Scotch on top of the stove.

'Be my guest.'

In spite of its storing place, the cold Scotch was thick and oily. Killigrew knocked it back before it froze in the mug.

'No luck catching Bruin so far?' asked Strachan.

'Not yet. I think I'll call it off for today. Visibility's dropping out there. Soon Osborne and the others won't be able to see their hands in front of their faces.' He indicated the log Strachan was poring over. 'Interesting reading?'

'In a way. It's queer: even the ramblings of a madman have their own kind of twisted, perverted logic.'

Killigrew put down his mug. 'I'm going back aboard the *Venturer* for dinner. Coming?'

'In a minute. I've just got a couple of pages to go.'

The lieutenant replaced his cap and went out again, buttoning his coat. The fog had thickened more rapidly than he had expected and even the *Venturer* – less than seventy yards from the door of the observatory – was hidden, with only a slight paleness in the surrounding opacity revealing the presence of lights. He cursed. As soon as he got back on board, he would have Unstead pipe Bähr and the marines back to the ship. It was too dangerous to be out in this weather with a polar bear on the prowl.

Pettifer was still ranting and the huskies still barked, both more frenziedly than ever now. Killigrew watched his footing as he ascended the gangplank, saw McLellan's footprints in the film of light snow that had fallen earlier that afternoon, and beneath those . . .

'Christ!'

He went up the gangplank as fast as he could, his boots slipping and sliding on the ice, gauntlets scrabbling awkwardly for purchase on the lifeline. At the top of the gangplank he saw blood seeping out from under the wadding tilt awning, lots of blood, black against white in the dim light, quickly thickening and freezing.

He tore open the fastenings at the opening, parted the flaps and came face to face with the bear.

XVII

The Hunt

Killigrew had seen polar bears before, at the Zoological Gardens in Regent's Park. At the time, they had struck him as big, powerful creatures, albeit rather cuddly with all their shaggy cream-coloured fur. Compared to this monster they looked scrawny.

There was nothing cuddly about Bruin. His chops were smeared with blood and from the expression on his snarling face he did not like to be interrupted in the middle of a meal. The meal was what was left of McLellan, his bloody face still recognisable at one end of the gory mess.

Killigrew stood frozen stock-still, mesmerised by the beast's feral gaze. Then the bear reared up on its hind legs with a roar. Its ears brushed the awning, about eleven and a half feet above. O'Houlihan had been exaggerating when he said the bear was twelve feet long, but not by much: it had to weigh at least nine-tenths of a ton.

It lunged.

Killigrew stepped back instinctively through the opening and raised his hands in a futile, instinctive gesture to protect his head. He felt the deck shake beneath his feet as those massive paws smashed down, felt the beast's rank breath in his face, and then it smashed into him. He was tossed aside, the rope of the gangplank's handrail biting into his buttocks. The world spun around him. White, black, a shaggy hindquarter, the wind chill on his face, and then something smashed against his head and

313

lights exploded inside his skull. Not quite in the same instant, but so close as to make it impossible to tell whether it came before or after, something else smashed against his body.

He was lying on the ice. That meant he was a sitting duck. He remembered his first fight to the death, a skirmish on the deck of a Barbary corsair off the coast of North Africa – sun, sand, did such things really exist or had he imagined them? Curved swords flashing in the mêlée, shouts and screams, blood everywhere, something crashing against his skull and his legs buckling, face down on the deck, feet trampling him, then Jory Spargo's strong hands lifting him up, get up, *get up*!

Killigrew stood up. At once his legs gave way beneath him and he sank to his hands and knees. His head swam and a darkness sought to overwhelm him. He fought it off. *You can't faint now . . . Where am I, what's going on? Danger . . . polar bear . . . Christ, a big bastard . . . Where is it now, where, where?*

He looked around woozily. It was impossible to tell where the Arctic fog ended and the mist behind his eyes began. No bear . . . shouts, shots, light falling over him from behind, voices making no sense.

'There's someone down there!'

Down where?

'He's moving, he's still alive!'

'Who is it?'

'Can't tell.'

Footsteps, thump thump thump thump. Killigrew's elbows buckled beneath him and snow burst under the peak of his cap, stinging his cheek. Strong hands lifting him. *Good old Jory.*

'It's Mr Killigrew!'

'Well, don't just stand there! Get him to the sick-berth. Where the hell's the pill-roller?'

Faces, footsteps, more faces, surrounding him, concern in their eyes. He knew the faces but he could not think where from.

'You oh-kay, sir?'

'I'm fine.' His own voice came from ten thousand miles away, all the way back in England. *Good old England.* Hands holding him, gently leading him up the gangplank. No, he didn't want to go up there, but there were too many to resist and he felt too weak. Then the dim oil-lanterns slung beneath the awning dazzled him and he averted his eyes only to see the mangled remains of McLellan, ribs white against the crimson of torn flesh.

'Don't look, sir. You can't do anything more for him.'

Able Seaman Erlend McLellan. Dead. But you're still alive. Why? Because the bear had already sated its appetite, it wasn't interested in you, it only wanted to get away and you stood in its path. But supposing it had not been sated, supposing it had attacked you? That could be you lying down there with your entrails ripped out.

Killigrew pictured himself lying there. His stomach lurched and his knees gave way again, but the men surrounding him caught him. They helped him down to the sick-berth, sat him in a chair, and Strachan crouched before him.

'Are you all right?'

Killigrew nodded and then winced at the pain that lanced up his neck and into his skull.

'How many fingers am I holding up?'

Killigrew saw six, but he was not fooled. 'Three.'

'Good. All right, Ågård, help me get his coat off. The rest of you get out of here, give the man some room to breathe.' Ågård took off Killigrew's coat and Strachan explored the back of his head with tentative fingers.

'Ouch!' said Killigrew.

'Hmm. Well, there's a lump on the back of your head so large I've half a mind to stick a Union Flag in it and claim it for Queen Victoria as a new-found continent. But I don't think your skull's fractured. What happened?'

'Had a bit of a tussle with our pal Bruin. Must've fallen off the gangplank and cracked my head on the ice.'

'You were fortunate.'

'More fortunate than poor McLellan. I sent him to his death, Strachan. You were there. *I sent him to his death.*'

'Where the devil do you think you're going?' Strachan demanded furiously the next morning.

'To kill the bear.' Killigrew descended the gangplank to where Boatswain's Mate Unstead was trying to harness six of the dogs to one of the dog sledges – and making a proper pig's ear of it, by the look of things. As well as the smaller dog sledge, they were taking one of the larger sledges, which would be hauled by Killigrew, Bähr, Bombardier Osborne and Privates Jenkins, Phillips and Walsh. They had loaded up the two sledges the previous evening with everything they would need for the hunt: guns – including the makeshift bomb-gun – ammunition, food supplies, a portable cooking stove and a tent.

'You're in no condition to go anywhere, let alone go chasing bears across the Arctic,' protested Strachan.

Killigrew shook his head. It still throbbed dully, but he had taken a powder and the pain was less intense than it had been when he had woken up a couple of hours earlier. 'I did a lot of thinking last night. It's time to carry the fight to the enemy.'

'Fight him on his own turf, you mean?'

Killigrew smiled wanly. 'Wherever we fight him, it'll be on his own turf. But it's time the hunter became the hunted.'

'At least wait a couple of days, until you're feeling better.'

'I'm feeling better now,' lied Killigrew. 'And so far the weather's been with us.' He shone the beam of a bull's-eye to where the bear's tracks still stood out in the snow, showing there had been no snowfall during the night – not that there was much difference between night and day, now that the sun had finally sunk beneath the horizon for the last time that year. 'We have to go now, while the tracks are still there to be followed.'

'Then stay behind and let someone else go in your place.'

'Not my style.'

'Assistant surgeon's orders, Killigrew.'

'Sorry, Strachan. You may be the medical officer, but I'm the acting commander. This is something only I can do. With a little help from Bähr, Unstead and our jollies.'

'Sounds like gammon to me.' The assistant surgeon grinned lop-sidedly. 'Always got to be the hero, haven't you?'

'Not much choice in the matter, Strachan. I'll explain when I get back.'

'*If* you get back.'

'I'll be back,' said Killigrew. 'You realise, of course, that in my absence command falls to you?'

'Me!'

'Indeed, Mr Strachan. With me absent, Cavan dead, and Pettifer and Yelverton on the sick list, you're the next most senior.'

'But I'm just a civilian officer!'

'Nevertheless, you're next in command. Don't worry: I wouldn't drop such a big responsibility in your lap if I didn't think you were up to it. If you get stuck, you can always ask Yelverton for advice. And don't be afraid to lean on the petty officers. Ask 'em what they think, and if it makes more sense than anything you've been able to come up with, just nod sagely as if you'd known it all along, and were just testing them. They're not likely to be fooled for an instant, of course, but good form demands one keeps up a pretence of being in command.'

Strachan smiled thinly. 'I'll do my best.'

Ursula descended the gangplank, dressed once more in her Inuit clothing. 'Come to wish us good luck, Frau Weiss?' Killigrew asked her.

'I'm coming with you,' she said.

He barely stopped himself from laughing out loud. 'You, ma'am?'

'You need someone to drive the sledge now that Terregannoeuck's gone and McLellan is dead,' she pointed out reasonably.

'Unstead can drive the sledge,' said Killigrew. 'Isn't that right, Unstead?'

The boatswain's mate did not hear him: one of the huskies had run around his ankles, and now he was struggling to disentangle himself from the traces.

Ursula arched an eyebrow sceptically.

'He'll get the hang of it soon enough,' Killigrew said defensively.

Behind him there was a thud as Unstead fell over.

'Really?'

'I'm sorry, ma'am. It's too dangerous for a woman where we're going.'

'You think I'll be any safer on board the *Venturer*, after what happened to McLellan yesterday? Besides, I can use a musket as well as any man.'

'I'm sure you can, ma'am . . .'

317

She turned to Phillips and indicated his rifled musket. 'May I?'

The marine glanced at Killigrew. 'Go on, let her have it,' sighed Killigrew.

Ursula took the musket, raised it to her shoulder, and took aim at one of the iron pylons supporting the boundary rope, about fifty yards away in poor light. She fired. The bullet spanged audibly against the pylon, and the rope jumped as it was knocked away at an angle. Impressed, Phillips let out a low whistle.

'Belay that, Phillips,' said Killigrew.

Unstead was yelling now as the huskies leaped all over him, thinking it was some kind of game.

'I know the Arctic better than you or any of the men going with you,' Ursula pointed out. 'You need me, Herr Killigrew.'

He glanced down, and then looked up at her with his hands on his hips. 'Are you sure you know how to drive a team of dogs?'

'Watch me.'

'It isn't going to be easy, you know. We're going to have to move fast. We can only carry enough supplies to last the six of us for two weeks; so if we don't catch the bear after one week, we'll have to turn back. You'll be sharing a tent with us, living on a pound and a half of salt pork and pemmican per day, cold, wet, unable to get dry for day after day . . .'

'I am familiar with the conditions in the Arctic. I want to see that bear killed every bit as much as you, Herr Killigrew. Herr Ziegler was a friend of mine. Besides, if you should fail, then sooner or later the bear will come back here for the rest of us.'

He sighed. 'Stand down, Unstead.'

'Sir?'

'You heard me. You're staying behind.'

The boatswain's mate did not seem to be disappointed at being taken off the expedition; if anything, his expression was one of relief.

'Good God, man!' exploded Bähr, who was checking his hunting rifle and making sure his ammunition had been properly stowed on the sledge. 'You're not seriously going to let her come with us?'

'You heard her,' said Killigrew. 'She knows the Arctic better

318

than any of us; and she's the only one who can drive the dog sledge.'

'But . . . damn it all, she's a woman!'

'I'm well aware of the fact. But we need her; more than we need you, perhaps. If you don't like it, you can stay behind and Molineaux can go in your place: he's every bit as good a shot as you are.'

Grumbling, Bähr acceded. As much as he disapproved of taking a woman on an expedition like this, it was clear that having a chance to be the one to kill the bear meant more to him.

'Good luck, sir,' said Latimer, and grinned. 'My money's on you killing the bear rather than vice versa.'

'What sort of odds did you get?'

'Good ones, sir.'

'From whose point of view, Latimer? Ours or yours?'

The clerk flushed, but did not answer.

Finally Molineaux brought Killigrew his Norwegian snow-shoes and push-poles. 'Wish you'd let me come with you, sir.'

'Thank you.' Killigrew lowered his voice as he crouched down to fasten the snow-shoes on to his boots: the gliding 'ski' under his left foot nearly ten feet long, the other shorter, wrapped in sealskin to give him traction as he pushed himself over the snow-covered ice. 'Part of me wishes you were coming with us, Molineaux. But if the worst comes to the worst and we don't come back, someone's got to stay behind and get the others to safety. Strachan's a good man, but he's no sailor.'

Molineaux nodded and glanced across to where the assistant surgeon stood. 'Don't you worry about that, sir. I'll look after him. But I'm hoping the worst doesn't come to the worst. We'll all be going back to England, with you on my damned back if I have to carry you all the way from here to Montreal.'

'That's the spirit. Remember, if we're not back within two weeks—'

'I'll see you then, sir,' Molineaux said firmly, and produced his Bowie knife. 'Would you take this with you, sir? Just in case?'

'Thank you.' Killigrew pulled up the skirt of his greatcoat and tucked the knife in the small of his back. Ursula had freed Unstead and untangled the traces of the huskies' harnesses.

Killigrew slithered across to where Bähr, Osborne, Jenkins, Walsh and Phillips were shrugging on their knapsacks.

'All right, let's go!' Killigrew gestured them forward with a ski-pole and pushed off, blazing the trail as he followed the bear's massive paw-prints in the soft snow.

Molineaux found Fischbein sitting at one of the tables on the mess deck, staring into space. He put a mug of cocoa down in front of the half-deck boy, but Fischbein did not seem to notice it.

'It would have worked, Ignatz,' said Molineaux. 'The bomb-gun, I mean. It's not Jenkins' fault he didn't see the bear in the fog. We'll get it next time.'

Fischbein did not respond. Molineaux snapped his fingers in front of the youth's face. 'Ahoy there! Anyone in?'

Fischbein looked up sharply, then shook his head. '*Entschuldigung*! I was just thinking if the *Carl Gustaf* had not been nipped, I would be back in Hamburg by now.'

'You got family waiting for you there? A frow, maybe?'

Fischbein smiled. 'A *Fräulein*. Luise Grünholz. I only met her a year ago. There was an *Aufruhr*... In English you would say ...? Men fighting in streets, industrial workers protesting, throwing bricks at the soldiers ...'

'A riot?'

'Yes, a riot. I went down to the *Rathaus* with some mates – we're not *Radikaleren*, but we heard there was going to be a protest, and we never pass up the opportunity for a chance to fight with the police. Anyhow, Luise was there with her mother. They went out shopping and got caught up in the *Aufruhr*, the riot. I helped get them to safety. Luise's parents are very wealthy, her father is a teacher ...'

Molineaux arched an eyebrow. 'A wealthy teacher?'

'More wealthy than me, anyhow. And you know how teachers look down on those of us who have never been to school. I thought a girl like Luise wouldn't give a *Kerl* like me a second glance. But a girl that beautiful – I knew I'd regret it the rest of my life if I did not ask if I could call on her. Can you believe my surprise when she said yes?'

'I've been there, shipmate.'

'We've been . . . what is the word, when a man and a woman get together?'

'Chauvering?'

Fischbein had been living on the lower deck long enough to know what *that* meant. He scowled. 'Luise is not that sort of girl.'

'Oh! Courting, you mean.'

'Yes, courting. Of course, her parents do not know about us. If they did . . .' Fischbein shook his head.

'You've been seeing her over a year and you still haven't mounted her?' Molineaux exclaimed incredulously. 'I don't know whether to admire your restraint or damn you for a booby. I couldn't go out with a blower for one week if I wasn't getting my oats, never mind one year!'

Fischbein grinned. 'What can I say? I'm in love. Sickening, is it not?'

'Very! So you're pretty serious about this Luise, then?'

The youth nodded. 'I'm going to marry her.'

'You don't think her parents might have something to say about that?'

'I'm more worried about what Luise will say. If she's willing, I think she would be happy to *durchgehen*. . . run away with me?'

'Elope?'

'Yes, elope. But I want to do the right thing. I thought, if I could get enough money from one more voyage on a whaling ship, I could put on a show, impress her parents.'

'It's worth a try,' acknowledged Molineaux.

Fischbein gestured around the mess deck. 'Alas, the best laid plans . . .'

'Don't you worry about this, Ignatz. We'll get you safely back to your Luise, never fear.'

'Yes, but with empty pockets.'

'But richer in spirit. Think about it, shipmate. You'll be a hero. All the men that go on Arctic expeditions are heroes when they go home. I used to know this seaman called John Hepburn; he went on one of Franklin's earlier expeditions – you know, the one where they had to eat their boots? You should've seen him in the waterfront gatherings when he got back. With the stories he

321

used to tell, he didn't have to pay for his own drinks for a year. And he couldn't fight the blowers off with a big stick – not that he tried! So you get back to Hamburg and tell your Luise about your adventures, and she'll run away to Timbuctoo with you, if you ask her.'

Fischbein smiled. 'Is that why you volunteered for this expedition? For the girls?'

'For the money,' said Molineaux. 'There's double pay on discovery service, and I need every penny. Besides, I've already got a gal.'

'Yes?'

'Yur – she's a Hamburger too, come to think of it. There's a lot of German gals in Whitechapel. Hold on, I've got a picture somewhere.' He stood up to lift the lid of his seat-locker, and took out his copy of *Beowulf*. The dog-eared calotype of Lulu was tucked between the pages as a bookmark. He handed it to Fischbein.

The youth regarded the calotype incredulously. 'This is your sweetheart?'

Molineaux grinned. 'Yur. I like that picture of her: makes her look like a duchess, don't it? Them ain't her real togs – she borrowed them from the costume basket of the penny-gaff where she sings, to pose for that calotype. Maybe you've heard of her? Lulu Kisswetter?'

Fischbein shook his head.

'Tell you what: when we get back to England, I'll take you to the penny-gaff where she sings; you can catch her act before you sail for Hamburg. She's not much of a singer, but . . . well, she makes up for it in other ways, if you catch my drift.' Molineaux winked, and Fischbein blushed.

Molineaux stared at the calotype wistfully. 'I still don't know what she's doing with a cove like me. We met five years ago: I'd just got back from the Guinea Coast with a wounded leg; I was getting around on crutches. I got knocked down by a gang of rampaging medical students, the next thing I knew there was this angel crouching over me. We've been dabbing it up ever since. I ain't green enough to fool myself into thinking she's faithful to me when I'm at sea – she's got bills to pay, after all, and I can't honestly say that I'm faithful to her . . . Well, you're a sailor, you know how it is. But when I'm back in London, it's just the two of us.' He tucked the picture back in his book and slipped it into his locker once more.

Fischbein sipped his cocoa. 'You really think we'll make it back home?'

'Don't you worry. Me and Tom Tidley have faced worse dangers than the Arctic. We'll make it, never fear. It'll take more than some mangy old bear to get the better of Tom Tidley, believe you me.'

'This is lunacy,' said Killigrew. 'We travelled four and a half thousand miles to search for Franklin and his missing crew, and what are we doing now that we're here? Searching for a damned polar bear!'

'A damned bear that's killed five of your men,' Bähr reminded him. 'A damned bear that will come back to kill again and again, unless we get it first.'

'Slim hope of that. I don't know how fast polar bears travel, but I'll lay odds it's a damned sight faster than the twelve miles a day we've averaged so far.'

There had been no heavy falls of snow since the day the bear had killed McLellan, and the sledge party had followed its tracks without difficulty. Occasionally Killigrew would travel ahead on his skis, blazing the trail with Ursula on the dog sledge where the tracks became hard to follow, but most of the time his skis were strapped to the large sledge and he hauled on the harness along with the rest of the men. By his reckoning they had covered nearly fifty miles in the four days since they had left the *Venturer*, but the bear had led them on a meandering, circuitous route: due east across the neck of land that connected Boothia to the Canadian mainland.

They were yoked to the sledge in tandem, one pair behind another, Killigrew leading the way with Bähr beside him. Behind them were Osborne and Walsh, while Jenkins and Phillips brought up the rear.

Ursula drove the smaller dog sledge up ahead of them. Killigrew had not been entirely comfortable with the idea of using dogs as beasts of burden at first. But they had hauled the sledge with such enthusiasm under Ursula's skilful handling, he had realised that they had been born and bred for such work, and were a lot happier hauling a sledge across the wide, open spaces of the Arctic than they would ever be cooped up in their kennels on board the *Venturer*.

They travelled from seven in the morning until six in the evening, resting for ten minutes in every hour and for an hour between noon and one; not that time as they understood it had much meaning in a world that hovered between the dusk of midday and the pitch black of midnight. Yet even the thin light of the stars, reflected blue off the snow and ice all around them, was enough to guide their way. On some days, when the trail led over the relatively smooth ice of frozen lakes, they covered as much as seventeen miles; on others, when the way led through rocky hills, they were lucky to cover four, and at night crawled into their chrysalis bags exhausted. But at least their exhaustion allowed them to sleep soundly in spite of the freezing temperatures inside their tent. And as the days progressed and they consumed more of their rations, the large sledge they hauled behind them became perceptibly lighter.

They were moving across the sea again now.

'Where the devil's it going, anyhow?' Killigrew panted in exasperation. 'It seems to be roaming all over the place.'

'Terregannoeuck told me that the Esquimaux call polar bears *pisugtooq*, "the great wanderer",' said Bähr.

'I can't help wondering if this bear is simply trying to wear us out before—' Killigrew broke off abruptly.

'Sir!' Phillips hissed urgently. '*Look!*'

Killigrew glanced over his shoulder and saw that the marine was pointing up ahead of them. Following the direction he indicated, the lieutenant saw something on the ridge ahead of them where the rise of the land suggested the coast; with snow and ice covering everything, sometimes it was impossible to tell where land ended and the water began. At first Killigrew thought it was nothing more than a rock, poised on the low ridge overlooking the coast ahead, silhouetted against the indigo sky. Then the rock moved, and he realised it was an animal of some kind.

'Is it . . .?' asked Phillips.

Killigrew took out his pocket telescope, rubbed the palm of

his gauntlet over the eyepiece to take the chill off it – he did not want it freezing to his face and pulling his eyelids away when he lowered it – and looked at the animal.

'It's a polar bear, all right,' he confirmed. 'Whether or not it's the one we're after—'

'Of course it's the one we're after,' said Bähr. 'The tracks lead that way, don't they?'

Killigrew was not convinced. 'How we managed to keep up with it . . .' He trailed off. The bear was looking back at him. Impossible to tell what it was thinking, at that distance in that light, but the lieutenant was willing to hazard a guess.

Ursula was some way up ahead of them, following the bear's tracks where they curved round to the west before approaching the shore below the ridge where the bear stood watching them. She had not seen the bear itself.

'Frau Weiss!' Killigrew called, as loud as he dared. He did not want to frighten off the bear, but at the same time he did not want her to blunder into a messy death in the bear's paws. Fortunately she heard him, and glanced back in his direction. He indicated the bear. She glanced in that direction, nodded, and reined in the dogs with a cry of 'Whoa!', waiting to see what Killigrew and the other men would do next.

Phillips unslung his rifle and levelled it at the bear, but Osborne knocked the barrel of his rifle up. 'Don't waste your shot, lad. Even you couldn't hit it from here.'

Then the bear turned abruptly and trotted on, disappearing out of sight on the other side of the ridge.

It hit Killigrew all at once: 'He's leading us into a trap.'

'Don't talk nonsense,' said Bähr. 'What, do you think he's got half a dozen of his ursine friends waiting for us on the other side of that ridge? He's just a dumb animal, Killigrew.'

The lieutenant saw the sense of what Bähr was saying, but all the same he could not help thinking that something was not right.

'There are six of us, armed with shotguns and rifled muskets,' persisted the doctor. Killigrew could only presume he was discounting Ursula in the event of a violent encounter. 'The devil take it! Even if there *were* six of them, we'd be a match for them.'

'There were thirty-five of us when we first reached Horsehead Bay, but that didn't stop Bruin from killing five of us on his own,' Killigrew pointed out. Nonetheless, he knew they had come this far to kill the bear; they could not turn back now, not when they had come so close.

There was nothing except smooth ice between them and where they had seen the bear to their right. Killigrew led them straight across to the shore, loading a shell into each of the barrels of his Verney-Carron shotgun as his shoulders took the strain of his sledge harness.

'We'll drag the sledge as far as the lake shore, then leave it there with Osborne and Ursula while the rest of us spread out to go after the bear,' he decided. 'Don't anyone shoot until we get closer. We want to kill it, not frighten it off.'

'Don't you worry,' said Bähr. 'This bear may think it's rather clever, but so far it's just been lucky. I've got a feeling that its luck is about to run out—'

'Halt!' said Killigrew.

The six of them came to an abrupt stop. 'Now what's the matter?' demanded Bähr.

'Did anyone else hear that?'

'Hear what?'

Crack!

'That.'

They exchanged nervous glances and then, as realisation set in, slowly and apprehensively lowered their gaze to the ice beneath their feet.

Crack – crack!

'Down!' Killigrew grabbed Bähr's arm and dragged him down after him as he threw himself flat. 'Down on the ice, fast! Spread yourselves out!'

The six of them sprawled on the ice, breathing hard. In the silence that followed, as they strained their ears for further sounds of the ice cracking beneath them, Killigrew could feel his heart pounding.

'Is everyone all right?' he asked. They murmured their assent. 'All right, this is what we're going to do. Slowly, carefully, inch by inch if we have to, we're going to make our way to the land.'

326

'On our bellies?' protested Bähr. 'It's got to be at least half a mile!'

'It's probably only a few fathoms to the bottom of the sea, Doctor. Would you rather go that way?'

'This is daft.' Jenkins pushed himself to his feet. 'The ice supported the weight of the bear, didn't it? If it can support the weight of a two-thousand-pound bear, it's not going to break under our weight, is it?'

'Get down, Ted!' gasped Phillips.

'Look – I'll prove it.'

To Killigrew's horror, Jenkins started to jump up and down on the ice. He expected to see the marine drop straight through into the freezing waters below. 'Belay that, Jenkins, damn you! Get down, like I told you!'

But Jenkins' confidence in the ice proved well founded. 'See? I'm probably the heaviest one here, and it's more than strong enough to support my weight. You five can crawl on your bellies if you like, but I'm walking to the shore on my feet.' He made as if to shrug off his harness.

Crack . . . crack . . . crack!

Killigrew's eyes were focused on Jenkins, expecting the ice to open up under the marine. But the ice was solid beneath his feet; the lieutenant realised belatedly it was not the marine, but the sledge – the one they were all harnessed to, with their tent, chrysalis bags, victuals, cooking apparatus, dry clothes, spare ammunition and tools – that was sinking.

Chunks of ice tilted up all around the sledge as it settled slowly down, and then disappeared abruptly. The strain snapped at their harnesses. Jenkins was pulled on to his back, while Killigrew felt himself being dragged across the ice towards the hole where the sledge had sunk. Walsh squirmed out of his harness and picked himself up, sprinting for the shore.

'Walsh!' roared Osborne. 'Come back here, you damned coward!' On his back, the bombardier tried to grip the harness with his mittened hands while the heels of his boots sought purchase on the ice. But Walsh was already dozens of yards away and showed no intention of returning.

Still holding his shotgun in one hand, Killigrew scrabbled at the ice with his other hand and his toecaps, but he felt himself being pulled back inexorably with the others towards the gaping hole in the ice. If only he had had the ice-axe . . . but the axe was on the sledge, with the rest of the tools.

Phillips was at the edge of the hole now. 'Cut through the harnesses, lad!' gasped Osborne.

'I can't do that, Bomb. We'll never make it back to the *Venturer* without what's on that sledge!'

Killigrew knew that the young marine was right. But if they followed the sledge into the freezing water, whether or not they could make it back to the *Venturer* would become a moot point.

Crack . . . crack . . .

The ice splintered under Phillips at the edge of the hole, and then he too was pulled under. Killigrew could see his mittened hands waving frantically over the surface, fumbling for purchase were there was none to be had. *Cut the harness, lad*, Killigrew found himself thinking. Even though to lose the large sledge would mean death for them all, he could not help willing Phillips to cut the harness before he drowned in that freezing water.

Now Bähr and Osborne were at the edge of the hole and being dragged closer and closer every second.

Killigrew remembered the shotgun in his hands. He reversed his grip on it and rammed the twin muzzles against the ice. They skittered off the slippery surface.

The four of them were dragged closer to the edge. He brought the shotgun down again, and this time the muzzles bit into the ice, deep enough to give him purchase. As his shoulders took up the strain, it required all his strength to hold the shotgun in place. Their headlong slide to the hole halted, he was able to scrabble about with his feet until they too could find purchase.

If the bear attacked now, they were all as good as dead.

'Doctor! Take the knife from my belt and use that as an ice-axe!'

Bähr nodded and complied, digging the blade into the ice. Once he had taken up some of the strain, Killigrew risked taking the shotgun away again, relying only on the purchase of his feet. He rammed the muzzles against the ice, a few inches further away this time, and pulled himself after it, until he was taking the strain of the harness once more. Then it was Bähr's turn to inch forward a few inches. Behind them, Osborne and Jenkins did their best to help. Phillips' hands still flailed in the water behind them.

Then Ursula arrived with the dog sledge, heedless of her own safety on the thin ice. Keeping a firm grip on the huskies' harnesses with one hand, she unfastened them dextrously from the smaller sledge with the other, and tied them to Killigrew's and Bähr's harnesses.

'*Marche! Marche!*'

The huskies took up the strain. It made all the difference; Killigrew knew they could not have done it without them. Inch by agonising inch, they pulled Phillips and the sledge up after them. When Phillips' head and shoulders emerged from the hole, his searching hands were grasped by those of Osborne and Jenkins, and they hauled him up out of the water. Then all five of them pulled the sledge up after them.

It took them three attempts. Each time they got the sledge out again, the ice cracked beneath it and it sank once more, almost pulling them after it. But at last the six of them were able to manhandle it to an area of thicker, stronger ice. They lay there, drained, frozen and exhausted, Phillips' teeth chattering audibly. Killigrew could happily have sprawled there until his strength returned, or until the cold sapped the last of his strength and he slipped into a deep and endless sleep. But he knew he could not let down the others; besides, it was not in his nature to give up, not ever.

'We'll make for the shore,' he gasped. 'We'll make camp there for the night—'

'With the bear so close?' asked Bähr.

'What do you want us to do, doctor? Walk another ten miles? Phillips is going to freeze to death if we don't get him warm and in some dry clothes in a brace of shakes. How are you feeling, Phillips?'

'C-cold, sir. B-but I'll b-be all right.'

Killigrew was sceptical: it was hard to tell in the dim light of the stars, but it looked as if the marine was turning blue.

'Maybe we should put him on the sledge and drag him with the rest of the supplies,' suggested Bähr.

'And make the sledge even heavier?' asked Osborne. 'Not a good idea, sir.'

'We'll get the sledge to the shore quicker if I help,' said Phillips. 'And it'll help warm me up if I keep moving.'

'Good for you, Phillips.' Killigrew felt only anguish at having to expect anything more from the marine after the ordeal he had just been through, but he knew they had no other choice: everything depended on their reaching the safety of the shore. Besides, Phillips was right: his best chance of keeping warm lay in staying active.

Crawling on their hands and knees, shuffling along on their bottoms, they moved painstakingly across the 850 yards to the coast, dragging the sledge behind them. The water saturating Phillips' clothes froze solid and crackled with his every movement. When they were only a couple of hundred yards from the shore, their confidence in the thickness of the ice grew more assured, and they dragged the sledge on foot for the final furlong.

'How come the ice was so thin there, when it's so thick everywhere else?' asked Phillips. 'Shouldn't it be the same thickness everywhere?'

'There must be a hot spring underwater below,' said Killigrew. 'What do they call them?'

'A polynya,' said Ursula.

He nodded. 'A polynya. Bruin avoided it; we weren't so clever.'

'You don't suppose . . .?' she asked.

'That he planned it that way?' Killigrew shook his head, trying to convince himself as much as Ursula. 'Animals don't make plans. Not like that.'

Osborne took the portable stove from the sledge and filled the reservoir with spirits of wine to make some tea for Phillips. As the ice he used for water was melting over the thin flame, he looked about. 'Where's that gutless bastard – pardon my French, ma'am – Walsh?'

'Probably too ashamed to show his face, I should imagine,' said Bähr.

'What's that?' Ursula indicated a dark shape a few hundred yards away, clearly silhouetted against the dusting of white snow on the land.

'Wait here,' Killigrew told the others, before setting out to investigate the shape. He paused after a few steps, and turned back to Osborne. 'Keep a sharp lookout in case Bruin returns.'

The bombardier nodded and reached for the makeshift bomb-gun he had constructed with Kracht.

Killigrew checked the shotgun as he ascended the ridge. The muzzles were choked with snow; all he could do for now was to poke it out with the stub of a pencil, and hope the damned thing did not blow up in his face when he tried to use it.

Ever since Ursula had pointed out the shape, Killigrew had known in his heart what it must be, but there was always that hope that he might be mistaken. The bloody mess he found on the ice might have been a wandering Esquimau or even the carcass of a seal, for all that Killigrew could tell from the half-devoured remains, except for the scraps of Walsh's Royal marine uniform beneath his shredded box-cloth jacket, and the rosary still clutched in a dismembered hand.

Killigrew crouched over the remains and sighed. If they had made it back to the *Venturer*, the marine would have been in for a severe reprimand, probably a week in the lazaretto on bread and water. But he had not deserved to die for his cowardice, least of all like this.

He raised his eyes and gazed about the icescape around him, searching for the bear. He could see no sign of it, but in a very unscientific manner Strachan would not have approved of, he sensed it was watching him.

He rose slowly to his feet. '*Come on out and show yourself, you bastard!*' he roared. '*You want a fight? Then fight me!*'

His words of defiance echoed back hollowly from the empty wilderness around him.

The aurora borealis put in its first appearance at nine twenty in the evening on 2 December.

Molineaux had heard about it from Ågård, of course, but the ex-spouter had been unable to describe it adequately, only giving him the impression that by not having seen it he had missed out on something spectacular. During the voyage from England, Molineaux had wondered if he might not be disappointed by the reality of the phenomenon; but now, as he

331

patrolled the perimeter with a rifled musket in his hands, he realised that if anything Ågård had understated its wondrous nature.

First a narrow streak of light stretched across the heavens, terminating in a feather, and then four green-tinged masses of cumulus-shaped light appeared, seeming to reach down to the ground as they pulsated in the sky, rippling like the swell of the ocean on a gentle summer's day, more beautiful than any fireworks he had ever seen. For a moment, all he had been through seemed to have been worth it, just to see this spectacle: then he remembered that eight men had died since they had left England, including Ziegler.

He knew he ought to go back on board and alert the others, so that they too could see this. Yelverton, he knew, was particularly keen to see the aurora, and he was aware Strachan had instructions to take magnetic and electrical readings from his equipment to try to establish what caused the phenomenon. Doubtless the scientificer had his own theory, but even if Molineaux did not believe in God himself, he preferred to live in a magical world where some things were beyond explaining. Life was to be enjoyed, not explained away. So he lingered on the ice, torn between summoning the others and enjoying this moment of peace by himself. It was almost as if the heavens had put on this display for his benefit alone.

A paw landed on his shoulder. The petty officer jumped nearly a foot in the air, and whirled to see Terregannoeuck standing behind him.

'Jesus, Terry! Don't creep up on me like that! Where the hell have you been, anyhow?'

'Terregannoeuck go to bottom of sea, talk to Nuliayuq.'

'Ask a silly question.'

'Killigrew in trouble. We go save him.'

'What do you mean, he's in trouble? You saw him?'

Terregannoeuck shook his head. 'Nuliayuq tell me.'

'When you were chatting to him at the bottom of the sea.'

The Inuk laughed. 'You very stupid! Nuliayuq not man; Nuliayuq woman. You not know anything?'

'I guess not.'

'You waste time. Killigrew and others die if we not get there

332

in time. Kokogiaq stalk them, lead them into trap. We get dogs and sledge quickly, go warn them.' Terregannoeuck started walking across the ice towards the *Venturer*.

'Now hold your huskies, Terry! If I go and tell Mr Strachan that we need to take a sledge and the only remaining team of dogs to rescue Mr Killigrew and the others on the say-so of some blower you were chaffing with at the bottom of the sea, he's going to laugh in my phizog. And then certify me nuts along with Pettifer.'

'Then we not tell him we go,' Terregannoeuck replied, without so much as a backward glance.

Molineaux lingered at his post, staring after the Inuk's broad back. Then he swore crudely under his breath, and set off after him. 'Hold up, Terry! Wait for me!'

XVIII

Bait

Killigrew and the others dragged the sledge – even heavier now that all their gear was waterlogged – across one of the many frozen lakes that littered the neck of the Boothia Peninsula. Unlike the frozen seas, the ice of the lakes was relatively smooth and free of pressure ridges, but there were other obstacles to be negotiated: thousands of fracture lines that crisscrossed the surface. Some were only a few inches wide and could be stepped over with ease, the sledge sliding across them without difficulty. Others were broad crevasses that necessitated wide detours.

Like the one that blocked their path now, almost ten feet wide. Standing on the edge, Killigrew struck a match to light his bull's-eye and flashed the beam into the blackness below. The chasm angled back underneath them, so that all he could see was the far wall of ice, glittering where it caught the rays of the lantern. Unlike the salt-water sea, which rarely froze to a depth of more than seven feet, the freshwater lakes could sometimes freeze all the way to their bottoms. There was no telling how deep the crevasse might be. Perhaps they could jump it, had any of them cared to try it, but there was no way of getting the sledge across.

'Perhaps there's another way around,' suggested Bähr.

Osborne shook his head, and nodded towards Phillips. 'He's beat, sir. He can't walk another step.'

'We're all tired, Osborne.' Killigrew cast the beam of his bull's-eye about and directed it towards an outcrop of rock over by the lake shore, about forty yards away. 'That looks like a likely spot. Your turn to make supper, Jenkins. Bähr, perhaps you could help Osborne get the tent up?'

Ursula fed the dogs with herrings, after which they settled down by burrowing shallow beds for themselves in the snow. Killigrew wound up the chronometer they had brought with them and then wrote up the day's occurrences in his journal by the light of his bull's-eye. 'Looks as if a storm's coming in,' Ursula remarked as a rising wind whipped at the pages of the journal.

He nodded and passed his day's workings to Bähr. 'Would you mind double-checking my calculations, doctor?'

'By all means,' Bähr said with relish.

Never mind the wind, the cold, the wet and the aching ankles after skiing for miles and miles over the ice; for Killigrew the most painful part of the sledging expedition was having Bähr check his calculations. Killigrew had a dirty secret: he was hopeless at arithmetic. If he had had to retake his examination for lieutenant in 1852, now that examinations were proper, fully thought-out tests, he would probably have failed on navigation; as it was, he had been promoted five years ago, and by a board composed of old-school captains who thought more of a man's seamanship than his knowledge of sines and cosines. It did not matter on board the *Venturer*, where Yelverton was able to check his workings and discreetly correct them without anyone else on board being any the wiser; but Bähr took great relish in setting him straight in front of Osborne, Jenkins and Phillips. His secret was very much out.

'Oh, dear me!' chuckled the doctor. 'Look here, you've forgotten to carry the one; and the logarithm of forty-two is one-point-six-two-three-two. How on earth did you get nought-point-nine-treble-nought? Don't you know how to use a slide rule?'

'My hand must've slipped.'

'See here, you've put us eleven miles west of our actual position. Don't they teach you trigonometry in the Royal Navy?'

'Geometry was never my strong point.'

'I should say not!' Bähr handed back the chart they had drawn. 'That's where I put us.'

Killigrew glanced over the doctor's workings – if only for form's sake – and as usual could not fault them.

'It's been six days since we left the *Venturer*,' said Bähr. 'If we don't catch Bruin by tomorrow evening, we'll have to turn back.'

Killigrew had been hoping that the bear would lead them in an arc away from the *Venturer*, so that they would not be all that far from their base, but instead he had only led them further and further away. He wondered if the bear knew they were on its trail, and was deliberately leading them to the limit of their resources.

They washed supper down with weak, tepid tea, and then crawled into the chrysalis bags. Osborne, who was on the roster for cooking duties tomorrow, settled down by the mouth, where he could crawl out to prepare breakfast first thing in the morning without disturbing any of the others.

'Shouldn't we set someone on guard, sir?' asked the bombardier. 'Keep an eye out for the bear?'

'The dogs will do that,' said Bähr. 'If they scent a bear, they'll start howling fit to wake the dead—'

The dogs started barking. Everyone in the tent exchanged nervous glances.

'Want me to take a look-see, sir?' offered Osborne.

'We'll both go.' Killigrew took his shotgun, handed the bombardier a rifle, and lit a bull's-eye with a match. The two of them pulled their greatcoats on over their clothes – they had all gone to bed fully dressed – and slipped out of the tent.

A blizzard had blown in from the north-east, and the fat snowflakes danced in the beam of the lantern. The huskies were all on their feet, barking furiously through the swirling snow at something in the darkness. Killigrew pointed the beam of the bull's-eye in that direction. 'See anything?' he shouted at Osborne above the howling wind.

The bombardier shook his head. 'Is it the bear?'

Then Killigrew saw it: the light of the bull's-eye reflected in a pair of eyes. He dropped the lantern, brought up the shotgun and fired both barrels in quick succession. The eyes disappeared and he heard a heavy body fall to the snow with a soft thump.

'I think you got it, sir!' said Osborne.

Killigrew reloaded both barrels of the shotgun and crouched to relight the bull's-eye. He clipped it to his belt and the two of them advanced cautiously until they found the body.

A dead reindeer.

'Sir!' Osborne protested accusingly, with a grin. 'You shot Prancer!'

Killigrew sighed, feeling the tension gush out of him like blood from a severed artery. 'Come on, let's get back to the tent.'

The two of them crawled back inside. 'What was it?' asked Bähr. 'We heard a couple of shots.'

'False alarm,' Killigrew said truculently, feeling foolish. 'Just a stray reindeer.' He squirmed back into his chrysalis bag, but outside the dogs were still barking. 'Now what?' he sighed. 'An Arctic vole?'

'They can probably smell the blood from that reindeer,' said Osborne.

'Perhaps we should give them something to eat,' said Ursula.

Osborne nodded. 'I'll cut up the reindeer and let them have it.'

'Go with him, Jenkins,' ordered Killigrew. 'Just in case.'

'Very good, sir.'

The two marines crawled out of the tent, lacing the flaps behind them.

Killigrew glanced across to where Ursula watched anxiously over the shivering Phillips. 'How is he?'

'Not good,' she said. 'If we don't get him warm soon, he'll freeze to death.'

Killigrew nodded. 'We'll start back for the *Venturer* tomorrow.'

'But we're so close!' persisted Bähr.

'We'll start back for the *Venturer* tomorrow,' Killigrew repeated firmly. 'I've already lost one man today; I don't intend to lose any more on this expedition. This was a foolish notion, anyhow. Thinking we could hunt Bruin down on his own territory. If we can get over the ridge to the west in the morning and travel down to the sea that way, we can be back at Horsehead Bay by Monday.'

Outside, the dogs started to bark even more frenziedly; presumably excited by the fresh meat Osborne and Jenkins were giving them. Then, one by one, they fell silent: they had better manners than to bark with their mouths full.

Killigrew rolled on to his side to go to sleep, and found Ursula's face barely inches from his own. He smiled reassuringly at her, and she surreptitiously felt for his gloved hand, clasping it tightly.

The dogs were all silent now: the only sounds were the wind outside, their own rasping breath, and Phillips' teeth chattering. Killigrew braced himself for the blast of cold wind that would follow Osborne and Jenkins back into the tent.

It never came.

A nasty feeling stirred in the pit of his stomach. He crawled out of his chrysalis bag and reached for his shotgun and bull's-eye once more. 'What's wrong?' asked Ursula.

'I'll just go see what's taking Osborne and Jenkins so long.'

He crawled out of the tent, pausing to flash the bull's-eye beam through the snow before lacing the tent flaps behind him. There was no sign of the two marines. Surely the damned fools had not wandered off and got lost? It would not be difficult in this blizzard . . .

He walked over to where the huskies lay and his stomach lurched when he saw their mangled, bloody corpses.

He levelled the shotgun and flashed the beam of the bull's-eye around. Still no sign of the marines. 'Osborne! Jenkins!'

No reply. He retreated to the tent and crouched by the entrance, still flashing his light through the snow. 'Dr Bähr? Could you come out here and take a look at this?'

'What is it?'

'You'd best come and see for yourself. And bring your rifle.'

Killigrew heard Bähr grumbling in German. He still kept an eye open before him, his back to the tent. The doctor emerged, clutching his hunting rifle. 'Well? What is it?'

The lieutenant indicated the dogs. Bähr crawled out of the tent and Killigrew fastened the flaps behind him while the doctor went across to examine them.

'Oh!'

Killigrew followed him across, flashing the beam of his bull's-eye all around as he did so.

'That's rum,' said Bähr.

'What?'

'They've been torn apart, and yet . . . as far as I can see, there's no flesh missing. Whoever – *what*ever killed them, it hasn't . . . um . . . feasted. Where are Osborne and Jenkins?'

Killigrew flashed the bull's-eye beam on to the snow until he found tracks: paw-prints, a bloodstained furrow, and footprints following them.

'The bear must've grabbed one of them, and then the other went after them.'

Killigrew started to follow the tracks, but Bähr grabbed him by the arm. 'Where are you going?'

'One of them might still be alive.'

'Don't be a fool, man! You'll just get yourself killed like them.'

Killigrew shook his head. 'I came out here to kill that bear; I'm not going to give up now that I know it's close—'

A scream sounded above the howling wind. The sound – unmistakably human – sent a shudder of horror down Killigrew's spine. He broke into a run, following the tracks. Bähr followed him after a momentary hesitation. The two of them stumbled through the whirling snowflakes, clutching their guns. The screams were not far off when they stopped abruptly.

They found Jenkins a few yards further on, his skull crushed, his stomach ripped open and one leg chewed to tatters. The blood-stained snow on the ground was kicked up in all directions – by footprints and paw-prints – and in the limited visibility it was impossible to tell which way the bear had gone.

'Where's Bruin?' asked Bähr.

'We must have frightened him off! Besides, perhaps Osborne's still alive.'

'We'll spread out!'

'No! We stick together, and stick close. If we get separated, Bruin will just pick us off separately—'

A bestial roar sounded – close by, too close for comfort. Killigrew whirled, bringing up the shotgun, but in the beam of his bull's-eye he could see only dancing snowflakes, getting thicker with each passing moment. Then another roar sounded, even closer this time. He whirled again – with the wind howling about his ears, it was impossible to tell which direction the sound came from.

'He's here!' he screamed at Bähr. 'Bruin's right here!'

The lieutenant was almost hysterical with terror, his guts squirming and his mouth dry. He was no stranger to fear, but that was a fear he could cope with: fear of things like pirates and slavers, things he could fight by conventional means. This was a wild animal; it did not fight as men fought, and it seemed possessed of a supernatural cunning. A product of the Age of Reason, Killigrew knew that was nonsense, but against his rational mind was weighed the evidence of his own eyes. They could not defeat this bear; it was vain of them even to attempt.

Bähr grabbed him by the shoulders and shook him vigorously. 'For God's sake, Lieutenant! Get a grip on yourself. It's just a wild animal! Now come on, and look sharp. These buggers can move fast when they want to. Give me the bull's-eye.'

Bähr lit their way and soon found the bear's tracks again. After meandering for a few hundred yards, they led to a bloody corpse in the snow. 'Osborne?' asked Bähr.

Killigrew shook his head. 'Jenkins.' He recognised the insignia on the private's uniform. 'Bruin's leading us in circles.'

'He must've doubled back on himself.'

The two of them stared at one another.

'Ursula!' gasped Killigrew. Clutching his shotgun, he started to run back in the direction he thought the tent lay, but Bähr caught him by the arm.

'You go back and make sure the others are all right. I'm staying out here until I know that bear is dead.'

'On your own?'

'Trust me! I've been hunting big game since you were a gleam in your father's eye. Go on, go! Ursula might be in danger. Here, take the bull's-eye.'

Killigrew wanted to argue, but there was no time. He took the lantern from the doctor and sprinted off through the swirling snow.

Bähr watched the light of the bull's-eye dance away through the snow until it was barely visible, and then started to follow with his hunting rifle cradled in his arms. *That's it, you bugger*, he thought. *Run – and let Bruin see your light and come to investigate*. The doctor had read that polar bears were insatiably curious. It was a fact he intended to use against this one. The bear had had the element of surprise on its side in all its attacks so far. This way, Bähr hoped, he would turn the tables and get the drop on the bear.

A pity he had to use the young officer as live bait, but it had to be done. With any luck, when the bear made an appearance and charged, Bähr would be able to shoot it before it reached the lieutenant. And if not – well, he would certainly kill it afterwards. Better to sacrifice one than for them all to die.

But Killigrew made it to the tent without incident. Bähr took shelter behind a hummock of snow and settled down to wait. When the bear came, it would head straight for the tent and the doctor would have a clear shot at it. He did not mind the cold and snow; he could wait for hours, if need be, without stirring a muscle. He had come to the Arctic to bag a bear, and this was his chance. A far superior specimen to the two cubs he had killed a couple of months ago. And what a tale to tell visitors to his home when he showed them the trophies in his library! It would be the centrepiece of his collection.

He heard a roar off to his left, bloodcurdling in its savagery. But Bähr was not frightened. *Roar all you like, my beauty. A bullet in the brain will silence you soon enough.*

Another roar, closer this time. Bähr glanced in that direction and glimpsed a pale shape moving through the swirling blizzard, away from him. Grinning, he started to crawl through the snow after it. *What do you want to be, Bruin? Mounted on the wall, or a hearthrug?*

He found the bear's tracks and followed them over a ridge into a shallow gully. Sensing he was close to his quarry, he quickened his pace, his eyes searching the blizzard. A specimen like this would be wasted if it were wall-mounted or reduced to a hearthrug. He wondered if he could drag the whole carcase back to the *Venturer* and stuff it and mount it himself, in a realistic and frightening pose. It would look splendid in a corner of the library in his house in Hannover.

He stopped. He should have caught the bear by now; something was wrong. A tiny niggle of doubt stirred at the back of his mind, a faint *frisson* of fear. Could it be he had underestimated his quarry?

A snuffling sound directly behind him made the hairs prickle on the back of his neck and his blood ran cold. He started to turn.

His last words in the mortal realm were spoken with an almost fatalistic calmness:

'*Ach, Scheiße—*'

Killigrew thrust his head inside the tent and was relieved to see Ursula watching over Phillips, just as he had left them. 'Are you all right?' he asked.

She nodded. 'Where are Dr Bähr, and Jenkins and Osborne?'

Killigrew fastened the laces of the tent flap behind him. 'They're still out there, somewhere.' It was true enough: no point in worrying her now by telling her about Jenkins' death. 'Bähr thinks he can kill the bear; I was worried it might have turned back and come for you.'

She shook her head. 'I have seen nothing.'

A long, growling howl sounded, full of bestial rage and savagery. He looked up with a fearful shudder and levelled his shotgun at the mouth of the tent, before realising that the howl had been some distance off.

The next growl was much closer. It made Killigrew jump, and Ursula clutched at him fearfully.

The wind battered against the sides of the tent. The roaring and howling of the wind sounded like the bear; or perhaps the bear sounded like the roaring of the wind.

Even as the breath billowed from his mouth in clouds of condensation, Killigrew could feel the sweat dripping from under his arms.

Then the wind stopped as abruptly as if someone had closed a door. Killigrew could hear Phillips' teeth chattering, Ursula's frightened panting, his own breath issuing raggedly through his clenched teeth, and his heart thudding.

'What's happening?' moaned Ursula.

'I don't know.' Killigrew took her by the hand and dragged her towards the mouth of the tent. 'But I know this much – we'll be a lot safer outside the tent than inside.' He reached for the laces fastening the tent flap when five long claws lacerated the holland fabric.

Killigrew leaped back, pushing Ursula back behind him. He

expected the bear to burst inside, but then all was still again.

Long seconds ticked by. The back of his hand stung, and when he was able to drag his eyes away from the mouth of the tent and look down he saw that his gauntlet had been slashed, the blood weeping from a scratch in the hand beneath.

He heard a snuffling outside, and promptly blasted in that direction with the shotgun, blowing a hole through the fabric of the tent. Gun smoke mingled with their misty breath in the tent, and was torn apart where the wind blew flakes of snow through the hole.

An outraged howl came from outside. Killigrew blasted at it, tearing a second hole in the tent. Then all was silent once more.

'Did you get it?' asked Ursula.

Killigrew reached into his pocket for some fresh shells for his shotgun, only to remember that all the spare ammunition was on the large sledge; besides, it was probably useless after its soaking earlier. He edged carefully towards the second of the two holes he had blasted, the fabric still smouldering at the edges, and peered out, squinting through the swirling snow. There was no sign of the bear. Perhaps he had wounded it; perhaps it had crawled off to die somewhere. But there was no sign of any blood.

That was when the bear lunged through the front of the tent.

Killigrew barely had time to push Ursula one way before he threw himself the other as the bear charged between them. He rolled to his right seconds before a massive, clawed paw came down where his head had been. The guy ropes snapped and the whole tent was whipped away from over their heads.

He stood up and blinked, blinded by the snow that was driven in his face. The tent was flapping away through the night like some huge winged spirit, the small sledge caught up in its guy ropes bumping along behind it. Killigrew saw Phillips sprawled in the open, half out of his chrysalis bag, and when he crouched over him to examine him saw that the marine's throat had been ripped open.

He heard a scream, looked up and saw Ursula dashing off into the night, the bear loping after her. Killigrew snatched up one of the boarding pikes they had used as a tent pole, but cut down to four and a half feet in length, its steel head long since removed, it was about as effective a weapon against 2,000 pounds of polar bear as a feather duster.

Killigrew started to run after the bear, but it quickly became apparent that the bear would reach Ursula long before he caught up with either of them. 'Leave her alone, you goddamned son of a bitch!'

As the bear bore down on Ursula, its paws only a couple of feet behind her heels, Killigrew saw its muscles tense, ready for a final pounce.

And then Ursula disappeared.

Too late Killigrew realised that she had unwittingly fled in the direction of the crevasse. In her panic, she had failed to see it until it was too late.

'*No!*'

The bear skidded to a halt at the lip of the crevasse. Hearing Killigrew's anguished scream, it turned and drew its dark lips back to reveal its long fangs.

Killigrew stopped and brandished the tent pole.

The bear advanced slowly, taking its time, knowing that it had eliminated all of its enemies except one. If it relished this moment, there was no telling from the expression on its face: a feral snarl, twisted in an animalistic hatred that went beyond a savage need for food. Perhaps when the bear had attacked its first human, it had done so out of hunger, but there was no need to kill Killigrew for food with the bodies of Jenkins, Bähr and Phillips in the vicinity. The bloodlust was on the beast now, and it would not rest until it had been sated.

It advanced with its head lowered, its dark eyes boring into Killigrew's skull. As the lieutenant backed away, it reared up, towering over him. As it descended towards him, Killigrew swung at its wedge-shaped head with the tent pole. The bear caught the stick between its teeth and tore it from the lieutenant's grip.

Killigrew turned and ran.

The bear charged after him. He did not need to glance over his shoulder to know this, did not dare to: the ice seemed to shudder beneath his feet with each thud of the bear's steps. Killigrew saw the crevasse up ahead; some of the haversacks from the small sledge were scattered on the far side where the tent had deposited them as it was whipped away into the night by the howling gale. And one of those haversacks, he remembered, had his pepperboxes in them.

If he could have redoubled his efforts he would have done, but with the bear literally breathing down his neck he was running flat out as it was. He measured the remaining steps towards the lip of the crevasse.

Only ten feet wide, he told himself. Jumping over a sandpit, ten feet was nothing. Jumping over a yawning, bottomless abyss, however . . .

As he launched himself from the lip of the crevasse, his foot – the snow compacted against the soles negating the effect of the crampons – slipped.

He sailed out into space with his heart in his mouth, clawing at the wind with his hands. At first he thought he might make it – the other side was hurtling towards him – and then he was dropping, down, down, into the abyss . . .

The far side slammed against his chest, driving the breath from his lungs. His eyes filled with tears as he tried to claw at the surface of the lake, his feet scrabbling for purchase at the wall of ice below him and sliding over frictionless ice in a futile search for a foothold.

A few yards to his right, the bear sauntered up to the edge of the crevasse and leaped over with almost delicate ease. It began to circle around to where Killigrew clung to the lip.

A haversack lay in the snow only a few feet from where he hung on for dear life, one of the straps less than two feet away. Killigrew reached for it, and his fingers came up less than an inch short.

The bear was closing in now. If ever a bear looked confident, this one did. With a supreme effort, Killigrew lunged for the strap, straining his muscles. His fingers hooked themselves over the strap and then he slipped. He dropped down a foot, and his arm was almost torn from his socket as the fingers of his left hand caught on the lip. He tucked his head in as the haversack dropped on him, bouncing on his shoulder and then falling to dangle by its strap in his right hand. The sudden jerk almost pulled the grip of his other hand free.

Sobbing for breath, Killigrew dangled there. Somehow he

managed to draw up the haversack until he could balance it on his left shoulder.

Above him, he could hear the bear snuffling as it approached. 'Come on, you bastard,' he mumbled, working the buckles of the haversack with his right hand and his teeth. 'Kit's got a little surprise for you . . .'

The bear appeared immediately above him, peering down at him curiously. Then it seemed to remember it was looking at an enemy, and it drew back its lips in a snarl.

The buckle came free, the contents of the bag spilling out all over Killigrew: boxes of ammunition, signal rockets, pepper-boxes, all tumbling down into the darkness below. He let go of the haversack and clutched frantically at one of the pistols as it fell, even managed to brush it with his fingertips, and then it was gone.

His heart sank to the bottom of the abyss with the pepperboxes.

He remembered Osborne's screams as the bear tore him to shreds. Better to plunge to his death than to die like that. But he could not relinquish his life just by letting go with his left hand: no matter how desperate the situation, he was not ready to give up and die.

He raised his head and glared back at the bear, his own eyes boring into the beast's skull now. 'You want to eat me?' he snarled. 'You can't eat me while I'm hanging down here.' He raised his right hand and waved it temptingly before the bear's snout. 'You've got to pull me up, you hear? You've got to take my hand and drag me out of this crevasse! Take my hand, damn you!' Once out of the crevasse, he would be able to fight the bear with both hands; he still had Molineaux's Bowie knife tucked in the small of his back, and he would fight the bear with his bare hands if he had to. He would gouge its eyes out with his thumbs; throttle it if all else failed. He knew that if Latimer could have seen him, the clerk would not have given much for his chances, but whatever else happened Kit Killigrew was going to die fighting.

The bear followed the movements of his hand with its whole head. It looked sorely tempted; then it seemed to change its mind. It reared up on its hind legs, and then brought its forepaws crashing down against the edge of the crevasse, on either side of Killigrew's fingers.

'What the hell are you doing? Take my hand, damn you! You want to taste my blood, you're going to have to take my hand!'

Again the bear reared up and crashed its paws down again, and again. And then the chunk of ice from which Killigrew dangled broke away from the lip of the crevasse and he was falling, down, down into an oblivion far darker than any midnight in an Arctic winter.

'Cheer up, lads,' said Riggs, joining his messmates at one of the tables in the mess deck. 'Only three weeks to Christmas.'

'I must remember to order a goose from the local butchers,' said Ågård.

With the marines out with Killigrew, Bähr and Ursula, Molineaux adrift, and Armitage still on the sick list, there were only eleven of them eating in the mess deck now: Ågård and Riggs, Qualtrough, Unstead, Stokers Butterwick and Gargrave, Seamen Endicott, Hughes and Smith, Ignatz Fischbein and Jakob Kracht. With so many vacant places, the mess deck was starting to look empty.

Smith and Gargrave, mess cooks for the day, doled out the food to the respective messmates: salt pork and split peas again.

Hughes indicated his plate with his knife. 'What's this?' he asked Smith.

'Mr Latimer's cress. Same as you had for dinner today, same as you had for supper yesterday, same as you had for dinner the day before that.'

'Exactly,' said Hughes. 'I've had enough cress to last me a lifetime. I don't even like normal cress, but this stuff – it's disgusting!'

Hughes was being a little unfair about Latimer's cress-farming efforts. True, the cress was a pallid yellow from the lack of sunlight, and it might not have been as crisp as the stuff that grew in England, but it was palatable enough for all that.

'He'd want it soon enough if only the officers ate it,' said Endicott, and there was a general murmur of agreement all around the mess deck.

'I'll have it if you divven't want it,' said Butterwick. 'I love cress, me.'

'You're welcome to it.' Hughes held his plate across the aisle between their tables so the stoker could fork the cress onto his own plate, but Ågård took the plate from him and put it back in front of him.

'Everyone eats their own portion of cress,' said the ice quartermaster. 'Them's orders. Got to eat your fresh greens. You don't want scurvy, do you?'

'That's all my eye and Betty Martin, if you ask me,' said Hughes. 'You can't tell me the Esquimaux eat cress – or any other greens, for that matter. You don't see them dying of scurvy, do you?'

'That's because they eat plenty of fresh, raw meat,' said Qualtrough.

'I can arrange for you to get your ration of meat uncooked, if you prefer,' Ågård told Hughes. 'No? Didn't think so. Now eat your cress, or I'll see to it you get no grog ration tonight.'

'You know what? You can take your cress – and your bloody grog ration – and stick them up your bum.' Hughes stood up, picked up his plate, and hurled it across the mess deck. '*I hate cress!*'

The plate shattered against the bulkhead beside the door leading aft just as Sørensen stepped through. There was a sharp intake of breath from everyone as the brawny harpooner paused to take in the mess. 'Is there a problem, Jake?'

'Red won't eat his cress, Bjørn,' said Unstead.

'So I see. Or his pork or split peas, by the look of it.' Everyone else shrank back as Sørensen crossed to where Hughes stood up. 'You know what's wrong with you, Red? You don't know what's good for you.'

'It's not cress, Mr Sørensen, I know that much.'

'If you want to go without cress, Red, it can be arranged. We'll put you in irons in the lazaretto, and you can go without cress and everything else but bread and water for a week. How does that suit you?'

Hughes muttered something under his breath. Sørensen hauled him out of his chair and sent him staggering across the mess deck with a well-placed boot to the backside, towards where the shattered remains of the broken plate lay at the foot of the bulkhead. 'You want any supper tonight, Red, you can lick that mess off the deck. Otherwise you go without, hoist in? Then clean up the mess. I'll be back at two bells to make sure you've done a good job; and if you haven't, it will be the lazaretto for you whether you like it or not! And if I catch any of the rest of you slipping him food tonight when you think no one's looking, I'll have him on extra duties from now until Christmas!' He stalked back the way he had come.

'Capitalist lapdog!' muttered Hughes, glaring after Sørensen.

Ågård shook his head sadly. 'You never bloody learn, do you?' he told Hughes. He sighed, and glanced across to where Butterwick was stuffing the last of his salt pork and split peas into his gullet. 'At least someone's got a hearty appetite.'

After supper, Ågård and Kracht made their way up on deck for guard duty. 'Still no sign of Herr Killigrew and the others,' remarked the blacksmith.

'It's only been five days,' Ågård said mildly. 'It could be another nine before they get back.'

'What if they don't come back? What if the bear gets them, or they get lost and freeze to death out there?'

'They'll be back.'

'But what if they're not? You really think that when the spring thaw comes – if it comes at all – we'll be able to sail this ship out of here, with Herr Strachan in command? Don't misunderstand me – he seems a fine fellow – but . . . a sailor?' Kracht shook his head sadly.

'That's where you and I come in, Jakob,' Ågård told him. 'We'll get them all safely home to their mamas. But never you fear: Mr Killigrew will be back with the others.'

'How can you be so sure?'

'Fifteen years I've known him, and I can tell you this: his tendency to get himself into tight corners is matched only by his skill at getting himself out of them again. If I know Mr Killigrew, he's probably already on his way back here even now, with a completed chart of the North-West Passage in his back pocket, Franklin and the others in tow, and Bruin's carcass on the sledge ready to be stuffed and mounted. Wherever Mr Killigrew is right now, you can be sure he's on top of things.'

★ ★ ★

Killigrew was running from the bear, but his legs felt as though they had been carved from blocks of ice and would not obey him. Realising that he could not escape, he turned just in time to see the bear pounce. Its jaws closed over his face, its teeth slicing through his skin like a thousand red-hot, razor-sharp knives. He parted his lips to cry out, and snow fell into his mouth. The bear's teeth were melting, turning into water that dripped over his cheeks, and then some part of his nightmare-fuddled mind grasped the reality: he was unconscious, and dreaming.

The realisation shattered the dream like a rock hurled through the film of ice on a freshly frozen pond. But the wet, burning sensation on his cheeks did not go away. Someone was rubbing snow in his face. He spat it out of his mouth and jerked his head back with a gasp, shuffling away from his assailant. Except that when he tried to put his left hand down behind him it met nothing but cold air. He sprawled on his back in the snow, with nothing beneath his head and shoulders.

'Don't move!'

Groping beneath him with his left hand and finding nothing but the edge of an icy ledge that he hung over, he decided it would be a good idea to obey the voice. 'Ursula? I thought you were dead!'

'I was beginning to think the same about you. Be careful – there's a drop to the right – your left, I mean.'

'So I see.' Not that Killigrew could see anything: after the dazzling wash of light in his nightmare, this new hell seemed pitch-black at first. He eased himself to his right, and after moving only a couple of inches in that direction met a wall of ice, smooth and sheer. 'Clearly this isn't heaven, and it's too cold for hell.'

He took off his gauntlets, tucking them in the front of his coat so he would not lose them, and fumbled for his box of matches with numb fingers. He massaged them and tried to get the blood flowing. When the sensation started to return he fumbled for his matches again. He struck one with trembling fingers and then blinked as its searing light blinded him. The flame settled down and he blinked away the tears. The yellow flame reflected only

351

cold, glittering blueness. They were in a crevasse, with sheer walls of ice rising on either side of them. The ledge they sat on was littered with objects from the haversack that Killigrew had inadvertently emptied while clinging to the lip of the crevasse above.

He glanced up. The single flame did not provide enough light to illuminate the walls of the crevasse all the way to the top, but Killigrew doubted it could be more than twenty feet; even with the snow banked on the ledge to break his fall, a further plunge would surely have broken his neck. As it was, as far as he could tell he had sustained no injuries worse than a throbbing shoulder and a large bump rising on the back of his aching head.

The match burned down to his fingers, but they were so frozen it was some seconds before he realised it and dropped it with a gasp. The flame sailed down into the darkness below, until the angle of the crevasse hid it from sight altogether. Its light was reflected from the icy walls for a few seconds more, slowly fading until there was nothing but blackness left.

Moving carefully, he stood up on the ledge and explored the side of the crevasse with his fingers. It was not quite vertical, but so smooth and devoid of hand- and foot-holds it might as well have been.

Ursula must have heard him moving around. 'What are you doing?'

'Trying to find a way up.'

'There isn't one.' Her voice was bleak, dispassionate, as if she had already abandoned all hope of escaping. 'I tried calling for Phillips, but he didn't come.'

'No, he wouldn't.'

Ursula was silent for a while as the implication of Killigrew's words sank in.

'How long was I unconscious for?'

'No more than a minute or two, I think.'

'So the chances are that Bruin's still sniffing around up there, waiting for us.' *And gorging himself on the bodies of the others while he waits.*

'Our situation would not appear to be enviable.'

'Oh, I wouldn't go so far as to say that.' Killigrew tried to inject a breezy note into his voice. 'At least we're out of the wind.'

'Do you always look for the bright side in a hopeless situation?'

'Always. I find it helps immensely. *Nil desperandum*: the fact that this isn't the first time I've been in a hopeless situation should tell you that things are never quite as hopeless as they seem.'

'You have a plan for getting us out of here?'

'I'm working on it.' He struck another match and used it to collect all the bits and pieces that had fallen out of the haversack: a box of shells for the shotgun, two signal rockets, a bottle of spirits of wine. Not much help there.

The match burned down. He took out a notebook, tore out a page, twisted it tightly and set it in the snow before lighting it with another match. By the flickering light he emptied his pockets and added the contents to the meagre pile of objects: Molineaux's Bowie knife; his hip flask and cheroot case; his fob watch; pencil stub; miniature pocket telescope; his clasp knife; and the five-inch length of fuse he had had left over when they had blown a dock in the ice in the Middle Pack, what seemed like a lifetime ago. He really had to clean his pockets out more often. Apart from some lint, that was all. None of it much help at all in their present situation.

He took a swig from the hip flask. The Irish whiskey burned a fiery trail down his throat, warming him from inside. He proffered the flask to Ursula. 'Take a swig of this. It'll help warm you up.'

'Dr Bähr says that the warmth is just an illusion.'

'At this moment in time we need all the illusions we can get.'

She took a swig and handed the flask back to Killigrew. 'Could we send up a signal rocket?'

'Easily. But we're more than thirty miles from the *Venturer*. Even if anyone did happen to be looking in the right direction, I doubt they'd notice it.' He glanced at her face in the light of the makeshift candle. Perhaps it was just the eerie, flickering illumination, but she looked even paler than usual. 'Massage your face,' he told her. 'Got to keep frostbite at bay.' He moved closer to her and put an arm gently around her shoulders, drawing her

353

against him. 'Pardon the familiarity, ma'am, but we'll stand a better chance of survival if we share our body heat.'

'Under the circumstances, I think you may call me Ursula. Or Urse – that's what my sisters called me. Is this something they teach you in naval officer school?'

He chuckled. 'Something Strachan mentioned in one of his lectures – "Arctic Survival", I think it was. I'm just glad it's you with me right now, and not one of the others.'

She smiled wanly. 'I wish I could say the same. Not that I find you repellent!' she added hurriedly.

'You're too kind!'

'I mean, I would rather it was someone else trapped down here in my place. But if I must be here, I'd rather it was with you than anyone else.'

The torn page flickered and went out, leaving them in darkness. She clung to him even more tightly, and they bumped noses.

'*Entschuldigung!*'

'That's the way the Esquimaux kiss,' said Killigrew. 'Rubbing noses.'

'I prefer the European way.'

'Me too.'

He kissed her: tentatively at first, not sure if she would push him away and slap him. But her mouth opened into his at once and their tongues met, searching less for mutual lust as for the warmth of human contact: a reminder that for now, at least, they were both still able to enjoy mortal pleasures.

He pushed her away with reluctance. 'First things first. Let's see if we can get out of this chasm.' He fumbled for the ice chisel. 'Stand with your back to the ice. I'm going to have to stand on your shoulders, I hope you don't mind . . .?'

'What are you going to do?'

'Cut hand-holds in the ice.'

'But that will take for ever!'

'Time would seem to be the one commodity we have in abundance.'

XIX

Stage Fright

Molineaux sat on the sledge, following the tracks made by Killigrew and the others nearly a week ago with the beam of a bull's-eye, while Terregannoeuck stood on the back and drove the dogs. The snowfall grew thicker and thicker until the lantern could no longer pick out the tracks through the swirling flurries.

'It's no good!' Molineaux yelled over his shoulder. 'I'll have to go ahead of the sledge on foot!'

Terregannoeuck nodded and reined in the huskies. Molineaux climbed off and walked past the dogs. The tracks were still discernible, but the heavy snow was quickly covering them. If they did not find Killigrew and the others soon, they never would.

Molineaux trudged through the snow while Terregannoeuck followed him, leading the huskies by the muzzle of the lead dog, so that they would not overtake Molineaux in their enthusiasm while they dragged the sledge.

Even in his Arctic clothing, Molineaux felt frozen. He had to remind himself that while he had only been out here for three days; Killigrew and the others had been gone for twice as long. How cold must he be? Molineaux had to go on, because he knew that the lieutenant would have done the same for him.

The tracks they were following grew fainter and fainter, until Molineaux was not sure if he was following genuine traces or just seeing what he wanted to see. Eventually the blanket of snow became so thick he could not even kid himself there was anything to follow.

The snow swirled thickly around them. 'We never find them this way!' said Terregannoeuck.

Molineaux looked around in desperation. 'Sir?' he yelled, cupping mittened hands around his mouth. 'Mr Killigrew, sir! Are you out there? Where are you?'

Nothing. Just snow, ice, the howling of the wind and the panting of the dogs.

Molineaux reached under his jacket, took out his boatswain's call and blew 'All hands to quarters'. Then he listened again, trying to penetrate the snowstorm with his ears, straining for any sound that might have been a man calling for help. But there was nothing.

'We make camp,' Terregannoeuck decided, and led the dogs and the sledge into the lee of a twenty-foot high pressure ridge. Molineaux looked around in agitation. It was not in his nature to give up, but he could not see what else he could do.

Terregannoeuck sat down in the snow and took a swig from the gourd he wore on a thong around his neck. 'What's in there?' asked Molineaux. 'Rum?'

The Inuk ignored him and closed his eyes.

'Fine. You hog it to yourself. I'll make some scran, shall I?' Molineaux took the portable stove from the sledge and managed to get it going. 'Tomato soup do you?'

Terregannoeuck was rocking from side to side, making an odd humming noise.

Molineaux eyed him nervously. 'You oh-kay?'

The Inuk just went on rocking himself from side to side. It was giving Molineaux a creepy feeling. He decided the best thing to do was to ignore it. He hacked the lid off a tin of soup with an ice-axe. The soup was frozen in the tin. He put the tin on the portable stove until it had melted enough for him to tip it into a saucepan in a solid cylinder and then sat and watched it slowly melt.

After a while Terregannoeuck became perfectly still. Molineaux stared at him, and then got up and crossed over to shake him by the shoulders. 'Hey, don't go to sleep! The pill-roller says it's a bad notion to fall asleep in the snow. He says you won't wake up.'

Terregannoeuck could not be roused.

'Wake up, wake up!'

This was crazy! Sure, it was cold – damned cold – but if a London boy like Molineaux could take it, then surely an Inuk would not succumb? 'Don't do this to me, Terry. Mr Killigrew needs you. Christ, *I* need you!' Molineaux was not sure that he could find his way back to the *Venturer* without the Inuk. He raised his eyes to the heavens, wondering if he could navigate his way back to the ship by the stars. There was a rent in the clouds somewhere off to his left, but the only constellation he could see was Ursa Major. Not a good omen.

'Hot food,' Molineaux muttered to himself, concentrating on the melting soup. 'That's what you need, Terry, some hot soup inside you . . .'

Somewhere not too far away, he heard a wild, bestial roar. Molineaux stood stock-still for a second, and then ran across to the sledge to retrieve the shotgun. He checked both barrels were primed and loaded, and peered into the thick snow all around them. No sign of the bear, but the snow was coming down so thick it could have been ten yards away and he still would not have seen it.

He tried shaking Terregannoeuck awake again. 'Come on, Terry!' he persisted. 'Don't do this to me!'

But the Inuk remained in a trance.

Molineaux paced up and down, cradling the shotgun in his arms, jumping at every shadow. At last the soup was melted. It looked as if it was steaming. He tasted a little, but it was still tepid. Well, that would have to do. 'Come on, Terry, have some . . .'

He glanced across to where the Inuk had been sitting, but Terregannoeuck had vanished. Molineaux gasped in shock and looked around to see him striding across to the sledge. 'We go!'

'Don't you want some soup?'

'We go!' insisted Terregannoeuck.

With 2,000 pounds of savage carnivore wandering about out there somewhere, Molineaux was not inclined to argue. He put out the stove and carried it back to the sledge. 'Are we going back to the *Venturer*?' He hated to think of abandoning Killigrew, but he could not see what else they could do.

'Get on.'

Molineaux climbed on the sledge.

'*Marche!*' The dogs took up the strain and once again they raced over the snow. Molineaux illuminated the way as best he could with the bull's-eye. Terregannoeuck seemed to know where they were going. Back to the *Venturer*? Molineaux had no idea. Normally he was pretty good at keeping his bearings, but in this blizzard it was hopeless.

They had gone about half a mile over the snow before Terregannoeuck stopped the sledge again, in the middle of nowhere. 'What are we doing here?' demanded Molineaux.

Ignoring him, Terregannoeuck climbed down from the sledge and walked a few yards through the snow until he came to a low hummock in the ice, about six feet long. He started to dig into it with his hands.

Molineaux took a shovel from the sledge and went to help him, but Terregannoeuck had already uncovered something. It took the petty officer a moment to work out what it was he was looking at, still half-buried beneath the recent snowfall. When he recognised it, his stomach lurched. He reeled in horror, and his heel tapped something else buried in the snow.

Terregannoeuck indicated the corpse he had uncovered. 'Marine?'

Molineaux nodded. 'Osborne.' His face was unrecognisable, but there were still scraps of uniform left on the chewed cadaver, enough to distinguish the wearer as a bombardier in the Royal Marine Artillery.

'Something bad happen here,' said Terregannoeuck.

'You don't have to be an *angakok* to know that!' Molineaux started to dig in the snow to exhume the object his heel had brushed, terrified of finding the corpse of one of the others. Instead he found the makeshift bomb-gun. It had not even been fired. The petty officer had no love for marines, but he could not help feeling sorry for Osborne: the poor bastard had never stood a chance.

One of the huskies started to bark frantically, then they were all at it, staring off through the snow like pointers. 'What the hell's got into them?' Molineaux asked Terregannoeuck.

'*Nanuq* near.'

Those two words sent a chill down the petty officer's spine. As Terregannoeuck crossed back to the sledge and unstrapped his harpoon, Molineaux removed the percussion cap from the bomb-gun and replaced it with a fresh one from his cartouche box. For all he knew, Osborne had had time to aim and squeeze the trigger, but had been betrayed to death by a faulty cap. If it was the bear out there, Molineaux wanted to avoid having a misfire at the worst possible moment.

Terregannoeuck crouched by the dogs and unfastened their harnesses one by one. Tensed and panting eagerly, nonetheless they waited until the Inuk had released the last dog. He gave them an order in his native tongue, and as one they all sprang off into the snow in a pack. Clutching his spear, Terregannoeuck scurried after them, and in the blink of an eye Molineaux was left standing on his own by the sledge. Realising there was no one left to watch his back, he glanced fearfully over his shoulder, and then hurried off in the direction Terregannoeuck had gone after the dogs.

The driving snow blinded him, but he only had to follow the sound of the dogs. A second noise was soon added to the cacophony: the snarling of a large creature. He almost bumped into Terregannoeuck, poised to throw his spear, although at what Molineaux could not tell. He could just make out the dogs, formed into a rough semi-circle, all barking at something amidst them, and then . . .

'Jesus Christ!'

The bear was huge, well over ten feet tall on its hind legs. It lunged towards one of the huskies with a sudden access of speed, seizing it in its powerful jaws and twisting its head this way and that while the dog yelped pitifully and the barking of its companions became all the more frenzied. Only when the husky's yelps were silenced did the bear toss its limp corpse to one side.

Molineaux levelled the bomb-gun, bracing the stock against his shoulder. He aimed at where the bear reared up, less than fifteen yards from where he stood, and squeezed the trigger.

There was a loud bang, the stock slammed into his shoulder, and he was thrown back into a snowdrift behind him as a whooshing sound filled his ears. His first thought was that the gun had exploded, but then there was a small explosion, a blossoming of bright orange amidst the swirling black and white of the winter snowstorm. He raised his head, saw the bear still standing between him and where the bomb had exploded, and realised with a sick feeling that he had missed.

But the explosion had distracted the bear. It half turned, and that was when Terregannoeuck ran in under the guard of its massive paws and drove the tip of the spear deep into his chest. Blood dribbled down its white fur. It raised its head to the heavens, gave one last agonised roar and toppled sideways, forcing two of the remaining huskies to get out of the way sharpish, or else be crushed beneath its massive weight.

Terregannoeuck backed off, panting hard. The dogs continued to bark, as if they feared the bear was playing possum. Molineaux could not blame them. He picked himself up out of the snow and crossed to where the bear lay. He prodded it with the empty muzzle of the bomb-gun, fearing it might burst back into savage life and wishing he had a fresh bomb handy to reload the gun with. The bear did not twitch a muscle. Molineaux gave it a savage kick, then ran away a few feet and turned. The bear lay still.

Terregannoeuck approached the bear and pulled his spear from its chest. A little more blood spilled from the wound, not much. The Inuk crouched by the massive body.

'Easy, Terry!' warned Molineaux.

Terregannoeuck placed his hand against the bear's chest, over its heart. 'Him dead.'

'You sure?'

'Terregannoeuck sure. No heartbeat,'

The truth of the matter finally sank in. Molineaux let out an exultant whoop of joy. 'You sonuvagun! You actually killed it!'

The Inuk began to pray over the carcass in his own tongue – thanking it for allowing him to slay it, Molineaux supposed. 'Say one for me, Terry,' he said, feeling equally grateful. The reign of terror that had begun two months ago and claimed the lives of at least five of his shipmates – not to mention Ziegler and perhaps Killigrew and the others as well – was finally over.

Another whoosh sounded off to Molineaux's right, and he turned to see something shooting through the night sky, little more than a rising glow behind the flurries of snow. *Signal rocket.* He ran across the ice in the direction he guessed it had come, swinging his bull's-eye to light his path and blowing shrilly on his boatswain's call.

'. . . er . . .ere!' A faint voice, whipped away on the wind.

'Who's there?' demanded Molineaux, still running through the snow. 'Where are you? I can't see you!'

'Over here!' The voice was closer now, but oddly muffled.

Molineaux took a couple more steps, and then paused. 'Is that you, Mr Killigrew? Where are you?'

'*Stop!* Don't . . . take . . . another . . . step!'

Molineaux realised that the voice was coming up from his feet. Glancing down, he saw the chasm that loomed beneath him, and stepped back hurriedly. He advanced more cautiously and peered down, shining his bull's-eye into the chasm. In the darkness below, he could just make out Killigrew and Frau Weiss standing on a ledge below him.

'Mr Killigrew? That you? Boy, am I glad to see you!'

'Not half as glad as we are to see you, Molineaux, I can assure you,' Killigrew called back up weakly.

'Hang on, sir, I'll get you out!'

Molineaux dashed back to the sledge only to meet Terregannoeuck coming in the opposite direction, leading the five surviving dogs dragging the sledge. They had not brought any rope with them from the *Venturer*, so they unfastened the dogs from the harness and used that instead, lowering it down to Killigrew and Ursula. First they brought up Ursula, and then the lieutenant. Both their faces were blue with cold. Molineaux quickly bundled them in buffalo robes and heated some soup for them over the portable stove while Terregannoeuck started to construct an *iglu* for them, carving blocks of ice from the frozen lake with a special ice-cutting knife. He worked so quickly and efficiently, the *iglu* was finished by the time Molineaux had heated the soup until it was tepid enough to eat.

With its low entrance facing away from the prevailing winds that howled across the landscape, it was surprisingly cosy inside the *iglu*, and it was not long before Killigrew and Ursula started to show signs of improvement. Still, they both shivered too much to feed themselves, so Molineaux and Terregannoeuck spoon-fed them.

'We found Osborne,' said Molineaux.

'Dead?' Killigrew stammered through chattering teeth.

Molineaux nodded. 'What about the others? Bähr and the other marines?'

Killigrew shook his head, a haunted look on his face. 'The bear got them. How in the world did you manage to find us?'

'I don't know, sir. We followed your tracks for the first couple of days, but then the snow started to cover them. How we found you after that I'll never know. It was a miracle . . .' Molineaux glanced across to the Inuk, who shrugged.

'Just lucky, Terregannoeuck reckon.' His face as impassive as ever, nonetheless he winked at Molineaux.

The petty officer was about to protest, when he realised that Killigrew would never believe it. Molineaux did not believe it himself. He shook his head dismissively. It was like Terregannoeuck had said: just lucky. *Yur, in a pig's eye.* He had been at sea for fourteen years, travelled the world over from the Orient to . . . well, to here, the North Pole, near as damn it, and he had seen some weird things in his time, but this one beat the band. He shivered, and not just because of the intense cold. 'We still wouldn't have found you if you hadn't sent up that signal rocket when you did. How did you know to fire one off then?'

'Heard an explosion. Kracht's bomb-gun?'

Molineaux nodded.

'What were you shooting at?'

'The bear.'

'It's still around?'

Molineaux grinned. 'He won't be going anywhere in a hurry. You should've seen it, sir, it was incredible. The dogs had it at bay, but it picks one of 'em up in its jaws and worries the poor bugger to death. I takes a shot at it with the bomb-gun, and miss, like a goddamned cack-handed greenhorn . . .'

'You missed?' said Killigrew, and managed a wan smile. 'I find that difficult to believe.'

'Happens to the best of us, sir,' Molineaux said philosophically. 'Wasn't ready for the recoil, was I? That thing's got a kick like a sixty-eight pounder! Anyhow, just when I'm thinking

362

we've had it for sure, Terry here just runs up to the bugger and stabs it in the heart with his pig-sticker and . . . blap! Down it goes.'

'So it's over?' asked Ursula.

'It's over,' said Molineaux.

'Indeed,' said Killigrew. 'All we have to do now is get back to the *Venturer*, hope the ice thaws enough to get back to Lancaster Sound in the spring, and sail four and a half thousand miles back to England.'

'After what we've come through?' Molineaux grinned. 'Easy as caz! We'll start back for the *Venturer* tomorrow morning. We'll be there by Wednesday.'

'Only one small problem,' said Terregannoeuck. 'Very small problem . . .' He held up one hand with the thumb and forefinger a fraction of an inch apart so they could see just how minuscule the problem was. 'I kill wrong *nanuq*.'

'How are you feeling?' asked Strachan.

'First-rate, thanks,' said Killigrew. 'As a matter of fact, I think I'm ready to get out of my bunk now.'

'Oh, no you don't!' Strachan pushed him back down against the pillow. 'You'll get up when I say you can, and not a moment before. We don't want you having a relapse, and, incredible though it may seem, I can manage perfectly well without you for now. But we want you back on your feet when the spring thaw happens, so you can get us back to safety.'

'I hope I'm on my feet long before then!'

'I'm sure you will be – provided you don't try to rush things now.' He laid the back of his hand against Killigrew's forehead. 'Looks as though your fever's finally broken. Here: put this under your tongue.' He thrust a thermometer into the lieutenant's mouth.

It was Friday 10 December, two days since Molineaux and Terregannoeuck had brought Killigrew and Ursula back on board – not that Killigrew could remember much about the journey back to Horsehead Bay. The last thing he recalled was Molineaux and Terregannoeuck bickering over whether or not it was Bruin the Inuk had killed. The petty officer had insisted that the polar icecap was not big enough for two such massive bears, but Terregannoeuck had stuck by his quietly stated but firm conviction that it had been some other polar bear.

After that, moments of lucidity – bundled up on the sledge next to Ursula while Molineaux and Terregannoeuck drove them back to the *Venturer* beneath the aurora borealis – had alternated with delirious, disturbing dreams. Back in the comfort of his cabin – so cold and chilly before he had set out on the bear hunt, so warm and cosy now – it was all too good to be true, and he still half expected the scene to melt into another nightmare.

Strachan removed the thermometer and glanced at it. 'Well, your temperature is almost back to normal. We'll see how you're doing this time tomorrow, and then I'll decide whether or not you're fit to return to your duties.'

'How's Ursula?'

'Doing fine. Better than you, even. Don't believe any of that gammon they'll tell you about women being weak, delicate, sickly creatures: they're as tough as old boots, most of 'em. You ask anyone who's ever done any midwifery.'

'Uh-huhn. What was that godawful caterwauling I heard a few minutes ago?'

'Stoker Butterwick auditioning for Latimer's Christmas Eve concert party.'

'Latimer's still going ahead with that?'

'Most definitely. With so many men dead, there's never been a greater need to keep morale up. There could be a long, hard winter ahead of us. Oh, there have been a few changes to the programme: instead of having the crew perform the whole of *The Winter's Tale*, Latimer's just going to read a few soliloquies. Molineaux's going to do some prestidigitation and a comic song, while Terregannoeuck's agreed to give us a display of Esquimaux singing and dancing. Endicott offered to sing "Shiverand Shakery, The Man that Couldn't Get Warm", but I vetoed that. Thought it might be bad for morale.'

'I should damned well think so. Everything else all right? How's Yelverton?'

'Much improved; better than he deserves to be.'

'What about Pettifer?'

'He seems to be better, too. Calmer, at any rate.'

'You think he's fit to return to his duties?'

Strachan grimaced. 'I wouldn't want to take responsibility for a decision like that. I've heard of too many lunatics who could feign sanity to lull their doctors into releasing them, only to prove themselves more deranged than ever. If you want my opinion, Killigrew, you should keep him restrained until you can get a second opinion from a doctor who specialises in cases of insanity.'

'Now where am I going to find such a doctor around here?'

'Exactly! And you can have that counsel in writing, if you want it.'

'It's all right, your word is good enough for me. How's Armitage?'

'Up and about; but not much good in the galley with only one thumb, I'm afraid. Molineaux's taken over his duties, so at least our food is edible again.'

'Who did the cooking while Molineaux was out looking for Ursula and me?'

'Butterwick and Gargrave. They don't have many duties while the ship is overwintering, barring keeping the stoves coaled. I thought it would keep them out of trouble.'

'Did it?'

'Hardly. Butterwick set fire to the galley twice and Gargrave burned every meal he had a hand in. So now Molineaux's back – by popular demand.'

'How does he feel about it?' While Killigrew knew that the petty officer enjoyed cooking for himself, he preferred to avoid acting as ship's cook, which he saw as subservient.

'You know Molineaux. He'd rather do a job himself than let someone else do it badly. Especially when he's got to eat the results.' Strachan hesitated, as if there was something else he wanted to discuss with Killigrew, but was reluctant even to broach the topic before he was certain the lieutenant was fully recovered from his ordeal. He took a deep breath. 'There is one other thing . . .'

'Go on.'

'Well, Terregannoeuck brought back the bladder of the bear he killed while he was out with Molineaux. He's hung it up over the upper deck.'

'I hope no one's going to order that one taken down!'

'Faiks, no! Not that I believe in that sort of superstitious nonsense, you understand,' Strachan added hurriedly. 'But I appreciate how superstitious sailors can be, and I couldn't see any harm in it. Well, there wasn't room on the sledge to bring back the rest of the bear's carcass as well as you and Ursula, but Molineaux did have the wit to cut off one of the bear's paws and bring it back so I could compare it with my plaster casts. He even managed to get the right paw. You know Terregannoeuck's been saying that the bear he killed wasn't the bear that's been giving us so much trouble, but Molineaux's convinced it was? He thought I could prove him right.'

'And?'

Strachan took another deep breath. 'I'm afraid I had to prove Molineaux wrong and Terregannoeuck right.'

'So Bruin's still out there, somewhere?'

'Apparently. I'm sure it's nothing to worry about. You probably scared it off, chasing it all that way and setting off bomb-guns and the like—'

'Having faced that bear twice now, I find it hard to believe it could be scared of anything.'

'Aye, well, we'll just have to wait and see, won't we? Anyhow, now that it's got the bodies of – well, you know – to satiate it, I doubt we'll be seeing it again for another ten weeks or so. That takes us well into the New Year.'

'Unless the Arctic foxes start raiding his larder. I'm starting to have my doubts about your theory that it gets hungry every two weeks, Strachan. The way that bear came after me when it had already killed Walsh, Jenkins, Osborne, Bähr and Phillips . . . it's no normal bear.'

'Och, don't you start turning all superstitious on me! No' you, of all people!'

'I'm not saying it's some supernatural spirit seeking to avenge the deaths of mate and cubs,' Killigrew assured him. 'But there's something not right about that bear, Strachan. Something . . . evil.'

'*Evil!* Crivvens! Will you listen to yourself, Killigrew? How can a bear be evil? It just obeys its natural instincts, that's all. It's a bear. All it does is hunt, eat, wander about the icecap, and make little cubs. You know, in its way it's really a remarkable creature. Perfectly suited to survive and thrive in the inhospitable environment of the Arctic.'

'You sound as if you admire it.'

'I suppose I do, in a way. I admire its . . . *purity*.'

Killigrew shook his head. 'There's nothing pure about this bear, Strachan. There's something wrong with it. You tell me that polar bears only behave in a certain way, yet everything we know about the way they behave is based on anecdotal evidence and the limited observations of a few specimens by zoologists like Pennant. Suppose you were a polar bear zoologist studying human beings . . .'

'Now you're just talking daft!'

'Humour me. Suppose you based your observations on a few humans like . . . oh, I don't know . . . say, the men on the lower deck. From those you drew your theories about human behaviour. It would be a fairly accurate reflection of the behaviour of the breed *Homo maritimus*, wouldn't it?'

Strachan chuckled. 'I suppose so.'

'Would it prepare you for the way that Pettifer started behaving?'

'An insane bear? That's all we need!'

'Not necessarily insane. Just . . . an aberration. You can look for your patterns in nature if you like, lay down your scientific rules about the way the laws of nature work, but you know in your heart as well as I that there are always anomalies. Specimens that are flawed in some way, that fail to match up to nature's perfect blueprint.'

'The exception that proves the rule, you mean?'

'Precisely.'

Strachan rubbed his jaw. 'I don't know. It's something to think about, I suppose.' The assistant surgeon stood up. 'But it's nothing to lose any sleep over, I assure you. Aberration or no, that's a mortal bear, and a bullet in its skull will end its life, the same as it would mine or yours. And we're keeping sentries posted at all hours, just in case. So don't you worry: you get some rest, and I'll look in on you tomorrow, see how you're doing.'

Molineaux concluded his magic act by singing a song of his own composition. It was a ballad about a sailor who found the North Pole and carried it back to London, where he enjoyed a variety of amorous misadventures with the aid of the abstract rod. In the style of the penny gaffs, but toned down out of consideration for the presence of the officers and Frau Weiss, the succession of single *entendres* nonetheless left little to the imagination.

The crew had set up a stage on the forecastle with a backcloth of wadding tilt, and Molineaux sat on a stool, singing his song while he strummed his guitar by the light of a single oil-lamp. A misty layer of condensation hung about six feet off the deck, so that from the audience's point of view Molineaux was hidden from the neck up, but they had seen his face before and knew they were not missing all that much. He was not much of a singer, either, but he played the guitar beautifully.

Rows of benches and chairs had been set up facing the stage to form a makeshift auditorium. The crew listened and guffawed. Killigrew sat in the front row with Latimer, who giggled like a naughty schoolboy – Killigrew had the impression that the clerk was an aficionado of penny-gaff entertainments – and Ursula, who tried to pretend she did not understand the words, although the effect was marred by the smile of amusement that played on her face. Next to her sat Yelverton, who had obtained Strachan's permission to drag himself out of bed for the Christmas Eve concert. The long rest seemed to have done him some good, and there was colour back in his cheeks now, although a fierce coughing fit during one of the earlier acts had worried Killigrew. He wanted to ask Strachan's opinion, but the seat he had saved for the assistant surgeon was empty.

Saturday the eighteenth of December had come and gone without incident. Despite Strachan's theory that even if the bear did attack again, it was unlikely to do so before the New Year, the hands in the forecastle had got it into their heads that the bear attacked every fortnight. Since the eighteenth was exactly two weeks after the bear had killed Walsh, Jenkins, Bähr and Phillips, the eighteenth must be the date on which Bruin would return to the *Venturer*. As the fatal day approached, everyone had become increasingly nervous: even Killigrew had been infected by their trepidation, and although Strachan had professed such fears foolish, the lieutenant had had his doubts that his friend had been entirely free of fear.

The eighteenth had come and gone. So had the nineteenth, and the twentieth. On the twenty-first, Latimer – whose remarks were not always in the best of taste – had jokingly said that he was going to miss Bruin. Now it was Christmas Eve, and Killigrew dared to let himself wonder if Strachan might not be right: perhaps they had seen the last of the bear. It was just a bear, after all. Only the horror of its repeated attacks had built it up into something it was not, some mystical creature against which they were powerless. The more superstitious amongst the crew argued that the bear had been out for revenge for the murder of its cubs, and since Bähr – who had killed the cubs – was now dead, Bruin was satisfied that justice had been done.

When Molineaux had finished the song everyone applauded and the seaman stood up and took a bow. There was a brief hiatus while they waited for the next act to come on and do his turn.

'Oh, Lor'!' exclaimed Latimer, seated next to Killigrew. 'I'd clean forgotten I was next! Excuse me!' He leaped to his feet and dashed behind the backcloth to get changed. The seamen started to talk amongst themselves and Strachan took the place so recently vacated by Latimer.

'Where've you been?' asked Killigrew, mildly annoyed. He knew that the men in tonight's performance had put a lot of effort into preparing this concert – rehearsals, costumes, scenery, not to mention putting up with Latimer's stage-direction – and it was the least the officers could do to be seen enjoying it.

'Standing at the back. I didn't want to disturb Molineaux's performance. What's wrong with you? You're like a bear with a sore head.'

'Very droll.'

'Well, how is your head?'

'Fine. Haven't had a headache since Sunday morning.'

'And he was sinking the whiskeys fast enough on Saturday night,' Yelverton put in with a grin. Killigrew scowled.

Latimer swept aside the backcloth with a flourish and stepped out on to the makeshift stage, dressed in a vague approximation of Elizabethan clothing, carrying a bundle that was supposed to represent a baby. Everyone clapped and he took a bow, lapping it up. 'Thank you, ladies and gentlemen, thank you. My first soliloquy is from Shakespeare's *The Winter's Tale*,' he announced with a smirk.

Cue boos and raspberries from the hands.

'Picture the scene: Bohemia, a desert country near the sea. I am Antigonus, a lord of Sicilia.' He cleared his throat and launched into the soliloquy without further ado about nothing.

' "Come, poor babe. I have heard, but not believ'd, the spirits o' the dead May walk again. If such a thing be, thy mother Appear'd to me last night; for ne'er was a dream So like a waking. To me comes a creature . . ." '

'*The Winter's Tale*?' muttered Yelverton. 'I'd've thought *Ham*let would've been more appropriate.'

'Shh!' said Killigrew, who privately agreed but considered heckling despicably rude.

' " . . .I never saw a vessel of like sorrow . . ." '

'Ah, now that's more like it,' muttered Yelverton. 'Much more pertinent, I think.'

Killigrew shot him a dirty look, but the master was oblivious.

'Oh, cheer up, Killigrew,' murmured Strachan, as Latimer droned on. 'No one's seen hide nor hair – no pun intended – of our friend Bruin for nearly three weeks. The longest night is behind us now.'

'We're still in the longest night,' Killigrew reminded him. 'The sun won't return until February, weather permitting.'

'You know what I mean. February's not far off. First the sun comes back, then the ice melts and before you know it we'll be free to sail back to England. I really don't see what can happen to us which hasn't happened already.'

' " . . .Affrighted much, I did in time collect myself, and thought This was so and no slumber. Dreams are toys; Yet, for this once, yea, superstitiously, I will be squar'd by this. I do believe Hermione hath suffer'd death; and that Apollo would, this being indeed the issue Of King Polixenes, it should here be laid, Either for life or death, upon the earth Of its right father . . ." '

The fore and aft spars that supported the awning creaked softly. Killigrew wondered how great the weight of snow above them was. They had allowed it to build up to act as insulation, but he suddenly found himself wondering if they had not let it get too deep.

' " . . .Farewell! The day frowns more and more. Thou art like to have A lullaby too rough; I never saw the heavens so dim by day . . ." '

'Now he's hit the mark,' muttered Yelverton.

' "A savage clamour! Well may I get aboard! This is the—'

Latimer never finished the soliloquy, for there came the sound of rending cloth and a great mass of snow came crashing through the awning. The single lantern flickered as the howling gale roared through the upper deck, carrying with it great gusts of snow and a vicious, merciless wind.

Killigrew leaped to his feet. 'All right, everyone stay calm. It's just the—'

He broke off in horror. It was not 'just' anything.

Bruin had made an unscripted entrance.

XX

Fire in the Night

The great bear stood there, as stunned by his sudden fall through the awning as the seamen around him. Someone made a sound – half yell, half scream, all terror – and the bear responded, rising on its hind legs with a dreadful roar.

The next few minutes would stay with Killigrew for the rest of his life.

Everything happened at once: the men scattering, dashing for the hatches, the bear swiping its terrible claws left and right, unable to miss in the crowd of bodies that panicked around it, the bang of Ågård's pistol as he fired at the bear, feet thundering on the deck, Molineaux's beloved guitar trampled underfoot. The bear roared, men screamed, blood splashed on the deck, on the awning, on the makeshift stage and the backdrop.

Finding the bear between himself and the hatchway, Jacko Smith scrambled up the foremast as nimble as a monkey and clung to one of the yards that formed a ridge-pole beneath the wadding tilt awning, but in doing so he managed to catch the bear's eye. It reared up on its hindquarters and sank its jaws into one of the seaman's dangling ankles, dragging him back screaming to the deck. As Smith tried to crawl away, the bear batted at him with its massive paws like a cat playing with a mouse.

Killigrew shouted for everyone to stay calm, realising the futility of such an order even as he gave it. At the front of the audience, he was swept before the press of bodes and carried down the forward hatch. He dashed across the mess deck in time to meet the stampede of people descending the main hatch.

'Out of my way! Out of my way!' He threw himself at the crowd like a ship trying to break through the ice and managed to get down to the spirit room. Aware that every precious second would mean more deaths, his hands trembled as he took a brace of Deane & Adams revolvers from one of the racks.

By the time he re-emerged things seemed quieter. He glimpsed a few men hiding underneath the tables on the mess deck, a few more level-headed ones – Molineaux amongst them – appearing with muskets. The rest must have gone down to the orlop deck in the bowels of the ship, hiding amongst the trays of cress, where even the bear could not get them, or at least so they hoped. At that moment Killigrew would not have put anything past it.

He ran up the companion way to the upper deck with Molineaux and Ågård hard on his heels. In the confusion the lamp had crashed to the deck and spread a pool of burning oil on the forecastle. The blaze was the only source of illumination, the flickering flames torn and shaken by the wind that blew in through the tear in the awning. Killigrew searched the scene by the eerie light of that hellish blaze. He could see only two bodies: one of those still stirring, although the man's trousers were torn to shreds and soaked with his blood. Even with great flurries of snow being swept beneath the awning, something as big as the bear should not have been that difficult to spot.

Then he saw it, or at least its hind quarters, disappearing through a fresh rent it had slashed in the awning with its razor-like claws. He levelled one of his revolvers, fired, and then the bear was gone.

'Someone put that fire out!' he yelled as he ran across to the rent in the awning. He reached it in time to see the bear lope off into the blizzard, dragging something along beside it. Killigrew realised that the object was one of the men, one ankle clamped between the bear's jaws, his leg twisted at an impossible angle as he bounced along at the bear's side.

And he was still alive.

Killigrew pushed through the rent and at once plunged chest-deep into the snowdrift banked against the side of the hull. Fighting his way through the snow, he raised both revolvers. He knew that in firing at the bear there was a danger he would hit the man it dragged away, and yet at the same time he knew that if he did not stop it, the man was doomed to die a horrible death, torn limb from limb. If he could have killed the man outright with one shot, it would have been a mercy killing. He fired both revolvers alternately, until all ten chambers were empty and the bear had vanished. On either side of him both Molineaux and Ågård fired their rifled muskets. At that range surely one of them must have hit it?

'Who was it?' he asked them.

'Don't know, sir,' said Ågård.

'Unstead,' said Molineaux, shaken by the death of his fellow boatswain's mate. 'Jake Unstead.'

Killigrew stared in the direction the bear had disappeared in stunned amazement. *It's only an animal*, he told himself. And yet surrounded by men – and solid Jack Tars at that – it had wreaked bloody havoc, seemingly invulnerable to the modern firearms held by Killigrew and the others. Man, created in God's image, was supposed to be master of the globe, and yet the species that had brought about the technological marvels of the industrial revolution seemed powerless to defend itself against one polar bear.

The bear was gone now, frightened off – or at least it had taken what it had come for, and saw no reason to linger. But Killigrew's problems were a long way from being over. He made his way around the hull with Molineaux and Ågård, and the three of them ascended the gangplank to find the blaze of the oil-lamp had spread like wildfire, eating up everything in its path: wood, ropes, wadding tilt, everything.

'Form a human chain!' he ordered Sørensen. 'From here to the fire hole.'

The harpooner glanced helplessly at the dozen men standing on deck. 'There aren't enough of us.'

'Then get down to the orlop deck and roust out the others!' They had held fire drills in the first few weeks after their arrival at Horsehead Bay, but the men had forgotten their quarters in their panic and besides, there were so many fewer of them now to tackle the blaze.

Strachan was crouching over the wounded man: Stoker

Gargrave. The dead man was Jacko Smith, his head all but torn from his shoulders by one swipe of the bear's paw. Killigrew glanced around, but no other bodies caught his eye. If the final toll was two dead and one wounded, they could count themselves lucky. 'Endicott, Hughes – carry Gargrave to the observatory so that Mr Strachan can attend to him properly.'

'What can I do to help?' asked Ursula.

'Ever done any nursing?'

She laughed, without much humour. 'A woman on board a whaler? Can a duck swim?'

'Good. Go help Strachan tend to Gargrave in the observatory. Orsini! Search around for other wounded – make sure we didn't miss anyone.'

The steward nodded and started to check around the upper deck, heedless of the blaze that raged on the forecastle. Ågård seemed to take for ever to get his human chain formed, while the fire continued to spread until the whole of the forecastle was a raging inferno. Finally the hands started to pour up on deck, realising that the ship was imperilled and with it their chances of survival. Then it was a case of too many cooks and everyone milled around uselessly, wanting to help without knowing what to do.

'Starboard watch form a human chain!' ordered Killigrew. He had to shout to make himself heard above the roar of the flames fanned by the gusting wind. 'Messes two and four of the port watch shift the wounded, the rest of you get yourselves out of the way!'

Armitage stumped up on deck, his face blackened by smoke. 'Sick-berth deck head's on fire, sir!'

Killigrew turned to Fischbein. 'Run to the observatory, tell Strachan the sick-berth's on fire. Tell him to come back and get everything he needs.'

'*Jawohl, mein Herr.*'

While Fischbein ran to the entry port, Killigrew remained with the men fighting the fire on the forecastle, directing them where to pour each pail of water as it came. The water thrown over the flames every few seconds was having no appreciable effect and Killigrew – who had learned to make contingency plans as soon as contingencies occurred to him – realised he would have to start to think about what to do in the event of the unthinkable happening. If the *Venturer* burned and left them stranded on the ice there would be nothing left for them to do but shoot themselves to ensure a swift death, so much more preferable to a long, agonising, drawn-out death by exposure and starvation. But he would never give up hope, not while there was breath left in his body and perhaps not even when there was not. They had to do something, to be ready for the worst.

Strachan returned from the observatory. 'Fischbein said you wanted me?' he shouted above the roar of the blaze.

'Get down to the sick-berth and get out anything you may need. Medicines, bandages, surgical equipment—'

'My notebooks! My photographical paraphernalia . . .'

'Forget them! This is life and death, man!'

Strachan stared at him stupidly.

'Go, man, go!' roared Killigrew, his angry tone sparking Strachan into action. 'Give him a hand, Latimer,' he added to the clerk, who looked dazed and was only getting in the way of everyone else. 'Go with them, Butterwick,' Killigrew added to the stoker as the two civilian officers hurried down the fore hatch. If either Strachan or Latimer was overcome by the smoke then Butterwick, used to working in a hot and smoky environment, would be the best person to pull him out.

'Anything I can do?' asked Yelverton.

'Yes! Get the chronometers off the ship. And charts, logs, navigational instruments, anything we need to find our way home that Pettifer hasn't already destroyed: get them off the ship and put them somewhere safe.'

'You think it's that bad?'

'Just a precaution.'

From the look on Yelverton's face, the master did not believe a word of it. The lieutenant did not blame him: he did not believe it himself.

Ågård had slashed a hole in the awning so that the empty buckets and pails could be thrown over the side down to where they were refilled at the fire hole. But as the flames advanced up the deck he had to retreat before the heat and cut another rent further away from the blaze, further away from the fire hole: more time wasted in ferrying the empty buckets to the fire hole.

As the flames ate away the awning above, great clumps of snow would drop through onto the flames, melting and steaming without seeming to have any effect on the fire.

Butterwick emerged from the main hatch dragging an unconscious Strachan under the armpits. 'Where's Latimer?' demanded Killigrew.

'Right behind us, sir,' said Butterwick.

Killigrew glanced down at the hatch. Thick smoke billowed out of it. At least the wind that fanned the flames on the upper deck was keeping it clear of smoke, but below decks it would be a different story entirely and he was not reassured by Butterwick's words. 'All right, take him out into the fresh air, revive him and then put him in the observatory with Gargrave.' Only time would tell whether Strachan would be in the observatory to minister to the wounded stoker or to be a casualty himself.

Killigrew glanced to where the hands tackled the blaze that now reached past the fore hatch. They were doing the best they could, though he feared it would not be enough. But there was nothing he could do to help: Ågård and Molineaux were doing everything they could to direct the fire-fighting operations and needed no help from Killigrew. Feeling like a spare part, he glanced at the smoke that now billowed thickly from the main hatch.

He took a deep breath and descended the companion way.

It was dark on the lower deck, the thick smoke blotting out everything. It stung his eyes and clawed at the back of his throat. He stumbled across the mess deck with his eyes closed, unable to rely on anything but touch and memory. The deck head above was ablaze, but he only knew that from the searing heat as he passed below. He opened his eyes, saw the orange glow through the suffocating smoke that brought tears to his eyes.

'Latimer! Mr Latimer!'

There was no reply, but the roaring blaze and the crackling of the timbers might have drowned out his words. Not that it mattered: if Latimer was conscious he would have got out of there; nothing could survive for long in that airless space.

The door to the sick-berth was an arch of fire. Killigrew crooked an arm over his brow and dashed through. On the other side he stumbled over something and pitched head-first on the deck.

He looked up. There was more air down there, but what he saw did not instil him with any sense of hope. Everything was ablaze: the deck head, the bulkheads, the drawers and the cots, the timbers of the hull itself. The searing heat blistered his flesh. As he wiped tears from his eyes a burning timber crashed down in a shower of sparks only a few feet from where he lay. Glancing up at the charred, flaming timbers above he saw that the whole deck above him was ready to collapse, and even as he watched it shifted and bulged with an ominous crackle.

He glanced back to see what he had tripped over and saw Latimer lying there, unconscious. Killigrew got up on his hands and knees and crawled back to him. There was no point in trying to revive the lad: the best thing to do was to get him out into the fresh air as quickly as possible; for them both to get out into the fresh air, before they suffocated or were crushed beneath falling timbers.

He managed to get Latimer on his shoulders – the clerk weighed a ton – and pushed himself to his feet. As he re-emerged on to the mess deck he found it as much ablaze as the sick-berth had been. Stumbling under Latimer's weight, he tried to find a route to the companion way, disorientated by the smoke and flames. Then, with a loud crack, the timbers in front of him fell from the deck head. For one panicky moment he thought his way would be blocked, but the timbers stayed there, suspended about six feet above the deck by something he could not see.

'This way, *min herre*!' Sørensen's Danish accent. 'Quickly!'

A gust of wind from somewhere tore a rent in the swirling smoke and revealed the harpooner standing with a blazing beam supported in his hands, the fire quickly blistering and charring his hands.

The fresh air on his face revived Killigrew enough to take the last few steps to the companion way and he dashed under the beam. He heard a crash behind him and turned to see that the beam had finally fallen, smashing a hole through the deck and carrying the blaze into the orlop deck below. Sørensen was gone. No point in going back for him.

Killigrew staggered up the companion way on to the deck where Riggs and Kracht quickly came forward to relieve him of his burden. 'You all right, sir?' asked Riggs.

The lieutenant nodded, and then doubled up, retching.

'Get outside!' yelled Yelverton. 'Get some fresh air. There's nothing you can do here which isn't already being done.'

'Warm clothes!' rasped Killigrew. 'We'll need warm clothes, otherwise we'll freeze to death on the ice!'

'It's been taken care of. Go, man, go!'

Killigrew squeezed down the gangplank past the chain of men who passed slopping buckets of water on to the deck. After the searing heat of the fire, the bitter wind outside was so cold it numbed his exposed flesh at once. Every so often a man would be carried down from the *Venturer*'s upper deck, overcome by smoke inhalation. At least someone had thought to release the huskies from their kennels and now they ran around on the ice, barking at the burning ship as if they could extinguish the flames that way. But they were only getting under everyone's feet.

'Terregannoeuck! Tie those damned dogs up, for God's sake!'

Dazed by the nightmarish scene, Killigrew turned back to stare at the burning ship. The entire front half was ablaze now. Varrow's squat figure appeared at the top of the gangplank, silhouetted by the flames behind him, and staggered down to where Killigrew stood. 'The coals in the bunkers are on fire now, sir,' he reported. 'We'll never get it out! It's reached the after hatch on the orlop deck.'

Killigrew's stomach lurched as the implication hit him. 'The spirit room! There's enough powder in there to blow the ship sky-high! Get Qualtrough, Ibbott and Hughes to help you.'

'How are we supposed to get to the spirit room if the after hatch is on fire?' asked Hughes.

'There's a scuttle from the wardroom,' Killigrew reminded him impatiently. How Hughes had even been rated able seaman was a mystery: the fellow seemed to lack any initiative. 'Take Riggs. Once you're in the spirit room, cut a hole in the side and take the powder out through the sail roof. A hole in the hull we can repair, if it's above the waterline.'

'Through all that extra planking?' Riggs said dubiously.

'*Try*, damn it! If the whole ship goes up, we're as good as dead!'

'Is there anything I can do?' asked Kracht.

'No,' said Killigrew. There was nothing anyone could do to help now. It would have taken a tidal wave to put the fire out. But there was no tidal wave in the offing; even the flurries of snow that descended from the heavens had thinned out. This was why ships never cruised alone through the Arctic. If there were two ships and one burned or was crushed in the ice, at least the crew would have a chance of getting back to civilisation on the other. But Pettifer, madman that he was, had insisted on going ahead without awaiting the rest of Belcher's squadron.

Pettifer. The light was on in the porthole of his cabin towards the ship's stern. Perhaps it would serve him right if he died in the blaze, but Killigrew knew it was not his place to make such judgements.

'Kracht! Help me fetch the captain!'

'*Jawohl, mein Herr*.' The blacksmith followed him round to the stern. As they approached, Killigrew could hear Horatia barking frantically inside; at least there was someone alive in there to save.

'Give me a bunk up,' said Killigrew. Kracht stood beneath the gallery window and clasped his hands together before him. Killigrew smashed in one of the panes of glass in the gallery window with the butt of a revolver and then he reached through, opened the window, and climbed into the captain's day-room. Even here, in the aftermost part of the ship, the insidious smoke had drifted under the door to fill the air with its acrid haze. Horatia barked at him as if it was his fault the ship was on fire. Killigrew scooped up the dachshund – and was bitten on the hand for his pains – and handed Horatia down to Kracht, who received similarly rough treatment from her.

Killigrew crossed the deck quickly and opened the door to the cabin where Pettifer was bound hand and foot on the bunk. He looked up at Killigrew with placid eyes.

' "Hail and fire mingled with blood," ' he said, nodding to himself, as if he had foreseen this. ' "A great mountain burning with fire was cast into the sea; and the third part of the sea became blood." '

381

'If I untie you, are you going to behave yourself?'

' "The third part of the creatures which were in the sea, and had life, died; and the third part of the ships were destroyed." '

Killigrew sighed and cut through Pettifer's bonds with his clasp-knife, keeping the revolver on him the whole time. One false move and he would shoot Pettifer dead; but, aside from his ravings, the captain seemed calm enough.

' "Her plagues shall come in one day: death, and mourning, and famine; and she shall be utterly burned with fire: for strong is the Lord God who judges her!" '

They crossed the deck to the gallery window and Killigrew helped Pettifer climb down to where Kracht waited anxiously. The blacksmith led Pettifer across the ice and Killigrew jumped down from the window to follow them.

' "Alas, alas, that great city, that was clothed in fine linen, and purple, and scarlet, and decked with gold, and precious stones, and pearls," ' said Pettifer. ' "For in one hour so great riches is come to naught. And every shipmaster and all the sailors stood afar off and cried when they saw the smoke of her burning." '

'Tie his hands behind his back,' Killigrew told Kracht. They had enough problems to cope with, without a homicidal madman on the loose. 'Get him under cover.'

He turned back to the ship and watched it burn. The whole of the upper deck was ablaze now, the awning long gone, and it was all the men could do to stand around her sides throwing buckets of water at the blaze. Then three figures – Varrow's stocky shape among them – jumped down from the gallery window, rolled on the ice and picked themselves up at once, sprinting away from the ship as if their lives depended on it. 'Get back, get back!' roared Varrow. 'The fire's reached the burning fluid. She's gannin' to blow!'

'You heard him!' yelled Killigrew. 'Everyone get back!'

They turned and ran to what they judged was a safe distance. When Killigrew stopped and turned back, the ship was a huge beacon of fire in the Arctic night, but there was no sign of any explosion. He wondered if the engineer had misjudged the situation in the spirit room. Perhaps there was still a chance that the ship could be saved. The alternative was unthinkable . . .

A muffled *wumph* came from inside the bowels of the ship:

that would be Latimer's cheap but highly volatile burning fluid exploding, spraying blazing liquid in all directions.

'*Dio mio!*' moaned Orsini, and pointed. 'Look!'

A burning figure appeared at the gallery window. Killigrew watched in horror as the human torch jumped down to the ice and rolled in the snow, trying to extinguish the flames that wreathed his body.

Killigrew broke into a run.

'Get back, sir!' yelled Varrow. 'She'll go up any moment now!'

The lieutenant unbuttoned his coat and tore it off as he ran to where the burning man lay immediately below the stern. He threw the coat over the man to smother the flames and then rolled him over and over in the snow until his clothes were extinguished. Then he picked him up, threw him over his shoulder, and started to stagger to where the others waited a short distance from the ship. Ågård came running to meet him, and with the brawny Swede to help him Killigrew made better progress across the ice. They were almost fifty yards from the ship when it exploded.

A hot wall of air slammed into Killigrew's back, throwing him down on the ice with Ågård and the burned man. A roaring sound filled his ears and he twisted on to his back to see a great ball of fire tear the ship apart from within. The flames roared up to the dark heavens, and then Killigrew had to roll on to his front and protect his head with his arms as pieces of debris rained down on the ice all around them.

When he looked up again, there was nothing left of the *Venturer* but a charred hole in the ice.

Killigrew cast his tired eyes over the faces of the eighteen men and one woman who huddled in the observatory with him. None of them had slept much that night, and their faces were lined with exhaustion and worry, their eyes sunk deep in their smoke-blackened faces, but none looked as used-up as Strachan, who had been hard at work all night tending to the injured. Despite the assistant surgeon's best efforts, Ibbott – the man who had been so badly burned trying to get the gunpowder out of the spirit room before it was too late – had died in the small hours of the morning, and his body had been carried outside to rest with that of Jacko Smith. Considering the pain he must have been in from his burns, it had probably been a mercy.

Killigrew was more worried about the living: he knew that before they reached safety, all of them might find themselves envying those who had died last night.

Strachan's fob watch – one of the new 'repeaters' – chimed the hour. Killigrew checked his own watch: it was six o'clock in the morning. He pushed himself wearily to his feet. 'All right, let's get to work,' he said. 'Latimer, how are you feeling this morning?'

'Much better, thank you, sir. My lungs hardly hurt at all.'

'Is he fit to work, Strachan?'

'Light duties only.'

'That's all I want from him this morning. Latimer, I want you to take an inventory of everything we have left: food, clothing, equipment, everything.' The *Venturer* might be destroyed, but everything that had been in the depot on the ice – victuals, spare spars and sails, and various other pieces of equipment – was intact, along with anything else they had managed to salvage from the ship before it had exploded. 'Molineaux, you can help him.'

'Aye, aye, sir.' If the boatswain's mate was tired, he was not letting it show. He followed Latimer outside.

'Ågård, I want you to form a work party and dig two graves: one for Ibbott and one for Smith.'

'What about Sørensen, sir?' asked the ice quartermaster.

There was nothing left of the harpooner to bury: his burned body had been blown to smithereens. Under more propitious circumstances, Killigrew would have ordered an empty grave dug for him. Seamen were superstitious enough to prefer spending an hour digging an empty grave to leaving a dead shipmate unburied. But he knew that in the weeks ahead they were going to need every last ounce of strength if they were going to live to see England again, and could not afford to waste it digging empty graves. 'Belay that, Ågård. Sørensen's memorial will have to wait for another time.'

'Aye, aye, sir. Right, lads, I want four volunteers. You, you, you and you!' He picked out Qualtrough, Endicott, Hughes and

Butterwick. 'Fetch picks and shovels and come with me.'

'I could make them headboards, sir,' offered Riggs.

'There'll be no headboards, Chips. We lost our remaining sledges in the fire last night, so you and Kracht are going to be busy today making new ones. We'll need three large sledges – eleven feet long, three broad and a foot high – and a smaller sledge for the dogs to draw. Take a look around and see what material you can find, then let me know what you want to break up for wood before you do anything: I might have other plans for it.'

'Aye, aye, sir.' Riggs and Kracht went out.

'Are there any portable stoves left, Orsini?'

'*Sí, signore*. Two.'

'Good. You can make breakfast for everyone. Something hot. And cocoa all around. Fischbein, you can help him. Strachan, how's Gargrave?'

'Not good.' The assistant surgeon's tone made it clear he wanted to say more, but was not prepared to discuss it in front of the others.

'All right. Frau Weiss, you stay with Gargrave, try to make him as comfortable as possible.' Killigrew looked about to see who was left: if he kept the men busy, it would help take their minds off the hopelessness of their predicament. 'Armitage?'

'Sir?'

'Stand guard over Captain Pettifer. If he so much as looks as though he's thinking about giving us any trouble, you have my permission to shoot him.'

'Aye, aye, sir.'

'Yelverton, Strachan, Varrow and Terregannoeuck: you four come with me.'

The five of them stepped out into the dark of the Arctic morning. A pall of smoke hung over the scene, unable to rise in the frozen air, and the stench of death filled Killigrew's nostrils. He thought of the men who had died, and the men who were still alive but who would surely die long before they reached safety. The dogs howled mournfully, as if sensing the atmosphere of despair.

Killigrew led the way into the wash-house and the five of them stood and faced one another awkwardly. Everyone knew what they had to discuss, but no one wanted to be the first to broach the subject. It was difficult to know where to begin. Killigrew lit one of his cheroots – he only had three left, the rest had gone up in smoke with the *Venturer* – before starting. After this, he would save one for New Year's Eve, and the other to celebrate with once they had reached safety. Between now and then he might be able to sleep occasionally, but he knew he would not be able to rest properly.

He took a deep breath. 'The way I see it, we have three choices.' He tried to keep the tremor out of his voice. 'The first is to wait here and hope that someone comes to rescue us. In its favour, we've got plenty of food here: we won't know the exact figures until Latimer's completed his inventory, but I'd guess we've got more than enough food to keep the twenty of us alive for a year, perhaps even two.

'Against this, we have to bear in mind that the chances of anyone coming to look for us are so small as to be non-existent. No one knows where we are, and thanks to Pettifer no one even knows in which direction we were headed. Given that the rest of the squadron may not even have made it through the Middle Pack, it may be that no one even *knows* we're missing – and we may not be listed as missing for another two or three years. Even if the rest of the squadron *did* make it as far as Beechey Island and are looking for us even now, they have hundreds of thousands of miles of coastline to search. There are thousands of miles of ice between them and us. For all we know they're trapped in the ice. For all we know they're worse off than we are. For all we know they've already turned back and gone home. It's no good our waiting here for rescue, because it isn't coming. The only people we can rely on to get us out of here is ourselves.'

'Reckon there's another good reason for not biding here, sir,' said Varrow. 'Bruin. He attacked again last night, despite Mr Strachan's assurances to the contrary.' The engineer glanced at the assistant surgeon, who flushed and hung his head. 'I think we can be sure he'll be back. Again and again and again, until there's nay reason left for him to come here.'

'And if we move off and try to get back to civilisation?' Strachan asked Varrow. 'Do you think he won't follow us?'

'Pipe down, the pair of you!' said Killigrew. 'What's done is done. Whether we stay here or set out for safety, I'm sure the one thing we can all agree on is that Bruin is still a factor to be taken into account. But first I want us all to agree that we can't stay here.'

The others nodded. 'What are our other choices?' asked Yelverton.

'Secondly, we can head north, across Boothia and North Somerset, to Beechey Island. That's only about four hundred miles from here, and the chances are that when we get to Barrow Strait the sea will still be sufficiently frozen for us to cross on foot.'

'And if it isn't?' asked Yelverton. 'If we reach the north coast of North Somerset and meet with open water? Worse, what if we make it as far as Beechey Island and find that the rest of the squadron never got that far? We'll be even worse off than we are now, another four hundred miles from civilisation.'

Killigrew nodded. 'Which brings us to our third – and to my mind our only – option. We head south-west, to Fort Hope on the Great Slave Lake.'

'Fort Hope!' exploded Yelverton, and was at once seized by another fit of coughing. 'That's nearly a thousand miles away!' he wheezed.

'Eight hundred, according to my calculations,' Killigrew said mildly.

'What's at Fort Hope?' asked Strachan.

'It's a Hudson's Bay Company outpost,' explained Killigrew. 'Ever since Franklin disappeared, the company has been keeping its outermost trading posts well stocked with stores of food in case Franklin and his men pitched up there. There may even be traders at Fort Hope – voyageurs, fur trappers – who can help us on our way, show us the easiest routes back to civilisation.'

'And you think the twenty of us can walk eight hundred miles across the most inhospitable terrain on earth, in the dead of the Arctic winter, to Fort Hope?' asked Yelverton.

'You have any better suggestions?'

'It would be hard to think of a worse one. We'll run out of food before we get halfway there! Even dragging our victuals behind us on sledges, we can only carry enough food to keep us

387

going for forty days at the most. Even if we average twelve miles a day – which I very much doubt – that'll still only take us four hundred and eighty miles. What do we do when our food runs out?'

'If we go on six-upon-four, we can spin out our rations for seven hundred and twenty miles.'

'The men can't drag the sledges seven hundred and twenty miles on six-upon-four.'

'The further we go, the lighter the sledges will become.'

'And the shortfall of eighty miles?'

'We've got two factors on our side: we're heading south, and we're heading into spring. There'll be more game: reindeer, musk-ox, ptarmigan. We'll be able to live off the land.'

'What do you think, Mr Terregannoeuck?' asked Strachan. It was some indication of how desperate their straits were that the scientificer was prepared to admit they had to rely on the 'primitive savage' for advice on how to survive in the wilderness.

'It only way,' the Inuk said grimly. 'Small chance – but small chance better than no chance at all.'

'Then it's settled,' said Killigrew. 'I'll tell the men at once. The sooner they know we've got a plan – that there *is* hope – the sooner their morale will start to lift. We can't do this unless we *believe* we can do it.'

'Then I'm doomed from the outset,' said the master.

'Don't give up on me now, Yelverton. We need you. I can't navigate from here to Fort Hope without you.'

'What makes you think I can do it? The closest thing I could find to a chart was a map in a book from the ship's library.'

'We have chronometers, don't we? Compasses? Navigational instruments? All we have to do is reach the Great Fish River and follow it upstream to Lake Aylmer. From there it can't be more than ninety miles due south to the eastern arm of the Great Slave Lake.'

The master sighed. 'I'll do what I can.'

Killigrew clapped him on the shoulder. 'Good. Plot us a course for Fort Hope, Yelverton.'

The master went out, followed by Strachan and Varrow. Only the Inuk lingered in the wash-house with Killigrew. 'What are our chances, Mr Terregannoeuck? Can we really make it?'

'Twenty too many to live off land. If strongest of you leave rest – ten at most – there is chance you make it back by living off land as you go.'

'And abandon the others, you mean?'

'Otherwise you *all* die.'

Killigrew shook his head. 'I can't abandon them; not any of them. When I assumed command of the *Venturer* and her crew I became responsible for every man on board.'

'Then stay behind. Send others. At least give some of your men chance of life.'

'No. We're all going.' He hesitated. 'Mr Terregannoeuck, you're not a member of the ship's crew. If you want to take your own chances – and I know they'll be better than if you stay with us – I shan't think any the less of you.'

The Inuk grinned, the first smile Killigrew had seen all morning. 'You never make it back to your own people without Terregannoeuck.'

'We're not your responsibility.'

'You become responsibility of Terregannoeuck when he agree to come with you. Terregannoeuck cannot live with guilt if he abandon you now when you have greatest need of him.'

Killigrew wondered if the Inuk spoke from experience. Perhaps he felt guilty that he had abandoned Franklin and the others to their deaths; perhaps that was why he had agreed to join the crew of the *Venturer*. Perhaps, for him, this was an act of atonement.

'Then you understand why I cannot leave any of these men to perish. No matter how hopeless it may seem, I must try.'

Terregannoeuck nodded and went out.

As soon as Killigrew was alone, his expression crumpled. He splashed cold water on his face, but now that talking his desperate plan through with the others had put everything in perspective, the reality of their situation finally hit home.

They were all going to die.

He stumbled across to the latrines and vomited.

He had faced death before plenty of times, but not like this. Before there was always hope, a chance that he could outwit his enemies or, if the worst came to the worst, overcome them by sheer grit and determination. But there was no escaping their situation now. No amount of cunning and ingenuity was going to take them all the way to Fort Hope.

'Are you all right?' Ursula's voice asked behind him.

He took out his handkerchief and wiped his face before straightening and turning to her. 'Still feel a bit all-overish from all that smoke I inhaled last night.'

'We are in trouble, are we not?'

There was no point in lying to her: she would see through it in an instant. 'It doesn't look good.' He chuckled softly, without much humour. 'It's rum, when you think about it. You know the real reason I volunteered for this expedition? It wasn't to find Franklin and the others – I know as well as you that they're all dead by now – and it wasn't to find the North-West Passage, either. It was to find out if I was up to it. To find out if I could follow in Franklin's footsteps and survive where he died. To prove myself a man.' He smiled wanly. 'Queer, ain't it? I'm intelligent enough to know how stupid that sort of behaviour is, yet still I fall a prey to it.'

'You can't help it. You're a man.'

'Well, I suppose now I have my answer. I was the one who got Yelverton, Cavan, Strachan, Ågård, Molineaux, Dawton, Endicott and O'Houlihan berths on this expedition. Now Cavan, Dawton and O'Houlihan are dead, thanks to me, and the rest of us are doomed. Because I wanted to prove myself man enough to face down the Arctic, and win.'

'I could tell you that they were all grown men capable of making their own decisions – that it was their own choice to come on this expedition – but I do not suppose that would cut much ice with you.'

He shook his head. 'I'm their commanding officer now. They're my responsibility.'

'Then *take* responsibility for them! Instead of feeling sorry for yourself, get out there and reassure them. Give them the one thing you've got left to give: hope. Remember what you said to me when we were trapped on that ledge in the ice crevasse? *Nil desperandum*: things are never quite as hopeless as they seem. You want to believe you're the one who got these men into this situation? Very well. Then be the one who gets them out of it.'

XXI

A Single Step

'All right, lads, gather round.' Killigrew felt sick to look on those smoke-blackened, frost-bitten, defeated faces. He had to put hope in these men, give them the strength to follow him out of this wilderness. Even Moses would have balked at such a task. But Moses, he reminded himself ruefully, had not held Her Britannic Majesty's commission.

'Now, I'm not going to lie to you and pretend that everything's all right. So first the bad news, to get it out of the way. We're eight hundred miles from the closest outpost of civilisation: Fort Hope, on the shores of the Great Slave Lake. It's the dead of winter, and the weather's going to get colder before it turns. I'd say it's going to take us about three months to make the journey through the most inhospitable climate on the face of God's creation. And I'll tell you now that some of us won't make it. But I believe some of us will. And I can tell you which ones will make it: those of you who have the *will* to live. Those of you who aren't prepared to give in, not now, and not later, when the going starts to get tough. Because get tough it will, I can assure you.

'That's the worst of it. Now the good news. The summer thaw is still several months away, so if there are any stretches of water between here and the mainland we can just walk right over them. The further south we travel, the easier the going will get. The sun will return, the weather will improve, there'll be more wildlife for us to hunt, more food for us to eat. And we've got plenty of food to keep us going until then.' He took a deep breath. 'Now this is the way it's going to be. Once we set out we'll be back on six-upon-four—'

The men groaned.

'Yes, that's right, six-upon-four. We've got a lot of ground to cover and for the first few hundred miles the only food we're likely to find is what we take with us. Six-upon-four will weaken us, but it'll last half as long again. Same goes for the officers. We eat the same rations and we share the work of pully-hauly, Mr Yelverton excepted . . .'

'If it's all the same with you, Killigrew, I'd rather do my fair share,' protested the master.

'It's not all the same with me, Mr Yelverton. You're in no condition for pully-hauly. When you agreed that I assume command of this company, you put yourself under my orders. Well, I'm giving you an order now. Have the sledges loaded, Mr Yelverton. We'll need victuals, stoves, spirits of wine, tents, chrysalis bags, changes of clothes and spare boots.' Killigrew had a feeling they would be needing the spare boots. 'The sooner we get going the better.' He turned away and headed for the observatory.

'Mr Killigrew?' called Butterwick. 'Sir?'

The lieutenant turned back. 'Yes, stoker?'

'Merry Christmas, sir.'

Killigrew stared at him, wondering if he was being sarcastic. Butterwick flushed. 'Well, it's Christmas Day, isn't it, sir?'

'That it is, Butterwick,' Killigrew said wryly. 'That it is.' He continued on his way to the observatory and motioned for Strachan to accompany him. 'How's Gargrave?' he asked the assistant surgeon in a low voice.

'Not good. You realise, of course, that he can't walk, let alone haul a sledge? His leg's broken in a dozen places. He'll probably never walk again.'

'I know.'

'We can't drag him on one of the sledges. Not if we're going to take enough food to get us even halfway to Fort Hope. Besides, no matter what we do, no matter how warmly we wrap him up, those injuries will become frost-bitten. Then they'll turn gangrenous. Then the only chance of saving his life will be to amputate, and even that's no guarantee.'

'You mean to tell me that with all the advances that medicine has made in the past few years—?'

'Damn it, Killigrew! I'm an apothecary with surgical training, not a miracle worker.'

'You realise what you're saying, don't you?'

Strachan nodded. 'You can put him on a sledge and drag him, but the chances are he'll be dead before we've covered fifty miles. And in the meantime he'll be taking up space which could be used for precious food.' The assistant surgeon looked more haggard than ever when he met the lieutenant's gaze. 'You know why people like me become medical men, Killigrew?'

'To help people?'

Strachan shook his head. 'That's what I told myself when I began my studies. But I was wrong. We want to play God, Killigrew. That book you loaned me, *Frankenstein*? He wanted to create life. All I ever wanted to do is preserve it, to say: "This man will live." But a man who can say who lives also has to say who dies.'

'It's my decision. I'm in command here, it's my responsibility.'

Strachan grinned sourly. 'If it makes you feel noble to take that responsibility on yourself, don't let me stop you. But don't think it will make me feel any better.'

'You're gannin' to leave him, aren't you?' Varrow stood in front of the door to the observatory with his arms folded. 'If you leave him, he'll die.'

'If we take him with us, he'll probably die anyhow,' said Killigrew.

'You canna know that for sure.'

'We can be pretty sure,' said Strachan. 'At least if we leave him, we'll have more room for supplies, a better chance for the rest of us to make it back.'

Varrow suddenly produced a revolver. Killigrew thought he was going to threaten them with it, but instead he reversed his grip on it and held it grip-first towards Strachan. 'Then you do it, if you find it so easy to make a decision like that. 'Cause it'll be a bloody sight quicker and cleaner than leaving him to starve or freeze to death. So you gan in there and put that pistol to Bob

Gargrave's forehead and look into his eyes when you pull the trigger.'

Strachan stared at him, and then reached for the gun, but Killigrew got there first. 'That's enough of that, Mr Varrow. If you think that either myself or Mr Strachan has reached this decision without a great deal of soul-searching, or that it won't weigh on our consciences and haunt our nightmares for the rest of our lives, you've got another think coming.'

Varrow flushed. 'Sir, at least someone should stay behind to make his last hours more comfortable.'

'Leave a second man behind to die with him? Out of the question. Stand aside, Mr Varrow.'

'I'm volunteering, sir. He's one of my lads. I'm not leaving him.'

Killigrew hesitated. For Gargrave, it would be the humane thing to do. But for Varrow . . .? 'No.'

'I'm not leaving him, sir. You can if you want, but I'm staying right here.'

'You'll go back and help the others to load the sledges, Mr Varrow. That's an order.'

'I know the rules, Mr Killigrew. Once the ship is destroyed, we're not part of the crew nay more. The ship nay longer exists. We divven't get paid, and I divven't have to take orders from you.'

'If I might make a suggestion, gentlemen?' said Yelverton, crunching across the snow towards them with his hands thrust deep in the pockets of his greatcoat, shoulders hunched against the wind.

Killigrew could see what was coming next. '*No.*'

'Mr Varrow is no spring chicken, I'll admit, but he's still got plenty of years left in him. I, on the other hand, find my days are numbered.'

'That's nonsense,' said Strachan.

'You said so yourself: I might fall down dead at any moment.'

'You might also live to a ripe old age.'

Yelverton appealed to Killigrew. 'You know this is what I want . . .'

'What you want is no concern of mine, Mr Yelverton. You think I don't know how you both feel? That you'd rather die than

394

abandon one man to his fate? You think I don't feel the same way?' He shook his head. 'Gargrave's already dead. As officers of Her Majesty's navy, our foremost duty is to the living. One more man is enough, more than enough. I've already seen too many men sacrificed on the altar of Arctic exploration, though I dare say I'll see a few more before we make it back to civilisation. Besides, you've got a family waiting for you back in Yarmouth.'

'My screaming triplets, you mean? My horrible in-laws?'

'Like them you may not, Mr Yelverton, but you still have a responsibility to them. Just the same as I have a responsibility for all of you, regardless of whether or not the *Venturer* is still in commission. Now be about your duties, the pair of you, otherwise I'll have you both court-martialled for mutiny when we get back to England; you see if I don't!'

'You're bloody nuts, you are!' grumbled Varrow. 'You canna give me orders nay more.'

'You know something? You're absolutely right. I must be mad. If I was rational, I'd abandon the whole damned lot of you to your fates, leave you behind while I struck out for Fort Hope on my own. One man could make his way to Fort Hope by living off the land, with a little sand and determination. But I'm staying because it's my duty. Now be about yours.' Killigrew held out his hand. 'Give me the gun, Varrow.'

The engineer turned the gun on him.

'I shan't ask you again.'

Varrow looked as though he might actually pull the trigger. Then he slammed the revolver into Killigrew's hand, and turned and marched back to where the others were loading the three sledges, christened Faith, Hope and Charity by the men. If ever there was a time they had needed God on their side, this was it.

Strachan looked at the gun in Killigrew's hand. 'You want me to . . .?'

'No. My responsibility.' He jerked his head after the others. 'Go and lend them a hand, Strachan.'

The assistant surgeon nodded and walked away without looking back. Killigrew watched him, then stepped into the observatory. Gargrave looked up at him.

Killigrew did not know what to say. What did one say to a

man you were about to kill? It was easy when you hated them, felt nothing but contempt for them and knew you would be making the world a better place by dispatching them from it; but this man had served him well and faithfully. He should be thanking him, not snuffing out his life. What could he say? Apologise? Beg his forgiveness? Pray with him? The last of these filled him with revulsion. There was no scriptural justification for what he was about to do, only cold, callous logic, a kind of inverted humanity at best. He could not, would not hide behind his religion.

As a child Killigrew had been encouraged to study the works of Francis Hutcheson, amongst others, and that worthy had once written: 'That action is best, which procures the greatest happiness for the greatest numbers.' But Hutcheson had never stood on the icecap with a gun in one hand and a wounded man waiting for him to kill him.

'Close your eyes, Gargrave.'

The stoker understood, and shook his head. 'Please, sir, no . . .'

'I'm sorry, Gargrave . . .'

'I can make it, sir, I know I can . . .' Gargrave tried to get up, but his strength failed him.

Could Strachan be sure that Gargrave could not make it? Supposing the assistant surgeon had made a mistake?'

'Please, sir!' Gargrave was sobbing now. 'I divven't want to die! I divven't want to die!'

Killigrew hated him then, hated him for making a difficult job more difficult. Why couldn't he accept what had to be with strength and fortitude? But if Killigrew were in Gargrave's place, would he have been any different? He seized his rage like a drowning man clutching at a straw and put the muzzle to the stoker's forehead.

'God forgive me,' he whispered, and fired. Again and again, until there was only one bullet left inside the cylinder. The air inside the observatory was acrid with the reek of gun smoke and Gargrave's face was unrecognisable.

Killigrew put the muzzle inside his own mouth. The tangy metal felt hot against his lips and tasted of gunpowder. It would be so easy just to pull the trigger, end it all. Then he would not have to live with the guilt of the killing, the recriminations of the other men, or face the arduous, impossible journey that lay ahead of them.

He took the muzzle from his mouth. Someone had to lead the men to safety, or at least die trying. It was his responsibility. If he failed in that, then he would be as guilty of killing them as he was of killing Gargrave. He dropped the revolver and sank to his knees with a sob, staring at Gargrave's body. He had done this, he knew. He could not shift the blame, he could not lessen its weight by sharing it, but share it he would. All those people back in England who thrilled to read of Arctic adventures, who pressured the Admiralty into sending more and more men to their deaths in quest of the chimerical North-West Passage – they had all played a part in this tragedy. He would go back and face them all, tell them what had happened here, tell them not of the nobility of one man's sacrifice but of the pitiful pleadings of another. Public opinion would condemn him, but the same public opinion had condemned these men to die in this God-forsaken place.

He pushed himself to his feet, brushed the fast-freezing tears from his cheeks and dusted himself down, emerging from the observatory with a semblance of dignity while his own self-respect lay in tatters within. No one met his gaze, the men pretending to be hard at work loading the sledges and the boats.

Then it finally sank into Butterwick's thick skull what had happened. He broke away from the others and snatched up an ice-axe, charging at Killigrew. 'No! Murderer!'

Ågård tripped the stoker up before he even got halfway to the lieutenant, who was too dazed to defend himself. Butterwick slid on the ice and the axe flew from his hand. He tried to get up again, but Ågård put a foot on the back of his neck. 'It had to be done, Jemmy. It was the kindest thing to do. Bob were a dead man; at least this way he didn't suffer.' He helped the stoker to his feet and dusted him down.

Butterwick cuffed tears from his cheeks with a mittened hand. 'He was my mate, was Bob. He looked out for me.'

'I'm sorry for it, Jemmy. We're all sorry for it. Mr Killigrew not least. But it couldn't be helped.' He led Butterwick back to the sledges and put him to work to keep his mind off his grief.

Only Terregannoeuck had any words of consolation for the lieutenant. 'You do right thing.'

Killigrew regarded him coldly. 'Oh?'

'That man not die of cold or hunger.' The Inuk nodded to the horizon where a low, pale shape was visible in the starlight: Bruin, seated on his haunches, watching them intently.

Killigrew froze. 'I thought you said that if a polar bear didn't want us to see it, we wouldn't?'

'That's right. But *nanuq* not care if we see him. He know he get us sooner or later. So you see what happen to Stoker Bob if you leave him behind alive?' Terregannoeuck toyed with the bear-tooth that hung against his chest as he spoke. 'He come for Stoker Bob anyhow, but at least now Stoker Bob not live to see it, to feel *nanuq*'s claws tear his flesh, his teeth snap his bones.'

Killigrew felt a shudder run down his spine. He hurried across to where Ågård and some of the others were fashioning harnesses to drag the sledges with. There were only nineteen of them left now, nineteen out of the thirty-seven who had sailed through Lancaster Sound: Commander Pettifer, his hands still bound behind his back; Killigrew, Strachan and Latimer; the consumptive Yelverton, leaning on a walking stick for support; Terregannoeuck with his charms and potions; Mr Varrow and Stoker Butterwick; peg-leg Armitage, with his left hand still bandaged where his thumb had been, and Steward Orsini; Riggs the carpenter's mate; Ice Quartermasters Ågård and Qualtrough; and Molineaux and Able Seamen Endicott and Hughes. And the last survivors of the *Carl Gustaf*: Ursula, Kracht and Fischbein. How many of them would make it to Fort Hope?

Molineaux had seen the bear too. 'Want me to fetch a musket, sir?'

'Don't bother,' said Terregannoeuck. 'You not hit him, this distance. You go nearer, he see you come with gun and turn and run. By the time you reach crest of ridge, *nanuq* be even further away.'

'It's just a bear,' Killigrew insisted dully. 'It doesn't know what a gun is.'

'He knows,' said Terregannoeuck. 'He watch us long time now. He know everything about us.'

Again Killigrew felt a shudder run down his spine, as if

someone or something had walked over his grave. He cast a final glance at the charred remains of the *Venturer*. 'All right,' he said. 'Let's get going. A journey of a thousand miles starts with a single step.'

'*Marche!*' The five remaining huskies took up the strain as Terregannoeuck blazed the trail on the dog sledge. The rest of them slipped the harnesses on, each of three teams of six men towing one of the larger sledges. Killigrew led one team, Yelverton another and Strachan the third.

A single step, Killigrew told himself. The harness bit into his shoulders as he took up the strain. His foot slithered on the ice, and then the sledge shifted forwards a few inches.

Again. Just one step, then another, and another. That's all it takes.

The sledge began to move forwards, jerkily at first, and then more smoothly as the men found their own rhythm.

There, that's not so difficult, is it? Now all you have to do is keep it up.

For the next eight hundred miles.

The first thirty miles were easy – across smooth bay ice, perfect for pully-hauly – and on the first day they managed to cover not eight but seventeen miles. It was only towards the end of the second day, when they rounded the cape that formed the western arm of Horsehead Bay, that they ran into their first pressure ridge. Sixty feet high, it ran across their path as far as the eye could see in either direction, a towering mass of slabs and chunks of ice, thrust together by the pack around them and cemented with the snow that had been driven into its crevices.

'What do you think?' asked Strachan. 'If we head in one direction, we're bound to find a way around sooner or later.'

'Aye,' agreed Yelverton. 'My concern is it will be later rather than sooner. I say we climb it.'

Killigrew glanced across to where Molineaux stood, gazing up the side of the ridge with a speculative expression on his face. 'It'll take a couple of hours to get all four sledges over, and the dogs,' said the lieutenant.

'It could take days to find another way round,' pointed out Yelverton. 'For all we know this ridge could stretch for dozens of miles in either direction. And we haven't got days to spare, if we're going to reach Fort Hope before our victuals run out.'

The master was right, of course. 'All right,' said Killigrew. 'But we'll climb it in the morning, while we're still fresh. We'll make camp tonight, and look for an easy place to climb it tomorrow.'

But by the time Killigrew emerged from his tent the following morning a storm had blown in from the north. There was no rain or snow, but the gusting wind swept ice spicules against his face like a million airborne needles. Combined with the darkness, the storm reduced visibility to a few feet and there was no way of scouting an easy path up the side of the pressure ridge.

'No chance of climbing it now,' he told Yelverton. 'We'll have to wait until this storm dies down.'

'How long is that likely to be?' asked the master, reminding him that time was not on their side.

'Nothing else for it,' said Killigrew. 'I wouldn't try climbing up there in this visibility, and I'm not going to send a man up there to do what I wouldn't.'

Sitting in one of the tents with Ågård, Qualtrough, Endicott and Hughes eating a breakfast of boiled bacon and ship's biscuits, Molineaux overheard them. He thrust his head out of the tent, blinking at the driving ice spicules. 'Sir?'

Killigrew and Yelverton turned. 'What is it, Molineaux?' asked the lieutenant.

'Begging your pardon, sir, but if you ask me this is a job for Cowcumber Henson.'

'Who the devil is Cowcumber Henson?' demanded Yelverton.

'He is,' said Killigrew. 'Or was, at any rate. It's a long story. Thank you for the offer, Molineaux, but climbing up the side of a sixty-foot pressure ridge in the middle of an Arctic storm is a different kettle of fish from burgling a house.'

'Not as different as all that.' Molineaux crawled out of the tent, pulling his wire-mesh goggles down over his eyes. 'I've climbed houses in London Particulars. As long as you've planned your way up beforehand, don't matter if you do it in pitch-darkness.'

'And did you get a chance to plan a way up last night?'

'Force of habit, sir.' Molineaux shrugged. 'I guess I knew I'd end up being the one to climb it.'

'I was planning to try myself, as it happens.'

'That's very noble of you, sir, but you know as well as me there's no one here better suited for this job than me. And at least it ain't straight up, like the side of a house.' He grinned. 'Pity there ain't no drainpipe, but I wouldn't get to look like a hero if it was too easy, would I?'

'All right. But for goodness' sake, be careful!'

Molineaux took a coil of rope from one of the sledges, an ice-axe, and attached some ice-anchors to his belt. 'Mind if I swap my mittens for your gloves, sir? I'm going to need all my fingers for this one.'

'Of course.' Killigrew stripped off his gauntlets and swapped them for the petty officer's mittens. 'When you get to the top, drive one of those anchors into the ice as a belaying point and lower a rope down to us.'

Molineaux nodded and approached the ridge, trying to find the foot of the route up he had surveyed the night before. He found a familiar formation in one of the lower ice blocks and began to climb. Somewhere above him, he knew, a large slab of ice had been broken in two at right angles, snapped by the pressure of the pack, creating a rough-hewn chimney with plenty of handholds that led almost to the top. If he could get that far, it would be as easy as caz.

It was straightforward at the bottom: the slabs at the base of the ridge were almost horizontal, and after slipping a couple of times he discovered a technique for ramming his cramponed feet against the ice to give him some purchase. Then a second slab lying across the first blocked his path, and he had to bury the tip of the ice-axe in its surface to give him enough purchase to pull himself over.

From there on it was all hands and feet. When he was almost halfway up, he paused to get his bearings. The chimney should have been immediately above him, but there was no sign of it, just a wall of sheer-sided ice. Then he glanced to his right and recognised an unmistakable column of ice running up the side of the ridge. The chimney was on the other side of that.

But getting to it was going to be no easy task, without climbing back down and starting all over again. There was nothing to grip on to while swinging himself around the column, so he braced his back against a block of ice behind him and attacked the ice with his axe, carving out both a handhold and a foothold. He stood up, got one foot on to the tiny ledge he had carved, and reached around the column. He embraced it, found his centre of balance, and started to grope for a handhold. There was none.

He could see a ledge about a foot to his right. He buried the axe in the ice above and to his right and used it for support while taking his right foot from the foothold, bracing it against the ledge, and moving his left foot to where his right had been. Then the foothold started to crack, and he had to lunge with his whole body for a spur of ice. He tugged the axe out from its hold and was about to bury it somewhere firmer when his sudden movement startled an auk that had been sheltering from the storm in a crevice amongst the jumbled blocks of ice.

There was always one. It was Molineaux's First Law of Climbing, a variant of Sod's law: whatever you were climbing, be it a town house in London, a cliff on the coast of a Mediterranean island or a volcano in New Zealand, there was always a pigeon/seagull/kea waiting for the worst possible moment to break cover and catch you off guard.

He was so startled by the tiny, flapping wings that he had to put a foot back on the foothold he had carved. It crumbled beneath his weight and he found himself sliding back down an almost sheer slope.

He hacked at it with the axe, but its head just bounced off the iron-hard ice. Then his legs shot out over a precipice. He hooked his left arm over a spur of ice and dangled there, his legs and body hanging in space.

He swore, and glanced down – heights had never troubled him – but the ice spicules in the air concealed everything below him from sight. It could not be far to the pack ice below – no more than twenty feet – but he would probably break a leg on landing. And he was not going to get far on a broken leg. Then Killigrew would have to put a bullet in his brain, the same as he had done with Gargrave; and it would be the right, kind thing to do, but Molineaux would not have cared for it one little bit.

'Everything all right up there, Molineaux?' Killigrew yelled from somewhere below.

'Oh, yur, sir. Just plummy!' he called down scathingly.

'Then stop hanging around and get a move on!'

'Use your axe, Wes!' Riggs called up helpfully. The carpenter's mate could always be relied upon to come up with unneeded, unwanted advice.

Use my axe, Molineaux thought sourly. *What does he think I'm using, my jockum?* 'I'll use my axe, Jerry! I'll use it on your bloody noddle, if you don't shut your trap! You think this is easy? You want to come up here and have a stab at it?'

He swung the axe at the smooth slope above him, but it failed to bite into the ice. The spur he clung to with his left arm was starting to crumble. He swung the axe, and this time it bit: not deep enough for him to be happy about trusting his weight to it, but he did not have much choice.

Then the spur broke away and went spinning into space, leaving Molineaux hanging from the ice-axe. 'Watch under!' he yelled, and in the same instant heard the chunk of ice shatter below.

Gripping the shaft of the axe with one hand, scrabbling for purchase with the other, he managed to draw his legs up until he could get the soles of his boots against the ice and his crampons bit. He wormed his way up a couple of feet, swung the axe against the ice further up, and then inched his way up to the chimney. There, bracing his back against one wall and the soles of his feet against the other, he was able to squirm his way slowly and painstakingly to the top.

From the crest of the ridge he could see nothing, just the ice spicules driving out of the darkness at him. He dug a hole in the ice with the axe, buried the hook of an ice-anchor into it, then unlooped the coil of rope from his shoulders, rove one end through the anchor and belayed it before dropping the other end down the side of the ridge.

Killigrew climbed up after him, followed by Ågård, Qualtrough, Riggs and Kracht. Endicott tied pylons, anchors and tools to the end of the rope and they drew them up next. They managed to rig a cat's cradle and then dragged the first sledge up. The sledge weighed close to fifteen hundred pounds and it took all six of the men on the crest of the ridge to draw it up. It got stuck against the underside of a projecting slab of ice. They lowered it a foot, tried to lift it again, but again it got caught.

Molineaux sighed, belayed his rope to an ice-anchor, then tied another rope to another anchor and rappelled down the side of the ridge to where the sledge was stuck.

'Give me some slack!' he yelled up to Killigrew.

The others lowered the sledge a foot. Molineaux wedged himself beneath it and pushed it out from beneath the slab of ice so they could pull it up over the projection. Then it was all they could do to hold it in place until Molineaux had climbed back up to the ridge to help them. They hauled it up the rest of the way, grunting with the effort.

Orsini and Butterwick climbed up next, and Riggs and Kracht rappelled down to the pack on the other side of the ridge, where at least there was some shelter from the driving wind. The men left on the ridge lowered the sledge to them, and the carpenter's mate and the blacksmith untied the ropes. Killigrew and the others drew the ropes up and then threw them down on the other side so Endicott and Hughes could belay them to the second sledge.

Getting the other three sledges over was no easier, and it took them two hours of back-breaking work in those appalling conditions to get sledges, dogs and people over the ridge. Inevitably, the weather waited until they were almost done before easing off, and visibility improved to the extent that they could see the pack ice below from the ridge. Ågård and Molineaux were the last to climb down from the ridge, pausing to remove all anchors and pylons from the crest. Molineaux tested a spur of ice for strength, and then doubled the last rope around it, so they could climb down without leaving anything behind: they might need it again before their long trek was over.

'Thank God that's over,' said Ågård, preparing to precede Molineaux down to the pack ice below. 'I wouldn't want to go through all that again.'

As the starlit sky cleared, Molineaux glanced to southwards and saw something that made his heart sink. Half a mile away across the pack, he could see another pressure ridge in the ice. And behind that, another. And behind that, another. Ridge after ridge, stretching away as far as the eye could see beneath the starlit sky.

XXII

A Frightful Fiend

'How far have we come?' Killigrew asked Yelverton as they set up camp in the lee of another pressure ridge on the ice pack four days later.

'Thirty-eight miles since we set out on Christmas Day,' said the master. 'That's an average of six and one-third miles a day.'

'Not quite the twelve miles a day I'd been hoping for. What's our average been since we reached the first of the pressure ridges?'

Yelverton lowered his voice. 'Two miles a day.'

Killigrew swore. 'And how long's it going to take us to reach Fort Hope at that rate?'

'One year, two weeks and two days, I should say. But it can't be much more than another twenty miles before we reach the mainland. No more pressure ridges – we'll make much better time.'

'We'll have to: at this rate it'll be another ten days before we even reach the mainland! How many more days' rations have we got, Latimer?'

'At our current rate? Fifty-four days.'

'Which gives us forty-four days to get from the coast to Fort Hope,' mused Killigrew. 'How many miles a day will we have to cover to make up for lost time, Yelverton?'

'If my guess that there's another twenty miles between us and the coast is correct, then that leaves seven hundred and thirty-eight miles to Fort Hope. Divide seven hundred and thirty-eight by forty-four days . . .' He looked up at Killigrew with worried eyes. 'Seventeen miles a day, near as damn it.'

Killigrew felt a tightness in his stomach, and not just because he had been on six-upon-four rations with the rest of them. 'Seventeen miles a day is nothing.' He tried to sound blasé. 'That's from Falmouth to Truro. I used to do it all the time when I was a boy.'

'That's seventeen miles a day after having been on six-upon-four for over a month,' Yelverton reminded him gently. 'Dragging sledges behind us through some of the worst conditions known to man.'

'The sledges will get lighter the further we go. As soon as we've used up enough of our victuals, we'll take all the equipment off Charity, divide it between Faith and Hope, and abandon Charity. Then we'll be nine men to a sledge instead of six. Besides, the further south we go, the more wildlife we'll be able to hunt to supplement our victuals.'

'I'm afraid food might turn out to be the least of our problems,' said Latimer.

Their hardships had aged them all since they had entered the Arctic, but sometimes the young clerk looked positively decrepit. His once-rubicund face was permanently ashen. He hardly spoke at all now, and sometimes when they bedded down for the night in their tents Killigrew heard him quietly sobbing himself to sleep. Latimer needed keeping an eye on: he was going to be the first to break, and it would happen soon. 'We're getting through bottles of spirits of wine at an appalling rate. When that runs out, we won't be able to cook any food or even melt snow into drinking water.'

Killigrew stared at him. 'You told me we had more than enough spirits of wine to see us to Fort Hope.'

Latimer flushed. 'I'm rather afraid I miscalculated.'

'You miscalculated?' Varrow asked incredulously, rising to his feet. 'You *miscalculated*? Well, that's bloody champion, that is! We're all gannin' to die, because this bloody quill-driver miscalculated!' He grabbed Latimer by the lapels and hauled him to his feet. 'Maybe we should send you back to the depot on foot to fetch some more bottles!'

'All right, Mr Varrow, let go of him,' Killigrew said firmly.

The engineer complied.

Latimer straightened his clothing with as much dignity as he could muster. 'There was nothing wrong with my figures. I calculated the amount of spirits of wine we'd get through on the basis used up per man for each of the sledging expeditions. We're using up more now, that's all.'

'Of course we are,' said Strachan. 'The weather's that much colder: it takes that much more fuel to thaw food out before we eat it.'

'It can't be helped,' sighed Killigrew. 'We'll just have to wait for the sun to return, that's all. And in the meantime, we treat spirits of wine like liquid gold: no more wasting it to melt snow into drinking water. From now on, if anyone wants a drink, he can scoop snow into his water bottle and wear it next to his body until it melts.'

Molineaux came across with a couple of mugs in each hand. 'I made you some cocoa, sir. I'm afraid it's not very warm, but . . . drink it up, before it freezes.'

Killigrew gulped the tepid cocoa down. 'God bless you, Molineaux.'

'Happy New Year, sir.'

'Good God, is it New Year already?'

'I wonder what eighteen fifty-three has in store for us?' mused Strachan.

'More snow and ice, for the next three months at least,' Yelverton said morosely.

Killigrew shook his head. 'The world we left behind is still waiting for us, gentlemen. A world of warmth and sunlight. That's what we're heading for. I know it seems like a long-forgotten dream now, but it was real enough once, and it will be again.'

Strachan sang a chorus of 'Auld Lang Syne' softly, and the others joined in the refrain, without much enthusiasm. 'So, any New Year's resolutions, anyone?' Strachan asked when they had finished.

'If we get out of this, I'm going to start going to church every Sunday,' said Latimer. 'Because it'll be thanks to the grace of God and God alone.'

'Mr Yelverton?' prompted Strachan.

'Mr Yelverton's going to admit himself to a hospital the

409

moment we get back to Britain,' said Killigrew. 'Isn't that so, Giles?'

'The devil it is,' said Yelverton. 'Since every minute may be my last, I'm going to live life as if that was the case. That's my New Year's resolution. What about you, Mr Strachan? In my experience, a man who asks others what their New Year's resolution is only does so in the hope they'll ask him his.'

Strachan made a pretence of thinking about it. 'My New Year's resolution? Never to go on another expedition to the Arctic so long as I live.'

As the others crawled into their tents one by one, Killigrew lingered outside to celebrate the New Year with his penultimate cheroot. Ursula joined him. With no one else close by, she felt confident enough to slide her arm through his and the two of them leaned against one another companionably. 'What are you thinking about?' she asked him.

'I was just thinking about what I'd be doing right now if I was in London instead of here in the Arctic.'

'And what *would* you be doing, if you were in London right now instead of in the Arctic?'

He checked his fob watch. 'Let's see now: it's just after three in the morning in England. This time last year, I was passed out on my bed in my chambers . . .'

'Alone?'

'That's not the sort of question a gentleman answers,' he replied primly. 'I woke up at ten o'clock and went for a swim in the Serpentine to clear my head.'

'In the middle of winter?'

'Very invigorating. And believe me, it's a lot warmer in London at this time of year than it is in the Arctic.'

'I have never been to London,' she said wistfully. 'I should have liked to have seen it, before I died.'

He clasped her hand in his. 'And so you shall. Why, London's the finest city in the world! Everyone should see it once. Perhaps you should make that your New Year's resolution.'

'My New Year's resolution is the same as Herr Yelverton's: to live each day as if it were my last. It's strange – I feel as if I've woken up from a dream, after ten years.'

'Ten years?'

'Ever since I married Wolfgang,' she explained. 'When you are a woman, your whole life seems to build up towards marriage; one should be forgiven for thinking that once that goal is reached, all one's problems will be solved.'

'Instead you found you had a whole new parcel of problems to cope with?'

She nodded. 'I found myself trying to become what he wanted, rather than being myself. Somewhere along the line I forgot what it was like to enjoy life. As terrifying as these past few months have been, I've felt more alive than I can ever remember having been before. Strange, that I should have come to the dead world of the Arctic to rediscover the pleasure of being alive.'

'When we get back to England, I'll take you around London, show you the sights: the Royal Opera, the British Museum, the Great Globe, the Royal Academy, the Tower, the Zoological Gardens . . . I hear they've got a polar bear, if you're interested in seeing one?'

She elbowed him in the ribs. 'No, thank you! I have seen all the polar bears I ever want to see.'

'Then there's the Crystal Palace . . .'

'I thought they had taken that down?'

'They were going to re-erect it somewhere, the last I heard. It'll probably be open again by the time we get back. Let's see, it'll be summer by the time we're there. You want to live? You haven't lived until you've been boating on the Serpentine at high summer.'

'But still you have not told me your New Year's resolution.'

'Mine? To get us back to safety; every last one of us.'

Molineaux was awoken by the dogs barking furiously. He peeped out from under the flap of the tent he shared with Yelverton, Latimer, Hughes, Orsini and Fischbein. Outside it was still dark.

But the first signs of returning light were already visible, already the sky was starting to grow lighter at noon, and if Yelverton was to be believed they would catch their first glimpse of the returning sun within a week.

He nudged the man snoring next to him until he stopped

snoring: Hughes. 'Is it morning already?' the Welshman mumbled.

'I don't know,' whispered Molineaux. 'What time is it?'

'How should I know?' Hughes grumbled, and turned over to go back to sleep.

Ågård had been supposed to rouse Molineaux at two in the morning when it was Molineaux's turn to stand guard, yet the boatswain's mate was certain he had been asleep for a lot longer than two hours. He crawled out of the tent and stretched stiff and aching limbs, his torso sore where the ropes of his harness chaffed it. What he would not give for just one night in a hammock! Or, since he was fantasising, a night in a nice cosy bed with Lulu.

He glanced about the encampment in the moonlight. There were the other two tents, the black patch between them, where the camp-fire had burned out. By the dog sledge, the huskies barked into the darkness.

Then he saw the sledges, saw that something was not right. He rummaged through the stores until he found a bull's-eye, lit it with a match and cursed in horror and disbelief at the sight that greeted his eyes. Faith and Hope remained as they had been left the night before, with their victuals and equipment neatly bundled and strapped on. But Charity had been overturned, the Halkett boat ripped to shreds, crates broken open, tins of food torn apart, their contents scattered. Even the sledge itself had been broken up.

Killigrew emerged from one of the tents, stretching stiff and aching limbs, and headed briskly away from the encampment.

'Sir?'

'One moment, Molineaux.' His back to the petty officer, Killigrew relieved himself into the snow.

'Better come and take a look at this, sir,' said Molineaux, as the lieutenant buttoned his flies.

'What's the matter?'

Molineaux directed the beam of the bull's-eye at the mess.

'Oh, Christ! How the devil did this happen?'

By way of reply, the petty officer played the beam over the snow on the ice. It did not take him long to find what he was looking for: the paw-prints of an enormous bear.

'Jesus! Who was supposed to be on watch?'

'What time is it, sir?'

Killigrew checked his fob watch. 'Nearly six o'clock.'

'Hughes' turn, then.'

'Where the deuce is he?'

'Still sleeping, I expect. I was supposed to wake him at four, at the end of my watch. I didn't, because Ågård was supposed to wake me at two.'

'Where is Ågård?'

That was a good question. 'Ollie?' Molineaux called softly; and then, realising that if anyone had not been woken by the dogs, they were hardly likely to be awoken by him calling out. 'Ollie!'

Killigrew indicated a dark shape lying in the snow, and Molineaux directed the bull's-eye at it: a musket.

'Ollie's musket.'

There were more paw-prints leading to where the musket lay, and drag-marks leading away; just a few spots of something dark, which might have been blood spattering the snow.

Everyone else was crawling out from the tents now. Molineaux picked up the musket and gave it a cursory examination. It had not been fired; Molineaux would have heard the shot. And Ågård had not cried out. The bear had got so close it could kill him or knock him out before he was aware of it, and then dragged him away just as it had dragged off Thwaites and Unstead.

'It followed us?' asked Latimer, as Terregannoeuck studied the paw-prints. 'For thirty-eight miles, it followed us?'

'Don't be ridiculous,' said Strachan. 'It isn't the only polar bear in the Arctic.'

Terregannoeuck rose to his feet. 'It same one. When winter bad, *nanuq* often follow reindeer for hundreds of miles. And this winter very bad.'

'Oh, *no*!' Latimer had seen the mess that the bear had made of the stores on Charity. 'Oh, Jesus, no!'

'It didn't touch the stores on Faith or Hope,' observed Molineaux. 'I wonder why not?'

'Maybe it's curiosity was sated by what was on Charity,' said Strachan. 'Who knows what goes through that crazy bear's head?'

413

'Evidently it prefers fresh meat to tinned mutton,' said Varrow.

'How much food have we lost?' Killigrew asked quietly.

'I'd have to take a full inventory of what's left to know for certain . . .'

'*How much*, Latimer?'

The clerk took a deep breath. 'About ten days' worth.'

'Jesus!' said Butterwick.

'We're going to end up eating our boots, just like Franklin and the others,' moaned Hughes. 'I just *know* it. It's going to be the Donner Party all over again!'

'All right, it's not the end of the world . . .' said Latimer.

'Might as well be,' sniffed Varrow.

'. . . We'll just have to head back to Horsehead Bay and collect more victuals, build another sledge, that's all.'

Killigrew looked at the faces of the men. Tired, drawn, blackened with soot from the smoky lamps they used in the tents at night and from lack of washing. There was more to this than the simple arithmetic of victualling. Now they were at their lowest ebb; at least, he hoped this was their lowest ebb. If he told them now that the distance they had covered already – those gruelling thirty-two miles over pressure ridge after pressure ridge – was going to have to be covered all over again, not once but twice, he was going to have a dozen men with broken spirits on his hands; and it was going to take spirit as much as food to get them to Fort Hope.

'There'll be no turning back,' he said, and the relief on the men's faces was plain to see.

'But we've only got forty-four days' of food left,' protested Latimer.

'It will have to do. The worst is behind us now: once we reach the mainland, the going should get easier. We're not wasting another twelve days climbing back over all those pressure ridges – twice – when for all we know we'll probably get to Horsehead Bay to find that Bruin did the same thing to the food there as he's done here. We'll press on. Down house, break up. I want you all to take everything you can salvage from Charity and divide it between Faith and Hope. Leave one of the tents – it'll make things a bit cosier at night, but it's crucial we keep the weight down. Strachan, you're in charge of Hope from now on;

414

I'll take Faith. The rest of you, your teams are as follows: Latimer, Frau Weiss, Molineaux, Riggs, Orsini, Endicott and Kracht; you're on Hope. Mr Varrow, Qualtrough, Armitage, Butterwick, Hughes and Fischbein: you're on Faith.'

'What about the cap'n, sir?' Armitage indicated Pettifer. His hands bound all but permanently, the commander had hauled on his sledge harness along with the rest of them, and more tireless and uncomplaining than any of them.

'He's on Faith with you, Armitage. Keep a close watch on him.'

'Aye, aye, sir.'

'Terregannoeuck, you can drive the dog sledge. Now let's get the tents packed up back on the sledges and be on our way. We can stop for breakfast once we've got another pressure ridge under our belts.'

'Wait a minute, sir!' protested Molineaux. 'What about Ågård?'

'What about him?' Killigrew answered bleakly.

'Aren't we even going to look for him? He might be wounded, dying . . .'

'He's dead.'

Molineaux shook his head in disbelief. Not Ollie Ågård. They had known each other for nearly five years now, serving together in the Orient, the South Seas, and now in the Arctic. Ågård had always been dependable, invincible, the one who could keep a cool head in a crisis, a constant tower of strength. And now Molineaux was supposed to believe he was dead, killed by a god-damned bear?

And what about Killigrew? He had known Ågård even longer. Even if the relationship between an officer and a rating was by definition different to that between two ratings, surely Killigrew must have felt something at the death of a man who had served with him loyally for what, fifteen years? But even if it had been Frau Weiss who had been dragged off by the bear, Molineaux knew that whatever Killigrew was feeling he would have kept it bottled up tight inside. This was not a time for hysterics. They needed to save their strength for the gruelling journey ahead of them.

He put on his harness and they set off once more. As he

trudged over the ice, the words of Coleridge came once more unbidden to his lips, the rhythm of the verse fitting the ponderous tread of his feet:

> Like one, that on a lonesome road
> Doth walk in fear and dread,
> And having once turned round walks on,
> And turns no more his head;
> Because he knows, a frightful fiend
> Doth close behind him tread.

Throughout the next week the sky became imperceptibly lighter towards noon, until on the ninth they got their first sight of the sun in over a month. When its first appearance was heralded by Kracht, who saw it from the crest of the pressure ridge they were in the process of traversing, the others all scrambled up – even those who had already climbed down on the other side – to see for themselves, to reassure themselves it was real. Raised prematurely from its hibernation by the refraction of the cold air, its thin rays were enough to impart a hint of warmth to their bodies, and a promise of brighter days to come. It did not fully rise, of course, and the segment that showed itself was gone after a couple of minutes, but those two minutes had been enough to give them hope. The next day the sun came fully above the horizon formed by the next pressure ridge, and stayed in the pale Arctic sky for a full thirty minutes.

Killigrew surveyed the scene as he ate breakfast the following morning. The pressure ridges had become lower and easier to traverse, the closer to the coast they came. Here they were no more than thirty feet high, and less steep; as often as not, they could get the sledges across without even taking off their harnesses.

He turned to Terregannoeuck. 'Will this do?'

'It as good a place as any,' said the Inuk.

'Good for what?' asked Latimer.

Killigrew took a cartouche box from one of the sledges and loaded a rifled musket. 'Varrow, I want you to take charge of Faith from here on,' he said. Latimer was senior to Varrow, but despite the engineer's grumbling, Killigrew knew he was tougher and would drive the men on long after the clerk had given up. 'Ursula, I want you to drive the dog sledge.'

'Terregannoeuck can drive it better than I can.'

'You can drive it well enough. Terregannoeuck's staying behind with me.'

'What for?' asked Latimer.

'What do you think?' said Yelverton. 'They're going to try to ambush the bear.'

Ursula clutched Killigrew's arm. 'Don't do it, please. It's madness! You'll be killed for sure. You tried this before, remember? When Bähr and the marines were killed?'

'This time it's going to be different,' he told her. 'For one thing, I won't have you to worry about. And for another, I'll have Terregannoeuck with me.'

'And what about that time you tried to bait him with those herrings?' asked Strachan.

'We used the wrong bait.'

'What are you going to use this time?'

'Ourselves.' Killigrew checked a musket and passed it to Terregannoeuck. 'We know Bruin likes the taste of human flesh. We know he's following us. While the rest of you continue on your way, Terregannoeuck and I will wait here for it. I've a feeling it won't keep us waiting long. If all goes well, we'll put our Norwegian snow-shoes on and catch you up before you make camp for the night.'

'And what if all doesn't go well?' demanded Yelverton.

'I'll have done my bit. From then on it will be up to you.'

'And supposing he sees you waiting for him and just gives you a wide berth without either of you being any the wiser?' asked Strachan. 'You'll just be waiting here for an eternity while the bear continues to hunt us down one by one.'

Killigrew pursed his lips. 'That is a possibility,' he allowed. 'Which is why you mustn't wait for us. Just keep moving, and keep your eyes open and your guard up at all times. But put yourself in Bruin's place. He sees us split into two parties: one of two men; and one of fifteen men, a woman, five huskies and a dachshund. Which one would you deal with first?'

Strachan nodded.

Killigrew lowered his voice so that only the assistant surgeon could hear him. 'And whatever happens, don't give up. For me. If I'm going to make the ultimate sacrifice, I don't care for it to be in vain, understand?'

Ursula approached again. 'You know what you're doing is crazy, don't you?'

Killigrew nodded. 'Perhaps. But this is the way it must be. I've already lost too many men because of that damned bear, and if we keep on like this he'll just pick us off one by one until none of us is left. It has to stop, and Terregannoeuck and I are going to end it here.' He gave her hand a surreptitious squeeze. 'Don't worry. I made a promise to you, and I'm a man who likes to keep his promises.'

'Which promise was that?'

'Boating on the Serpentine, remember?'

She wiped her runny nose on the back of a frost-rimed mitten, and managed a wan smile.

Killigrew turned to Molineaux. 'This is where our ways part, Molineaux. Good luck to you; and thank you, for everything. It's been an honour and a privilege.'

'The privilege was all mine, sir. You know me: I ain't got much time for gentry coves, officers least of all, but . . . you're oh-kay, sir.'

Killigrew smiled. 'From you I'll take that as praise indeed.'

'It's meant as such, sir.'

The other men crowded around him and shook his hand – a few even deigned to shake Terregannoeuck's hand as well – and then they waved and set off across the ice once more, dragging the sledges behind them, Ursula driving the dog sledge.

Killigrew and Terregannoeuck stood just below the crest of the last ice ridge and watched them go. The others disappeared over the next ice ridge, and a few minutes later were seen cresting the one beyond, and then they had disappeared from sight for good. The lieutenant and the Inuk checked their weapons again and settled down behind the crest of the ridge, watching the unending sea of ridges that stretched out behind them beneath the midday sun. The sky was clear and everything had a razor-sharp clarity to it, as if they could see for miles. Perhaps they could: the only thing to give them any sense of perspective was their own tracks in the snow behind them,

418

visible on the crest of each ridge.

Killigrew wished he had a sip of whiskey left in his hip flask, or a cheroot to calm his nerves. But he only had one cheroot left, and he had promised himself he would not smoke that one until he had seen the others to safety. Not much chance of that now, he told himself, and got as far as putting the cheroot between his lips and striking a match when something made him stop, shake out the match and return the cheroot to his case. He was not ready to give up on any promises yet.

He gripped his musket tightly and strained his eyes watching the landscape behind them, waiting for the bear to show up. He would not shoot it at once; he would hold his fire, wait for it to get closer, and then make sure of his shot.

Terregannoeuck waited placidly, as if his whole life had been building up to this moment and now he was ready for it. Killigrew suddenly realised how little he knew about the Inuk. 'Have you got a wife waiting for you back in Greenland, Terregannoeuck?'

'No. I used to have woman, but I leave her.'

'Why?'

'It was time to move on.'

Killigrew nodded. He had heard that sharks had to keep moving constantly, otherwise they sank to the bottom of the sea and drowned. Some people were like that too, constantly driven onwards by some inner demon, like Coleridge's Ancient Mariner. He wondered if he himself were such a man, doomed to sail the seas for eternity, or would he one day settle down and raise a family? Once he had been convinced that he would live for ever, but his twenties seemed to have flashed by without him being aware of it and now, in a couple of years, he would be thirty. When he had been a midshipman in his teens, he had looked at the older officers on board his ship and envied them their age and experience, their responsibility, and wished he could be as old as they. Thirty had seemed like a good age then. Now it was almost upon him, he wished he could be in his teens again. It was nine months since he had sailed from Woolwich on this senseless mission, a year wasted, and it would be many months before he returned to England.

If only he could live through today.

A thought popped into his head, a question he had been wanting to ask the Inuk for some time, and this seemed as good a time as any. 'Terregannoeuck, that time I went out with Frau Weiss, Dr Bähr and the others, and Frau Weiss and I fell down that crevasse . . . how did you find us?'

'Wes knew you were not dead.'

'Yes, but . . . how did you find me? By then the snow had covered over our tracks, you could hardly see your hand in front of your face in that blizzard. But still you managed to follow us closely enough for you to see the rocket we sent up.'

Terregannoeuck grinned. 'It was magic.'

'I don't believe in magic.'

'I would not believe in the power of your steam engines, if I had not seen them for myself. Your culture has the *kabloonas'* magic, just as mine has ours.'

'Seeing is believing,' said Killigrew, not believing a word of such damned superstitious nonsense, but unwilling to insult Terregannoeuck by saying as much. Besides, if it had not been magic, then what had it been? Some kind of native trick, he supposed. The snow might have hidden the tracks from a white man's eyes – and a black man's eyes, for that matter – but perhaps traces had remained that an Inuk, living his whole life in this world of snow and ice, could pick out.

Terregannoeuck suddenly took off the bear's tooth he wore on a thong around his neck and proffered it to Killigrew. 'Wear this,' he said gravely. 'It will protect you.'

More superstitious nonsense. 'I couldn't. You killed that bear, you earned it. Besides, don't you need protection, too?'

Terregannoeuck insisted on looping the thong over Killigrew's head. 'I have Nuliayuq to protect me, just as you have your *kabloona* god.'

Killigrew thought about what Strachan had told him when he had dissected the sow Molineaux had shot. Was the Bible wrong? Was Christianity no more than the same superstitious nonsense that so many unenlightened heathens around the world indulged in? Seeing was believing. What had Killigrew ever seen to convince him that there was a God? Precious little. But that was the essence of Christianity: faith. Without faith . . . he caught himself. If Christianity was so much gammon, then all

420

this nonsense about needing faith was the perfect cloak.

What do you *believe in, Kit Killigrew? God, or science?*

'I've no idea how this is going to turn out,' he told Terregannoeuck. 'But I want to thank you for helping us, staying with us so long. Even though we didn't always heed your advice. I find it hard to believe that this bear is after us because we didn't honour the she-bear's *tatkoq*, but there are some things in life even Mr Strachan's beloved science can't explain . . .' Killigrew grimaced, knowing that as an apology it sounded lame.

The Inuk shook his head. 'No need to thank Terregannoeuck. He should thank you.'

'Thank us? Why?'

'For letting him accompany *kabloonas*. For giving him chance to put right what he once fail to do.'

'That story you told us . . . about the Esquimau Hooterock—'

'Hoeootoerock,' the Inuk corrected him. 'Terregannoeuck's brother.'

Killigrew nodded. At last he understood. 'He asked you to accompany him when he went off to face the Kokogiaq?'

'And Terregannoeuck refuse. Say Hoeootoerock dishonour Kokogiaq, responsibility to appease Kokogiaq belong to Hoeootoerock. But Terregannoeuck have responsibility to brother, too. But Terregannoeuck afraid. When Hoeootoerock not return, other people look at Terregannoeuck, smell his fear, blame him also. Terregannoeuck leave own people, wander ice like *pisugtooq*, lonely hunter.'

'And if you kill this bear? Will you be able to face your own people again?'

The Inuk shrugged. 'Terregannoeuck not know. But it not matter. Terregannoeuck must prove courage to Terregannoeuck, let others think what they may.' His leathery face cracked into a grin. 'Sound crazy to you?'

Killigrew smiled, and shook his head. 'No, I think I understand exactly what you mean—'

Terregannoeuck tensed suddenly.

'What is it?'

Disdaining one of the muskets, the Inuk reached for his spear. '*Nanuq* is here.'

Killigrew searched the landscape beyond the crest of the ridge but saw nothing. 'Where?'

'Behind us.'

They both whirled and saw the bear standing on the next ridge, outlined against the moonlit landscape, about fifty yards away. Killigrew brought the stock of his musket up to his shoulder and took aim, but did not fire at once. *Come on, you sonavabitch. Just a bit closer...*

Then he realised that Terregannoeuck was no longer beside him, but racing down the side of the ridge with his spear poised to thrust, letting out a wild yell.

The bear responded with a terrible roar and charged down its own ridge to meet him at an appalling rate: deceptively swift, ponderous, inexorably powerful.

The Inuk was going to get himself killed. 'No!' yelled Killigrew, and fired.

He missed.

In the trough between the two ice ridges, only a few yards separated Terregannoeuck and the bear now. Killigrew snatched up the second musket, took aim, and pulled the trigger. At that range, in such good light, he could not miss.

The hammer came down on the percussion cap with a snap: a misfire.

The bear reared up, slashing with its paws. Terregannoeuck thrust the spear at its heart, but the bear's left paw snapped off the whalebone tip. Then the right claw scythed across and Terregannoeuck staggered back as his blood splashed on the snow.

Killigrew slung the musket across his back and drew both the revolvers he was carrying, blazing away as he charged down the side of the ridge. '*No!*'

Terregannoeuck was on his back now. He raised his arms to protect his head, and the bear clamped its jaw over one. Killigrew heard the bone snap. The Inuk screamed.

Both of Killigrew's guns were empty. He threw them away and unslung the empty musket. 'Come on, you bastard! You want to fight someone, fight me!'

The bear left off tearing at Terregannoeuck's flesh and reared up, facing Killigrew now. The lieutenant swung the musket like a club and cracked the bear across the snout with the stock. It roared in fury. He swung at its head again, but this time the bear's jaws clamped down on the musket and snapped the stock clean off.

Killigrew stood there, disarmed, paralysed with fear, and waited for the bear to finish him.

Five shots rang out in quick succession, two dark bursts of crimson blossoming in the bear's side. The bear yelped in wounded agony and fell back onto all fours. It ran off a short distance, limping now, blood dripping in its wake Near the crest of the ridge it turned back to snarl furiously at Killigrew, and then it loped out of sight.

Gasping for breath, Killigrew turned to where Terregannoeuck lay on the ice, holding another revolver. Even as the lieutenant turned, the gun fell from the Inuk's limp fingers and his arm fell back on to the ice. Killigrew ran across to him and dropped on to his knees at his side.

Terregannoeuck grinned weakly, his teeth flecked with blood. 'A present from Mr Latimer. *Kabloona* magic is strong indeed.'

The bear's claws had slashed through his jacket, through the shirt and flesh beneath, exposing his ribs that gleamed with slick blood. His arm was barely recognisable as such, a mangled mess. 'Is it dead?'

'Dead or dying,' said Killigrew. 'You killed it, Terregannoeuck. You killed the polar bear.'

'Good. I go on a long journey now, to meet Nuliayuq. You go rejoin your friends now, *kabloona*. Your heart is strong, you will lead them to safety.' With his left arm, he gripped Killigrew's jacket tightly as a spasm seized his body and he retched, coughing up blood, and then lay still.

Feeling sick, Killigrew drew down the man's eyelids. He pushed himself wearily to his feet, crossed back to where he had left the other musket, and reloaded it. Perhaps the bear was dying, but he wanted to be sure. Gripping the musket, he ran up the ridge in the bear's tracks and in the trough behind he saw . . .

Nothing.

He looked around wildly. Even the trail of blood seemed to have petered out.

Sick fear gripped him. It could not have disappeared: it was wounded, bleeding. But there was the evidence of his own eyes: it had vanished, as if by magic.

And it was still out there.

He walked back to where they had left their skis, slung the musket over his back, bound the skis to his feet, and got the hell out of there.

A few miles further on he caught up with the others.

'Did you get it?' asked Yelverton.

'No.'

'Terregannoeuck?'

Killigrew shook his head wearily.

The next day they left the sea ice behind and climbed through a band of low, peculiar-looking hills, like volcanic plugs. Even though they were still in uncharted territory, Killigrew was confident that at their current latitude this, at last, must be the North American mainland. On their current heading – south-west, towards Fort Hope – Yelverton calculated that they would cross the Arctic Circle within two weeks. Now they had completed the first sixty miles of their long trek to safety. All they had to do was keep on walking.

For another 740 miles.

They trudged slowly across the Canadian tundra, a harsh, rocky, iron-hard landscape. If anything the weather seemed to get colder and colder. Each exhaled cloud of condensating breath turned at once into tiny ice crystals in the air before their faces, falling to the snow at their feet. Their beards became rimed with frost. They moved like old men, bent against the weight of the harnesses with which they hauled the sledges, exhausted, hungry and weak. Their one consolation – and it was cold comfort indeed – was that the load they hauled grew progressively lighter each day. They were running low on food, and lower on fuel for the portable stoves.

Within five days Yelverton was able to place them on the map torn out of a book in place of a proper chart: back on *terra cognita*, on the east side of Chantry Inlet. Nine days later they reached the mouth of the Great Fish River. A little over 630 miles still to go.

Then, when it seemed things could not get any worse, the blizzard descended on them.

They pushed on as hard as they could, the storm whipping the thick snow against their backs until their clothes were weighed down with a thick coat of ice. Feet in flapping boots trudged through thick drifts, ankle-deep, knee-deep, waist-deep. Armitage, stumping along on his wooden leg, was the first to collapse.

'It's no good!' Strachan had to yell to make himself heard against the howling wind that screamed across the tundra. 'We can't go on!'

Killigrew knew they *had* to go on. They had to make it south, to where the wildlife was more abundant, where at least stunted trees would help them replenish their dwindling supplies of fuel for cooking. Every day they lingered would bring them closer to death. But Strachan was right. They had to rest.

They erected the two remaining tents and crawled under them to wait for the blizzard to pass. Strachan was in the other tent, but he crawled in Killigrew's to check the rest of the men for signs of frostbite or other physical infirmities.

'There's not a man-jack amongst us who isn't showing some signs of scurvy, frostbite and starvation,' he told Killigrew in a low voice. 'And there's not a damned thing I can do about it. It's Armitage that worries me most of all. The damn' fool should have said something.'

'About what?'

'His wooden leg. It's been chafing against his stump, a sore's developed and now he's got gangrene. What am I supposed to do, amputate the rest of his leg?' They had been talking in whispers, and now Strachan lowered his voice even further so that Yelverton, at the far end of the tent, could not hear him. 'And Yelverton's suffering. He'd never admit it, but I can see it in his eyes.'

'All right,' said Killigrew. 'When the blizzard clears we'll take all the victuals and equipment off the dog sledge and distribute them between Faith and Hope. Then at least Armitage can ride on the dog sledge.'

'At least we won't have to worry about Bruin any more.'

'What makes you so sure?'

'Polar bears never stray far from the sea. I think we've put enough miles between us and the coast to make sure he doesn't try to follow us any further.'

For three days they huddled in their tents, using the last of their stocks of spirit oil to heat their portable stoves to make cocoa, chewing on pemmican frozen rock-solid. One night, as Killigrew lay listening to the wind howling across the landscape outside, he thought he heard the polar bear snuffling around outside. He knew he should go out to check on the men in the other tent, but what could he do? He told himself it was only his imagination. After all, it had been five weeks since the bear's last attack; surely they had given it the slip by now?

He heard a voice singing softly in the darkness:

> *'She'd an ankle like an antelope and a step like a deer,*
> *A voice like a blackbird, so mellow and clear,*
> *Her hair hung in ringlets so beautiful and long,*
> *I thought that she loved me but found I was wrong.*
>
> *'She was as beautiful as a butterfly*
> *And as proud as a queen*
> *Was pretty little Polly Perkins*
> *Of Paddington Green.'*

Killigrew was surprised to recognise the voice as Pettifer's. For such a big man, his singing voice could be surprisingly melodious.

Latimer was less charitable. 'Stop it! Make him stop it!' he screeched. 'Shut up, damn you, shut up! Shut up, shut up, shut up!' Before anyone realised what was happening, the clerk had launched himself at Pettifer and tried to throttle him, the captain prevented from defending himself with his hands tied together.

It took both Killigrew and Strachan to pull Latimer off Pettifer. Struggling between them, the clerk screamed and sobbed until Strachan slapped him.

'Sorry, Latimer, but it's for your own good.'

The clerk stopped screaming and crawled off into a corner to weep quietly to himself.

'You're all going to die,' said Pettifer. He sounded saner than he had done in a long while, and he was making sense for a change. 'You realise that, don't you?'

'If we die, you die with us,' Killigrew said softly.

Pettifer grinned. 'Not I. My father will protect me.'

'Your father?'

'Why, God, of course.'

'The Good Lord is father to all of us,' said Yelverton.

Pettifer shook his head. 'Not that one,' he said, nodding at Killigrew. 'Don't you see? He's the Anti-Christ. He will lead you all to perdition. Turn back! Turn back to the path of righteousness, before it is too late!'

'Oh, stow your damned gaff, for heaven's sake!' exclaimed Yelverton. 'What with Mr Latimer blubbering on one side of me and you ranting and raving on the other, I don't know which way to turn! We may end up having to eat the dogs, but if it were up to me we'd eat you first, you loony!'

'No one's going to have to eat anyone,' Killigrew said firmly. 'We've made good progress so far; all we have to do is keep it up for another two months, and we'll be toasting ourselves in front of a warm fire at Fort Hope. Now everyone pipe down and get some sleep. We'll need it for the rest of our journey when this blizzard clears.'

The rest of their journey. Even the nightmare of the *Venturer*, trapped in the ice, seemed little more than a blissful, half-forgotten dream. And they were not yet even a third of the way to Fort Hope.

In the darkness, Pettifer went on singing softly to himself:

'When I'd rattle in a morning and cry, "Milk below",
At the sound of my milk cans her face she would show
With a smile upon her countenance and a laugh in her eye,
If I'd thought she'd've loved me, I'd've laid down to
die . . .

'She was as beautiful as a butterfly

And as proud as a queen
Was pretty little Polly Perkins
Of Paddington Green.'

XXIII

The River

They were down to their last match by the end of the week. It rattled pathetically in its box until Molineaux pulled off a mitten to pick it out with numb, frozen fingers.

'Careful, now,' said Riggs, as they huddled around the unlit camp-fire. 'Don't waste it.'

Molineaux glared at him. 'You think so? I was thinking of just throwing it away without lighting it, you great noddy!' Scowling, he struck the match. It flared into life, and a moment later a gust of wind blew it out again.

Everyone groaned. 'What did I tell you?' demanded Riggs.

'What, you think I did that on purpose?' Molineaux retorted angrily.

'All right, everyone, simmer down,' ordered Killigrew. 'We've just got to think around the problem, that's all. Man made fire long before the invention of matches. I don't see why we can't do the same.'

'We could try rubbing sticks together!' said Latimer.

'No trees,' said Yelverton.

Killigrew picked up a fistful of snow and scrunched it together in his hands, squeezing and moulding it. 'A little application of science is all it takes,' he explained. 'Have none of you ever used a magnifying glass to start a fire with?'

'I don't suppose you've got a magnifying glass on you, have you, sir?' asked Molineaux.

'No. But we can make a lens.'

'What with?'

'Snow.' Killigrew went on squeezing and moulding the ice between his palms. 'All we need to do is compact it into ice, then fashion it into a convex lens to concentrate the sun's rays—'

'Killigrew?'

'Not now, Strachan, I'm busy. Where was I?'

'You were fashioning a lump of snow into a convex lens to concentrate the sun's rays,' said Molineaux.

'Will that work?' Qualtrough sounded dubious.

'In theory.'

'Killigrew!' The assistant surgeon's voice was more insistent this time.

'Please, Strachan! Can't you see I have my hands full?' Killigrew looked at the lump of ice he had made. It was about the right shape, but far too opaque to be of any use. He went on squeezing it and moulding it.

'I really think you ought to see what the pill-roller's got for you, sir,' said Molineaux.

The lieutenant glanced up at him, and then turned to where Strachan was holding out his magnifying glass with an apologetic expression on his face.

'You might find it easier with this.'

Onwards they trudged, dragging Faith and Hope behind them, Armitage riding on the dog sledge driven by Ursula. But the cook's gangrene was spreading. When he became feverish Strachan realised he could not wait any longer before amputating. There was no chloroform to use as an anaesthetic, not enough alcohol to do it the old-fashioned way. While Molineaux stood by with an iron heated up into a laughable approximation of red-hot, ready to cauterise the stump, Strachan tied a tourniquet tightly about midway up the thigh. In the absence of a scalpel, he cut away flaps of Armitage's skin from the thigh, exposing the muscle and bone below, while Qualtrough and Kracht held the cook down. Ursula could not bring herself to watch.

The closest thing Strachan could find to a surgical saw was an axe. He tried to heft the tool in his hand and a look of despair crossed his face.

'I can't do it,' he whimpered to Killigrew.

'Come on, man. I've seen you perform amputations before now.'

Strachan shook his head. 'It's not that. I mean, I haven't got the strength to do it. Not in one blow.'

'Just get on with it, for Christ's sake!' groaned Armitage.

'Let me do it, sir,' offered Molineaux, swapping the iron for the axe.

'Sure you can do it?' asked Strachan.

'Only one way to find out.' Molineaux took a deep breath. 'You ready for this, Tommo?'

'Just do it!'

'Hey, Tommo, you remember when we stopped at that hot-pie shop in Greenwich and you—' Molineaux broke off in mid-sentence and smashed the axe down, shearing through flesh, sinew and bone with one powerful blow. Armitage gave a hoarse gasp and blood gouted on to the snow.

Strachan sewed the flaps of skin over the stump. There were no bandages, so they had to wrap it up with rags that quickly soaked through with blood.

Armitage died the following night, from shock, loss of blood, whatever. Everyone was too exhausted to care any more. The next morning they put Yelverton on the dog sledge, while the remaining sixteen of them hauled their dwindling stock of tinned food and pemmican on the two sledges.

Onwards and onwards, week after week, day after day, hour after hour, minute after minute, each second a lifetime of weary pain and suffering. By 2 February they had used up enough of their victuals to abandon Faith and cram everything that was left on Hope. Killigrew regretted the choice of names now, because he knew that eventually they would have to abandon the other sledge, too, and the seamen would see it as a bad omen when they abandoned Hope. He cut their daily rations from six-upon-four to six-upon-three in the hope of spinning them out a few more days, knowing it was hopeless. Barely enough food for another three weeks, and still 580 miles to go. They were covering about eight miles a day. The mathematics of their situation was inescapable.

Two weeks later he cut their rations again, to eight-upon-two.

They ate one meal a day: a sliver of pemmican, a ship's biscuit, a couple of one-ounce squares of chocolate, and a mug of weak, tepid tea fortified with a spoonful of sugar, and a tablespoon of rum on Saturdays.

Days merged into weeks, weeks into months. They threw away their boots, put on their spares, and started to wear those out too. They crossed a wide, frozen lake where a recent fall of rain had melted the surface into a honeycomb of razor-sharp ridges, which slashed through boots and the feet beneath, men and dogs alike leaving a trail of blood in their wake. Bellies tight, limbs like lead, every step of the way meant more pain.

One step equals eighteen inches, Killigrew told himself. *Two steps one yard. One thousand, seven hundred and sixty yards in a mile. Only four hundred miles to go now, halfway there. How many steps is that? One million, four hundred and eight thousand. Another step. Now only one million, four hundred and seven thousand, nine hundred and ninety-nine to go. One million, four hundred and seven thousand, nine hundred and ninety-eight. You can do it, you're eating up the miles now. Just keep plodding on, one foot in front of the other, left, right, left, right, oh Jesus, how much more of this? Doesn't this landscape ever end? What the hell was God thinking of when he made this benighted land? So cold, and so hungry, where's all the wildlife that Terregannoeuck promised us? Can't keep this up, not for another four hundred miles, damn it, haven't we suffered enough?*

What's the point? Every step hurts, every step, on and on, damn the monotony, what's the point? You'll never make it, why make the suffering worse? Less painful just to lie down and die right here. There are worse ways of dying than just falling asleep in the snow.

Come on, man, get a grip on yourself. You're Kit Killigrew, you never give up.

But I've never been in a situation as hopeless as this before.

You're going to give up now? Look at the others. They can do it, so can you. You're a British officer, you're in command, it's up to you to set the example.

Why? Why should I be responsible for them?

Because that's what you signed up for when you accepted the

432

Queen's commission. Now come on, get a grip. Just keep moving, it's not that difficult, one foot in front of the other . . .

A body thudded against the snow behind him. He turned, saw Latimer lying down in imminent danger of being run over by the sledge, and quickly called a halt.

'Has he fainted?' asked Strachan.

Killigrew rolled Latimer on his back. The young man was conscious, but his cheeks were streaked with tears. 'What's up, lad?'

'It's no good, sir. I can't go on.'

'Yes, you can. We're all tired, Latimer. We all have sore feet and aching bones. We're all weary. But we must go on.'

'It's no good, I can't.'

'You're a British officer. You don't know the meaning of the word "can't".'

'Just leave me here, all right? I just need to rest for a few minutes and catch my breath.'

Killigrew knew that if they left him behind they would never see him again. 'No can do, Latimer. Come on, man, on your feet, damn you! Get up! That's an order, Latimer!'

'It's no good, sir. It's hopeless!'

'There's still breath in our bodies, isn't there? Then there's hope. We've just got to keep moving. Remember New Year's Eve, when we were all exhausted and we realised that all we'd covered was thirty-eight miles in six days? Well, we've got fewer than four hundred to cover now. That's *four hundred* behind us. Did you ever think we'd get this far back then?'

Latimer shook his head.

'No. But we did it, didn't we? Well, if we can cover four hundred miles, can't we cover another four hundred? Just an eensy, teensy four hundred miles?'

Latimer managed a weak smile. They both knew it was not as simple as that. Their bodies ravaged by malnutrition, scurvy and frostbite, every mile seemed like a hundred now.

'That's the spirit,' said Killigrew. 'If you can smile, you can walk another four hundred miles. That's nothing after what we've come through together, a stroll in the park. It's *ground*, Latimer, that's all it is. And we can conquer it just by putting one foot in front of the other.'

The clerk tried to get up. Killigrew took his arm and helped him to his feet.

'That's it, lad. You can do it.'

They took up the strain. The sledge behind them slithered and ground over the ice. More miles, mile after mile after mile. What if Latimer was right? What if it *was* hopeless? Of course it was hopeless. Even on half-rations, they did not have enough food left to last them a fortnight. Well, so what? What could they do? Lie down and die? At least this way they would die trying; that had to be better than just lying down in the snow and giving up.

They waded through snow lying a foot thick on the ground, frequently stumbling on the loose stones concealed beneath. Where the snow covered marshes, their feet would break through the thin covering of ice and they would sink in up to their knees. Pettifer, of all people, was a tower of strength. Half-rations seemed to have no effect on his energy. He led the way, hauling mightily, tirelessly, sometimes singing shanties to set the pace, at other times muttering darkly to himself, but never once suggesting they should give up.

They ran out of spirits of wine and threw away the portable stoves as good for nothing, an unnecessary encumbrance. Soon afterwards they saw their first trees in eleven months: curious, stunted things, dwarf firs, few and far between but plentiful enough for a camp-fire. The food stocks ran so low it became easier to abandon the last of the sledges – no one was referring to it as 'Hope' now – and stuff the supplies that remained into their knapsacks. Endicott and Hughes carried a tent each, Molineaux the poles and ropes for them.

Then, with another 236 miles still to go, the last of the victuals were gone. 'Now what are we gannin' to eat?' asked Butterwick, who had been concerned enough about where his next meal was coming from even before they had set out on this desperate trek.

Killigrew glanced towards the huskies.

'Oh, no!' protested Strachan.

'Oh, yes,' said Killigrew. 'Sorry, Strachan: it's them or us.'

Qualtrough sighed. 'I'll do it,' he offered. 'Which is the weakest?' he asked Ursula.

She shook her head, unwilling to have any part of it.

Qualtrough used his own judgement and separated one dog out from the rest, leading it behind a snow hummock with an ice-axe in one hand. The dog did not even get a chance to yelp before it died.

They were all reluctant to take the first bite, but after subsisting on pemmican for weeks a taste of fresh meat reminded them all – as if they could ever forget – just how hungry they were.

The first dog kept the sixteen of them going a couple more days. When they ate the second, there were only three huskies left, not enough to pull the dog sledge. From there on, Yelverton had to walk with the rest of them. Only 170 miles left to go; a fraction of what they had faced when they started out.

After they killed the final husky there was nothing for it but to tighten their belts for a couple of days. But it was April now, spring – such as it was – returning to the tundra and with it came a miracle: a herd of migrating reindeer. They shot enough of the beasts to last them another week, expending four times as much ammunition as it would have taken healthy men whose hands would not have trembled so much just to hold their muskets up. Ammunition was running low; they could not afford to be so prodigious with their bullets and cartridges. But they could not afford to let the reindeer go past. They skinned the animals, feasted on the flesh and wrapped the hides around their feet in place of the tatters that had been their boots.

It took them two weeks to cover the next eighty-two miles. Two weeks of stumbling in a daze, too hungry and exhausted to think straight. They ate the last of the reindeer meat, trudged onwards for two more days in hope of finding another herd. A flock of ptarmigan flew overhead and they blazed away with their muskets. Two birds fell to the earth: hardly enough for a mouthful each and the taste left them feeling even hungrier than before.

The next night they dined a little more substantially, a couple of mouthfuls of fresh meat each. Molineaux crouched by Pettifer to spoon-feed the commander: no one wanted to untie his wrists. 'Mmm, good!' Pettifer said enthusiastically. 'I thought we killed the last of the huskies three weeks ago?'

The others exchanged nervous glances. Pettifer narrowed his eyes suspiciously: insane he might be, but he was still intelligent

435

enough to know that something was going on.

'Where's Horatia?'

The dachshund had followed them for 720 miles, trotting along in the little woollen coat Pettifer's wife had knitted for her, eating her share of the rations without contributing to helping them in their journey as the huskies had. As the men became more and more broken by cold, exhaustion and malnutrition, Horatia seemed to have a limitless supply of energy, running off on her own sometimes, or nipping at the heels of the men pulling the sledges until they kicked her away. Now she was noticeable by her absence.

Someone had to tell Pettifer: sooner or later he was going to guess anyway. Better it be broken to him gently.

It had been Killigrew's decision. 'She gave her life so that we might live,' he explained.

Pettifer stared at him, his jaw slowing as it worked up and down, chewing the mouthful of fresh meat Molineaux had just spooned between his lips. Then he spat it out – straight in Molineaux's eyes – and butted the petty officer on the bridge of the nose. As Molineaux fell, Pettifer was on his feet in an instant and charged across to where Killigrew sat.

The lieutenant barely had time to rise to his feet. Then, his hands still bound before him, Pettifer managed to get his massive fists around Killigrew's neck and the two of them went down in the snow.

In spite of his bound hands, the commander was still able to bring all of his bulk to bear, and Killigrew, weakened by the arduous trek, was hard-pressed to defend himself. Their limited rations did not seem to have robbed Pettifer of his strength – or if they had, his insane rage gave him new energy. He fought like a wild thing, clawing at Killigrew's eyes, trying to sink his teeth into the lieutenant's neck but only getting a mouthful of his woollen comforter.

Kracht was the first to reach them, bringing the stock of a musket down against the back of Pettifer's head: once, twice, three times. Only after the third blow did Pettifer's eyes roll up in his skull and he slumped. Endicott and Hughes pulled his body off Killigrew and Strachan hurried across.

'Are you all right?'

Killigrew nodded, feeling shaken by the savagery of Pettifer's attack. 'Molineaux?'

The boatswain's mate was gingerly fingering the bridge of his nose, opening and squeezing his eyes shut as if he was having difficulty focusing. There was blood all over his upper lip and chin. 'I'll be all right, sir. Just a bit dazed, that's all. Sorry about that – I should've seen it coming.'

'So should I,' admitted Killigrew. The cold was numbing his brain, robbing him of his ability to think things through properly. 'No harm done.'

Strachan crouched over Pettifer.

'Is he dead?' asked Killigrew, trying not to sound too hopeful. The rational part of him wished the commander no ill will – it was not his fault he was insane, he was not responsible for his actions – but it was difficult to summon much sympathy for a man who had just tried to kill him, and come too close for comfort. Besides, sooner or later Killigrew knew that he was going to have to face a court martial if he ever got back to England, and if Pettifer recovered his senses or was even lucid long enough to give evidence, the lieutenant knew that he would be lucky if being dismissed the service was the worst thing they did to him.

But now was not the time to worry about what would happen when they got back to England: it would be nothing short of a miracle if they made it as far as Fort Hope.

'He'll live,' announced Strachan.

'From now on we'll keep his hands tied behind his back, I think.'

Pettifer stirred, opened his eyes and glared at Killigrew with insane rage in them. 'I'm going to kill you,' he said matter-of-factly.

The lieutenant shrugged, almost indifferent to the threat in his weariness. 'Perhaps you've already killed us all.'

Sixty-seven miles to go. The only edible thing they could find was *tripe de roche*, the lichen that had sustained Franklin's party on his first overland expedition. They scraped it from the rocks and boiled it. It was bitterly foul and it gave them bellyaches, but at least the action of chewing and swallowing fooled them into thinking they might not die of starvation.

In spite of the *tripe de roche*, scurvy began to take its toll on them. Livid red blotches and brown and purple skin haemorrhages appeared all over their bodies. Their legs swelled up to twice their size and excruciating pain stabbed at their joints with every step. The insides of their mouths became bubbled with lesions; the gums reddened and receded: soon they would turn black and their teeth would fall out.

The returning sun, which took the edge off the wind as it spent more and more time above the horizon each passing day, brought with it new tortures: sunburn and snow blindness. Reflected off the whiteness all around them, the sun burned their faces, the insides of their nostrils and mouths, even the undersides of their eyelids. Even with their snow-goggles on, the dull ache in their eyes grew in intensity until it felt as though they had grit in them. Their vision became tinged pink, then blood red, until their eyes watered so much they could barely see at all. Strachan treated their eyes with glycerine and Killigrew decided that from then on they would travel at night and sleep by day. By now they were all so exhausted and malnourished it was all they could manage to cover five miles a day.

Killigrew knew they were all dying.

One foot in front of the other. Just keep going. Think of all that lovely food waiting for you at Fort Hope.

Old age had killed the musk-ox, or some disease perhaps. It looked as if it had been dead for some time: weeks, months, perhaps even years. Doubtless the cold had helped to preserve it, but the cold could not protect it from the attentions of the sand flies that buzzed over it in a cloud, or the evidence that scavenger birds had picked over it. And shortly after its death, its own body heat had allowed some decomposition: the putrid stench of decay was overpowering.

'We have to do it,' mumbled Strachan. A mumble was all any of them could manage, when they felt they had the breath left in their bodies to be squandered on speech.

Killigrew nodded. 'Perhaps if we cook it—'

'Eat that?' gasped Varrow. 'It's putrid, man! One nibble at that would kill an elephant with food poisoning!'

'We have to risk it,' said Killigrew. 'Apart from *tripe de roche*, it's the only food we've seen in a fortnight. It could be the last meat we'll see between here and Fort Hope.'

'We might see another herd of reindeer tomorrow!'

'We might not. We can't take that chance. We'll be dead in another week.' Killigrew turned to Endicott and Hughes. 'Gather up some firewood.' Over the past forty miles the trees had become thicker and larger and finding fuel for their camp-fires had ceased to be a problem.

Molineaux licked scabby lips. 'I'll make a stew,' he decided.

Strachan – the least squeamish of them – undertook the task of butchering the carcass. Even he gagged at the stench. He cut off the least rancid parts of the meat and Molineaux boiled them up in a pannikin, adding *tripe de roche* for seasoning. Stomachs growled while he allowed it to simmer for a long, long time, hunger battling with revulsion. At last mess tins were filled, handed out. Killigrew stared at the contents of his. It smelled all right, but that had to be balanced against the knowledge of where it had come from. He glanced at the others. Most of them also hesitated. Even Molineaux, dubious about his own skill in turning a putrid musk-ox into a feast, was clearly having second thoughts. Only Butterwick tucked in at once, eating as heartily as if it were his favourite, salmagundi served up on the mess deck of the *Venturer*.

'How is it?' Varrow asked him.

'Good,' Butterwick mumbled enthusiastically, speaking with his mouth full, trying to spoon in another mouthful before he had swallowed the first.

Molineaux eased a tiny nibble into his mouth, then another. Strachan tried it, and did not retch.

Gagging, Killigrew took a deep breath, and spooned it into his mouth. Sancho Panza had been right: hunger was the best sauce in the world. The stew tasted better than the finest game served at Rules.

Everyone had seconds.

The meat gave them the strength to go on. They were still weakened, their bodies ravaged by malnutrition, and it took them two days to cover the next nine miles, but those were nine

439

miles behind them now and suddenly they had only fifty-four miles to go.

And that was when they came to the river. A river where no river was marked on the map. Fifty feet wide and swollen by the melt waters of the spring thaw. Back in England, Killigrew could have swum it without a second thought. But that had been a thousand years ago when he had been a young man, not the decrepit, starved octogenarian who gazed at those ice-cold, fast-flowing waters and felt only despair. If they had still had the Halkett boat, they might have crossed it; but as if anticipating they would need it, the bear had destroyed the boat along with Charity over three months ago.

They walked along the bank for a couple of miles, but there was no way across. The river barred their path.

'Fifty-four miles,' said Molineaux, as they slumped to the ground. 'Fifty-four *bloody* miles.'

'We tried,' sighed Yelverton. 'Dear God, how we tried.'

They had come so far, got so close, and yet they were all so far gone with hunger Killigrew could see they were ready to give up. But there had to be a way across, there *had* to be! He looked around, but there were no trees they could cut down to create a bridge or make a raft, just stunted bushes. Not that any of them had the strength to cut down any trees.

'Mr Latimer, would you be so good as to hold these for me for a minute?' said Strachan.

Latimer accepted the spectacles the assistant surgeon handed him. Strachan picked up a rope and tied one end to a rock.

'What are you going to do?' Killigrew asked him.

Strachan ignored him and tied the other end of the rope around his waist.

The assistant surgeon's intentions finally dawned on Killigrew's hunger-dulled brain. 'No!' he tried to run across to grab Strachan, but his legs collapsed beneath him and he fell to his knees. 'You'll never make it! You'll freeze to death, man! Stop him, someone!'

Yelverton tried to grab him, but Strachan just ran out into the water. He gasped at its icy touch, then waded out until he was waist-deep. He plunged into it and began swimming.

'Haul him in, for God's sake!' said Killigrew. 'The fool's going to kill himself!' He crawled over to where Strachan had tied the rope to a boulder, but Molineaux stopped him.

'It's a done thing now, sir. Either he makes it, or he doesn't. If he doesn't, we're all going to die anyhow.'

They watched from the bank as Strachan paddled pathetically across the mill-race. He had never been the strongest of them, and their arduous trek from the polar seas had taken its toll on him as much as anyone. If Killigrew had had to pick someone to swim the river, Strachan would not have been high on his list.

The current in mid-stream caught the assistant surgeon and threatened to sweep him away. He fought it, his desperation giving him new strength. Then he was through the worst of it and it looked as though he was going to make it.

The next moment he had disappeared.

The men watching groaned. Killigrew waited for him to resurface. He had come so close: if he had only gone under momentarily, then to drag him back now would mean all his efforts had been in vain, and he would never have the strength to make a second attempt; if he had not . . .

Seconds passed. Killigrew scanned the foaming white water. Strachan did not resurface. 'All right, that's enough. Pull him in.'

'Hold on, sir,' said Molineaux. 'Just give him a few more moments . . .'

'Pull him in *now*, damn it! He's drowning!'

'No he isn't, by God! Look!' Yelverton pointed downstream, to the left of where Killigrew had been watching. Strachan had resurfaced and still struggled to reach the shallows on the far side.

'Come on, sir!' Molineaux yelled hoarsely. 'Just a few more feet!'

'You can do it, sir!' shouted Endicott.

Killigrew had seen men in the final stages of exhaustion and he could see that Strachan was well beyond those stages, drawing on reserves of endurance that no man could have any right to. At last the assistant surgeon was wading up out of the shallows, staggering like a dying man; which, Killigrew thought grimly, was probably what he was. Strachan splashed out of the water, clambered up the rocks on the far bank, took two more steps and then collapsed in the snow.

He had earned a rest, of course, but he could not afford to

pause, not now, not until he had tied that rope to one of the rocks on the far side. Until he had done that, there was nothing anyone on the north bank could do for him. If he fell asleep where he lay – and what man could not, after what he had just been through? – then he would never wake up.

Killigrew was about to call out to him when he saw Strachan slowly push himself to his feet, untie the rope from around his waist, and loop it around a rock. He tied it off and then collapsed once more.

On the north bank, Molineaux and Endicott drew in the slack and made the rope fast. Killigrew took the rope in both hands and was about to wade into the water when Molineaux laid a hand on his arm. 'You think the pill-roller's rope-work is any better than his needlework?' he asked, with a nod to where Strachan had tied off the other end of the rope.

'Only one way to find out.' Killigrew stepped into the river.

The water looked icy, but appearances were deceptive: it was so cold, it burned. Killigrew realised at once that Strachan had had the right idea: get across as quickly as possible, before the cold seeped into his bones to paralyse his muscles with agonising cramp. With the rope to help him, it was a lot easier than it had been for Strachan. He was through the mill-race in midstream when the rope gave a little and he glanced across to see the knot where Strachan had tied it coming adrift. With a lunge of desperation, he pushed on. The rope shifted again and he lost his footing and went under. Only the rope saved him, but as he pulled himself up it shifted even more. There were only a couple of inches left beyond the knot, sliding through inexorably, and just when it seemed that the knot must come adrift Strachan appeared on his feet once more and hauled it tight again. He kept on hauling on it until Killigrew was able to let go of the rope and wade out of the shallows.

Strachan's teeth were chattering too fiercely for him to be able to speak. Killigrew retied the rope with a proper seaman's knot and then went to gather some firewood while Qualtrough entered the water behind him. They had to untie Pettifer's hands so he could haul himself across, while Qualtrough kept him covered with a musket. There were no muskets with dry powder on the south bank, but by the time Pettifer hauled himself out of the water, he was too exhausted to resist as Molineaux bound his hands once more.

Most of them were across by the time he had got a fire going by the time-honoured method of rubbing two sticks together.

'What the hell were you playing at?' Killigrew asked Strachan, not unkindly.

The assistant surgeon managed to grin through chattering teeth. 'You always get to be the hero. Thought it was my turn.'

Killigrew returned his grin, and then caught sight of the crimson stain spreading through the snow around Strachan's right foot and the smiled faded from his face. 'What happened to your foot?'

'Must've stepped on something under the water,' said Strachan. 'Thought it was cramp. So cold . . . hardly felt a thing . . . Is it bad?'

Killigrew unwrapped the rags the assistant surgeon wore in place of a boot. They were soaked with blood, and underneath the flesh was lacerated to the bone. 'It's not good,' he admitted. It might only be fifty-four miles to Fort Hope, but Strachan was not going to get far with his foot in that condition. Worse, without proper medical attention, that wound was going to fester and become gangrenous.

'Jesus!' hissed Molineaux. At first Killigrew thought he too had seen the state of Strachan's foot, but then the seaman raised his voice in a hoarse yell of panic. 'Mr Yelverton! Look out behind you, sir!'

Killigrew looked up. Kracht was the last man but one to cross the river, hauling himself strongly through the torrent. Behind him, Yelverton was on the verge of following him into the water. At Molineaux's yell, he turned in time to see the bear charging towards him.

The men on the south bank reached for their guns, guns rendered useless by the water that soaked the cartridges. Yelverton froze, reached for his knife, and then thought better of it and splashed into the water. The bear followed him unhesitatingly, diving from the bank with remarkable agility. It swam confidently after Yelverton, seemed to rise up on top of him, and then they both went under. The water foamed red, and then the bear was swimming back to the north bank, dragging Yelverton with his leg in its jaws.

The ultimate horror was that the master was still alive. He screamed horribly while Killigrew and the others watched helplessly from the far side of the river. At that moment the lieutenant would have given anything for dry powder so he could put his old friend out of his misery.

The bear dragged Yelverton out of the water and then, growing weary of his struggles and screams, smashed his skull with a casual swipe of one paw. Glowering across the river at the others, the bear backed out of sight, dragging Yelverton's corpse behind it.

'Dear God!' sobbed Latimer. 'You don't think it was the same one . . .?'

'How many polar bears that big do you think there are in the world?' Varrow retorted sharply.

'Yes, but to follow us for nearly *eight hundred* miles . . .'

It was inconceivable that anything in God's creation, man or beast, could show such single-minded determination, but Killigrew was sure the engineer was right. There had been two dark specks on the bear's side, and Killigrew did not doubt they were the scars where Terregannoeuck had shot it. He felt grief: grief for an old friend he had sailed with for many years, grief for the family back in Yarmouth whom he would have to tell in person that their husband and father was dead – and tell the old, old lie that he had not suffered. But more punishing than that was the fear. The fear that the same fate awaited him somewhere along the last fifty miles of their trek. Bullets had not killed the bear, nor dissuaded it from following them 746 miles.

'You remember what Terry told us,' said Molineaux. 'They go where the food is, trailing herds of reindeer for hundreds of miles.'

'Not inland,' said Latimer, and rounded on Strachan. 'You said it wouldn't follow us inland!'

The assistant surgeon grinned weakly, without humour. 'I think we must have made it really, *really* angry.'

Killigrew sighed. He could not accept that the bear had followed them hundreds of miles inland just to settle a grudge, and yet there it had been. 'Come on, let's get organised,' he

444

said. 'Our guns will be useless until the powder dries, so we'll have to make alternative weapons. There are more than enough saplings around here for every man to make a spear, so let's look lively.'

No one had much strength for cutting down trees and sharpening them to wicked points, but they had less taste for being killed by the bear, so they went to work. Killigrew hoped that its latest kill would sate its hunger until they could reach Fort Hope – how long would that take, a fortnight? – where, with any luck, help would be at hand. Nonetheless, there was no need to appoint anyone to stand guard that night: no one felt much like sleeping. Molineaux spent the night sewing stitches in Strachan's foot, at the doctor's insistence. Strachan never once cried out, although Killigrew feared this was less a reflection of his fortitude – already proven beyond question – than of the fact that his foot was numbed with frostbite.

Dawn came – what a luxury it was to see the sun rise in the mornings again! – and they set off once more. Strachan hobbled along on a makeshift crutch that Riggs had fashioned for him from a stout sapling. The weather favoured them, but that was about all. The next day Killigrew saw a couple of stray reindeer some distance off and he and Molineaux went after them with muskets, but the reindeer eluded them easily and they rejoined the others empty-handed. That night they dined as usual on the vile, indigestion-inducing *tripe de roche*.

A week later they had to cross a rocky defile. It was hard-going, and when Qualtrough was about halfway down he lost his footing, fell a few feet, and rolled the rest of the way to the bottom. Killigrew wanted to hasten down after him to make sure he was all right, but he knew that that way he would only risk breaking his own neck.

'Qualtrough? Are you all right?' Killigrew's raised voice, hoarse as it was, sounded strange as it echoed off the rocks.

'I'm fine,' the ice quartermaster called back.

It took Killigrew another five minutes to climb to the bottom and find Qualtrough sitting up in the lee of a boulder. The ice quartermaster had been lying: he was not fine at all. He was conscious and in no immediate pain, to all intents and purposes in good spirits, but Killigrew did not need to wait for Molineaux and Butterwick to finish helping Strachan down the steep slope to find out that Qualtrough had a compound fracture of the left leg. As Strachan did what he could to make the quartermaster comfortable, Killigrew announced that they would make camp there for the night. Afterwards Strachan took him aside.

'He's never going to get to Fort Hope on that leg.'

'Then we'll have to carry him,' Killigrew said simply. 'I'm not leaving anyone behind. Damn it, there were thirty-seven of us on board the *Venturer* when we left Beechey Island, and how many are left now? Fifteen!'

Strachan shook his head. 'See sense, Killigrew. Look at us. The fittest of us will be lucky to make it to Fort Hope. If anyone tries to carry him, they'll die along with Qualtrough himself.'

'Then what do you suggest?' Killigrew hissed angrily. 'That we leave him here to make another meal for Bruin?'

Strachan shook his head wearily. 'I don't know. God help me, Killigrew, I just don't know.'

Killigrew cursed. He reckoned they had covered nearly thirty miles in the ten days since they had crossed the river. Only twenty-two miles left to go, but as they staggered along they were covering an average of three miles a day. They would be lucky to reach Fort Hope in a week.

'All right,' he said. 'Perhaps if we sent a couple of the stronger ones ahead to Fort Hope to send help back here. Say, six days for someone to get there, a day or two for a party of fit and healthy men to make it back here; the rest would only have to wait eight days at the most, if this weather holds up.'

Strachan shook his head. 'You know it makes more sense for the majority to go on, Killigrew. Less food for a rescue party to bring back to the survivors. I'll wait here with Qualtrough. I don't think I can go much further with this damned foot of mine.'

'No can do,' said Killigrew. 'What if Bruin comes back?'

'Leave us a couple of muskets. We'll have to take our own chances. There's no point in us holding back the rest of you.'

Killigrew shook his head. He could not leave his friend and Qualtrough at the mercy of the bear. 'Then I'll stay with you.'

Strachan grasped him by the arm. 'No! The others *need* you,

Killigrew. I know it's only a few miles to Fort Hope, but they'll never make it without you. They're ready to give up, they'd all have given up a long time ago if it wasn't for you.'

'And what will you eat while you're waiting for us to send food back to you? You're in no condition to go foraging for *tripe de roche*.'

'I'll stay with them, sir,' said Molineaux, who was sitting nearby. 'I can get them food, keep a fire going; and if Bruin comes sniffing around, I'll soon settle his hash,' he added with a grin, patting the barrel of the musket he was cleaning.

Killigrew shook his head. He knew that if he left anyone behind he would be leaving him to die. It was bad enough even to contemplate leaving his friend Strachan behind, but to leave Molineaux as well, who was also . . . yes, damn it, his friend . . . It was curious to think of a rating as a friend, but Killigrew knew of few men of his own class he could rely on the way he could depend on Molineaux. Both the assistant surgeon and the petty officer had helped him so much in the past; he owed his life and his career to them both.

Molineaux stood up and came across to join them. 'I'll look after 'em, sir. That's a promise.'

Killigrew stared hard at him and realised that if any man could fulfil that promise, he stood before him now. He hated to do it, as much as he had hated to put Gargrave out of his misery; but once again it was the only sensible solution.

He took a deep breath. 'Thank you, Molineaux. But I'll be obliged if you'll keep that promise.'

'Have I ever let you down in the past, sir?'

'Never.'

'Well, then.'

The next day it was eleven men and one woman who set out from the camp site, leaving three behind them. Killigrew was too choked up to find anything to say to his friends as he left them, so he just shook their hands.

'Don't you worry, sir,' said Molineaux. 'We'll see you at Fort Hope in a couple of weeks.'

'Thank you, Molineaux. God be with you.'

'And with you, sir.'

The rest trudged on. At the mouth of the defile Killigrew

stopped and glanced back. Molineaux was already too busy building a fresh fire to notice but, despite the petty officer's apparent self-confidence, Killigrew could not shrug off the feeling that he was looking at his friends for the last time.

XXIV

A Taste of Pork

Towards evening Killigrew, Ursula and the other ten men passed through a patch of open ground where *tripe de roche* were so plentiful they had no difficulty in eating their fill, or at least as much of the disgustingly bitter lichen as they could cram between their blistered lips. If only Qualtrough and Strachan could have kept going this far, Killigrew would not have had to worry about them finding enough to eat until a rescue party could reach them, but it was too late now. He thought about sending someone back to tell them about this spot; but every one of the men who had come with him was so far gone they would be lucky to cover the remaining twenty miles to Fort Hope, without making them cover the additional four miles there and back to where they had left Strachan, Molineaux and Qual-trough.

It was Kracht's turn to build a fire. 'May I have Herr Strachan's *Vergrö Berungslas, mein Herr?*' he asked Killigrew. He snapped his fingers and grimaced, trying to remember the English word. 'For making fire?'

'The magnifying glass, you mean.'

Killigrew reached into the pocket of his coat but found only his clasp-knife and what felt like a piece of string. 'Must be in my knapsack.' He gestured to where he had put down his pack a few feet away after shrugging it off, too exhausted to fetch the magnifying glass himself. 'Help yourself.'

As Kracht rummaged in his pack, Killigrew drew out the

piece of string and looked at it: that five-inch length of safety fuse he had never got around to tidying out of his pockets. Not much use to him now. He toyed with it, tying and untying knots.

Kracht drew out one of the metal canisters Killigrew had brought with him and removed the stopper, sniffing inside as if he thought it might contain food. 'Message canister,' Killigrew told him.

'Why the devil did you lug one of those all this way, sir?' asked Latimer. 'I thought we were supposed to leave anything extraneous behind.'

'To leave a final message,' said Varrow, 'so that whoever finds our bodies will know what happened to us.'

The engineer had guessed correctly, but Killigrew would have preferred it if he had kept such negative thoughts to himself. He glanced at the others to see how they were taking it, but the truth was they had no illusions about their chances and could not possibly be any more dispirited than they were now. 'How did you guess?' he asked Varrow with a thin smile.

The engineer pulled a matching canister from his own knapsack. 'Had the same idea meself.'

Kracht was gazing at the length of fuse in Killigrew's hands. '*Zündschnur*?' he asked.

'Pardon?'

'Fuse,' said Ursula.

'Oh. Yes, that's right.'

'May I?' Kracht held out his hand. Killigrew gave him the fuse.

The blacksmith picked up the ice-axe and used it to puncture a hole in the lid of the canister. Then he removed it and started breaking open cartridges. They had plenty of cartridges – it was bullets they were running out of – so Killigrew did not object. The others started to gather round, watching curiously.

'A grenade?' guessed Killigrew.

Filling the canister with gunpowder, Kracht nodded. 'In case the bear comes back.' He tied a knot in one end of the fuse, poked it through the hole in the lid, and replaced it on the canister.

'And just how do you plan to light the fuse?' asked Varrow.

Kracht held up the magnifying glass by way of reply.

'Well, that's champion, that is,' said Varrow. 'Let's just hope the next time Bruin attacks he does it during the day – a day when there's nay cloud cover, like.'

'And that he stands and waits while you try to light the fuse with the magnifying glass,' put in Killigrew.

Red-faced, Kracht pushed himself to his feet. 'You have a better idea, *mein Herr*?' he demanded hotly.

Killigrew shook his head. 'No,' he admitted. 'I haven't. It's a good idea.'

To judge from the expression on the blacksmith's face, he was not mollified.

They ate their supper and crawled into their tents. Just how far gone the men were was brought home to Killigrew the next morning when he tried to rouse them. Most of them pushed themselves to their feet, moving like clumsy, ill-made automatons; it had been many weeks since any of them had even had the energy to grumble, and now when Butterwick protested they could not go any further, Killigrew could only believe it. 'It's nay good, sir. I canna gan on.'

Killigrew shook his head. It was bad enough leaving the others behind; was he to leave a string of men, too weak to go on, from here to Fort Hope? 'Surely you can, Butterwick. It's only twenty miles, for heaven's sake. Twenty miles, out of eight hundred! Don't tell me you're going to give up now?'

Butterwick just shook his head sadly. 'I canna, sir. Not another step.'

'Me too, *mein Herr*,' said Fischbein. 'I'm exhausted.'

Killigrew had more sympathy for the half-deck boy. Unlike the brawny, simple-minded stoker – and indeed all the seamen – Ignatz Fischbein had never been a big strong man, and if Killigrew had had to put any money on one of them not making it to Fort Hope, it would have been Fischbein. But the half-deck boy had made it this far, and done so as uncomplainingly as any of the seamen. 'Very well,' he relented at last, seeing from the sullen look in Butterwick's eyes that the stoker was not going to back down, and that here perhaps was a way to kill two birds with one stone. 'If you can't make it to Fort Hope, do you think you could make it as far as where we left Mr Strachan, Qualtrough and Molineaux yesterday? It can't be more than two miles.'

'I can try, *mein Herr*.'

'What about you, Butterwick?'

'I s'pose so.'

'I suppose so, *sir*,' Killigrew chided him. No matter how desperate the situation, one could not afford to let discipline slide, and he did not care for the look in Butterwick's eye.

'Aye, aye, sir.'

'That's more like it. Do you think you can go back to the others, and bring them this far?' He indicated the *tripe de roche* on the rocks around them.

'We'll do our best, *mein Herr*.'

'That's good enough for me,' said Killigrew, and gave Fischbein his shotgun. Molineaux, Butterwick and Fischbein together would have a better chance of defending Strachan and Qualtrough from the bear than just Molineaux alone.

He watched Butterwick and Fischbein shamble slowly back the way they had come the day before, and then signalled for the rest of them to continue onwards. 'One last effort, my buckoes,' he told them, trying to sound hearty but only croaking like a decrepit crow. 'Only twenty miles to go. We can be there before the end of the week!'

Nine men and one woman left, and twenty miles to go. Killigrew could not help wondering how many of them would be left by the time they reached Fort Hope.

'There you go, gents.' Molineaux handed out the boiled *tripe de roche* to Strachan and Qualtrough. 'Get that little lot inside you. Just the thing to warm you up on a cold winter's day.'

'Except it's the middle of spring,' grumbled Strachan.

'And what culinary delights have you prepared for us this evening?' asked Qualtrough. 'Lobster thermidor? Steak château-briand, perhaps? Oh, no, it's more *tripe de roche*. Well, there's a surprise.'

Molineaux could not blame them for grumbling. He was getting sick of *tripe de roche* himself. No, he corrected himself, he had been sick of *tripe de roche* after his first mouthful. But they had to eat to stay alive. He had got his start at sea as a galley assistant and had become quite a proficient cook, priding

452

himself on his ability to knock together an appetising meal from the most humdrum ingredients – God knows, there was rarely a shortage of humdrum ingredients on Her Majesty's ships – but he doubted even his ability to prepare something appetising from *tripe de roche*, even if he had had the best condiments that Fortnum and Mason's could supply to spice it up.

'When I was at school,' mused Strachan, 'they used to give us liver on Thursdays. Every Thursday, without fail. I used to dread it. I hate liver. "Eat it up, Strachan minor," they'd say. "There are starving children in India who would be grateful for that liver." "Then let them have it," I retorted once. I got six of the best off the head prefect for that; my backside still smarts to think of it.'

Molineaux and Qualtrough managed a smile. It was not too difficult to imagine the young assistant surgeon as a schoolboy.

'It wasn't enough to make me eat that disgusting liver, though. They wouldn't let us out of the dining hall until our plates were cleared, so on Thursdays I'd try to get a seat by the window so I could chuck it out when no one was looking. If I couldn't, I'd slip it in my pockets and dispose of it later. My greatest recollection of being a schoolboy was having pockets permanently greasy with gravy. I'll tell you one thing, though: what I wouldn't give for some of that liver now!'

In the silence that followed, a twig snapped amongst the trees at the mouth of the defile. Molineaux quickly snatched up one of the muskets and levelled it, but it was only Butterwick. The boatswain's mate lowered the musket and exchanged glances with Strachan and Qualtrough as the stoker came across to join them.

'All right?' was the only explanation Butterwick would offer them.

'Jemmy?' said Molineaux. 'What are you doing here?'

'Couldn't gan on, not all the way to Fort Hope.' Butterwick sat down by the fire and warmed his hands. 'Mr Killigrew said as how me and Ignatz could come back and join you. We found a big patch of that moss stuff, what's it, treep durrosh? It's about two mile down the way, if you can make it that far.'

'Maybe tomorrow, when I've had a rest,' said Strachan. 'But I don't think Qualtrough is going to be able to make it on that broken leg of his.'

'Reckon he will, with me and Jemmy to carry him,' said Molineaux.

'What!' spluttered the stoker. 'You want me to help you carry 'im two miles? You must be bloody joking. I only came back 'cos I were so knocked up. Anyhow, we divven't need to now. I found a dead wolf on the way back, I brought you some meat. You can eat that instead. It's only about half a mile from here. I reckon there's enough meat on it to keep us going until Mr Killigrew and the others can send a rescue party from Fort Hope.'

'Meat!' said Qualtrough. 'Give it here! I don't care if it's wolf meat, right now I could eat a warthog's scabby bum!'

'Are you no gannin' to cook it first?' Butterwick asked dubiously, as Strachan, Qualtrough and Molineaux gorged themselves on the raw flesh.

'Cook it!' Molineaux exclaimed, talking with his mouth full. 'Who can wait?'

Strachan nodded, wiping blood from his lips. 'The last time I tasted meat it was that damned putrid musk-ox. At least this is fresh.'

They slumped down around the fire with a blissful feeling of indigestion.

'Where's Ignatz?' asked Qualtrough.

'Eh?' said Butterwick.

'You said Mr Killigrew gave both you and Ignatz permission to come back and join us. Well? I don't see him.'

'We got separated. In the blizzard.'

Qualtrough nodded. A sudden blizzard had sprung up during the afternoon, and the three of them had had to huddle in the lee of the rocks to shelter from the worst of it. It was easy enough to imagine Butterwick and Fischbein becoming separated in it. 'Still, he should be here by now,' said Qualtrough.

'You calling me a liar?' Butterwick demanded with an aggressive thrust of his jaw.

Qualtrough blinked, as surprised by the stoker's violent reaction to his statement as Strachan was. 'No. I'm just worried about him, that's all.'

'He must've lost his way in the blizzard.'

'Maybe I should go and look for him,' offered Molineaux.

'Nay!' yelped Butterwick. 'I mean . . . what if that polar bear comes back, like? You're not leaving us here on us own, are you?' In their present conditions, neither Qualtrough nor Strachan counted for much.

'He's got a good point, Molineaux,' said Strachan. 'Perhaps it's better if we all stick together.'

'But what about Ignatz?' demanded Qualtrough. 'For God's sake! The poor lad could be dying out there!'

'Maybe that's why he's not found his way here yet,' said Butterwick. 'Maybe the bear got him.'

On which disquieting note, they wrapped themselves up in their furs and tried to get to sleep, leaving the sullen stoker on watch with the shotgun across his knees.

After the brief but violent blizzard it was a relief when the next day dawned bright and clear. Molineaux got the fire going again and they dined on the last of the meat that Butterwick had brought them. 'I never thought that meat could taste so good,' said Qualtrough. 'Especially not wolf-meat.'

'It's plummy,' agreed Molineaux, wiping grease from his chops with a sleeve. 'Reminds me of something – I can't quite put my finger on it. If wolves weren't such vicious brutes, I'll bet you could make a fortune from farming them for their meat.'

'Pork,' said Strachan.

Molineaux stopped chewing. 'Pardon?'

'That's what it tastes like,' Strachan mumbled with his mouth full. 'Pork chops.'

The petty officer stared at him for several seconds, and then spat out his mouthful, choking and retching.

'You're not Muslim, are you?'

Molineaux shook his head. He looked sick and haggard.

'What's the matter?' Butterwick demanded surlily, toying with the shotgun on his lap. 'Divven't you like it?'

Molineaux transferred his attention to the stoker. A number of emotions seemed to cross his face in the space of a second or two, and then he mastered himself and put on the blank expression of a man who wanted to give nothing away.

'It's . . . it's plummy,' he stammered. 'But my crammer feels so tight after going without too long, I'm worried I might do meself an injury by eating too much. I think I read something about the members of Sir John Franklin's expedition overeating after having gone without for too long, and only succeeding in making themselves sick. I think,' he added, with a hard glare at Strachan and Qualtrough, 'that we've eaten enough.'

'Speak for yourself,' said Qualtrough, still gorging himself. 'I don't care how ill I make myself, I can't possibly feel any worse than I do now.'

Strachan looked at Molineaux. He could tell the petty officer was hiding something, and while he knew that Molineaux would not lie without good reason, he was at a loss to know what that reason was. Nevertheless he put down the last of his meat, in spite of the pangs of hunger that still troubled him.

'Are you nay gannin' to eat it, either?' asked Butterwick.

Strachan shrugged. 'Molineaux's got a good point. It's dangerous to overindulge after a prolonged period of enforced abstinence.'

'Well I like that!' grumbled Butterwick. 'After all the trouble I went to to kill that wolf, so you'd have summat to eat.'

'You killed it?' said Strachan.

'Why aye, man! That's what I said, isn't it?'

'No. Yesterday you said you and Fischbein found it already dead, before the two of you became separated in the blizzard.'

'You calling me a liar?'

'I'm confused, that's all,' said Strachan. 'First you say one thing, then you say another. What the deuce is the matter with you, Butterwick?'

'If Jemmy says he killed the wolf, that's good enough for me,' Molineaux said quickly, with a glance in Strachan's direction that warned him to let the matter drop.

Something was going on which Strachan did not know about, that much was obvious. Not only Butterwick but now also Molineaux was acting damned rum. Strachan wanted to quiz him, but not in the stoker's presence, and there was no subtle way he could take the petty officer to one side. Then a thought occurred to him. 'Molineaux, do you want to help me make a litter for Qualtrough here, so you and Butterwick can carry him between you?'

'I'll help you,' Butterwick jumped in, as if he had guessed that Strachan wanted to talk to Molineaux in private and was determined not to allow it.

'It's all right, Butterwick. Molineaux can help.'

'I said: *I'll help*.' Butterwick's tone advised Strachan against quarrelling with a man holding a shotgun.

They cut down a couple of saplings with an ice-axe and then used them as the poles for a stretcher, tying a fur between them. They managed to get Qualtrough on the stretcher. Molineaux reached for his musket but Butterwick got there first.

'I'll carry that,' he said.

This was getting worse and worse. Something in Butterwick's manner warned Strachan against letting the stoker have both guns, but again Butterwick had the shotgun and the assistant surgeon thought better of arguing.

They picked up the stretcher between them and carried Qualtrough, while Strachan hobbled along behind them with his crutch. The pace was agonisingly slow, and after a couple of miles that took six hours to cover, Butterwick sank to his knees in the snow, almost toppling Qualtrough from the stretcher as he did so. The ice quartermaster cried out in agony from his broken leg, and Strachan quickly attended to him, although there was not much the assistant surgeon could do but clasp Qualtrough's hand and tell him everything was going to be all right.

'We'll stop here for the night,' said Butterwick. 'I canna carry him nay further.'

'What about that patch of *tripe de roche* you came across the day before yesterday?' asked Molineaux. 'How much further is it from here?'

'I divven't know!' snapped Butterwick. 'One mile, ten miles, a hundred miles – what difference does it make? We're gannin' to die anyhow. You might as well kill me and eat me.'

'What?' spluttered Strachan. 'What the deuce has got into you, Butterwick?' The stoker had always been simple-minded, but now he was acting unbalanced. Strachan was beginning to suspect that the only difference between Pettifer and Butterwick was that while the captain had lost his mind, the stoker had never had much of a mind to lose in the first place.

Butterwick levelled the shotgun at him, more in a casual way than a deliberate, conscious act of aggression. 'Are you nay gannin' to build a fire, then?'

'Sure, Jemmy, sure.' Molineaux backed out of the glade.

Left alone with Butterwick and the silently weeping Qualtrough, Strachan started to feel nervous. The stoker sat down and toyed with the musket, his back to the assistant surgeon. Strachan picked up his makeshift crutch and limped out of the clearing, glancing over his shoulder every other painful step to see if Butterwick had noticed, but the stoker seemed to be in a world of his own.

Strachan gulped breaths of razor-sharp air into his lungs as soon as he was safely out of the line of fire. Whatever had got into the stoker, the next thing to do was to take those guns from him.

He found Molineaux gathering dead wood amongst the trees. When the petty officer heard his shuffling footsteps he whirled, Bowie knife in hand, but he relaxed when he recognised Strachan.

The assistant surgeon glanced back towards the camp. They were far enough away to talk normally without Butterwick overhearing them. 'All right, Molineaux. Would you mind telling me what the deuce is going on?'

'I don't know what wolf-meat tastes like, sir, but I'm willing to bet it ain't pork.'

'What do you mean?'

'Remember when we were in the South Seas three years back, we met that cove Paddon?'

'The sandalwood trader? Of course. He got you and Killigrew out of a tight spot, didn't he?'

Molineaux nodded. 'On the voyage back to Aneiteium we got talking about the natives over a bottle of whiskey. I asked him how he was able to trade with them without them trying to kill him, and he told me he'd won their trust by attending one of their feasts. They'd just won a battle against a rival tribe, and . . . well, you know what the natives of Erromango did with their captives.'

'You mean he . . . he actually consumed human flesh?'

'He weren't proud of it, sir. Don't reckon he'd've told me at all, if we hadn't sunk a few drinks between us. He had no

458

choice, see? Otherwise they might just have eaten *him* for afters.'

'All right, Molineaux. But I hardly see what that's got to do with—'

'I asked him what it tasted like, sir, and you know what he said?'

Strachan had a sick feeling he already knew the answer, but he merely nodded for the petty officer to continue, the taste of bile in his mouth.

'Like *pork*, sir. He said it tasted like pork.'

Even though Strachan had seen it coming, the final confirmation hit him like a kick in the stomach. He doubled up, retching, but there was nothing left undigested in his stomach to bring up, which only made the spasms all the more painful.

Finally he straightened, wiping tears from his cheeks.

'What are we going to do, Molineaux?'

'We've got to get those guns off him.'

'How?'

Before Molineaux could reply, the sound of a musket shot echoed through the trees.

Molineaux broke into a stumbling run, leaving the crippled assistant surgeon behind as he careered wildly through the trees, feet slipping and sliding in the snow, mindful of the fact that the only weapon he carried, apart from the Bowie knife sheathed in the small of his back, was the ice-axe dangling from his haversack. When he reached the camp site everything was exactly as he had left it, except that now Butterwick was reloading the musket and a large, ugly hole had been smashed through Qualtrough's forehead.

Molineaux skidded to a halt, gasping for breath.

'What happened?'

'He shot hissel,' said Butterwick, as coolly as if remarking upon the price of bread.

Molineaux glanced at Qualtrough's corpse with a shudder. There were no powder burns around the wound, which there should have been if he had shot himself. Not that he believed that for a minute.

Strachan hobbled into the clearing and came to an abrupt halt when he saw Qualtrough's corpse. He regarded Molineaux quizzically.

'Qualtrough shot himself,' the petty officer said carefully.

Strachan's eyes searched Molineaux's face and nodded. He no more believed it than Molineaux did himself.

Butterwick yawned. 'Oh, well. Our mam allus used to say every cloud has a silver lining.'

'What do you mean?' Molineaux half expected Butterwick to suggest that they eat Qualtrough next.

'At least now we divven't have to carry him,' explained Butterwick.

Is that why you killed him, you crazy sonuvabitch? wondered Molineaux. *Because he was too goddamned* heavy?

No one got any sleep that night. Butterwick insisted on keeping guard all night long and sat by the fire with the musket slung across his back and the shotgun in his lap. Molineaux watched him, waiting for him to let his guard drop long enough to be overpowered, at the same time terrified that if he himself went to sleep the deranged stoker might see to it that he never woke up again.

The next morning, when they got ready to set off the rest of the way to the patch of *tripe de roche*, Butterwick went off to relieve himself amongst the trees. He took the shotgun with him, but left the musket. Seeing his chance, Molineaux snatched it up, but then Butterwick returned before he had a chance to formulate a plan of attack with Strachan. Butterwick did not even seem to notice the musket was now slung from Molineaux's shoulder next to his haversack.

'Coming?' Molineaux asked him.

'You two gan on ahead,' said Butterwick. He was toying with the shotgun now, breaking open the breech to check the chambers. 'I'll catch you up.'

Molineaux and Strachan exchanged glances and set off, the petty officer walking slowly to match his pace to that of the crippled assistant surgeon, even though he expected Butterwick to shoot them both in the back at any moment.

But the shots never came.

As soon as they were out of sight of Butterwick, Strachan nodded to the musket. 'Good work, Molineaux. Now all we have to do is take that other gun from him.'

'And then what, sir?'

'What do you mean? Without poor Qualtrough to weigh us down, I think we can make it to Fort Hope. We'll let Mr Killigrew decide what's to be done with Butterwick. The poor fellow's clearly lost his mind.'

'It'll take us several days to make it to Fort Hope, sir, even if we can pick up the trail. That means several nights alone in a camp with Butterwick. What do we do with him? Keep him bound hand and foot?'

'We can take it in turns to stand guard over him . . .'

'Come on, sir. What if whoever's on guard falls asleep and leaves us both at Butterwick's mercy? No disrespect to you, sir, but I'm so tired I couldn't promise to stay awake and alert.'

'Then what do you suggest?'

'Sir, is there any doubt in your mind that Butterwick killed Fischbein? Or that he murdered Qualtrough?'

'No.'

'And that he'll prob'ly kill us next?'

Strachan hesitated before replying, although there was only one answer he could give. 'No.'

'Then you know what's got to be done.'

Strachan looked distraught. 'But . . . what right have we? To make such a decision, I mean?'

'We know we're making the same decision that twelve good men and true would make back in England. And I'd say the fact we'd be acting in self-defence would give us more right than any jury.'

Strachan sighed. 'You're right, of course. Give me the gun, Molineaux. As the only officer present, it's only right that I should take full responsibility for this.'

Molineaux refused to relinquish the musket. 'I appreciate that, sir, but have you ever killed a man before?'

'Not intentionally.'

'There's one shot in that musket, sir, and then it has to be reloaded . . .'

'I realise that, Molineaux.'

'Are you a good shot, sir? Because if you miss, you won't have time to reload. Butterwick's got two shots in the shotgun, and if you miss he'll be able to take his time . . .'

'Nonetheless, it's my responsibility . . .'

They heard a sound behind them and turned to see Butterwick striding towards them, trampling over their footprints, the shotgun in his hands.

Molineaux hesitated. Butterwick was still fifty yards away, but even at that distance the petty officer could see there was murder in his eyes. He unslung the musket and raised the stock to his shoulder. Butterwick still had the shotgun lowered towards the ground in front of him. Molineaux wondered if he had mistaken the stoker's intention.

'Put the gun down, Jemmy.'

Butterwick did not seem to have heard him.

'Drop it, Jemmy. We know you burked Qualtrough, and prob'ly Ignatz as well. Drop it, or 'swelp me God I'll croak you where you stand.'

Butterwick was thirty yards away now, and still advancing purposefully.

'Stop right where you are! I don't want to kill, but I will if you don't stop right there and put the shotgun on the ground.'

Butterwick grinned evilly. 'Better make sure you kill us, then, 'cause I won't give you a second chance.'

'God damn it, Jemmy! Do you *want* me to shoot you? Is that what you want?'

Butterwick was less than twenty yards away when he brought up the double-barrels of the shotgun. Molineaux could not wait any longer: he already had a bead drawn on Butterwick's forehead; all he had to do was pull the trigger.

The hammer snapped against an empty chamber and Butterwick's grin became even broader. Molineaux realised that the stoker had intended this all along, had left the musket unloaded and allowed him to pick it up so he could later claim he had acted in self-defence. He cursed himself for not having thought to check if the musket was loaded.

Butterwick halted, fifteen feet away, and took careful aim. Molineaux pushed Strachan to the ground and followed him down as the first barrel boomed. Something stung him in the buttocks. He ripped the ice-axe from its thong and flung it. The axe tumbled over and over through the air. It seemed to take for ever, and all the time Molineaux was staring down the second barrel of the shotgun that gaped like the maw of hell.

The ice-axe came to an abrupt halt, firmly embedded in Butterwick's forehead. The stoker blinked at the blood that trickled down from the awful wound, sank to his knees, and fell on his face in the snow, which rapidly turned crimson beneath his head.

Nought miles.

'It should be here,' said Killigrew, for once at a loss.

'It isn't,' said Varrow.

They gazed about the trees around them. They had left the tundra behind them and here the firs were close-packed, like in any normal forest. The problem was that Fort Hope might be within a quarter of a mile and they would not know about it.

Ill equipped, they had travelled over 800 miles on foot, dragging three heavily laden sledges for much of the distance. If Killigrew had stopped to think about it when they had first set out, he would never have believed they could have made it; which was why he had been at pains not to think of it, either at the wreck of the *Venturer* or on any one of the hundreds of miles of inhospitable, frozen wasteland they had crossed. Yet they had done it; in spite of all the odds they had done it, and while Killigrew felt keenly the loss of every man who had died on the way, he was amazed that so many of them – ten now, and he was not yet prepared to give up on Strachan, Qualtrough, Butterwick and Fischbein while they had Molineaux with them – had made it.

And now their long trek was over they could not find Fort Hope.

To set out from an uncertain starting point to navigate across uncharted territory with only the stars to guide them was a task that few men other than naval officers would have undertaken without misgivings. Yelverton would have been able to do it within a mile or two under normal circumstances, but Yelverton was dead and Killigrew's geometry left a great deal to be desired. Besides, a mile or two was not close enough; and what if Yelverton, in his debilitated condition, had made a miscalculation? Killigrew would not have blamed him if he had. But it was quite possible they were a good deal more than a couple of miles from Fort Hope. It was quite possible they were dozens of miles from the fort. If that was the case, then Killigrew knew they would never make it, for they had been ready to drop for a long time now. They had come through so much, they deserved to survive now; they had earned a hearty meal and a good rest. But fate had been cruel to them so far, and might yet have one last trick to play.

'All right,' he said, no longer making any attempt to sound chirpy. 'All we have to do is find the lake. Find the lake, and we'll find the fort. We'll split up and search in different directions. We know it isn't behind us, so we'll split into three teams. Mr Varrow, you take Endicott and Orsini and go west. Mr Latimer, you take Chips and Hughes and go east. Frau Weiss, Commander Pettifer and Kracht will come with me. We'll meet back here in two hours, unless one of you sees the fort. In that event, let off one shot into the air to signal the rest of us, and another shot five minutes after that, and so on, until we're all together again.'

'We're running low on cartridges,' said Varrow, his hoarse voice little more than a whisper now. 'If we divven't find the fort, we may need every shot for hunting.'

'Then pray we find the fort,' Killigrew said simply. Because if they did not, they were dead.

They set off in their appointed directions. Killigrew handed one of his revolvers to the blacksmith and nodded at Pettifer. 'Keep an eye on the commander, Kracht. Make sure he doesn't do himself – or anyone else – an injury.'

'*Jawohl, mein Herr.*'

The four of them trudged south, the boughs above their heads heavy with snow. Everything was silent but for the crunch of the snow beneath their feet and the strenuous rasp of their breath. They were dying, they had pushed themselves too far too hard, but with salvation perhaps close at hand they could not give up now.

Then Killigrew thought he heard another sound. He signalled a halt.

'What is it, *mein Herr*?' asked Kracht.

'Shh!'

They listened. Nothing but silence. Not even the birds were singing in the trees, which was odd. Killigrew decided that he must have imagined it and was about to say as much when he heard it again: a distant tap, tap, tap. He had heard that sound somewhere before, although he could not place it. he was sure of one thing, however: it was not a natural sound.

'You heard that?' he asked Ursula.

She nodded. 'It seemed to come from over there.' She pointed off to their right.

Tap, tap, tap. Tap, tap, tap.

'There it goes again!'

This time Killigrew had been able to pin down the direction of the strange sound more precisely, although it was possible the wind had thrown him off. They set off in that direction anyway, and after another fifty yards they emerged from the trees on to the banks of a frozen lake, the north-east arm of the Great Slave Lake. A hump in the flat surface of the lake betrayed the presence of a low island, and on the crest of that hump stood a stockade with two low watch-towers at diametrically opposite corners and the roofs of three buildings visible within.

Fort Hope.

It was the first man-made structure Killigrew had seen since they had set out on their trek. He wanted to weep with joy. Instead he took his other revolver, aimed it into the ground, and fired.

The other three were already staggering across the frozen lake. Killigrew tried to break into a run, but he did not have the energy. He stumbled and sank to his knees in the snow, then got up again and forced himself to go on. His goal was in sight. He had never thought he would live to see this, and now he forced himself to enjoy his enforced slowness, relishing the moment. When he reached the shore of the island he forgot his pain, his hunger, his exhaustion, and staggered the last few paces to salvation.

No one came out to meet them, in spite of the shot. The gate was ajar, which was just as well, because snow had drifted against it and if it had been shut they would never have got it open in their weakened condition, even if a feast fit for the Lord Mayor's Banquet had awaited them on the other side.

The four of them stumbled through.

There were three log cabins within the stockade: the main hall and a windowless building that was probably a storehouse in the centre, and the voyageurs' quarters up against the palisade. The place was clearly deserted and presumably had been so all winter. That did not matter, so long as the Hudson's Bay Company had been true to its promise to keep the place stocked with a depot of food in case Franklin and his men, in similar straits, should ever find their way here. There was plenty of firewood stacked against the storehouse. As Killigrew and the others stared about the deserted compound, the wind moaned eerily and the tap, tap, tap sounded again close to hand, a halyard banging against a bare flagpole in the breeze.

'No one at home,' said Killigrew. 'Ursula, see how much food is in the store. Kracht, you come with me. Bring the captain.'

As Ursula trudged across to the storehouse, Killigrew tried the door to the main hall. It was stiff, perhaps frozen. Putting his shoulder to it had no effect. He had no more strength.

He heard Kracht cock the hammer of the musket and turned, but the blacksmith was only levelling it at Pettifer who had moved forwards. Killigrew moved aside and Pettifer threw his shoulder against the door. It gave on the third attempt.

'Thank you, sir,' Killigrew said softly.

They stepped inside. A faint, musty smell of decay filled the place. There were a couple of cots against one wall, a wood-burning stove in one corner with a kettle and a couple of mugs on top of it, and a chest. An oil-lamp hung from the low ceiling. He took it down and shook it: empty. He glanced around, saw some whale-oil bottles on a shelf, and a box of matches. The bottles were all empty, but there were a dozen matches left in the box: that was something, at least. He pocketed the matches and opened the chest. It contained some rough blankets and a few medical supplies: dressings, scissors, some numbered bottles of pills and medicines, and a bottle of rubbing alcohol.

He took the stopper out of the bottle of alcohol, sniffed it, and took a swig.

'You know that stuff is for external use only?' Kracht asked with a grin.

Killigrew gasped: it was like drinking sulphuric acid, but after feeling so numb for so long it was good to experience sensation again. 'I've tasted worse.' He proffered it to Kracht, but the blacksmith shook his head.

Killigrew put the bottle on the shelf and gave his other revolver to Kracht in exchange for the musket. 'Keep an eye on the captain, Kracht. I'll bring some firewood in and we'll see if we can get a fire going in the stove.'

'*Jawohl, mein Herr.*'

Killigrew stepped out of the stockade and looked around for the others. There was still no sign of them, and judging it was about five minutes since he had fired the first shot, he discharged the musket into the air.

He checked inside the voyageurs' quarters: more cots and blankets, another stove, a box of tools, a half-empty cask of nails, some pots of paint, brushes, a bottle of turpentine and a pot of glue.

He made his way across to the storehouse. The door was open now, so he supposed Ursula had got in without difficulty. He laid the musket against the side of the building, brushed snow from the first pile of logs and was about to pick one up – he did not think he had the strength to carry more than one at a time – when he heard sobbing from inside.

He crossed to the door and looked inside. Ursula was sprawled on the dirt floor, weeping.

The storehouse was empty.

XXV

Hand-to-Paw Combat

Strachan examined his wounded foot by the camp-fire Molineaux had built. 'Is that what I think it is?' asked Molineaux, wrinkling his nose at the stench.

The assistant surgeon nodded. He was too weary to feel any emotion about it. 'Gangrene. That foot is going to have to come off.'

'If that's the way it's got to be, that's the way it's got to be.' Molineaux checked that the musket was unloaded and put it so that the barrel was in the fire.

'What are you doing?' asked Strachan.

'The only thing I can use to cauterise the stump,' said Molineaux.

'Forget it. How far do you think I'm going to get on one leg? Save yourself, Molineaux. You can make it from here without me to slow you down.'

'Now there's no need for that kind of talk, sir. It's only six more miles or so, I reckon. You'll make it, if I have to carry you on my back every step of the way.' He waited until the barrel of the musket glowed red-hot and then tied a tourniquet around Strachan's ankle.

'You do that well,' said Strachan, astonished by how calm he felt.

'Seen you do it enough times, sir.' Molineaux picked up the axe. 'Ready?'

'As I'll ever be.' Strachan laid a hand on Molineaux's arm to stay the blow. 'There's a kind of poetic justice to this, if you think about it, isn't there?'

'Sir?'

'I mean, I've amputated enough limbs in my time. Now I'm getting a taste of my own medicine. Literally.'

'Close your eyes, sir. Best not to look.'

Strachan squeezed his eyes shut and heard the thunk of the ice-axe. 'Don't waste your strength with a practice swing, just get on with it,' he groaned.

'That wasn't a practice blow, sir,' said Molineaux, and Strachan heard a sizzling sound. 'It's done.'

The smell of charred meat reached Strachan's nostrils and he opened his eyes to see his own dismembered foot lying in the snow: a part of him, but no longer part of him.

He fainted.

Killigrew sank to his knees. He felt as if he had been kicked in the stomach by a mule. All his hopes had been pinned on this, on Fort Hope, and they had made it so far only to find that it was a false hope. The cupboard was well and truly bare.

The next nearest outpost of civilisation was Fort Chipewyan, almost another three hundred miles to the south.

At length he crawled across to where Ursula lay sobbing and gently put a hand on her shoulder. 'You know, when we get back to London I'm going to have some harsh words to say about the board of directors of the Hudson's Bay Company concerning this.'

Ursula managed to chuckle through her tears in spite of everything, although Killigrew could tell her heart was not in it. 'This is it, isn't it? We're going to die here, aren't we?'

Killigrew said nothing, because to say anything other than a simple 'yes' would have been an outright lie.

He slowly pushed himself to his feet, took Ursula by the arm and pulled her up after him. 'Come on,' he said. He was not looking forward to telling Kracht – and the others when they arrived – about the empty storehouse, but it had to be done.

They were halfway across the compound when they heard sounds of a struggle from inside the log cabin. There was a loud crash – someone falling against the stove – and the door to the

abin opened. Pettifer stood there, his wrists untied, a revolver in
ither hand.

Under the circumstances, the logical thing to do would have
een to stand still and allow Pettifer to blow their brains out: a
ar more merciful death than the one by slow starvation that
nust inevitably follow. But human instinct does not understand
nercy; only survival.

Killigrew and Ursula ducked behind the storehouse as Pettifer
aised one of the revolvers and fired. A bullet soughed past
Killigrew's ear, and then another bit into one of the logs that
ormed the walls of the storehouse as the two of them ducked
ehind cover.

They stumbled round the back of the storehouse and Ursula
eeped over the logs stacked against the wall. Another shot
ounded and she cried out. Killigrew hauled her back, thinking
he had been hit, but all that had happened was that splinters
rom one of the logs had been driven into her cheek by a
ullet.

The two of them sat against the wall of the storehouse,
gasping for breath. There was nowhere to run, nowhere to hide.
On the other side of the storehouse, Pettifer started singing to
aimself in a melancholy voice:

'The words that she uttered went straight through my heart,
I sobbed, I sighed, and straight did depart;
With a tear on my eyelid as big as a bean,
Bidding goodbye to Polly and Paddington Green . . .'

Come out, come out, wherever you are!' he added jovially.

Killigrew looked about in desperation. About ten yards of
pen ground lay between them and the back of the main hall.
Think you can make it to the gate?' he asked Ursula in a
vhisper.

She nodded. 'What about you?'

Killigrew grimaced. 'It's me he's after. I'll try and draw his
ire, you run to the others. They must be close by now.'

Ursula nodded tearfully, wiping her nose on her sleeve.

'Ready?' asked Killigrew. 'On the count of three . . . one . . .
wo . . . *three*!'

The two of them burst from cover, Killigrew running in on
direction, Ursula in the other. More shots echoed in the com
pound. Killigrew was aware of the captain's bulk outside th
storehouse but could not tell which direction he was shooting i

His emaciated legs feeling wobbly, Killigrew stumbled behin
the main building. He wondered if Ursula had made it to th
gate. The important thing to do was to keep Pettifer fro
pursuing her. 'Commander Pettifer?' he shouted hoarsely. 'Ar
you there?'

Pettifer replied by singing:

> 'She was as beautiful as a butterfly
> And as proud as a queen
> Was pretty little Polly Perkins
> Of Paddington Green.'

Killigrew peered cautiously round the far side of the mai
building. Seeing no sign of Pettifer, he crossed back and peere
behind the back wall in case the lunatic was trying to creep u
on him. No sign of him there either. Killigrew crept round to on
of the windows of the cabin and peered through the crac
between the shutters. Only Kracht was in there, slumped again
the stove, a livid purple bruise rising on his temple. There wa
no way of telling if he was dead or alive.

Pettifer resumed singing, and Killigrew whirled.

> 'In six months she married – the hard-hearted girl –
> But it was not a viscount, and it was not an earl,
> It was not a baronet, but a shade or two wuss,
> It was a bow-legged conductor of a twopenny 'bus.'

The voice echoed eerily about the compound, one momer
strangely distant, the next so close Killigrew whirled in alarr
expecting to see Pettifer right behind him. Was the derange
captain inside the stockade, or had he followed Ursula out?

Killigrew crossed to where he had left the musket propped u
against the wall of the storehouse. Much good it would do hin
unloaded, but if he could get close enough to Pettifer perhaps h
could use it as a club.

But first he had to find him.

He crossed to the gate and peered out across the clearing. There was no sign of Pettifer, no sign of Ursula, no sign of anyone. What the devil was going on? Surely the others must have been drawn by the shooting by now?

He heard a creak behind him and turned in time to see Pettifer emerge from the storehouse. One of the revolvers blazed, and a stinging pain in Killigrew's upper arm made him drop the musket with a cry. He slumped to the ground and tried to crawl away, his blood dripping on to the snow.

Pettifer advanced, singing, punctuating each line with a shot from one of the revolvers. Each shot missed, but landed close enough to let Killigrew know the captain was toying with him now.

> *'She was as beautiful as a butterfly*
> *And as proud as a queen*
> *Was pretty little Polly Perkins*
> *Of Paddington Green.'*

Killigrew had reached one of the corners of the stockade now. With nowhere left to go, he rolled painfully on to his back and found Pettifer standing over him. The captain levelled the revolver in his right hand at Killigrew's forehead. The lieutenant squeezed his eyes shut as Pettifer squeezed the trigger.

The hammer fell on an empty chamber.

Killigrew opened his eyes. If he had had any strength left, he would have lunged for Pettifer now, but what he saw behind the commander sapped the last of his reserves.

Pettifer was oblivious to anything behind him. 'All gone!' he said, like a child. He tossed aside the revolver in his right hand and took his time transferring the other from his left. He took aim once more. 'It is written in the Good Book that the legions of righteousness must triumph over the workings of the evil one in the final chapter. So let it be. Amen.'

Killigrew finally found his tongue. 'You've got a bear behind—'

'Eh?'

The polar bear reared up on its hind legs with a roar. Pettifer began to turn and in the next instant his head bounced off the palisade, slashed clean from his body by the bear's powerful claws. The bear sank its teeth into Pettifer's thigh and shook his decapitated body like a dog playing with a rag doll.

Killigrew forced himself on to his feet and reached for where the loaded revolver had fallen in the snow, less than a foot from where the bear was occupied in ripping Pettifer's body to bloody shreds. The bear sharply swung its head round in his direction with a threatening growl. Killigrew quickly backed away without the revolver, hoping the bear would return to its feast. It did not, but steadily advanced on him.

He turned and ran. The very ground seemed to shake beneath the bear's massive paws as it lumbered in pursuit. Killigrew stumbled through the open door of the log cabin and slammed it behind him. Seconds later it was splintered by a blow from the bear, one of the planks flying across the room to clip the lieutenant on the temple. Dazed, he staggered back against the rear wall of the cabin, sank to the floor next to Kracht and waited to die.

The bear's head and forequarters came through the door, flecks of blood on its lips and jagged teeth. Its breath stank of rancid meat. Then it stopped. Its hips were too broad to pass through the narrow door. It roared in frustration, and pushed, but it could not get through.

Fighting for breath, Killigrew pushed himself to his feet and took out his clasp-knife: better than nothing in a fight against another man, but against a bear . . .?

The whole cabin seemed to shudder as the beast strained against the doorposts. Killigrew opened the blade of the knife and advanced cautiously. He jabbed at one of the bear's eyes, but the bear was fast and almost caught his hand in its jaws as it snapped at him. Killigrew jerked his hand back, and thrust again. Another jerk of the bear's head preserved its eye, but this time Killigrew got close enough to score a line of blood across the beast's snout. The bear roared and retreated.

Killigrew stayed inside the cabin, wondering what to do. He could still hear the bear snuffling about outside, although he could not see it through the open door.

'Herr Killigrew?'

The lieutenant turned, saw Kracht had regained consciousness and was rummaging about inside his knapsack. He pulled out his home-made grenade. 'Try this,' he said, and tossed it at the lieutenant. Killigrew caught it and tucked it under one arm while he took out the matches he had found and struck one. He applied it to the fuse and it spluttered into life.

And then the bear's head lunged through the window, its jaws snapping at Killigrew. He jumped aside, sprawled on the floor, the grenade rolling from his hand, the fuse sputtering. He swore, crawled across, retrieved it and threw it at the window. It bounced off the bear's haunches and dropped to the ground. Killigrew could hear the fuse fizz, see smoke rising between the bear's legs. The bear lowered its head to sniff at the grenade, then looked at Killigrew again and snarled. Then it moved away from the window.

The grenade exploded against the side of the log cabin with a flat crack.

Killigrew picked himself up and edged cautiously towards the window once more: no sign of the bear, just a small crater in the snow surrounded by the jagged pieces of brass that had been thrown in all directions.

'Did you get it?' asked Kracht.

Killigrew shook his head and edged closer to the door. He peered across the compound to where the loaded revolver lay. It was only fifteen feet away: if he could just . . .

The bear's head lunged through the door once more, its bloody snout smashing against Killigrew's wounded arm but at the same time saving his life as it knocked him clear of its snapping jaws. It started to claw at the wood around the door, tearing at the logs, shredding them, smashing them. The whole cabin shuddered under the impact. As it fought to widen the opening, Killigrew realised it would only be a few more seconds before it succeeded.

'Out the window, quick!' he yelled at Kracht. 'Make for one of the watch-towers!'

The blacksmith nodded, picked himself up and climbed out.

With one final effort, the bear knocked a couple of logs free and squeezed through.

Killigrew was too terrified to listen to the protests of exhausted, emaciated limbs. He flung himself through the window, rolling in the snow outside.

His whole body was an ocean of pain. He wanted to lie there and die, let the bear come and finish this nightmare. *Get up, get up!* Jory Spargo's voice. Killigrew forced himself up on to his knees. There was Kracht, climbing up the ladder to one of the watch-towers; and there was the bear, squeezing itself out of the main hall once more and blocking Killigrew's path. The only other refuges were the voyageurs' quarters and the storehouse, but the bear could smash its way into those just as easily as it had broken into the main hall.

He ran around the back of the cabin and jumped up at the low eaves. A fit and healthy Killigrew could have done it without even thinking about it, but that had been a thousand miles away, a million lifetimes ago. He barely managed to get his arms on the shingles, his legs dangling over the eaves, flailing wildly within reach of the bear's jaws. His fingers clawed at the snow-covered roof and the rags on his feet scrabbled against the logs below. Somehow he managed to pull himself up towards the apex of the roof.

The bear jumped effortlessly up after him.

Killigrew backed towards the far end of the roof. The bear advanced, putting one paw in front of the other, as surefooted as a cat, its head lowered aggressively, teeth bared in a snarl.

Killigrew ran out of roof. There was a drop of about twelve feet to the ground, and even if he managed to jump down without breaking a leg then the bear would be on him in an instant. He took out the clasp-knife once more and slashed its nose. The bear fixed him in its gaze, inviting him to drop his guard just for one split second.

'Kit!' Ursula's voice, God bless her. 'I'm here, Kit!'

'There's a revolver down there somewhere! Use it, girl!'

'Where?'

'Down there, somewhere!' Killigrew dared not take his eyes off the bear to give Ursula directions.

'Got it!' Killigrew heard the click, click of a hammer falling on spent percussion caps. 'It's empty!'

'The other one!'

476

The bear snapped at Killigrew's hand, but he managed to pull it clear in time and stabbed the bear in a nostril. The bear howled, backed off a couple of feet, and then started to inch forwards, head lowered.

Five shots sounded in quick succession, five wounds blossomed in the bear's left side. It let out a roar of fury and at once leaped down from the roof, turning its attention on Ursula. The five bullets in it did not even seem to slow it. Ursula threw the empty revolver at its head and ran for the other watch-tower. The bear lumbered after her. She scrambled nimbly up the ladder. The bear leaped up after her, but she pulled into the shelter at the top only inches ahead of its snapping jaws.

Killigrew slid down the roof of the main hall, pitched forward on his face in the snow and dropped the knife. He wasted precious seconds scrabbling for it.

The bear stood on its hind legs, looking up at the watch-tower where Ursula had taken refuge. The shelter was about twenty feet off the ground, too high up for the bear to reach, and it could not climb up. With a snarl of frustration, it dropped back to the ground, looked around, and saw Killigrew.

He picked himself up and ran to the watch-tower where Kracht watched anxiously. He reached the ladder, hauled himself up the rungs, and had almost reached the shelter when something clamped itself over his foot.

The pain was excruciating. He glanced down and saw that the bear had seized his ankle in its jaws. He wrapped his arms around the ladder as the bear tried to pull him down, clinging on for dear life.

Kracht scraped some snow off the roof of the shelter, moulded it into a ball, and flung it at the bear's head. It exploded in the bear's eyes, and the beast was startled enough to let go of Killigrew's ankle. Kracht hauled the lieutenant up through the entrance to the shelter.

Sobbing with pain and exhaustion, Killigrew crawled across into the corner to examine his foot. Miraculously, the bone was not broken, but there was a nasty puncture mark where one of the bear's incisors had pierced the flesh. He took out a handkerchief and used it to bind the wound as best he could. 'Any sign of the others?'

Kracht looked across to the shore of the lake, and shook his head.

Killigrew stood up. The bear was trotting back and forth between the two watch-towers, growling with frustration.

'We're safe for now,' he told Kracht. 'Even Bruin can't climb up here. All we've got to do is wait for the others to arrive.'

'Unless Bruin has already killed them.' Kracht glanced at the other watch-tower, and his face fell. 'Oh, no!'

'What?' Killigrew turned to see for himself.

Bruin had settled at the base of Ursula's watch-tower and was chewing at one of the legs supporting the shelter.

'It can't possibly chew through that support . . .'

The wood snapped with a splinter. The bear spat out a mouthful of wood chips, and crossed to the next leg. Ursula clung to one of the stanchions supporting the roof of her shelter, and looked across pleadingly to Killigrew and Kracht. The lieutenant racked his brains, but could not think of anything.

'There must be something we can do!' moaned Kracht.

Killigrew shook his head. The bear would chew through the legs of the watch-tower until it collapsed, and when it had finished feasting on Ursula it would come for the two men in the other tower. And there was not a damned thing they could do about it.

'Damn it to hell!' Killigrew started to climb down the ladder to the ground.

'Where are you going?'

'To finish this business!'

Taking his clasp-knife from his pocket, he limped across the stockade. Bruin was too busy chewing through the leg on the watch-tower to notice his approach. 'Here! Here, you big bastard!' he sobbed hoarsely. 'Fight me! Let's finish it!'

The bear turned, saw Killigrew, left off chewing the leg, and charged.

Killigrew turned and ran, hobbling on his wounded ankle. He had almost made it to the foot of the watch-tower when the bear caught him, swiping at him with a paw. The claws tore through his coat, the clothes underneath, the flesh of his shoulder, slamming him against the side of the voyageurs' quarters. He managed to crawl through the open door before the bear seized him in its jaws. It tried to follow him, but once again its broad haunches would not let it through. Killigrew backed into one corner, only inches from the bear's swiping paws, and his foot knocked against a pot of paint with a brush in it. He snatched up the pot and tried to dash it into the bear's eyes, but the paint was solid, either frozen or dried up, the paintbrush embedded in it. He threw the pot. It bounced off the bear's skull and the beast retreated, shaking its head muzzily.

Killigrew looked around for a weapon. He took a saw from the toolbox, glanced at it and threw it away. Then he picked out a hammer. If he could just get close enough, perhaps . . .

Then he saw the bottle of turps. Oil of turpentine, to be precise, also known as . . . *camphene.*

He crossed to the door. The bear had gone back to chewing on the legs of Ursula's tower: the structure looked as though it was going to collapse at any moment. Killigrew snatched up the bottle of turps and limped across to the main hall. He took one of the mugs off the stove, tipped out the dead spider inside, and poured turps into it until it was one-fifth full. Then he took the bottle of rubbing alcohol and topped up the mixture, stirring it with a finger.

He took down the oil-lamp from the ceiling and poured the burning fluid into the reservoir. It was a delicate operation: he was not sure there would be enough in the mug as it was, without spilling any.

A crash sounded outside and he glanced up to see that Ursula's tower had collapsed, pitching her into the snow. She rolled over and picked herself up, much to Killigrew's relief, but the bear lumbered towards her. There was no time for her to make it to Kracht's tower. She retreated into a corner of the palisade. The bear swiped at her with its claws, but the angle was too tight for it to reach her. It tried to sink its fangs into her waist. Sobbing in terror, she kicked at the bear, caught it on the snout and knocked its head away. It roared in annoyance.

Killigrew replaced the stopper on the lamp's reservoir and scrabbled for the matches he had dropped earlier, when he had lit the grenade. He struck one, and applied it to the lamp's twin wicks. It took a few seconds for the wicks to soak up the burning fluid, but when they did they burned with a bright, clear flame.

Ursula screamed in terrible agony. Sick with fear for her, he picked up the lamp and crossed to the door. The bear had seized one of her legs between its powerful jaws. She beat at its head with her tiny fists, but it would not let go.

There was no chance for her to get out of the way: he could only hope the bulk of the bear's body would protect her. If he didn't act now, she was dead.

Killigrew flung the lamp with all his might. 'Put this in your pipe, and smoke it!'

The lamp smashed against the ground at the bear's feet and sprayed it with flaming burning fluid.

Its fur caught fire at once. Roaring in agony, the bear let go of Ursula's leg and ran out of the stockade, trailing flames and smoke.

Killigrew hobbled across to where Ursula lay. 'Are you all right?'

She nodded, but her leg was a mess. He helped her to her feet and the two of them limped to the gateway.

Its roars now high-pitched and pitiful – more like a whimper – the bear rolled over and over in the snow, trying to put out the flames, but the burning fluid would not be extinguished. The bear writhed about, its screams disturbingly human, and Killigrew suddenly felt a pang of pity for the beast.

Kracht joined Killigrew and Ursula at the gateway. The bear lay still now, but the low moans issuing from its lips told them it was still alive as the flames now consumed the blubber of its fat body.

Killigrew limped back to the voyageurs' quarters, fetched the hammer, and made his way out of the stockade. 'Be careful!' Ursula urged him, as he approached the bear.

The acrid stench of burning fur and flesh filled the air. As Killigrew approached the dying beast, he saw that this bear would never kill anyone again. Its dark eyes looked at him pleadingly, as if he could put a stop to the terrible agony it suffered.

Tears spilled down his cheeks, tears of relief mixed with pity. Now he no longer had cause to fear it, he was able to view the animal dispassionately and recognise it for what it was: a magnificent beast, ideally formed to live in the harsh environment of the Arctic, skilful and clever enough to run rings around the crew of one of Her Majesty's exploring ships for the best part of eight months. In a way, it had only been defending itself, for they were the ones who had invaded its territory and wantonly slaughtered its kind. He had killed many men in the course of his duties – pirates and slavers – and when he acted in self-defence he lost no sleep over it. He could claim self-defence today, but had he not been foolish enough to come on this expedition, perhaps there would have been no need for him to kill it.

'Thank you,' he murmured to the bear, 'for allowing us to slay you.'

A spasm of pain shot through his torn right shoulder as he raised the hammer – he could feel his own hot blood seeping through his clothes – and he brought it down against the bear's skull with all his might.

It was over.

He turned away, wiping tears from his face with his sleeve as he walked a few paces away, and told himself it was the smoke that made him cry so. He slumped to the snow, feeling ashamed.

On the shore of the lake, Varrow, Endicott and Orsini emerged from the trees. The three of them stumbled across to where Killigrew lay a few yards from the bear's burning carcass.

'*Dio mio!*' exclaimed the steward. 'Is that . . .?'

'Aye,' said Varrow. 'Supper!'

Jog . . . jog . . . jog . . . jog.

It was like being on horseback. Strachan remembered going for a ride in the hills of Hong Kong. Funny thing to remember. He wondered where he was. Not Hong Kong, he was certain of that. Hong Kong was hot and humid, but he was cold. His shoulders ached, his arms felt like they were being slowly torn from their sockets, but the jogging motion was strangely comforting. Perhaps his nanny had jogged him to sleep when he had been a bairn.

He opened his eyes and found himself gazing into a black ear hole. Molineaux's ear hole. With all due respect to the seaman, it was not the prettiest sight he had ever woken up to. He tried to move his hands, but his wrists were tied together with what felt like strips of fur.

'Molineaux?'

'Back with us, are you, sir?' Molineaux was carrying Strachan piggy-back fashion.

'What are you doing?'

'Said I'd carry you the rest of the way if I had to.' Molineaux tried to sound cheerful, but there was no disguising the strain in his voice. 'I made Mr Killigrew a promise, remember? I've already let him down by leaving Qualtrough behind: I don't intend to do the same with you. I know he'd never let me down like that; I don't know how I'd ever look him in the eye again.'

'Don't be a fool, Molineaux. You'll never make it. Leave me, for any favour!'

'I'll make it, sir. Reckon I've already covered five miles today. I've picked up the others' trail; we should be there soon. Now, you don't mind if I save my breath, do you?'

They jogged on. The pace slowed. Molineaux was weakening. 'Don't be a fool, man!' groaned Strachan. 'You'll kill yourself!'

'I can do it, sir. I'm an Englishman. I can do anything.' Molineaux fell silent again. He was staggering now. 'Talk to me, sir,' he gasped.

'About what?'

'About anything. Tell me about ortho-whatsit.'

'Orthogenesis?'

'Yur . . . you mentioned it in one of your lectures last year. Linnaeus and his great chain of being, Lamarck's theory, about how all animals are related to a common ancestor.'

'So you do pay attention in my lectures, then?'

''Course I do, sir. You never know, one day I might learn something useful!' Molineaux was silent for a few paces, struggling to catch his breath while he plodded along. 'Tell me . . . about . . . how it is . . . that one kind of animal . . . can change . . . into another.'

'Well, no one understands the precise nature of the mechanism. Lamarck suggested that the natural environment influenced the nature of the changing species. Thanks to the work of Mr Lyall and other geologists, we know that the natural environment has undergone constant change over the aeons. Perhaps the species on our planet have changed in some way to adapt to changes in their natural environment.'

'It's a . . . harsh world . . . sir. Got to be . . . fit . . . to survive in it.'

'Indeed one must, Molineaux.' The petty officer's words triggered a spark inside Strachan's weakened brain. He grasped for it, but it was like chasing a will-o'-the-wisp through a foggy night. He shook his head. No good trying to recall it . . . Best not to think about it, and it would come back to him in time.

He smiled sadly. 'I've learned one thing on this expedition, Molineaux.'

'What would . . . that be . . . sir?'

'I'm poorly adapted to the Arctic environment.'

'Aren't we all? Look up ahead, sir: smoke. Reckon we're about there.'

Molineaux pressed on with renewed energy and ten minutes later he kicked open the door to the main hall at Fort Hope.

The sight that greeted them appalled Strachan. The others lay about, too ill even to get up: Latimer, Varrow, Riggs, Orsini, Kracht, Endicott and Hughes. Their bearded, blistered, smoke-blackened faces had the haggard look of men who had given up hope. Ursula, ashen-faced, had her leg bound up with bloody strips of bear-fur. Just ten of them in total, out of the thirty-seven who had been on board the *Venturer* when it had sailed from Beechey Island.

Only Varrow seemed to have strength enough to stand and he did so at once, creating enough space for Molineaux to lay Strachan down. 'Mr Strachan! And Molineaux! We'd given you up for dead. Where's Qualtrough?'

'He didn't make it,' Molineaux said curtly.

'What about Butterwick and Fischbein? We sent them back to meet you. Did they not find you?'

Molineaux exchanged glances with Strachan. They had discussed how much of the details of their adventure they should reveal and decided to tell all to Killigrew, let him make his mind up about the matter. For now he evaded the question. 'Where's Mr Killigrew?'

'Dead,' said Hughes.

'Mr Killigrew's gone for help,' said Endicott.

'Help? Where from?'

'Fort Chipewyan, I suppose.'

Latimer nodded. 'Another three hundred miles away.'

'He'll never make it,' said Riggs. 'He could barely walk when he left.'

'He'll make it,' said Molineaux. The idea of Killigrew failing in anything he set his mind to was just unacceptable. 'Any chance of some vittles? I've about had my fill of *tripe de roche*.'

'There's no food,' said Latimer.

'What?'

'When we got here, the place was empty. The only reason we're alive now is because the bear turned up and Killigrew managed to kill it. The last of the bear-meat ran out two days ago. We've been living off its bone-marrow since then.'

Molineaux stared at him as the full gravity of the situation dawned on him. Then he set his jaw. 'You think if a man can kill a bear like that, three hundred miles of open country is going to be a problem to him?'

'You bloody fool!' Hughes yelled hoarsely. 'He'll never make it! He just went out to die! Don't you see? It's over! We're all going to die!'

Molineaux seized the Welshman by the shoulders and shook him. 'Now you hold on to yourself, Red. Mr Killigrew will manage something, you'll see. He got us this far, didn't he?'

'Your faith in Mr Killigrew is touching, Molineaux,' said Latimer. 'But I fear Hughes has grasped the nub of the situation.'

'Oh, bloody hell!' Varrow said suddenly. Molineaux glanced at the engineer and saw he was peering out through a crack in one of the shutters.

'What is it, Mr V?'

'You'd better come and take a squint at this.'

Molineaux joined him at the window. Beyond the gates of the stockade he could see three copper-skinned figures bundled in furs flitting across the snow towards them in the gloom of the gathering dusk. 'Christ! As if we didn't have enough to worry about!'

'What is it?' asked Latimer.

'Savages, sir,' said Varrow.

'Oh, God!' moaned the clerk. 'We're going to be scalped, I know it! That's what Indians do to people; I read it in a book. They cut their scalps off as trophies!'

'Well, we'll just have to defend ourselves, that's all,' said Molineaux.

'What with? There's no ammunition left . . .'

Molineaux took out his Bowie knife. As he moved to the door his legs almost buckled under him. He knew he was in no condition to fight three savages with nothing but a Bowie knife, but he was damned if he would give up his scalp without a fight.

The door was jerked open and the three Native Americans stood there, their angular faces terrifyingly impassive. Molineaux moved quickly to block their entrance. One of them caught his wrist in a vice-like grip and effortlessly disarmed him. Then the three of them pushed past him into the cabin and took bundles from their backs. Molineaux watched helplessly as they set about the men on the floor, giving them . . . *food*?

'Hey, you!' protested Molineaux. 'Speakee English?'

One of them looked at him, and then reached inside his furs and pulled out a scrap of paper torn from a notebook. He thrust it into Molineaux's hand.

'What is it?' Latimer asked through a mouthful of pemmican.

'It's a letter,' Molineaux said in wonder. 'From Mr Killigrew.'

'Killigrew! What does he say?'

' "Dear all, Hope this letter finds you well. I stumbled into a hunting party of Yellowknife Indians, they are a little rough, but splendid fellows once you get to know them. None of them speaks any English, but by using signs I think I have made them understand your predicament and even as I write they seem to be bundling up some food to bring to you. Treat them courteously . . ." – Christ, hope it's not too late for a fresh start – "as they have not much food themselves. I am certain there is no need to tell you to eat everything they bring you! Hope to see you soon, yours *et cetera*, Lt Christopher I. Killigrew, RN . . ." '

Epilogue

August 1853

Killigrew stared at his reflection in the tarnished mirror that the Hudson's Bay Company factor at Fort Chipewyan had loaned him, and hardly recognised himself. A little over a year since he had set sail from England with the rest of Sir Edward Belcher's squadron, a young lieutenant of seven-and-twenty, full of hopes and dreams with what seemed like his whole career ahead of him. The face that stared back at him was that of a decrepit old man of twenty-eight going on eighty, his once-smooth brow creased with worry lines, eyes shrunk deep in his emaciated face. But as dreadful as he looked now, he remembered how sick his companions had looked when the Indians had brought them into their camp, and how much they had improved since.

They had spent a month with the Indians, rebuilding their strength, having their injuries tended. Strachan had sniffed at the primitive and superstitious techniques they had used to tend Killigrew's shoulder, arm and ankle, Ursula's leg, even the stump of his own foot; but there was no denying they had all healed.

After that the Indians had brought them here in easy stages: across the frozen Great Slave Lake – Ursula and Strachan dragged on travois – and then up the Slave River by canoe to Fort Chipewyan on the shores of Lake Athabasca, where the factor had been first astonished by the wild appearance of the ten men and one woman who had walked out of the wilderness, and then grovellingly apologetic, blaming the head office in London, the Indians, the French-Canadian voyageurs – indeed, anyone but himself – when Killigrew had mentioned the absence of any food at Fort Hope.

Killigrew hung the looking-glass from a nail on the wall and tried to glance over his shoulder at the bear's claw-marks on his back: they were healing nicely, although the scars would be a permanent reminder of his Arctic adventure, as if he would ever need one; more likely he would spend the rest of his days trying to put the nightmare behind him.

Now he was eating properly his health was returning gradually, although it would be many months – if not years – before he or any of the other survivors were fully recovered from their ordeal. Indeed, it was such a miracle that any of them had made it, everything that had happened since he had reached the Indians' camp seemed unreal. He expected to wake up and find himself back in the Arctic Circle, somewhere between Horsehead Bay and Chantry Inlet, with the bulk of their journey still to be completed and the bear alive, out there somewhere, waiting for a chance to pick them off one by one.

But they were well enough to travel now. Killigrew was in no hurry: he had already sent off a dispatch to the Admiralty, telling them what had happened. Tomorrow they would set out with a party of voyageurs for the York Factory on the coast of Hudson Bay – a journey of another 750 miles overland, but with plenty of food now, the weather more clement, game plentiful. With any luck there would be a ship to take them home, and Hudson Strait would still be ice-free; they might see England again before the autumn was out.

He finished shaving, splashed water on his face and dressed, emerging from the log cabin into the wide compound of Fort Chipewyan. Unlike Fort Hope, this place was all hustle and bustle: traders, fur-trappers, voyageurs and Indians. A far-flung outpost on the furthermost reaches of the British Empire, but after Killigrew's long sojourn in the wilderness it seemed like a metropolis.

He saw Ursula come through the gates, still using a crutch to support her injured leg, but dressed in European clothing now. He waved to her, and she saw him and waved back with a smile.

And that was when the polar bear came through the gate behind her.

Everyone scattered, everyone except Ursula. She seemed oblivious to the panic. Killigrew fought to get to her before the bear did, but the tide of fleeing people held him back. He shouted a warning, but no sound would come.

The bear reached her. She turned, tried to beat at it with her crutch. Killigrew was still a hundred yards away. The bear swiped at her, its long claws tearing through her gown, shredding her stomach, eviscerating her. Killigrew saw her entrails spill out, blood red on the compacted snow of the compound, and let out a howl of animal despair . . .

'Lieutenant Killigrew?'

Hands shaking him. He opened his eyes, blinked up at the flag lieutenant standing over him.

'Are you all right, Lieutenant?'

It took Killigrew a moment to adjust to his surroundings: a chair in the waiting room at the Admiralty. The flag lieutenant immaculate in his dress uniform. Dust motes dancing in the warm summer sunshine. The clop of horses' hoofs and the rattle of carriages and hansoms on Whitehall. The bellow of a sergeant-major drilling troopers on the parade ground outside Horse Guards. The whistle of a steam boat plying the Thames in the distance.

He rubbed his eyes wearily. 'I'm fine. It was just a nightmare, that's all.'

The flag lieutenant regarded him with a mixture of pity and contempt. 'If you're ready, Sir James will see you now.'

Killigrew straightened his full-dress uniform, adjusted his cocked hat on his head, and was ushered into a high-ceilinged office with rococo furniture and paintings of famous admirals on the walls: Cochrane, Hornblower, Nelson. He remembered that Nelson had once taken part in an Arctic expedition as a midshipman, and wondered if the great admiral had been troubled by nightmares afterwards.

There were two men seated behind the table at the far side of the room. Killigrew recognised one – plump, elderly, balding, Mr Pickwick in naval uniform – as Rear Admiral Sir Francis 'Windy' Beaufort, the head of the navy's Hydrographic

Department. The other man, in civilian clothing, could only be the Right Honourable Sir James Graham, First Lord of the Admiralty.

The flag lieutenant closed the door behind him. Killigrew limped across the room, half-boots clacking on the polished floor, stood to attention before the table and saluted.

To his astonishment, both Sir James and Admiral Beaufort rose from their seats and came around the table to shake him vigorously by the hand. 'Lieutenant Killigrew!' exclaimed the First Lord. 'Heard a good deal about you. Congratulations, young man. You're a hero!'

'I am?'

'The press certainly seem to think so. Leading ten men and a woman eleven hundred miles across the most inhospitable terrain to safety, against all the odds? Remarkable achievement, sir, remarkable achievement!'

'I don't know where they got the story from, sir – certainly neither I nor any of my men, or Frau Weiss or Herr Kracht, have spoken to anyone from the press.'

'I briefed Mr Delany of *The Times* when I received your dispatch from Fort Chipewyan. Of course I did not let him have the full story – I thought it only proper that the hero himself should tell his own story to the press – just enough to satisfy the public's demand for knowledge.'

Killigrew nodded. 'I doubt I'll be seen as a hero when the full facts of the story get out, sir.'

Sir James exchanged glances with Beaufort. 'That's exactly what we want to talk to you about today,' said the First Lord. 'But where are my manners?' he gestured to the chair in front of the table. 'Sit down, sit down! You must be exhausted.'

Killigrew took off his cocked hat, tucked it under one arm, and sat down stiffly.

Graham opened the cigar box on the table. 'Cheroot? Rear Admiral Napier tells me you prefer Trincomalee tobacco.' Sir James crossed to the sideboard and poured brandy from a decanter, returning to thrust the glass into Killigrew's hand. 'Have a drink. You look as if you could do with one.'

Killigrew thought this must be another dream: the First Lord of the Admiralty and the Navy's Hydrographer-in-Chief waiting on him hand and foot, plying him with cheroots and brandy. Eighteen months ago he would have declined politely, not wanting to give the impression that he was a hard-drinking smoker – it was not in Killigrew's nature to be toady, but these men could make or break his career, after all, and there was no shortage of men who disapproved of such vices – but now he did not give a damn about any of them. He was just glad to be alive. Besides, if this was a dream, he could tell the pair of them to jump into the Thames; but he restrained himself, out of politeness; besides, there was the off-chance that this was really happening. So he accepted the light that Graham struck him for the cheroot, sipped his brandy, and waited to see what they would say next.

Graham and Beaufort resumed their seats behind the table. 'Now, you understand, there will have to be a court martial concerning the loss of Her Majesty's exploring ship *Venturer*?' asked Beaufort. 'That's unavoidable.'

'Purely a formality,' Graham said hurriedly. 'I'm confident that the court martial will show both Lieutenant Killigrew and Commander Pettifer – and indeed the service as a whole – in the best possible light.'

'I wish I could say that was likely to happen, sir. But when the subject of Commander Pettifer's insanity comes up—'

Graham grimaced. 'Ah, yes. Commander Pettifer's insanity.'

'*Alleged* insanity,' Beaufort corrected him.

'Yes, that's right,' agreed Graham. '*Alleged* insanity. Very good, Sir Francis.' The First Lord turned back to Killigrew. 'In your dispatch you mentioned something about a letter that Mr Strachan wrote for you, recommending that you relieve the captain of command. You brought it with you?'

'Yes, sir.' Killigrew took out the letter and passed it across the table.

Graham picked up the letter, perused it thoughtfully – Killigrew saw his eyes scan the lines twice – and then struck a match. He dropped the burning letter into the large crystal ashtray.

Killigrew felt as though he had been gut-punched. The only evidence he had that he had been right to relieve Pettifer of command . . . No, damn it. Strachan was still alive, he could still testify. So would every one of the survivors.

'There will be no mention of Commander Pettifer's insanity . . . *alleged* insanity . . . at the court martial,' Graham said firmly.

'But then how am I to justify my actions in relieving him of command, sir?'

'There will be no mention of the fact that you mutinied.'

Finally Killigrew understood. 'You're asking me to lie, sir?'

' "Lie" is a very ugly word, Lieutenant,'' said Graham. 'We're merely suggesting that certain facts be . . . *omitted*. After all, Commander Pettifer left a widow. I see no reason why his name should be dragged in the mud unnecessarily.'

'Then there's the good of the service to be considered,' said Beaufort.

'As you're probably aware, everyone's up in arms about this business with Russia invading the Danubian principalities,' said Graham. 'The possibility that it may come to war cannot be ruled out. In the event of a war, the navy will be of vital importance in keeping the Russian fleet bottled up in the Baltic, and we cannot rely on the press gang to bring the fleet back to a wartime footing. Even if I were in favour of the reintroduction of the press gang – and I most certainly am not – Parliament would never accept it. So we'll have to rely on volunteers. And men aren't going to be willing to come forward if they think they're going to be put under the command of . . . ahem . . . reckless lunatics who'll throw their lives away in pursuit of vainglory.'

'So we need to make sure that whatever story comes out at the court martial, it's one that inspires men to want to belong to the finest navy in the world,' said Beaufort. 'And you do believe that the Royal Navy is, always has been, and always will be the finest in the world, don't you, Lieutenant?'

'I'd like to think so, sir. But the finest navy in the world isn't necessarily perfect.'

'We'll see to it that the prosecuting counsel doesn't ask you any, shall we say, awkward questions,' said Graham. 'And of course we'll rely on your discretion in not reporting any extraneous, unpleasant details to the press.'

'Play your cards right, Lieutenant, and there might even be a promotion to commander for you in this,' said Beaufort.

'And if I refuse?'

Graham's face hardened. 'Then the Admiralty will need a

scapegoat, Lieutenant. A living one, so you can forget all about blaming it on Commander Pettifer.'

'I'm willing to take that chance.'

'For what? For the truth? Suppose the whole story did come out. You'd be court-martialled for mutiny. At best dismissed the service, at worst . . . you could be shot. *Cui bono*, Mr Killigrew? Who benefits?'

'The men whose lives are spared when the Royal Navy is forced to abandon its programme of Arctic exploration.'

'There will be no more expeditions to the Arctic, once Sir Edward returns with the rest of the squadron,' said Graham. 'Not for a while, at any rate. If this trouble in the Balkans cannot be controlled, I've a feeling the navy will have more pressing matters to attend to. But your squadron was sent out under the orders of my predecessor.' Graham smiled nastily. 'It is no skin off *my* nose if you seek to embarrass *him*.'

'You've got a promising career as a naval officer ahead of you,' said Beaufort. 'Don't throw it away over a point of principle.'

'What do you say?' asked Graham.

'I need some time to think about it, sir.'

'Of course,' said Beaufort. 'You can have all the time you need.'

'As long as you let us know your decision by the end of the week,' added Graham. 'The court martial is set for next Monday, and we need to brief the prosecuting counsel. Thank you for your time, Lieutenant. I await your decision with interest.'

Killigrew rose to his feet, saluted, crossed to the door and hesitated before opening it. He turned back to the two men at the table.

'Even if I were to agree to such a whitewash, I cannot guarantee that any of the other men who survived will not speak to the press about some of the more embarrassing aspects of our voyage.'

'Then you must persuade them, Lieutenant Killigrew.' Graham smirked. 'Or should I say, *Commander* Killigrew?'

Killigrew licked his lips. 'Those men are all destitute now, sir. I know the navy doesn't pay its crews a penny after the destruction of their ships, but they might be more amenable to keeping quiet if they were paid some kind on honorarium to cover the period from the destruction of the *Venturer* to thei. arrival back in England.'

'It would be highly irregular . . . but I'll see what I can do. The First Lord smiled. 'I do believe we'll make a politician ou of you yet, Mr Killigrew.'

'God forbid!' Killigrew replied with some feeling.

'Hyde Park Corner, please,' Killigrew told the cabbie of the hansom waiting outside. He climbed in and sat down next to Ursula.

'How did it go?'

'They're going to promote me to commander.'

'But that is wonderful!'

'No it isn't. The court martial is going to be a whitewash. I ge a promotion as long as I keep quiet about anything that migh. embarrass the navy.'

'You rejected their offer?'

'I told them I'd think about it.' As the hansom rattled down Pall Mall and up St James's Street on to Piccadilly, he told he about the deal he had been offered.

'What will you do?'

Killigrew took a deep breath. 'Accept, I expect. Oh, I'll wai. until the last minute before I let those bastards know – make 'em sweat a bit. A petty revenge, but all I can manage. For now Besides, they've got me over a barrel and they know it. If the full facts did come out, I'd be the one with the most to lose. They'd see to it I was found guilty of mutiny. I don't believe they'd have me shot, but I'd be dismissed the service – and when you come from a long line of naval officers, it amounts to much the same thing.'

'I do not think anyone could blame you for accepting.'

'No one,' he agreed, 'except myself. I'd be lying if I denie wanting that promotion to commander, but . . . Lor' to get it like this!' He shook his head, filled with self-loathing.

The cabbie dropped them off at Hyde Park Corner. Killigrew paid him, told him to keep the change, and escorted Ursula into the park. The Crystal Palace had been dismantled now, and the riders were out on Rotten Row. Killigrew and Ursula made thei way to the Serpentine where the lieutenant hired a boat from the attendant. Even those turgid waters sparkled beneath the glorious sunshine, and their Arctic ordeal seemed little more than a half-remembered nightmare. Ursula made herself comfortable on the cushions on the bottom boards and Killigrew rowed her out into the middle of the lake. Then he shipped his oars and stared off into the middle distance.

'You kept your promise,' she said. 'To take me boating on the Serpentine.'

He grunted non-committally.

'What's wrong?'

'Perhaps I didn't let you down, but I can't help thinking of the others . . . the ones I left behind,' he said bitterly. 'And for what? We didn't find the North-West Passage; we didn't even find any traces of the Franklin Expedition. Twenty-six men dead, Strachan missing a foot . . .'

'I saw him earlier this morning. Out and about on crutches, showing off the wooden foot that Riggs carved for him. He seemed very . . . *heiter*. In English you would say "chipper"?'

Killigrew managed a faint smile. 'That sounds like Strachan. How's *your* leg?'

She sighed. 'I'll always have the scars. But I like them. Something to remember you by.'

"I'll give you something to remember me by.' He lay down beside her in the boat and kissed her.

She tried to push him away. 'Kit! Someone will see us!'

'Don't be silly. We're right out in the middle of the lake. Who's going to see us here?'

'Ahoy there!' The familiar voice came from a second rowboat that headed towards them. 'Is that you, Killigrew?'

He cursed under his breath and sat up to see Rear Admiral Sir Charles Napier sitting up in the stern of the boat while a midshipman rowed him from the bank.

'Mr Latimer told me I might find you here,' Napier said when he was nearer. The admiral looked the same as ever: civilian clothes hopelessly dishevelled, a dusting of snuff all down the front of his frock coat.

'*Did* he!' Killigrew muttered in a tone that boded no good for the clerk.

'I read your dispatch to the Admiralty with interest,' Napier continued as his boat came alongside. 'One hopes that now they'll see sense and stop wasting men on Arctic exploration. There are plenty of more important jobs for you to do. Surveying enemy waters, for one thing. As you've probably gathered since your return, there's a lot of gammon about how we're going to have to go to war with the Russians over this spot of bother in the Balkans.'

'The Mediterranean, sir?' Killigrew said hopefully. 'The Black Sea?'

'Ah, actually, that's already in hand. I've been saving something special for a man with your particular experience with ice.'

'Ice!' exclaimed Killigrew. 'Don't talk to me about ice, sir. After the Arctic, I don't think I shall be able to look at even so much as a sorbet again so long as I live.'

'Ah,' Napier said dubiously. 'It's just that we do need a survey of Russian fortifications at Murmansk and Archangel to be carried out, and I was wondering . . .?'

'*Nyet!*' Killigrew seized up his oars, pushed off from Napier's boat, and began rowing strongly for the southern shore of the lake.

Afterword

The Truth about Polar Bears, and Other Matters

In the years after the defeat of Napoleon, the Royal Navy searched for alternative spheres of endeavour and found one in exploration: not only of the Arctic, but also of the Antarctic and the interior of Africa. One only has to glance at maps of the polar regions to see the names of the leaders of these expeditions commemorated for all time: the Ross Ice Shelf, Cape Parry, Franklin Bay, McClure Strait and McClintock Channel. Not that they were so egotistical as to name geographical features after themselves, but they did have a tendency to name them after one another, which served the purpose equally well. To be fair, they were more inclined to name things after patrons: hence Victoria Island, Prince Albert Peninsula, Boothia Peninsula, Barrow Strait and Viscount Melville Sound; although I'm not entirely sure how the lovely young Swedish opera singer Jenny Lind came to have an island named after her.

The most famous of these was Franklin, perhaps because of the mystique of his disappearance and the subsequent search. We shall never know for certain what happened on his third, final and fatal expedition, but Francis McClintock's expedition of 1857–59 revealed the most clues, including a message in a cairn on King William Island that told how Franklin himself, along with twenty-three other members of the expedition, had already died. What they died of is not specified, but an autopsy carried out on the bodies of Braine, Hartnell and Torrington, frozen in the permafrost off Beechey Island, found excessive

497

levels of lead in bone and hair samples, suggesting that lead poisoning from the solder on the tin canisters might have contributed to their deaths. Not that they had any idea there was such a thing as lead poisoning in the 1850s – they used the damned stuff to make pipes for supplying drinking water. In those days, lead was perfectly harmless, to the best of scientific knowledge (just as genetically modified food is today).

According to the message McClintock found, one of Franklin's ships was sunk, and the other was thrust on shore by the moving ice. The next senior officer of the expedition, Captain Crozier, decided they should try to strike out for the mainland. Further on, McClintock found a boat that the survivors of the Franklin expedition had dragged there, with two corpses in it. It was this discovery that must have inspired Julius von Payer's splendidly gothic painting of the final episode of the Franklin expedition: a ship's boat half-buried in snow, while bearded figures lie all around, dead or dying; one man, still alert, clutches a shotgun and watches with condensation billowing from his mouth as a particularly savage-looking polar bear stalks towards him. It's a long way from Raymond Briggs' cartoons of cuddly animals but, one suspects, slightly closer to the truth about polar bears.

To be fair to that noble animal *Ursus maritimus*, contrary to Thomas Pennant's claim, polar bears do not have an unquenchable thirst for human blood. Humans are not their staple food, and it is very rare for a polar bear to attack a human; two of the most well-documented attacks by bears in the last century, which resulted in fatalities, were a hobo who attracted the bear's attention by carrying meat in his pocket, and one of a gang of teenagers in Churchill, Manitoba, who thought it would be fun to aggravate one of Bruin's descendants. How wrong they were.

Most male polar bears measure between 8 feet 2 inches and 9 feet 8 inches in length, and weigh between 772 and 1,433 pounds, although a specimen measuring 12 feet and weighing 2,209 pounds has been recorded. Polar bears are extremely curious, and know little fear – I've seen footage of a polar bear in the wild that ran *towards* a landing helicopter, and have even read of a mother bear trying to attack a hovering helicopter that she thought was threatening her cubs – but on the whole they prefer to avoid the company of humans. On the other hand, there is no reason to doubt the hellish accounts of the polar bear attacks on Barents' expeditions. That a polar bear can easily run off with a man's body clamped between its jaws is attested to by two bear attacks at oil-drilling installations in the Beaufort Sea in 1983. Pennant's account suggests that polar bears were more savage in the days before they learned to fear mankind. If one should cross your path, try not to aggravate it. Remember: if you're in the Arctic, you're on Bruin's territory, so treat your host with respect.

If the *Erebus* and *Terror* were never seen again, then the crews of the *Enterprise* and the *Investigator* were more fortunate. They had already become separated by the time they reached the Bering Strait, Captain Robert McClure racing ahead in the *Investigator*, determined to be the first to find the North-West Passage. She became trapped in the ice where McClure proved to be indifferent to the sufferings of his men, ordering the rations cut to two-thirds, and later to half, contrary to the advice of his surgeon. After three winters in the Arctic, many members of the crew had to be confined to their beds suffering from physical or mental illness, and while McClure clung on to his sanity Mate Robert Wyniatt became so crazed and despondent at one stage that he often howled all night long in his cabin. He threatened to kill McClure three times, and on one occasion had to be lowered to the ice, screaming, in an attempt to calm him down. So much for the British stiff upper lip.

By New Year 1853, everyone on board the *Investigator* had scurvy, and twenty men were on the sick list, two of them close to death. In April, when conditions on board were looking increasingly desperate, McClure spotted a figure moving over the ice. At first he thought it must be a musk-ox, then an Inuk. But in fact it turned out to be Lieutenant Bedford Pim of HMS *Resolute*, one of the ships of Sir Edward Belcher's squadron. Pim had sledged over from Dealy Island where the *Resolute* and the *Intrepid* were wintering and discovered a cairn left by McClure the previous autumn, detailing the *Investigator*'s predicament and location.

McClure reluctantly agreed for himself and his crew to abandon the *Investigator* – he thought he could still sail through the North-West Passage, although when he asked his crew for volunteers to stay behind with him to make the attempt, only four men stepped forward – and they made the journey across the ice to the *Resolute*, in time becoming the first men to complete the North-West Passage.

While the men of the *Investigator* joined the crews of the *Resolute* and the *Intrepid*, however, they found it was a case of out of the frying pan and into the fire. Before they could escape from the Arctic the seas froze around them again. Belcher's flagship *Assistance*, meanwhile, was ice-bound in Wellington Channel with the *Pioneer*. Sir Edward Belcher was a martinet who quarrelled constantly with his subordinates and ended up falling out with all of them. The only ship he had that was free was the *North Star*, and he abandoned his other ships – unnecessarily, in the opinion of many of his subordinates – and sailed back to Britain in 1854.

HMS *Enterprise*, meanwhile, returned to Britain in 1855, Captain Richard Collinson having spent most of his command drunk and falling out with his officers. He placed his first, second and third officers under arrest, as well as his second ice-master. When they got back to Britain he called for them all to be court-martialled, while they were, unsurprisingly, keen for him to be brought to trial, calling him a liar, a tyrant, a bully, a coward and a drunkard.

All in all, the exploration of the Arctic in the early 1850s was far from being the most glorious episode in the history of the Royal Navy. By 1854, however, the Admiralty had other fish to fry: war had broken out with Russia, and further Arctic exploration was put on the back burner. The Royal Navy resumed Arctic exploration after the war, but the first ship to sail through the North-West Passage did so over a number of seasons, from 1903 to 1906, captained by a certain Norwegian named Roald Amundsen.

A postscript: in 1855 the abandoned HMS *Resolute* broke free from the ice and floated, unmanned, down Lancaster Sound. The crew of an American whaler salvaged her and, when the British waived all claim to her, she was purchased by the United States Congress for $40,000 and returned, fully restored, to Queen Victoria as a gesture of goodwill. In 1880 the *Resolute* was broken up at Chatham, and a desk was made from her timbers that Victoria had shipped to Washington as a gift for President Rutherford B. Hayes. John F. Kennedy is supposed to have discovered this same desk in the cellars of the White House and had it moved to the Oval Office. It was under this same desk that Monica Lewinsky made a name for herself, and yet while George 'Dubya' Bush had every other piece of furniture in the Oval Office removed when he took over from Bill Clinton, the desk was kept; and for all I know remains there to this day.

Now you can buy any of these other bestselling
Headline books from your bookshop or
direct from the publisher.

FREE P&P AND UK DELIVERY
(Overseas and Ireland £3.50 per book)

Vale Valhalla	Joy Chambers	£5.99
The Journal of Mrs Pepys	Sara George	£6.99
The Last Great Dance on Earth	Sandra Gulland	£6.99
Killigrew and the Incorrigibles	Jonathan Lunn	£5.99
Virgin	Robin Maxwell	£6.99
The One Thing More	Anne Perry	£5.9
A History of Insects	Yvonne Roberts	£6.9
The Eagle's Conquest	Simon Scarrow	£5.9
The Kindly Ones	Caroline Stickland	£5.9
The Seventh Son	Reay Tannahill	£6.9
Bone House	Betsy Tobin	£6.9
The Loveday Trials	Kate Tremayne	£6.9
The Passion of Artemisia	Susan Vreeland	£6.9

TO ORDER SIMPLY CALL THIS NUMBER

01235 400 414

or visit our website: www.madaboutbooks.com

Prices and availability subject to change without notic